The Television Late Night Horror Omnibus
GREAT TALES FROM TV ANTHOLOGY SERIES

By the same editor:

The Television Detectives' Omnibus

The Television
LATE NIGHT HORROR
Omnibus

GREAT TALES FROM TV ANTHOLOGY SERIES

Edited by
PETER HAINING

ARTUS BOOKS,
LONDON

First published in Great Britain in 1993 by Orion.
This 1994 edition published by Artus Books
Orion Publishing Group, Orion House, 5 Upper St Martin's Lane,
London WC2H 9EA

ISBN 1 898799 03 2

Printed in England by Clays Ltd, St Ives plc

In Memory of
VALENTINE DYALL
'The Man in Black'

CONTENTS

INTRODUCTION

'Honeee, I'm home!' Jack Nicholson screams in a scene from Stephen King's story *The Shining* (1978) as he leers through a door he has smashed with an axe into millions of television sets in the living rooms of the world. That image, and the equally familiar ones of Franken-stein, Dracula and the maniacal dead-alive killer Freddy Krueger, are typical of the archetypes that are now an integral part of late night horror viewing on the small screen. Though all of this quartet were, of course, made originally as cinema movies, they have been shown with equal impact – some might say with even more – on television, and by so doing become a part of a tradition that stretches back to the black and white infancy of the medium in the years immediately after World War Two.

Each of us, I suspect, has a memory of his introduction to terror on television. My own was in the early Fifties when British TV was still divided into adult and children's programmes. It was a time when youngsters watched their own special broadcasts until the witching hour of 6 p.m., after which news, entertainment and drama shows for the older generation took over. An actual break in transmission when the screen went blank often marked this gulf – no doubt, we children thought, to make it easier for parents to send reluctant off-spring to bed. Each family made its own decision about when the heretofore hidden delights of 'adult' viewing should be revealed to young eyes and impressionable minds.

In my case, the decision to let me stay up to watch an adult production on BBC (then, in fact, the only channel on the air) was accorded to Robert Louis Stevenson's great horror classic, *Dr Jekyll and Mr Hyde*. *Why* it should have been this story with its undertones of schizophrenia and the triumph of evil over good when it takes up human habitation, my parents have never been able to satisfactorily explain, beyond a fairly sweeping statement, 'Well, the story *is* literature.' For me, though, watching the flickering images of Jekyll being transformed into the hideous figure of Hyde on an eight by ten inch screen in a room with the curtains drawn against the evening light, was a profoundly affecting experience – and almost certainly the one that inspired what has since become a lifetime's fascination with the macabre in print and on the screen.

I cannot recall who starred in that production of the Stevenson novel, or even who directed it or wrote the script – and I suspect that some, if not all, of my memories of that night could well be spoiled if I did. For the actors' very names might dispel some of the terrors that for years I have associated with the transmission, just as the production itself which was acted live in front of our very eyes may well have been beset by the sort of problems that were commonplace in many dramas of the time. Actors missing their cues, the camera catching unexpected views of the sound booms, or, horror of horrors, a member of the cast apparently dead getting up before a scene had dissolved. All these faults – and more – I recall from other Fifties' TV programmes; and I have no wish to find, forty years later, that they were a part of that very special and cathartic experience.

It was also at this time in my life that I discovered on the radio a weekly, half-an-hour mystery and suspense series, *Appointment with Fear*, narrated by the sinister-sounding 'Man in Black', who the *Radio Times* informed me, was played by an actor with the resonant name of Valentine Dyall. Here, too, there were horrors to be enjoyed from the 'Wireless set' as murderers and madmen infused with the same fiendish delight as Jack Nicholson pursued their hapless victims against the background of howling winds and creaking doors. You couldn't of course see their leering faces, though the actors' lugubrious voices sometimes suggested as much – but the pictures in the mind were, if anything, more frightening still. In time, *Appointment With Fear* also appeared on television, as did a number of other popular British and American radio thriller shows.

This, then, was my introduction to late night horror on TV. An experience halfway between pleasure and fear that became a fascination and later a profession when I started to write about the supernatural and the paranormal, and to edit collections of fantasy and horror stories. In time, too, like millions of others, I began to watch the anthology series which blossomed in the late Fifties and Sixties when television producers realised that there was a public on the other side of the screen who really enjoyed a little frisson of fear in the comfort of their armchairs. From its fairly crude origins, the late night horror show developed quickly thanks to the advances in television technology, special effects and better production standards.

The arrival of colour further helped establish it as one of the most popular genres. Series such as *Thriller*, *Alfred Hitchcock Presents*, *Out of the Unknown*, *The Twilight Zone*, *Night Gallery*, *Tales of the Unexpected*, and many more became hugely successful with audiences on both sides of the Atlantic. Some now enjoy cult status, while the best of the rest are reshown to new generations of viewers who have similarly come to appreciate the special, often unique, qualities they possess.

This collection is an attempt to reflect some forty years of late night horror viewing as it has been shown in the anthology series. And, as short stories were a prime source for many of these programmes, what better way to recapture their appeal than by reprinting the very best of these that have been adapted for the various series? The book, in fact, ranges from those tales which were used in the very first live, black and white dramas of the Fifties to today's multi-million-dollar special-effects productions made for both public and cable viewers. Many are the work of the leading writers of horror fiction, and not a few have long been out of print or difficult to obtain. Assembling this book has been like a journey into my own past, reviving memories of TV series that I enjoyed and which, I hope, will strike a chord in the memory of many readers, too.

One of the bonuses of my long-standing interest in late night horror has been the invitations to work as story consultant on a number of recent series including Granada's Seventies' production, *Haunted*, and *Tales of the Unexpected* which Anglia produced in the Eighties. The research for these particular series not only gave me an insight into the production of anthology shows generally, but also opened the doors to a wealth of information about the actors, producers and directors who have worked in the genre. These facts I am happy to share in the introductions to the stories which you will find in the pages that follow.

Make yourself comfortable, then, and unless the real thing is about to start on your television, please prepare yourself to enter the weird, uncanny and often frightening world of late night horror . . .

PETER HAINING,
March 1993

Vampire Tower

BY JOHN DICKSON CARR

The first late night programme specifically devoted to horrifying its audience was Appointment with Fear *which began its broadcasting career as a half-hour BBC radio programme in September 1943 – going out at ten-thirty* PM *– and six years later made a successful transition to television. The series, which was narrated by 'The Man in Black' (Valentine Dyall) was the brainchild of John Dickson Carr (1906–1977), an American mystery writer who specialized in stories of impossible murders taking place in locked rooms which he then logically explained. Born in Pennsylvania, Carr had met and married an English girl and decided to settle in England in the Thirties. Such a success did* Appointment With Fear *prove that when Carr was in danger of being called up to serve in the American armed forces, the producers Val Geilgud and Martyn C. Webster appealed to the US Authorities that the scripts were his 'war work' and essential to the morale of the British listening public! Their effrontery paid off and Carr was allowed to remain in the country, continuing to write for the show until its final transmission in 1955. His contributions earned him the accolade of being 'a literary necromancer' from critic Douglas C. Greene. Apart from Carr's stories, the show also featured adaptations of classic horror tales such as Poe's 'The Pit and the Pendulum' (featuring Marius Goring) and 'The Body Snatchers' by Robert Louis Stevenson (with Sir Cedric Hardwicke) as well as contemporary creepy dramas like 'The Man Who Died Twice' (starring Peter Lorre) and the great Sidney Greenstreet in 'The Hangman Won't Wait'. All the adaptations, though, benefited enormously from the sepulchral tones of Valentine Dyall whose voice, according to one reviewer, 'sent more chills up wartime listeners' spines than the ensuing play.' Dyall* introduced each broadcast with a short monologue – a trademark that was to be copied later by many similar shows in Britain and America. A typical such address began: 'This is your storyteller, The Man in Black. Have you ever been alone in a haunted house, with the firelight flickering uneasily on the walls? No? Well, when I tell you that Camilla was sleeping in a Victorian bed in an old farmhouse we hope we keep our promise to bring you . . . an appointment with fear!' Such was Dyall's fame that in 1949 BBC radio gave him his own series, The Man in Black, to which John Dickson Carr also contributed during its two-year run.

It was in 1949 that BBC TV presented a short season of Apppointment With Fear stories produced by Michael Carreras, who would later become famous as the driving force behind Hammer Films. Once again Valentine Dyall appeared as the narrator, more often than not becoming involved in the weird and uncanny events that ensued. Several of the stories which had been broadcast on the radio series were adapted for TV including 'The Ghost of Rashmon Hall', 'The Man With a Cloak' and 'Vampire Tower' a John Dickson Carr tale first broadcast on 11 May 1944. It was directed by Denis Kavanagh and starred Alec Faversham and Anne Howard as the hero and heroine of a grisly tale of murder in a sealed room. Carr had himself adapted the episode from one of his own short stories, 'Terror's Dark Tower', which is reprinted below. It is something of a landmark, too, as one of the very first stories to introduce late night horror viewing to television audiences way back in December 1949 . . .

L OUISE turned her lovely face so that her dark, troubled eyes looked directly into my own.

'Could you believe,' she said, 'that though a woman locked and barred herself into a room beyond any possible attack, nevertheless something came from the air and tore out her eyes?'

They were wild words to have been said at that time and place – and yet they were spoken so quietly!

We sat in a rustic summerhouse down the slope of the hill. The oak trees had gone dull scarlet with October, but the leaves under-foot were yellow, and a wet wind stirred them. On an autumn afternoon there is no place in England more mournful than this brown fold of the hills where Somerset becomes Devon, and northward the waters of Bristol Channel make a chilly gleam. My arm was around Louise, and I felt her shiver. She got up suddenly. She went to the door, and stood staring at the brown road that wound up the hill to Moat Hall.

'I don't know whether I believe it,' she went on quietly. 'But if you marry me, you marry a family curse. And I do know that I'm horribly afraid.'

She had never spoken like this before. The words were all the more startling because they had come in the midst of a happiness such as I had never known before, when Louise's eyes and Louise's cheek were close against my shoulder. I had ridden over that afternoon, singing aloud in the joyous air, from Sir James Fenwick's place on Exmoor. Singing – because Louise would meet me when I tethered my horse by the little spring they called Goblin Water.

Her dark hair would be blown back like the gray scarf around her neck, her hazel eyes shining, and her lips parted in that half smile which had completely upset my universe when I first met her a month ago. Then we would walk up the brown hill to our summerhouse. Well, I had asked my question, and had been answered. So the whole dark afternoon had turned to gold – until now. For here was Louise staring at me with a white, serious face.

'Do you mean what you're saying?' I asked. 'Afraid? What have you to be afraid of?'

'I'm afraid for my sister Anne. You met her, remember? Yes, and I'm afraid for myself too. Afraid that something will come and tear out our eyes. No, no, please don't think I've gone mad!' Her face became whiter yet as I got up and took her hands. 'You see, it isn't merely a thing like a curse. But Anne is to be married next week. She's marrying a very decent chap, one of the Gordons of Hope Grange. My Uncle Harry is furious – I shouldn't mind that, if he didn't keep on smiling. He says nothing, and makes no objection. He simply smiles.'

'Object? Why should he object?'

She did not answer. I looked at the dull-red brick house on the hill, with its latticed windows winking in the afternoon light, and its broad moat where the swans floated. A crooked tower rose from it like a deformity. Louise Mortlake was no product of that gloom. But there had been Mortlakes at Moat Hall since the reign of Queen Elizabeth. The line had decayed; they had closed themselves in behind shutters; the clean winds that blew across the moors did not touch them. With my friend Sir James Fenwick, I had dined there one night – it was the night I first met Louise.

We dined in shabby pomp, under the oak panelling and candles. Besides Louise, there were four in the family. There was her quiet sister Anne. There was a high-nosed Aunt Kate, with a dark face like an old painting. There was an eighteen-year-old cousin Richard. But most of all I remembered Henry Mortlake, fat and sweating and soft-voiced, smiling as he cracked walnuts with a big fist.

'Anne is to be married a week from today,' Louise went on blankly, without answering my question. 'If the thing should creep up and catch her this evening, as Uncle Harry says it might –'

'You've got to stop this!' I said, and gripped her shoulders hard, for she was trembling on the edge of hysterical tears. 'The place has poisoned you. Shall I tell you what we'll do? I'll swing you up on that horse and we'll ride over and put you in the charge of Lady Fenwick. They have such things as special licences in England, haven't they? Tomorrow Sir James and I will see about getting one. Then I will come back and undertake the pleasant task of telling Uncle Harry exactly where he can jump in the moat.'

She smiled, shakily. 'All right; I'll be good. But I want you to listen to something. I want you to listen as carefully as though you were reading evidence in a court case. For it *is* evidence. This isn't the legend and the curse. It's something that happened less than fifty years ago, and there are people alive who can swear to it.'

'Yes?'

'You see that tower?' She pointed. 'At the top of that tower there is one room. It is a bare brick room, with no furniture except a table and a chair. There is one door, and one window. The window faces this way; it is heavily barred, and below there is a smooth face of brick sixty feet down. You can see that from here.'

'In June 1886, one evening just a week before her wedding day, my grandfather's sister Ellen went into that room alone. The door isn't of the ordinary sort; since that room occupies the whole top of the tower, it's a trap door in the ceiling of the room below. You understand, don't you? Like going up into a loft. You must use a ladder for it.

'Well, Ellen Mortlake climbed up there. She shut and bolted the trap door on the inside. Just below her, watching the trap door all the time, were four people whose truthfulness is beyond question. She had been there only ten minutes when they heard her scream, horribly, and the table overturn. When they got a ladder and smashed in the bolted trap, they found her lying in the middle of the room with both eyes jaggedly torn out. She died of shock, without speaking, only a few minutes later.'

Louise was speaking very quietly, her lips barely moving in the gloom of the summerhouse, and the hazel eyes never left my face. She went on: 'Oh, do you think they didn't try to make it a police case? They did. But what could they find out? . . . There was nobody in that room except poor Ellen. Nobody! Not even a place to hide, and they searched immediately. There was nothing in the room that could have given her such wounds. Nobody left the room while they were searching. There was no such foolish thing as a secret entrance or panel; they examined every inch of the room. They even took the table and chair apart, looking for a possible weapon. Nothing! Yet the door was bolted and watched by four people. The window was solidly barred, and sixty feet up a wall that a fly couldn't have climbed. Tom, no human murderer could have done it. But it was done.'

Now the wind rose in a great gust through tattered oaks, and the yellow evening light struck full across on the tower up the hill. I felt that from happiness I had slipped into a nightmare. For Louise believed this. The thing had to be gripped and faced.

'And you really believe,' I said, trying to keep my voice steady, 'that a curse did that? What was the woman doing in that room?'

'*She* didn't believe in the legend. She was trying to show it was all nonsense.'

'What is the legend?'

Louise turned away to look at the road. 'I – can't tell you all of it now. But this much you ought to know, Tom. A horrible thing was done three hundred years ago, by a woman who wanted her own way. Her name was Vivian Mortlake; she was a shrew and a beauty. Because she hated a man whom her family wanted her to marry, she had him killed in such a way that the crows of the field tore out his eyes while he was still alive.'

'Go on,' I said. 'Give me your hand. At least it will do you good to talk.'

'Before he died, he said that if she ever married, he would pay her a visit a week before the wedding. She watched for him from that tower window. A week before her wedding, the crows came to her –' Louise drew a deep breath. 'You see, it was said she saw him coming back from his grave, groping his way up this road in the twilight, with the blood soaking out of his empty eye sockets, and the great crows clustered on him like pets. Anyway, Vivian Mortlake went mad with blindness and pain.'

She swung round to face me.

'And this is the tale, Tom: that if any Mortlake girl marries against the will of her family, as Vivian did, those blind things shall fly from the air and stab out her eyes . . . Don't laugh. Whatever you do, in God's name don't laugh! I don't know anything, except that it *has happened*. My sister, you see, will be marrying against the family's will.'

I had no inclination to laugh. I wanted only to curse 'Uncle Henry'

Mortlake's smug and unctuous ghost stories, his poisoning of two girls in a lonely house as surely as though he had done it with cyanide.

'And he doesn't want you to marry, either?' I asked.

'No. You see – both Anne and I have a little money held in trust for us till we marry. As it is, the money supports all of us . . .'

'Held in trust by him?'

'Yes.'

'Damn his soul,' I said. 'He can have all the money he wants, crammed down his throat. But there are other things to settle with him.'

'There are,' spoke up a great voice in the road behind us, 'if it's not too late to do any good.'

It was the familiar, quiet, curt voice of Sir James Fenwick. Neither of us had heard him ride up, though Queen of Clubs was blown as though from a long gallop. He sat motionless on the great horse, outlined against the yellow sunset, but his voice shook like the hand on his bridle rein. He wore his old tweed cap and coat; in his big lined face the eyeglass was stuck in his left eye, and the corners of his mouth were turned down. He took one look at us.

'So,' he said. 'She's told you about the bogey, eh? Then you're just in time to hear the latest development.' He stabbed his finger towards the house. 'Louise, did they tell you that Henry M. has persuaded – or goaded – Anne to try her luck in the tower room? No, by God, they wouldn't! Well, he has. She's there now. Your cousin Dick just telephoned me on the quiet to come and do something about it. He's too afraid of Henry to put in a word. He tried to get in touch with Anne's fiancé, but young Gordon's in London – and I was the only one left.'

'You mean . . .' said Louise. 'No! No!'

'I mean some deviltry. Come on! I'm off to see if I can –'

The great horse reared, monstrous in the twilight, but not from his urging. It was sixty yards up the hill to Moat Hall, yet we heard the screams plainly. A woman in the tower room was screaming in such hideous pain or terror that it dislodged wheeling birds in a fluttering cloud from the eaves. The screams abruptly stopped. Fenwick cursed only once. His horse pawed the air, came down with a strike of sparks from the flints, and was off like thunder up the road.

II

Louise and I ran hard. When we reached Moat Hall, the startled swans were still flapping the water in the moat. Fenwick was already across the stone causeway; he was standing at the big door furiously banging its knocker. Nobody answered. But it was unlocked, and Louise led us inside. In the dark oak hallway there was – I don't know how to describe it – a kind of ringing stillness, as of evil sinking back after it strikes. A dim figure almost walked into us, and my heart rose in my throat.

Then the figure began to laugh hysterically. It was the eighteen-year-old cousin, Richard. His callow, sensitive face, with the shrunken good looks of the Mortlakes, rocked back and forth in the gloom.

'You're too late,' he said. 'The crows dug through into the brain. She's dead.'

I thought Louise was going to faint. She turned round and put her head against my shoulder. It was Fenwick's strong presence that kept us sane; he had Richard by the collar, choking off his laughter.

'Pull yourself together,' he said harshly. 'Quiet, do you hear? Now tell me: Why was she fool enough to let Henry persuade her to . . . go in there?'

Richard looked at Louise. 'She did it for you,' he answered. 'She said you had found somebody you had fallen in love with. She said that she wouldn't have you terrified, and she was going to break the curse forever. You see, there's trust and honour – even among the Mortlakes.'

'Henry is in there now, is he?' asked Fenwick, after a silence. 'And your Aunt Kate too?'

'Yes. If they were the only ones!' said the other bitterly. 'But they're not. There's Mr Walters, and Dr Porter, and Squire Brixley; the vicar, the doctor, and the chief magistrate of the county. All men whose word is above reproach. They were summoned to see it. They can swear – we'll all have to swear – they saw an impossible thing done. Anne went up the ladder, she bolted the trap; we never took our eyes off it. All those men can testify . . .'

'His witnesses,' Fenwick groaned. 'And yet nobody tried to stop it?'

Richard stopped, as though he had said too much. His head was shaking with a terrible motion like a paralytic's.

'The vicar tried to. But Anne insisted. Also, Dr Porter said it was a lot of damned nonsense, and Squire Brixley was half drunk and didn't care a hoot either way. So she went in. I – I can't stand this. You see, she trusted me. You'd better go upstairs.'

Two minutes more, and we were climbing the stone staircase that curved up into the tower. We emerged into the room where the watchers had waited, the one just below the room of the curse. A ladder ran up to a trap in the ceiling; the trap door was splintered through where they had smashed it in. From the room above we could hear footsteps moving about, and the mutter of voices.

This lower room was square, with diamond-paned windows through which the sunset light had turned reddish. The furniture was black Jacobean oak, and the silver candlesticks caught a glitter. Beside the table sat Kate Mortlake, Henry's wife, with her high-bridged nose and darkish face. Her hands were folded quietly, as though the matter did not concern her.

'Good evening,' said Henry Mortlake's smooth voice from the western window. 'Ah, but isn't it sad – sad! Louise, my dear, I am sorry to tell you that your poor sister is . . . gone. I warned her, but she was foolish and headstrong. I ask you to remember that she did this of her own free will.'

He was standing by the open window, big and shapeless, with the reddish light shining on his face, and he was smiling. On his face there was a thin oil of sweat. He was eating walnuts; I saw his black fingernails as he broke a walnut in one hand, and delicately shook out the kernel. His little eye gleamed like a crumb of glass. Although he tried to be impassive, he could not keep the loose mouth from broadening into a grin.

'Gone,' echoed Aunt Kate, without inflection.

'Mortlake,' said Sir James Fenwick calmly, 'I think you know what I believe. It's not necessary to go into that now . . .'

'Yes, yes! By all means tell me what you believe,' said the other, with agreeable surprise. 'Please tell me. Then I can institute a suit for slander, and the court will award me several thousand pounds. Eh, Kate? My niece Anne chose to disobey my orders about marriage. So she suffered – but not through me. No human intelligence can explain how she was struck down in an empty, sealed room. Three unprejudiced men will swear that the room was both empty and sealed. They will tell you that all the while I stood before their eyes, and did not move from here. Eh?' He smiled again, and spoke very softly as he thrust out his head. 'So? You are James Fenwick, late of India, and retired chief of the Indian secret police? Then see if you can explain the magic of the supernatural . . . You poor bloody fool, if you so much as dare mention what you may be thinking, I'll go to court and have the very shirt off your back.'

He chuckled. Fenwick's face was grey, and he was gripping his riding crop hard. Mortlake's indifferent eye turned round towards me.

'And now I hear,' he added pleasantly, 'that there is talk of more marriages against my express wish. An American visitor comes and makes love to our little Louise. Can I humbly ask you to take a warning? Louise has pretty eyes too –'

12

There was a riding crop slung by a loop round my own wrist. I gripped the butt and took a step forward, but Fenwick seized my arm.

'Don't do it!' he snapped. His voice broke the mist of wrath that had taken all of us. 'Don't you see you'd be doing exactly what he wants you to?'

'There is talk of a marriage,' I said, releasing the crop. 'Have you any objections?'

'I? *I*? Of course not. You do not understand, I fear. But then you Americans, who have not even any grandparents you can identify, would not understand such things, would you? There is a blight on that girl. It is a part of her; it is in her blood, and her destiny, and the sticks and stones of this house. If she will not obey our wishes, then it will –'

'I don't think it'll have the chance.'

'Well, I'm going up there now, in any case,' said Louise, and her eyes brimmed over. 'She did that for me.'

She was climbing the ladder before anybody could stop her. But we did not realize the worst of the business until we stood in the bare black room above. The evening light was almost gone. A wet wind blew through the bars of the one small window, and made a vast seething in the trees below. It was not merely what we saw there . . .

Dr Porter was bending over the body on the floor, and at first we did not see the ruined face. At one side stood the lean old vicar, Walters, in his clerical black; at the other side was the stout Major Brixley, in dark riding clothes, and now quite sober. They looked themselves like three birds of prey.

Dr Porter held up his hand. 'Don't look, Louise,' he cried, but he was too late.

Anne Mortlake had been a small, fragile girl, dressed in grey silk. I need not describe her injuries, except to say they were such that Louise could not remain very long, and Major Brixley had to take her downstairs. After Anne had been attacked, she had evidently run and stumbled wildly round the room in her blindness – there were stains on the wall in several places – before she fell. Her dress was stained, and ripped down from the shoulder as though she had torn loose from something. But this was not the terror which made our skins crawl. It was the realization that this attack must have been conjured up by powers from hell, because it could not have been done by man.

It was Dr Porter, with his black pointed beard and his Ascot tie, who spoke first.

'I don't believe it!' he said wildly, and stared round. 'I see it, and yet I don't believe it. Look round you. Blank walls – not even a place for a rat to hide. No furniture – not even the chair and table they talked about. There was nobody here before she came up – we saw that. There was nobody here when we smashed that trap door after she screamed. And we never took our eyes off that trap door, either. As for the window, look at it! Bars too close for a midget to get through, set solid in stone, and sixty feet up a wall smooth as glass. Well?'

'You've tested the walls?' asked Fenwick sharply.

'Been over every inch of 'em,' nodded the doctor, and Walters agreed. 'The ceiling too. There's no secret entrance, and no hocus-pocus mechanical device to attack her, if that's what you're thinking.'

The old clergyman rubbed blurred eyes.

'This is my fault,' he said with an unsteady look round. 'I protested, but I should have done something . . . something . . . You see, I was a boy when Ellen Mortlake died here nearly fifty years ago. I remember it well. It was exactly like this.'

'So I've heard. That,' said Fenwick, 'is what makes me wonder. But suppose we get things straight, gentlemen, before we have to send for the police. I suppose you're all provided with . . . alibis?'

'Eh? Alibis?' said Porter, startled. 'Good God, yes! That is, I suppose so. We were all together down there. None of us came up with her.'

'You were all down there, including Mr Henry Mortlake?'

'Yes, certainly.'

'Thank you,' said a smooth, fat voice from the trap door. 'Thanks very much.' Mortlake's head appeared in the opening. 'It will set the good Sir James's doubts at rest. Would you like to telephone the police now?'

And he laughed in our faces.

III

'Have you gone mad?' cried Walters. 'Do you realize, or don't you, that your niece is . . . ?'

Mortlake became contrite, with a sudden change like fear. 'Excuse me, gentlemen. Of course I am sorry. But you d-don't understand. She paid a penalty, that is all.'

'You honestly believe that?' snapped the doctor.

'Can you prove anything different? Prove it, I said?' the other asked composedly. 'I advise you to be careful.'

'We'll try,' said Fenwick grimly. He paused as the thin, drawn face of Richard Mortlake appeared in the trap. 'To get this in order, doctor: when did Anne come up to this room?'

Porter looked at his watch. 'About half an hour ago. Say six o'clock or thereabouts.'

'Did anybody come up here with her?'

'No. Not up here. Except that . . .'

'Yes?'

'Well,' grunted the doctor uncomfortably, 'as she was climbing up the ladder, Dick Mortlake here climbed up a few rungs and whispered something to her.'

The young man, who was climbing over the edge of the trap, stumbled. His face went white with the implications of this.

'I didn't have anything to do with it!' he cried. 'Don't look at me like that! I – I was trying to help her. All I said was not to worry, and that I had telephoned Sir James to come up as soon as he could –'

'So,' interrupted Henry, and showed his teeth, 'you are the reason why our estimable neighbour pays us this visit, eh? I shall remember that.'

Fenwick kept his eyes on Porter. 'But he didn't actually come up into this room with her?'

'Oh, no.'

'Was anything else said to her before she went up?'

Porter hesitated. 'Henry here said, "If you see Rupert and his pets coming up the road, my dear . . ." '

'What did he mean by that?'

'You had better let me explain that,' nodded Henry, and giggled.

He moved over softly against the grey light from the window. The wall was very thick, so that the window sloped outward, and the bars – set three inches apart – were fixed immovably in stone. Nevertheless Henry made a great show of shaking them and winking at us.

'It is a pretty story, gentlemen,' he went on. 'Some of you may have heard it. It does not concern the modern crow, but the carrion crows of 1621, which were used to gorging themselves on battlefields. In 1621 Rupert Henley was the suitor of Vivian Mortlake, the red-haired devil, and he was the man her family – her wise family, gentlemen – ordered her to marry. She hated him. She even hated him for his devotion. It is evil blood, I tell you, in the women of our race!'

He pointed at us. His face was like pale butter in the gloom.

'She would scream at him, "Will you never tire of following me wherever I go?" And he would answer, "Madam, love has four faces, like a compass; and I am the needle to be drawn wherever you are. You will never be rid of me."

'Do you know what she had done to him? He was waylaid one night when he rode home past the great acres of cornfields that used to lie at the bottom of this hill. He was stripped of his clothes, and bound round in surgical bandages and splints so that he could not even move

15

his body. He was a living mummy. Even his head was bound in splints, with only the eyes and nose showing. Then they dressed him in the rags and straw and hood of a scarecrow, and propped him up on sticks high in the field. All the world could pass by and see him, yet no one would know the scarecrow was a living man. The exposed part of his face was slashed so that the blood should be there to attract the carrion crows . . .

'The next day she could sit in this tower room and look out to where the scarecrow hung in the blaze of sun. She sang at her needlework, and jabbed her needle as the cloud of crows came down there. It is said he endured two days of it, while nobody ever knew. They did notice, however, that the crows swarmed in such fashion that the head of the scarecrow seemed to be covered in moving black fur. And thus it was discovered. When two farm hands came to beat them away, they discovered . . .

'Still he was not quite dead. He never betrayed her, and nobody at the time knew she had been responsible. He only said to tell Milady Mortlake that if she ever married, he would visit her a week before the wedding. "And she will find," he said, "that death has four faces too." '

Henry drew a deep breath. Then his voice rose almost to a scream.

'Can anybody deny the truth of that? You blind fools, don't you know that the Devil is as real in this world as the beef you eat at dinner or the lamp that lights your room? The Devil is real. I have seen him lurk behind the hedges. Can you deny that he sent a dead Rupert Henley riding up that road on a dead horse, with his blind eye sockets fixed on this tower; and that the cloud of crows left his head to fly up here through this window and covered Vivian Mortlake's face as though with moving black fur?

'And if you do not believe that,' he said, very softly now, 'remember what happened tonight. You all heard it. We were down there listening. And just as Anne screamed, can you in your sober senses deny that we all heard a *great beating of wings*?'

We had all drawn back. The man was cool and smiling now, mopping at the oil of sweat on his face, but his smirk looked more fanatical than any rage. Dr Porter looked hard at him.

'I'm not sure,' said the doctor, 'whether it ought to be Walters or myself who prescribes for you. I don't know whether you need a doctor or a clergyman. . . . Beating of wings! Yes, we heard it. But I know what it was. It was the swans down below, that got a scare when she screamed; I heard them splashing as well, and I can swear to that. You ought to know. You were standing by the window down there.'

'So,' said Fenwick, in such a queer voice that we all whirled round. 'He was standing by the window, was he?'

Fenwick's big face was impassive, but he stared straight at the trap door in the floor near Mortlake.

'He was,' said Porter. 'But what of it?'

'Mr Walters,' Fenwick went on, and turned to the vicar without raising his voice, 'you said that you were a young man when Ellen Mortlake died in this room in 1886, and that you remember the case? Good. Who objected to Ellen Mortlake's marriage? Her father?'

'Her . . . ?' The vicar seemed sunk in apathy, and he raised his white head vacantly. 'Her father? No. He was dead. The one who objected was her brother Henry. Come to think of it, he was the father of Mr Henry Mortlake here.'

'And what,' asked Fenwick in a curious tone, 'was his profession?'

'I believe he was a jeweller.'

Fenwick slashed his riding crop across his knee. 'It tells us nothing! Damnation, he could not have been a jeweller! I tell you he couldn't –' He broke off as Mortlake's assured, contemptuous grin defied him to do anything whatever. But I noticed that Fenwick had caught my eye as though asking me to agree with anything he said. He went on: 'Now shall I tell you something, Mortlake? The curse is broken. Your poor little bogey is smashed to blazes, and we can laugh at it. Do you know why? Louise came into this room a while ago, and was unharmed . . .'

'Naturally,' said Mortlake. 'We must patiently wait – and I hope she enjoys the prospect – until a week before her wedding.'

'It is just a week before her wedding,' said Fenwick politely. 'Didn't you know that she and my friend Tom Brocklin had arranged this afternoon to be married on the same day as Anne and her fiancé?'

At this thumping lie, Mortlake's loose mouth fell open a little.

'It's against all decency,' Fenwick's cold voice went on, 'with Anne dead, but you might be interested to hear that they are going through with it. Why? To save Louise's reason. To show that this tuppenny curse can be smashed for the turnip ghost it is. Better violate a few conventions rather than have Louise in a madhouse . . . But you didn't know that, did you? And your ghosts didn't know it, either. This is the last night Louise will spend under your roof. Good afternoon, gentlemen.'

He strode across and began to descend the ladder. I followed him. We were in the room below before Mortlake stuck his head down the trap.

'A last word, my friend,' he said silkily, and pointed with the stained point of the walnut pick. 'Put a guard of police round me, if you like.

Let every move I make be watched. Put her into a room with all the doors and windows bolted, and a guard around her. *They* will come after her just the same. As for you, dear Mr Brocklin –'

'Don't answer him,' snapped Fenwick, and dragged me away from that reddish face peering down, while Mortlake went on smiling. Fenwick and I were going down in the gloom of the tower stairs before my friend spoke.

'God help us, Tom. I mean that in a literal sense. I'm afraid he will keep his word.'

'You mean Louise . . . ?'

'Yes.'

'But the man's not supernatural!' I cried. 'He can't command black magic and turn loose a cloud of devils. Or can he? He can't commit murder in a locked and sealed room while he's still standing before the eyes of all those witnesses! Unless, of course, the witnesses were lying.'

'The witnesses were not lying,' said Fenwick quietly. 'But if it's any consolation to you I think I can tell you there's nothing supernatural about it. It's only a very brilliant and very horrible trick. But he may work it again.'

'You mean a device hidden in that room?'

'No, Tom. The room is as harmless as – as a nursery; there's nothing there. But don't be confident when you learn it's not supernatural. There are worse things. I think that Mortlake already had a crack in his brain, for the dark world to press through. It split wide when I challenged him; he'll go to any lengths now, and it's our only chance to catch him. Don't argue! We must find Louise.'

We found her in the dusky lower hall.

'I'm sorry I was weak,' she said, and took my hand like a child. 'It was . . . everything at once. I am strong now.'

'That,' said Fenwick quietly, 'that is good news. Because, Louise, I am going to ask you to be stronger still. Tonight, after the police have gone, I am going to ask you to go up into the tower room alone.'

IV

Even as he said it, I realized that the whispering old house was not so quiet as we had thought. Somewhere, on the stairs or in one of the tapestry-hung rooms, there was the sound of a footfall: a creaking as someone stalked us. It was as though the whole house were listening.

But I heard for only an instant – and then forgot, for Fenwick's words were too startling to allow anything else to remain in my mind.

'Go up into that room alone tonight?' I said. 'Look here, have you gone crazy too? If she ever goes up into that room alone, there's just one precaution we'll take first: we'll strangle Uncle Henry.'

Fenwick turned round. I saw the gleam of his eyeglass, but his lips did not move against tightened jaws when we heard the whisper: '*Agree with anything I say, you fool.*' He turned back to Louise, and spoke in an audible mutter.

'Now listen carefully, and whatever you do, don't fail me in any particular if you value your life or your reason. Got it? Got that? I don't want you to go up there to break the curse. I want you to go because it's the highest point in this house, and the only place from which you can see across the moor to Fenwick House.'

'Your own place?'

'My own place. At eleven o'clock I want you to go up to the tower room. The police will have gone by then; and until then you'll be safe. You will take no light, understand? But you will be armed. Go up there and watch for my signal. At eleven I'll put a lamp in the highest window of the east wing of my house. If you see one light, that means that no matter what happens, you are to remain absolutely still in that room until . . . something happens. But if you see two lights, that will mean my plan has miscarried. In that case you are to get out of the house instantly, and shoot without question anyone who tries to stop you.'

He paused, staring straight at her.

'I know it's a lot to ask, Louise. I know it would break the nerve of anybody with less at stake than you have. Believe me, I should not ask you to trust me blindly –'

'Blindly,' said Louise in a low voice.

'That,' said Fenwick, and made a fierce gesture, 'was the wrong word. I should not ask you to trust me if I did not know – *know*, do you hear? – that it's the only way to bring you out of the shadow and into clean air . . . Well?'

'She did it for me,' Louise answered, after a pause, and nodded. 'It's the least I can do for her. Of course I will. I – I – What now?'

'Outside,' he muttered. 'Both of you. Quickly!'

We hurried out on the causeway in the thickening dusk. Fenwick made certain the big door was shut, and then peered up and down the moat.

'We were overheard,' I said. 'You knew that?'

'Of course. I intended that we should be.'

'Then the plans are changed?' Louise asked quickly.

'Not at all. Do just as I told you, with one addition. You are to conceal Tom somewhere in the house. Can you do that? Good! Tom, you know the way up to the tower room. You are to get up there, secretly, at least fifteen minutes before she does. Show no light, and watch. If everything goes well . . . Ah! Found it! Look there, both of you!'

Abruptly he pointed up the shadowy stretch of the moat, now grey and ruffled in its fringe of reeds. He indicated a point at a great distance away from the big tower, and I could see only a white blur on the water. We followed him round to look at it from the bank. It floated shapeless and dead: a swan whose long neck was outstretched snakily, and whose head was severed in a red pulp that still stained the water. Nothing brought out the intrinsic horror breathing from this house more than that sodden white mass floating in the dusk.

'Someone's chopped off –' muttered Louise, and stopped. 'Uncle Harry is very fond of the swans. He has names for all of them.'

'It's the last link,' said Fenwick, closing his fist. 'The last piece of evidence we need. First, the direction of the sun this afternoon. Second, the fact that his father was a jeweller. Third, that dead swan. Does he have names for all of them? By God, he ought to call that one Justice. It is going to hang him.'

That laugh went echoing and twisting in my mind through all the long hours between then and eleven o'clock. As each clock tick drew us nearer the time for Louise's vigil, my own fear grew to more grotesque shapes.

Worst of all, I could not see Louise during those hours. She had hidden me in a little back library, where neither of the two old servants ever came. She went about her tasks with a white face but a steady smile. Hidden away in her bureau upstairs, she said, she had a Browning .22 for pot shots at rabbits. Meanwhile the police had been summoned from Porlock, the nearest town.

So I waited in the dark, not daring to smoke and hardly daring to move, while the phantoms gathered. When a clock out in the hall chimed ten-thirty, I almost jumped out of a crawling skin.

I allowed five minutes more, and then crept out. I groped my way upstairs, keeping to the wall and testing every tread. The closer I crept to the tower door, the more hot grew my fear of discovery. Nearly there! Watch out for chairs. Ten feet more, and bear to the right –

I climbed the tower stairs, slipped into the lower tower room, and groped for the ladder. Two seconds more, and I was in the loft, where the rain blew through open bars. No gleam yet showed across the moor in the direction of Fenwick House. This rain, I realized, would play the devil about seeing that signal. I crouched back against one wall away from the trap, and waited.

The direction of the sun, a jeweller, and a dead swan ... These strangely unrelated things hammered over and over in my brain, but they conjured up a thousand incredible shapes in the dark for the Death with Four Faces. . . .

Somebody was coming up the ladder. I heard it above the splashing of the rain, a mere rustle of sound. A shadow moved on lighter blackness; the shattered trap door creaked slightly.

'Tom . . .' whispered Louise's voice, and something wrenched in my throat.

'Take it easy,' I whispered. Those threads of sound moved and crossed.

Only blackness showed at the window. If Fenwick failed us now . . .

'I asked,' she whispered, 'because, Tom, there was somebody following me up the tower stairs.'

The roar of the rain grew, but it did not quite blot out the noise of someone crossing the floor of the room below. Whoever it was, I was a little surprised to find that he was not trying to walk softly. The ladder shook, just as Louise seized my arm and seemed gesturing towards the window. Far down the hill and out across the moorland, there was a blurry gleam.

Someone was climbing the ladder. I motioned Louise to the far side of the room, and crouched ready behind the trap. A head came through. The beam of a flashlight struck across the room on Louise's face.

'It's all right!' came an agonized whisper. 'Louise! Are you there? It's all right! – I know about it! Sir James told me. It's Dick.'

'What do you want?' she whispered. 'Don't you know you'll break up –'

'I had to help you! Don't you know you'll never see that light in this rain unless . . .' He held out his hand, and there was a dark gleam. 'I've brought you a pair of binoculars – night glasses. You'll be able to pick it up now.'

'Thanks, Dick. Give them here, quick! It's past elev –'

She screamed.

Out of the dark a few feet to my right sprang the straight white glare of a bull's-eye lantern. It fastened on young Mortlake's fallen jaw as he whirled round with the small binoculars in his hands.

'Don't touch those glasses,' said the voice of Sir James Fenwick. *'That's what killed Anne. Grab him, Tom, and don't let him yell for help. Steady, now.'*

V

Richard Mortlake showed no fight. He backed against one wall, pushing his hands out feebly before him, like a child under hypnosis. Fenwick kept the light steadily in his eyes propping the man's own flashlight on the floor.

'Oh, no,' said Fenwick, who himself was breathing heavily, 'he's not the king devil, though he may hang for all of that. You see, he was too afraid of Henry to refuse. But our young friend was used because Anne trusted him. He planted the glasses. Like to see how the damnable trick was worked? . . . Give me those glasses!'

Richard Mortlake handed them over. His thin chest heaved, and his tongue seemed too big for his mouth, so that he could not speak.

'Somebody gives you a pair of binoculars, or you find them on a window ledge,' Fenwick went on, very quietly. 'You put them to your eyes, and you can see only a blur. What do you immediately do? While you keep on looking, you put your hand up and start to turn the focus wheel in the middle, to put the glasses into focus. Only, in this case . . .

'There's a good reason why you see a blur. It's worked on the principle of a compressed air gun, and only a touch of the focus wheel is necessary, like a trigger. When you turn it, two jagged steel points about an inch and a half long strike out from the lenses and drive through your eyes. There's your bogey and your curse, Louise, and that's *all* there is to it.'

Louise could not speak, but her breath came in a shuddering gasp.

'And yet,' Fenwick went on evenly, 'no glasses were found in this room afterwards. That's the brilliant part of the whole scheme. Without it, there would have been no curse and no mystery when Henry Mortlake's father took advantage of an old curse and devised these glasses to kill his sister fifty years ago. And since a jeweller is usually also an optician . . .

'Think how it was done! A woman is told to watch a road for a phantom rider coming up a road towards evening, and she finds a pair of binoculars conveniently left there . . . You see, what young Dick really whispered to Anne – when she was going up the ladder – was that he had left a pair of glasses up there for her. And she trusted him . . . Well, what happens? Strong evening light is beating straight through that window into her eyes. She can't see very well. But suddenly she notices, far down the evening road, a horseman. She sees –'

'She sees *you*,' Louise interrupted, and in the shock of realization our eyes turned – I don't know why – to a slobbering Richard Mortlake.

Fenwick passed a hand over his eyes. His voice was heavy and bitter.

'She sees me – for I have been summoned, just at the right time, by a telephone call. The recollection of that, the knowledge that *I* was responsible for that girl's death . . . ! But to explain. Let's suppose you saw, dimly against the sun, just that. You want a good look. But though you can get a shaded look with those binoculars, *the bars are in your way* and impede the glasses. What do you do?'

I felt a little sick. By turning those glasses sideways, they could be passed out through the bars.

'In that case,' I said, 'you'd pass those glasses *out* through the three-inch space between the bars. You'd hold the middle part of the nose against one bar, with the eyepieces outside the bar on either side, and look through. But when you turned the wheel –'

'We needn't dwell on it,' said Fenwick savagely. 'I only dwell on it now to show Louise what thin tissue paper all the terrors were built of. Oh, evil enough! But not supernatural. The steel points go through. In that sudden blast of agony, the victim releases the glasses. They go down, sixty feet, and sink to the bottom of the moat. Any splash they may make – which is carefully listened for by Henry Mortlake, standing by an open window to make sure his plan has succeeded – any splash is explained by the beating of the swans. As it happened, those glasses smashed off the head of a swan when they fell. It was simple enough; all clues led straight to the moat. But we had to get a confession. We had to find somebody tonight fishing up those glasses from the moat. And last of all we had to catch somebody, before witnesses, handing those glasses to Louise. Hence my scheme to misdirect attention to the lights at my house.

'As for you,' he snapped, and walked slowly towards Dick, 'I rather thought your excellent master and devil's advocate would be too canny to do the work himself. So we can't implicate him, eh? Well, *you're* going to implicate him now, unless you want to swing for murder.'

Dick was wiping a hand aimlessly across his mouth, his eyes roving. But when he heard this he burst out. It was to Louise he spoke.

'You – you don't understand,' he said, in a shaky voice that was like a child's puzzled hesitation. 'I – yes, I admit I did that. I couldn't help myself. He's mad. He'd have sneaked in, if I refused; he'd have sneaked in, while I was sleeping, and put those glasses over my eyes. I was going to kill myself, anyway, after what I did to Anne. But you don't understand, Louise. I was going to save your life. I tried to save your life. Honestly and truly, Louise, I was going to –'

'You're going to talk,' said Fenwick. 'Speak up! Do you admit, before witnesses, what I've just been saying?'

'Yes!'

'Then we'll round it out. Why was Henry standing by the window all the time? Wasn't it because he wanted to see the glasses fall? And if by any chance his scheme didn't work, and the glasses fell inside the room, he had a duplicate harmless pair in his pocket? He was going to be the first to rush up that ladder, and substitute the harmless ones for the others? Is that right?'

'Yes!'

'And if I write all this down, here and now; you'll sign it?'

'Yes!'

A soft, heavy voice spoke behind us.

'That, of course, is open to debate,' it said. 'No, I wouldn't move, if I were you.'

We had not even heard him come up the ladder, or seen his light. He was squatting beside the trap, smirking and wagging his head over a lantern before him. It outlined every bloated feature of the moist face; it made monstrous the flabby bald head, and threw a slow-wagging distortion of shadow on the wall behind. I got Louise behind me. But we looked into his eyes, and we saw death.

'I have here,' he said, opening his eyes wide, 'an air pistol. I think it is more powerful than the German type you remember from the war, although it is much older. My father made it, as he made that air-gun mechanism in those glasses. It is almost noiseless. It also fires an expanding bullet, and I shall be able to blow your guts wide open if any of you so much as moves a finger. Is that clear?' he put his tongue in his cheek and smiled thoughtfully. He was in no hurry. 'I have said,' he went on, 'that this is a more powerful air pistol than the German. Let's test it, shall we?'

I don't know what happened, except that I saw the thing come round in a half circle. I cannot remember any sound at all, although there must have been one. The lantern light spun sideways and seemed to pitch forward. The full weight of my shoulder had come down on the floor, and I was looking at that broad reddish face from underneath. They say there is no pain, which is a lie. It went over my brain in a sick heat like sunstroke.

'Don't try to get up,' said Mortlake. 'Your right leg is smashed just below the knee. But you will be feeling a trifle dizzy now ... I am not going to hurt any of you, with bullets. You will simply be put out of commission, until I can make you ... look at the stars through my telescope. Eh? Eh? You know, I rather fancy myself as a humorist. Eh?'

'No, you won't hang,' Fenwick observed. 'Unfortunately I think you'll only go to Broadmoor. In case you don't know it, that's where they put the criminally insane.'

'I shouldn't talk like that, if I were you,' said Mortlake coolly, and pulled the trigger again.

I heard a scraping noise on the wall, as though Fenwick were trying to hold himself up. He said nothing, but I heard the little tinkle as his eyeglass broke on the floor.

'That was a worse one,' Mortlake said, 'but still not serious. You'd better let go that wall, my poor bloody friend, the head of the secret police, or I shall have to give you another.' A snarl suddenly came up behind his grin. 'You're all going to look through my telescope, you know. As for you, Louise, don't try to use that little toy pistol. I unloaded it early this evening.'

His voice rose querulously.

'Do you think I didn't know what you were plaining? I prepared for it. Something had to be done. I could see the great Sir J. had spotted my little optical device. We might as well have a banquet, eh? And if you had every policeman in the West Country surrounding the place at this moment, I fail to see how it could help you – do you?'

I was thinking that if I could get any leverage for my body in my wobbling arms, I might pitch forward into him and carry him through the trap door. Unfortunately, he saw the intention just as I jumped. Something else went into my arms. He lowered the air gun and got to his feet.

'It's all right, Dick,' he said to that stricken young man, who was praying now. 'Take it easy, and you may not be hurt – yet. Don't be a fool like this one. Will you obey me now?'

'Yes!' The boy meant it; we all knew that.

'There is just one thing I should like to know. *You!*' He screeched the word at Fenwick, and I thought he was going to fire again. 'What did you mean by that little trick and fancy with those lights at your place? What do you mean by it? Eh?'

'Suppose,' Fenwick's voice said coolly, 'you try to find out.'

'I will. *These* glasses,' said Mortlake, tapping the case at his side, 'are harmless. We'll have a look. We –' He screamed.

I could not see him where he was, but something grimy yellow spilled across my line of sight just as there was a metallic crash on the floor. The yellow blur became distorted, seemed to strike the floor and roll from side to side before it lay breathing but unconscious. Over that room where the terrors had lately choked and blasted, there was now only the cool rush of the rain. Two people spoke.

Fenwick said: 'Pick up that gun of his, Louise. Take it easy, now. He'll give very little trouble.'

And, rising to the breaking point, Dick Mortlake's voice went on in its puzzled babble; 'I told you I tried to save your life. Honestly, I tried to save your life. You see, Louise, I wasn't lying. Tonight, before I came up here, and when he didn't know it, *I switched the two pairs of glasses.*'

I remember grinning at Louise, who was running towards me. Then it is possible that the whole nightmare ended in a bad faint.

The Corpse and the Kid

BY CORNELL WOOLRICH

The first American programme to extensively feature late night horror was Suspense *which, like* Appointment with Fear, *began life as a radio series in 1942 and then transferred to CBS TV in 1949 where it was to remain a feature until 1964. It was also linked to its British counterpart in that John Dickson Carr was a frequent contributor in the Forties and Fifties. The radio show had already earned a prestigious Peabody Award and a special citation from the Mystery Writers of America, so that it came to the small screen with an enviable reputation. It proceeded to live up to this with stories of people in dangerous and threatening situations – producing many a memorable half-hour adaptation which went out on Tuesday evenings at 9.30 p.m. Amongst these can be numbered 'The Waxworks' starring William Prince; 'The Tortured Hand' with Peter Lorre; and a version of that tale which so affected me,* Dr Jekyll and Mr Hyde, *made in 1950 with Ralph Bell and then repeated a year later with Basil Rathbone. In its early years the show was transmitted 'live' from New York (it would be filmed from 1954 onwards) and consequently could draw on the leading Broadway actors as well as movie favourites such as Nina Foch, Barry Sullivan, John Carradine, Henry Hull and Boris Karloff. Among the horror story writers whose work was featured on* Suspense *were Edgar Allan Poe, H.P. Lovecraft and Cornell Woolrich (1903–1968) who, like the other members of this trio was a tortured, alcoholic, reclusive man, and about whom Chris Steinbrunner and Otto Penzler have written in their* Encyclopedia of Mystery & Detection, *'His ability to create an atmosphere of terror has been equalled only by that of Poe.'*
A number of Cornell Woolrich's stories were snapped up for

Suspense *almost as soon as it went onto television – adaptations of no less than four being screened in the first year: 'Three O'Clock', 'The Man Upstairs', 'After-Dinner Story' and 'Post-Mortem'. Their appeal to viewers can be judged by the fact that in subsequent years other late night horror shows including* Thriller, Alfred Hitchcock Presents *and* Dark Room *have made extensive use of his work. Boris Karloff also starred in an excellent version of Woolrich's novel,* Rendezvous in Black, *made by Playhouse 90 in 1956. Admirers of the author's short stories, though, believe that the best adaptation of all was for 'The Corpse and the Kid' screened on Suspense in 1951. This tale of a young man travelling up a lonely highway with a gruesome burden over his shoulder was published in Dime Detective Magazine in September 1935 and adapted for TV by Donald S. Sandford. It was directed by Herschel Daugherty and starred Larry Pennell, Edward C. Platt, Jody Fair and Chris Seitz. Of the production itself, Woolrich's biographer, Francis M. Nevins has written, 'Despite a censorial last-minute reversal of Woolrich's ironic ending, this is one of the very best adaptations, with a superb Jerry Goldsmith score.' The story itself is also haunted by the sensations of psychological terror – and appears here complete with that original ending which American television was afraid to show . . .*

L ARRY didn't even know his father was in the house until he met him coming down the stairs. It was a little after five and he'd just come in from the beach. 'Hello Dad,' he said and held his hand out in welcome. 'You didn't tell us you were coming down from New York tonight!' Then he said: 'Gee, you look white! Been working too hard?'

Larry idolized his father and worried continually about the way he kept slaving to provide for and indulge his family. Not that they weren't comfortably well off now – but the doctor had told the elder Weeks that with that heart of his – it was only a matter of months now.

Mr Weeks didn't answer, nor did he take his son's outstretched hand. Instead he sat down suddenly in the middle of the staircase and hid his face behind his own hands. 'Don't go upstairs, kid!' he groaned hollowly. 'Keep away from there!'

Larry did just the opposite. His own face grown white in dread premonition, he leapt past his father and ran on up. He turned down the cottage's short upper hallway and threw open the door at the end of it and looked in. It was the first room he'd come to. It was the right room.

*

She lay partly across the bed with her head hanging down above the floor and her light brown hair sweeping the carpet. One arm was twisted behind her back; the other one flailed out stiff and straight, reaching desperately for the help that had never come. She was his father's wife, Larry's stepmother. The dread he had felt on the stairs became a certainty now as he looked in. He had expected something like this sooner or later.

He turned her over, lifted her up, tried to rouse her by shaking her, by working her lower jaw back and forth with his hand. It was too late. Her eyes stared at him unblinkingly, her head rolled around like a rubber ball. Her neck had been broken. There were livid purple marks on her throat where fingers had pressed inward.

Larry let her drop back again like a rag doll, left the room and closed the door behind him. He stumbled down the hall to the head of the stairs. His father was still sitting there halfway down, his head bowed low over his knees. Larry slumped down beside him. After a while he put one hand on his father's shoulder, then let it slip off again. 'I'm with you,' he said.

His father lifted his head. 'She gone?'

Larry nodded.

'I knew she must be,' his father said, 'I heard it crack.' He shuddered and covered his ears, as though he were afraid of hearing it over again.

'She asked for it and she got it,' Larry remarked bitterly.

His father looked up sharply. 'You knew?'

'All the time. He used to come down weekends and she'd meet him at the Berkeley-Carteret.'

'Why didn't you tell me?'

'She was your wife,' Larry said. 'Wouldn't I have looked great.'

On a little table down at the foot of the stairs the telephone started to ring, and they both stiffened and their pale faces grew even paler. They turned and looked at each other without a word while it went on shattering the ominous stillness of the house with its loud pealing.

'I'll get it,' Larry said suddenly. 'I know all the answers.' He got up and went down to it, while his father gazed after him fearfully. He waited a minute to brace himself, then swiftly unhooked the receiver. 'Hello,' he said tensely. Then with a quick let-down of relief, 'No, she hasn't come back from the beach yet.' He exchanged a glance with his father, halfway up the stairs. 'Why don't you pick her up there instead of calling for her here at the house? You know where to find her. She won't be back for hours yet, and you'd only have to hang around here waiting.' Then he added: 'No, I don't mean to be inhospitable, only I thought it would save time. 'Bye.' He puffed his cheeks and blew out his breath with relief as he hung up. A couple of crystal drops oozed out on his forehead. 'Helen's boyfriend,' he said, turning to the man on the stairs. Helen was his sister. 'If he does what I told him, it'll give us a couple of hours at least.'

The older man spoke without his lifting his head at all. 'What's the use? Better phone the police and get it over with.'

Larry said: 'No.' Then he yelled it at the top of his voice. 'No, I tell you! You're my father – I can't, I won't let you! She wasn't worth your life! You know what the doctors said. You haven't much time anyway – Oh, God.' He went close and jabbed his knee at Weeks to bring him to. 'Pull yourself together. We've got to get her out of here. I don't care where it happened, only it didn't happen here – it happened some place else.'

Twenty-one years of energy pulled forty-two years of apathy to its feet by the shoulders. 'You – you were in New York. You *are* in New York right now, do you get me? You didn't come down here, just as none of us expected you to.' He began to shake his father, to help the words and the idea that was behind them to sink in. 'Did anyone see you on the train, at the depot just now, or coming into the house? Anyone who knows you by sight? Think hard, try to remember, will you Dad?'

Weeks ran his hand across his forehead. 'Coming in, no,' he said. 'The street was dead, they were all down at the beach or on the boardwalk. The depot I'm not sure about, some of the redcaps might know me by sight –'

'But they only see you one day every week. They might get mixed up after a day or two in remembering just the exact day. We gotta take a chance. And make sure they see you tomorrow when you *do* come down, that'll cover today. Talk to one of them, lose something, stumble and get helped up, anything at all. Now about the train. The conductor must know you by sight –'

Weeks face brightened all of a sudden, as the idea began to catch on, take hold of him. The self-preservation instinct isn't easily suppressed. He grasped his son by the lapel of his coat. 'Larry,' he said eagerly, 'I just remembered – my commutation ticket –'

Larry's face paled again. 'And I,' he groaned, 'forgot all about that. The date'll be punched – we can't get around that –'

'No, wait a minute. Just today – something that never happened before all summer – my mind was haywire I guess on account of what I'd found out – but when I got to Penn Station I found I didn't have it with me, I'd left it at the office. I had to buy an ordinary ticket to get down here –'

'Then it's a pushover!' exclaimed Larry. 'It's a Godsend. It'd be a crime not to take advantage of a break like that. Doesn't it convince you what the best thing to do is? If I were superstitious I'd call it –' He stopped short. 'Wait a minute, round-trip I hope? Or will you have to step up and buy a return ticket at this end?'

'It's here,' panted Weeks, fumbling in his coat. 'I was burning so, I didn't even notice –' He dragged it out and they both gave a simultaneous sigh of relief. 'Swell,' said Larry. 'That unpunched commutation ticket is going to be an A-one alibi in itself. Hang onto it whatever you do. But we'll fix it all up brown. Can you get hold of someone in the city to pass the evening with you – or better still two or three of your friends?'

'I can get in touch with Fred German. He always rolls up a gang of stay-outs as he goes along.'

'Go to a show with 'em, bend the elbow, get a little lit, stay with them as late as you possibly can manage it. And before you leave them – not after but *before*, so they all can see and hear you – call me long-distance down here. That means your name'll go down on the company's records from that end. I'll have your cue ready for you by that time. If she's not dead yet, then the rotgut made you sentimental and you wanted to talk to your family, that's all. But if I have everything under control by that time, then I'll have bad news for you then and there. You can stage a cloudburst in front of them and continue under your own speed from that point on. But until that happens, watch your step. Keep the soft pedal on. Don't be jerky and nervous and punchy. Don't give 'em an idea you've got anything on your mind. The better you know people, the better they can tell when something's wrong with you. Now all that is your job. Mine' – he drew in his breath – 'is upstairs. Got your hat? ' He took out his watch. 'Get back to the station, the six o'clock pulls out in ten minutes. They're starting to drift back from the beach, so go to Charlton Street, one over, and keep your head down. Don't look at anyone. Thank God she wasn't much on getting acquainted with her neighbours –' He was leading him toward the door as he spoke.

'What're you going to do?' asked Weeks with bated voice.

'I don't know,' said Larry, 'but I don't want an audience for it, whatever it is. All I need is darkness, and thinking how swell you've been to me all my life – and I can do the rest, I'll pull through. Stand behind the door a minute till I take a squint.' He opened the door, sauntered out on the bungalow doorstep, and looked casually up in one direction, then down in the other, as though seeking a breath of air. Then suddenly he was back in again, pushing his father irresistibly before him. 'Hurry up, not a living soul in sight. It may not be this way again for the rest of the evening. They all sit on their porches after dark –'

Weeks' body suddenly stiffened, held back. 'No, I can't do it, can't let you! What am I thinking of anyway, letting my own son hold the bag for me. If they nab you doing this they'll hang it on you –'

'Do you want to die at Trenton?' Larry asked him fiercely. The answer was on Weeks' face, would have been on anyone's face. 'Then lemme do it my way!' They gripped hands for a second. Something like a sob sounded in Weeks' throat. Then he was over the threshold and Larry was pushing the door silently after him.

Just before it met the frame Weeks pivoted abruptly, jumped back, and rammed his foot into the opening. There was a new urgency in his voice. 'Helen. I see her coming! She just turned the corner!'

'Get back in!' snapped Larry. 'Can't make it now. Her eyes are too good, she'll spot you even from a distance.' He closed the door on the two of them. 'He with her?'

'No.'

'Then they missed connections. I'll send her right out again after him.' He swore viciously. 'If you're not out of here in five minutes, you don't make that train – and the later you get back the riskier it gets. As it is, you have three hours you can't account for. Here – the clothes closet – be ready to light out the first chance you get. It's just a step to the door.'

Weeks, pulling the door of the hall closet after him, murmured: 'Don't you think the kid would –'

All Larry said was: 'She was pretty chummy with Doris.'

Her key was already jiggling in the front door. Larry seemed to be coming toward it as she got it open and they met face to face. She was in her bathing suit. He'd overlooked that when he'd spoken to her boy friend. He swore again, silently this time.

'Who was that came to the door just now, before I got here?' she asked.

'Me,' he said curtly. 'Who'd you think?'

'I know, I saw you, but I thought I saw someone else too, a minute later. It looked like two people from where I was.'

'Well it wasn't,' he snapped. 'Whatta ya been drinking?'

'Oh, grouchy again.' She started for the stairs. 'Doris back yet?'

'No,' he said firmly.

'Good, then I can swipe some of her face powder while she's out.' She ran lightly up the stairs. He went cold for a minute, then he passed her like a bullet passing an arrow. He was standing in front of the door with his back to it when she turned down the upstairs corridor. 'What's the matter with *you*?' she asked drily. 'Feel playful?' She tried to elbow him aside.

'Lay off,' he said huskily. 'She raised Cain just before she went out about your helping yourself to her things, said she wants it stopped.' He got the key out of the door behind his back and dropped it into his back pocket.

'I don't believe it,' she said. 'That isn't like her at all. I'm going to ask her to her face when she comes ba—' She rattled the doorknob unsuccessfully, gave him a surprised look.

'See, what'd I tell you?' he murmured. 'She must have locked it and taken the key with her.' He moved down the hall again, as if going to his own room.

'If it was already locked,' she called after him, 'why did you jump up here in such a hurry to keep me out?'

He had an answer for that one though, too. 'I didn't want you to find out. It's hell when trouble starts between the women of a family.'

'Maybe I'm crazy,' she said, 'but I have the funniest feeling that there's something going on around here today – everything's suddenly different from what it is other days. What was the idea freezing Gordon out when he tried to call for me?'

She had stopped before her own door, which was next to their stepmother's. He was nearer the stair – well than she was, almost directly over it. From below came the faint double click of a door as it opened then shut again. Even he could hardly hear it, she certainly couldn't. The front door – he'd made it. Larry straight-armed himself against the stair railing and let a lot of air out of his lungs. He was trembling in strange places, at the wrists and in back of his knees. It was his job now. He was scared sick of it, but he was going to do it.

Without turning his head he knew she was standing there up the hall, watching him, waiting. What the hell was she waiting for? Oh, yes, she'd asked him a question, she was waiting for the answer. That was it. Absently he gave it to her. 'You weren't here, I only told him where to find you.' She went into her room and banged the door shut.

And with that sound something suddenly exploded in his brain. The connecting bathroom, between her room and Doris's! She could get in through there! Not only could but most certainly would, out of sheer stubbornness now, because she thought Doris was trying to keep her out. Women were that way. And when she did – there in full view upon the bed, what *he* had seen, what his own loyalty had been strong enough to condone, but what might prove too much for hers. He

33

couldn't take the chance. His father's life was at stake, he couldn't gamble with that. It had to be a sure thing –

He dove back to that door again and whipped the key from his pocket. He got the door open as quietly as he could, but he was in too much of a hurry and it was too close to her own room to be an altogether soundless operation. Then, when he was in, with the twisted body in full view, he saw what had covered him. She was in the bathroom already, but she had the water roaring into the washbasin and that kept her from hearing. But the door between was already open about a foot, must have been that way all afternoon. Just one look was all that was needed, just one look in without even opening it any more than it already was. She hadn't given that look yet. He could be sure of that because her scream would have told him, but any minute now, any fraction of a second . . . He could see her in the mirror. She had the straps of her bathing suit down and was rinsing her face with cold water.

There was no time to get the body out of the room altogether. He didn't dare try. That much movement, the mere lifting and carrying of it, would surely attract her attention. And the long hall outside – where could he take it? The thought of trying deftly to compose and rearrange it where it lay, into the semblance of taking a nap, came to him for a moment and was rejected too. There wasn't time enough even for that, and anyway he'd already told her she was out. All this in the two or three stealthy cat-like steps that took him from the door to the side of the bed.

As he reached it he already knew what the only possible thing to do was, for the time being. Even to get it into the clothes closet was out of the question. It meant crossing the room with it, and then clothes hangers have a way of rattling and clicking.

He dropped to his knees, crouched below the level of the bed on the side away from the bathroom, pulled the corpse toward him by one wrist and one ankle, and as it dropped off the side, his own body broke its fall. It dropped heavily athwart his thighs. The way the arms and legs retained their posture betokened rigor mortis already, but made it easier to handle if anything. From where it was, across his lap, two good shoves got it under the bed, and he left it there. It was a big enough bed to conceal it completely, unless you got down on the floor where he was.

Under and beyond the bed, on a level with his eyes, he could see the threshold of the bathroom. While he looked, and before there was any chance to scurry across the room to the hall door, Helen's feet and

34

ankles came into view. They paused there for a moment, toes pointed his way, and he quickly flattened himself out, chin on floor. She was looking in. But she couldn't see under the bed, nor beyond it to the other side where he was, without bending over. And only old maids, he thought with a dismal chuckle, look under beds the first thing when they come into a room.

He held his breath. Maybe she'd go away again, now that she'd glanced in. But she didn't. The bare ankles in house-slippers crossed the threshold into the room. They came directly over toward him, growing bigger, like in a nightmare, as they drew nearer. They stopped on the other side of the bed from him, so close that her knees must be touching it. And one slipper was an inch away from Doris's rigidly outstretched hand. Oh my God, he thought, if she looks down at the floor – or if she comes around to this side!

What did she want there by the bed, what did she see, what was she looking at? Was there blood on it? No, there couldn't be, no skin had been broken, only her neck. Had something belonging to the dead woman been left on the bed, something he'd overlooked, a ring maybe or a necklace?

The bedclothes on his side brushed his face suddenly, moved upward a little. The danger signal went all over his body like an electric shock, until he understood. Oh, that was it! In dislodging the body he'd dragged them down a little. Womanlike she was smoothing the covers out again, tugging them back in place. Her feet shifted down toward the foot a little, then back toward the head again, as she completed her task. Momentarily he expected to see one of them go in too far and come down on the dead flesh of that upturned palm. Momentarily he expected her to come around to his side. Or even see him over the top of the bed, if she leaned too far across it. He lived hours in those few seconds. But she didn't do any of those things.

The feet turned, showed him their heels, and started back across the room growing smaller again. He was too prostrated even to sigh, he just lay there with his mouth open like a fish. She didn't go out, though. The feet skipped the opening to the bathroom and stopped before Doris's dresser over to one side. Helping herself to the face powder. But now she had a mirror in front of her, damn it! And he knew what mirrors were. If, for instance, it was tilted at a slight angle, it would show her the floor behind her – better than she could see it herself. Like a periscope in reverse, it might even reveal what lay under the bed, what her own unaided eyes would never have shown her.

He heard the thud of Doris's powder-box as she put it down again. He waited for the scream that would surely come as she raised her eyes

35

to the quicksilver before her. He lay there tense, as rigid as that other form next to him even if a little warmer. He wondered why he didn't get it over with by jumping up and showing himself, saying, 'Yes, I'm here – and look what's beside me!' But he didn't. The time to do that had been when she first came in downstairs. That time was past now. There was no going back.

And then just when he'd quit hoping, there was a little shuffling sound and her feet had carried her back over the threshold and out of the room, and he was alone with the dead.

He couldn't get up for a while – even though he knew that right now was the best time, while she was busy dressing in her own room, to get out of there. He felt weak all over. When he finally did totter upright it wasn't to the outside door that he went but to the one to the bathroom.

He carefully eased it shut and locked it on his side. Let her suspect what she wanted, she wasn't going to get back in there again until the grisly evidence was out of the way! And that would have to wait until she was out of the house. He cursed her bitterly, and her pal Gordon even more so, for unknowingly adding to his troubles like this. He even cursed the dead woman for not dissolving into thin air once she were dead. He cursed everyone but the man who was by now speeding back to New York and safety; he was loyal to him to the last breath in his body. He went out into the hall and once more locked the dead woman's door behind him, once more extracted the key.

Just as he got in the clear once more, the phone started downstairs. It wasn't New York yet, too early. The train hadn't even got there yet. Helen stuck her head out of her room and called: 'If it's Gordon, tell him I'm ready to leave now, not to be so impatient!' But it wasn't Gordon. It was an older voice, asking for Doris. The masculine 'hello' Larry gave it seemed to leave it at a loss. Larry caught right on; he did some quick thinking. She'd been ready to leave an hour ago, she'd been going to this voice, and had never got there because death had stopped her in her own room. Still, an hour isn't much to a pretty woman – or to the man who's smitten with her.

Larry thought savagely, 'It was your party. You're going to pay for it!' He tried to make his voice sound boyish, cordial. 'She's gone out,' he said with a cheerful ring, 'but she left a message in case anyone called up for her. Only I don't know if you're the right party –'

'Who is this speaking?' said the voice suspiciously.

'I'm Helen's boy friend.' That ought to be all right. He must know by now that Doris had been pretty thick with Helen, that therefore any friends of the latter would be neutral, not hostile like himself.

36

The voice was still cagey though. 'How is it you're there alone?'

'I'm not. Helen's here with me, but she's upstairs dressing. Can't come to the phone, so she asked me to give the message –'

'What is it? This is the right party,' the voice bit in.

'Well, Mrs Weeks was called out this afternoon. Some people dropped in from the city and she couldn't get away from them. She said if anyone called, to say she'd gone to the Pine Tree Inn for dinner. You know where that is?' Why wouldn't he? Larry himself had seen the two of them dancing there more than once, and had promptly backed out again in a hurry each time.

But the voice wasn't committing itself. 'I think so – it's a little way out on the road to Lakewood, isn't it?'

'You can't miss it,' said Larry pointedly. 'It's got a great big sign that lights up the road.'

The voice caught on. 'Oh, then she's going to wai – Then she'll be there?'

'These people are only passing through, they're not staying. She'll be free at about nine-thirty. You see they're not bringing her back, so she thought if you wanted to pick her up with your car out there – Otherwise she'd have to phone for a taxi and wait until it got out there.'

'Yeah, I could do that,' said the voice hesitantly. 'Y'sure she said she'll be – free by nine-thirty?' Alone, was the word he wanted to use, Larry, knew.

'That's the time Helen told me to say,' he reassured. 'Oh, and I nearly forgot –' Like hell he had! It was more important than everything else put together, but it had to be dished out carefully so not to awaken suspicion. 'She said you don't have to drive right up to the place if you don't feel like it, you can sound your horn from that clump of pines down the road. You can wait there. She'll come out to you.'

He would go for that idea, Larry felt, if only to avoid getting stuck with any possible bill that she might have run up in the roadhouse. That clump of pines wasn't new to him anyway. Larry'd already seen his car berthed in it while they were inside dancing – all to get out of paying the extra fifty cents the inn charged for parking. He'd known whose it was because he'd seen them both go back to it once to smoke a cigarette out under the stars.

He heard Helen coming down the stairs, dressed at last and ready to clear out, yet he didn't dare break the connection too abruptly.

'Who you talking to?' she said in her clear, shrill voice and stopped beside him. But he'd counted on her saying something, and the mouthpiece was already buried against his shirt-front by the time she spoke. Her voice couldn't reach it.

'Sweetie of mine,' he said limply. 'Have a heart, don't listen –' His eyes stared tensely at her. While she stood there he couldn't uncover the thing and speak into it himself. One peep from her and the voice at the other end would ask to speak to her, and she wasn't in on the set-up. On the other hand he had to keep talking, couldn't just stand there like that. Cold feet can be awfully catching, even over a wire.

'All right, son,' the voice sounded into his ear. 'I'll do that. You sure you got the message straight now?'

'Looks like you've got a bad case of it,' said Helen derisively. 'Your eyes are staring out of your head. I wish you could see yourself –' But she moved away, started for the front door.

'Absolutely. Just like I told you,' he said into the instrument.

'All right, thanks a lot,' the voice came back. There was a click at the other end. He felt himself caving in at his middle.

'Give her my love,' Helen was saying from the open doorway.

'There's a fresh dame here sends you her love, honey,' he said into the dead phone. 'But she's not as pretty as you are.'

As his sister banged the front door after her, the fake grin left his face with it. He parked the phone and leaned his head weakly against the wall for a minute or two. He'd been through too much in just one hour, too much to take without leaning against something. And there was lots to come yet, he knew. Plenty.

He was alone in the house now with the body of a murdered woman. That didn't frighten him. It was getting it out of there that worried him – with a double row of porches to buck in either direction, porches jammed with the rocking-chair brigade on sentinel duty. Yet out it must go, and not cut up small in any valise either. That body had a date with its own murder. It had to travel to get there, and it had to travel whole. Though at this very minute it was already as dead as it would ever be, its murder was still several hours off and a good distance away. Nine-thirty, in a clump of trees near Pine Tree Inn, just as a starting-point. Details could come later. The important thing was to get it away from this house, where no murder had ever taken place, and have it meet up with its murderer, who didn't know that was what he was yet, and wasn't expecting to kill.

Let him worry about getting rid of it after that! Let him find out how much harder it is to shake off the embrace of dead arms than it is of living ones! Let him try to explain what he was doing with it in a lonely clump of trees at the side of the road, at that hour and that far from town – and see if he'd be believed! That is, if he had guts enough to do the only thing there was for him to do – raise a holler, report it then and there, brazen it out, let himself in for it. But he wouldn't, he was in too deep himself. He'd lose his head like a thousand others had before him. He'd leave it where it was and beat it like the very devil to save his own skin. Or else he'd take it with him and try to dump it somewhere, cover it somehow. Anything to shake himself free of it. And once he did that, woe betide him!

The eyes of the living were going to be on hand tonight, at just the wrong time for him – just when he was pulling out of that clump of trees, or just as he went flashing past the noon-bright glare in front of the inn on the road away from Asbury, to get rid of her in the dark open country somewhere beyond.

She would be reported missing the first thing in the morning, or even before – when his father phoned – Larry would see to that. Not many people had seen them dancing together and lapping their Martinis together and smoking cigarettes in a parked car together – but just enough of them had to do the damage. A waiter here, a gas-station attendant there, a bellboy somewhere else. Larry'd know just which ones to get.

He said to himself again what he'd said when he answered the man's phone-call. 'It was your party; you're gonna pay for it, not Dan. She's gonna be around your neck tonight choking you, like he choked her!'

Only a minute had gone by since Helen had banged the front door after her. Larry didn't move, he was still standing there leaning his head against the wall. She might come back, she might find out she'd forgotten something. He gave her time to get as far as the Boardwalk, two blocks over. Once she got that far she wouldn't come back any more, even if she had forgotten something. She'd be out until twelve now with Gordon. Three minutes went by – five. She'd hit the Boardwalk now.

He took his head away from the wall but he didn't move. He took out a cigarette and lit it. He had all the time in the world and he wanted that last silvery gleam of twilight out of the sky before he got going. It was a lot safer here in the house with her than out in the open under those pine trees. He smoked the cigarette down to its last inch, slowly not nervously. He'd needed that. Now he felt better, felt up to what was ahead of him. He took a tuck in his belt and moved away from the wall. Anyone who had seen him would have called him just a lazy young fellow slouching around the house on a summer evening.

He wasn't bothering with any fake alibi for himself. His father had a peach and that was all he cared about. If, through some unforeseen slip-up the thing boomeranged back to their own doorstep in spite of everything, then he'd take it on – himself. He didn't give a rap, as long as it wasn't fastened on his father. His own alibi, if worst came to worst, would be simply the truth – that he'd been in the house here the whole time. And, he told himself wisely, when you don't bother tinkering with an alibi is usually when you don't need one anyway.

He pulled down all the shades on all the windows. Then he lit just one light, so he could see on the stairs. From the street it would look like no one was home and a night-light had been left burning. Then he went upstairs and got her out from under the bed.

He was surprised at how little she weighed. The first thing he did was carry her downstairs and stretch her on the floor, over to one side of the stairs. To go out she had to leave by the ground floor anyway. Then he sat down next to her, on the lowest step of the stairs, and for a long time nothing else happened. He was thinking. The quarter hour chimed from somewhere outside. Eight-fifteen that was. He still had loads of time. But he'd better be starting soon now, the Pine Tree Inn wasn't any five minutes away from here. The thing was – how to go about it.

It was right there under his eyes the whole time, while he'd been racking his brains out. A spark from his cigarette did it – he'd lit another one. It fell down next to her, and he had to put his foot on it to make it go out. That made him notice the rug she was lying on. About eight by ten it was, a light-weight bright-coloured summer rug. He got up and beat it over to the phone directory and looked under *Carpet Cleaners*.

He called a number, then another, then another, and another. Finally he got a tumble from someone called Saroukian. 'How late do you stay open tonight?'

They closed at six, but they'd call for the article the first thing in the morning.

'Well, look,' he said, 'if I bring it over myself tonight, won't there be someone there to take it in? I'll just leave it with you tonight, and you don't need to start work on it until you're ready.'

They evidently lived right in back of, or right over, their cleaning shop. At first they tried to argue him out of it. Finally they told him he could bring it around and ring the bell, but they wouldn't be responsible for it.

'That's OK,' he said. 'I won't have time in the morning and it's gotta be attended to.' He hung up and went over to get it ready for them.

He moved her over right into the middle of it, the long way. Then he got his fountain pen out, shoved back the plunger, and wrecked the border with it until there was no more ink in the thing. It took ink beautifully, that rug. He went and got some good strong twine, and he rolled the rug around her tight as a corset and tied it at both ends, at about where her ankles were and at about where her broken neck was. It bulged a little in the middle, so he tied it there too and evened it out. When he got through it wasn't much thicker than a length of sewer pipe. Her loosened hair was still spilling out at one end though, and there was another round opening down where her feet were. He shoved the hair all back in on top of her head where it belonged, and got two small cushions off the sofa and wedged one in at each end, rammed it down with all his might. They could stand cleaning too, just like the rug. That was the beauty of a bloodless murder, you weren't afraid to leave anything at the cleaner's. He hoisted the long pillar up onto his shoulder to try it out. It wasn't too heavy, he could make it. No heavier than carrying a light-weight canoe.

He put it down again and went upstairs to the room where it had happened, and lit up and looked around for the last time. Under the bed and on top of it and all over, to make sure nothing had been overlooked. There wasn't a speck of anything. He went to her jewel case and rummaged through it. Most of the gadgets just had initials, but there was a wristwatch there that had her name in full on the inside of the case. He slipped that in his pocket. He also took a powder compact, and slipped a small snapshot of herself she'd had taken in an automatic machine under the lid, just for luck. He wanted to make it as easy for them as he could.

He put out the lights and went down. He opened the front door wide and went back in again. 'From now on,' he told himself, 'I don't think; I let my reflexes work for me!' He picked the long cylinder up with both arms, got it to the porch, and propped it upright against the side of the door for a minute while he closed the door after him. Then he heaved it up onto his right shoulder and kept it in place with one upraised arm, and that was all there was to it. It dipped a little at both ends, but any rolled-up rug would have. Cleopatra had gone to meet Caesar like this, he remembered. The present occupant was going to keep a blind date with her murderer – three or four hours after her own death.

Someone on the porch of the next cottage was strumming *Here Comes Cookie* on a ukelele as he stepped down to the sidewalk level with the body transverse to his own. He started up the street with it,

41

with his head to one side to give it room on his shoulder. He came to the first street light and its snowy glare picked him out for a minute, then handed him back to the gloom. He wasn't walking fast, just trudging along. He was doing just what he'd said he'd do: not thinking about it, letting his reflexes work for him. He wasn't nervous and he wasn't frightened, therefore he didn't look nervous and he didn't look frightened.

'This is a rug,' he kept repeating. 'I'm taking it to the cleaners. People taking rugs to the cleaners don't go along scared of their shadows.'

A rocking chair squeaked on one of the wooden platforms and a woman's nasal voice said: 'Good evening, Larry. What on earth are you doing, trying to reduce?'

He showed his teeth in the gloom. 'Gotta get this rug to the cleaners.'

'My stars, at this hour?' she queried.

'I'll catch it if I don't,' he said. 'I was filling my fountain pen just now and I got ink all over it.' He had deliberately stopped for a moment, set the thing down, shifted it to his other shoulder. He gave her another flash of his teeth. 'See you later,' he said, and was on his way again.

She gave a comfortable motherly laugh. 'Nice young fellow,' he heard her say under her breath to someone beside her. 'But that stepmother of his –' The sibilant whispers faded out behind him.

So Doris was already getting a bad name among the summer residents – good. 'Go to it!' he thought. 'You'll have more to talk about in a little while.'

Every porch was tenanted. It was like running the gauntlet. But he wasn't running, just strolling past like on any other summer evening. He saw two glowing cigarette ends coming toward him along an unlighted stretch of the sidewalk. As they passed under the next light he identified one – a girl he knew, a beach acquaintance, and her escort. He'd have to stop. He would have stopped if he only had a rug with him, so he'd have to stop now. The timing wasn't quite right though. Instead of coming up to them in one of the black stretches between lights, the three of them met face to face in one of the glaring white patches right at the foot of a street lamp.

'Hello old-timer.'

'Hello babe.' He tilted his burden forward, caught it with both arms, and eased it perpendicularly to the pavement.

'Johnny, this is Larry.' Then she said: 'What in the world have you got there?'

'Rug,' he said. 'I just got ink all over it and I thought I could get it taken out before I get bawled out.'

'Oh, they'll charge like the dickens for that,' she said helpfully. 'Lemme look, maybe I could do it for you, we've got a can of wonderful stuff over at our house.' She put out her hand toward the top opening and felt one of the wedged-in cushions.

He could feel his hair going up. 'Nah, I don't want to undo it,' he said. 'I'll never get it together again if I do.' He didn't, however, make the mistake of pushing her hand away, or immediately trying to tip the thing back on his shoulders again. He was too busy getting his windpipe open.

'What's that in the middle there?' she said, poking her hand at the cushion.

'Sofa pillows,' he said. 'They got all spotted, too.' He didn't follow the direction of her eyes in time.

'How come you didn't get it all over your hands?' she said innocently.

'I was holding the pen out in front of me,' he said, 'and it squirted all over everything.' He didn't let a twitch get past his cuff and shake the hand she was looking at, although there were plenty of them stored up waiting to go to work.

Her escort came to his aid; he didn't like it because Larry'd called her 'babe'. 'Come on, I thought you wanted to go to the movies –'

He started to pull her away.

Larry tapped his pockets with his free hand; all he felt was Doris's wristwatch. 'One of you got a cigarette?' he asked. 'I came out without mine.' The escort supplied him, also the match. Larry wanted them to break away first. They'd put him through too much, he couldn't afford to seem anxious to get rid of them.

'My, your face is just dripping!' said the girl, as the orange glare swept across it.

Larry said: 'You try toting this on a warm night and see how it feels.'

' 'Bye,' she called back, and they moved off into the shadows.

He stood there and blew a long cloud of smoke to get into gear again. 'That was the closest yet,' he thought. 'If I got away with that, I can get away with anything.'

He got back under the thing again and trudged on, cigarette in mouth. The houses began to thin out; the paved middle of the street began to turn into the road that led out toward Pine Tree Inn, shorn of its two sidewalks. But it was still a long hike off, he wasn't even halfway there yet. He was hugging the side of the roadway now, salt marshes spiked with reeds on all sides of him as far as the eye could reach. A car or two went whizzing by. He could have got rid of her easy enough along here by just dropping her into the ooze. But that wasn't the answer, that wouldn't be making him pay for his party.

There was another thing to be considered though. Those occasional cars tearing past. Their headlights soaked him each time. It had been riskier back further where the houses were, maybe, but it hadn't looked so strange to be carrying a rug there. The surroundings stood for it. It was a peculiar thing to be doing this far out. The biggest risk of all might be the safest in the end; anything was better than attracting the attention of each separate driver as he sped by. A big rumbling noise came up slowly behind him, and he turned and thumbed it with his free hand. The reflexes would look out for him, he hoped, like they had so far.

The truck slowed down and came to a stop a foot or two ahead; it only had a single driver. 'Get in,' he said facetiously. 'Going camping?' But it had been a rug back further, so it was still going to be a rug now, and not a tent or anything. Switching stories didn't pay. Only instead of going to the cleaners it would have to be coming from there now; there weren't any cottages around Pine Tree Inn.

'Nah,' Larry said. 'I gotta get this rug out to Pine Tree Inn, for the manager's office. Somebody got sick all over it and he had to send it in to be cleaned. Now he's raising hell, can't wait till tomorrow, wants it back right tonight.'

He handed it up to the driver and the man stood it upright against the double seat. Larry followed it in and sat down beside it, holding it in place with his body. It shook all over when the truck got going and that wasn't any too good for the way it was rolled up. Nor could he jump down right in front of the inn with it, in the glare of all the lights and under the eyes of the parking attendants.

'Who do you work for?' said the driver after a while.

'Saroukian, an Armenian firm.'

'What's matter, ain't they even got their own delivery truck?'

'Nah, we used to,' said Larry professionally, 'but we gave it up. Business been bad.'

The ground grew higher as they got back inland; the marshes gave way to isolated thickets and clumps of trees. The truck ate up the road. 'Got the time?' said Larry. 'I'm supposed to get it there by nine-thirty.'

'It's about nine now,' said the driver. 'Quarter to when I started.' Then he looked over at Larry across the obstacle between them. 'Who d'ya think you're kidding?' he said suddenly.

Larry froze. 'I don't get you.'

44

'You ain't delivering that nowhere. Whatever it is, it's hot. You swiped it. You're taking it somewhere to sell it.'

'How do you figure that?' said Larry, and curled his arm around it protectively.

'I wasn't born yestidday,' sneered the driver.

Larry suddenly hauled it over his way, across his own lap, and gave it a shove with his whole body that sent it hurtling out the side of the truck. It dropped by the roadside and rolled over a couple of times. He got out on the step to go after it. 'Thanks for the lift,' he said. 'I'll be leaving you here.'

'All right, bud, if that's how you feel about it,' agreed the driver. 'Hell, it's not my look-out, I wasn't going to take it away from you –' Without slowing up he reached out and gave Larry a shove that sent him flying sideways out into the night. His red tail-lights went twinkling merrily up the road and disappeared in the dark.

Larry had fortunately cleared the asphalt roadbed and landed in the soft turf alongside. None too soft at that, but nothing was broken, his palms and knees were just skinned a little. He picked himself up and went back to where the rug was. Before he bent for it he looked around. And then his swearing stopped. Even this hadn't gone wrong, had come out right, very much right. He was so close to the inn that the reflection of its lights could be seen above the treetops off to one side. And the clump of pines would be even nearer, a five-minute walk from where he was. All that driver had done was save him the necessity of getting out in front of it and giving himself away.

But now, as he stooped over his grisly burden he was horrified to see that one of the cords had parted, that a pillow had fallen to the road and that the body had slid down till the forehead and eyes showed beneath the blond hair that cascaded over the roadway. Larry looked up as a pair of approaching headlights floated around a distant corner. Hurriedly he worked the body back into position, shielding it with his own form from any curious glances that might be directed at him from the oncoming car. He had managed to get the pillow stuffed back in position and was retying the burst cord as the car whizzed by without even a pause of interest. Larry heaved a sigh of relief and shouldering the load got going again. This time he kept away from the side of the road, going deeper and deeper among the trees. It made the going tougher, but he wasn't coming up the front way if he could help it.

The glare from the roadhouse grew stronger and kept him from losing his bearings. After a while a whisper of dance music came floating to him through the trees, and he knew he was there. He edged back a little closer toward the road again, until he could see the circular clearing in the pines just ahead of him. It was just big enough to hold a single car, but there wasn't any car in it. He sank down out of sight with what he'd carried all the way out here, and got to work undoing the cords that bound it. By the time he was through, the rug and the two pillows were tightly rolled up again and shoved out of the way, and the body of the woman who had died at five that afternoon lay beside him. He just squatted there on the ground next to it, waiting. In life, he knew, Doris had never been the kind of woman who was stood up; he wondered if she would be in death.

When it felt like half the night was gone – actually only about twenty minutes had passed – a sudden flash of blinding light exploded among the trees as a car turned into the nearby clearing from the road. He was glad he hadn't gone any nearer to it than he had. As it was he had to duck his head, chin almost touching the ground, for the far-flung headlight beams to pass harmlessly above him. They missed him by only two good feet. The lights swept around in a big arc as the car half turned, then they snapped out and the engine died. He couldn't see anything for a minute, but neither could whoever was in that car. Nothing more happened after that. When his eyes readjusted themselves he knew by its outline that it was the right car. Then there was a spurt of orange as the occupant lit a cigarette, and that gave his face away. Same face Larry had seen with Doris. It was the right man, too.

Larry stayed where he was, didn't move an inch. To do so would only have made every twig and pine needle around him snap and rustle. He couldn't do anything anyway while the man stayed there at the wheel; the first move would have to come from him. True, he might get tired of waiting and light out again – but Larry didn't think he would. Not after coming all the way out here to get her. No one likes to be made a fool of, not even by a pretty woman. When she didn't show up he'd probably boil over, climb out and go up to the inn himself to see what was keeping her. It became a case of seeing which one of them would get tired waiting first. Larry knew it wasn't going to be himself.

The cushions of the roadster creaked as the man shifted his hips around. Larry could see the red dot of his cigarette through the trees, and even get a whiff of the smoke now and then. He folded his lapels close over his shirt-front and held them that way so the white wouldn't gleam out and give him away. The red dot went out. The leather creaked again. The man was getting restless now. About ten minutes had passed. The creaking became more frequent.

All of a sudden there was a loud honking blast, repeated three times.

Larry jumped and nearly passed out. He was giving her the horn, trying to attract her attention. Then the door of the car cracked open, slammed shut again, and he was standing on the ground, swearing audibly. Larry got the head of the corpse up off the ground and held it on his lap, waiting. About a minute more now.

Scuffling, crackling footsteps moved away from the car and out onto the road. He stood there looking down it toward the inn. Larry couldn't see him but the silence told him that. No sign of her coming toward him. Then the soft scrape of shoe leather came from the asphalt, moving away toward the inn. He was going up to the entrance to take a look in. Larry waited long enough to let him get out of earshot. Then he reared up, caught the body under the arms, and began to struggle toward the car with it, half carrying and half dragging it. The car was a roadster and Larry had known for a long time what he was going to do. The underbrush crackled and sang out, but the music playing at the inn would cover that.

When he got up to the car Larry let the body go for a minute and climbed up and got the rumble-seat open. It was capacious, but he had a hard time getting the stiffened form into it. He put her in feet first, and she stuck out like a jack-in-the-box. Then he climbed up after her, bent her over double, and shoved her down underneath. He dug the wristwatch with her name on it out of his pocket and tossed it in after her. Then he closed the rumble seat and she was gone.

'You're set for your last joyride, Doris,' he muttered. He would have locked the rumble, to delay discovery as long as possible, if he had had the key. He took the powder-compact with her snapshot under the lid and dropped it on the ground in back of the car. Let him deny that he'd been here with her! Then he moved off under the trees and was lost to sight.

A few minutes later he showed up at the door of the inn, as though he'd just come out from inside. The doorman was just returning to his post, as though someone had called him out to the roadway to question him. Larry saw a figure moving down the road toward the clump of pines he'd just come from. 'What was his grief?' he asked, as though he'd overheard the whole thing.

'Got stood up,' the doorman grinned. He went back inside and Larry went down to the edge of the road. The headlights suddenly flared out in the middle of the pines and an engine whined as it warmed up. A minute later the roadster came out into the open backwards, straightened itself. It stayed where it was a moment. A taxi came up to the inn and disgorged a party of six. Larry got in. 'Back to town,' he said, 'and slow up going past that car down there.'

47

The man in the roadster, as they came abreast of it, was tilting a whiskey bottle to his lips. Larry leaned out the window of the cab and called: 'Need any help? Or are you too cheap to go in and buy yourself a chaser?'

The solitary drinker stopped long enough to give Larry a four-letter word describing what he could do with himself, then resumed.

'Step on it,' Larry told the driver, 'I'm expecting a phone call.'

When he let himself into the house once more, something stopped him before he was even over the threshold. Something was wrong here. He hadn't left that many lights turned on, he'd only left one dim one burning, and now – He pulled himself together, closed the door, and went forward. Then as he turned into the living room he recoiled. He came face to face with his father, who'd just gotten up out of a chair.

Weeks looked very tired, all in, but not frightened any more. 'I took the next train back,' he said quietly. 'I'd come to my senses by the time I got there. What kind of a heel do you take me for anyway? I couldn't go through with it, let you shoulder the blame that way.'

Larry just hung his head. 'My God, and I've been through all that,' he groaned, 'for nothing!' Then he looked up quickly. 'You haven't phoned in yet, or anything – have you?'

'No. I was waiting for you to come back. I thought maybe you'd walk over to the station-house with me. I'm not much of a hero,' he admitted. Then he straightened up. 'No use arguing about it, my mind's made up. If you won't come with me, then I'll go alone.'

'I'll go with you,' said Larry bitterly. 'Might as well – I made a mess of it anyway. I see that now! It never would have held together. The whole thing came out wrong. I left the rug I carried her in, there under the trees. A dozen people saw me with it. I showed myself at the inn. I even told the taxi driver I was expecting a phone call. That alone would have damaged your alibi. How was I supposed to know you were going to call, if it wasn't a set-up? And last of all my prints are all over her powder-compact and her wristwatch. A big help I turned out to be!' He gave a crooked smile. 'Let's go. And do me a favour, kick me every step of the way getting there, will you?'

When they got to the steps of the headquarters building, they stopped and looked at each other. Larry rested his hand on his father's shoulder for a minute. 'Wait here, why don't you,' he said in a choked voice. 'I'll go in and break it for you. That'll be the easiest way.' He went in alone.

The sergeant on duty looked at him across the desk. 'Well, young feller, what's your trouble?'

'The name is Weeks,' said Larry, 'and it's about Doris Weeks, my stepmother –'

The sergeant shook his head as though he pitied him. 'Came to report her missing, is that it?' And before Larry could answer the mystifying question, 'Recognize this?' He was looking at the wrist-watch he'd dropped into the rumble seat less than an hour ago.

Larry's face froze. 'That's hers,' he managed to say.

'Yeah,' agreed the sergeant, 'the name's on it. That's the only thing we had to go by.' He dropped his eyes. 'She's pretty badly hurt, young feller,' he said unwillingly.

'She's dead!' Larry exclaimed, gripping the edge of the desk with both hands.

The sergeant seemed to mistake it for apprehension and not the statement of a known fact. 'Yeah,' he sighed, 'she is. I didn't want to tell you too suddenly, but you may as well know. Car smash-up only half an hour ago. Guy with her must have been driving stewed or without lights. Anyway a truck hit them and they turned over. He was thrown clear but he died instantly of a broken neck. She was caught under the car, and it caught fire, and – well there wasn't very much to go by after it was over except this wristwatch, which fell out on the roadway in some way –'

Larry said: 'My father's outside, I guess I'd better tell him what you told me –' and he went weaving crazily out the doorway.

'It sure must be tough,' thought the sergeant, 'to come and find out a thing like that!'

The Hollow Man

BY THOMAS BURKE

Lights Out *was another American series featuring stories of mystery and the supernatural which had begun life as a successful radio series in 1934 and then been transferred to the television medium in 1946 with four 'Specials' produced by Fred Coe. So well received were these live shows, that in July 1949 a weekly, half-hour series was put out by NBC at nine* PM *each Tuesday night with Jack LaRue as host. Viewers were left in no doubt about the contents of the show as each episode began with a close-up of a pair of eyes, followed by a bloody hand reaching out to turn off the lights. An eerie laugh would follow and a sonorous voice intoned, 'Lights out, everybody . . .'*

Some of the stories in the series were adaptations of classic short horror tales, although a number were especially commissioned. Tales about haunted houses, the dead returning, and ghastly encounters on lonely country roads were familiar themes during the three years of Lights Out. *Because of budget restrictions, few of the actors and actresses used in the early episodes were familiar names, but as the ratings shot up in 1950 an increasing number of guest stars began to be featured including Leslie Nielson, Basil Rathbone, Raymond Massey, Yvonne De Carlo, Burgess Meredith and Boris Karloff who enlivened the series' run. Among the best performances were those of Billie Burke in an adaptation of Nathaniel Hawthorne's creepy, 'Dr Heidegger's Experiment'; Helmut Dantine in a surprisingly lavish version of 'The Fall of the House of Usher' by Edgar Allan Poe; and William Bendix in the chilling story of 'The Hollow Man'. The transmissions were also enhanced by the special eerie musical effects of Arlo Hults on an organ and Doris Johnson on a harp.*

Bendix, with his large skull and heavy jaw, made a career playing either dumb and brutish, or kindly but simple characters. For years he worked on radio and then broke into television, becoming best known for his weekly series, Life of Riley. *He was ideally cast for the leading role in the* Lights Out *adaptation of 'The Hollow Man' by the English novelist, Thomas Burke (1886–1945), who had popularized the dark and mysterious reaches of London in books such as* Limehouse Nights *(1916) and* Twinkletoes *(1926), both of which had been filmed in the Twenties. Burke's stories were, in fact, to be used in a number of later horror anthology series – including* Alfred Hitchcock Presents *– but the 1950 version of 'The Hollow Man' is said to have been the most faithful and compelling to watch of them all. Although no copy of William Bendix's performance exists today, the next few pages give a very clear indication of the power of the story . . .*

HE came up one of the narrow streets which lead from the docks, and turned into a road whose farther end was gay with the light of London. At the end of this road he went deep into the lights of London, and sometimes into its shadows, farther and farther away from the river, and did not pause until he had reached a poor quarter near the centre.

He was a tall, spare figure, wearing a black mackintosh. Below this could be seen brown dungaree trousers. A peaked cap hid most of his face; the little that was exposed was white and sharp. In the autumn mist that filled the lighted streets as well as the dark he seemed a wraith, and some of those who passed him looked again, not sure whether they had indeed seen a living man. One or two of them moved their shoulders, as though shrinking from something.

His legs were long, but he walked with the short, deliberate steps of a blind man, though he was not blind. His eyes were open; and he stared straight ahead; but he seemed to see nothing and hear nothing.

Neither the mournful hooting of sirens across the black water of the river, nor the genial windows of the shops in the big streets near the centre drew his head to right or left. He walked as though he had no destination in mind, yet constantly, at this corner or that, he turned. It seemed that an unseen hand was guiding him to a given point of whose location he was himself ignorant.

He was searching for a friend of fifteen years ago, and the unseen hand, or some dog-instinct, had led him from Africa to London, and was now leading him, along the last mile of his search, to a certain little eating-house. He did not know that he was going to the eating-house of his friend Nameless, but he did know, from the time he left Africa, that he was journeying towards Nameless, and he now knew that he was very near to Nameless.

Nameless didn't know that his old friend was anywhere near *him*, though, had he observed conditions that evening, he might have wondered why he was sitting up an hour later than usual. He was seated in one of the pews of his prosperous little workmen's dining-rooms – a little gold-mine his wife's relations called it – and he was smoking and looking at nothing.

He had added up the till and written the copies of the bill of fare for next day, and there was nothing to keep him out of bed after his fifteen hours' attention to business. Had he been asked why he was sitting up later than usual, he would first have answered that he didn't know that he was, and would then have explained, in default of any other explanation, that it was for the purpose of having a last pipe. He was quite unaware that he was sitting up and keeping the door unlatched because a long-parted friend from Africa was seeking him and slowly approaching him, and needed his services.

He was quite unaware that he had left the door unlatched at that late hour – half-past eleven – to admit pain and woe.

But even as many bells sent dolefully across the night from their steeples their disagreement as to the point of half-past eleven, pain and woe were but two streets away from him. The mackintosh and dungarees and the sharp white face were coming nearer every moment.

There was silence in the house and in the streets; a heavy silence, broken, or sometimes stressed, by the occasional night-noises – motor horns, back-firing of lorries, shunting at a distant terminus. That silence seemed to envelop the house, but he did not notice it. He did not notice the bells, and he did not even notice the lagging step that approached his shop, and passed – and returned – and passed again – and halted. He was aware of nothing save that he was smoking a last pipe, and he was sitting in that state of hazy reverie which he called thinking, deaf and blind to anything not in his immediate neighbour-hood.

But when a hand was laid on the latch, and the latch was lifted, he did hear that, and he looked up. And he saw the door open, and got up and went to it. And there, just within the door, he came face to face with the thin figure of pain and woe.

To kill a fellow-creature is a frightful thing. At the time the act is committed the murderer may have sound and convincing reasons (to him) for his act. But time and reflection may bring regret; even remorse; and this may live with him for many years. Examined in wakeful hours of the night or early morning, the reasons for the act may shed their cold logic, and may cease to be reasons and become mere excuses.

And these naked excuses may strip the murderer and show him to himself as he is. They may begin to hunt his soul, and to run into every little corner of his mind and every little nerve, in search of it.

And if to kill a fellow-creature and to suffer the recurrent regret for an act of heated blood is a frightful thing, it is still more frightful to kill a fellow-creature and bury his body deep in an African jungle, and then, fifteen years later, at about midnight, to see the latch of your door lifted by the hand you had stilled and to see the man, looking much as he did fifteen years ago, walk into your home and claim your hospitality.

When the man in mackintosh and dungarees walked into the dining-rooms Nameless stood still; stared; staggered against a table; supported himself by a hand, and said 'Oh!'

The other man said 'Nameless!'

Then they looked at each other; Nameless with head thrust forward, mouth dropped, eyes wide; the visitor with a dull, glazed expression. If Nameless had not been the man he was – thick, bovine and costive – he would have flung up his arms and screamed. At that moment he felt the need of some such outlet, but did not know how to find it. The only dramatic expression he gave to the situation was to whisper instead of speak.

Twenty emotions came to life in his head and spine, and wrestled there. But they showed themselves only in his staring eyes and his whisper. His first thought, or rather, spasm, was Ghosts-Indigestion-Nervous-Breakdown. His second, when he saw that the figure was substantial and real, was Impersonation. But a slight movement on the part of the visitor dismissed that.

It was a little habitual movement which belonged only to that man; an unconscious twitching of the third finger of the left hand. He knew then that it was Gopak. Gopak, a little changed, but still, miraculously, thirty-two. Gopak, alive, breathing and real. No ghost. No phantom of the stomach. He was as certain of that as he was that fifteen years ago he had killed Gopak stone-dead and buried him.

The Blackness of the moment was lightened by Gopak. In thin, flat tones he asked, 'May I sit down? I'm tired.' He sat down, and said: 'So tired. So tired.'

Nameless still held the table. He whispered: 'Gopak . . . Gopak . . .

But I – I *killed* you. I killed you in the jungle. You were dead. I know you were.'

Gopak passed his hand across his face. He seemed about to cry. 'I know you did. I know. That's all I can remember – about this earth. You killed me.' The voice became thinner and flatter. 'And I was so comfortable. So comfortable. It was – such a rest. Such a rest as you don't know. And then they came and – disturbed me. They woke me up. And brought me back.' He sat with shoulders sagged, arms drooping, hands hanging between knees. After the first recognition he did not look at Nameless; he looked at the floor.

'Came and disturbed you?' Nameless leaned forward and whispered the words. 'Woke you up? Who?'

'The Leopard Men.'

'The what?'

'The Leopard Men.' The watery voice said it as casually as if it were saying 'the night watchman'.

'The Leopard Men?' Nameless stared, and his fat face crinkled in an effort to take in the situation of a midnight visitation from a dead man, and the dead man talking nonsense. He felt his blood moving out of its course. He looked at his own hand to see if it was his own hand. He looked at the table to see if it was his table. The hand and the table were facts, and if the dead man was a fact – and he was – his story might be a fact. It seemed anyway as sensible as the dead man's presence. He gave a heavy sigh from the stomach. 'A-ah . . . The Leopard Men . . . Yes, I heard about them out there. Tales!'

Gopak slowly wagged his head. 'Not tales. They're real. If they weren't real – I wouldn't be here. Would I? I'd be at rest.'

Nameless had to admit this. He had heard many tales 'out there' about the Leopard Men, and had dismissed them as jungle yarns. But now, it seemed, jungle yarns had become commonplace fact in a little London shop.

The watery voice went on. 'They do it. I saw them. I came back in the middle of a circle of them. They killed a nigger to put his life into me. They wanted a white man – for their farm. So they brought me back. You may not believe it. You wouldn't *want* to believe it. You wouldn't want to – see or know anything like them. And I wouldn't want any man to. But it's true. That's how I'm here.'

'But I left you absolutely dead. I made every test. It was three days before I buried you. And I buried you deep.'

'I know. But that wouldn't make any difference to them. It was a long time after when they came and brought me back. And I'm still dead, you know. It's only my body they brought back.' The voice trailed into a thread. 'And I'm so tired. So tired. I want to go back – to rest.'

Sitting in his prosperous eating-house, Nameless was in the presence of an achieved miracle, but the everyday, solid appointments of the eating-house wouldn't let him fully comprehend it. Foolishly, as he realized when he had spoken, he asked Gopak to explain what had happened. Asked a man who couldn't really be alive to explain how he came to be alive. It was like asking Nothing to explain Everything.

Constantly, as he talked, he felt his grasp on his own mind slipping. The surprise of a sudden visitor at a late hour; the shock of the arrival of a long-dead man; and the realization that this long-dead man was not a wraith, were too much for him.

During the next half-hour he found himself talking to Gopak as to the Gopak he had known seventeen years ago when they were partners. Then he would be halted by the freezing knowledge that he was talking to a dead man, and that a dead man was faintly answering him. He felt that the thing couldn't really have happened, but in the interchange of talk he kept forgetting the improbable side of it, and accepting it. With each recollection of the truth, his mind would clear and settle in one thought – 'I've got to get rid of him. How am I going to get rid of him?'

'But how did you get here?'

'I escaped.' The words came slowly and thinly, and out of the body rather than the mouth.

'How.'

'I don't – know. I don't remember anything – except our quarrel. And being at rest.'

'But why come all the way here ? Why didn't you stay on the coast?'

'I don't – know. But you're the only man I know. The only man I can remember.'

'But how did you find me?'

'I don't know. But I had to – find you. You're the only man – who can help me.'

'But how can I help you?'

The head turned weakly from side to side. 'I don't – know. But nobody else – can.'

Nameless stared through the window, looking on to the lamplit street and seeing nothing of it. The everyday being which had been his half an hour ago had been annihilated; the everyday beliefs and disbeliefs shattered and mixed together. But some shred of his old sense and his old standard remained. He must handle this situation. 'Well – what you want to do? What you going to do? I don't see how I can help you. And you can't stay here, obviously.' A demon of perversity sent a facetious notion into his head – introducing Gopak to his wife – 'This is my dead friend.'

But on his last spoken remark Gopak made the effort of raising his head and staring with the glazed eyes at Nameless. 'But I *must* stay here. There's nowhere else I can stay. I must stay here. That's why I came. You got to help me.'

'But you can't stay here. I got no room. All occupied. Nowhere for you to sleep.'

The wan voice said: 'That doesn't matter. I *don't* sleep.'

'Eh?'

'I *don't* sleep. I haven't slept since they brought me back. I can sit here – till you can think of some way of helping me.'

'But how *can* I?'

He again forgot the background of the situation, and began to get angry at the vision of a dead man sitting about the place waiting for him to think of something. 'How *can* I if you don't tell me how?'

'I don't – know. But you got to. You killed me. And I was dead – and comfortable. As it all came from you – killing me – you're responsible for me being – like this. So, you got to – help me. That's why I – came to you.'

'But what do you want me to do?'

'I don't – know. I can't – think. But nobody but you can help me. I had to come to you. Something brought me – straight to you. That means that you're the one – that can help me. Now I'm with you, something will – happen to help me. I feel it will. In time you'll – think of something.'

Nameless found his legs suddenly weak. He sat down and stared with a sick scowl at the hideous and the incomprehensible. Here was a dead man in his house – a man he had murdered in a moment of black temper – and he knew in his heart that he couldn't turn the man out. For one thing, he would have been afraid to touch him; he couldn't see himself touching him. For another, faced with the miracle of the presence of a fifteen-years-dead man, he doubted whether physical force or any material agency would be effectual in moving the man.

His soul shivered, as all men's souls shiver at the demonstration of forces outside their mental or spiritual horizon. He had murdered this man, and often, in fifteen years, he had repented the act. If the man's appalling story were true, then he had some sort of right to turn to Nameless. Nameless recognised that, and knew that whatever happened he couldn't turn him out. His hot-tempered sin had literally come home to him.

56

The wan voice broke into his nightmare. 'You go to rest, Nameless. I'll sit here. You go to rest.' He put his face down to his hands and uttered a little moan. 'Oh, why can't I rest? Why can't I go back to my beautiful rest?'

Nameless came down early next morning with a half-hope that Gopak would not be there. But he was there, seated where Nameless had left him last night. Nameless made some tea, and showed him where he might wash. He washed listlessly, and crawled back to his seat, and listlessly drank the tea which Nameless brought to him.

To his wife and the kitchen helpers Nameless mentioned him as an old friend who had had a bit of a shock. 'Ship-wrecked and knocked on the head. But quite harmless, and he won't be staying long. He's waiting for admission to a home. A good pal to me in the past, and it's the least I can do to let him stay here a few days. Suffers from sleeplessness and prefers to sit up at night. Quite harmless.'

But Gopak stayed more than a few days. He outstayed everybody. Even when the customers had gone Gopak was still there.

On the first morning of his visit when the regular customers came in at mid-day, they looked at the odd, white figure sitting vacantly in the first pew, then stared, then moved away.

All avoided the pew in which he sat. Nameless explained him to them, but his explanation did not seem to relieve the slight tension which settled on the dining-room. The atmosphere was not so brisk and chatty as usual. Even those who had their backs to the stranger seemed to be affected by his presence.

At the end of the first day Nameless, noticing this, told him that he had arranged a nice corner of the front room upstairs, where he could sit by the window and took his arm to take him upstairs. But Gopak feebly shook the hand away, and sat where he was. 'No. I don't want to go. I'll stay here. I'll stay here. I don't want to move.'

And he wouldn't move. After a few more pleadings Nameless realized with dismay that his refusal was definite; that it would be futile to press him or force him; that he was going to sit in that dining-room for ever. He was as weak as a child and as firm as a rock.

He continued to sit in that first pew, and the customers continued to avoid it, and to give queer glances at it. It seemed that they half-recognised that he was something more than a fellow who had had a shock.

During the second week of his stay three of the regular customers were missing, and more than one of those that remained made acidly facetious suggestions to Nameless that he park his lively friend somewhere else. He made things too exciting for them; all that whoopee took them off their work, and interfered with digestion. Nameless told them he would be staying only a day or so longer, but they found that this was untrue, and at the end of the second week eight of the regulars had found another place.

Each day, when the dinner-hour came, Nameless tried to get him to take a little walk, but always he refused.

He would go out only at night, and then never more than two hundred yards from the shop. For the rest, he sat in his pew, sometimes dozing in the afternoon, at other times staring at the floor. He took his food abstractedly, and never knew whether he had had food or not. He spoke only when questioned, and the burden of his talk was 'I'm so tired. So tired.'

One thing only seemed to arouse any light of interest in him; one thing only drew his eyes from the floor. That was the seventeen-year-old daughter of his host, who was known as Bubbles, and who helped with the waiting. And Bubbles seemed to be the only member of the shop and its customers who did not shrink from him.

She knew nothing of the truth about him, but she seemed to understand him, and the only response he ever gave to anything was to her childish sympathy. She sat and chatted foolish chatter to him – 'bringing him out of himself' she called it – and sometimes he would be brought out to the extent of a watery smile. He came to recognise her step and would look up before she entered the room. Once or twice in the evening, when the shop was empty, and Nameless was sitting miserably with him, he would ask, without lifting his eyes, 'Where's Bubbles?' and would be told that Bubbles had gone to the pictures or was out at a dance, and would relapse into deeper vacancy.

Nameless didn't like this. He was already visited by a curse which, in four weeks, had destroyed most of his business. Regular customers had dropped off two by two, and no new customers came to take their place. Strangers who dropped in once for a meal did not come again; they could not keep their eyes or their minds off the forbidding, white-faced figure sitting motionless in the first pew. At mid-day, when the place had been crowded and late-comers had to wait for a seat, it was now two-thirds empty; only a few of the most thick-skinned remained faithful.

And on top of this there was the interest of the dead man in his daughter, an interest which seemed to be having an unpleasant effect. Nameless hadn't noticed it, but his wife had. 'Bubbles don't seem as bright and lively as she was. You noticed it lately? She's getting quiet – and a bit slack. Sits about a lot. Paler than she used to be.'

'Her age, perhaps.'

'No. She's not one of these thin dark sort. No – it's something else. Just the last week or two I've noticed it. Off her food. Sits about doing nothing. No interest. May be nothing; just out of sorts, perhaps . . . How much longer's that horrible friend of yours going to stay?'

The horrible friend stayed some weeks longer – ten weeks in all – while Nameless watched his business drop to nothing and his daughter get pale and peevish. He knew the cause of it. There was no home in all England like his: no home that had a dead man sitting in it for ten weeks. A dead man brought, after a long time, from the grave, to sit and disturb his customers and take the vitality from his daughter. He couldn't tell this to anybody. Nobody would believe such nonsense.

But he *knew* that he was entertaining a dead man, and, knowing that a long-dead man was walking the earth, he could believe in any result of that fact. He could believe almost anything that he would have derided ten weeks ago. His customers had abandoned his shop, not because of the presence of a silent, white-faced man, but because of the presence of a dead-living man.

Their minds might not know it, but their blood knew it. And, as his business had been destroyed, so, he believed, would his daughter be destroyed. Her blood was not warming her; her blood told her only that this was a long-ago friend of her father's, and she was drawn to him.

It was at this point that Nameless, having no work to do, began to drink. And it was well that he did so. For out of the drink came an idea, and with that idea he freed himself from the curse upon him and his house.

The shop now served scarcely half a dozen customers at mid-day. It had become ill-kept and dusty, and the service and the food were bad. Nameless took no trouble to be civil to his few customers. Often, when he was notably under drink, he went to the trouble of being very rude to them. They talked about this. They talked about the decline of his business and the dustiness of the shop and the bad food. They talked about his drinking, and, of course, exaggerated it.

And they talked about the queer fellow who sat there day after day and gave everybody the creeps. A few outsiders, hearing the gossip, came to the dining-rooms to see the queer fellow and the always-tight proprietor; but they did not come again, and there were not enough of the curious to keep the place busy. It went down until it served scarcely two customers a day. And Nameless went down with it into drink.

Then, one evening, out of the drink he fished an inspiration.

He took it downstairs to Gopak, who was sitting in his usual seat, hands hanging, eyes on the floor. 'Gopak – listen. You came here because I was the only man who could help you in your trouble. You listening?'

A faint 'Yes' was his answer.

'Well, now. You told me I'd got to think of something. I've thought of something. . . . Listen. You say I'm responsible for your condition and got to get you out of it, because I killed you. I did. We had a row. You made me wild. You dared me. And what with that sun and the jungle and the insects, I wasn't myself. I killed you. The moment it was done I could a-cut me right hand off. Because you and me were pals. I could a-cut me right hand off.'

'I know. I felt that directly it was over. I knew you were suffering.'

'Ah! . . . I have suffered. And I'm suffering now. Well, this is what I've thought. All your present trouble comes from me killing you in that jungle and burying you. An idea came to me. Do you think it would help you – do you think it would put you back to rest if I – if I – if I – killed you again?'

For some seconds Gopak continued to stare at the floor. Then his shoulders moved. Then, while Nameless watched every little response to his idea, the watery voice began. 'Yes. Yes. That's it. That's what I was waiting for. That's why I came here. I can see now. That's why I had to get here. Nobody else could kill me. Only you. I've got to be killed again. Yes, I see. But nobody else – would be able – to kill me. Only the man who first killed me. . . . Yes, you've found – what we're both – waiting for. Anybody else could shoot me – stab me – hang me – but they couldn't kill me. Only you. That's why I managed to get here and find you.'

The watery voice rose to a thin strength. 'That's it. And you must do it. Do it now. You don't want to, I know. But you must. You *must*.'

His head drooped and he stared at the floor. Nameless, too, stared at the floor. He was seeing things. He had murdered a man and had escaped all punishment save that of his own mind, which had been terrible enough. But now he was going to murder him again – not in a jungle but in a city; and he saw the slow points of the result.

He saw the arrest. He saw the first hearing. He saw the trial. He saw the cell. He saw the rope. He shuddered.

Then he saw the alternative – the breakdown of his life – a ruined business, poverty, the poorhouse, a daughter robbed of her health and perhaps dying, and always the curse of the dead-living man, who might follow him to the poorhouse. Better to end it all, he thought. Rid himself of the curse which Gopak had brought upon him and his

60

family, and then rid his family of himself with a revolver. Better to follow up his idea.

He got stiffly to his feet. The hour was late evening – half-past ten – and the streets were quiet. He had pulled down the shop-blinds and locked the door. The room was lit by one light at the further end. He moved about uncertainly and looked at Gopak. 'Er – how would you – how shall I –'

Gopak said, 'You did it with a knife. Just under the heart. You must do it that way again.'

Nameless stood and looked at him for some seconds. Then, with an air of resolve, he shook himself. He walked quickly to the kitchen.

Three minutes later his wife and daughter heard a crash, as though a table had been overturned. They called but got no answer. When they came down they found him sitting in one of the pews, wiping sweat from his forehead. He was white and shaking, and appeared to be recovering from a faint.

'Whatever's the matter? You all right?'

He waved them away. 'Yes, I'm all right. Touch of giddiness. Smoking too much, I think.'

'Mmmm. Or drinking. . . . Where's your friend? Out for a walk?'

'No. He's gone off. Said he wouldn't impose any longer, and had to go and find an infirmary.' He spoke weakly and found trouble in picking words. 'Didn't you hear that bang – when he shut the door?'

'I thought that was you fell down.'

'No. It was him when he went. I couldn't stop him.'

'Mmmm. Just as well, I think.' She looked about her.

'Things seem to a-gone wrong since he's been here.'

There was a general air of dustiness about the place. The table-cloths were dirty, not from use but from disuse. The windows were dim. A long knife, very dusty, was lying on the table under the window. In a corner by the door leading to the kitchen, unseen by her, lay a dusty mackintosh and dungaree, which appeared to have been tossed there. But it was over by the main door, near the first pew, that the dust was thickest – a long trail of it – greyish-white dust.

'Really this place gets more and more slapdash. Why can't you attend to business? You didn't use to be like this. No wonder it's gone down, letting the place get into this state. Why don't you pull yourself together. Just look at that dust by the door. Looks as though somebody's been spilling ashes all over the place.'

Nameless looked at it, and his hands shook a little. But he answered, more firmly than before: 'Yes, I know. I'll have a proper clean-up to-morrow. I'll put it all to rights tomorrow. I been getting a bit slack.'

For the first time in ten weeks he smiled at them; a thin, haggard smile, but a smile.

What Price Murder?

BY STEVE FISHER

Murder and psychological terror were the main ingredients of Danger, *CBS's half hour weekly excursion into late night horror in the early Fifties – also screened on Tuesday evenings, but not starting transmission until ten* PM. *Broadcast live from New York from the autumn of 1950 until May 1955, the show has become more famous in TV history for some of the directors and stars it launched rather than the undoubted quality of the episodes it broadcast. Yul Brynner, for instance, who began his career in television, was the first director of the series, to be followed by Sidney Lumet and later John Frankenheimer. On the other side of the camera, careers were just beginning for Charlton Heston, Paul Newman, Grace Kelly, Walter Matthau, Rod Steiger, Carroll Baker, Anthony Quinn, Jack Lemon, Nina Foch, John Cassavetes and the young James Dean. The episodes in which this galaxy-of-talent-to-be featured were all narrated by the host, Richard Stark.*

Many of the stories for Danger *were specially commissioned, with titles featuring the words 'Murder' and 'Death' being almost mandatory. A regular contributor was Steve Fisher (1912–) a prolific writer of hardboiled pulp fiction in the Thirties for magazines like* Black Mask, *who then turned to scriptwriting for television and films. He wrote several novels including* Satan's Angel *(1935) and* I Wake Up Screaming *(1941), the latter of which was filmed twice: first in 1941 with Betty Grable and Victor Mature, and then in 1953 with Jeanne Crain and Elliott Reid. Fisher's best work, though, was undoubtedly for the small screen – a fact underlined by the five Emmy Award nominations he has received. Occasionally, he drew on some of his old pulp fiction stories as the basis for his contributions to* Danger, *including the next item, 'What Price Murder?' (Detective Tales, September 1936) which was telecast in December 1953 with Anthony Quinn and Kim Stanley in the leading roles.*

AS Joe shuffled into the dark alley he could feel the gravel scraping beneath the paper soles of his shoes. His suit was clean, but it was frayed and threadbare, and he was afraid it would go to pieces. He was at a low ebb, but a bitter smile twisted his pale face, and there was a strange glow in his dark eyes. After a year of going straight, he was tackling his first crooked job. But he'd be able to eat now. And with money, be able to see Judith.

He jammed his hands in his pockets, the faint notes of a song whistled from his lips. Swank cafés backed on the alley, and from the front of them he could hear music playing. Crooners bleating out their love songs. He could see in his mind's eye, the dancing couples, the white-clad waiters. Soon he'd be in one of those places with Judith.

Fire crackers snapped from somewhere near. Rockets shot into the sky and burst, all red, yellow, and green. Joe could not help but feel happy. He'd been sprung from the Big House a year ago. For twelve months he'd tried to go straight, tried to get ahead enough money so he could call Judith and tell her he was back in town. She had never known about his trip to Sing Sing – thought he was in Europe. Whenever he had been with her he had been well heeled. She wouldn't, he imagined, have anything to do with a guy who didn't have the sugar. Month after month he had gone crazy thinking about that. And now, just for pulling a little job – two hundred and fifty dollars. Enough to rent a tux, hire taxis. . . . What'd it matter if it was a step backward toward the old life he'd renounced? Two hours with Judith was worth eternity!

Fourth of July . . . A snub-nosed automatic lying in his coat pocket. A short job. He turned suddenly and entered a back door. He said something to the Chink just inside. In a moment he was ushered into Moreland's office.

He didn't like the way Moreland was looking at him. Of course, that conversation on the phone had given the crime boss no indication of Joe's appearance. He had a right to be surprised, but he didn't have to stare like that. Moreland with his shiny bald head and his dark burning eyes. Joe watched him rub his hawkish nose.

'Well, you ain't lookin' so good, Joey.'

'I've been on the shelf for a year,' Joe said. 'But I'm willing to work now.'

Moreland smirked, waved his hand in dismissal of the Chink who had brought Joe in. He turned in his swivel chair and drew a box of cigars close to him. He did not offer Joe one, but stuck a stogie in his own mouth, bit off the end, then lit up.

'You ain't going to work for me, Joe. I've heard about how you've been livin'. Sleepin' on park benches, and singin' for your doughnuts down at the mission. I don't want any heels like that around here!'

Joe's face burned, and he became cold. 'If you don't want me – why'd you call?'

Moreland puffed at the cigar, took it out of his mouth and looked at it. There was a queer glint in his hard eyes. 'Oh, I've got one job for you if you want it. You see, I gotta get it done cheap.'

'I've been damned straight for a year,' Joe said suddenly. 'If –'

Moreland waved his hand. 'Don't worry. This ain't hard, and you don't have to actually do anything crooked. You're a punk that ain't got guts enough to do anything hard.'

Joe's lips were tight. 'You didn't used to talk to me like that. You thought I was pretty good once. I've seen you crawl, Moreland. Now can the big shot chatter and get down to business.'

Moreland drummed his fingers on the desk. 'We're having a little trouble with a certain alderman,' he said slowly. 'We want to scare him.'

'Sure you mean *scare*?'

'Sure.' His eyes flickered. 'You stand across the street, see? In front of a rooming house, the door of which is open. You watch the alderman's house, and when he comes out, you plug a shot at him.' Moreland sucked in his breath. 'Of course you miss a mile, and –'

Joe watched the big crook for a moment, saw the crafty expression in his face. Then fury seized him. Because he knew from past experiences that Moreland was a double-crossing rat, he knew now what the set-up was. Plug a shot at the city official – run out through the back of a rooming house! Sure! And Moreland would have the cops waiting for him in the alley. Joe's shot would miss, all right. But someone else would fire, and they wouldn't miss. Joe would be the goat. It was as plain as day. Moreland must have taken him for an awful damn fool!

He moved forward, conscious now that he was sweating, and that his eyes were burning hot in their sockets. His fingers worked in and out.

65

'Moreland,' he snarled, 'You're nothing but a rotten, yellow-bellied punk. You're trying to use me as a fall guy. You know damn well they'll nab me and I'll burn for the job!'

'But I said to miss him!'

Joe laughed gratingly. 'Sure. I miss. But somebody else hits. I'm the only guy they see shoot. What the hell kind of a rube do you take me for?'

Moreland turned a little pale. He put his cigar on the edge of the desk and got up. 'If you don't want the job –'

'Want it?' Joe growled. 'You said you had something easy for me! I ought to beat the living daylights out of you, you two-timing punk!'

A gun appeared into the bald man's hand, his finger tight on the trigger. 'If we don't do business,' he said coolly, 'the interview is finished.'

Joe stared into Moreland's livid eyes, and saw the treachery that was in them. God, how they try and heel over when you're down! They sneer and hold their filthy blood money over your head as if they know you'll do anything to get it. He hated them. He had vowed he was through being a thug. He had only come back to accept a job so he could be with Judith . . . Well, the hell with it. He wouldn't see her.

He turned and went slowly to the door. He could feel Moreland's eyes following him. Suddenly Moreland spoke.

'By the way, Joe,' he said sneeringly, 'ever think of that ex-flame of yours?'

Joe stiffened, his body was like ice, yet he dripped with sweat. When he answered, his tongue felt like wood.

'Not much, why?'

Moreland held his gun steady. His eyes were mocking. 'Oh, I just wondered. Thought you might be interested in knowing that her father died – sort of suddenly. An accident, they say. I'm her guardian now.'

Joe's life blood seemed to run out of him. He stared at Moreland dumbly. Stammered:

'You – you mean Judith Lawrence?'

'Yes . . . That's her. Thought you'd remember.'

Joe thought that he must be hearing wrong. He was stunned. He could not move from the spot on which he was standing. Judith – her father dead – Moreland her guardian. He stared at the cool, smirking bald-headed man, and then rage seized him.

'You haven't any right to –'

Moreland yawned, looked at his wristwatch. 'That's all I have to say, Joe. Don't slam the door, will you?'

Don't slam the door! Joe moved toward Moreland. The gun didn't matter, somehow. Nothing mattered. Moreland robbing Judith of what money she had left. When he got through with her she'd end up on a boat headed for South America. Joe knew all about Moreland's little games. But a kid like Judith . . . A haze of purple rage swam before his eyes.

He charged forward. Moreland fired, but the bullet missed by inches. Joe's hand dove to his pocket, and the snubnosed automatic came out popping yellow flames.

Moreland grasped his side. Joe stood watching him, transfixed. He saw the crook's legs buckle beneath him, and he saw the hot blood sticky on his fingers.

For a moment he didn't know what to do. He just stood there. He could hear the confusion in the front of the club. The body guards, waiters, and customers breaking their necks to get back here. Then his eyes fell upon Moreland's safe. It was open a crack, and he could see green bills stacked inside. Money! Money meant only one thing to Joe – Judith.

He turned, started for the window that opened onto the alley. He shoved it open. Then for a fraction of a second he wavered. It was blood money. Moreland had gotten it crookedly. If Joe could use just enough of it – enough to see Judith before the cops got him for this killing.

The door was crashing open when he dove back at the safe, swung open the little vault and scooped up handfuls of the green bills. In the next instant he was out the alley window. He heard a clatter of feet, the shouts of men behind him. A revolver crashed.

Joe ran down the alley. He could still hear the fire crackers, see the rockets all green and red and yellow. The music of the swank clubs droned into his ears. He kept running, breathless, desperate. From somewhere a siren screamed. Shots blazed through the darkness after him.

Time was precious. He couldn't evade the law long. The Chink had seen him enter the club, others would know that Moreland had had an appointment with him. They'd get him, all right. But he must first have his evening with Judith.

He sat now, adjusting the bow tie. A French tailor walked in circles gesturing approval with his hands. Joe was cleanly shaven, he'd had a bath. Top to bottom, he was spic and span, decked out in white vest, tails, and top hat.

At last he got to his feet, paid the tailor with a handfull of bills, and left the shop. A taxi swerved to the curb at sight of him, and Joe climbed into it.

'Wellinglex Hotel,' he said grandly.

He sat back then, lighting a gold-tipped cigarette. He glanced at a watch strapped about his wrist. It still shone with the jeweller's polish. Joe, the little crook who had tried the straight and narrow, was coming back for a glimpse of Heaven. A killer in coat and tails – the ragged clothes of yesterday heaped in an ash can.

He climbed out of the cab, gave the driver a bill, tipped the doorman, and entered through the revolving doors. He walked to the desk.

'Came in town for the theatre,' he said, 'and I'm staying over. I want the best suite in the house.'

'Yes sir,' the clerk snapped.

Joe's eyes were gleaming, his ruddy face was flushed hot with anticipation. Before long now, he would be talking to Judith. After that, well, he closed his eyes, because he didn't like to think about it.

The elevator took him speedily to the twenty-third floor where he followed a uniformed bell boy down to his suite. Joe tipped him.

When the door closed, he turned and went to the phone. He was cold now, and his hands were trembling. There was an eternity of waiting – then a low feminine voice came on the wire. Something akin to an electric shock ran through Joe. His body was tingling.

'This Judith?'

'Yes. Who is this?'

'Joe. You remember me, don't you?'

'Joe!' she cried. 'Joe, where are you? Is this really you?'

Tears welled into his eyes. Hot, burning tears that seared down his face. Her voice was so tender, and so full of alarm, surprise and happiness. He assured her that it was he, that he had just arrived in town, back from Europe. Could he have a date? Certainly? That was fine! Yes, he'd missed her all right. Would it be good to see her? He hoped to shout it would! In an hour then, he could pick her up? He hung up the receiver. Judith – her own lovely voice! She still loved him! He could tell that by the way she had spoken.

He paced the floor nervously, smoking one cigarette after another. At last he settled down. Faced the grim business to which he would sooner or later have to resign himself. He was tired of being down and out – a bum. He didn't want the life of a fugitive hunted for murder. There was no use trying to evade the cops, they'd catch him sooner or later. He wanted only to see Judith – after that, well it didn't matter a hell of a lot, and he might as well make a clean breast of it!

He went to the window and stared out. He kept smoking, thinking. At last he made up his mind. He would turn himself over! He'd better call now, though. If he didn't he might not have guts enough to do it later – after he saw Judith. He didn't want to back down the last minute; he wanted to be a man about it. He went doggedly to the phone, his face white.

His hand trembled as he touched the receiver. He lifted it, put it to his ear. His voice was husky.

'Police department . . .' He waited. Then: 'Thirty-first? I want Detective Harry Ryan. Yeah, Ryan of the homicide.'

Again he waited. It was Ryan who had gathered the evidence against him to send him up the first time. Ryan to whom he had been reporting for twelve months while on parole. Ryan who had kept smiling and patting him on the back and telling him to *keep* going straight, that he wouldn't be sorry.

'Ryan speaking.'

'Hello,' Joe said, 'I guess you know who this is speaking.' He chuckled hoarsely. 'Looking for a killer, Ryan?'

'I sure am, Joe,' the detective said in a low voice.

'Listen, then, and take my word for it. I'd rather see you get credit for the capture. In two and a half hours show up at the club Ritz – not before, see, or you'll gum up the works. I'm on the level with you Ryan. In two and a half hours. What about it?'

'Sure, if –'

'Don't come sooner, will you? If you do – well, you'll spoil everything.'

Ryan's voice lowered. 'I get you, Joe. I'll be there.'

'Okay,' Joe said, and hung up.

His face was covered with sweat now, and he sponged it away with a silk handkerchief. He picked up his top hat and put it on his head. He straightened his jacket, then left the room.

Judith's hair was in a beautiful cluster about her face. A golden cluster, it was, and it gave illumination to her wide blue eyes, her delicate nose, and the thin crimson lines of her lips.

'Aw gee,' she sighed, 'it's wonderful to be with you again, Joe!'

Joe was lost. He was glad that he had called the cops first, telling them to take him away after it was over, because if he hadn't, he never would have had the guts to do it after seeing Judith, being with her. The music was playing softly. Balloons floated above the dancing couples. Gay coloured confetti littered the floor. It was Fourth of July, happiness, joy – and perhaps love.

Joe looked at the girl he loved. 'It doesn't seem that we've been together for almost two hours, does it?'

She shook her head, and laughed. 'I should say it doesn't. And I want it to go on forever.'

Joe frowned, looked at his watch. 'I'm sorry to tell you this Judy, believe me, I am. It has to end.'

Her face sobered, her blue eyes were levelled on him, a curious, hurt expression flushed in her face.

'What do you mean?'

'Well, there are things you don't understand, I have to go back to Europe.'

'Joe,' she said, 'let's not fool each other. You were a crook in the old days. I found found that out, and it was awfully hard for me to believe. You got out of jail a year ago. Since then you've been honest. And during that I've realized that I love you. That I'd love you no matter what you were!'

He stared at her, groped for his cocktail glass, gulped down some of the liquid. The music was playing, couples dancing, and soon his time would be up. She knew. How?

'My guardian told me about you,' she said, as if she had read his thoughts. 'He calls himself my guardian. Father died in an accident, and it was discovered that this man – a Mr Moreland – was named in father's will. It is all very technical. A lawyer explained it once. But that doesn't matter. If I could have found you, Joe, I would have come to you. No matter how poor you were, nothing in the world could have stopped me!'

'Wait a minute,' he said hoarsely. He leaned across the table. 'You mean that – even though I was broke, a bum – you would love me, as long as I was on the level. Wasn't a crook?'

'Of course,' she breathed softly. 'It isn't money, darling, it's you.'

Joe drew back in his chair. It was hot now, and he had begun sweating again. What a fool he had been! If only he had known that earlier. Could have known before he let his finger squeeze the trigger of the gun. He twisted his fingers around the cocktail glass and broke it. His lips were drawn back.

'Joe,' Judith said, 'what's the matter?'

'Nothing – nothing at all.' He said, and his face was grey. 'I was just thinking about how ironic life can be sometimes. They say a square shooter gets the breaks.' He stared at her steadily for a moment, then his eyes dropped. His fingers were trembling when he lit the cigarette that he put in his mouth. He puffed, glanced at his watch.

Judith put out her cigarette. The waiter came over and she ordered some more drinks. There would never be time to finish them, Joe thought. He would have to go. Ryan would be waiting.

'Mr Moreland was in a little trouble this evening,' Judith said.

Joe stiffened.

'Someone shot him,' she went on. 'But it was just a crease along his ribs, and he said he'd be all right. He is going to meet me here tonight.'

Joe's tongue stuck to the roof of his mouth. 'He's going to – meet you – *here?*'

'Yes, he wanted to know where I was going, and I told him.'

Joe gulped, dropped his cigarette into his drink. 'You didn't tell him with whom you were going?'

'Sure, I did. He was not very surprised. He said he thought you were going to get in touch with me, and that he'll be glad to see you.'

'Yeah,' Joe said. 'Yeah, he will be.'

At that moment he saw three tall, tuxedo-garbed men stride in through the foyer. Two others followed shortly behind them. A minute passed, and another two entered. Seven men. The foremost one was Moreland. His shiny bald head was gleaming, his face was like a clay mask – a mask of grim hatred.

Joe felt the snub-nosed automatic in his back pocket. His shaking fingers snaked back for it.

Joe saw one of the men head down the side of the room to where the main light switch was. He could visualize how simple the murder – his murder – would be. Lights out. Shots. When the lights went on again the seven men would be sitting at tables, and a waiter, tipped off in twenties, would be carting the smoking guns out to the garbage heap.

'Joe,' Judith said, 'what's the matter,'

Moreland was weaving in and out through the tables. His lieutenants were on his heels.

'Joe,' Judith said, 'what's the matter, you look as if you've seen a ghost.'

'I have,' Joe said steadily. 'Don't turn around, but when I get out of my chair, duck under the table. Hear me? Duck, for God's sake, Judy – and don't ask any questions. Just do as I tell you.'

There was a hard, brittleness in his tone that defied her to disobey. She nodded, her blue eyes filled with fear.

'*Now!*' Joe snapped. Judith obeyed. People turned and stared at her.

Joe had acted first – beat them to the draw, because he had seen a familiar figure cross the foyer. Ryan of the Homicide! Three burly dicks were with him.

'Ryan!' Joe shrieked, '*here*'

At that moment a gun roared at him. The lights went out. Screams echoed throughout the room. Tables were overturned. Joe sent a hell-bent bullet straight in the direction Moreland had been coming. He followed it with another shot.

One of the dicks had sprinted to the lights and in the next moment they were back on. Joe saw Moreland crumpling, a black, blood-filled hole in his forehead. Joe saw, also, a gunman drawing a bead on him.

Quickly, Joe fired. The gunman clutched his heart, sank to the floor. Three of the others were running toward the exit. Ryan stopped them. The other dicks were slapping handcuffs on the remaining two.

The action had taken place in less than two minutes. The orchestra began playing again. Waiters were shouting that everything was under control.

Joe helped Judith to her feet. She was shaking, and crying. 'Joe, are you all right? Are you hurt?'

'No, but he is.' He thumbed toward Moreland.

She stared down for only a moment. Her breath was sucked in huskily.

'I – I'm glad,' she whispered. 'I was afraid of him – terribly afraid . . . '

Joe was aware of a firm hand grasping his shoulder. He looked up into Detective Harry Ryan's tanned, smiling face.

'You're looking good, Joe. Hope you keep that way. Thanks for the tip on Moreland. He was laying low on a murder charge, all right. We had just collected the evidence having to do with the so-called accidental death of a financeer named Lawrence. Moreland bumped him.'

Judith was staring. Ryan evidently did not know Lawrence was her father.

'So when I got your tip,' the detective went on, 'I took your word for it and showed up in two hours . . . '

Joe could scarcely speak. 'I meant – that to be me. I thought I was the killer. Thought I had killed Moreland!'

Ryan laughed. 'Well, you have. And thanks for it. You saved the state some electric current and a board bill in the death house for three months!'

The music caught on in a fast tune. The balloons were still floating lazily over head. Outside, Fourth of July rockets were zooming skyward.

Judith looked up at Joe. 'I – I'm going to need a guardian,' she said, 'I wouldn't be safe alone, do you think?'

Joe turned and looked at her. 'I should say you wouldn't.' He gripped her hand and started pulling her toward the door.

'Hey,' she cried, 'where we going?'

'To Harrison,' Joe said, 'they give out marriage certificates fast up there, and we've even enough of your guardian's money for cocktails afterward!'

The Crystal Egg

BY H. G. WELLS

Tales of Tomorrow *which ran on ABC TV in America from 1951 to 1953 has been described as 'one of television's earliest adult Science Fiction series', a slight misnomer because it also featured some excellent horror and mystery episodes. Among enthusiasts of the anthology, two episodes are legendary: 'The Dark Angel' in which Meg Mundy starred as an eternally young woman; and 'Frankenstein' in which Lon Chaney Jnr. appeared as the creature wearing horrific make-up designed by Vincent Kehoe. It was as well that the series occupied a nine-thirty* PM *to ten* PM *slot on Friday evenings! The producers, Mort Abrahams and George Foley Jnr., mixed classic and modern tales of strange and supernatural happenings – and among typical episodes were 'The Monsters', 'The Flying Saucer' and a bold two-part version of Jules Verne's* 20,000 Leagues Under the Sea. *Top actors appeared in the series, too, Franchot Tone, Veronica Lake, Boris Karloff, Eva Gabor, Leslie Neilson and Lee J. Cobb to name just a few. Such, indeed, was the popularity of* Tales of Tomorrow, *that for a time during 1953 a radio version was also being broadcast to American audiences.*

A top fantasy offering from Tales of Tomorrow *was 'The Crystal Egg' by H.G. Wells (1866–1946), who apart from his work as the 'Founding Father' of SF, also wrote horror and supernatural stories such as 'The Cone', a gruesome tale of revenge, and the amusing 'Story of the Inexperienced Ghost'. The thirty-minute adaptation of 'The Crystal Egg' was transmitted in October 1951 and starred Franchot Tone as Mr Cave the mild-mannered little antiquarian shopkeeper who possesses a most unusual and coveted item . . .*

THERE was, until a year ago, a little and very grimy-looking shop near Seven Dials, over which, in weatherworn yellow lettering, the name of 'C. Cave, Naturalist and Dealer in Antiquities', was inscribed. The contents of its window were curiously varied. They comprised some elephant tusks and an imperfect set of chessmen, beads and weapons, a box of eyes, two skulls of tigers and one human, several moth-eaten stuffed monkeys (one holding a lamp), an old-fashioned cabinet, a fly-blown ostrich egg or so, some fishing-tackle, and an extraordinarily dirty, empty glass fish-tank. There was also, at the moment the story begins, a mass of crystal, worked into the shape of an egg and brilliantly polished. And at that two people, who stood outside the window, were looking, one of them a tall, thin clergyman, the other a black-bearded young man of dusky complexion and unobtrusive costume. The dusky young man spoke with eager gesticulation, and seemed anxious for his companion to purchase the article.

While they were there, Mr Cave came into his shop, his beard still wagging with the bread and butter of his tea. When he saw these men and the object of their regard, his countenance fell. He glanced guiltily over his shoulder, and softly shut the door. He was a little old man, with pale face and peculiar watery blue eyes; his hair was a dirty grey, and he wore a shabby blue frock-coat, an ancient silk hat, and carpet slippers very much down at heel. He remained watching the two men as they talked. The clergyman went deep into his trouser pocket, examined a handful of money, and showed his teeth in an agreeable smile. Mr Cave seemed still more depressed when they came into the shop.

The clergyman, without any ceremony, asked the price of the crystal egg. Mr Cave danced glanced nervously towards the door leading into the parlour, and said five pounds. The clergyman protested that the price was high, to his companion as well as to Mr Cave – it was, indeed, very much more than Mr Cave had intended to ask, when he had stocked the article – and an attempt at bargaining ensued. Mr Cave stepped to the shop door, and held it open. 'Five pounds is my price,' he said, as though he wished to save himself the trouble of unprofitable discussion. As he did so, the upper portion of a woman's face appeared above the blind in the glass upper-panel of the door leading into the parlour, and stared curiously at the two customers. 'Five pounds is my price,' said Mr Cave, with a quiver in his voice.

The swarthy young man had so far remained a spectator, watching Cave keenly. Now he spoke. 'Give him five pounds,' he said. The clergyman glanced at him to see if he were in earnest, and, when he looked at Mr Cave again, he saw that the latter's face was white. 'It's a lot of money,' said the clergyman, and, diving into his pocket, began counting his resources. He had little more than thirty shillings, and he appealed to his companion, with whom he seemed to be on terms of considerable intimacy. This gave Mr Cave an opportunity of collecting his thoughts, and he began to explain in an agitated manner that the crystal was not, as a matter of fact, entirely free for sale. His two customers were naturally surprised at this, and inquired why he had not thought of that before he began to bargain. Mr Cave became confused, but he stuck to his story, that the crystal was not in the market that afternoon, that a probable purchaser of it had already appeared. The two, treating this as an attempt to raise the price still further, made as if they would leave the shop. But at this point the parlour door opened, and the owner of the dark fringe and the little eyes appeared.

She was a coarse-featured, corpulent woman, younger and very much larger than Mr Cave; she walked heavily, and her face was flushed. 'That crystal *is* for sale,' she said. 'And five pounds is a good enough price for it. I can't think what you're about, Cave, not to take the gentleman's offer!'

Mr Cave, greatly perturbed by the irruption, looked angrily at her over the rims of his spectacles, and, without excessive assurance, asserted his right to manage his business in his own way. An altercation began. The two customers watched the scene with interest and some amusement, occasionally assisting Mrs Cave with suggestions. Mr Cave, had driven, persisted in a confused and impossible story of an inquiry for the crystal that morning, and his agitation became painful. But he stuck to his point with extraordinary persistence. It was the young Oriental who ended this curious controversy. He proposed that they should call again in the course of two days – so as to give the alleged inquirer a fair chance. 'And then we must insist,' said the clergyman. 'Five pounds.' Mrs Cave took it on herself to apologize for her husband, explaining that he was sometimes 'a little odd,' and as the two customers left, the couple prepared for a free discussion of the incident in all its bearings.

Mrs Cave talked to her husband with singular directness. The poor little man, quivering with emotion, muddled himself between his stories, maintaining on the one hand that he had another customer in view, and on the other asserting that the crystal was honestly worth ten guineas. 'Why did you ask five pounds?' said his wife. '*Do* let me manage my business my own way!' said Mr Cave.

Mr Cave had living with him a step-daughter and a step-son, and at supper that night the transaction was rediscussed. None of them had a high opinion of Mr Cave's business methods, and this action seemed a culminating folly.

'It's my opinion he's refused that crystal before,' said the step-son, a loose-limbed lout of eighteen.

'But *Five Pounds*!' said the step-daughter, an argumentative young woman of six-and-twenty.

Mr Cave's answers were wretched; he could only mumble weak assertions that he knew his own business best. They drove him from his half-eaten supper into the shop to close it for the night, his ears aflame and tears of vexation behind his spectacles. 'Why had he left the crystal in the window so long? The folly of it!' That was the trouble closest in his mind. For a time he could see no way of evading sale.

After supper his step-daughter and step-son smartened themselves up and went out and his wife retired upstairs to reflect upon the business aspects of the crystal, over a little sugar and lemon and so forth in hot water. Mr Cave went into the shop, and stayed there until late, ostensibly to make ornamental rockeries for goldfish cases but really for a private purpose that will be better explained later. The next day Mrs Cave found that the crystal had been removed from the window, and was lying behind some second-hand books on angling. She replaced it in a conspicuous position. But she did not argue further about it, as a nervous headache disinclined her from debate. Mr Cave was always disinclined. The day passed disagreeably. Mr Cave was, if anything, more absent-minded than usual, and uncommonly irritable withal. In the afternoon, when his wife was taking her customary sleep, he removed the crystal from the window again.

The next day Mr Cave had to deliver a consignment of dog-fish at one of the hospital schools, where they were needed for dissection. In his absence Mrs Cave's mind reverted to the topic of the crystal, and the methods of expenditure suitable to a windfall of five pounds. She had already devised some very agreeable expedients, among others a dress of green silk for herself and a trip to Richmond, when a jangling of the front door bell summoned her into the shop. The customer was an examination coach who came to complain of the non-delivery of certain frogs asked for the previous day. Mrs Cave did not approve of this particular branch of Mr Cave's business, and the gentleman, who had called in a somewhat aggressive mood, retired after a brief exchange of words – entirely civil so far as he was concerned. Mrs Cave's eye then naturally turned to the window; for the sight of the crystal was an assurance of the five pounds and of her dreams. What was her surprise to find it gone!

She went to the place behind the locker on the counter, where she had discovered it the day before. It was not there; and she immediately began an eager search about the shop.

When Mr Cave returned from his business with the dog-fish, about a quarter to two in the afternoon, he found the shop in some confusion, and his wife, extremely exasperated and on her knees behind the counter, routing among his taxidermic material. Her face came up hot and angry over the counter, as the jangling bell announced his return, and she forthwith accused him of 'hiding it'.

'Hid *what*?' asked Mr Cave.

'The crystal!'

At that Mr Cave, apparently much surprised, rushed to the window. 'Isn't it here?' he said. 'Great Heavens! what has become of it?'

Just then, Mr Cave's step-son reentered the shop from the inner room – he had come home a minute or so before Mr Cave – and he was blaspheming freely. He was apprenticed to a second-hand furniture dealer down the road, but he had his meals at home, and he was naturally annoyed to find no dinner ready.

But, when he heard of the loss of the crystal, he forgot his meal, and his anger was diverted from his mother to his step-father. Their first idea, of course, was that he had hidden it. But Mr Cave stoutly denied all knowledge of its fate – freely offering his bedabbled affidavit in the matter – and at last was worked up to the point of accusing, first, his wife and then his step-son of having taken it with a view to a private sale. So began an exceedingly acrimonious and emotional discussion, which ended for Mrs Cave in a peculiar nervous condition midway between hysterics and amuck, and caused the step-son to be half-an-hour late at the furniture establishment in the afternoon. Mr Cave took refuge from his wife's emotions in the shop.

In the evening the matter was resumed, with less passion and in a judicial spirit, under the presidency of the step-daughter. The supper passed unhappily and culminated in a painful scene. Mr Cave gave way at last to extreme exasperation, and went out banging the front door violently. The rest of the family, having discussed him with the freedom his absence warranted, hunted the house from garret to cellar, hoping to light upon the crystal.

The next day the two customers called again. They were received by Mrs Cave almost in tears. It transpired that no one *could* imagine all that she had stood from Cave at various times in her married pilgrimage. . . . She also gave a garbled account of the disappearance. The clergyman and the Oriental laughed silently at one another, and said it was very extraordinary. As Mrs Cave seemed disposed to give them the complete history of her life they made to leave the shop. Thereupon Mrs Cave, still clinging to hope, asked for the clergyman's address, so that, if she could get anything out of Cave, she might communicate it. The address was duly given, but apparently was afterwards mislaid. Mrs Cave can remember nothing about it.

In the evening of that day, the Caves seem to have exhausted their emotions, and Mr Cave, who had been out in the afternoon, supped in a gloomy isolation that contrasted pleasantly with the impassioned controversy of the previous days. For some time matters were very badly strained in the Cave household, but neither crystal nor customer reappeared.

Now, without mincing the matter, we must admit that Mr Cave was a liar. He new knew perfectly well where the crystal was. It was in the rooms of Mr Jacoby Wace, Assistant Demonstrator at St Catherine's, Westbourne Hospital, Westbourne Street. It stood on the sideboard partially covered by a black velvet cloth, and beside a decanter of American whisky. It is from Mr Wace, indeed, that the particulars upon which this narrative is based were derived. Cave had taken off the thing to the hospital hidden in the dog-fish sack, and there had pressed the young investigator to keep it for him. Mr Wace was a little dubious at first. His relationship to Cave was peculiar. He had a taste for singular characters, and he had more than once invited the old man to smoke and drink in his rooms, and to unfold his rather amusing views of life in general and of his wife in particular. Mr Wace had encountered Mrs Cave, too, on occasions when Mr Cave was not at home to attend to him. He knew the constant interference to which Cave was subjected, and having weighed the story judicially, he decided to give the crystal a refuge. Mr Cave promised to explain the reasons for his remarkable affection for the crystal more fully on a later occasion, but he spoke distinctly of seeing visions therein. He called on Mr Wace the same evening.

He told a complicated story. The crystal he said had come into his possession with other oddments at the forced sale of another curiosity dealer's effects, and not knowing what its value might be, he had ticketed it at ten shillings. It had hung upon his hands at that price for some months, and he was thinking of 'reducing the figure', when he made a singular discovery.

At that time his health was very bad – and it must be borne in mind that, throughout all this experience, his physical condition was one of ebb – and he was in considerable distress by reason of the negligence, the positive ill-treatment even, he received from his wife and step-children. His wife was vain, extravagant, unfeeling, and had a growing taste for private drinking; his step-daughter was mean and over-reaching; and his step-son had conceived a violent dislike for him, and lost no chance of showing it. The requirements of his business pressed heavily upon him, and Mr Wace does not think that he was altogether free from occasional intemperance. He had begun life in a comfortable position, he was a man of fair education, and he suffered, for weeks at a stretch, from melancholia and insomnia. Afraid to disturb his family, he would slip quietly from his wife's side, when his thoughts became intolerable, and wander about the house. And about three o'clock one morning, late in August, chance directed him into the shop.

The dirty little place was impenetrably black except in one spot, where he perceived an unusual glow of light. Approaching this, he discovered it to be the crystal egg, which was standing on the corner of the counter towards the window. A thin ray smote through a crack in the shutters, impinged upon the object, and seemed as it were to fill its entire interior.

It occurred to Mr Cave that this was not in accordance with the laws of optics as he had known them in his younger days. He could understand the rays being refracted by the crystal and coming to a focus in its interior, but this diffusion jarred with his physical conceptions. He approached the crystal nearly, peering into it and round it, with a transient revival of the scientific curiosity that in his youth had determined his choice of a calling. He was surprised to find the light not steady, but writhing within the substance of the egg, as though that object was a hollow sphere of some luminous vapour. In moving about to get different points of view, he suddenly found that he had come between it and the ray, and that the crystal none the less remained luminous. Greatly astonished, he lifted it out of the light ray and carried it to the darkest part of the shop. It remained bright for some four or five minutes, when it slowly faded and went out. He placed it in the thin streak of daylight, and its luminousness was almost immediately restored.

So far, at least, Mr Wace was able to verify the remarkable story of Mr Cave. He has himself repeatedly held this crystal in a ray of light (which had to be of a less diameter than one millimetre). And in a perfect darkness, such as could be produced by velvet wrapping, the crystal did undoubtedly appear very faintly phosphorescent. It would seem, however, that the luminousness was of some exceptional sort, and not equally visible to all eyes; for Mr Harbinger – whose name will be familiar to the scientific reader in connection with the Pasteur Institute – was quite unable to see any light whatever. And Mr Wace's own capacity for its appreciation was out of comparison inferior to that of Mr Cave's. Even with Mr Cave the power varied very considerably: his vision was most vivid during states of extreme weakness and fatigue.

Now from the outset this light in the crystal exercised an irresistible fascination upon Mr Cave. And it says more for his loneliness of soul than a volume of pathetic writing could do, that he told no human being of his curious observations. He seems to have been living in such an atmosphere of petty spite that to admit the existence of a pleasure would have been to risk the loss of it. He found that as the dawn advanced, and the amount of diffused light increased, the crystal became to all appearance non-luminous. And for some time he was unable to see anything in it, except at night-time, in dark corners of the shop.

But the use of an old velvet cloth, which he used as a background for a collection of minerals, occurred to him, and by doubling this, and putting it over his head and hands, he was able to get a sight of the luminous movement within the crystal even in the day-time. He was very cautious lest he should be thus discovered by his wife, and he practised this occupation only in the afternoons, while she was asleep upstairs, and then circumspectly in a hollow under the counter. And one day, turning the crystal about in his hands, he saw something. It came and went like a flash, but it gave him the impression that the object had for a moment opened to him the view of a wide and spacious and strange country, and turning it about, he did, just as the light faded, see the same vision again.

Now, it would be tedious and unnecessary to state all the phases of Mr Cave's discovery from this point. Suffice that the effect was this: the crystal, being peered into at an angle of about 137 degrees from the direction of the illuminating ray, gave a clear and consistent picture of a wide and peculiar country-side. It was not dream-like at all; it produced a definite impression of reality, and the better the light the more real and solid it seemed. It was a moving picture: that is to say, certain objects moved in it, but slowly in an orderly manner like real things, and according as the direction of the lighting and vision changed, the picture changed also. It must, indeed, have been like looking through an oval glass at a view, and turning the glass about to get at different aspects.

Mr Cave's statements, Mr Wace assures me, were extremely circumstantial, and entirely free from any of that emotional quality that taints hallucinatory impressions. But it must be remembered that all the efforts of Mr Wace to see any similar clarity in the faint opalescence of the crystal were wholly unsuccessful, try as he would.

The difference in intensity of the impressions received by the two men was very great, and it is quite conceivable that what was a view to Mr Cave was a mere blurred nebulosity to Mr Wace.

The view as Mr Cave described it, was invariably of an extensive plain, and he seemed always to be looking at it from a considerable height, as if from a tower or a mast. To the east and to the west the plain was bounded at a remote distance by vast reddish cliffs, which reminded him of those he had seen in some picture; but what the picture was Mr Wace was unable to ascertain. These cliffs passed north and south – he could tell the points of the compass by the stars that were visible of a night – receding in an almost illimitable perspective and fading into the mists of the distance before they met. He was nearer the eastern set of cliffs, on the occasion of his first vision the sun was rising over them, and black against the sunlight and pale against their shadow appeared a multitude of soaring forms that Mr Cave regarded as birds. A vast range of buildings spread below him; he seemed to be looking down upon them; and, as they approached the blurred and refracted edge of the picture, they became indistinct. There were also trees curious in shape, and in colouring, a deep mossy green and an exquisite grey, beside a wide and shining canal. And something great and brilliantly coloured flew across the picture. But the first time Mr Cave saw these pictures he saw only in flashes, his hands shook, his head moved, the vision came and went, and grew foggy and indistinct. And at first he had the greatest difficulty in finding the picture again once the direction of it was lost.

His next clear vision, which came about a week after the first, the interval having yielded nothing but tantalizing glimpses and some useful experience, showed him the view down the length of the valley. The view was different, but he had a curious persuasion, which his subsequent observations abundantly confirmed, that he was regarding this strange world from exactly the same spot, although he was looking in a different direction. The long façade of the great building, whose roof he had looked down upon before, was now receding in perspective. He recognized the roof. In the front of the façade was a terrace of massive proportions and extraordinary length, and down the middle of the terrace, at certain intervals, stood huge but very graceful masts, bearing small shiny objects which reflected the setting sun. The import of these small objects did not occur to Mr Cave until some time after, as he was describing the scene to Mr Wace. The terrace overhung a thicket of the most luxuriant and graceful vegetation, and beyond this was a wide grassy lawn on which certain broad creatures, in form like beetles but enormously larger, reposed.

Beyond this again was a richly decorated causeway of pinkish stone; and beyond that, and lined with dense *red* weeds, and passing up the valley exactly parallel with the distant cliffs, was a broad and mirror-like expanse of water. The air seemed full of squadrons of great birds, manoeuvring in stately curves; and across the river was a multitude of splendid buildings, richly coloured and glittering with metallic tracery and facets, among a forest of moss-like and lichenous trees. And suddenly something flapped repeatedly across the vision, like the fluttering of a jewelled fan or the beating of a wing, and a face, or rather the upper part of a face with very large eyes, came as it were close to his own and as if on the other side of the crystal. Mr Cave was so startled and so impressed by the absolute reality of these eyes, that he drew his head back from the crystal to look behind it. He had become so absorbed in watching that he was quite surprised to find himself in the cool darkness of his little shop, with its familiar odour of methyl mustiness, and decay. And, as he blinked about him, the glowing crystal faded, and went out.

Such were the first general impressions of Mr Cave. The story is curiously direct and circumstantial. From the outset, when the valley first flashed momentarily on his senses, his imagination was strangely affected, and, as he began to appreciate the details of the scenes he saw, his wonder rose to the point of a passion. He went about his business listless and distraught, thinking only of the time when he should be able to return to his watching. And then a few weeks after his first sight of the valley came the two customers, the stress and excitement of their offer, and the narrow escape of the crystal from sale, as I have already told.

Now while the thing was Mr Cave's secret, it remained a mere wonder, a thing to creep to covertly and peep at, as a child might peep upon a forbidden garden. But Mr Wace has, for a young scientific investigator, a particularly lucid and consecutive habit of mind. Directly the crystal and its story came to him, and he had satisfied himself, by seeing the phosphorescence with his own eyes, that there really was a certain evidence for Mr Cave's statements, he proceeded to develop the matter systematically. Mr Cave was only too eager to come and feast his eyes on this wonderland he saw, and he came every night from half-past eight until half-past ten, and sometimes, in Mr Wace's absence, during the day. On Sunday afternoons, also, he came. From the outset, Mr Wace made copious notes, and it was due to his scientific method that the relation between the direction from which the initiating ray entered the crystal and the orientation of the picture was proved. And, by covering the crystal in a box perforated only with a small aperture to admit the exciting ray, and by substituting black holland for his buff blinds, he greatly improved the conditions of the observations; so that in a little while they were able to survey the valley in any direction they desired.

So having cleared the way, we may give a brief account of this visionary world within the crystal. The things were in all cases seen by Mr Cave, and the method of working was invariably for him to watch the crystal and report what he saw, while Mr Wace (who as a science student had learnt the trick of writing in the dark) wrote a brief note of his report. When the crystal faded, it was put into its box in the proper position and the electric light turned on. Mr Wace asked questions, and suggested observations to clear up difficult points. Nothing, indeed, could have been less visionary and more matter-of-fact.

The attention of Mr Cave had been speedily directed to the bird-like creatures he had seen so abundantly present in each of his earlier visions. His first impression was soon corrected, and he considered for a time that they might represent a diurnal species of bat. Then he thought, grotesquely enough, that they might be cherubs. Their heads were round, and curiously human, and it was the eyes of one of them that had so startled him on his second observation. They had broad, silvery wings not feathered, but glistening almost as brilliantly as new-killed fish and with the same subtle play of colour, and these wings were not built on the plan of bird wing or bat, Mr Wace learned, but supported by curved ribs radiating from the body. (A sort of butterfly wing with curved ribs seems best to express their appearance.) The body was small, but fitted with two bunches of prehensile organs, like long tentacles, immediately under the mouth. Incredible as it appeared to Mr Wace, the persuasion at last became irresistible, that it was these creatures which owned the great quasi-human buildings and the magnificent garden that made the broad valley so splendid. And Mr Cave perceived that the buildings, with other peculiarities, no doors, but that the great circular windows, which opened freely, gave the creatures egress and entrance. They would alight upon their tentacles, fold their wings to a smallness almost rod-like, and hop into the interior. But among them was a multitude of smaller-winged creatures, like great dragonflies and moths and flying beetles, and across the greensward brilliantly coloured gigantic ground beetles crawled lazily to and fro. Moreover, on the causeways and terraces, large-headed creatures similar to the greater winged flies, but wingless, were visible, hopping busily upon their hand-like tangle of tentacles.

Allusion has already been made to the glittering objects upon masts

84

that stood upon the terrace of the nearer building. It dawned upon Mr Cave, after regarding one of these masts very fixedly on one particular vivid day, that the glittering object there was a crystal exactly like that into which he peered. And a still more careful scrutiny convinced him that each one in a vista of nearly twenty carried a similar object.

Occasionally one of the larger flying creatures would flutter up to one, and, folding its wings and coiling a number of its tentacles about the mast, would regard the crystal fixedly for a space – sometimes as long as fifteen minutes. And a series of observations, made at the suggestions of Mr Wace, convinced both watchers that, so far as this visionary world was concerned, the crystal into which they peered actually stood at the summit of the end-most mast on the terrace, and that on one occasion at least one of these inhabitants of this other world had looked into Mr Cave's face while he was making these observations.

So much for the essential facts of this very singular story. Unless we dismiss it all as the ingenious fabrication of Mr Wace, we have to believe one of two things: either that Mr Cave's crystal was in two worlds at once, and that, while it was carried about in one, it remained stationary in the other, which seems altogether absurd; or else that it had some peculiar relation of sympathy with another and exactly similar crystal in this other world, so that what was seen in the interior of the one in this world was, under suitable conditions, visible to an observer in the corresponding crystal in the other world; and *vice versa*. At present, indeed, we do not know of any way in which two crystals could so come *en rapport*, but nowadays we know enough to understand that the thing is not altogether impossible. This view of the crystals as *en rapport* was the supposition that occurred to Mr Wace, and to me at least it seems extremely plausible. . . .

And where was this other world? On this, also, the alert intelligence of Mr Wace speedily threw light. After sunset, the sky darkened rapidly – there was a very brief twilight interval indeed – and the stars shone out. They were recognizably the same as those we see, arranged in the same constellations. Mr Cave recognized the Bear, the Pleiades, Aldebaran, and Sirius: so that the other world must be somewhere in the solar system, and, at the utmost, only a few hundreds of millions of miles from our own. Following up this clue, Mr Wace learned that the midnight sky was a darker blue even than our midwinter sky, and that the sun seemed a little smaller. *And there were two small moons!* 'like our moon but smaller, and quite differently marked,' one of which moved so rapidly that its motion was clearly visible as one regarded it. These moons were never high in the sky, but vanished as they rose:

that is, every time they revolved they were eclipsed because they were so near their primary planet. And all this answers quite completely, although Mr Cave did not know it, to what must be the condition of things on Mars.

Indeed, it seems an exceedingly plausible conclusion that peering into this crystal Mr Cave did actually see the planet Mars and its inhabitants. And, if that be the case, then the evening star that shone so brilliantly in the sky of that distant vision was neither more nor less than our own familiar earth.

For a time the Martians – if they were Martians – do not seem to have known of Mr Cave's inspection. Once or twice one would come to peer, and go away very shortly to some other mast, as though the vision was unsatisfactory. During this time Mr Cave was able to watch the proceedings of these winged people without being disturbed by their attentions, and, although his report is necessarily vague and fragmentary, it is nevertheless very suggestive. Imagine the impression of humanity a Martian observer would get who, after a difficult process of preparation and with considerable fatigue to the eyes, was able to peer at London from the steeple of St Martin's Church for stretches, at longest, of four minutes at a time. Mr Cave was unable to ascertain if the winged Martians were the same as the Martians who hopped about the causeways and terraces, and if the latter could put on wings at will. He several times saw certain clumsy bipeds, dimly suggestive of apes, white and partially translucent, feeding among certain of the lichenous trees, and once some of these fled before one of the hopping, round-headed Martians. The latter caught one in its tentacles, and then the picture faded suddenly and left Mr Cave most tantalizingly in the dark. On another occasion a vast thing, that Mr Cave thought at first was some gigantic insect, appeared advancing along the causeway beside the canal with extraordinary rapidity. As this drew nearer Mr Cave perceived that it was a mechanism of shining metals and of extraordinary complexity. And then, when he looked again, it had passed out of sight.

After a time Mr Wace aspired to attract the attention of the Martians, and the next time that the strange eyes of one of them appeared close to the crystal Mr Cave cried out and sprang away, and they immediately turned on the light and began to gesticulate in a manner suggestive of signalling. But when at last Mr Cave examined the crystal again the Martian had departed.

Thus far these observations had progressed in early November, and then Mr Cave, feeling that the suspicions of his family about the crystal were allayed, began to take it to and fro with him in order that, as occasion arose in the daytime or night, he might comfort himself with what was fast becoming the most real thing in his existence.

In December Mr Wace's work in connection with a forthcoming examination became heavy, the sittings were reluctantly suspended for a week, and for ten or eleven days – he is not quite sure which – he saw nothing of Cave. He then grew anxious to resume these investigations, and, the stress of his seasonal labours being abated, he went down to Seven Dials. At the corner he noticed a shutter before a bird fancier's window, and then another at a cobbler's. Mr Cave's shop was closed.

He rapped and the door was opened by the step-son in black. He at once called Mrs Cave, who was, Mr Wace could not but observe, in cheap but ample widow's weeds of the most imposing pattern. Without any very great surprise Mr Wace learnt that Cave was dead and already buried. She was in tears, and her voice was a little thick. She had just returned from Highgate. Her mind seemed occupied with her own prospects and the honourable details of the obsequies, but Mr Wace was at last able to learn the particulars of Cave's death. He had been found dead in his shop in the early morning, the day after his last visit to Mr Wace, and the crystal had been clasped in his stone-cold hands. His face was smiling, said Mrs Cave, and the velvet cloth from the minerals lay on the floor at his feet. He must have been dead five or six hours when he was found.

This came as a great shock to Wace, and he began to reproach himself bitterly for having neglected the plain symptoms of the old man's ill-health. But his chief thought was of the crystal. He approached that topic in a gingerly manner, because he knew Mrs Cave's peculiarities. He was dumbfounded to learn that it was sold.

Mrs Cave's first impulse, directly Cave's body had been taken upstairs, had been to write to the mad clergyman who had offered five pounds for the crystal, informing him of its recovery; but after a violent hunt in which her daughter joined her, they were convinced of the loss of his address. As they were without the means required to mourn and bury Cave in the elaborate style the dignity of an old Seven Dials inhabitant demands, they had appealed to a friendly fellow-tradesman in Great Portland Street. He had very kindly taken over a portion of the stock at a valuation. The valuation was his own and the crystal egg was included in one of the lots. Mr Wace, after a few suitable consolatory observations, a little off-handedly proffered perhaps, hurried at once to Great Portland Street. But there he learned that the crystal egg had already been sold to a tall, dark man in grey. And there the material facts in this curious, and to me at least very suggestive, story come abruptly to an end. The Great Portland Street dealer did not know who the tall dark man in grey was, nor had he observed him with sufficient attention to describe him minutely. He did not even know which way this person had gone after leaving the shop. For a time Mr Wace remained in the shop, trying the dealer's patience with hopeless questions, venting his own exasperation. And at last, realizing abruptly that the whole thing had passed out of his hands, had vanished like a vision of the night, he returned to his own rooms, a little astonished to find the notes he had made still tangible and visible upon his untidy table.

His annoyance and disappointment were naturally very great. He made a second call (equally ineffectual) upon the Great Portland Street dealer, and he resorted to advertisements in such periodicals as were likely to come into the hands of a bric-à-brac collector. He also wrote letters to *The Daily Chronicle* and *Nature*, but both those periodicals, suspecting a hoax, asked him to reconsider his action before they printed, and he was advised that such a strange story, unfortunately so bare of supporting evidence, might imperil his reputation as an investigator. Moreover, the calls of his proper work were urgent. So that after a month or so, save for an occasional reminder to certain dealers, he had reluctantly to abandon the quest of the crystal egg, and from that day to this it remains undiscovered. Occasionally, however, he tells me, and I can quite believe him, he has bursts of zeal in which he abandons his more urgent occupation and resumes the search.

Whether or not it will remain lost for ever, with the material and origin of it, are things equally speculative at the present time. If the present purchaser is a collector, one would have expected the inquiries of Mr Wace to have reached him through the dealers. He has been able to discover Mr Cave's clergyman and 'Oriental' – no other than the Rev. James Parker and the young Prince of Bosso-Kuni in Java. I am obliged to them for certain particulars. The object of the Prince was simply curiosity – and extravagance. He was so eager to buy, because Cave was so oddly reluctant to sell. It is just as possible that the buyer in the second instance was simply a casual purchaser and not a collector at all, and the crystal egg, for all I know, may at the present moment be within a mile of me, decorating a drawing-room or serving as a paper-weight – its remarkable functions all unknown. Indeed, it is partly with the idea of such a possibility that I have thrown this narrative into a form that will give it a chance of being read by the ordinary consumer of fiction.

My own ideas in the matter are practically identical with those of Mr Wace. I believe the crystal on the mast in Mars and the crystal egg of Mr Cave's to be in some physical, but at present quite inexplicable, way *en rapport*, and we both believe further that the terrestrial crystal must have been – possibly at some remote date – sent hither from that planet, in order to give the Martians a near view of our affairs. Possibly fellows to the crystals in the other masts are also on our globe. No theory of hallucination suffices for the facts.

Back for Christmas

BY JOHN COLLIER

There was probably no series that did more to establish the tradition of late night horror on television than Alfred Hitchcock Presents *which the maestro of menace introduced on CBS in the autumn of 1955. Unlike its predecessors, the series was pre-filmed for transmission and consequently achieved a high level of technical and acting quality as well as being able to overcome the problems that so often beset live TV. The stories invariably had a twist in the tail and as the villains quite frequently came out on top, the ethical code of the time demanded that Hitchcock sign off with an epilogue emphasizing their moral misdemeanours. The series in fact continued with phenomenal success until 1961, when it was switched to NBC and, retitled* The Alfred Hitchcock Hour, *ran for another ninety-three episodes, finally ending in 1964. Twenty years later, in 1985, NBC re-launched the programme in colour, remaking a number of the earlier stories and adding some new material. Hitchcock himself was dead by that time – he had passed away in 1980 – but computor-coloured versions of his original monologues were used to preface each story. As Leslie Halliwell commented, 'It was a macabre joke that Hitchcock would have appreciated!' The unmistakeable theme tune, Gounod's Funeral March of a Marionette, was also retained the second time around. Though it is true that Hitch himself directed very few of the episodes in the series, he nonetheless made an important contribution to them all – and the development of series of this kind in general – by stamping his own distinct personality and penchant for the gruesome upon each and every one. Among episodes that are especially remembered in this context are 'Voodoo' about the pickling of heads; 'Arthur' about a chicken farmer who turns his unfaithful wife into bird feed; and 'Man from the South' in which Peter Lorre gambled with the youthful Steve McQueen for . . . the fingers of his right hand.*

With quality in the writing of paramount importance, short stories by a number of the leading writers in the horror and mystery genre were adapted for Alfred Hitchcock Presents *– men such as John Keir Cross, Cornell Woolrich, Roald Dahl, John Wyndham, Ray Bradbury and Robert Bloch, all of whom were to provide material for other later horror anthology series. Perhaps not altogether surprisingly, Hitchcock liked work by English writers, and one author he used more than most was John Collier (1901–1980) who had been born in England but moved to Hollywood as a scriptwriter where he made his name working on* I Am a Camera *and* The African Queen. *But Collier was also a writer of exquisite short tales of the macabre – as well as a classic novel,* His Monkey Wife *(1930) – and a lot of his stories have been rightly compared to the best of Saki. Among Collier's contributions to* Alfred Hitchcock Presents, *'Back For Christmas' enjoys a special place of pre-eminence as being one of the handful of episodes actually directed by Hitch himself. The adaptation of the story was by Francis Cockrell and starred John Williams, Isobel Elsom and Gavin Muir. Interestingly, the story was used again on TV in 1980 in* Tales of the Unexpected *when Richard Johnson played the man whose seemingly perfect plan to murder his wife (Sian Phillips) proves to have just one flaw . . .*

'DOCTOR,' said Major Sinclair, 'we certainly must have you with us for Christmas.' Tea was being poured, and the Carpenters' living-room was filled with friends who had come to say last-minute farewells to the Doctor and his wife.

'He shall be back,' said Mrs Carpenter. 'I promise you.'

'It's hardly certain,' said Dr Carpenter. 'I'd like nothing better, of course.'

'After all,' said Mr Hewitt, 'you've contracted to lecture only for three months.'

'Anything may happen,' said Dr Carpenter.

'Whatever happens,' said Mrs Carpenter, beaming at them, 'he shall be back in England for Christmas. You may all believe me.'

They all believed her. The Doctor himself almost believed her. For ten years she had been promising him for dinner parties, garden parties, committees, heaven knows what, and the promises had always been kept.

The farewells began. There was a fluting of compliments on dear

Hermione's marvellous arrangements. She and her husband would drive to Southampton that evening. They would embark the following day. No trains, no bustle, no last-minute worries. Certain the Doctor was marvellously looked after. He would be a great success in America. Especially with Hermione to see to everything. She would have a wonderful time, too. She would see the skyscrapers. Nothing like that in Little Godwearing. But she must be very sure to bring him back. 'Yes, I will bring him back. You may rely upon it.' He mustn't be persuaded. No extensions. No wonderful post at some super-American hospital. Our infirmary needs him. And he must be back by Christmas. 'Yes,' Mrs Carpenter called to the last departing guest, 'I shall see to it. He shall be back by Christmas.'

The final arrangements for closing the house were very well managed. The maids soon had the tea things washed up; they came in, said goodbye, and were in time to catch the afternoon bus to Devizes.

Nothing remained but odds and ends, locking doors, seeing that everything was tidy. 'Go upstairs,' said Hermione, 'and change into your brown tweeds. Empty the pockets of that suit before you put it in your bag. I'll see to everything else. All you have to do is not to get in the way.'

The Doctor went upstairs and took off the suit he was wearing, but instead of the brown tweeds, he put on an old, dirty bath gown, which he took from the back of his wardrobe. Then, after making one or two little arrangements, he leaned over the head of the stairs and called to his wife, 'Hermione! Have you a moment to spare?'

'Of course, dear. I'm just finished.'

'Just come up here for a moment. There's something rather extraordinary up here.'

Hermione immediately came up. 'Good heavens, my dear man!' she said when she saw her husband. 'What are you lounging about in that filthy old thing for? I told you to have it burned long ago.'

'Who in the world,' said the Doctor, 'has dropped a gold chain down the bathtub drain?'

'Nobody has, of course,' said Hermione. 'Nobody wears such a thing.'

'Then what is it doing there?' said the Doctor. 'Take this flashlight. If you lean right over, you can see it shining, deep down.'

'Some Woolworth's bangle off one of the maids,' said Hermione. 'It can be nothing else.' However, she took the flashlight and leaned over, squinting into the drain. The Doctor, raising a short length of lead pipe, struck two or three times with great force and precision, and tilting the body by the knees, tumbled it into the tub.

He then slipped off the bathrobe and, standing completely naked, unwrapped a towel full of implements and put them into the washbasin. He spread several sheets of newspaper on the floor and turned once more to his victim.

She was dead, of course – horribly doubled up, like a somersaulter, at one end of the tub. He stood looking at her for a very long time, thinking of absolutely nothing at all. Then he saw how much blood there was and his mind began to move again.

First he pushed and pulled until she lay straight in the bath, then he removed her clothing. In a narrow bathtub this was an extremely clumsy business, but he managed it at last and then turned on the taps. The water rushed into the tub, then dwindled, then died away, and the last of it gurgled down the drain.

'Good God!' he said. 'She turned it off at the main.'

There was only one thing to do: the Doctor hastily wiped his hands on a towel, opened the bathroom door with a clean corner of the towel, threw it back onto the bath stool, and ran downstairs, barefoot, light as a cat. The cellar door was in a corner of the entrance hall, under the stairs. He knew just where the cut-off was. He had reason to: he had been pottering about down there for some time past – trying to scrape out a bin for wine, he had told Hermione. He pushed open the cellar door, went down the steep steps, and just before the closing door plunged the cellar into pitch darkness, he put his hand on the tap and turned it on. Then he felt his way back along the grimy wall till he came to the steps. He was about to ascend them when the bell rang.

The Doctor was scarcely aware of the ringing as a sound. It was like a spike of iron pushed slowly up through his stomach. It went on until it reached his brain. Then something broke. He threw himself down in the coal dust on the floor and said, 'I'm through. I'm through!'

'They've got no *right* to come,' he said. Then he heard himself panting. 'None of this,' he said to himself. 'None of this.'

He began to revive. He got to his feet, and when the bell rang again the sound passed through him almost painlessly. 'Let them go away,' he said. Then he heard the front door open. He said, 'I don't care.' His shoulder came up, like that of a boxer, to shield his face. 'I give up,' he said.

He heard people calling. 'Herbert!' 'Hermione!' It was the Wallingfords. 'Damn them! They come butting in. People anxious to get off. All naked! And blood and coal dust! I'm done! I'm through! I can't do it.'

'Herbert!'

'Hermione!'

'Where the dickens can they be?'

'The car's there.'

'Maybe they've popped round to Mrs Liddell's.'

'We must see them.'

'Or to the shops, maybe. Something at the last minute.'

'Not Hermione. I say, listen! Isn't that someone having a bath? Shall I shout? What about whanging on the door?'

'Sh-h-h! Don't. It might not be tactful.'

'No harm in a shout.'

'Look, dear. Let's come in on our way back. Hermione said they wouldn't be leaving before seven. They're dining on the way, in Salisbury.'

'Think so? All right. Only I want a last drink with old Herbert. He'd be hurt.'

'Let's hurry. We can be back by half-past six.'

The Doctor heard them walk out and the front door close quietly behind them. He thought, 'Half-past six. I can do it.'

He crossed the hall, sprang the latch of the front door, went upstairs, and taking his instruments from the washbasin, finished what he had to do. He came down again, clad in his bath gown, carrying parcel after parcel of towelling or newspaper neatly secured with safety pins. These he packed carefully into the narrow, deep hole he had made in the corner of the cellar, shovelled in the soil, spread coal dust over all, satisfied himself that everything was in order, and went upstairs again. He then thoroughly cleansed the bath, and himself, and the bath again, dressed, and took his wife's clothing and his bath gown to the incinerator.

One or two more little touches and everything was in order. It was only quarter past six. The Wallingfords were always late; he had only to get into the car and drive off. It was a pity he couldn't wait till after dusk, but he could make a detour to avoid passing through the main street, and even if he was seen driving alone, people would only think Hermione had gone on ahead for some reason and they would forget about it.

Still, he was glad when he had finally got away, entirely unobserved, on the open road, driving into the gathering dusk. He had to drive very carefully; he found himself unable to judge distances, his reactions were abnormally delayed, but that was a detail. When it was quite dark he allowed himself to stop the car on the top of the downs, in order to think.

The stars were superb. He could see the lights of one or two little towns far away on the plain below him. He was exultant. Everything that was to follow was perfectly simple. Marion was waiting in Chicago. She already believed him to be a widower. The lecture people could be put off with a word. He had nothing to do but establish himself in some thriving out-of-the-way town in America and he was safe for ever. There were Hermione's clothes, of course, in the suitcases; they could be disposed of through the porthole. Thank heaven she wrote her letters on the typewriter – a little thing like handwriting might have prevented everything. 'But there you are,' he said. 'She was up-to-date, efficient all along the line. Managed everything. Managed herself to death, damn her!'

'There's no reason to get excited,' he thought. 'I'll write a few letters for her, then fewer and fewer. Write myself – always expecting to get back, never quite able to. Keep the house one year, then another, then another; they'll get used to it. Might even come back alone in a year or two and clear it up properly. Nothing easier. But not for Christmas!' He started up the engine and was off.

In New York he felt free at last, really free. He was safe. He could look back with pleasure – at least after a meal, lighting his cigarette, he could look back with a sort of pleasure – to the minute he had passed in the cellar listening to the bell, the door, and the voices. He could look forward to Marion.

As he strolled through the lobby of his hotel, the Clerk, smiling, held up letters for him. It was the first batch from England. Well, what did that matter? It would be fun dashing off the typewritten sheets in Hermione's downright style, signing them with her squiggle, telling everyone what a success his first lecture had been, how thrilled he was with America but how certainly she'd bring him back for Christmas. Doubts could creep in later.

He glanced over the letters. Most were for Hermione. From the Sinclairs, the Wallingfords, the vicar, and a business letter from Holt & Sons, Builders and Decorators.

He stood in the lounge, people brushing by him. He opened the letters with his thumb, reading here and there, smiling. They all seemed very confident he would be back for Christmas. They relied on Hermione. 'That's where they make their big mistake,' said the Doctor, who had taken to American phrases. The builders' letter he kept to the last. Some bill, probably. It was:

Dear Madam,
 We are in receipt of your kind acceptance of estimate as below and also of key.
 We beg to repeat you may have every confidence in same being ready in

ample time for Christmas present as stated. We are setting men to work this week.

    We are, Madam,

Yours faithfully,
PAUL HOLT & SONS

    To excavating, building up, suitably lining one sunken wine bin in cellar as indicated, using best materials, making good, etc.

. . . .£18/0/0

The Hand

BY LARRY MARCUS

The Hollywood studio MGM and producer Collier Young were responsible for making the excellent series One Step Beyond *which was launched in January 1959. Screened at ten PM. on ABC, it was hosted by John Newland who would enquire of his viewers, 'Have you ever walked down a street and had the feeling that you knew what lay beyond the unturned corner?' Such was its appeal that the show subsequently ran for over three years and was even briefly revived in colour in 1978. The stated aim of Collier Young was to 'probe into the dark and mysterious world of the unknown' and many episodes were claimed to be based on actual case histories of supernatural phenomena and the occult. Such artistic licence when patently not true caused a number of complaints to be made to ABC – but these did nothing to affect the ratings success of the show. Confrontations with ghosts and various forms of precognition and the paranormal were frequently the themes of the half-hour episodes, and all were produced with a suitably eerie and mysterious air – underlined by John Newland's mild and reserved demeanour. Newland was also the director of the series, which chalked up a first for television production by using limbo sets and having the narrator walk in and out of the action. One story, 'If You See Sally', about a ghostly little girl who is given a lift by a sympathetic truck driver, had the unexpected effect of generating dozens of letters from viewers who had had similar experiences. Conversely, 'Doomsday' and 'Night of the Kill' about the legend of the Bigfoot creature were presented in such a matter-of-fact manner as to give younger viewers nightmares! The slightly bizarre and moody style of* One Step Beyond *was undoubtedly a forerunner of the immensely successful* Twilight Zone *series which followed – yet it also promoted fond memories which led to a second series, The Next Step Beyond, in 1978. John Newland was once more the host, but somehow the fact that the series was now in colour seemed to detract from the unique black and white qualities of the original. It lasted just one season and left the reputation of its predecessor unsurpassed. Among the stars who appeared in the episodes were Cornel Wilde, Janet Blair, John Cassavetes, Jack Carson, Cliff Robertson, Agnes Moorhead, Walter Slezak and Gary Merrill. According to English TV historian, Philip Purser, some episodes were remade in Britain in 1960–61 by Associated Rediffusion using local actors, 'but with John Newland still inviting the audience in his New England tones to explore with me the amazing world of the unknown and take that Wan Stup Beyahnd'.*

Among the top voted episodes of One Step Beyond was 'The Hand' in which John Cassavetes played Tom Grant a piano player whose act of murder is revealed in a totally unexpected manner. The story was written by Larry Marcus (1930–) a former Hollywood reporter turned scriptwriter who created a number of the best episodes in the series.

THE bus boys were beginning to stack the chairs on the tables as Johnny Lane and his Combo sweated through the last chorus of 'Midnight Sun'. It was almost three AM in the Jazz Cellar, one of New Orleans' less glittering late, late spots. It had its share of regulars, though, attracted by its pleasant dinginess and the solid beat of the band.

The band was tired now, having played all night. The boys were eager for a cigarette, a drink, and a chair. They wanted the break to pass quickly, too. Then they could finish the set and get the hell out.

Tom Grant, of course, had constant access to the comforts of the break. A tall Scotch and a burning cigarette were always within reach on his piano. It was good to know they were there, especially when the band demanded only a faking background rhythm. Then he would reach for the glass and take a deep swallow, pushing the image of Alma out of focus, at least temporarily. It was better, though, when the spotlight was on him. Then he couldn't see the people out there. Not even Alma. And then he could pound hard and furiously on the keys, and the ache and tension inside would lessen.

Tonight had been the climax of several miserable weeks in the life of Tom Grant, weeks during which he had vascillated between trying to shut the face and body of Alma out of his mind for ever and pursuing her with a compulsion that seemed capable of destroying him as it drove him.

When he left her unanswered door or hung up the phone after he had listened several minutes to the futile buzzing at the other end of the line, he would be weak with self-loathing, for the awful choking pride was there at every turn of the hopeless pursuit.

Yet even as his pride raged and filled him with hatred for the girl whom he pictured ignoring the phone's ringing while she lay in the arms of another man, he would persuade himself that he had dialled the wrong number and pick up the phone again.

It had not always been thus, for Tom Grant at twenty-eight was not unattractive to women. He was tall, thin, ordinary-looking, actually, but he had powerful white hands which obeyed his will at the piano, and many women who listened found themselves wanting to know the touch of those hands.

Such a one was Nina Olsen, a trim little red-head, who swayed in the dark now murmuring 'Yes, Tommy. Oh, yes, Tommy. Yes, oh, yes . . .'

But the Nina Olsens were a dime a dozen, easy to have and hard to get rid of, and he had made a policy of staying clear even when there hadn't been the magnet of Alma to draw toward herself all his animal hungers.

Alma was a would-be singer of small talent, a pretty Creole, a girl who had run away from home. Perhaps girls like her were a dime a dozen, too, but she had a careless, aloof kind of sensuality that got to a man – especially a man like Tom Grant, who was accustomed to finding in his ash-tray mash notes folded in dollar bills.

Alma, on the other hand, warned you with her eyes and her body to stay away even as she beckoned, and there was a challenge in her movements to satisfy her strange hungers if you could. Of course you couldn't, yet you felt you had to try and in the trying you became consumed with a need apart from and a part of hers which drove you back and back.

Now, tonight, after weeks of avoiding him, Alma had decided to make the scene . . . with another man. He supposed it was her idea of a joke; he was familiar with her fondness for playing cat and mouse. All during the set she had been laughing ostentatiously at her tipsy escort's whispered stories, sparing Tom a glance now and then that flashed the old gleam of defiance.

Tom played his heart out during his solo, and reached limply for his Scotch as the spotlight shifted to Johnny for the finale. Johnny blew hot and cool and high in a long, whining coda and took the trumpet from his lips. He was the casual type MC.

'A ten-minute break to mop our fevered brows,' he said into the mike, 'and then we'll be back for our last session. Don't nobody go away, you hear? There ain't many of you, but you're quality.'

As Johnny talked, Alma reached into her companion's jacket and plucked out a dollar bill. She sauntered over to Tom at the piano and slipped the crumpled bill into his ash-tray.

'For you, piano man,' she said with an ironical smile, and before he could speak she was gone.

Tom waited until Johnny was through with his announcement, then picked up the bill and stuffed it into his pocket. As the men moved off the bandstand, Nina called out, 'Tom, when you come back, play "How High the Moon" just once more, willya?'

But he was already out of the door, leaving her humming sadly to the accompaniment of her empty glass drumming on the table. Nina was loaded.

Alma and her gentleman friend were in a warm embrace against a brick wall in the alley a few doors up from the Jazz Cellar.

'Don't you know a girl has to breathe?' asked Alma, finally breaking loose.

'Do all your breathin' while I get the car,' he told her.

'I'll honk for you.'

He wove up the street and Alma took out her compact to repair the damage he'd done.

This was how Tom found her. He flung the dollar bill at her feet.

'When you put the knife in, you like to twist it, don't you, Alma?'

She glanced coolly down at the bill. She didn't pick it up.

'You played real good tonight, Tommy,' she said.

'How could you tell? You were so busy laughing.'

'The fellow I'm with likes a girl to laugh. I heard a buck's worth.'

Tom couldn't sustain the bitterness, at least the show of it. The need of her was still there, strong and compelling, and she was before him.

'Where've you been, Alma?' he asked brokenly. 'I've been pounding on every door in New Orleans.'

'You shouldn't pound on anything but those black and white keys, honey,' she said, taking a cigarette from her purse. She handed the matches to Tom. As he struck a light, she cupped her hands around his strong white ones.

'You want to know something, piano man?' she asked archly. 'This is what I fell for. You got a beautiful pair of hands. I could still almost go for 'em.'

What a kick it was for her to torment him! 'Alma, I've got to see you,' Tom said desperately.

Alma went on as if she hadn't heard:

'Do you suppose you could leave me those hands in your will?' she wondered. 'You know, like people do with eyes? I'd mount 'em, like wild tigers, and put 'em in the nicest room in the house, and dust 'em every day.'

'Will you shut up and listen to me?'

'What can you say I haven't heard?'

'Honey, I'm crazy about you!'

'It's one-sided, piano man. As far as I'm concerned, you're just a face in the crowd.'

'But you never gave me a chance. You left without even –'

'Where's that man with the car?' Alma inquired, tired of the game.

Another sort of pain hit Tom in the belly. 'Who is he?' he asked unsteadily.

'His name escapes me,' Alma shrugged. 'Shaeffer or something. He's got a lot of funny stories.'

She was turned away from him, looking towards the neck of the alley. He grabbed her and spun her around to face him.

'Alma, you must listen to me. I'm dead without you!'

She looked down at the strong hands she had admired. It amused her that they were really ineffectual – like him – because they weren't going to convince her to go with him; not now, not ever.

'Save the hands for the piano,' she remarked coldly.

Just then a horn sounded not far away.

'That's my comedian friend. You'll have to excuse me.'

Tom's hands still clutched her arms, even more fiercely.

'Let go!' she snapped.

'Alma, I can't let go,' he moaned, nevertheless slackening his grip. 'Please give me a chance.'

His hold was sufficiently infirm to enable her to fling herself free and he fell against a barrel.

'I hate you when you start that whining!' she snarled, giving full vent to her scorn. And she started away from him up the alley.

Tom's left hand had landed upon a broken bottle in the trash-filled barrel. He gripped it unthinkingly, almost shattering it with the strength that seemed suddenly to have entered his fingers. Alma had made him feel weak and small and helpless again, and now she was going to that creep's room or taking him to her – it didn't matter which; she'd be with him. If she thought of him – Tom Grant – at all, it would be to joke about him. She'd tell her comedian friend how ridiculous he had been, and they'd laugh like hyenas as they drank and necked a little to tease each other.

Throw him away, would she? Laugh at him and spit on him? She wouldn't get away with it. *They* wouldn't get away with it. Strength seemed to flow from his hands to his body as he gripped the broken bottle. He lunged up the alley after Alma, overtaking her before she got to the street.

Alma didn't even have a chance to scream. Tom stared down in horror at the body at his feet. The fresh blood was vermilion against her skin, which shone chalk-white in the glare of the street lamp. Her black eyes stared vacantly up at him, like a doll's.

'Hey, girl!' came the drunken voice of the man whose name was probably Shaeffer. Tom dropped the jagged bottleneck to the ground.

He looked at his hand. It was bloody: he dug a handkerchief from his pocket and wiped it clean.

'*You want to know something, piano man?*' Somewhere back in his brain a tiny record of Alma's voice seemed to be playing over and over: '*You got a beautiful pair of hands.*'

A car door opened somewhere.

'What the hell is keeping you, Alma girl?' The voice of Shaeffer was nearer. Tom picked up the bottleneck and fled up the dark alley.

He snared the dollar where it lay on the pavement and stuffed it into his pocket. He hid the bottleneck in the trash barrel. Then he made a dash for the back door of the club.

The band was just playing the tag end of a number as he came in. Johnny looked at him questioningly, but Tom avoided his eyes and made for the piano. As he sat down, a Scotch was placed on top of the piano by Nina.

'Lucky you came back,' she said thickly. 'I jus' about got up and played all by myself.'

'Huh?'

' "How High the Moon". You promised your lil friend, namely, me.'

'Okay, okay,' and he forced himself to look at Johnny.

Johnny reached for the mike.

'For the little lady of the twenty-seven Scotch and sodas – "How High the Moon", featuring the answer to her prayers: Tom Grant.'

The spotlight swung to Tom and he managed a glassy grin. As he began to play, he heard the whine of a siren swelling from far to near, and his left hand reached nervously for the Scotch Nina had left for him. Having taken a calming swig, he lifted it back to set it down again on top of the piano. His eye caught the glass in its upward arc, and his hand froze in mid-air. Through the amber liquid he could see his hand holding the glass. It was bloody!

The glass crashed to the floor, and Tom pounded out some loud chords to cover the sound. But he was even more shook up when he looked down at the keyboard. Of course, the white keys. They, too. were smudged with bloody fingerprints.

Tom slammed the lid over the keys and stood up unsteadily.

'I – I don't feel so hot,' he muttered to Johnny, who had moved over to him and was looking at him curiously. He bolted to the washroom, leaving the rest of the band to fend for themselves through the number that was supposed to be his.

He leaned over the basin, washing his hands with the careful attention of a surgeon about to operate. He examined them closely. They were perfectly clean.

As he reached for the roller towel, there was a knock at the door.

'Tom? You in there?'

'Yeah, yeah.'

'Come on out. Something's happened.'

Tom didn't reply. He was staring, horrified, at the roller towel. It couldn't be true, he thought, it couldn't be. His hands had been perfectly clean when he dried them. But now the white towel was stained with bright crimson.

'Tom?' insisted Johnny's voice.

He held the left hand up to the light. It was spotless! With his right hand, Tom frantically began to roll the towel around so that the stained part would be hidden. He took a deep breath, and reached for the doorknob.

Wait – what if . . . ? He looked down. There it was: the bloody evidence left by his closing the door a moment ago.

Desperately, his eyes combed the small lavatory for something with which to remove these stains. In the wastebasket he spied a newspaper. Tremblingly, he tore off a page and wiped the doorknob with it.

'Tom, you all right?'

'I'll be right with you.'

Tom shoved the crumpled newspaper into his pocket, unhooked the latch – remembering to keep his left hand in his pocket – and joined Johnnny.

The musicians, waiters and customers were clustered together, buzzing with excitement. With Johnny was a heavy-set man in his early fifties. Johnny introduced the two men: 'Tom Grant – Police Detective Harmon.'

Tom knew, of course, the nature of his mission, but it still wasn't easy to hear it. He turned away. overcome with emotion – partly because he was afraid for himself, but mostly because he felt a genuine aching grief for the girl he had killed.

'We know who did it,' said Harmon.

Tom turned slowly to face the detective.

'The guy she came in here with,' he went on. 'He was standing over the body. Oh, he claims he didn't, but he's so drunk he doesn't know whether it's five o'clock or Thursday.'

Harmon had taken out a packet of cigarettes, removed one for himself, and offered the packet to Tom. Out of habit, Tom took the packet with his left hand and dug out a cigarette with his right.

'How long did you know this girl?' Harmon asked him.

'Long enough.'

'What did she do for a living?'

'Tried singing for a while, but she wasn't much good at it.'

From the bandstand came the sound of someone fooling around with the piano. Tom whirled to see Nina drunkenly picking out an uncertain tune.

'Did she have any folks that you knew about?' There was no answer. 'Mr Grant.'

Tom was nervous about what Nina may have noticed on the piano keys.

'Huh? Oh, yeah . . . her old man . . . he farms a little land upstate.'

'They tell me you and she went around together for a time –'

'I don't want to talk about it,' Tom said heatedly, and started for the bandstand to get Nina away from the piano.

'Hey, wait a minute!' said Harmon. 'Where do you think you're going with my cigarettes?'

Tom stopped dead. He realized that he was holding the packet in his left hand. He knew what that meant. Harmon looked at the limp packet in Tom's fist and grinned good-naturedly.

'You crushed 'em pretty good,' he said. 'Well, there was only a couple left – keep 'em.'

'Thanks,' said Tom resuming his trip to the piano.

'And tell that broad to lay off with the 'Chopsticks' and come on over here,' Harmon told him.

Nina held a glass of whisky in one hand and devoted the other to the piano. She was so crocked and so involved with her glass and its contents that Tom couldn't be sure she had noticed or understood the meaning of the stained keys.

'Betcha if I had a few lessons I could play as good as anybody,' she said.

'Sure you could.'

His tone carefully humoured her so that she wouldn't give him a hard time as he closed the keyboard. Nevertheless, she did.

'Now wait a minute, wait just a lil old minute,' she said, making a cacaphonous chord as she pushed a hand stubbornly against the keys.

'The detective wants to see you.' Tom told her.

'About what?'

'About what happened.'

Harmon was almost upon them and Tom was frantically eager to get the keyboard closed.

'Would *you* give me lessons?'

'Why not?' said Tom absently.

Thank God, she stood up. Now if she'd just keep her hands off him.

'If I could play, jus' play a lil bit like you,' she gushed, making a giddy run up his sleeve with two fingers, 'I'd be the happiest girl in town.'

Tom had his chance. As he stood with his back to the piano, suffering Nina's clinging, he closed the keyboard behind him with his right hand.

'I haven't talked to you yet, have I, Miss?'

'Mrs is my name,' she giggled. 'Mrs Nina Olsen. Mr Olsen is a rat, but I still respect the name. I will answer any and all questions to the best of my ability, Inspector Sir. You *are* from Scotland Yard, aren't you?'

Harmon paused. 'I guess you can go, Mrs Olsen,' he said.

'No questions, Mr Inspector?'

'No thanks.'

'Oh, you're quite welcome, I'm sure,' Nina chuckled, pleased with herself. 'So if you will all excuse me – I will pick up all my little thingies . . . and be on my way.'

Her purse was on top of the piano, its contents half spilled on the surface. With ridiculous precision, she began to refill the bag.

'She's really blind, huh?' said Harmon, under his breath.

Tom would have liked to think so, but as Nina turned to leave, her eye caught Tom's and she gave him a deliberate wink. Quite unmistakably it said: 'We share a secret, don't we?'

Tom was eager to follow her to find out if it was the secret he feared that she alluded to, but Harmon got in his way.

'I didn't get your address,' he said.

'1812 Baker Street. Why?' replied Tom, still more concerned about Nina than with the detective's interest in him.

'They'll need you tomorrow for the preliminary hearing. I'll get in touch with you first thing in the morning and tell you where and when. What's your phone number?'

Tom repeated it hastily, half on the run. He wanted to waylay Nina.

However, when he reached the street, he found it empty, and the side streets, too. He decided to give up on her and go home.

It wasn't much: a room with a pull-down bed, a rented upright piano in the corner, a two-burner gas plate. A bathroom of his own, anyway. He'd always been grateful for that.

He stood at the sink, pouring a disinfectant on his left hand. The veins in his forehead stood out and he clenched his teeth as the liquid bit into the skin. He pressed the hand down on the newspaper he'd put on the top of the water closet. Tears of despair came to his eyes when he took the hand away. There across the page, as vividly as before, was a red hand-print soaking into the paper. In his anguish he buried his face in both hands, realizing in an instant what he had done.

He tore his hands away and looked at himself in the mirror. A crimson palm print streaked the left side of his face. With his right hand he grabbed a towel and violently rubbed his face until the stains disappeared.

Just then, the doorbell sounded. He stuffed the towel into the clothes hamper, and approached the door cautiously.

'Who is it?' he asked, without opening the door.

'Me. Nina Olsen.'

Tom opened the door quickly and there she was all right. At least, she was relatively sober now. She walked in boldly and gave the place the once-over.

'What do you want?' asked Tom, apprehension in his voice.

'What do you think I want?' she challenged. She walked over to the piano and ran her fingers over the keys deliberately.

'Look,' Tom said nervously, 'whatever you say – whatever you think . . .'

'You said you would,' Nina interrupted.

'Said I would what?'

'Give me lessons . . .'

'Lessons!' he repeated, stunned.

'That's what you said. Don't you remember?'

'Are you nuts?' Tom wanted to know. 'It's after three o'clock.'

Nina shrugged. 'I can't sleep – you can't sleep – so what's the diff?'

'Will you go home?' Tom said, repressing his anger with effort.

'You're no fun at all.'

'I mean it – get out.'

Nina strolled, unaffected, to the door. 'I hope you didn't hurt it bad,' she said idly.

Their eyes met, but Tom didn't have anything to say.

'Your hand,' explained Nina.

'I – I don't know . . .' stammered Tom.

'You cut it when you dropped that glass, didn't you?' Tom tried to hide his relief.

'Yes,' he said.

'You sure made a mess of that piano.'

'It's okay now.'

'Let me look at it.'

'No!'

His hand had been in his pocket all the while. He kept it there.

'I took a course in first aid once,' Nina coaxed. 'I got a button to prove it.'

'Come on, now,' said Tom, crossing to the door, 'go home, will you?' As he opened the door, however, he found more complications. There was Johnny, his hand raised about to knock. Behind him were the other members of the band, smiling, cheerful, and loaded down with beer and groceries.

'Now, that's what I call instant service,' said Johnny. And before Tom could protest, they were all crowding into the room.

'What are you guys up to?' Tom demanded.

'We decided to rent our ole buddy's place for a little clean and sincere poker,' explained Johnny. Then he spied Nina. 'Well, look who's here. Miss How-High-the-Moon herself!'

'Hiya!' acknowledged Nina, delighted for the delay in being bounced.

'How do you like this guy!' said Johnny. 'We came here to cheer you up, you rascal you!'

The boys were making themselves at home. Frank, the drummer, was unloading the groceries. He pulled out a redolent salami.

'Take a whiff of this,' he said happily. 'Five hundred years old – knock your head off!'

A loaf of French bread, bags of potato chips, packages of cheese, and cans of beer soon littered the small cupboard by the gas plate.

'Can I stay?' asked Nina.

'Can you make sandwiches?' Frank wanted to know.

'Sure!'

'Stay.'

Tom was beside himself.

'Listen,' he began, 'can't you guys understand? I've got to be alone.' Nina was attacking the French bread with a knife she'd found in the cupboard. 'Will you get outa here?' Tom added to her.

'But I've been invited,' she replied, continuing to saw blithely at the

107

bread. Frank joined her at the cupboard, while the others set up the table for the game.

'Look,' pleaded Tom, 'I know why you guys are doing this – to get my mind off what's happened. I appreciate it, but I swear I've got to be by myself.'

Harry, the sax man, was dealing five places, 'Now, why don't everybody stop talking and pull up a chair. Table stakes – jacks or better. Lady, be good to me and all my creditors.'

The others took seats around the table, including Frank, a tremendous salami and cheese sandwich in his fist.

'Sit down, kid,' Johnny advised. 'Come on – pick up your hand.'

Suddenly Tom whirled and dashed out of the room, leaving everyone open-mouthed.

'He's taking it pretty hard,' observed Johnny. 'Guess he was really crazy about Alma.'

Frank turned up the cards that had been dealt to Tom. 'He shoulda stayed.' he said. 'Full house.'

Tom ran up the street as if pursued by the hounds of hell. He stopped once to catch his breath. The wall by the sidewalk was plastered with advertising posters. Slowly he walked towards the wall, almost as if hypnotized. He held his left hand aloft and let his arm guide it toward the poster. He pressed it against the white background, holding it there for a long moment as he shut his eyes and let his head drop forward. He wanted to stay that way, supported by the wall, his palm outstretched in just that position. Never, never to move. Not to look, not to know.

But he had to. He pulled away weakly and made himself examine the place his palm had been. There it was – the bloody claw!

Nothing but panic now. No empowering anger, no feat to inspire action, no despair to bring a moment's anguish reconnoitering – only panic and flight. It didn't even seem to matter that he was out of breath, he simply ran on and on, without direction, gracelessly, mindlessly.

Yet the body would give out and thus permit some minimal return of rationality. He sagged against a lamp-post, his chest heaving. He hugged the post as if it were his mother and the metal against which his cheek rested cooled the tears that made new salty tracks on his hot sweaty face.

A yellow sign ahead blinked on and off. The letters, seen through his tears, thickened and dripped like those on a birthday cake. It blinked on again. He'd read it right. It said: 'Emergency Hospital'.

An idea flashed with the sudden glow of the sign. Tom pulled himself together as much as possible and made his way to the entrance.

There was only a seedy old first-aid man named Harris on duty and that suited Tom just fine. He was afraid of too much professionalism.

Harris shone a light on the hand that had brought in this wild one. He was puzzled. 'No cuts . . . no breaks in the skin,' he mused.

'There must be slivers of glass. Something,' insisted Tom.

'No, not a thing. Just shaky.' Harris looked up. 'What made you think anything was wrong?'

'Well . . .'

'Does it hurt you?'

'No.' Tom was guarded.

'Well, does it tingle – ache like rheumatism?'

'No.'

'Now, there must have been something to bring you here.'

'Can your hand . . . bleed without a wound or a sore?' Tom blurted.

Harris looked at Tom strangely.

'Now, how could it do that?' This late duty brought in some weirdies all right. 'You ought to get a regular doctor first thing tomorrow. Meanwhile, I can give you something to make you sleep.'

'What can a regular doctor do for me that you can't?'

'Sounds to me like a bad case of nerves.'

Tom was defensive. 'You mean you think I'm losing my mind.'

'Now did I say that?'

The man reached into a drawer and pulled a couple of pills into an envelope.

'I don't want any pills,' Tom said stubbornly.

Harris was getting impatient. 'Okay by me, mister. That'll be five dollars.'

Tom took out his wallet with his right hand and put it on the table so that he could open it without using his left.

Observing this, Harris commented: 'There's nothing wrong with your hand. If you don't use it, you're going to have real trouble.'

'How'd you like to make another ten bucks?' Tom said suddenly.

'What for?' Harris was suspicious.

'I want you to bandage my hand.'

'But there's no reason to!'

'Is that the worst thing you've ever done in this crummy joint?' Tom exploded. 'Stop acting like you were some fancy doctor or something!'

The man shrugged.

'All right. Guess there's no law against a man having his hand bandaged if he wants to.'

He began to take gauze and adhesive tape out of a wall cabinet.

'I want you to bandage it good – plenty of tape and padding,' Tom was saying.

'If you want to hide your hand so bad,' said Harris, 'why don't you wear gloves?'

'In the middle of summer wear gloves?' Tom snorted. 'Oh, that's a wonderful idea. People really would think I was nuts.'

'What do you care?' wondered Harris. He was becoming mildly interested in this one.

'Just bandage it, will you?' snapped Tom.

Harris followed his orders. 'You from New Orleans?' he inquired. 'Yeah.'

'What do you do for a living?'

'Just fix the hand!'

The man had suddenly stopped winding the gauze. He looked at the hand in amazement. The bandage was gradually turning crimson.

'It looks like blood,' he said.

Come on, hurry up!'

'But how can it be?' Harris fretted. 'There's no abrasion – nothing. When did it start?'

'Will you just put the bandage on!'

'Maybe there is something wrong,' said Harris, moving toward the phone. 'I want somebody else to look at this.'

'No!'

'But it should be X-rayed,' protested the first-aid man.

'Maybe I missed something. Let me run you over to the General Hospital.'

Before he could reach the phone, Tom was out the door. When the man said 'X-ray', it was as though he'd pulled the trigger for a race.

Tom's pull-out bed remained on its stanchions through the night and morning. Oblivious to his surroundings, as well as his condition, Tom sat huddled in a chair. The room was a shambles and he didn't care. Nina had confined herself last night to serving the uninvited guests. Surrounded by empty beer cans, dirty dishes, and left-over food, Tom sat haggard and numb and staring. Nor did he move or change expression when the knocking began.

The vigorous pounding on the door sounded far, far away to him, hardly worthy of his notice. Much closer and louder was the voice of Alma:

'This is what I fell for . . . You got a beautiful pair of hands . . . '

Through the transom came the voices of Detective Harmon and Tom's landlady.

'But I saw him come in a few hours ago when I got the morning milk,' she said.

'Why do you suppose he doesn't answer?'

'He didn't look at all well,' she confided. 'And not so much as a good morning. I was going to say something about his friends staying half the night and making so much noise, but he just went on past.'

'You have a pass key?'

'Of course.'

The key turned in the lock and Detective Harmon confronted the grimy facsimile of Tom Grant.

'Are you all right?' inquired Harmon.

'What do you want?' Tom's voice was flat and listless.

'That preliminary hearing I told you about last night. You've got to be there.'

'Why?'

'Because the fellows in the prosecutor's office want you. They want as good a case against this guy as they can present. So far it's all circumstantial.'

'What can I tell them?'

'Something about the girl herself.'

'I can't go. I'm not feeling well.'

Harmon reached into his pocket. He felt sorry for this poor slob, but he had a job to do. He handed Tom the subpoena.

Tom didn't take it. He kept his fists tightly clenched and said nothing.

'Now, look, you can't get out of this unless the police doctor examines you and says what's wrong,' Harmon pointed out.

'I don't want any doctor,' Tom muttered.

Harmon still couldn't be tough on the guy. He wanted to tell him that no dame was worth all this – especially one who would get herself bumped off by a shifty character she had picked up in a night club. But he knew he would only make matters worse by sounding off.

'Maybe you'd feel better if you had a cup of coffee,' he said instead.

There was no response.

'A preliminary hearing's not much,' he went on reassuringly. 'The whole thing's over in about half an hour. They'll just ask you a few questions about the girl and then you come home. I'll drive you down and back in the squad car.'

Tom sat motionless.

111

'If you don't come along, I'll have to call the doctor,' Harmon warned.

Tom didn't seem to hear him.

'You mind if I use your phone?' asked Harmon. He picked it up without waiting for a reply.

'Wait,' Tom said.

He slowly pushed himself to his feet. His left hand was in his jacket pocket.

'You want to wash up and put on a clean shirt? We got a few minutes,' said Harmon.

Tom shook his head and walked out the door without a word. It was Harmon who closed and locked the door.

The hearing had already started when they arrived, and there were a few people in the spectator rows Alma's friend sat at the defence table – nervous, sober now, badly frightened.

A police officer was testifying. Tom sat with Harmon, his hand still in his pocket, conspicuously so, as if he were holding something valuable that he was afraid someone would steal. Harmon was beginning to become naggingly curious about the man's behaviour, which didn't conform precisely with that one might expect of a grieving lover.

'Will Thomas Grant take the stand,' said the clerk. Harmon had to nudge him to get him off the bench and on his way to the witness box.

'Raise your right hand,' recited the clerk. 'Put your left hand on the Bible and repeat after me, "I promise to tell the truth, the whole truth, and nothing but . . ." '

The clerk paused momentarily. He had recited this piece a thousand times without incident, but Tom had made no move to comply.

'Mr Grant?' he said.

Tom looked dazed.

'The oath, Mr Grant,' said the clerk. 'Raise your right hand, put your left on the Bible.'

Tom's eyes reluctantly focused on the Bible reposing on the ledge. He looked at it as if it were some sort of grotesque jack-in-the-box.

'Raise your right hand,' repeated the clerk.

Slowly, painfully, Tom did as he was told.

'And now your left hand on the Bible.'

Tom looked at the Book with mounting horror.

'Mr Grant,' urged the clerk. 'Please.'

The courtroom was alive with chatter, but Tom was oblivious to it. His entire attention was focused on *The Book*, toward which his hand began to grope drunkenly.

It had been said that a man's entire life flashes before his mind's eye at the moment he realizes he is going to die. In the minutes that Tom's guilty hand reached toward the Bible, the quality, if not all the incidents, of his wild and wonderful month with Alma were thus relived. *Her* words, too, echoed again in his head: the maddening taunt that had prefaced his savage impulse – '*You want to know something, piano man? This is what I fell for. You got a beautiful pair of hands. I could still almost go for 'em.*'

He remembered how it had been when he'd had her, when she'd been his woman, when he'd hoped he could keep it like that always. There had been about Alma a curious kind of dependence, a needing to cling, underneath her free and easy manner. He'd hoped he could make her need him enough so that she wouldn't leave, as he constantly feared she would when she discovered his own need.

And it had happened as he had feared it would, but not only because she felt contempt for his need. She was driven by her own hungers from man to man. She would be drawn to a man for some one thing, some crazy thing – like the way he sang, or the way he told stories, or the cut of his clothes – any one of a number of things. His hands, say, and the way he played the piano. And then she would get bored, after the initial attraction had palled: and if she knew he still wanted her, wanted her terribly, she'd move on.

If he could convince her that he didn't want her, not that much, not so much that he thought he could do without her, she'd stick around even after the particular charm had dulled . . . for a while.

But if she was certain she had him where she wanted him, she would skip and return only when her appetite for blood, for causing pain, had not recently been satisfied.

Tom had often reflected painfully in the weeks after Alma walked out that she would have left him sooner or later, no matter what he did, or avoided doing, to hold her.

Yet, even now, he held this knowledge not as a conviction. Even now he wondered if he could have had her again if he hadn't cried for her, if he had taken her boldly and fiercely. Perhaps then she would have cried out herself and clung to him like a child as she had done at first. And now it was too late, for ever too late, by his own doing, his own hand!

Suddenly everything exploded inside him. 'I can't . . . I can't . . . I can't . . .' he groaned.

The buzzing that had begun in the courtroom at Tom's strange performance became tumult. Detective Harmon adjusted immediately to the new situation; he was not unaccustomed to such changes of pace, and his suspicions had been aroused. Immediately he was at Tom's side.

'Do you have something you would like to say?' he asked.

'Yes. Quickly!' Tom muttered.

Harmon nodded to a uniformed policeman who had approached the witness box, and the three men retired to an office across the hall, leaving the courtroom to rejoice with the exonerated man.

'I went out the back door after Alma left the club with Shaeffer,' Tom began.

A stenotypist had been called in. His fingers flew over the keys, finding it easy to keep up with Tom's halting account of last night's events.

'. . . and she just lay there, on her back, looking up at me blankly. I knew she was dead,' he finished with a choked sigh.

He leaned back in his chair as the stenotypist left the room to type up final copies of the confession. He was suddenly very tired. It wasn't hard to go to sleep now. He went out like a light and stayed unconscious until Detective Harmon roused him. The document was ready for his signature.

Tom reached for a pen and began to sign immediately. His left hand pressed heavily against the white blotter on the desk.

'You better read it first,' advised Harmon. 'A confession's nothing to take so lightly.'

Tom paid no attention. He let the pen drop as he crossed the final 't' in his name.

'Now get a doctor and find out how to stop this blood,' he said.

'What blood?' asked Harmon.

Tom removed his left hand from the blotter and flashed Harmon a look of bitterness.

'Do you think I'd ever have told you that happened if it wasn't for *this*?'

'What are you talking about?' Harmon demanded, looking at the blotter.

Tom, too, looked then at the white blotter, where his left hand had been pressing.

The blotter was still white – just as white as new-fallen snow.

Where Is Everybody?

BY ROD SERLING

The Twilight Zone *is probably the most celebrated and influential of all late night horror anthology shows. From its modest origins as the brainchild of the radio and TV scriptwriter, Rod Serling (1924–75), it has become an unprecedented cult series, frequently reshown, and the inspiration of a sequel and a full-length movie, as well as a magazine, comic books and various souvenir spin-offs such as games and records. Launched on CBS in October 1959 as a half-hour series, it was briefly expanded to an ill-omened thirteen hour-long episodes, before reverting to thirty minutes for the remainder of its five-year run until 1964. Serling's basic concept was for a fantasy series, but elements of horror and SF inevitably crept in, helped by several of his leading co-writers including Charles Beaumont, Richard Matheson, George Clayton Johnson and Ray Bradbury. In all, 156 episodes of* The Twilight Zone *were produced, and at its peak the series attracted an audience of well over twenty million viewers and won three Emmy awards. It also made the phrase 'the twilight zone' part of the English language and prompted one interviewer to ask Serling where it had come from. 'I thought I'd made it up,' Rod replied, 'but I've heard since that there is an Air Force term relating to a moment when a plane is coming down on approach and it cannot see the horizon, it's called the twilight zone, but it's an obscure term which I had not heard before.' Interestingly, too, Serling was not originally intended to be the narrator of the series. One suggestion had been the veteran Westbrook Van Voorhis, famous for his big voice; another was Orson Welles, but his fee was considered too expensive for the budget. Although the network was initially sceptical, Serling's dedication to the idea plus his intimate knowledge of the material – he actually wrote ninety-two of the episodes himself – overruled any argument. The measured words which he delivered to camera are now a part of television folklore: 'There is a fifth dimension beyond that which is known to man. It is a dimension as vast as space and as timeless as infinity. It is the middle ground between light and shadow – between science and superstition; between the pit of man's fears and the summit of his knowledge. It is an area we call . . . The Twilight Zone.'*

There is probably no more suitable story to include in this collection than the very first of the series, 'Where Is Everybody?' – which Rod himself wrote and which, after it had been screened on 2 October 1959, ensured the success of the programme. 'It was a stunning plot,' reviewer Ira Steiner was to say later, 'but it was still a little freaky in terms of the kind of show that was then showing on TV.' The story concerns a young man who wakes up in a deserted town where all the signs are that the inhabitants have just left – but where to and why? Directed by Robert Stephens from Serling's own script, 'Where Is Everybody?' starred Earl Holliman in a personal acting tour de force climaxed by the kind of surprise ending which became one of the show's trademarks. Rod had obtained part of the original idea from an article in Time *magazine about isolation experiments – and the rest from a harrowing personal experience when he became trapped in a telephone booth! In 1962 he adapted the script into a short story and I am pleased to include it here as a fitting tribute to one of the greatest of all television series. It is also prefaced by a short essay by Rod about* The Twilight Zone *which has not previously appeared in book form.*

MY BELIEFS ABOUT THE REAL TWILIGHT ZONE

by Rod Serling

I think it was an actor who wrote that every writer is a frustrated actor who recites his lines in the hidden auditorium of his skull. I think that statement is applicable to all writers. They really want to be actors. That is the reason they are writers.

Although I have been successful, I also know about failures. My bathroom walls are papered with rejection slips, but the TV show has lasted many years and the re-run of episodes still seem to stand up.

One of the interesting things is that psychiatrists used to consult me. I used to get a lot of correspondence, letters from doctors whose patients had mentioned seeing the show. This was particularly true with young people with mental illnesses and neurotic problems who had seen the show and would talk to their doctors about a certain episode which had moved them or hurt them or jarred them in some way. They identified. They related to the situation. Sometimes they would willingly discuss a particular problem they had if our show had dealt with a similar area – death, life after death, hatred, fears – many of these things.

Very often kids are basic, real, sensitive people. I used to get a sense of desperate, heavy responsibility because I had the feeling that probably, every time I went on the air, there was an unseen audience of millions of people who probably hated my guts – parents, for instance, because I kept their kids awake – I made them nervous – I made them ill. It worried me and I was glad when the *Twilight Zone* series was completed.

Doing a television series involves a back-breaking, frustrating schedule. Doing a dramatic series has a special difficult quality all its own. You have your own problem doing a show like this as often as you do them but to try to create qualitative, consistently good shows each week for five years is next to impossible. It's up to younger men now. I'm going to pass to that group. No more for me.

Many of the far-out things we used as subjects for episodes I believe in. Take flying saucers, for example. I think there is enough documented evidence to support the existence of extra-terrestrial people.

I know there is a file in the Air Force offices in Washington that compiles all the documented sightings of unidentified flying objects, UFO's which have never been explained. Too often they come from well-trained professional people such as airline pilots. There are at least two or three on file over populated areas in which the sighting was reconfirmed by numerous people.

There is one story that is wild. It occurred sometime in the middle 1940s. Right after the war an American airline pilot over the National Airport in Washington, DC sighted a flying saucer and followed it for forty-five seconds. He took pictures of the UFO which I know are on file. Since then they have been essentially reproduced and released to the public but no one has ever explained that event.

I don't know whether or not I believe in ghosts, seances, calling back the dead, or reincarnation, but as to the extra-terrestrial life, visitations from other planets, existences of other lives on other planets – this I believe.

The universe is so large. The stars and planets are so multitudinous that they are like grains of sand and we are just one of them.

It would be idiotic and presumptuous to assume that in a universe which is infinite, containing millions and millions of planets that we on earth are the only ones with a civilized order.

I once received a true story from a woman in Berkeley, California. She is involved in a science project there and told me about some maps they found in a cave in southern Florida. These were maps of the eastern seaboard of the United States roughly as it exists today. By the nature of the paper the maps were proven to be at least 3000 years old. It took some smarty, through a spasm of understanding, to realize and to point out that the only way those maps could have been drawn was from the air.

The maps are currently in the possession of people in Berkeley so you can guess the amount of excitement that will happen one of these days when the treasure is opened for the public.

* * *

THE sensation was unrelated to anything he'd ever felt before. He awoke, but had no recollection of ever having gone to sleep. And, to mystify him further, he was not in a bed. He was walking down a road, a two-lane black macadam with a vivid white stripe running down the centre. He stopped, stared up at a blue sky, a hot, mid-morning sun. Then he looked around at a rural landscape, high, full-leafed trees flanking the road. Beyond the trees were fields of wheat, golden and rippling.

Like Ohio, he thought. Or maybe Indiana. Or parts of upstate New York. Suddenly he was conscious of the words being thought. Ohio. Indiana. New York. It immediately occurred to him that he didn't know where he was. A new thought followed quickly – he didn't know *who* he was, either! He looked down at himself, fingering the green, one-piece set of coveralls he was wearing, the heavy, high shoes, the zippered front that went from neck to crotch. He touched his face and then his hair. An inventory. Trying to piece together items of familiarity. An orientation through the tips of his fingers. He felt a light beard stubble, a nose slightly indented at the bridge, moderately heavy eyebrows, close-cropped hair. Not quite a butch – but close. He was young. Reasonably young, anyway. And he felt good. Healthy. At peace. He was confused as hell, but not at all frightened.

He walked over to the side of the road, took out a cigarette and lit it. He stood there leaning in the shade of one of the giant oaks that flanked the road. And he thought: I don't know who I am. I don't know where I am. But it's summer and I'm out in the country some place and this must be some kind of amnesia or something.

He drew deeply and enjoyably on the cigarette. As he took it out of his mouth and held it between his fingers, he looked at it. King-sized and filtered. Phrases came to him. 'Winstons taste good like a cigarette should.' 'You get a lot to like in a Marlboro.' 'Are you smoking more now but enjoying it less?' That was for Camels – the kind you used to be willing to walk a mile for. He grinned and then laughed out loud. The power of advertising. He could stand there not knowing his name or where he was, but the twentieth-century poetry of the tobacco company cut across even the boundaries of amnesia. He stopped laughing and considered. Cigarettes and slogans meant America. So that's what he was – an American.

He flipped away the cigarette and walked on. A few hundred yards up the road he heard music coming from around the bend ahead. Loud trumpets. Good ones. There was a drum in the background and then a single, high-flying trumpet that rode an obbligato to the percussion. Swing. That's what it was, and again he was conscious of a word symbol that meant something to him. Swing. And this one he could relate to a specific time. It went with the 1930s. And this was beyond the thirties. This was the fifties. The 1950s. He let these facts pile up on top of one another. He felt like the key piece of a jigsaw puzzle, other pieces falling into place around him, forming a recognizable picture. And it was odd, he thought, how definite the pattern was, once they fell. Now he knew it was 1959. This was beyond doubt. Nineteen fifty-nine.

As he rounded the bend and saw the source of the music, he took a quick inventory of what he had discovered. He was an American, maybe in his twenties, it was summer, and here he was.

In front of him was a diner, a small, rectangular clapboard building with a sign on the front door which read, 'OPEN'. Music was pouring out the front door. He went inside and got an impression of familiarity. He'd been to places like this before, this much he knew definitely. A long counter studded with ketchup bottles and napkin holders; a back wall plastered with hand-written signs announcing kinds of sandwiches, soups, pie à la mode, and a dozen other items. There were a couple of large posters with girls in bathing suits holding up Coke bottles, and at the far end of the room was what he knew to be a juke box, the source of the music.

He walked the length of the counter, swinging a couple of seats around as he passed. Behind the counter an open swinging door led to the kitchen where he could see a big restaurant stove, a pot of coffee perking on it. The gurgling sound of the coffee was familiar and comforting and sent an aroma of breakfast and morning into the room.

The young man smiled as if seeing an old friend, or better, *feeling* the presence of an old friend. He sat down on the last stool so that he could see into the kitchen. There were shelves laden with canned goods, a big double-door refrigerator, a wooden chopping table, a screen door. He looked up at the signs on the wall. The Denver sandwich. The hamburger. Cheeseburger. Ham and eggs. Again he was aware of the phenomenon of having to associate obviously familiar words with what they represented. What was a Denver sandwich, for example? And what was pie à la mode? Then, after a few moments of reflection, a picture came into his mind along with a taste. He had an odd thought then, that he was like an infant who was being exposed to the maturing process in a fantastically telescoped, jet-propelled way.

The music on the juke box broke through his thoughts, loud and intrusive.

He called out, toward the kitchen, 'That loud enough for you, is it?'

There was a silence. Only the music answered him.

He raised his voice, 'Can you hear it okay?'

Still no response. He went over to the machine, pushed it out a few inches from the wall and found a small volume-knob near the base. He turned it. The music fell away from him and the room seemed quieter and more comfortable. He pushed the machine back against the wall and returned to his stool. He picked up the cardboard menu that was leaning against the napkin-holder and studied it, occasionally looking up into the kitchen. He could see four pies browning nicely through the glass door of the oven and again there was the sense of something familiar, something friendly that he could respond to.

He called out again: 'I think I'll have ham and eggs. Eggs up and easy and some hash browns.'

Still there was no movement from the kitchen and no answering voice.

'I saw a sign that there was a town up ahead. What's the name of it?'

Coffee bubbled in the big enamelled pot, the steam rising into the air. A light wind moved the screen door in a creaking four-inch arc back and forth, and the juke box continued to play quietly. The young man was getting hungry now and felt a little nudge of irritation.

'Hey,' he called out, 'I asked you a question in there. What's the name of the town up ahead?'

He waited for a moment and when there was no answer he got up from the stool, vaulted the counter, pushed the swinging door open and went into the kitchen. It was empty. He walked through to the screen door, pulled it open and went outside. There was a big gravel back yard, unpunctuated by anything but a row of garbage cans, one of which had tipped over, littering the ground with a collection of tin cans, coffee grounds, egg shells and some empty cereal boxes; some orange crates; a broken, partially spokeless wheel; three or four piles of old newspapers. He was about to go back inside when something made him stop dead. He looked again at the garbage cans. There was something missing. An element not there that should have been there. He didn't know what it was. It was just a minute tilt to the dial inside his head that registered balance and reason. Something was wrong and he didn't know what it was. It left him with a tiny feeling of disquiet which he pushed into the back of his mind.

He returned to the kitchen, went over to the coffeepot, smelled it again, carried it over to the chopping table. He found a mug and poured himself a cup of hot coffee. He leaned against the back of the chopping table and sipped the coffee, enjoying it, liking its familiarity.

Then he went into the other room and took a large doughnut from a glass jar. He carried it back to the kitchen, and leaned against the jamb of the swinging door so that he could survey both rooms. He munched slowly on the doughnut, sipped at the coffee, and reflected. Whoever ran this place, he thought, is either in the basement or maybe his wife's having a baby. Or maybe the guy's sick. Maybe he's had a coronary or something. Maybe he should look around and find a basement door. He looked over at the cash register behind the counter. What an easy set-up for a heist. Or for a free meal. Or for anything, for that matter.

The young man reached in his pocket and pulled out a handful of coins and a dollar bill.

'American money,' he said aloud. 'That settles that. No question about it. I *am* an American. Two half-dollars. A quarter. A dime. Four pennies and a dollar bill. That's American money.'

He went into the kitchen again, looking up at the cereal boxes with the familiar names. The Campbell soup cans. Was that the one with the fifty-seven varieties? Again he reflected on who he was and where he was. On the disjointed *non sequiturs* that passed through his consciousness; his knowledge of music, the colloquialisms he spoke, the menu that he read and understood perfectly. Ham and eggs and hash browns – things he could relate to appearance and taste and smell. And then a phalanx of questions marched by. Exactly who was he? What the hell was he doing there? And where was 'there'? And why? That was the *big* question. Why did he suddenly wake up on a road and not know who he was? And why wasn't anyone in the diner? Where was the owner or the cook or the counterman? Why weren't they there? And again the little germ of disquiet that he'd felt outside stirred inside him.

He chewed the last piece of doughnut, swigged it down with what remained of the coffee, and went back into the other room. Once again he vaulted over the counter; tossed a quarter on top of it. At the front door, he turned and surveyed the room again. Damn it, but it was normal, it was real, it was natural looking. The words, the place, the smell, the look. He put his hand on the knob of the door and pulled it open. He was about to step outside when a thought hit him. Suddenly he knew what had disturbed him about the garbage cans. He carried this disquiet with him as he walked out into the hot morning.

He knew what was the missing element and the knowledge gave him a cold apprehension that he hadn't felt before. It did little jarring things to his nerve endings because suddenly something formed and entered into his thoughts. Something that couldn't be understood. Something beyond the norm. Beyond the word symbols, past the realm of logic that had been supporting him and answering his questions and giving him a link to reality.

There were no flies.

He walked around the corner of the building to stare again at the back yard with its row of garbage cans. There were no flies. There was a silence and nothing stirred and there were no flies.

He walked slowly back toward the highway, suddenly conscious of what was wrong. The trees were real and the highway and the diner with everything in it. The smell of the coffee was real and the taste of the doughnut and the cereals had the right names and Coca Cola came in a bottle and cost a nickel. It was all right and proper and everything was in its right place. *But there was no life to it!* This was the missing element – activity! This was the thought he carried down the highway past a sign which said, 'Carsville, 1 mile'.

He entered the town and it spread out in front of him, neat and attractive. A small main street circled a village park that lay in the centre of everything. Set back in the middle of this park area was a large school. On the circular main street were a row of stores, a movie theatre, more stores and a police station. Further down was a church, a residential street that lay beyond and finally a drugstore on the corner. There was a book store, a confectionery, a grocery store and out in front of it, a small sign which read 'Bus Stop'. It lay there quietly and prettily in the mid-morning sun and it was quiet. There was no sound at all.

He walked down the sidewalk peering into the windows. All of the stores were open. The bakery had fresh cake and cookies. The book store was running a special sale. The movie theatre advertised a picture out front having to do with war in the air. There was a three-storey office building that told of lawyers inside, public notary and a real estate firm. Further down there was a glass-enclosed public telephone and then a department store with a delivery entrance blocked off from the street by a wire mesh fence.

Once again he reflected on the phenomena. There were the stores, the park, the bus stop, the whole works, but there were no people. There wasn't a soul to be seen. He leaned against the side of the bank building and scanned the street left to right, as if somehow he could find something stirring if he looked hard enough.

It was when his eyes reached the fence fronting the department store delivery entrance directly across the street, that he saw the girl. She was sitting in a truck parked inside the yard, plain as day – the very first person he'd seen. He felt his heart jump as he nervously stepped off the curb and started walking toward her. Halfway across the street he stopped, feeling his palms wet. He had an impulse to run like hell over to the truck or to stand there and shout questions at the girl. He forced a matter-of-factness into his tone, made himself smile.

'Hey, Miss! Miss, over here.' He felt his voice rising higher and again he made an effort to keep it low and conversational. 'Miss, I wonder if you could help me. I was wondering if you knew where everyone was. Doesn't seem to be anyone around. Literally . . . not a soul.'

Now he took what he hoped was a sauntering walk across the street toward her, noticing that she continued to look straight at him from inside the cab of the truck. He reached the other side of the street, stopped a few feet from the wire mesh gate and smiled at her again.

'It's a crazy thing,' he said. 'Crazy, odd-ball thing. When I woke up this morning –' He stopped and he thought this over. 'Well, I didn't exactly wake up,' he said. 'I just sort of – just sort of found myself walking down the road.'

He reached the sidewalk, went through the half-open gate to the passenger side of the truck. The girl inside wasn't looking at him any longer. She was staring straight out through the front windshield and he saw her profile. Beautiful woman. Long blonde hair. But pale. He tried to think where he'd seen features like that – so immobile, so without expression. Bland, yes, but more than bland. Spiritless.

'Look, Miss,' he said, 'I don't want to frighten you, but there must be somebody around here who could tell me –'

His hand had opened the truck door when his voice was cut off by the girl's body as she slumped over, past the wide, amazed eyes of the young man, and down, hitting the sidewalk with a loud, almost metallic clank. He stared down at the upturned face, then became aware of words on the panel of the truck, 'Resnick's Store Mannequins'. He looked back at her face – the wooden, lifeless face with the painted cheeks and the painted mouth and the fixed half-smile, with the eyes that were wide open and showed nothing, told nothing. Eyes that looked exactly what they were – holes in a dummy's face. Something of the humour of it struck him now. He grinned, scratched his jaw, then slowly slid down, his back against the side of the truck till he was sitting next to the mannequin who lay there staring up at the blue sky and the hot sun.

The young man nudged her hard wooden arm, winked, clucked his tongue and said, 'You'll forgive me, babe, but at no time did I mean to be so upsetting. As a matter of fact' – he nudged her again – 'I've always had kind of a secret yen for the quiet type.' Now he reached over to pinch the unyielding cheek and laughed again. 'Get what I mean, babe?'

He picked up the dummy, and carefully deposited her back in the cab of the truck, pulling her dress down to a modest point over the knees. He closed the cab door, then turned and took a few aimless steps away from the truck. On the other side of the mesh gate was the circular main street with the small park in the middle. He went to the fence and let his eyes move left to right once more, taking in every one of the stores, as if by some unique concentration he might find a sign of life. But the street lay empty, the stores were unoccupied, the silence was persistent.

He went toward the service entrance of the department store beyond the truck, stuck his head into a dark hall, loaded with mannequins piled nude on top of one another. The thought hit him that it was like World War Two pictures of the gas ovens at the concentration camps, the way they were piled on top of one another. He was disturbed by the similarity and hurriedly backed out into the delivery yard. Then he shouted toward the open door.

'Hey! Anybody here? Anybody hear me?'

He went to the truck again and looked inside. There was no key in the ignition. He grinned at the lifeless face of the mannequin.

'How about it, babe? You wouldn't know where the ignition keys would be, would you?'

The mannequin stared straight ahead at the windshield.

It was then he heard the sound. The first he'd heard outside the diner. At first it made no sense to him. It was unrelated to anything he knew or could associate with the stillness. Then he realized what the sound was. It was a phone ringing. He ran toward the fence, slamming himself against it, his fingers gripping the wire strands, his eyes darting around until he found what he was looking for. It was the glass enclosed public phone booth just across the street, a few yards into the park. The phone was still ringing.

The young man flung himself through the gate and raced across the street. He reached the booth at a dead run, flung open the glass door and almost pulled the phone out by the wire as he grabbed the receiver off the hook. He kicked the door shut behind him.

'Hello. Hello!' He jangled the receiver furiously. 'Hello! Operator? Operator?'

The phone was dead. He waited a moment, then slammed the receiver back on the cradle. He reached into his breast pocket and pulled out a dime. He shoved it in the slot and waited. Presently he heard his first voice, the colourless, astringently courteous tone of a telephone operator.

'The number you have reached,' the voice said, 'is not a working number –'

The young man was angry now. He shouted into the phone. 'Are you out of your minds down there? I didn't dial a number –'

'Please be sure you have the right number and are dialling it correctly.'

'I didn't dial a number, operator. The phone rang and I answered it.' Again he jiggled the hook wildly. 'Operator. Operator, will you listen to me, please? All I want to know is where I am. Understand? I just want to find out where I am and where the people are. Please, operator, listen –'

Again the operator's voice, impersonal, cold, as if from another planet. 'The number you have reached is not a working number. Please make sure you have the right number and are dialling it correctly.'

Then there was a long pause before the voice continued, 'This is a recording!'

The young man slowly replaced the receiver and stood there conscious now of the quiet town that surrounded him through the glass, terribly aware of the silence that hung over the place, a silence punctuated by what the operator had said. 'This is a recording.' The whole damn place was a recording. Sound put on wax. Pictures put on canvas. Things placed on a stage. But only for effect. But a voice – that was a lousy joke.

The inanimate things such as unattended coffeepots, mannequins, stores – these he could wonder at and walk away. But a human voice – he desperately needed to know that this was surrounded with flesh and blood. It was a cheat to have it any other way. It was a promise and then a withdrawal. It made him angry in addition to causing that tiny flutter of frightened concern. The phone book was hanging by a chain. He grabbed it, ripped it open, started to read through the pages. The names sprang up at him. Abel. Baker. Botsford. Carstairs. Cathers. Cepeda.

'Well, where are you people,' he shouted. 'Where do you hang out? Where do you live? Just in this God-damned book here?'

Again he rifled through the pages. The Dempseys. The Farvers. The Grannigans. And so on to a man named Zatelli who lived on North Front Street and whose first initial was A. The young man let the book drop from his hands. It swung back and forth on the chain. Slowly his head lifted until he stared out at the empty street.

'Look, boys,' he said softly. 'Who's watching the stores?' The glass windows looked back at him. *'Who's watching any of the stores?'*

He turned slowly, put his hand on the door and pushed. The door remained stationary. He pushed again. It was stuck tight. And now he had the feeling that it was a gag. A very big, complex, terribly unfunny gag. He pushed hard, throwing his shoulder against the door and still it did not move.

'Awright,' he shouted. 'Awright, it's a very funny joke. Very funny. I love your town. I love the sense of humour. But now it's not funny any more. Understand? Now it stinks. Who's the wise guy who locked me in here?' Now he kicked, shoved, pushed at the door until the sweat rolled down his face. He closed his eyes and leaned against the glass for a moment and then suddenly looked down to see the door hinge arched toward him. He gently pulled and the door swung open, bent and out of alignment, but open. He'd been pushing on it instead of pulling. It was as simple as that. He felt he should laugh or perhaps apologize to something or someone, but of course, there was no one to apologize to.

He stepped out into the sunlight and went across the park toward a building with a big glass globe in front with lettering on it which read 'Police'. He smiled to himself as he went toward it. Head for law and order, he thought. But more than just law and order – head for sanity. Maybe that's where to find it. When you're a little boy and lost, your mother tells you to go up to the nice policeman and tell him your name. Well, now he was a little boy and he was lost and there was no one else he could report to. And as to a name – someone would have to tell *him*.

The police station was dark and cool, split in half by a counter which ran the length of the room. Behind it was the sergeant's desk and chair and across the far wall a radio operator's table with microphone and a CW sending and receiving set. To the right was a barred door into a cell block. He went through the swinging door in the middle of the counter to the microphone. He picked it up, studying it, then illogically, as if it were expected of him to go along with the gag, he put on an official radio-car voice.

'Calling all cars. Calling all cars. Unknown man walking around police station. Very suspicious-looking egg. Probably wants to –'

His voice broke off. Across the room by the sergeant's desk, a thin column of smoke drifted lazily up toward the ceiling. He slowly put down the microphone and went to the desk. A big, quarter-smoked cigar was lying in an ash-tray, lighted and smoking. He picked it up, then put it down. He felt a tension, a fear, a sense of being watched and listened to. He whirled around as if to catch someone in the act of just that – staring and listening.

The room was empty. He opened the barred door. It creaked noisily. He went into the cell block. There were eight cells, four on each side, and they were all empty. Through the bars of the last cell on the right he could see a sink. Water was running. Hot water. He saw the steam. On a shelf was a razor, dripping wet and a shaving brush, full of lather. He closed his eyes for a moment because this was too much. This was far too much. Show me goblins, he thought, or ghosts or monsters. Show me dead people walking in a parade. Play shrill and discordant trumpet sounds on a funeral horn that jars the stillness of the morning – but stop frightening me with the grotesque normality of things. Don't show me cigar butts in ash-trays and water running in a sink and lather-covered shaving brushes. These are what shock more than apparitions.

He slowly entered the cell and went to the sink. He reached out a trembling hand and touched the lather on the brush. It was real. It felt warm. It smelled of soap. The water dripped into the sink. The razor said Gillette, and he thought of the World Series on television and the New York Giants taking four in a row from the Cleveland Indians. But God that must have been ten years ago. Or maybe it was last year. Or maybe it hadn't happened yet. Because now he had no base, no starting point, no date or time or place of reference. He was not conscious of the sound of the creaking cell door, as it slowly closed on him, until he saw the shadow of it on the wall inching across slowly, inexorably.

He let out a sob and flung himself across to the door, squeezing through just before it closed. He hung on to it for a moment, then backed away from the cell to lean against the door on the opposite side, and stare across at the now closed and locked door as if it were a kind of poisonous animal.

Something told him to run. Run. Run like hell. Get out. Take off. Get away. It was a whispered command in his inner ear. It was a last ditch order from an embattled mind, assaulted by nightmarish fear that could at any moment lock him rooted to the earth. It was all his instincts screaming at him in the name of safety and salvation. Get the hell out of here. Run! Run! *RUN!*

He was outside in the sun racing across the street, stumbling over the curb, scratching himself on a hedge as he ploughed head first into it. Then over the hedge and into the park, running, running, running. He saw the school building loom up in front of him and there was a statue in front. His motion carried him up the steps to the statue until suddenly he found himself clutching a metal leg of a heroic looking educator who died in 1911 and whose metal visage loomed up in front of him silhouetted against the blue sky. Then he began to cry. He looked up at the stillness, the stores, the movie theatre, and finally the statue, and he cried. 'Where is everybody? Please, for Christ's sake tell me . . . where is everybody?'

The young man sat on the curb in the late afternoon staring down at his shadow and the other shadows that flanked him. A store awning, a bus-stop sign, a streetlight post – formless globs of shadow that stretched across the sidewalk in a line. He slowly rose to his feet, looked briefly at the bus-stop sign and then down the street as if in some half-hearted, half-hopeless expectation of seeing a big red and white bus approach, open its doors, let out a crowd of people. People. That's what the young man wanted to see. His own kind.

The silence had been building all day. It had become an entity all of itself, a pressure on him, an oppressive, hot, itchy, wool-like thing that surrounded and covered him, that made him sweat and squirm and wish he could throw it off and crawl out.

He took a slow walk down the main street – his fortieth or fiftieth walk down that same street since morning. He passed the now familiar stores, looking into the now familiar doors, and it was the same. Counters, goods unattended.

He entered a bank for the fourth time that afternoon, and also for the fourth time, walked behind the tellers' cages, picking up handfuls of money and throwing them aside. Once he lit his cigarette from a hundred-dollar bill and laughed uproariously at it until suddenly, after he'd thrown the half-burnt bill down on the ground, he found himself unable to laugh any longer. All right, so a guy can light a cigarette from a hundred-dollar bill – but so what?

He walked out of the bank and then crossed the street and headed for the drugstore. There was a two-for-one sale announced on signs plastered across the window. Church bells rang from down the street and this jarred him. For a moment he flattened himself against the side of the drugstore staring wildly toward the sound until he realized what it was.

He walked into the drugstore, a big, square room surrounded by high counters and shelves with many glass display cases running in lines across the room. A big, mirror-backed fountain was at the rear, with pictures of floats and frappes and sodas and malts. He stopped by the cigar counter, helped himself to an expensive one, took off its paper and sniffed.

'A good cigar, that's what this country needs,' he said aloud as he walked toward the fountain. 'A good cigar. A couple of good cigars. And some people to smoke them.'

He put the cigar carefully in a breast pocket and went in back of the fountain. From there he scanned the room, the empty booths, the juke box selectors over each one. And felt the stillness of the place that was totally incongruous with what was in it. It was a room poised for action; a room on the verge of coming alive, but never quite doing so. Behind the fountain were the ice-cream containers. He picked up an ice-cream scoop, took a glass dish from a shelf near the mirror and put two large scoops of ice cream in it. He covered this with syrup, then with nuts, added a cherry and some whipped cream.

He looked up and said, 'How about it, anybody? Anybody for a sundae?' He paused and listened to the silence. 'Nobody, huh? Okay.'

He spooned up a large hunk of ice cream and cherry and whipped cream, put it in his mouth and liked the taste of it. For the first time he saw his reflection in the mirror and he was not surprised by what he saw. The face had a vaguely familiar look, not handsome, but not unpleasant. And young, he thought. It was quite young. It was the face of a man well under thirty. Maybe twenty-five or twenty-six, but no older. He studied the reflection. 'You'll forgive me, old pal,' he said to it, 'but I don't recollect the name. The face seems familiar, but the name escapes me.'

He took another bite of the ice cream, rolled it around in his mouth, melted it, and swallowed it, watching these actions in the mirror. He pointed the spoon very casually at the image.

'I'll tell you what my problem is. I'm in the middle of a nightmare that I can't wake up from. You're part of it. You and the ice cream and the cigar. The police station and the phone booth – that little mannequin.' He looked down at the ice cream and then around at the drugstore then back to his reflection.

'This whole bloody town – wherever it is – *whatever* it is –' He cocked his head to one side, suddenly remembering something and he grinned at the image.

'I just remembered something. Scrooge said it. You remember Scrooge, old buddy – Ebenezer Scrooge? It's what he said to the ghost, Jacob Marley. He said, "You may be an undigested bit of beef, a blot of mustard. A crumb of cheese. A fragment of an undone potato. But there's more of gravy about you than grave.'

He put the spoon down now and pushed the ice cream away. 'You see? That's what you are. That's what you all are. You're what I had for dinner last night.' Now the smile faded. Something intense crept into the voice. 'But I've had it now. I've had it. I want to wake up.' He turned from the mirror to the store and the empty booths. 'If I can't wake up I've got to find somebody to talk to. That much I've *got* to do. I've got to find somebody to talk to.'

For the first time he noticed a card standing on the counter. It was a basketball schedule of Carsville High School, announcing that on 15 September Carsville would play Corinth High. On twenty-first September, Carsville would play Leedsville. There'd be games on through December with six or seven other high schools – this was all announced matter-of-factly, quite officially, on the large poster.

'I must be a very imaginative guy,' the young man said at last. 'Very, very imaginative. Everything right down to the last detail. The last little detail.'

He left the fountain and crossed the room to where there were several revolving pocket-book racks. Titles on the book covers flicked briefly across his consciousness then disappeared. Murder stories, introduced on the covers by blondes in negligees, with titles like *The Brothel Death Watch*. Reprint of famous novels and gag books. Something called *Utterly Mad*, with a smiling half-wit face, captioned, 'Alfred E. Neuman says, "What, me worry?" Some of the books seemed familiar. Fragments of plots and characters made brief excursions into his mind. He absent-mindedly turned the racks as he walked by. They creaked around, sending titles, pictures and covers blurring in front of his eyes, until he saw one that made him reach forward, grab the rack to stop it.

The book's cover depicted a kind of vast desert with a tiny, almost undistinguishable figure of a human being standing in the middle of it, arms akimbo, staring up toward the sky. There was a dim range of mountains beyond and, seemingly rising from the mountaintops, was a single line title, *The Last Man on Earth*.

The young man riveted his eyes to these words, feeling a fusion taking place between mind and sight. The *Last Man on Earth*. There was something especially meaningful — something of particular significance — something that suddenly made him gasp and whirl the rack around, sending the title off into a blurred orbit.

But when the rack slowed down, the book cover took on clarity again and it was then that he discovered there were many of them. There were many books of the last man on earth. Row after row of tiny figures standing, arms outstretched, on vast deserts, each cover staring back at him as the rack slowed and finally stopped moving.

He backed away from the books, unable to take his eyes away from them, until he reached the front door and briefly saw his reflection in the mirror — a white-faced, youngish looking man who stood at the entrance to a drugstore, looking tired, lonely, desperate and — frightened.

He went out, assuming composure while both his body and his mind pulled and yanked at him. Halfway across the street, he stopped, turning round and round and round.

Suddenly he shouted, 'Hey? Hey! Hey, anybody? Anybody see me? Anybody hear me? Hey!'

An answer came after a moment. The deep throated, melodic bells of the church pealed out the notice of the passing day. They rang five times and then stopped. The echo lingered, and then this too faded away. The young man went down the street past the now familiar stores, no longer seeing them. His eyes were open but he saw nothing. He kept thinking of the book titles — *The Last Man on Earth*, and it did something to his insides. It was as if a heavy glob of indigestible food had gone protesting down his throat to settle, leaden and heavy, in his gut. *The Last Man on Earth*. The picture and the words stuck with frightening clarity in his consciousness. The tiny figure of the lone man in the desert, hands outstretched. The indistinct, lonely little figure whose fate was spread across the sky, across the mountain ranges beyond it — the last man on earth. He couldn't shake that picture or the words, as he headed toward the park.

He was quite unaware that the afternoon sun now looked pale and distant as it moved across the sky. It was on its way out for that day.

It was night and the young man sat on a park bench close to the statue in front of the school. He played tic-tac-toe with a stick in the dirt, winning game after game and then wiping out each victory with the heel of his shoe to begin all over again. He'd made himself a sandwich in a small restaurant. He'd walked through the department store and then through a Woolworth five-and-dime. He'd gone into the school, through empty classrooms and had stifled an impulse to scrawl obscenities on a blackboard. Anything to shock or jar or to defy. Anything in the way of a gesture to rip away at the façade of reality that surrounded him. He was sure it was a façade. He was sure it must be just the real quality of the unreal dream and if only he could erase it and reveal what was underneath! – but he couldn't.

A light shone on his hand. He looked up startled. Street lights were going on and lights in the park joined them. Light after light all over the town. Street lights. Store windows. And then the flickering of the marquee lights in front of the theatre.

He rose from the bench and went to the theatre and stopped by the tiny box office. A ticket was sticking out of the metal slot. He put it in his breast pocket and was about to go inside when he saw a poster announcing the movie inside. On the poster was a large blow-up of an air force pilot, profile to the sky, staring up at a flight of jet aircraft that streaked across and over him.

The young man took a step toward the poster. Slowly and unconsciously his hands touched the coveralls he was wearing and very gradually there was a bridge between himself and the man on the poster. And then it came to him. They were dressed alike. The coveralls were almost identical. The young man grew excited, and some of the fatigue washed away, leaving behind it an enthusiasm bordering on exultation. He reached out and touched the poster. Then he whirled around to look toward the empty streets and spoke aloud.

'I'm Air Force. That's it. I'm Air Force. I'm in the Air Force. That's right! I remember. I'm in the Air Force.' It was a tiny, insignificant skein to a crazy quilt blanket of unknowns – but it *was* something he could pick up and hold and analyse. It *was* a clue. And it was the first one. The only one.

'I'm in the Air Force,' he shouted. He headed into the theatre. 'I'm in the Air Force!' His voice reverberated through the empty lobby. 'Hey, anybody, everybody, somebody – I'm in the Air Force!' He yelled it into the theatre, the words banging through the air, over row after row of empty seats and hitting against the huge, white, motionless screen at the far end.

The young man sat down and found he was perspiring. He felt for a handkerchief, pulled it out, wiped his face. He felt the beard stubble, knowing that there were a thousand closed doors to his subconscious that he was close to opening.

'Air Force,' he said softly now. 'Air Force. But what does that mean? What does "Air Force" mean?' His head jerked upward. 'Was there a bomb? Is that it? That *must* have been it. A bomb –' He stopped, shaking his head. 'But if there'd been a bomb, everything would have been destroyed. And nothing's been destroyed. How could it have been a –'

The lights began to dim and a strong beam of light from a projectionist's booth somewhere in the rear of the theatre suddenly shone on the white screen. There was the sound of music, loud, blaring, martial music, and on the screen a B-52 bomber headed down a runway and suddenly screamed into the air over his head. There were more big B-52s and now they were in the sky, a flight of them, heading up leaving lines of vapour trails. And always the music blaring out underneath it.

The young man rose to his feet, his eyes wide, disbelieving. The beam of light disappeared into a small, blinking hole high above a balcony.

'Hey!' he screamed. 'Who's showing the picture? Somebody must be showing the picture! Hey! Do you see me? I'm down here. Hey, whoever's showing the picture – I'm down here!'

He ran up the aisle, through the lobby, and up the stairs to the balcony. He stumbled across the dark seats, falling several times and finally, not finding an aisle, he simply crawled and jumped and scrambled over the tops of seats toward the small bright hole in the wall at the far end. He threw his face against it, staring directly into the blinding, white light. It sent him reeling back in momentary blindness.

When he could see again he found another opening in the wall, higher than the first. He jumped up, and got a quick glimpse of an empty room, a giant projector and stacks of film cans. He was dimly aware of voices on the screen, loud, giant voices that filled the theatre. Once again he jumped up to look in the projectionist's booth and in the brief moment of one-sided combat with gravity, he again saw the empty room, the machine running smoothly, the hum of it heard dimly through the glass.

But when he landed back on his feet he knew there was no one up there. It was a machine running by itself. It was a picture showing itself. It was like the town and everything in it. Machines, items, things – all unattended. He backed away, banged against the back of the top row of seats and, losing his balance, sprawled head first.

The beam of light kept changing intensity as scenes altered on the screen. There was dialogue and music and it reverberated around the theatre. Voices of giants. Music of a million-piece band. And something inside the young man cracked. The small compartment in the back of his mind, where man closets his fears, ties them up, controls and commands them, broke open and they surged across brain and nerves and muscles – a nightmare flood in open rebellion.

The young man scrambled to his feet, sobbing, choking, screaming. He raced down the stairs, through the door, down the steps toward the lobby.

It was when he reached the foot of the steps that he saw the other person. He was directly across the lobby and approaching from a flight of stairs the young man hadn't noticed before. The young man didn't see him clearly nor did he try. He just ran toward him, dimly aware that the other person was running toward him at the same time. In the fraction of a moment that it took him to cross the lobby he had only one thought and that was to reach the other person, to touch him, to hold him. To follow him out to wherever he was going. Out of the building, off the streets, out of the city, because now he knew that he must get away.

It was this thought that filled his mind just before he hit the mirror – a full length mirror that hung on the opposite wall. And he hit it with the force of a hundred and seventy pounds, smashing into it at a dead run. The mirror seemed to explode into a thousand pieces. He found himself on the floor looking at little fragments of his reflection in the small and minute sections of mirror that remained on the wall. It was the picture of a hundred young men lying cut and dazed on the floor of a theatre lobby, staring up at what was left of a mirror. And then he lurched to his feet and, like a drunken man in a tilting ship in a heavy sea, he stumbled out of the lobby and out into the street.

Outside it was dark and misty; the streets were wet. The street lights were enveloped in fog and each shone like a dim moon hanging in vapour. He began to run along sidewalks and across streets. He tripped over a bicycle stand and landed on his face, but was on his feet in a moment continuing the mad, headlong, thoughtless, desperate race to no place in particular. He tripped over a curb near the drugstore and again fell on his face, conscious for a moment that he could still feel pain – a jarring, wrenching pain. But only for a moment. He pushed his palms against the sidewalk, forcing himself up and then fell over on his back.

For a moment he lay there, eyes closed. And then he opened them. A nightmare knocked at his head and asked to come in and ice flowed over his body. He started to scream. An eye was looking at him. A giant eye, bigger than the upper trunk of a man. An unblinking, cold-looking eye was staring at him and his scream never let up, even after he had floundered again to his feet and started to run back toward the park. He was like a human siren disappearing into the dark. Behind him the big painted eye on the optometrist's window stared after him — cold, inhuman and unblinking.

He fell, clutching against a street light. There was a panel with a button which his fingers touched, scrabbled at and finally kept pushing over and over again. A sign over it read, 'Push to turn green'. He didn't know the sign was there. He only knew he had to push the button and this he kept doing, while the light over the intersection turned red, then yellow, then green, over and over again, responding to the bleeding knuckles of the young man who kept pushing a button and moaning to himself in a soft, barely intelligible chant.

'Please – please, somebody – help me. Help me, somebody. Please. Please. Oh dear God – somebody help me! Won't somebody help me. Won't somebody come – can anyone hear me – ?'

The control room was dark and the figures of the uniformed men were silhouetted against the light that came from a small viewing screen on which could be seen the face and upper body of Sergeant Mike Ferris, a youngish looking man in coveralls who kept pushing a button to the right of the screen. Ferris' voice babbled out into the darkness of the control room pleading for help, for someone to listen, for someone to show themselves. It was the sobbing, pleading, supplicating voice of a man whose mind and body were laid bare on a block and the up-and-down intonation seemed naked and embarrassing, as if listened to through a keyhole, with an ear pressed against the door.

The brigadier-general rose, his face strained from long hours of protracted concentration. He was obviously disturbed by the face and voice of the man on the screen. His voice, however, was clipped and authoritative.

'All right, clock him and get him out of there,' the general commanded.

A lieutenant-colonel to the general's right reached over, pressed a button and spoke into a panel microphone.

'Release the subject on the double!'

Inside the vast, high ceilinged hangar, men sprang to their feet and ran toward the rectangular metal box that squatted impassively in the centre of the huge room. A metal door was swung open. Two non-coms entered followed by an Air Force doctor. Very gently the wires and electrodes were removed from Sergeant Ferris' body. The doctor's hands wandered over his wrists and then propped open his eyes to stare into the dilated pupils. His ear listened to the hollow thumping of an overworked heart. Then Ferris was lifted carefully out and placed on a stretcher.

The medical officer went to the general, where he stood with his staff, staring across the hangar toward the prostrate figure on the stretcher.

The medical officer said, 'He's all right, sir. Delusions of some sort, but he's responding all right now.'

The general nodded and said, 'Can I see him?'

The medical officer nodded and the eight uniformed men walked across the hangar, their feet making a clickety-clack against the concrete as they approached the stretcher. On each of their left shoulders was an insignia patch, indicating that they were members of the Space Technological Research Command, US Air Force. They reached the side of the stretcher and the general leaned over to look closely into the face of Sergeant Mike Ferris.

Ferris' eyes were open now. He turned his face to look up at the general and smiled slightly. The face was wan, pale, bearded. Anguish, loneliness, the misery of some two hundred-odd hours in solitary confinement in a metal box showed in his eyes and the lines of his face.

It was the post-shock look of every wounded man the general had ever seen and while he didn't know Ferris – that is, didn't know him personally except from sixty typewritten sheets in the man's file that he'd studied intensively before the test, he felt he knew him now. He'd been watching him for over two weeks on the small screen closely, more closely than any human being had been watched before.

The general reminded himself that there should be a medal in this for the sergeant. He had taken what no man had ever taken before. He had remained alone for two hundred and eighty-four hours on a simulated trip to the moon with almost every condition a man might have to face duplicated in the five-by-five box. The wires and electrodes had given a good indication of how the space traveller would react physically. They had charted his respiration, heart action, blood pressure. Beyond this, and most important, they had given a good idea of the point at which a man would break; of the moment a man would succumb to loneliness and try to battle his way out. It was at this moment that Sergeant Mike Ferris had pushed the release button inside his tiny confinement.

The general forced a grin as he leaned over Ferris and said, 'How you doing, Sergeant? Feeling better?'

Ferris nodded, 'Much better, sir, thank you.'

There was a moment's silence before the general spoke again. 'Ferris,' he asked, 'what was it like? Where'd you think you were?'

Ferris stared up toward the high ceiling of the hangar and reflected a moment before he spoke. 'A town, sir,' he answered. 'A town without people . . . without anybody. A place I don't want to go to again.' Then he turned to look back toward the general and he said, 'What was wrong with me, sir? Just off my rocker or something?'

The general turned toward the medical officer with a nod.

The medical officer said softly, 'Just a kind of nightmare your mind manufactured for you, Sergeant. You see, we can feed the stomach with concentrates. We can pump oxygen in and waste materials out. We can supply you with reading for recreation and try to keep your mind occupied.'

There was a silence now as the men surrounding the stretcher looked toward the medical officer.

'There's one thing we can't simulate,' he continued. 'And that's a very basic need. Man's hunger for companionship. That's a barrier we don't know how to breach yet. The barrier of loneliness.'

Four aid men lifted Mike Ferris up on the stretcher and carried him across the vast room to the giant doors at the opposite side. He was then carried out into the night where an ambulance had been pulled up and was waiting. Ferris looked up at a giant moon and thought to himself that the next time it would be for real. Not just a box in a hangar. But he was too tired to give it much thought.

They lifted him gently and were about to place him in the rear of the ambulance when Mike Ferris quite accidentally touched his breast pocket. He felt something stiff and took it out of his pocket. The doors of the ambulance shut on him and left him in the quiet darkness of the inside. He heard the engines start and felt the wheels underneath him and was much too tired to reflect on whatever was in his fingers, just a hand's length from his face.

Just a theatre ticket – that's all it was. A theatre ticket from a small movie house in an empty town. A theatre ticket, he thought to himself, and it was in his breast pocket and as the ambulance engines lulled him to sleep and the gently rolling wheels made him close his eyes, he held on to the ticket very tightly. In the morning he'd have to ask himself some questions. In the morning he would have to piece together some impossible fabric of dream and reality. But all that would have to come in the morning. Mike Ferris was much too tired now.

The Incredible Dr Markesan

BY AUGUST DERLETH

The year 1960 saw the debut of Thriller *a series devoted to horror stories and hosted by Boris Karloff at his sinister best. The fifty-minute adaptations of tales by a group of the best contemporary writers in the genre were stylishly filmed in black and white and NBC recruited an impressive roster of guest stars. Such, indeed, was the reputation of* Thriller *that the sixty-seven episodes which ran from 1960 to 1962 have subsequently been reshown a number of times on American TV, most recently in 1987 retitled* Boris Karloff Presents Thriller. *Among the stars who appeared were Leslie Neilsen, Jack Carson, William Shatner, Robert Vaughn, John Ireland, Ray Milland, John Carradine, Ursula Andress, and, occasionally, Boris Karloff himself. Of the series' writers, those whose names were most familiar to viewers were Charles Beaumont, Richard Matheson, Robert Arthur, Robert Bloch and August Derleth.*

The story remembered by most viewers for its genuinely chilling qualities was 'The Incredible Dr Markesan' by August Derleth (1909–71), a contributor to the legendary horror magazine, Weird Tales, *and editor of numerous horror anthologies. Derleth is, however, best remembered today for his activities as a publisher and being responsible for issuing the first book collections of the work of H.P. Lovecraft, Ray Bradbury, Robert Bloch and several more of the century's most important masters of the macabre. He was also principally responsible for generating the interest in the reclusive Lovecraft's work which has now made him a cult figure around the world. But Derleth was also a skilled writer of horror himself, as he demonstrates in the following story, which was one of several from his pen that were used in the series. Boris Karloff himself starred in the TV adaptation in which the Colonel Markesan of the original became Dr Markesan. One critic later described the episode as, 'an outrageous mad scientist tale jammed with Gothic trappings – a house with secret corridors, zombified cadavers resting inside open caskets in Markesan's workshop, and so on.' Robert Florey directed the story and there were excellent supporting performances from Dick Yorke and Carolyn Kearney. (As a matter of record, Karloff had been signed to make another horror anthology series,* The Veil, *before* Thriller *reached the screen. However, although he narrated the pilot film, none of the networks were prepared to finance the series and that one episode has remained unshown to this day.)*

I HESITATED to ring the bell.

Since that time I have thought many times how much better it would have been if I had not rung it, if I had gone away from that large lonely old house in the pine grove.

But I rang, and abruptly the door swung back.

Far back in the shadows of a darkened hall stood a tall, elderly man, dressed in a greenish black suit. The deep shadow flung across the doorway by the close-pressing trees and the darker blackness of the unlighted hall served to leave his outlines faint. He stood touching the door with an outstretched arm, and his strange, lustrous eyes were fixed upon me with disconcerting intensity.

'Can you direct me to Colonel Markesan's estate?' I asked.

'I am Colonel Markesan,' said the man in the hall, speaking in a soft, pleasant voice.

'I've come in answer to your advertisement for a caretaker,' I said.

'Come in,' said Colonel Markesan.

I stepped into the house, and the colonel began to walk down the hall, leaving me to close the door. 'Follow me, please,' he murmured, and led the way from the shadowy corridor into a library which was as dark and gloomy as the hall. A strong odour of long-settled dust and long-undisturbed wood and cloth hung in the air.

'Sit down, please,' said the colonel. He himself sat down as he spoke.

The room was so dark that I could see no more than the vague outlines of his head projecting over the chair, and the strange whiteness of his face and hands in the gloom.

'Your name?' asked Colonel Markeson

'Frederick Bancroft.'

'Age?'

'Twenty-seven.'

'Any chronic ill health? Or nervousness?'

'No.'

'Any experience?'

'None. I've been a school-teacher.'

A momentary flicker of interest crossed the colonel's face. He looked quickly away from me and for a moment said nothing. Presently he faced me again and asked, 'Have you any one depending on you?'

'No one but myself,' I replied.

'Very good,' said Colonel Markesan. 'I need a strong young man to keep the estate in good shape; it has gone somewhat to seed in my absence, and I haven't the strength to keep it up. It must be perfectly clear, however, that I shall not care to be asked questions regarding the estate or any of my activities. I am prepared to pay well.'

'What are the requirements?' I asked.

Colonel Markesan continued. 'I have an aversion for society; you are to be my sole link with the world, for I seldom go out. You will begin your duties today by going into Boston to pay for the advertisement which brought you. Since I own no machine and my carriage lacks horses to draw it, you will have to walk. Fortunately, it isn't far. You will also attend to any other possible applicants by sending them away at once.

'By day you are to take care of the house and grounds. You will find everything you need in the shed beyond the house. I don't care to have you venture out at night; you must either stay in your room from dusk to dawn, or leave the house entirely for the night. In such case, you must leave at once after dinner, which you will eat alone and prepare for yourself, since I employ no other person, and you must not return until after sunrise.' Colonel Markesan paused, as if awaiting protest from me. I made none. His requirements, which impressed me as those of a confirmed misanthrope, were not particularly difficult.

Since I said nothing, he went on. 'If my requirements seem odd, you must overlook that. If you can't, you may as well leave at once.'

'Your requirements do seem somewhat strange,' I replied, 'but I see no reason for not complying with them.'

Colonel Markesan nodded and rose. He walked noiselessly to a cabinet lost in the shadows save for a thin greenish light which penetrated the shutters of a near-by window and faintly outlined the surface of the old cabinet. This the colonel opened, and from it he took a packet of bills which he gave to me, saying, 'I think that will pay at least a month's expenses.'

After I had taken the money, he added, 'That concludes the

immediate business between us. Pray do not disturb me with any problems confronting you in the course of your duties; solve them as you please, as long as you don't infringe upon my fundamental rules.'

With this final instruction, Colonel Markesan turned on his heel and glided over the soft carpet to the almost hidden door of an adjoining room, through which he vanished into the blackness beyond.

I hesitated for a moment; then I made my way to a window, opened it, and pushed back the shutter. The sunlight fell on an old-fashioned red rug into which a large flower pattern had been woven, and the details of the room were brought to sudden, dusty life – a few very stiff, obviously antique chairs, a handsome table, the cabinet, and shelves lining the walls upon which books were evenly and neatly arranged, and obviously not much in use. The entire room showed little sign of usage, for it was devoid of any token of life. I looked at last at the packet of money in my hands and was faintly amused to find that the bills were still the old large kind which had gone out of circulation some years before. A later examination showed that not one of them had been printed later than 1907.

Shortly after, I left the house and caught a ride into Boston.

On my return to the Markesan estate, I put my bags down outside the front door and made my way around the house to the small wooden shed deep in the foliage of tall bushes where my gardening equipment was stored. The tools were apparently very old, and were rusted, though still usable. When I left the shed presently, I observed that the estate must run back a good distance, for as far as I could see through the woodland, no fence line broke the expanse. The vastness of the estate and its comparative silence brought a depressing feeling of loneliness which even the raucous cawing of a few crows in the pine trees could not dispel.

As I went down the hall with my bags I observed that a light was burning in the library, for the doorway of that room was limned in a strange, green glow, and shadows were flickering across the black, rug in the hall. I deposited my bags at the foot of the staircase and entered the library where I saw a solitary green candle alight on the table. Beneath the candle was a note, held down by a small bunch of keys.

The note was short:

'Mr Bancroft: I have been called away, and am not sure when I will return. Your room is at the head of the stairs. There you may do as you please. Molest nothing in the remaining rooms, excepting the kitchen. Avoid opening windows, please. Here are the keys of the house, also. Go to work on the grounds when you wish.

'Colonel Markesan.'

141

My room was bright and comfortable and in obvious readiness for a tenant. Though a bathroom adjoining the room lacked all electric fixtures. The single window of the room was set deep in the wall and protected by iron bars set recently from the outside. This discovery disconcerted me somewhat, and my trepidation was considerably increased when I discovered on leaving the room that my door was fitted with a bolt on the outside, making it possible for my employer to lock me in at his wish. Apparently Colonel Markesan was determined that I should have no chance to disregard his order and leave my room after once retiring in the evening.

When I had unpacked my bags, I went in search of the kitchen. I discovered that every cupboard and shelf was empty, a discovery which made necessary another immediate trip into Cambridge, where I purchased supplies for several days.

It was lunchtime when I returned, and I prepared my first meal. The colonel's promise that I would eat alone was borne out, for no one appeared then or during the remainder of that day, most of which I spent working on the grounds. When at last I retired to my room in accordance with instructions, Colonel Markesan had not reappeared.

I had been in my room scarcely a half-hour when I heard the sharp sound of iron grating on iron – the sound of a bolt sliding home just beyond my threshold. For a startled moment I sat listening; then, hearing nothing, I rose and cautiously tried the door. It was locked from the outside. I felt a chill apprehension upon reflecting that Colonel Markesan had certainly not been in the house when I had gone to my room, and I had not heard a sound to indicate that any one had since entered. Yet the Colonel must have returned.

I went to bed that night with reluctance.

Next morning someone had slipped the bolt on my door before dawn. There was no sign of my employer, nor did he appear during the forenoon. Yet, while I was working toward noon in the deeply shaded grounds just behind the house, I happened to look upward, and saw the unmistakable grey-white face and lustrous eyes of my employer gazing at me from a second-floor window! Even as I looked, he vanished from sight.

My momentary amazement, however, was dissipated when I reflected that Colonel Markesan could easily have returned to the house by the front way while I was engaged in the rear. For an instant I thought that he was for some reason in hiding in the house, but that that thought was groundless, I learned when I met him later in the day moving effortlessly along the lower hall. His eyes passing fleetly over my face as he nodded, left an inexplicable impression of something to be feared. Yet Colonel Markesan was outwardly an attractive man in his sixties, with firm and harmonious features, and there was no reason for the persistence of the sinister feeling my momentary encounter with him had inspired.

That night again I had hardly gone to my room when I heard the bolt slide to, but by this time I had come to the conclusion that my employer was an eccentric whose wages compensated me for whatever idiosyncrasies l was forced to tolerate.

In this fashion a week went by. Now and then I caught sight of my singular employer, but in all that time his sole conversation with me concerned his life in Virginia, from where he had evidently returned to Massachusetts, his native state. I learned, too, that the house in which we were living was over a century and a half old, and had always been the property of the Markesan family. I did not once encounter the colonel beyond the house. Meanwhile, my work went along well, and I lived pleasantly enough.

On the tenth night after I had taken up residence with Colonel Markesan, my sleep was disturbed by a sound from below, a sound that to my semiconscious ears bore a startling resemblance to a man's shout. I was awake instantly. The sound recurred, together with what seemed to be a woman's muffled scream. Following these sounds came a low murmur as of many voices whispering somewhere in the house. Apparently Colonel Markesan had visitors, though having visitors seemed incongruous with my employer's personality. I listened until the murmur from below ebbed from my consciousness and sleep overcame me.

In the morning I looked casually for any signs of the presence of others besides Colonel Markesan, but found none. Not a chair had been misplaced, not a footprint disturbed the dusty ground about the doors leading from the house. Yet there remained no doubt in my mind of what I had heard in the night. The memory troubled me all day, and when I began to put together the other strange factors relating to my employment – Colonel Markesan's odd appearances and disappearances, the conditions under which I remained nightly in my room, the colonel's uncanny personal appearance – I was alarmed and uneasy.

I brooded on the matter until my curiosity and vague fear mounted to such a degree that I could no longer rest. I had to know what went on in the house at night, and accordingly, I immediately went to work on my door, making an aperture between door and casement so that I could, by means of a thin steel rod, slip the bolt from within. That night, I determined, I would try to ascertain what went on below, even at the risk of discovery and discharge.

Shortly after I retired to my room, the bolt slipped to as usual. Again, despite the most intense concentration, I did not hear footfalls. However, since the stairs and halls of the old house were deeply carpeted, lightly treading feet would make little sound.

I waited. And then abruptly, the whispering began from below.

For a few minutes I listened with my ear against the door. Then I took off my shoes and manipulated the bolt; it slipped back without the slightest sound. I turned the knob, and pulled the door back, then slipped quietly out into the hall and made my way down the stairs to a landing. Then I looked down over the banister.

Below me, limned in the strange green light which once before had attracted my eye, was the entrance to the drawing-room, into which I could look easily. There were six people in the glow of the green candles. One of them was my employer, and of them all, he alone seemed to be enjoying himself, for his usually immobile face was broken by a smile. The faces of the others were indistinct, and one visitor, sitting far back from the light, caused me a thrill of horror, for it seemed as if he had no face. The source of the whispering was now perfectly clear, for as I watched I saw Colonel Markesan address one after the other of his visitors, and I waited with marked eagerness for their replies. It occurred to me uneasily that Colonel Markesan's guests were not in the house voluntarily, for there emanated from them an atmosphere of hostility so distinct that I felt it even on the stairs.

Suddenly one of the visitors rose and made for the door, forcing me back up the stairs and into my room, but not before I saw Colonel Markesan bar the way by occupying the threshold and heard his rasping voice, 'I am master – you can do nothing unless I will it!'

The face of the man who had tried to force his way from the room was familiar. I again slipped the bolt to, and in the quiet of my room searched my memory for clues to his identity – Symphony Hall – the Saturday evening concerts – the man who used to sit across the aisle from me – Doctor Merlin Grant, Harvard physicist! But Doctor Grant had been dead three months – had been drowned while on vacation at Annisquam. Horror ran suddenly through me, for my conviction was unshakeable: though dead, Merlin Grant was downstairs in Colonel Markesan's drawing-room!

That night I did not sleep.

As early as possible next morning I examined the dusty paths leading to the house – and there was no footprint save mine to mar the ground near the doors! My astonishment was unbounded, for certainly my employer had had guests in the night. Though, upon waking, I had momentarily thought that my glance of Doctor Grant the previous night was an illusion, I now began to reconsider cautiously. Suddenly a terrifying thought struck me – could it be that not only had I indeed not erred – that I had actually seen the dead Merlin Grant in the night, but that all those eerie visitors were as dead as he?

I thrust the horrible fear from me, yet I could not forget. That day I went into Boston and looked up Colonel Markesan in the Public Records Office and in newspaper files. Though I learned little about my employer, I was considerably agitated and shocked to find that he was the same Robert Crawford Markesan, the Harvard professor, who, after a scandalous affair precipitated by his avowal that he could raise the dead, was summarily dropped from Harvard's austere staff. His 'lapse' was quickly forgotten, and Professor Markesan had retired to Virginia, where he assumed the title of Colonel. Of his activities in recent years there was no information.

It was not until some hours had passed that my sluggish mind began to piece together a ghastly connection between what I had read and what I had seen the preceding night. The thought of returning to the house in the pine grove became every moment more unattractive, Yet, despite my strong impulse not to go back, I did return shortly after noon.

That night I watched again.

The bolt had hardly been closed before I prised it back and stepped into the deserted hall. As I stood there, I heard the rear door of the house close softly. I made my way rapidly down the stairs and cautiously opened the door.

The vague and shadowy figure of Colonel Markesan was visible in the dusk of the descending night. He was crossing the lawn under the trees, and had evidently struck out for a little path running through fields and private estates into Cambridge. But if he contemplated going into the city, why didn't he take the shorter highway running past the house?

For only a moment I hesitated. Then I stepped from the house, sped into the darkening shadows, and followed him. Fortunately, the path was heavily shrouded by bushes on either side, so that it was possible to vanish instantly into the brush. Colonel Markesan moved along at extraordinary speed, increasing as the distance from the house widened. He seemed no longer to walk, but to glide along in a queer flapping motion.

We had gone slightly over half a mile when Colonel Markesan abruptly left the path, and when I came to the spot where he had diverged, I was astonished to find that he had disappeared. There was but one place he might have gone – nearby Mount Auburn Cemetery, one of whose side gates was not ten steps from the path.

I ran forward silently and looked cautiously through the bars of the gate. Colonel Markesan was in the cemetery, walking slowly down a long lane cutting deep into the burial ground. I attempted to open the gate to follow, but I found it locked. However, my surprise was somewhat abated when I discovered a loose bar which would have enabled a man as thin as my employer to enter, though I reflected immediately that Colonel Markesan had accomplished his entrance in a remarkably short time. But my conjectures were abruptly dropped, for my employer had paused before a tomb not far from the side gate.

He stood for some moments in dead silence. Then he began to talk in his sibilant voice, now potent with sinister menace which sent a shudder through me. I crouched back against the stone wall.

Then, before my eyes, an extraordinary thing took place. As Colonel Markesan spoke, a faint radiance began to glow near the door of the vault, and as I watched, it began to take form, growing darker, apparently more solid. And then, in the space of a minute, a man stood at Colonel Markesan's side!

My horror mounted, but my impulse to flee was drowned in my curiosity. Colonel Markesan was moving forward, beckoning with one hand to the thing from the tomb, which followed obediently. The two of them stopped at a second tomb, where once again Colonel Markesan repeated his hellish procedure. This time a woman was drawn to join the man, and together those two went flapping after the colonel.

Then I turned and fled, the memory of those pathetic and terrible ghosts haunting my flight.

Back at the house, I bolted myself into my room. I wanted to go away, but I lacked the courage; I feared that Colonel Markesan might suspect and follow me into the city. Yet I could not again endure what went on below, knowing not what hellish sorcery drew the dead from their tombs! I solved the problem at last by taking two veronal tablets, and before any sound from below broke into my somnolence, I slept.

Despite what I had seen, I could not go in search of Colonel Markesan next morning and tell him I was leaving. I was held back, too, by the vague hope that I might somehow prevent him from exercising his magic powers. Thinking along this line, I formulated a plan, and as the first step, I went into Cambridge and called upon Professor Karl Hohlden of Harvard's science department, one of the men whose name had been linked with the Markesan scandal years before. Since I myself had done work under Hohlden some years ago he received me cordially.

I plunged at once into the story of the weird occurrences. At the mention of my employer's name, Hohlden went oddly pale.

'Did you say *Markesan?* You can't mean Professor Markesan?' he asked.

I nodded. 'He calls himself Colonel now,' I explained.

'Can you describe the man?'

I described Colonel Markesan briefly, and my description agitated Professor Hohlden very much.

'I'm afraid such things can't be, Bancroft,' he said when I had finished. 'They just don't happen. Perhaps you've been suffering from mental shock, or perhaps you've been reading about that affair at the university some years ago and have begun to imagine things.'

I laughed hollowly. 'Unfortunately, such is not the case.' I replied. 'I could wish it were. My experience has been too distressingly real.'

I saw abruptly that Professor Hohlden was not very firm in his disbelief in my story. He rose suddenly and left the room, murmuring something about sending a telegram.

When he returned, he seemed calmer.

With infinite patience, he went over the facts of my story with me, and in the end he admitted that if delusion were ruled out, then mine was the only explanation. But though outwardly he continued to think that everything I had seen was delusion bordering upon madness, there was in his words a strong suggestion of belief.

'I'm afraid you think I'm mad as a hatter,' I said at last. 'I could wish that, too. But I don't think I am. I want you to come out there with me tonight. I want you to stay through the night. I want you to *see!*'

At this moment a telegram was handed in to Professor Hohlden. Eagerly he ripped open the envelope and read the message. His face paled, and for a moment he stood with closed eyes. Then he turned to me and said, 'I'll go with you.'

At the same time he handed the telegram to me, saying, 'Read it. I was afraid of that.'

I took the telegram and read it:

'Colonel Markesan died three years ago. Buried on family estate outside Cambridge.'

I groaned. 'I should have known, if it weren't so impossible,' I said. For I knew now why Colonel Markesan kept to the darkest part of the house, why his footsteps were soundless, why he could vanish so quickly at will, why he left no tracks in the dust beyond the house. 'But what can we do now?' I asked. 'How can we find a dead man?'

'Wait,' cautioned Professor Hohlden. 'Wait until I've seen what's going on in his house.'

I called the Markesan house, but it was only after repeated trials that I heard my employer's voice on the wire. I asked him whether it would be all right for me to bring an old friend for the night, a friend who understood the conditions as I knew them. Colonel Markesan agreed only with a reluctance which he took no pains to conceal.

Thus it was that, shortly after dinner, which we had in Cambridge, Professor Hohlden and I arrived at the house, where we went immediately to my room. Colonel Markesan was not in evidence. Since it was not yet time for me to retire to my room for the night, Hohlden, realizing that he might be recognized by his old colleague if he ventured from the room, suggested that I go out to the family vault, and see if indeed the colonel rested there.

The vault was set in the close-pressing bushes beyond the shed at the rear of the house. I played safe, and went first into the shed, from which I looked warily back toward the house, searching every window. There was no one at watch, I felt sure. Then I slipped from the single window in the back wall of the shed, and under cover of the bushes made my way to the vault.

It opened easily enough. Inside, one wall was lined with a row of name-plates, marking coffins sealed in rock. I looked for that of Colonel Markesan, but failed to find it. As I turned to leave the vault, I caught sight of one of the name-plates which had been lifted out of place and set on the floor, and saw that the space for the coffin gaped empty. I turned the plate over and read:

Robert Crawford Markesan
Born 17 May 1867 – Died 7 April 1929

The coffin had obviously been removed to some other place on the estate, and so I pointed out to Professor Hohlden upon my return to my room. 'And that means an intensive search, for the estate is large,' I added.

But Professor Hohlden shook his head. 'I don't think so. I'm sure the coffin will be somewhere in the house; otherwise there could have been no better hiding-place than the vault.'

While we were sitting in silence shortly after, the bolt of my door slipped to. Hohlden was impressed at this first evidence of my strange story, and it was clear that his disbelief was fading rapidly. We took off our shoes and sat waiting.

About two hours after we had retired to my room, the sound of voices rose from below. I slipped back the bolt, and the professor and I went into the hall.

I led the way cautiously to the landing on the stairs. There we looked into the shadowy gathering below, seeing the weirdly green faces of men both of us knew to be long dead.

Almost at once Hohlden gripped my arm convulsively. 'Good God!' he exclaimed, '– Charing, Grant, Latimer!'

I warned him to be silent, but he did not hear me. 'Look,' he continued, '– the little man in the corner; he's Charing, my old colleague, dead eight years – he was one of us who forced Markesan out. They all belong to our group, every one of them.'

I saw Charing huddled in a chair, his grey-green face twisted with pain. As we watched, Markesan approached and began to taunt him. We caught references to the power of the mind over death and the souls and bodies of the dead. But the scene proved too much for Hohlden, who turned abruptly and retreated to my room. I followed, and found him collapsed in a chair.

'Charing, poor devil!' he murmured. 'And Grant, and Latimer, and the others! Bancroft, we've got to end this!'

'But how?' I asked.

'We must find Markesan's body and destroy it. Good God! who could have dreamed that he might be right – that he had control of some secret – magic or scientific – that gave him power over the dead? He goes to the graves, you said, and draws them forth. His power is probably hypnotic, and yet it's hard to tell. He's proved his original point – that the spirits of the dead do exist in some place beyond earth.'

A cry from below interrupted Hohlden. We sat looking at each other with haggard eyes.

'Now,' said Hohlden suddenly. 'We've got to do it now – we can't wait another minute. I can't stand the thought of this meaningless torture for the rest of the night.'

'But wait,' I cautioned. 'Markesan will see and recognize us.'

'Of course he will! That won't make any difference. He has no power over the living – he is master only over the dead.'

Snatching the lamp from the bureau, Hohlden flung back the door and strode out into the hall, his eyes gleaming fiercely. From the landing we saw that Colonel Markesan, having doubtless heard the sound of the door and Hohlden's careless footsteps, stood looking upward, his lustrous green eyes fixed balefully upon us.

I hesitated, but Hohlden did not. Straight down the stairs he went. Colonel Markesan came forward, and the two of them met at the threshold of the drawing-room. Colonel Markesan averted his face from the glare of the lamp.

'So Bancroft brought you, Hohlden,' he murmured.

'I've come to end this, Markesan,' said Hohlden harshly.

As he spoke he thrust the lamp rudely into Markesan's face, causing the colonel to stumble backward.

'You don't like the light, do you Markesan?' said Hohlden. 'You never did, I remember – always preferred the dark. You will have plenty of darkness soon.'

He had been advancing upon the colonel as Markesan was falling back into the room, and he continued to thrust thc lamp forward. Then suddenly Colonel Markesan flung himself backward and away through heavy portiers, between two bookcases.

His move came so suddenly that for a moment Hohlden was too surprised to pursue. Then he leapt forward, and I followed. But Colonel Markesan was not in the adjoining roonn. Frantically Hohlden ran the length of the room and out into the hall. Still there was no sign of Colonel Markesan.

'No use losing our heads,' said Hohlden then. 'He's in the house somewhere – We've got to find him I think if we can manage to decapitate him, we'll end his horrible undead existence. We've got to find the place where he hides.'

We began a systematic search through the entire house. I carried my revolver. Because we had at first looked only cursorily into the attic and cellar, we went over them a second time. And yet we did not find Colonel Markesan.

Finally we returned to the drawing-room. Dawn was penetrating the heavy pines around the house, and it would soon be light enough to aid our search. But as Hohlden preceded me into the drawing-room, he gave a sharp cry of dismay.

I peered over his shoulder and saw oddly crumpled bodies – most of which were not bodies at all, but weird masses of still white flesh. In our haste to capture the colonel, we had forgotten his unfortunate victims.

'Good God,' Hohlden muttered, 'how can we get these back to their graves? How can we explain – we can't!'

He turned on me in horror. 'And we can't leave them here! We've got to look until we find, Bancroft.'

'But we have looked everywhere,' I protested.

He nodded, disturbed. Then suddenly he turned. 'No, we haven't!' he exclaimed. 'We haven't looked behind the wood in the wood cellar!'

He bolted from the room and descended directly into the wood cellar.

'See,' he said, 'those fire-logs – how far out they're piled. He's here – he must be!'

He began to tear them away. He had not gone far when I saw the top of the coffin, standing on end behind the wood. We pulled away the logs until we had cleared the whole space before it.

But the most ghastly part of our task was yet before us. Even the professor hesitated a moment to attack the coffin with our only tool, an axe which stood against the wall, and which must later perform an even more disagreeable task of which I hesitated to think. We had little trouble with the coffin, for the lid swung open easily, and there before us was the body of Colonel Markesan!

The corpse was clothed in a stiff black suit that had turned a little green. The face was grey-white, the mouth and cheeks sunken, the eyes closed. A faint odour of medicine came from the coffin.

The professor motioned me to stand away, and raised the axe to strike. Then, to our horror, the eyelids of the corpse began to flutter, the corners of its mouth began to twitch, and arm moved slightly – the thing before us was coming to life!

Hohlden brought the axe downward, and at the same instant a stiff arm shot out from the coffin and clutched at the handle. Then Colonel Markesan came to furious life. His dark eyes fully open, he stumbled awkwardly from the confining coffin, tore the axe from Hohlden's nerveless fingers, and flung it into the woodpile. Then, with automatic precision, the dead man's arms reached for Hohlden.

How that dead thing fought! Like a machine, taking blow after blow without apparent injury, striking again and again. I do not know how long I stood frozen with horror, watching that unnatural battle, until my eyes fell upon the axe in the corner. Then I set the lamp on the woodpile, scrambled for the weapon, and struck blindly at the thing which was bearing Professor Hohlden to the floor.

My blow laid open the back of Colonel Markesan's neck. He fell, crumpling grotesquely, and a frightful greenish red liquid began to ooze from the cut.

Instantly the professor was at my side. He tore the axe from my hands and with one stroke decapitated the body. The head of Colonel Markesan rolled awkwardly away in a half-circle, coming to rest finally against Professor Hohlden's ankle. As Hohlden jerked his foot away, a sharp cry of pain escaped his lips.

Perhaps the professor was too quick in moving his leg, perhaps the ghastly life which had animated the body yet moved the severed head, for I saw that somehow Colonel Markesan's teeth had caught and ripped open the flesh of Hohlden's ankle.

For a fleeting moment I had the horrible impression that the awful eyes in the head were open – then I kicked the head frantically away.

'God! – let's get out of here,' I murmured.

Hohlden nodded weakly, took a step forward, and almost collapsed. Amazed, he looked down at the slight wound on his ankle. It was purpling rapidly.

'Good God!' muttered Hohlden, 'poison – whatever it was that gave Markesan his awful life –'

Hohlden grasped frantically at his throat, then pitched forward.

I came to my knees at his side, catching up his head. He opened his lips weakly, then his head lolled to one side. So lethal was the fluid in Colonel Markesan's body that Hohlden was dead within two minutes after having been bit.

For a moment I was too stunned to move. Then I thought of escape, came to my feet, and ran from the cellar. But I was only half-way up the stairs when I realized that I could never hope to tell anyone what had gone on here; that furthermore, I could not leave those pathetic remains in the drawing-room – I must destroy them, even as I must destroy the body of the fiend who had brought them here from their graves. And so, too, Professor Hohlden's death must be concealed.

Reluctantly, yet swiftly, I returned to the cellar. I took up the lamp and threw it with all my might against a pile of kindling, where it exploded and immediately set the wood on fire.

Then I fled the house, leaving that accursed building in the pines a roaring inferno of flames which consumed all that was mortal of Colonel Markesan and his unfortunate victims, and brought eternal rest to the tortured dead in Mount Auburn Cemetery.

The Machine Stops

BY E. M. FORSTER

Fresh from his success as the host of Thriller, *Boris Karloff crossed the Atlantic to his native England in July 1962 to act as host for one of the pioneer anthology shows on British TV,* Out of this World, *a fifty-minute, black and white series made by the independent television company, ABC. The man who played a major part in paving the way for such shows in the UK was the Canadian-born producer Sydney Newman who had made his name putting on live dramas for CBS and was then hired to come to England in 1958 to produce ABC's* Armchair Theatre. *In the next three years he revolutionized the production of plays on television, and his interest in fantasy – in particular H.G.Wells's novel,* The Time Machine *– lead him to sanction the making of* Out of this World, *and later, when he moved over to the BBC, inspired him to create the long-running space series,* Doctor Who. *Newman was also responsible for bringing Irene Shubik, a former academic historian, into ABC as a story editor – where one of her first assignments was with* Out of this World. *With producer Leonard White, Irene mixed literary fantasy with modern SF as well as encouraging scriptwriters to submit original material of their own. Terry Nation, later to become famous for his creation of the Daleks for* Doctor Who, *was the author of 'Botany Bay', one of the highlights of the series, which also included 'Imposter' by Philip K. Dick, 'Pictures Don't Lie' by Katherine MacLean and 'The Machine Stops' by E.M. Forster.*

Edward Morgan Foster (1879–1970), the English novelist and essayist – famous for A Passage to India *(adapted by the BBC in 1965, twenty years before David Lean's famous movie) – was also the author of a number of fantasy stories collected in* The Eternal Moment

(1912) and The Celestial Omnibus *(1914). Of these, 'The Machine Stops' – written in 1909 – has been described as a classic in the mould of Wells' The Time Machine. Small wonder Irene Shubik should have picked the story, and Sydney Newman approved of its use. Dramatised by Kenneth Cavander and Clive Donner, it starred Yvonne Mitchell and Michael Gothard in a production which was described by The Guardian as 'foreseeing a horrible future so accurately that it might have been written today newly for television.' Sadly, the series that it graced and which had such ambitious plans lasted only four months, and in September 1962 Karloff was back on a liner to America.*

I

IMAGINE if you can, a small room hexagonal in shape, like the cell of a bee. It is lighted neither by window nor by lamp, yet it is filled with a soft radiance. There are no apertures for ventilation, yet the air is fresh. There are no musical instruments, and yet, at the moment that my meditation opens, this room is throbbing with melodious sounds. An armchair is in the centre, by its side a reading-desk – that is all the furniture. And in the armchair there sits a swaddled lump of flesh – a woman, about five feet high, with a face as white as a fungus. It is to her that the little room belongs.

An electric bell rang.

The woman touched a switch and the music was silent.

'I suppose I must see who it is,' she thought, and set her chair in motion. The chair, like the music, was worked by machinery, and it rolled her to the other side of the room, where the bell still rang importunately.

'Who is it?' she called. Her voice was irritable, for she had been interrupted often since the music began. She knew several thousand people; in certain directions human intercourse had advanced enormously.

But when she listened into the receiver, her white face wrinkled into smiles, and she said:

'Very well. Let us talk, I will isolate myself. I do not expect anything important will happen for the next five minutes – for I can give you fully five minutes, Kuno. Then I must deliver my lecture on "Music during the Australian Period".'

She touched the isolation knob, so that no one else could speak to her. Then she touched the lighting apparatus, and the little room was plunged into darkness.

'Be quick!' she called, her irritation returning. 'Be quick, Kuno; here I am in the dark wasting my time.'

But it was fully fifteen seconds before the round plate that she held in her hands began to glow. A faint blue light shot across it, darkening to purple, and presently she could see the image of her son, who lived on the other side of the earth, and he could see her.

'Kuno, how slow you are.'

He smiled gravely.

'I really believe you enjoy dawdling.'

'I have called you before, mother, but you were always busy or isolated. I have something particular to say.'

'What is it, dearest boy? Be quick. Why could you not send it by pneumatic post?'

'Because I prefer saying such a thing. I want –'

'Well?'

'I want you to come and see me.'

Vashti watched his face in the blue plate.

'But I can see you!' she exclaimed. 'What more do you want?'

'I want to see you not through the Machine,' said Kuno. 'I want to speak to you not through the wearisome Machine.'

'Oh, hush!' said his mother, vaguely shocked. 'You mustn't say anything against the Machine.'

'Why not?'

'One mustn't.'

'You talk as if a god had made the Machine,' cried the other. 'I believe that you pray to it when you are unhappy. Men made it, do not forget that. Great men, but men. The Machine is much, but it is not everything. I see something like you in this plate, but I do not see you. I hear something like you through this telephone, but I do not hear you. That is why I want you to come. Pay me a visit, so that we can meet face to face, and talk about the hopes that are in my mind.'

She replied that she could scarcely spare the time for a visit.

'The air-ship barely takes two days to fly between me and you.'

'I dislike air-ships.'

'Why?'

'I dislike seeing the horrible brown earth, and the sea, and the stars when it is dark. I get no ideas in an air-ship.'

'I do not get them anywhere else.'

'What kind of ideas can the air give you?'

He paused for an instant.

'Do you not know four big stars that form an oblong, and three stars close together in the middle of the oblong, and hanging from these stars, three other stars?'

'No, I do not. I dislike the stars. But did they give you an idea? How interesting; tell me.'

'I had an idea that they were like a man.'

'I do not understand.'

'The four big stars are the man's shoulders and his knees. The three stars in the middle are like the belts that men wore once, and the three stars hanging are like a sword.'

'A sword?'

'Men carried swords about with them, to kill animals and other men.'

'It does not strike me as a very good idea, but it is certainly original. When did it come to you first?'

'In the air-ship –' He broke off, and she fancied that he looked sad. She could not be sure, for the Machine did not transmit *nuances* of expression. It only gave a general idea of people – an idea that was good enough for all practical purposes, Vashti thought. The imponderable bloom, declared by a discredited philosophy to be the actual essence of intercourse, was rightly ignored by the Machine, just as the imponderable bloom of the grape was ignored by the manufacturers of artificial fruit. Something 'good enough' had long since been accepted by our race.

'The truth is,' he continued, 'that I want to see these stars again. They are curious stars. I want to see them not from the air-ship, but from the surface of the earth, as our ancestors did, thousands of years ago. I want to visit the surface of the earth.'

She was shocked again.

'Mother, you must come, if only to explain to me what is the harm of visiting the surface of the earth.'

'No harm,' she replied, controlling herself. 'But no advantage. The surface of the earth is only dust and mud, no life remains on it, and you would need a respirator, or the cold of the outer air would kill you. One dies immediately in the outer air.'

'I know; of course I shall take all precautions.'

'And besides –'

'Well?'

She considered, and chose her words with care. Her son had a queer temper, and she wished to dissuade him from the expedition.

'It is contrary to the spirit of the age,' she asserted.

'Do you mean by that, contrary to the Machine?'

'In a sense, but –'

His image in the blue plate faded.

'Kuno!'

He had isolated himself.

For a moment Vashti felt lonely.

Then she generated the light, and the sight of her room, flooded with radiance and studded with electric buttons, revived her. There were buttons and switches everywhere – buttons to call for food, for music, for clothing. There was the hot-bath button, by pressure of which a basin of (imitation) marble rose out of the floor, filled to the brim with a warm deodorized liquid. There was the cold-bath button. There was the button that produced literature. And there were of course the buttons by which she communicated with her friends. The room, though it contained nothing, was in touch with all that she cared for in the world.

Vashti's next move was to turn off the isolation switch, and all the accumulations of the last three minutes burst upon her. The room was filled with the noise of bells, and speaking-tubes. What was the new food like? Could she recommend it? Has she had any ideas lately? Might one tell her one's own ideas? Would she make an engagement to visit the public nurseries at an early date? – say this day month.

To most of these questions she replied with irritation – a growing quality in that accelerated age. She said that the new food was horrible. That she could not visit the public nurseries through press of engagements. That she had no ideas of her own but had just been told one – that four stars and three in the middle were like a man: she doubted there was much in it.

Then she switched off her correspondence, for it was time to deliver her lecture on Australian music.

The clumsy system of public gatherings had been long since abandoned; neither Vashti nor her audience stirred from their rooms. Seated in her armchair she spoke, while they in their armchairs heard her, fairly well, and saw her, fairly well. She opened with a humorous account of music in the pre Mongolian epoch, and went on to describe the great outburst of song that followed the Chinese conquest. Remote and primaeval as were the methods of I-San-So and the Brisbane school, she yet felt (she said) that study of them might repay the musicians of today: they had freshness; they had, above all, ideas.

Her lecture, which lasted ten minutes, was well received, and at its conclusion she and many of her audience listened to a lecture on the sea; there were ideas to be got from the sea; the speaker had donned a respirator and visited it lately. Then she fed, talked to many friends, had a bath, talked again, and summoned her bed.

The bed was not to her liking. It was too large, and she had a feeling

157

for a small bed. Complaint was useless, for beds were of the same dimension all over the world, and to have had an alternative size would have involved vast alterations in the Machine. Vashti isolated herself – it was necessary, for neither day nor night existed under the ground – and reviewed all that had happened since she had summoned the bed last. Ideas? Scarcely any. Events – was Kuno's invitation an event?

By her side, on the little reading-desk, was a survival from the ages of litter – one book. This was the Book of the Machine. In it were instructions against every possible contingency. If she was hot or cold or dyspeptic or at a loss for a word, she went to the book, and it told her which button to press. The Central Committee published it. In accordance with a growing habit, it was richly bound.

Sitting up in the bed, she took it reverently in her hands. She glanced round the flowing room as if someone might be watching her. Then, half ashamed, half joyful, she murmured 'O Machine! O Machine!' and raised the volume to her lips. Thrice she kissed it, thrice inclined her head, thrice she felt the delirium of acquiescence. Her ritual performed, she turned to page 1367, which gave the times of the departure of the air-ships from the island in the southern hemisphere, under whose soil she lived, to the island in the northern hemisphere, whereunder lived her son.

She thought, 'I have not the time.'

She made the room dark and slept; she awoke and made the room light; she ate and exchanged ideas with her friends, and listened to music and attended lectures; she made the room dark and slept. Above her, beneath her, and around her, the Machine hummed eternally; she did not notice the noise, for she had been born with it in her ears. The earth, carrying her, hummed as it sped through silence, turning her now to the invisible sun, now to the invisible stars. She awoke and made the room light.

'Kuno!'

'I will not talk to you,' he answered, 'until you come.'

'Have you been on the surface of the earth since we spoke last?'

His image faded.

Again she consulted the book. She became very nervous and lay back in her chair palpitating. Think of her as without teeth or hair. Presently she directed the chair to the wall, and pressed an unfamiliar button. The wall swung apart slowly. Through the opening she saw a tunnel that curved slightly, so that its goal was not visible. Should she go to see her son, here was the beginning of the journey.

Of course she knew all about the communication-system. There was nothing mysterious in it. She would summon a car and it would fly with her down the tunnel until it reached the lift that communicated with the air-ship station: the system had been in use for many, many years, long before the universal establishment of the Machine. And of course she had studied the civilization that had immediately preceded her own – the civilization that had mistaken the functions of the system, and had used it for bringing people to things, instead of for bringing things to people. Those funny old days, when men went for change of air instead of changing the air in their rooms! And yet – she was frightened of the tunnel: she had not seen it since her last child was born. It curved – but not quite as she remembered; it was brilliant – but not quite as brilliant as a lecturer had suggested. Vashti was seized with the terrors of direct experience. She shrank back into the room, and the wall closed up again.

'Kuno,' she said, 'I cannot come to see you. I am not well.'

Immediately an enormous apparatus fell on to her out of the ceiling, a thermometer was automatically inserted between her lips, a stethoscope was automatically laid upon her heart. She lay powerless. Cool pads soothed her forehead. Kuno had telegraphed to her doctor.

So the human passions still blundered up and down in the Machine. Vashti drank the medicine that the doctor projected into her mouth, and the machinery retired into the ceiling. The voice of Kuno was heard asking how she felt.

'Better.' Then with irritation: 'But why do you not come to me instead?'

'Because I cannot leave this place.'

'Why?'

'Because, any moment, something tremendous may happen.'

'Have you been on the surface of the earth yet?'

'Not yet.'

'Then what is it?'

'I will not tell you through the Machine.'

She resumed her life.

But she thought of Kuno as a baby, his birth, his removal to the public nurseries, her one visit to him there, his visits to her – visits which stopped when the Machine had assigned him a room on the other side of the earth. 'Parents, duties of,' said the book of the Machine, 'cease at the moment of birth. P. 422327483.' True, but there was something special about Kuno – indeed there had been something special about all her children – and, after all, she must brave the journey if he desired it. And 'something tremendous might happen'. What did that mean? The nonsense of a youthful man, no doubt, but she must go. Again she pressed the unfamiliar button, again the wall swung back, and she saw the tunnel that curves out of sight. Clasping the Book, she rose, tottered on to the platform, and summoned the car. Her room closed behind her: the journey to the northern hemisphere had begun.

Of course it was perfectly easy. The car approached and in it she found armchairs exactly like her own. When she signalled, it stopped, and she tottered into the lift. One other passenger was in the lift, the first fellow creature she had seen face to face for months. Few travelled in these days, for, thanks to the advance of science, the earth was exactly alike all over. Rapid intercourse, from which the previous civilization had hoped so much, had ended by defeating itself. What was the good of going to Peking when it was just like Shrewsbury? Why return to Shrewsbury when it would all be like Peking? Men seldom moved their bodies; all unrest was concentrated in the soul.

The air-ship service was a relic from the former age. It was kept up, because it was easier to keep it up than to stop it or to diminish it, but it now far exceeded the wants of the population. Vessel after vessel would rise from the vomitories of Rye or of Christchurch (I use the antique names), would sail into the crowded sky, and would draw up at the wharves of the south – empty. So nicely adjusted was the system, so independent of meteorology, that the sky, whether calm or cloudy, resembled a vast kaleidoscope whereon the same patterns periodically recurred. The ship on which Vashti sailed started now at sunset, now at dawn. But always, as it passed above Rheims, it would neighbour the ship that served between Helsingfors and the Brazils, and, every third time it surmounted the Alps, the fleet of Palermo would cross its track behind. Night and day, winds and storm, tide and earthquake, impeded man no longer. He had harnessed Leviathan. All the old literature, with its praise of Nature, and its fear of Nature, rang false as the prattle of a child.

Yet as Vashti saw the vast flank of the ship, stained with exposure to the outer air, her horror of direct experience returned. It was not quite like the air-ship in the cinematrophote. For one thing it smelt – not strongly or unpleasantly, but it did smell, and with her eyes shut she should have known that a new thing was close to her. Then she had to walk to it from the lift, had to submit to glances from the other passengers. The man in front dropped his Book – no great matter, but it disquieted them all. In the rooms, if the Book was dropped, the floor raised it mechanically, but the gangway to the air-ship was not so prepared, and the sacred volume lay motionless. They stopped – the thing was unforeseen – and the man, instead of picking up his property, felt the muscles of his arm to see how they had failed him. Then someone actually said with direct utterance: 'We shall be late' — and they trooped on board, Vashti treading on the pages as she did so.

Inside, her anxiety increased. The arrangements were old-fashioned and rough. There was even a female attendant, to whom she would have to announce her wants during the voyage. Of course a revolving platform rang the length of the boat, but she was expected to walk from it to her cabin. Some cabins were better than others, and she did not get the best. She thought the attendant had been unfair, and spasms of rage shook her. The glass valves had closed, she could not go back. She saw, at the end of the vestibule, the lift in which she had ascended going quietly up and down, empty. Beneath those corridors of shining tiles were rooms, tier below tier, reaching far into the earth, and in each room there sat a human being, eating, or sleeping, or producing ideas. And buried deep in the hive was her own room. Vashti was afraid.

'O Machine! O Machine!' she murmured, and caressed her Book, and was comforted.

Then the sides of the vestibule seemed to melt together, as do the passages that we see in dreams, the lift vanished, the Book that had been dropped slid to the left and vanished, polished tiles rushed by like a stream of water, there was a slight jar, and the air-ship, issuing from its tunnel, soared above the waters of a tropical ocean.

It was night. For a moment she saw the coast of Sumatra edged by the phosphorescence of waves, and crowned by lighthouses, still sending forth their disregarded beams. These also vanished, and only the stars distracted her. They were not motionless, but swayed to and fro above her head, thronging out of one skylight into another, as if the universe and not the air-ship was careening. And, as often happens on clear nights, they seemed now to be in perspective, now on a plane; now piled tier beyond tier into the infinite heavens, now concealing infinity, a roof limiting for ever the visions of men. In either case they seemed intolerable. 'Are we to travel in the dark?' called the passengers angrily, and the attendant, who had been careless, generated the light, and pulled down the blinds of pliable metal. When the air-ships had been built, the desire to look direct at things still lingered in the world. Hence the extraordinary number of skylights and windows, and the proportionate discomfort to those who were civilized and refined. Even in Vashti's cabin one star peeped through a flaw in the blind, and after a few hours' uneasy slumber, she was disturbed by an unfamiliar glow, which was the dawn.

Quick as the ship had sped westwards, the earth had rolled

eastwards quicker still, and had dragged back Vashti and her companions towards the sun. Science could prolong the night, but only for a little, and those high hopes of neutralizing the earth's diurnal revolution had passed, together with hopes that were possibly higher. To 'keep pace with the sun', or even to outstrip it, had been the aim of the civilization preceding this. Racing aeroplanes had been built for the purpose, capable of enormous speed, and steered by the greatest intellects of the epoch. Round the globe they went, round and round, westward, westward, round and round, amidst humanity's applause. In vain. The globe went eastward quicker still, horrible accidents occurred, and the Committee of the Machine, at the time rising into prominence, declared the pursuit illegal, unmechanical, and punishable by Homelessness.

Of Homelessness more will be said later.

Doubtless the Committee was right. Yet the attempt to 'defeat the sun' aroused the last common interest that our race experienced about the heavenly bodies, or indeed about anything. It was the last time that men were compacted by thinking of a power outside the world. The sun had conquered, yet it was the end of his spiritual dominion. Dawn, midday, twilight, the zodiacal path, touched neither men's lives nor their hearts, and science retreated into the ground, to concentrate herself upon problems that she was certain of solving.

So when Vashti found her cabin invaded by a rosy finger of light, she was annoyed, and tried to adjust the blind. But the blind flew up altogether, and she saw through the skylight small pink clouds, swaying against a background of blue, and as the sun crept higher, its radiance direct, brimming down the wall, like a golden sea. It rose and fell with the air-ship's motion, just as waves rise and fall, but it advanced steadily, as a tide advances. Unless she was careful, it would strike her face. A spasm of horror shook her and she rang for the attendant. The attendant too was horrified, but she could do nothing; it was not her place to mend the blind. She could only suggest that the lady should change her cabin, which she accordingly prepared to do.

People were almost exactly alike all over the world, but the attendant of the air-ship, perhaps owing to her exceptional duties, had grown a little out of the common. She had often to address passengers with direct speech, and this had given her a certain roughness and originality of manner. When Vashti swerved away from the sunbeams with a cry, she behaved barbarically – she put out her hand to steady her.

'How dare you!' exclaimed the passenger. 'You forget yourself!'

The woman was confused, and apologized for not having let her fall. People never touched one another. The custom had become obsolete, owing to the Machine.

'Where are we now?' asked Vashti haughtily.

'We are over Asia,' said the attendant, anxious to be polite.

'Asia?'

'You must excuse my common way of speaking. I have got into the habit of calling places over which I pass by their unmechanical names.'

'Oh, I remember Asia. The Mongols came from it.'

'Beneath us, in the open air, stood a city that was once called Simla.'

' Have you ever heard of the Mongols and of the Brisbane school?'

'No.'

'Brisbane also stood in the open air.'

'Those mountains to the right – let me show you them.' She pushed back a metal blind. The main chain of the Himalayas was revealed.

'They were once called the Roof of the World, those mountains.'

'What a foolish name!'

'You must remember that, before the dawn of civilization, they seemed to be an impenetrable wall that touched the stars. It was supposed that no one but the gods could exist above their summits. How we have advanced, thanks to the Machine!'

'How we have advanced, thanks to the Machine!' said Vashti.

'How we have advanced, thanks to the Machine!' echoed the passenger who had dropped his Book the night before, and who was standing in the passage.

'And that white stuff in the cracks? – what is it?'

'I have forgotten its name.'

'Cover the window, please. These mountains give me no ideas.'

The northern aspect of the Himalayas was in deep shadow: on the Indian slope the sun had just prevailed. The forests had been destroyed during the literature epoch for the purpose of making newspaper-pulp, but the snows were awakening to their morning glory, and clouds still hung on the breasts of Kinchinjunga. In the plain were seen the ruins of cities, with diminished rivers creeping by their walls, and by the sides of these were sometimes the signs of vomitories, marking the cities of today. Over the whole prospect air-ships rushed, crossing the inter-crossing with incredible *aplomb*, and rising nonchalantly when they desired to escape the perturbations of the lower atmosphere and to traverse the Roof of the World.

'We have indeed advanced, thanks to the Machine,' repeated the attendant, and hid the Himalayas behind a metal blind.

The day dragged wearily forward. The passengers sat each in his cabin, avoiding one another with an almost physical repulsion and longing to be once more under the surface of the earth. There were eight or ten of them, mostly young males, sent out from the public nurseries to inhabit the rooms of those who had died in various parts of the earth. The man who had dropped his Book was on the homeward journey. He had been sent to Sumatra for the purpose of propagating the race. Vashti alone was travelling by her private will.

At midday she took a second glance at the earth. The air-ship was crossing another range of mountains, but she could see little, owing to clouds. Masses of black rock hovered below her, and merged indistinctly into grey. Their shapes were fantastic, one of them resembled a prostrate man.

'No ideas here,' murmured Vashti, and hid the Caucasus behind a metal blind.

In the evening she looked again. They were crossing a golden sea, in which lay many small islands and one peninsula.

She repeated, 'No ideas here,' and hid Greece behind a metal blind.

II

By a vestibule, by a lift, by a tubular railway, by a platform, by a sliding door – by reversing all the steps of her departure did Vashti arrive at her son's room, which exactly resembled her own. She might well declare that the visit was superfluous. The buttons, the knobs, the reading-desk with the Book, the temperature, the atmosphere, the illumination – all were exactly the same. And if Kuno himself, flesh of her flesh, stood close beside her at last, what profit was there in that? She was too well-bred to shake him by the hand.

Averting her eyes, she spoke as follows:

'Here I am. I have had the most terrible journey and greatly retarded the development of my soul. It is not worth it, Kuno, it is not worth it. My time is too precious. The sunlight almost touched me, and I have met the rudest people. I can only stop a few minutes. Say what you want to say, and then I must return.'

'I have been threatened with Homelessness,' said Kuno.

She looked at him now.

'I have been threatened with Homelessness, and I could not tell you such a thing through the Machine.'

Homelessness means death. The victim is exposed to the air, which kills him.

'I have been outside since I spoke to you last. The tremendous thing has happened, and they have discovered me.'

'But why shouldn't you go outside?' she exclaimed. 'It is perfectly legal, perfectly mechanical, to visit the surface of the earth. I have lately been to a lecture on the sea; there is no objection to that; one simply summons a respirator and gets an Egression-permit. It is not the kind of thing that spiritually-minded people do, and I begged you not to do it, but there is no legal objection to it.'

'I did not get an Egression-permit.'

'Then how did you get out?'

'I found out a way of my own.'

The phrase conveyed no meaning to her, and he had to repeat it.

'A way of your own?' she whispered. 'But that would be wrong.'

'Why?'

The question shocked her beyond measure.

'You are beginning to worship the Machine,' he said coldly. 'You think it irreligious of me to have found out a way of my own. It was just what the Committee thought, when they threatened me with Homelessness.'

At this she grew angry. 'I worship nothing!' she cried. 'I am most advanced. I don't think you irreligious, for there is no such thing as religion left. All the fear and the superstition that existed once have been destroyed by the Machine. I only meant that to find out a way of your own was – Besides, there is no new way out.'

'So it is always supposed.'

'Except through the vomitories, for which one must have an Egression-permit, it is impossible to get out. The Book says so.'

'Well, the Book's wrong, for I have been out on my feet.'

For Kuno was possessed of a certain physical strength.

By these days it was a demerit to be muscular. Each infant was examined at birth and all who promised undue strength were destroyed. Humanitarians may protest, but it would have been no true kindness to let an athlete live; he would never have been happy in that state of life to which the Machine had called him. He would have yearned for trees to climb, rivers to bathe in, meadows and hills against which he might measure his body. Man must be adapted to his surroundings, must he not? In the dawn of the world our weakly must be exposed on Mount Taygetus, in its twilight our strong will suffer euthanasia, that the Machine may progress, that the Machine may progress, that the Machine may progress eternally.

'You know that we have lost the sense of space. We say "space is annihilated", but we have annihilated not space, but the sense thereof. We have lost a part of ourselves. I determined to recover it, and I began by walking up and down the platform of the railway outside my room. Up and down, until I was tired, and so did recapture the meaning of

"Near" and "Far". "Near" is a place to which I can get quickly *on my feet*, not a place to which the train or the air-ship will take me quickly. "Far" is a place to which I cannot get quickly on my feet; the vomitory is "far", though I could be there in thirty-eight seconds by summoning the train. Man is the measure. That was my first lesson. Man's feet are the measure for distance, his hands are the measure for ownership, his body is the measure for all that is lovable and desirable and strong. Then I went further: it was then that I called to you for the first time, and you would not come.

'This city, as you know, is built deep beneath the surface of the earth, with only the vomitories protruding. Having placed the platform outside my own room, I took the lift to the next platform and paced that also, and so with each in turn, until I came to the topmost, above which begins the earth. All the platforms were exactly alike, and all that I gained by visiting them was to develop my sense of space and my muscles. I think I should have been content with this – it is not a little thing – but as I walked and brooded, it occurred to me that our cities had been built in the days when men still breathed the outer air, and that there had been ventilation shafts for the workmen. I could think of nothing but these ventilation shafts. Had they been destroyed by all the food-tubes and medicine-tubes and music-tubes that the Machine has evolved lately? Or did traces of them remain? One thing was certain. If I came upon them anywhere, it would be in the railway-tunnels of the topmost storey. Everywhere else, all space was accounted for.

'I am telling my story quickly, but don't think that I was not a coward or that your answers never depressed me. It is not the proper thing, it is not mechanical, it is not decent to walk along a railway-tunnel. I did not fear that I might tread upon a live rail and be killed. I feared something far more intangible – doing what was not contemplated by the Machine. Then I said to myself, "Man is the measure", and I went, and after many visits I found an opening.

'The tunnels, of course, were lighted. Everything is light, artificial light; darkness is the exception. So when I saw a black gap in the tiles, I knew that it was an exception, and rejoiced. I put in my arm – I could put in no more at first – and waved it round and round in ecstasy. I loosened another tile, and put in my head, and shouted into the darkness: "I am coming, I shall do it yet", and my voice reverberated down endless passages. I seemed to hear the spirits of those dead workmen who had returned each evening to the starlight and to their wives, and all the generations who had lived in the open air called back to me, "You will do it yet, you are coming." '

He paused, and, absurd as he was, his last words moved her. For Kuno had lately asked to be a father, and his request had been refused by the Committee. His was not a type that the Machine desired to hand on.

'Then a train passed. It brushed by me, but I thrust my head and arms into the hole. I had done enough for one day, so I crawled back to the platform, went down in the lift, and summoned my bed. Ah what dreams! And again I called you, and again you refused.'

She shook her head and said:

'Don't. Don't talk of these terrible things. You make me miserable. You are throwing civilization away.'

'But I had got back the sense of space and a man cannot rest then. I determined to get in at the hole and climb the shaft. And so I exercised my arms. Day after day I went through ridiculous movements, until my flesh ached, and I could hang by my hands and hold the pillow of my bed outstretched for many minutes. Then I summoned a respirator, and started.

'It was easy at first. The mortar had somehow rotted, and I soon pushed some more tiles in, and clambered after them into the darkness, and the spirits of the dead comforted me. I don't know what I mean by that. I just say what I felt. I felt, for the first time, that a protest had been lodged against corruption, and that even as the dead were comforting me, so I was comforting the unborn. I felt that humanity existed, and that is existed without clothes. How can I possibly explain this? It was naked, humanity seemed naked, and all these tubes and buttons and machineries neither came into the world with us, nor will they follow us out, nor do they matter supremely while we are here. Had I been strong, I would have torn off every garment I had, and gone out into the outer air unswaddled. But this is not for me, nor perhaps for my generation. I climbed with my respirator and my hygienic clothes and my dietetic tabloids! Better thus than not at all.

'There was a ladder, made of some primaeval metal. The light from the railway fell upon its lowest rungs, and I saw that it led straight upwards out of the rubble at the bottom of the shaft. Perhaps our ancestors ran up and down it a dozen times daily, in their building. As I climbed, the rough edges cut through my gloves so that my hands bled. The light helped me for a little, and then came darkness and, worse still, silence which pierced my ears like a sword. The Machine hums! Did you know that? Its hum penetrates our blood, and may even guide our thoughts. Who knows! I was getting beyond its power. Then I thought: "This silence means that I am doing wrong." But I heard voices in the silence, and again they strengthened me.' he laughed. 'I had need of them. The next moment I cracked my head against something.'

She sighed.

'I had reached one of those pneumatic stoppers that defend us from the outer air. You may have noticed them on the air-ship. Pitch dark, my feet on the rungs of an invisible ladder, my hands cut; I cannot explain how I lived through this part, but the voices still comforted me, and I felt for fastenings. The stopper, I suppose, was about eight feet across. I passed my hand over it as far as I could reach. It was perfectly smooth. I felt it almost to the centre. Not quite to the centre, for my arms was too short. Then the voice said: "Jump. It is worth it. There may be a handle in the centre, and you may catch hold of it and so come to us your own way. And if there is no handle, so that you may fall and are dashed to pieces – it is still worth it; you will still come to us your own way." So I jumped. There was a handle, and –'

He paused. Tears gathered in his mother's eyes. She knew that he was fated. If he did not die today he would die tomorrow. There was not room for such a person in the world. And with her pity disgust mingled. She was ashamed at having borne such a son, she who had always been so respectable and so full of ideas. Was he really the little boy to whom she had taught the use of his stops and buttons, and to whom she had given his first lessons in the Book? The very hair that disfigured his lip showed that he was reverting to some savage type. On atavism the Machine can have no mercy.

'There was a handle, and I did catch it. I hung tranced over the darkness and heard the hum of these workings as the last whisper in a dying dream. All the things I had cared about and all the people I had spoken to through tubes appeared infinitely little. Meanwhile the handle revolved. My weight had set something in motion and I spun slowly, and then –

'I cannot describe it. I was lying with my face to the sunshine. Blood poured from my nose and ears and I heard a tremendous roaring. The stopper, with me clinging to it, had simply been blown out of the earth, and the air that we make down here was escaping through the vent into the air above. It burst up like a fountain. I crawled back to it – for the upper air hurt – and, as it were, I took great sips from the edge. My respirator had flown goodness knows where, my clothes were torn. I just lay with my lips close to the hole, and I sipped until the bleeding stopped. You can imagine nothing so curious. This hollow in the grass – I will speak of it in a minute – the sun shining into it, not brilliantly but through marbled clouds – the peace, the nonchalance, the sense of space, and, brushing my cheek, the roaring fountain of our artificial air! Soon I spied my respirator, bobbing up and down in the current high above my head, and higher still were many air-ships. But no one ever looks out of air-ships, and in any case they could not have picked me up. There I was, stranded. The sun shone a little way down the shaft, and revealed the topmost rung of the ladder, but it was hopeless trying to reach it. I should either have been tossed up again by the escape, or else have fallen in, and died. I could only lie on the grass, sipping and sipping, and from time to time glancing around me.

'I knew that I was in Wessex, for I had taken care to go to a lecture on the subject before starting. Wessex lies above the room in which we are talking now. It was once an important state. Its kings held all the southern coast from the Andredswald to Cornwall, while the Wansdyke protected them on the north, running over the high ground. The lecturer was only concerned with the rise of Wessex, so I do not know how long it remained an international power, nor would the knowledge have assisted me. To tell the truth I could do nothing but laugh, during this part. There was I, with a pneumatic stopper by my side and a respirator bobbing over my head, imprisoned, all three of us, in a grass-grown hollow that was edged with fern.'

Then he grew grave again.

'Lucky for me that it was a hollow. For the air began to fall back into it and to fill it as water fills a bowl. I could crawl about. Presently I stood. I breathed a mixture, in which the air that hurts predominated whenever I tried to climb the sides. This was not so bad. I had not lost my tabloids and remained ridiculously cheerful, and as for the Machine, I forgot about it altogether. My one aim now was to get to the top, where the ferns were, and to view whatever objects lay beyond.

'I rushed the slope. The new air was still too bitter for me and I came rolling back, after a momentary vision of something grey. The sun grew very feeble, and I remembered that he was in Scorpio – I had been to a lecture on that too. If the sun is in Scorpio, and you are in Wessex, it means that you must be as quick as you can, or it will get too dark. (This is the first bit of useful information I have ever got from a lecture and I expect it will be the last.) It made me try frantically to breathe the new air, and to advance as far as I dared out of my pond. The hollow filled so slowly. My respirator seemed to dance nearer the earth; the roar was decreasing.'

He broke off.

'I don't think this is interesting you. The rest will interest you even less. There are no ideas in it, and I wish that I had not troubled you to come. We are too different, mother.'

She told him to continue.

'It was evening before I climbed the bank. The sun had very nearly slipped out of the sky by this time, and I could not get a good view. You, who have just crossed the Roof of the World, will not want to hear an account of the little hills that I saw – low colourless hills. But to me they were living and the turf that covered them was a skin, under which their muscles rippled, and I felt that those hills had called with incalculable force to men in the past, and that men had loved them. Now they sleep – perhaps for ever. They commune with humanity in dreams. Happy the man, happy the woman, who awakes the hills of Wessex. For though they sleep, they will never die.'

His voice rose passionately.

'Cannot you see, cannot all you lecturers see, that it is we that are dying, and that down here the only thing that really lives is the Machine? We created the Machine, to do our will, but we cannot make it do our will now. It has robbed us of the sense of space and of the sense of touch, it has blurred every human relation and narrowed down love to a carnal act, it has paralysed our bodies and our wills, and now it compels us to worship it. The Machine develops – but not on our lines. The Machine proceeds – but not to our goal. We only exist as the blood corpuscles that course through its arteries, and if it could work without us, it would let us die. Oh, I have no remedy – or, at least, only one – to tell men again and again that I have seen the hills of Wessex as Alfred saw them when he overthrew the Danes.

'So the sun set. I forgot to mention that a belt of mist lay between my hill and other hills, and that it was the colour of pearl.'

He broke off for the second time.

'Go on,' said his mother wearily.

He shook his head.

'Go on. Nothing that you saw can distress me now. I am hardened.'

'I had meant to tell you the rest, but I cannot: I know that I cannot: good-bye.'

Vashti stood irresolute. All her nerves were tingling with his blasphemies. But she was also inquisitive.

'This is unfair,' she complained. 'You have called me across the world to hear your story, and hear it I will. Tell me – as briefly as possible, for this is a disastrous waste of time – tell me how you returned to civilization.'

'Oh – that!' he said, starting. 'You would like to hear about civilization. Certainly. Had I got to where my respirator fell down?'

'No – but I understand everything now. You put on your respirator, and managed to walk along the surface of the earth to a vomitory, and there your conduct was reported to the Central Committee.'

'By no means.'

He passed his hand over his forehead, as if dispelling some strong impression. Then, resuming his narrative, he warmed to it again.

'My respirator fell about sunset. I had mentioned that the fountain seemed feebler, had I not?'

'Yes.'

'About sunset, it let the respirator fall. As I said, I had entirely forgotten about the Machine, and I paid no great attention at the time, being occupied with other things. I had my pool of air, into which I could dip when the outer keenness became intolerable, and which would possible remain for days, provided that no wind sprang up to disperse it. Not until it was too late did I realize what the stoppage of the escape implied. You see – the gap in the tunnel had been mended; the Mending Apparatus; the Mending Apparatus, was after me.

'One other warning I had, but I neglected it. The sky at night was clearer than it had been in the day, and the moon, which was about half the sky behind the sun, shone into the dell at moments quite brightly. I was in my usual place – on the boundary between the two atmospheres – when I thought I saw something dark move across the bottom of the dell, and vanish into the shaft. In my folly, I ran down. I bent over and listened, and I thought I heard a faint scraping noise in the depths.

'At this – but it was too late – I took alarm. I determined to put on my respirator and to walk out of the dell. But my respirator had gone. I knew exactly where it had fallen – between the stopper and the aperture – and I could even feel the mark that it had made in the turf. It had gone, and I realized that something evil was at work, and I had better escape to the other air, and, if I must die, die running towards the cloud that had been the colour of a pearl. I never started. Out of the shaft – it is too horrible. A worm, a long white worm, had crawled out of the shaft and was gliding over the moonlit grass.

'I screamed. I did everything that I should not have done, I stamped upon the creature instead of flying from it, and it at once curled round the ankle. Then we fought. The worm let me run all over the dell, but edged up my leg as I ran. "Help!" I cried. (That part is too awful. It belongs to the part that you will never know.) "Help!" I cried. (Why cannot we suffer in silence?) "Help!" I cried. When my feet were wound together, I fell, I was dragged away from the dear ferns and the living hills, and past the great metal stopper (I can tell you this part), and I thought it might save me again if I caught hold of the handle. It also was enwrapped, it also. Oh, the whole dell was full of the things. They were searching it in all directions, they were denuding it, and the white snouts of others peeped out of the hole, ready if needed. Everything that could be moved they brought – brushwood, bundles of fern, everything, and down we all went intertwined into hell. The last things that I saw, ere the stopper closed after us, were certain stars, and I felt that a man of my sort lived in the sky. For I did fight, I fought till the very end, and it was only my head hitting against the ladder that quieted me. I woke up in this room. The worms had vanished. I was surrounded by artificial air, artificial light, artificial peace, and my friends were calling to me down speaking-tubes to know whether I had come across any new ideas lately.'

Here his story ended. Discussion of it was impossible, and Vashti turned to go.

'It will end in Homelessness,' she said quietly.

'I wish it would,' retorted Kuno.

'The Machine has been most merciful.'

'I prefer the mercy of God.'

'By that superstitious phrase, do you mean that you could live in the outer air?'

'Yes.'

'Have you ever seen, round the vomitories, the bones of those who were extruded after the Great Rebellion?'

'Yes.'

'They were left where they perished for our edification. A few crawled away, but they perished, too – who can doubt it? And so with the Homeless of our own day. The surface of the earth supports life no longer.'

'Indeed.'

'Ferns and a little grass may survive, but all higher forms have perished. Has any air-ship detected them?'

'No.'

'Has any lecturer dealt with them?'

'No.'

'Then why this obstinacy?'

'Because I have seen them,' he exploded.

'Seen *what*?'

'Because I have seen her in the twilight – because she came to my help when I called – because she, too, was entangled by the worms, and, luckier than I, was killed by one of them piercing her throat.'

He was mad. Vashti departed, nor, in the troubles that followed, did she ever see his face again.

During the years that followed Kuno's escapade, two important developments took place in the Machine. On the surface they were revolutionary, but in either case men's minds had been prepared beforehand, and they did but express tendencies that were latent already.

The first of these was the abolition of respirators.

Advanced thinkers, like Vashti, had always held it foolish to visit the surface of the earth. Air-ships might be necessary, but what was the good of going out for mere curiosity and crawling along for a mile or two in a terrestrial motor? The habit was vulgar and perhaps faintly improper: it was unproductive of ideas, and had no connection with the habits that really mattered. So respirators were abolished, and with them, of course, the terrestrial motors, and except for a few lecturers, who complained that they were debarred access to their subject-matter, the development was accepted quietly. Those who still wanted to know what the earth was like had after all only to listen to some gramophone, or to look into some cinematophote. And even the lecturers acquiesced when they found that a lecture on the sea was none the less stimulating when compiled out of other lectures that had already been delivered on the same subject. 'Beware of first-hand ideas!' exclaimed one of the most advanced of them. 'First-hand ideas do not really exist. They are but the physical impressions produced by love and fear, and on this gross foundation who could erect a philosophy? Let your ideas be second-hand, and if possible tenth-hand, for then they will be far removed from that disturbing element – direct observation. Do not learn anything about this subject of mine – the French Revolution. Learn instead what I think that Enicharmon thought Urizen thought Gutch thought Ho-Yung thought Chi-Bo-Sing thought Lafcadio Hearn thought Carlyle thought Mirabeau said about the French Revolution. Through the medium of these ten great minds, the blood that was shed at Paris and the windows that were broken at Versailles will be clarified to an idea which you may employ most profitably in your daily lives. But be sure that the intermediates are many and varied, for in history one authority exists to counteract another. Urizen must counteract the scepticism of Ho-Yung and Enicharmon, I must myself counteract the impetuosity of Gutch. You who listen to me are in a better position to judge about the French Revolution than I am. Your descendants will be even in a better position than you, for they will learn what you think I think, and yet another intermediate will be added to the chain. And in time' – his voice rose – 'there will come a generation that has got beyond facts, beyond impressions, a generation absolutely colourless, a generation

seraphically free
From taint of personality

which will see the French Revolution not as it happened, nor as they would like it to have happened, but as it would have happened, had it taken place in the days of the Machine.'

Tremendous applause greeted this lecture, which did but voice a feeling already latent in the minds of men – a feeling that terrestrial facts must be ignored, and that the abolition of respirators was a positive gain. It was even suggested the air-ships should be abolished, too. This was not done, because air-ships had somehow worked themselves into the Machine's system. But year by year they were used less, and mentioned less by thoughtful men.

The second great development was the re-establishment of religion.

This, too, had been voiced in the celebrated lecture. No one could mistake the reverent tone in which the peroration had concluded, and it awakened a responsive echo in the heart of each. Those who had long worshipped silently, now began to talk. They described the strange feeling of peace that came over them when they handled the Book of the Machine, the pleasure that it was to repeat certain numerals out of it, however little meaning those numerals conveyed to the outward ear, the ecstasy of touching a button, however un-important, or of ringing an electric bell, however superfluously.

'The Machine,' they exclaimed, 'feeds us and clothes us and houses us; through it we speak to one another, through it we see one another, in it we have our being. The Machine is the friend of ideas and the enemy of superstition: the Machine is omnipotent, eternal; blessed is the Machine.' And before long this allocution was printed on the first page of the Book, and in subsequent editions the ritual swelled into a complicated system of praise and prayer. The word 'religion' was sedulously avoided, and in theory the Machine was still the creation and the implement of man. But in practice all, save a few retrogrades, worshipped it as divine. Nor was it worshipped in unity. One believer would be chiefly impressed by the blue optic plates, through which he saw other believers; another by the mending apparatus, which sinful Kuno had compared to worms; another by the lifts, another by the Book. And each would pray to this or to that, and ask it to intercede for him with the Machine as a whole. Persecution – that also was present. It did not break out, for reasons that will be set forward shortly. But it was latent, and all who did not accept the minimum known as 'undenominational Mechanism' lived in danger of Homelessness, which means death, as we know.

To attribute these two great developments to the Central Committee, is to take a very narrow view of civilization. The Central Committee announced the developments, it is true, but they were no more the cause of them than were the kings of the imperialistic period the cause of war. Rather did they yield to some invincible pressure, which came no one knew whither, and which, when gratified, was succeeded by some new pressure equally invincible. To such a state of affairs it is convenient to give the name of progress. No one confessed the Machine was out of hand. Year by year it was served with increased efficiency and decreased intelligence. The better a man knew his own duties upon it, the less he understood the duties of his neighbour, and in all the world there was not one who understood the monster as a whole. Those master brains had perished. They had left full directions, it is true, and their successors had each of them mastered a portion of those directions. But Humanity, in its desire for comfort, had overreached itself. It had exploited the riches of nature too far. Quietly and complacently, it was sinking into decadence, and progress had come to mean the progress of the Machine.

As for Vashti, her life went peacefully forward until the final disaster. She made her room dark and slept; she awoke and made the room light. She lectured and attended lectures. She exchanged ideas with her innumerable friends and believed she was growing more spiritual. At times a friend was granted Euthanasia, and left his or her room for the homelessness that is beyond all human conception. Vashti did not much mind. After an unsuccessful lecture, she would sometimes ask for Euthanasia herself. But the death-rate was not permitted to exceed the birth-rate, and the Machine had hitherto refused it to her.

The troubles began quietly, long before she was conscious of them.

One day she was astonished at receiving a message from her son. They never communicated, having nothing in common, and she had only heard indirectly that he was still alive, and had been transferred from the northern hemisphere, where he had behaved so mischievously, to the southern – indeed, to a room not far from her own.

'Does he want me to visit him?' she thought. 'Never again, never. And I have not the time.'

No, it was madness of another kind.

He refused to visualize his face upon the blue plate, and speaking out of the darkness with solemnity said:

'The Machine stops.'

'What do you say?'

'The Machine is stopping, I know it, I know the signs.'

She burst into a peal of laughter. He heard her and was angry, and they spoke no more.

'Can you imagine anything more absurd?' she cried to a friend. 'A man who was my son believes that the Machine is stopping. It would be impious if it was not mad.'

'The Machine is stopping?' her friend replied. 'What does that mean? The phrase conveys nothing to me.'

'Nor to me.'

'He does not refer, I suppose, to the trouble there has been lately with the music?'

'Oh no, of course not. Let us talk about music.'

'Have you complained to the authorities?'

'Yes, and they say it wants mending, and referred me to the Committee of the Mending Apparatus. I complained of those curious gasping sighs that disfigure the symphonies of the Brisbane school. They sound like someone in pain. The Committee of the Mending Apparatus say that it shall be remedied shortly.'

Obscurely worried, she resumed her life. For one thing, the defect in the music irritated her. For another thing, she could not forget Kuno's speech. If he had known that the music was out of repair – he could not know it, for he detested music – if he had known that it was wrong, 'the Machine stops' was exactly the venomous sort of remark he would have made. Of course he had made it at a venture, but the coincidence annoyed her, and she spoke with some petulance to the Committee of the Mending Apparatus.

They replied, as before, that the defect would be set right shortly.

'Shortly! At once!' she retorted. 'Why should I be worried by imperfect music? Things are always put right at once. If you not mend it at once, I shall complain to the Central Committee.'

'No personal complaints are received by the Central Committee,' the Committee of the Mending Apparatus replied.

'Through whom am I to make my complaint, then?'

'Through us.'

'I complain then.'

'Your complaint shall be forwarded in its turn.'

'Have others complained?'

This question was unmechanical, and the Committee of the Mending Apparatus refused to answer it.

'It is too bad!' she exclaimed to another of her friends. 'There never was such an unfortunate woman as myself. I can never be sure of my music now. It gets worse and worse each time I summon it.'

'I too have troubles,' the friend replied. 'Sometimes my ideas are interrupted by a slight jarring noise.'

'What is it?'

'I do not know whether it is inside my head, or inside the wall.'

'Complain, in either case.'

'I have complained, and my complaint will be forwarded in its turn to the Central Committee.'

Time passed, and they resented the defects no longer. The defects had not been remedied, but the human tissues in that latter day had become so subservient, that they readily adapted themselves to every caprice of the Machine. The sigh at the crisis of the Brisbane symphony no longer irritated Vashti; she accepted it as part of the melody. The jarring noise, whether in the head or in the wall, was no longer resented by her friend. And so with the mouldy artificial fruit, so with the bath water that began to stink, so with the defective rhymes that the poetry machine had taken to emit. All were bitterly complained of at first, and then acquiesced in and forgotten. Things went from bad to worse unchallenged.

It was otherwise with the failure of the sleeping apparatus. That was a more serious stoppage. There came a day when over the whole world – in Sumatra, in Wessex, in the innumerable cities of Courland and Brazil – the beds, when summoned by their tired owners, failed to appear. It may seem a ludicrous matter, but from it we may date the collapse of humanity. The Committee responsible for the failure was assailed by complaints, whom it referred, as usual, to the Committee of the Mending Apparatus, who in its turn assured them that their complaints would be forwarded to the Central Committee. But the discourse grew, for mankind was not yet sufficiently adaptable to do without sleeping.

'Someone is meddling with the Machine – they began.

'Someone is trying to make himself king, to reintroduce the personal element.'

'Punish that man with Homelessness.'

'To the rescue! Avenge the Machine! Avenge the Machine!'

'War! Kill the man!'

But the Committee of the Mending Apparatus now came forward, and allayed the panic with well-chosen words. It confessed that the Mending Apparatus was itself in need of repair.

The effect of this frank confession was admirable.

'Of course,' said a famous lecturer – he of the French Revolution, who gilded each new decay with splendour – 'of course we shall not press our complaints now. The Mending Apparatus has treated us so well in the past that we all sympathize with it, and will wait patiently for its recovery. In its own good time it will resume its duties. Meanwhile let us do without our beds, our tabloids, our other little wants. Such, I feel sure, would be the wish of the Machine.'

Thousands of miles away his audience applauded. The Machine still linked them. Under the seas, beneath the roots of the mountains, ran the wires through which they saw and heard, the enormous eyes and ears that were their heritage, and the hum of many workings clothed their thoughts in one garment of subserviency. Only the old and the sick remained ungrateful, for it was rumoured that Euthanasia, too, was out of order, and that pain had reappeared among men.

It became difficult to read. A blight entered the atmosphere and dulled its luminosity. At times Vashti could scarcely see across her room. The air, too, was foul. Loud were the complaints, impotent the remedies, heroic the tone of the lecturer as he cried: 'Courage! Courage! What matter so long as the Machine goes on? To it the darkness and the light are one.' And though things improved again after a time, the old brilliancy was never recaptured, and humanity never recovered from its entrance into twilight. There was an hysterical talk of 'measures', of 'provisional dictatorship', and the inhabitants of Sumatra were asked to familiarize themselves with the workings of the central power station, the said power station being situated in France. But for the most part panic reigned, and men spent their strength praying to their Books, tangible proofs of the Machine's omnipotence. There were gradations of terror – at times came rumours of hope – the Mending Apparatus was almost mended – the enemies of the Machine had been got under – new 'nerve- centres' were evolving which would do the work even more magnificently than before. But there came a day when, without the slightest warning, without any previous hint of feebleness, the entire communication-system broke down, all over the world, and the world as they understood it, ended.

Vashti was lecturing at the time and her earlier remarks had been punctuated with applause. As she proceeded the audience became silent, and at the conclusion there was no sound. Somewhat dis-pleased, she called to a friend who was a specialist in sympathy. No sound: doubtless the friend was sleeping. And so with the next friend whom she tried to summon, and so with the next, until she remembered Kuno's cryptic remark, 'The Machine stops.'

The phrase still conveyed nothing. If Eternity was stopping it would of course be set going shortly.

For example, there was still a little light and air – the atmosphere had improved a few hours previously. There was still the Book, and while there was the Book there was security.

Then she broke down, for with the cessation of activity came an unexpected terror – silence.

She had never known silence, and the coming of it nearly killed her – it did kill many thousands of people outright. Ever since her birth she had been surrounded by the steady hum. It was to the ear what artificial air was to the lungs, and agonizing pains shot across her head. And scarcely knowing what she did, she stumbled forward and pressed the unfamiliar button, the one that opened the door of her cell.

Now the door of the cell worked on a simple hinge of its own. It was not connected with the central power station, dying far away in France. It opened, rousing immoderate hopes in Vashti, for she thought that the Machine had been mended. It opened, and she saw the dim tunnel that curved far away towards freedom. One look, and then she shrank back. For the tunnel was full of people – she was almost the last in that city to have taken alarm.

People at any time repelled her, and these were nightmares from her worst dreams. People were crawling about, people were screaming, whimpering, gasping for breath, touching each other, vanishing in the dark, and ever and anon being pushed off the platform on to the live rail. Some were fighting round the electric bells, trying to summon trains which could not be summoned. Others were yelling for Euthanasia or for respirators, or blaspheming the Machine. Others stood at the doors of their cells fearing, like herself, either to stop in them or to leave them. And behind all the uproar was silence – the silence which is the voice of the earth and of the generations who have gone.

No – it was worse than solitude. She closed the door again and sat down to wait for the end. The disintegration went on, accompanied by horrible cracks and rumbling. The valves that restrained the Medical Apparatus must have been weakened, for it ruptured and hung hideously from the ceiling. The floor heaved and fell and flung her from her chair. A tube oozed towards her serpent fashion. And at last the final horror approached – light began to ebb, and she knew that civilization's long day was closing.

She whirled round, praying to be saved from this, at any rate, kissing the Book, pressing button after button. The uproar outside was increasing, and even penetrated the wall. Slowly the brilliancy of her cell was dimmed, the reflections faded from her metal switches. Now she could not see the reading-stand, now not the Book, though she held it in her hand. Light followed the flight of sound, air was following light, and the original void returned to the cavern from which it had been so long excluded. Vashti continued to whirl, like the devotees of an earlier religion, screaming, praying, striking at the buttons with bleeding hands.

It was thus that she opened her prison and escaped — escaped in the spirit: at least so it seems to me, ere my mediation closes. That she escapes in the body — I cannot perceive that. She struck, by chance, the switch that released the door, and the rush of foul air on her skin, the loud throbbing whispers in her ears, told her that she was facing the tunnel again, and that tremendous platform on which she had seen men fighting. They were not fighting now. Only the whispers remained, and the little whimpering groans. They were dying by hundreds out in the dark.

She burst into tears.

Tears answered her.

They wept for humanity, those two, not for themselves. They could not bear that this should be the end. Ere silence was completed their hearts were opened, and they knew what had been important on the earth. Man, the flower of all flesh, the noblest of all creatures visible, man who had once made god in his image, and had mirrored his strength on the constellations, beautiful naked man was dying, strangled in the garment that he had woven. Century after century had he toiled, and here was his reward. Truly the garment had seemed heavenly at first, shot with the colours of culture, sewn with the threads of self-denial. And heavenly it had been so long as it was a garment and no more, so long as man could shed it at will and live by the essence that is his soul, and the essence, equally divine, that is his body. The sin against the body — it was for that they wept in chief; the centuries of wrong against the muscles and the nerves, and those five portals by which we can alone apprehend — glossing it over with talk of evolution, until the body was white pap, the home of ideas as colourless, last sloshy stirrings of a spirit that had grasped the stars.

'Where are you?' she sobbed.

His voice in the darkness said, 'Here.'

'Is there any hope, Kuno?'

'None for us.'

'Where are you?'

She crawled towards him over the bodies of the dead. His blood spurted over her hands.

'Quicker,' he gasped, 'I am dying — but we touch, we talk, not through the Machine.'

180

He kissed her.

'We have come back to our own. We die, but we have recaptured life, as it was in Wessex, when Alfred overthrew the Danes. We know what they know outside, they who dwelt in the cloud that is the colour of a pearl.'

'But, Kuno, is it true? Are there still men on the surface of the earth? Is this – this tunnel, this poisoned darkness – really not the end?'

He replied:

'I have seen them, spoken to them, loved them. They are hiding in the mist and the ferns until our civilization stops. Today they are the Homeless – tomorrow –'

'Oh, tomorrow – some fool will start the Machine again, tomorrow.'

'Never,' said Kuno, 'never. Humanity has learnt its lesson.'

As he spoke, the whole city was broken like a honeycomb. An air-ship had sailed in through the vomitory into a ruined wharf. It crashed downwards, exploding as it went, rending gallery after gallery with its wings of steel. For a moment they saw the nations of the dead, and, before they joined them, scraps of the untainted sky.

Farewell Performance

BY H. RUSSELL WAKEFIELD

Moment of Fear on NBC was a curious mixture of live drama and filmed episodes drawn from other American anthology series. The premise of the series was character studies of people on the edge of fear and cornered by some life-threatening obstacle. A number of the 'live' tales were based on short stories by popular supernatural and mystery writers, while the filmed episodes – which came from shows like General Electric Theatre, Studio 57 and Pepsi Cola Playhouse – were all original screenplays which were included because they utilized the same elements of emotional crisis. On occasions, Moment of Fear would be divided into two segments separated by commercials: the first a story with a twist in the tail and the second an extract from a horror or mystery movie. Alfred Hitchcock appeared on Moment of Fear on several occasions to promote his pictures. Among the actors who were featured in the series were Hans Conried, Charles Bronson and Burgess Meredith.

'Farewell Performance' which was screened in December 1960 starred John Hoyt as a ventriloquist whose grip on reality starts to break up when his dummy threatens to betray the fact he is a murderer. The story was written by H. Russell Wakefield (1888–1964), a writer of supernatural stories which some experts have described as being the equal of those of M.R. James. Certainly, with stories such as 'Farewell Performance' he demonstrates a mastery of the weird and uncanny situation that remains long in the memory. It is a pity that there were so few other episodes of Moment of Fear about which the same could be said.

JACK Granger swung open the stage-door of the Wolverham Empire in the manner of one to whom stage-doors had no sanctity. The theatrical agent was a big fellow in his middle forties, rather overdressed. His mien suggested abounding self-confidence, acquisitiveness and competence; and that the elasticity of his conscience would meet any demands that might be made upon it.

'Mr Nimbo?' he said to the stage-door man.

'First on the right, top of the stairs.'

Granger took the flight in three strides and tapped on the designated door.

'Come in,' said a voice.

'Hullo, Gustave,' said Granger. 'So sorry to hear the bad news.'

Nimbo was lying back on a couch. On a table beside him was a bottle of whisky, a glass and water-pitcher. Bottle and glass were both half full.

The ventriloquist was ten years younger than his agent. In a way he was very good-looking. That is to say he appeared so in his photographs when something about his face was touched out; something that was not very easy to define, but something which caused persons of discernment instinctively to take a dislike to him. A look of furtive arrogance? Something like that. His father had been a Prussian and bad Prussians often wear that look. His mother had been English and he was completely anglicized. He was clad in a silk dressing-gown.

'I was in Brum on business when I heard about it. Very sudden, wasn't it?' said Granger.

'Not very,' answered Nimbo quickly. 'Sit down. Have a drink?'

'Not for me.'

'She'd been ailing for some time,' said Nimbo rather mechanically.

'Bad shock for you all the same,' said Granger. He had little more use for Nimbo than most people connected with the Profession, though they got on well enough; and he paid his rent and the upkeep of his car out of his percentage of Nimbo's earnings, for he topped most bills.

'Are you sure you're all right to go on?' asked Granger.

'I'm going to,' replied Nimbo, emptying his glass. The peg was stiff enough to contort his face slightly.

'May help to take your mind off it.'

'Off what?' asked Nimbo sharply.

Granger stared at him, puzzled.

'Your loss, of course.'

'Yes,' said Nimbo, pouring out another stiff drink.

'Ditto that stuff,' said Granger, 'but I shouldn't over-do it.'

'I'm all right,' said Nimbo irritably; he lay back and stared at the ceiling.

His doll, Nobby, was perched in a chair facing Granger. He was garbed as an infantry private and the condition of his kit reflected little credit on his corps. Nobby was famous and had cost a lot of money. He didn't look so funny, thought Granger, off stage and in repose. His set, sardonic grin, bulging red cheeks, round, staring eyes, were vaguely repulsive. He looked extraordinarily alive in a garish, bestial way. He was smirking knowingly at Granger, who looked away from him.

'You're sure you'll be okay?' he said. 'If you don't feel up to it, you've got a perfect alibi.'

'I'm going on,' said Nimbo, taking another drink.

'Well, you know best. I'll be in the front row of the stalls to lend you my support. Keep your chin up!'

'I'm all right,' said Nimbo. 'Thanks for coming.'

Granger went to the bar and sat down with a drink. He hadn't been reassured. Nimbo had a funny look about him; half-tight, of course, but something else, a sort of daft, strained, vague look; and ventriloquists had to have their wits about them. Oh well, artists nearly always pulled themselves together, drunk or sober, when they got out in front. He bought a programme. Mostly barturns except for the Midge Sisters and Nimbo, who came just before the interval, his invariable place, rather daringly and cleverly chosen.

Granger took his seat for the turn before Nimbo's:

'Ruggles Rowlock, the Ace of Chumps.'

Ruggles was a new one to Granger and might be worth a decco. The usual piece of cheese, however. Jokes as old and dirty as a tramp's pants; singing, septic; dancing, dud.

But he got a huge hand from the Wolverhamites of all ages, who obviously liked their sex raw.

Then the orchestra clanged out some introductory chords, the audience opened their mouths in a fixed grin and prepared to be mightily amused. A moment later Nimbo in his famous check plus-fives and wearing a monocle, came on to the stage, Nobby under his right arm. Nimbo acknowledged the vociferous greeting, sat down in his special gold chair, with a table beside it, arranged Nobby to his liking, adjusted his fingers to the loops and strings and lit a cigarette.

He didn't look too good, thought Granger; too full of whisky, wrong dope for ventriloquists.

'Well, Nobby,' said Nimbo, 'and how are you?'

'I'm okay,' squawked the doll, 'and you, Guv'nor?'

'Very well, thanks.'

'And the wife.'

Granger frowned. 'My God!' he exclaimed to himself, 'I'd have thought he'd cut that out! Whisky talking!' And indeed, a close observer might have noticed an odd look pass across the ventriloquist's face.

'She's well, too,' he muttered, pulling hard at his cigarette.

Nobby turned to the audience, pursed up his lips and winked his right eye in a highly impertinent and incredulous way.

'And how'd you like the army, Nobby?' asked Nimbo.

'I don't like it, Guv'nor. I don't like it!'

'Indeed. Why's that?'

'Always in trouble, Guv'nor. Always up to the gills in the 'ot connsommy.'

'What kind of trouble?'

'Impert'nence to officers.'

'Impertinence to officers! A very serious offence. What have you done?'

'I ain't done nuffin. It's like this 'ere. T'other mornin' we're 'avin' our chow when the ord'ly orficer comes around. An' 'e ses, "Any complaints?" an' I ses "Yussir", an' 'e ses, "Wha's the matter?" an' I ses, "It's the stew sir." "What abaht it?" ses 'e. "I don't fancy it," I ses. "Why not?" he ses.

' "It's the meat in it," I ses, "gives it a funny taste." 'E ses, "Ain't you the bloke what complains last week there ain't enough meat in it?" "Yussir," I ses. "Well," he ses, "we don't want many of your sort in the Dudshires. Owsoever I'll taste it." So 'e does and ses, "Excellent stew, never tasted better," and I ses, "You really likes it, sir?"

' "Yus," he ses, "I'll show yer", and 'e scoops up another spoonful, "Delishus", 'e ses, "an' don't let me 'ear no more complaints from you!"

' "Okay," I ses, "but you see that there spud a floating aroun' in that corner?"

' "What abaht it?" he ses.

' "Well," I ses, "there's a dead mouse unner it!" Well, you never did, Guv'nor! Anyone 'ud think I'd shoved some poison in it!'

Nimbo dropped his cigarette and again that odd, dazed expression came over his face.

'Shouldn't have attempted it,' thought Granger; 'he looks ghastly.'

'Then, Guv'nor, I gets sevin days CB,' said Nobby.

'You were confined to barracks?'

'Yus, Guv'nor, and sevin days EF.'

'What's that?'

'Extry fatigues, guv'nor, swabbin' out the cookhouse, an' sevin days BFU.'

'What's that?'

'Bloody fed-up, Guv'nor.'

'I've told you not to swear in front of me!' said Nimbo sternly. 'Never swear in front of a gentleman.'

'Are you a gentleman, Guv'nor?'

'Of course!'

'One of the Mayfair boys?'

'Certainly not!'

Nobby cocked his head round to the audience and seemed to mutter something.

'What did you say?' asked Nimbo in an urgent angry tone which made the audience roar.

'Nuffin', Guv'nor. An' then I gets anuffer packet. It's like this 'ere. When I joins hup, the serjunt bloke ses to hus: "If you wants a quiet life, you'll do just what you're tole, no more, no less, an' no back answers. Never let me 'ear you say, 'I thought', nor any tripe like that. You're not 'ere to do no thinkin'; and mos' of you ain't got the works to do it with." '

'That certainly applies to you, Nobby,' said Nimbo.

'Ho it does, does it! 'Ave you got brains, Guv'nor?'

'Most certainly I've got brains.'

'Is that 'ow you thinks of –?' and the doll leaned over and whispered something in Nimbo's ear. Nimbo shot his head back and his monocle clattered on to the table. Nobby faced the audience again, leered and winked.

' 'E didn't know I knows that one,' he squawked. 'Well, Guv'nor,' he continued, 'the Colonel, the 'ead bloke, comes up to me on the square one mornin' and ses, "Look 'ere, my man, d'you know where Corporal Twister is?" And I ses, "No, I doesn't, sir," an' 'e ses, "Possibly 'e's in the henseeos' mess. Go and see." So I goes there and finds this Corporal Twister a washin' 'is map; and I goes back an' tells the Colonel.

' "Didn't yer say I wants to see 'im?" he ses. "No, sir," I ses. "Well," he ses, "you're a most stupid and fat'eaded soldier," he ses, 'an' you'll never do for the Dudshires. Go an' tell 'im I wants to see 'im and put a jerk in it!" So I goes back and tells this Twister the Colonel bloke wants to see 'im. "Okey-dokey," 'e ses, "tell ole curried-guts I'll be there in 'arf a mo." So I goes back to this Colonel bloke an' 'e ses,

"Well, what did 'e say?" "'E said," I ses, "Okey-dokey, tell ole curried-guts I'll be there in 'arf a mo." Well, Guv'nor, you never see such a shine-up! Anyone 'ud think I'd done a murder!'

Nimbo seemed to start, so that the doll almost fell from his knee.

"'Ere, what's the gyme!' he squawked, 'if you does that again, you'll be givin' me conwulsions!'

'Imagine saying that!' thought Granger. 'He's not fit to be on. I'll tell him so when he goes off.'

'So I don't think I'm goin' to like the army, Guv'nor,' continued Nobby. 'Will yer buy me hout? Only thirty-five quid.'

'Certainly not! It'll be the making of you.'

'It'll be the death of me!' howled Nobby. 'An' I don't want to die, Gustave!' he added in a screaming falsetto.

Granger felt ripples of horrified dismay running down his spine.

'Her voice, too! He's completely lost control of himself. What had I better do?'

Nimbo stretched out a trembling hand and took and drained the glass of water on the table. The audience vaguely sensed this was wrong; the more perceptive became puzzled and uneasy. The giggling was fitful.

'D'you think we'll be sent abroad, Guv'nor?' asked Nobby.

'I expect so,' replied Nimbo mechanically.

'Where shall we go, Guv'nor?'

'Possibly to Aden.'

'Shove us in a den, Guv'nor!'

'And Lucknow.'

'What hat, Guv'nor?' asked Nobby peering round the theatre.

'Or Hong-Kong, perhaps, the Suez Canal or Khartoum.'

'Well, I'll be damned!' exclaimed Nobby. 'Sorry Guv'nor, mustn't say that! I'll be 'anged! That better, Guv'nor? So'll you, unless you 'as yer luck with yer! Fust we're shoved in a den. Then we 'as a date with King Kong, then we're bunged in Susie's Canal, and we ends up in a toom! Oh, must I die, Gustave!' And that high, feminine wail of despair came again.

Granger gritted his teeth. 'I can't stand much more of this,' he thought.

'Or you might be sent to Bombay,' said Nimbo monotonously.

'Bomb a what, Guv'nor?'

'Bombay is a city in India. I'm afraid you're terribly ignorant.'

'Am I, Guv'nor?'

'Terribly. Let's see if you know any geography.'

'Right, Guv'nor.'

'Where's Adelaide?'

'Dunno, Guv'nor. But yer left Gladys in Glasgie,' and the doll turned and faced the audience, grinning and winked. Nimbo half rose from his chair. The audience giggled no more. It seemed to their troubled minds that the roles of Nimbo and Nobby had been reversed, as if the doll was dictating the dialogue.

'Can I 'ave a fag, Guv'nor?' said Nobby.

Nimbo rather clumsily pushed a cigarette into a tube in the doll's mouth, and lit it.

'Shall I sing, Guv'nor?'

'If you like,' replied Nimbo vaguely.

The orchestra lightly suggested the accompaniment to "The Mountain of Mourne", and Nobby, puffing smoke and beating time with his right arm, burst into a raucous chant:

> 'In a very short time
> I'll be bung up the Pole,
> Right down on me huppers
> And drawin' the dole,
> For the 'angman'll soon be a cashin' 'is cheque,
> For shovin' a ro-ope around Nimbo's neck.'

Granger got up hurriedly and left the auditorium.

'Did yer like that, Guv'nor?' asked Nobby.

Nimbo did not answer and his face was contorted.

'We 'ad a bay'net practice this mornin', Guv'nor,' said Nobby. 'Narsty ole-fashioned way of killin' a bloke. Yer wouldn't do it that way, would yer, Guv'nor; you'd put a little white powder in 'er hoxo!'

Nimbo leapt to his feet. 'I didn't, you bloody little devil!' he cried, and flung the doll to the back of the stage. Then he staggered into the wings.

After a moment the curtain descended and the manager, looking worried, came on to the stage.

'Ladies and gentlemen,' he said, 'Mr Nimbo wishes to express his profound regret. The fact is he lost his wife yesterday. He pluckily tried to carry on, but the effort was too much for him. I'm sure you will all join with me in expressing our deep regret at his bereavement.'

By the time of the trial many myths and legends were current about that memorable half-hour. But there is a rather convincing body of testimony, supplied by those in the stalls, that just after the manager had spoken his last sentence, a derisive voice squawked from behind the curtain, 'Hi shud shay sho!'

The Terror of the Twins

BY ALGERNON BLACKWOOD

In March 1961, Associated Rediffusion announced the start of their series of 'Wednesday night creepies' based on the stories of Algernon Blackwood (1869–1951) who, until his death, had been familiar to British radio and television audiences. Blackwood's sombre features and deep voice coupled with his unique ability to relate supernatural stories with great authenticity had earned him the soubriquet, 'The Ghost Man'. Although he had worked on radio since the years of the Second World War, it was not until a few years before his death that he demonstrated the same mastery of the television medium. Had Blackwood still been alive, he would doubtless have made an ideal host for the series based on his work — but the role went instead to the saccarine — featured Scottish actor, John Laurie, who after a lifetime in films and on the stage, became famous as the gloomy undertaker in the hit BBC TV series, Dad's Army. *Laurie made an impressive job of hosting* Tales of Mystery, *flashing his eyes and rubbing his hands suggestively as he announced the ghoulish pleasures to follow.*

The series had a mixed reception from the press and public, however. Maurice Wiggin of the Sunday Times *was generally enthusiastic, commenting, 'Veteran viewers who remember the old man [Algernon Blackwood] telling his stories on BBC television and radio have a ready-made standard of reference.' Denis Thomas of the* Daily Mail, *on the other hand, shared the misgivings reviewers of the time often expressed about putting the supernatural on the screen. 'Television being a strictly literal medium,' he wrote, 'can add nothing to a cosy tale of death and diabolism without overdoing it. One way to cope with this difficulty might be to show less and suggest more.' Such comments notwithstanding, the adaptation of 'The Terror of the*

Twins', about a man who swears a terrible doom on one of his twin sons from beyond the grave, was atmospherically produced and offered Malcolm Russell in the lead role 'the chance to roll his eyes in a fine frenzy and to expire with a convincing death rattle,' according to the Daily Mail. *Those who remember watching the 'Wednesday night creepie' may well have memories of Russell's performance – which will certainly be vividly revived while reading the following pages . . .*

THAT the man's hopes had built upon a son to inherit his name and estates – a single son, that is – was to be expected; but no one could have foreseen the depth and bitterness of his disappointment, the cold, implacable fury, when there arrived instead – twins. For, though the elder legally must inherit, that other ran him so deadly close. A daughter would have been a more reasonable defeat. But twins –! To miss his dream by so feeble a device –!

The complete frustration of a hope deeply cherished for years may easily result in strange fevers of the soul, but the violence of the father's hatred, existing as it did side by side with a love he could not deny, was something to set psychologists thinking. More than unnatural, it was positively uncanny. Being a man of rigid self-control, however, it operated inwardly, and doubtless along some morbid line of weakness little suspected even by those nearest to him, preying upon his thought to such dreadful extent that finally the mind gave way. The suppressed rage and bitterness deprived him, so the family decided, of his reason, and he spent the last years of his life under restraint. He was possessed naturally of immense forces – of will, feeling, desire; his dynamic value truly tremendous, driving through life like a great engine; and the intensity of this concentrated and buried hatred was guessed by few. The twins themselves, however, knew it. They divined it, at least, for it operated ceaselessly against them side by side with the genuine soft love that occasionally sweetened it, to their great perplexity. They spoke of it only to each other, though.

'At twenty-one,' Edward, the elder, would remark sometimes, unhappily, 'we shall know more.' 'Too much,' Ernest would reply, with a rush of unreasoning terror the thought never failed to evoke – *in him.* 'Things father said always happened – in life.' And they paled perceptibly. For the hatred, thus compressed into a veritable bomb of psychic energy, had found at the last a singular expression in the cry of the father's distraught mind. On the occasion of their final visit to the asylum, preceding his death by a few hours only, very calmly, but with an intensity that drove the words into their hearts like points of burning metal, he had spoken. In the presence of the attendant, at the door of the dreadful padded cell, he said it: 'You are not two, but one. I still regard you as one. And at the coming of age, by hell, you shall find it out!'

The lads perhaps had never fully divined that icy hatred which lay so well concealed against them, but that this final sentence was a curse, backed by all the man's terrific force, they quite well realized; and accordingly, almost unknown to each other, they had come to dread the day inexpressibly. On the morning of that twenty-first birthday – their father gone these five years into the Unknown, yet still sometimes so strangely close to them – they shared the same biting, inner terror, just as they shared all other emotions of their life – intimately, without speech. During the daytime they managed to keep it at a distance, but when the dusk fell about the old house they knew the stealthy approach of a kind of panic sense. Their self-respect weakened swiftly . . . and they persuaded their old friend, and once tutor, the vicar, to sit up with them till midnight . . . He had humoured them to that extent, willing to forgo his sleep, and at the same time more than a little interested in their singular belief – that before the day was out, before midnight struck, that is, the curse of that terrible man would somehow come into operation against them.

Festivities over and the guests departed, they sat up in the library, the room usually occupied by their father, and little used since. Mr Curtice, a robust man of fifty-five, and a firm believer in spiritual principalities and powers, dark as well as good, affected (for their own good) to regard the youths' obsession with a kindly cynicism. 'I do not think it likely for one moment,' he said gravely, 'that such a thing would be permitted. All spirits are in the hands of God, and the violent ones more especially.' To which Edward made the extraordinary reply: 'Even if father does not come himself he will – *send!*' And Ernest agreed: 'All this time he's been making preparations for this very day. We've both known it for a long time – by odd things that have happened, by our dreams, by nasty little dark hints of various kinds, and by these persistent attacks of terror that come from nowhere, especially of late. Haven't we, Edward?' Edward assenting with a shudder. 'Father has been *at us* of late with renewed violence. Tonight it will be a regular assault upon our lives, or minds, or souls!'

'Strong personalities *may* possibly leave behind them forces that continue to act,' observed Mr Curtice with caution, while the brothers replied almost in the same breath: 'That's exactly what we feel so curiously. Though – nothing has actually happened yet, you know, and it's a good many years now since –'

This was the way the twins spoke of it all. And it was their profound conviction that had touched their old friend's sense of duty. The experiment should justify itself – and cure them. Meanwhile none of the family knew. Everything was planned secretly.

The library was the quietest room in the house. It had shuttered bow-windows, thick carpets, heavy doors. Books lined the walls, and there was a capacious open fireplace of brick in which the woodlogs blazed and roared, for the autumn night was chilly. Round this the three of them were grouped, the clergyman reading aloud from the Book of Job in low tones; Edward and Ernest, in dinner-jackets, occupying deep leather armchairs, listening. They looked exactly what they were – Cambridge 'undergrads', their faces pale against their dark hair, and alike as two peas. A shaded lamp behind the clergyman threw the rest of the room into shadow. The reading voice was steady, even monotonous, but something in it betrayed an underlying anxiety, and although the eyes rarely left the printed page, they took in every movement of the young men opposite, and noted every change upon their faces. It was his aim to produce an unexciting atmosphere, yet to miss nothing; if anything did occur to see it from the very beginning. Not to be taken by surprise was his main idea . . . And thus, upon this falsely peaceful scene, the minutes passed the hour of eleven and slipped rapidly along towards midnight.

The novel element in his account of this distressing and dreadful occurrence seems to be that what happened – happened without the slightest warning or preparation. There was no gradual presentiment of any horror; no strange blast of cold air; no dwindling of heat or light; no shaking of windows or mysterious tapping upon furniture. Without preliminaries it fell with its black trappings of terror upon the scene.

The clergyman had been reading aloud for some considerable time, one or other of the twins – Ernest usually – making occasional remarks, which proved that his sense of dread was disappearing. As the time grew short and nothing happened they grew more at their ease. Edward, indeed, actually nodded, dozed, and finally fell asleep. It was a few minutes before midnight. Ernest, slightly yawning, was stretching himself in the big chair. 'Nothing's going to happen,' he said aloud, in a pause. 'Your good influence has prevented it.' He even laughed now. 'What superstitious asses we've been, sir; haven't we –?'

Curtice, then, dropping his Bible, looked hard at him under the lamp. For in that second, even while the words sounded, there had come about a most abrupt and dreadful change; and so swiftly that the clergyman, in spite of himself, was taken utterly by surprise and had no time to think. There had swooped down upon the quiet library – so he puts it – an immense hushing silence, so profound that the peace already reigning there seemed clamour by comparison; and out of this enveloping stillness there rose through the space about them a living and abominable Invasion – soft, motionless, terrific. It was as though vast engines, working at full speed and pressure, yet too swift and delicate to be appreciable to any definite sense, had suddenly dropped down upon them – from nowhere. 'It made me think,' the vicar used to say afterwards, 'of the *Mauretania* machinery compressed into a nutshell, yet losing none of its awful power.'

'. . . haven't we?' repeated Ernest, still laughing. And Curtice, making no audible reply, heard the true answer in his heart: 'Because everything has *already happened* even as you feared.'

Yet, to the vicar's supreme astonishment, Ernest still noticed – nothing!

'Look,' the boy added, 'Eddy's sound asleep – sleeping like a pig. Doesn't say much for your reading, you know, sir!' And he laughed again – lightly, even foolishly. But that laughter jarred, for the clergyman understood now that the sleep of the elder twin was either feigned – or *unnatural*.

And while the easy words fell so lightly from his lips, the monstrous engines worked and pulsed against him and against his sleeping brother, all their huge energy concentrated down into points fine as Suggestion, delicate as Thought. The Invasion affected everything. The very objects in the room altered incredibly, revealing suddenly behind their normal exteriors horrid little hearts of darkness. It was truly amazing, this vile metamorphosis. Books, chairs, pictures, all yielded up their pleasant aspect, and betrayed, as with silent mocking laughter, their inner soul of blackness – their *decay*. This is how Curtice tries to body forth in words what he actually witnessed . . . And Ernest, yawning, talking lightly, half foolishly – still noticed nothing!

For all this, as described, came about in something like ten seconds; and with it swept into the clergyman's mind, like a blow, the memory of that sinister phrase used more than once by Edward: 'If father doesn't come, he will certainly – *send*.' And Curtice understood that he had done both – both sent and come himself . . . That violent mind, released from its spell of madness in the body, yet still retaining the old implacable hatred, was now directing the terrible, unseen assault. This silent room, so hushed and still, was charged to the brim. The horror of it, as he said later, 'seemed to peel the very skin from my back' . . . And, while Ernest noticed nothing, Edward slept! . . . The soul of the clergyman, strong with the desire to help or save, yet realizing that he was alone against a Legion, poured out in wordless prayer to his Deity. The clock just then, whirring before it struck, made itself audible.

'By Jove! It's all right, you see!' exclaimed Ernest, his voice oddly fainter and lower than before. 'There's midnight – and nothing's happened. Bally nonsense, all of it!' His voice had dwindled curiously in volume. 'I'll get the whisky and soda from the hall.' His relief was great and his manner showed it. But in him somewhere was a singular change. His voice, manner, gestures, his very tread as he moved over the thick carpet toward the door, all showed it. He seemed less *real*, less alive, reduced somehow to littleness, the voice without timbre or quality, the appearance of him diminished in some fashion quite ghastly. His presence, if not actually shrivelled, was at least impaired. Ernest had suffered a singular and horrible *decrease* . . .

The clock was still whirring before the strike. One heard the chain running up softly. Then the hammer fell upon the first stroke of midnight.

'I'm off,' he laughed faintly from the door; 'It's all been pure funk – on my part, at least . . . !' He passed out of sight into the hall. *The Power that throbbed so mightily about the room followed him out.* Almost at the same moment Edward woke up. But he woke with a tearing and indescribable cry of pain and anguish on his lips: 'Oh, oh, oh! But it hurts! It hurts! I can't hold you; leave me. It's breaking me asunder –'

The clergyman had sprung to his feet, but in the same instant everything had become normal once more – the room as it was before, the horror gone. There was nothing he could do or say, for there was no longer anything to put right, to defend, or to attack. Edward was speaking; his voice, deep and full as it never had been before: 'By Jove, how that sleep has refreshed me! I feel twice the chap I was before – twice the chap. I feel quite splendid. Your voice, sir, must have hypnotized me to sleep . . . ' He crossed the room with great vigour. 'Where's – er – where's – Ernie, by the bye?' he asked casually, hesitating – almost searching – for the name. And a shadow as of a vanished memory crossed his face and was gone. The tone conveyed the most complete indifference where once the least word or movement of his twin had wakened solicitude, love. 'Gone away, I suppose – gone to bed, I mean, of course.'

Curtice has never been able to describe the dreadful conviction that overwhelmed him as he stood there staring, his heart in his mouth – the conviction, the positive certainty, that Edward had changed interiorly, had suffered an incredible accession to his existing personality.

But he *knew* it as he watched. His mind, spirit, soul had most wonderfully increased. Something that hitherto the lad had known from the outside only, or by the magic of loving sympathy, had now passed, to be incorporated with his own being. And, being himself, it required no expression. Yet this visible increase was somehow terrible. Curtice shrank back from him. The instinct – he has never grasped the profound psychology of *that*, nor why it turned his soul dizzy with a kind of nausea – the instinct to strike him where he stood, passed, and a plaintive sound from the hall, stealing softly into the room between them, sent all that was left to him of self-possession onto his feet. He turned and ran. Edward followed him – very leisurely.

They found Ernest, or what had been Ernest, crouching behind the table in the hall, weeping foolishly to himself. On his face lay blackness. The mouth was open, the jaw dropped; he dribbled hopelessly; and from the face had passed all signs of intelligence – of spirit.

For a few weeks he lingered on, regaining no sign of spiritual or mental life before the poor body, hopelessly disorganised, released what was left of him, from pure inertia – from complete and utter loss of vitality.

And the horrible thing – so the distressed family thought, at least – was that all those weeks Edward showed an indifference that was singularly brutal and complete. He rarely even went to visit him. I believe, too, it is true that he only once spoke of him by name; and that was when he said –

'Ernie? Oh, but Ernie is much better and happier where he is –!'

William and Mary

BY ROALD DAHL

The CBS anthology series, Way Out, *which first appeared on Friday, 31 March 1961, came onto American TV screens in the half-hour slot immediately before* The Twilight Zone *offering viewers an uninterrupted hour of the weird and the macabre. Yet, despite the fact it was hosted by Roald Dahl, then living in America and already beginning to earn a reputation for his sinister, twist-in-the-tail stories about people in strange and unsettling situations, the show was taken off the air almost as dramatically as it had appeared after just fourteen remarkable episodes. It's sudden demise is regarded by aficionados as one of the saddest in the late night horror genre.*

The idea for Way Out *had sprung from New York producer David Susskind, an admirer of Roald Dahl's stories, who had met the towering Englishman with his wonderfully modulated voice and invited him to adapt some of his tales for TV and also host the programme. Dahl was immediately enthusiastic about the idea and, further, agreed to write the opening and closing remarks, tinging them with his inimitable brand of black humour. He would, for instance, give advice on how to murder a spouse, or reminisce on his childhood in Norway where, when somebody died, and the ground was frozen solid, they would sharpen the legs and hammer the body into the ground 'like an enormous nail'. Dahl's impact on viewers was instantaneous – a review of his first show describing him as 'a thin Alfred Hitchcock, an East Coast Rod Serling'. CBS, though, had set themselves a punishing schedule for* Way Out *– each episode had to be rehearsed and filmed in just three days in time for each Friday night's screening. Nevertheless, with a pool of versatile actors working in the New York theatre who were available to guest on the show – including*

Martin Balsam, Mark Leonard, Fritz Weaver, Mildred Dunnock and Charlotte Rae – the omens looked good. Until Friday the fourteenth. The reason for the cancellation did not emerge for a while, but was as simple as it was heartbreaking – Way Out had received excellent audience ratings in the metropolitan areas but failed nationwide. It was, as David Susskind remarked later, 'perhaps a little too odd for television'. Odd may not have been quite the right word for two episodes which genuinely made many viewers' flesh creep: 'False Face' in which Alfred Ryder, playing Quasimodo in a production of The Hunchback of Notre Dame, *found himself unable to remove his hideous make-up; and 'Soft Focus' where photographer Barry Morse changed his wife into an old hag by the use of a chemical solution on her photograph – and then accidentally spilled some on a portrait of himself . . . Citing these two stories in particular, critic Jeffrey Frentzen believes that Dahl's show was actually taken off the air because it 'shocked the censors'.*

Roald Dahl (1916–90), who, of course, went on to even greater things as a writer (especially for children) and in the Seventies inspired the highly successful British TV series, Tales of the Unexpected *(featured later in this collection), always remembered* Way Out *with great affection. 'I was a pretty young chap then,' he said in an interview in 1978, 'and it was amusing for me because it was my first thing on television.' Among the fourteen stories, the most highly praised was the first, which happened to be one of Dahl's own, about a wife's final revenge on her husband, 'William and Mary', which Marc Daniels directed with Henry Jones, Mildred Dunnock and Fritz Weaver. The impact of the final scene of a living human brain pulsating in a glass basin was given even greater frisson when Dahl, with a gentlemanly leer, offered comfort to his undoubtedly scared-stiff audience with the words, 'Goodnight . . . and sleep well.'*

WILLIAM Pearl did not leave a great deal of money when he died, and his will was a simple one. With the exception of a few small bequests to relatives, he left all his property to his wife.

The solicitor and Mrs Pearl went over it together in the solicitor's office, and when the business was completed, the widow got up to leave. At that point, the solicitor took a sealed envelope from the folder on his desk and held it out to his client.

'I have been instructed to give you this,' he said. 'Your husband sent it to us shortly before he passed away.' The solicitor was pale and prim, and out of respect for a widow he kept his head on one side as he spoke, looking downward. 'It appears that it might be something personal, Mrs Pearl. No doubt you'd like to take it home with you and read it in privacy.'

Mrs Pearl accepted the envelope and went out into the street. She paused on the pavement, feeling the thing with her fingers. A letter of farewell from William? Probably, yes. A formal letter. It was bound to be formal – stiff and formal. The man was incapable of acting otherwise. He had never done anything informal in his life.

> *My dear Mary, I trust that you will not permit my departure from this world to upset you too much, but you will continue to observe those precepts which have guided you so well during our partnership together. Be diligent and dignified in all things. Be thrifty with your money. Be very careful that you do not . . . et cetera, et cetera.*

A typical William letter.

Or was it possible that he might have broken down at the last moment and written her something beautiful? Maybe this was a beautiful tender message, a sort of love letter, a lovely warm note of thanks to her for giving him thirty years of her life and for ironing a million shirts and cooking a million meals and making a million beds, something that she could read over and over again, once a day at least, and she would keep it for ever in the box on her dressing-table together with her brooches.

There is no knowing what people will do when they are about to die, Mrs Pearl told herself, and she tucked the envelope under her arm and hurried home.

She let herself in the front door and went straight to the living-room and sat down on the sofa without removing her hat or coat. Then she opened the envelope and drew out the contents. These consisted, she saw, of some fifteen or twenty sheets of lined white paper, folded over once and held together at the top left-hand corner by a clip. Each sheet was covered with the small, neat, forward-sloping writing that she knew so well, but when she noticed how much of it there was, and in what a neat businesslike manner it was written, and how the first page didn't even begin in the nice way a letter should, she began to get suspicious.

She looked away. She lit herself a cigarette. She took one puff and laid the cigarette in the ashtray.

If this is about what I am beginning to suspect it is about, she told herself, then I don't want to read it.

Can one refuse to read a letter from the dead?

Yes.

Well . . .

She glanced over at William's empty chair on the other side of the fireplace. It was a big brown leather armchair, and there was a depression on the seat of it, made by his buttocks over the years. Higher up, on the backrest, there was a dark oval stain on the leather where his head had rested. He used to sit reading in that chair and she would be opposite him on the sofa, sewing on buttons or mending socks or putting a patch on the elbow of one of his jackets, and every now and then a pair of eyes would glance up from the book and settle on her, watchful, but strangely impersonal, as if calculating something. She had never liked those eyes. They were ice blue, cold, small, and rather close together, with two deep vertical lines of disapproval dividing them. All her life they had been watching her. And even now, after a week alone in the house, she sometimes had an uneasy feeling that they were still there, following her around, staring at her from doorways, from empty chairs, through a window at night.

Slowly she reached into her handbag and took out her spectacles and put them on. Then, holding the pages up high in front of her so that they caught the late afternoon light from the window behind, she started to read:

This note, *my dear Mary*, is entirely for you, and will be given you shortly after I am gone.

Do not be alarmed by the sight of all this writing. It is nothing but an attempt on my part to explain to you precisely what Landy is going to do to me, and why I have agreed that he should do it, and what are his theories and his hopes. You are my wife and you have a right to know these things. In fact you *must* know them. During the past few days I have tried very hard to speak with you about Landy, but you have steadfastly refused to give me a hearing. This, as I have already told you, is a very foolish attitude to take, and I find it not entirely an unselfish one either. It stems mostly from ignorance, and I am absolutely convinced that if only you were made aware of all the facts, you would immediately change your view. That is why I am hoping that when I am no longer with you, and your mind is less distracted, you will consent to listen to me more carefully through these pages. I swear to you that when you have read my story, your sense of antipathy will vanish, and enthusiasm will take its place. I even dare to hope that you will become a little proud of what I have done.

As you read on, you must forgive me, if you will, for the coolness of my style, but this is the only way I know of getting my message over to you clearly. You see, as my time draws near, it is natural that I begin to brim with every kind of sentimentality under the sun. Each day I grow more extravagantly wistful, especially in the evenings, and unless I watch myself closely my emotions will be overflowing onto these pages.

I have a wish, for example, to write something about you and what a satisfactory wife you have been to me through the years, and I am promising myself that if there is time, and I still have the strength, I shall do that next.

I have a yearning also to speak about this Oxford of mine where I have been living and teaching for the past seventeen years, to tell something about the glory of the place and to explain, if I can, a little of what it has meant to have been allowed to work in its midst. All the things and places that I loved so well keep crowding in on me now in this gloomy bedroom. They are bright and beautiful as they always were, and today, for some reason, I can see them more clearly than ever. The path around the lake in the gardens of Worcester College, where Lovelace used to walk. The gateway at Pembroke. The view westward over the town from Magdalen Tower. The great hall at Christchurch. The little rockery at St Johns where I have counted more than a dozen varieties of campanula, including the rare and dainty C. Waldsteiniana. But there, you see! I haven't even begun and already I'm falling into the trap. So let me get started now; and let you read it slowly, my dear, without any of that sense of sorrow or disapproval that might otherwise embarrass your understanding. Promise me now that you will read it slowly, and that you will put yourself in a cool and patient frame of mind before you begin.

The details of the illness that struck me down so suddenly in my middle life are known to you. I need not waste time upon them – except to admit at once how foolish I was not to have gone earlier to my doctor. Cancer is one of the few remaining diseases that these modern drugs cannot cure. A surgeon can operate if it has not spread too far; but with me, not only did I leave it too late, but the thing had the effrontery to attack me in the pancreas, making both surgery and survival equally impossible.

So here I was with somewhere between one and six months left to live, growing more melancholy every hour – and then, all of a sudden, in comes Landy.

That was six weeks ago, on a Tuesday morning, very early, long before your visiting time, and the moment he entered I knew there was some sort of madness in the wind. He didn't creep in on his toes, sheepish and embarrassed, not knowing what to say, like all my other visitors. He came in strong and smiling, and he strode up to the bed and stood there looking down at me with a wild bright glimmer in his eyes, and he said, 'William, my boy, this is perfect. You're just the one I want!'

Perhaps I should explain to you here that although John Landy has never been to our house, and you have seldom if ever met him, I myself have been friendly with him for at least nine years. I am, of course, primarily a teacher of philosophy, but as you know I've lately been dabbling a good deal in psychology as well. Landy's interests and mine have therefore slightly overlapped. He is a magnificent neurosurgeon, one of the finest, and recently he has been kind enough to let me study the results of some of his work, especially the varying effects of prefrontal lobotomies upon different types of psychopath. So you can see that when he suddenly burst in on me Tuesday morning we were by no means strangers to one another.

'Look,' he said, pulling up a chair beside the bed. 'In a few weeks you're going to be dead. Correct?'

Coming from Landy, the question didn't seem especially unkind. In a way it was refreshing to have a visitor brave enough to touch upon the forbidden subject.

'You're going to expire right here in this room, and then they'll take you out and cremate you.'

'Bury me,' I said.

'That's even worse. And then what? Do you believe you'll go to heaven?'

'I doubt it,' I said, 'though it would be comforting to think so.'

'Or hell, perhaps?'

'I don't really see why they should send me there.'

'You never know, my dear William.'

'What's all this about?' I asked.

'Well,' he said, and I could see him watching me carefully, 'personally, I don't believe that after you're dead you'll ever hear of yourself again – unless . . .' and here he paused and smiled and leaned closer '. . . unless, of course, you have the sense to put yourself into my hands. Would you care to consider a proposition?'

The way he was staring at me, and studying me, and appraising me with a queer kind of hungriness, I might have been a piece of prime beef on the counter and he had bought it and was waiting for them to wrap it up.

'I'm really serious about it, William. Would you care to consider a proposition?'

'I don't know what you're talking about.'

'Then listen and I'll tell you. Will you listen to me?'

'Go on then, if you like. I doubt I've got very much to lose by hearing it.'

'On the contrary, you have a great deal to gain – especially *after you're dead.*'

I am sure he was expecting me to jump when he said this, but for some reason I was ready for it. I lay quite still, watching his face and that slow white smile of his that always revealed the gold clasp of an upper denture curled around the canine on the left side of his mouth.

'This is a thing, William, that I've been working on quietly for some years. One or two others here at the hospital have been helping me, especially Morrison, and we've completed a number of fairly successful trials with laboratory animals. I'm at the stage now where I'm ready to have a go with a man. It's a big idea, and it may sound a bit farfetched at first, but from a surgical point of view there doesn't seem to be any reason why it shouldn't be more or less practicable.'

Landy leaned forward and placed both his hands on the edge of my bed. He has a good face, handsome in a bony sort of way, and with none of the usual doctor's look about it. You know that look, most of them have it. It glimmers at you out of their eyeballs like a dull electric sign and it reads *Only I can save you.* But John Landy's eyes were wide and bright and little sparks of excitement were dancing in the centres of them.

'Quite a long time ago,' he said, 'I saw a short medical film that had been brought over from Russia. It was a rather gruesome thing, but interesting. It showed a dog's head completely severed from the body, but with the normal blood supply being maintained through the arteries and veins by means of an artificial heart. Now the thing is this: that dog's head, sitting there all alone on a sort of tray, was *alive*. The brain was functioning. They proved it by several tests. For example, when food was smeared on the dog's lips, the tongue would come out and lick it away; and the eyes would follow a person moving across the room.

'It seemed reasonable to conclude from this that the head and the brain did not need to be attached to the rest of the body in order to remain alive – provided, of course, that a supply of properly oxygenated blood could be maintained.

'Now then. My own thought, which grew out of seeing this film, was to remove the brain from the skull of a human and keep it alive and functioning as an independent unit for an unlimited period after he is dead. *Your* brain, for example, after *you* are dead.'

'I don't like that,' I said.

'Don't interrupt, William. Let me finish. So far as I can tell from subsequent experiments, the brain is a peculiarly self-supporting object. It manufactures its own cerebrospinal fluid. The magic processes of thought and memory which go on inside it are manifestly not impaired by the absence of limbs or trunk or even of skull, provided, as I say, that you keep pumping in the right kind of oxygenated blood under the proper conditions.

'My dear William, just think for a moment of your own brain. It is in perfect shape. It is crammed full of a lifetime of learning. It has taken you years of work to make it what it is. It is just beginning to give out some first-rate original ideas. Yet soon it is going to have to die along with the rest of your body simply because your silly little pancreas is lousy with cancer.'

'No thank you,' I said to him. 'You can stop there. It's a repulsive idea, and even if you could do it, which I doubt, it would be quite pointless. What possible use is there in keeping my brain alive if I couldn't talk or see or hear or feel? Personally, I can think of nothing more unpleasant.'

'I believe that you *would* be able to communicate with us,' Landy said. 'And we might even succeed in giving you a certain amount of vision. But let's take this slowly. I'll come to all that later on. The fact remains that you're going to die fairly soon whatever happens; and my plans would not involve touching you at all until *after* you are dead. Come now, William. No true philosopher could object to lending his dead body to the cause of science.'

'That's not putting it quite straight,' I answered. 'It seems to me there'd be some doubt as to whether I were dead or alive by the time you'd finished with me.'

'Well,' he said, smiling a little, 'I suppose you're right about that. But I don't think you ought to turn me down quite so quickly, before you know a bit more about it.'

'I said I don't want to hear it.'

'Have a cigarette,' he said, holding out his case.

'I don't smoke, you know that.'

He took one himself and lit it with a tiny silver lighter that was no bigger than a shilling piece. 'A present from the people who make my instruments,' he said. 'Ingenious, isn't it?'

I examined the lighter, then handed it back.

'May I go on?' he asked.

'I'd rather you didn't.'

'Just lie still and listen. I think you'll find it quite interesting.'

There were some blue grapes on a plate beside my bed. I put the plate on my chest and began eating the grapes.

'At the very moment of death,' Landy said, 'I should have to be standing by so that I could step in immediately and try to keep your brain alive.'

'You mean leaving it in the head?'

'To start with, yes. I'd have to.'

'And where would you put it after that?'

'If you want to know, in a sort of basin.'

'Are you really serious about this?'

'Certainly I'm serious.'

'All right. Go on.'

'I suppose you know that when the heart stops and the brain is deprived of fresh blood and oxygen, its tissues die very rapidly. Anything from four to six minutes and the whole thing's dead. Even after three minutes you may get a certain amount of damage. So I should have to work rapidly to prevent this from happening. But with the help of the machine, it should all be quite simple.'

'What machine?'

'The artificial heart. We've got a nice adaptation here of the one originally devised by Alexis Carrel and Lindbergh. It oxygenates the blood, keeps it at the right temperature, pumps it in at the right pressure, and does a number of other little necessary things. It's really not at all complicated.'

'Tell me what you would do at the moment of death,' I said. 'What is the first thing you would do?'

'Do you know anything about the vascular and venous arrangements of the brain?'

'No.'

'Then listen. It's not difficult. The blood supply to the brain is derived from two main sources, the internal carotid arteries and the vertebral arteries. There are two of each, making four arteries in all. Got that?'

'Yes.'

'And the return system is even simpler. The blood is drained away by only two large veins, the internal jugulars. So you have four arteries going up – they go up the neck, of course – and two veins coming down. Around the brain itself they naturally branch out into other channels, but those don't concern us. We never touch them.'

'All right,' I said. 'Imagine that I've just died. Now what would you do?'

'I should immediately open your neck and locate the four arteries, the carotids and the vertebrals. I should then perfuse them, which means that I'd stick a large hollow needle into each. These four needles would be connected by tubes to the artificial heart.

'Then, working quickly, I would dissect out both the left and right internal jugular veins and hitch these also to the heart machine to complete the circuit. Now switch on the machine, which is already primed with the right type of blood, and there you are. The circulation through your brain would be restored.'

'I'd be like that Russian dog.'

'I don't think you would. For one thing, you'd certainly lose consciousness when you died, and I very much doubt whether you would come to again for quite a long time – if indeed you came to at all. But, conscious or not, you'd be in a rather interesting position, wouldn't you? You'd have a cold dead body and a living brain.'

Landy paused to savour this delightful prospect. The man was so entranced and bemused by the whole idea that he evidently found it impossible to believe I might not be feeling the same way.

'We could now afford to take our time,' he said. 'And believe me, we'd need it. The first thing we'd do would be to wheel you to the operating-room, accompanied of course by the machine, which must never stop pumping. The next problem . . .'

'All right,' I said. 'That's enough. I don't have to hear the details.'

'Oh, but you must,' he said. 'It is important that you should know precisely what is going to happen to you all the way through. You see, afterwards, when you regain consciousness, it will be much more satisfactory from your point of view if you are able to remember exactly *where* you are and *how* you came to be there. If only for your own peace of mind you should know that. You agree?'

I lay still on the bed, watching him.

'So the next problem would be to remove your brain, intact and undamaged, from your dead body. The body is useless. In fact it has already started to decay. The skull and the face are also useless. They are both encumbrances and I don't want them around. All I want is the brain, the clean beautiful brain, alive and perfect. So when I get you on the table I will take a saw, a small oscillating saw, and with this I shall proceed to remove the whole vault of your skull. You'd still be unconscious at that point so I wouldn't have to bother with anaesthetic.'

'Like hell you wouldn't,' I said.

'You'd be out cold, I promise you that, William. Don't forget you *died* just a few minutes before.'

'Nobody's sawing off the top of my skull without an anaesthetic,' I said.

Landy shrugged his shoulders. 'It makes no difference to me,' he said. 'I'll be glad to give you a little procaine if you want it. If it will make you any happier I'll infiltrate the whole scalp with procaine, the whole head, from the neck up.'

'Thanks very much,' I said.

'You know,' he went on, 'it's extraordinary what sometimes happens. Only last week a man was brought in unconscious, and I opened his head without any anaesthetic at all and removed a small blood clot. I was still working inside the skull when he woke up and began talking.

' "Where am I?" he asked.

' "You're in hospital."

' "Well," he said. "Fancy that."

' "Tell me," I asked him, "is this bothering you, what I'm doing?"

' "No," he answered. "Not at all. What *are* you doing?"

' "I'm just removing a blood clot from your brain."

' "You *are*?"

' "Just lie still. Don't move. I'm nearly finished."

' "So that's the bastard been giving me all those headaches," the man said.'

Landy paused and smiled, remembering the occasion. 'That's word for word what the man said,' he went on, 'although the next day he couldn't even recollect the incident. It's a funny thing, the brain.'

'I'll have the procaine,' I said.

'As you wish, William. And now, as I say, I'd take a small oscillating saw and carefully remove your complete calvarium – the whole vault of the skull. This would expose the top half of the brain, or rather the outer covering in which it is wrapped. You may or may not know that there are three separate coverings around the brain itself – the outer one called the dura mater or dura, the middle one called the arachnoid, and the inner one called the pia mater or pia. Most laymen seem to have the idea that the brain is a naked thing floating around in fluid in your head. But it isn't. It's wrapped up neatly in these three strong coverings, and the cerebrospinal fluid actually flows within the little gap between the two inner coverings, known as the subarachnoid space. As I told you before, this fluid is manufactured by the brain, and it drains off into the venous system by osmosis.

'I myself would leave all three coverings – don't they have lovely names, the dura, the arachnoid, and the pia? – I'd leave them all intact. There are many reasons for this, not least among them being the fact that within the dura run the venous channels that drain the blood from the brain into the jugular.

'Now,' he went on, 'we've got the upper half of your skull off so that the top of the brain, wrapped in its outer covering, is exposed. The next step is the really tricky one: to release the whole package so that it can be lifted cleanly away, leaving the stubs of the four supply arteries and the two veins hanging underneath ready to be re-connected to the machine. This is an immensely lengthy and complicated business involving the delicate chipping away of much bone, the severing of many nerves, and the cutting and tying of numerous blood vessels. The only way I could do it with any hope of success would be by taking a rongeur and slowly biting off the rest of your skull, peeling it off downward like an orange until the sides and underneath of the brain covering are fully exposed. The problems involved are highly technical and I won't go into them, but I feel fairly sure that the work can be done. It's simply a question of surgical skill and patience. And don't forget that I'd have plenty of time, as much as I wanted, because the artificial heart would be continually pumping away alongside the operating-table, keeping the brain alive.

'Now, let's assume that I've succeeded in peeling off your skull and removing everything else that surrounds the sides of the brain. That leaves it connected to the body only at the base, mainly by the spinal column and by the two large veins and the four arteries that are supplying it with blood. So what next?

'I would sever the spinal column just above the first cervical vertebra, taking great care not to harm the two vertebral arteries which are in that area. But you must remember that the dura or outer covering is open at this place to receive the spinal column, so I'd have to close this opening by sewing the edges of the dura together. There'd be no problem there.

'At this point, I would be ready for the final move. To one side, on a table, I'd have a basin of a special shape, and this would be filled with what we call Ringer's Solution. That is a special kind of fluid we use for irrigation in neurosurgery. I would now cut the brain completely loose by severing the supply arteries and the veins. Then I would simply pick it up in my hands and transfer it to the basin. This would be the only other time during the whole proceeding when the blood flow would be cut off; but once it was in the basin, it wouldn't take a moment to re-connect the stubs of the arteries and veins to the artificial heart.

'So there you are,' Landy said. 'Your brain is now in the basin, and still alive, and there isn't any reason why it shouldn't stay alive for a very long time, years and years perhaps, provided we looked after the blood and the machine.'

'But would it *function*?'

'My dear William, how should I know? I can't even tell you whether it would ever regain consciousness.'

'And if it did?'

'There now! That would be fascinating!'

'Would it?' I said, and I must admit I had my doubts.

'Of course it would! Lying there with all your thinking processes working beautifully, and your memory as well . . .'

'And not being able to see or feel or smell or hear or talk,' I said.

'Ah!' he cried. 'I knew I'd forgotten something! I never told you about the eye. Listen. I am going to try to leave one of your optic nerves intact, as well as the eye itself. The optic nerve is a little thing about the thickness of a clinical thermometer and about two inches in length as it stretches between the brain and the eye. The beauty of it is that it's not really a nerve at all. It's an outpouring of the brain itself, and the dura or brain covering extends along it and is attached to the eyeball. The back of the eye is therefore in very close contact with the brain, and cerebrospinal fluid flows right up to it.

'All this suits my purpose very well, and makes it reasonable to suppose that I could succeed in preserving one of your eyes. I've already constructed a small plastic case to contain the eyeball, instead of your own socket, and when the brain is in the basin, submerged in Ringer's Solution, the eyeball in its case will float on the surface of the liquid.'

'Staring at the ceiling,' I said.

'I suppose so, yes. I'm afraid there wouldn't be any muscles there to move it around. But it might be sort of fun to lie there so quietly and comfortably peering out at the world from your basin.'

'Hilarious,' I said. 'How about leaving me an ear as well?'

'I'd rather not try an ear this time.'

'I want an ear,' I said. 'I insist upon an ear.'

'No.'

'I want to listen to Bach.'

'You don't understand how difficult it would be,' Landy said gently. 'The hearing apparatus – the cochlea, as it's called – is a far more delicate mechanism than the eye. What's more, it is encased in bone. So is a part of the auditory nerve that connects it with the brain. I couldn't possibly chisel the whole thing out intact.'

'Couldn't you leave it encased in the bone and bring the bone to the basin?'

'No,' he said firmly. 'This thing is complicated enough already. And anyway, if the eye works, it doesn't matter all that much about your hearing. We can always hold up messages for you to read. You really must leave me to decide what is possible and what isn't.'

'I haven't yet said that I'm going to do it.'

'I know, William, I know.'

'I'm not sure I fancy the idea very much.'

'Would you rather be dead, altogether?'

'Perhaps I would. I don't know yet. I wouldn't be able to talk, would I?'

'Of course not.'

'Then how would I communicate with you? How would you know that I'm conscious?'

'It would be easy for us to know whether or not you regain consciousness,' Landy said. 'The ordinary electroencephalograph could tell us that. We'd attach the electrodes directly to the frontal lobes of your brain, there in the basin.'

'And you could actually tell?'

'Oh, definitely. Any hospital could do that part of it.'

'But *I* couldn't communicate with *you*.'

'As a matter of fact,' Landy said, 'I believe you could. There's a man up in London called Wertheimer who's doing some interesting work on the subject of thought communication, and I've been in touch with him. You know, don't you, that the thinking brain throws off electrical and chemical discharges? And that these discharges go out in the form of waves, rather like radio waves?'

'I know a bit about it,' I said.

'Well, Wertheimer has constructed an apparatus somewhat similar to the encephalograph, though far more sensitive, and he maintains that within certain narrow limits it can help him to interpret the actual things that a brain is thinking. It produces a kind of graph which is apparently decipherable into words or thoughts. Would you like me to ask Wertheimer to come and see you?'

'No,' I said. Landy was already taking it for granted that I was going to go through with this business, and I resented his attitude. 'Go away now and leave me alone,' I told him. 'You won't get anywhere by trying to rush me.'

He stood up at once and crossed to the door.

'One question,' I said.

He paused with a hand on the doorknob. 'Yes, William?'

'Simply this. Do you yourself honestly believe that when my brain is in that basin, my mind will be able to function exactly as it is doing at present? Do you believe that I will be able to think and reason as I can now? And will the power of memory remain?'

'I don't see why not,' he answered. 'It's the same brain. It's alive. It's undamaged. In fact, it's completely untouched. We haven't even opened the dura. The big difference, of course, would be that we've severed every single nerve that leads into it – except for the one optic nerve – and this means that your thinking would no longer be influenced by your senses. You'd be living in an extraordinarily pure and detached world. Nothing to bother you at all, not even pain. You couldn't possibly feel pain because there wouldn't be any nerves to feel it with. In a way, it would be an almost perfect situation. No worries or fears or pains or hunger or thirst. Not even any desires. Just your memories and your thoughts, and if the remaining eye happened to function, then you could read books as well. It all sounds rather pleasant to me.'

'It does, does it?'

'Yes, William, it does. And particularly for a Doctor of Philosophy. It would be a tremendous experience. You'd be able to reflect upon the ways of the world with a detachment and a serenity that no man had ever attained before. And who knows what might not happen then! Great thoughts and solutions might come to you, great ideas that could revolutionize our way of life! Try to imagine, if you can, the degree of concentration that you'd be able to achieve!'

'And the frustration,' I said.

'Nonsense. There couldn't be any frustration. You can't have frustration without desire, and you couldn't possibly have any desire. Not physical desire, anyway.'

'I should certainly be capable of remembering my previous life in the world, and I might desire to return to it.'

'What, to this mess! Out of your comfortable basin and back into this madhouse!'

'Answer one more question,' I said. 'How long do you believe you could keep it alive?'

'The brain? Who knows? Possibly for years and years. The conditions would be ideal. Most of the factors that cause deterioration would be absent, thanks to the artificial heart. The blood-pressure would remain constant at all times, an impossible condition in real life. The temperature would also be constant. The chemical composition of the blood would be near perfect. There would be no impurities in it, no virus, no bacteria nothing. Of course it's foolish to guess, but I believe that a brain might live for two or three hundred years in circumstances like these. Goodbye for now,' he said. 'I'll drop in and see you tomorrow.' He went out quickly, leaving me, as you might guess, in a fairly disturbed state of mind.

My immediate reaction after he had gone was one of revulsion toward the whole business. Somehow, it wasn't at all nice. There was something basically repulsive about the idea that I myself, with all my mental faculties intact, should be reduced to a small slimy grey blob lying in a pool of water. It was monstrous, obscene, unholy. Another thing that bothered me was the feeling of helplessness that I was bound to experience once Landy had got me into the basin. There could be no going back after that, no way of protesting or explaining. I would be committed for as long as they could keep me alive.

And what, for example, if I could not stand it? What if it turned out to be terribly painful? What if I became hysterical?

No legs to run away on. No voice to scream with. Nothing. I'd just have to grin and bear it for the next two centuries.

No mouth to grin with either.

At this point, a curious thought struck me, and it was this: Does not a man who has had a leg amputated often suffer from the delusion that the leg is still there? Does he not tell the nurse that the toes he doesn't have any more are itching like mad, and so on and so forth? I seemed to have heard something to that effect quite recently.

Very well. On the same premise, was it not possible that my brain, lying there alone in that basin, might not suffer from a similar delusion in regard to my body? In which case, all my usual aches and pains could come flooding over me and I wouldn't even be able to take an aspirin to relieve them. One moment I might be imagining that I had the most excruciating cramp in my leg, or a violent indigestion, and a few minutes later, I might easily get the feeling that my poor bladder – you know me – was so full that if I didn't get to emptying it soon it would burst.

Heaven forbid.

I lay there for a long time thinking these horrid thoughts. Then quite suddenly, round about midday, my mood began to change. I became less concerned with the unpleasant aspect of the affair and found myself able to examine Landy's proposals in a more reasonable light. Was there not, after all, I asked myself, something a bit comforting in the thought that my brain might not necessarily have to die and disappear in a few weeks' time? There was indeed. I am rather proud of my brain. It is a sensitive, lucid, and uberous organ. It contains a prodigious store of information, and it is still capable of producing imaginative and original theories. As brains go, it is a damn good one, though I say it myself. Whereas my body, my poor old body, the thing that Landy wants to throw away – well, even you, my dear Mary, will have to agree with me that there is really nothing about that which is worth preserving any more.

I was lying on my back eating a grape. Delicious it was, and there were three little seeds in it which I took out of my mouth and placed on the edge of the plate.

'I'm going to do it,' I said quietly. 'Yes, by God, I'm going to do it. When Landy comes back to see me tomorrow I shall tell him straight out that I'm going to do it.'

It was as quick as that. And from then on, I began to feel very much better. I surprised everyone by gobbling an enormous lunch, and shortly after that you came in to visit me as usual.

But how well I looked, you told me. How bright and well and chirpy. Had anything happened? Was there some good news?

Yes, I said, there was. And then, if you remember, I bade you sit down and make yourself comfortable, and I started out immediately to explain to you as gently as I could what was in the wind.

Alas, you would have none of it. I had hardly begun telling you the barest details when you flew into a fury and said that the thing was revolting, disgusting, horrible, unthinkable, and when I tried to go on, you marched out of the room.

Well, Mary, as you know, I have tried to discuss this subject with you many times since then, but you have consistently refused to give me a hearing. Hence this note, and I can only hope that you will have the good sense to permit yourself to read it. It has taken me a long time to write. Two weeks have gone by since I started to scribble the first sentence, and I'm now a good deal weaker than I was then. I doubt I have the strength to say much more. Certainly I won't say goodbye, because there's a chance, just a tiny chance, that if Landy succeeds in his work I may actually *see* you again later, that is if you can bring yourself to come and visit me.

I am giving orders that these pages shall not be delivered to you until a week after I am gone. By now, therefore, as you sit reading them, seven days have already elapsed since Landy did the deed. You yourself may even know what the outcome has been. If you don't, if you have purposely kept yourself apart and have refused to have anything to do with it – which I suspect may be the case – please change your mind now and give Landy a call to see how things went with me. That is the least you can do. I have told him that he may expect to hear from you on the seventh day.

Your faithful husband
William

P.S. Be good when I am gone, and always remember that it is harder to be a widow than a wife. Do not drink cocktails. Do not waste money. Do not smoke cigarettes. Do not eat pastry. Do not use lipstick. Do not buy a television apparatus. Keep my rose beds and my rockery well weeded in the summers. And incidentally I suggest that you have the telephone disconnected now that I shall have no further use for it.

W.

Mrs Pearl laid the last page of the manuscript slowly down on the sofa beside her. Her little mouth was pursed up tight and there was a whiteness around her nostrils.

But really! You would think a widow was entitled to a bit of peace after all these years.

The whole thing was just too awful to think about. Beastly and awful. It gave her the shudders.

She reached for her bag and found herself another cigarette. She lit it, inhaling the smoke deeply and blowing it out in clouds all over the room. Through the smoke she could see her lovely television set, brand new, lustrous, huge, crouching defiantly but also a little self-consciously on top of what used to be William's worktable.

What would he say, she wondered, if he could see that now?

She paused, to remember the last time he had caught her smoking a cigarette. That was about a year ago, and she was sitting in the kitchen by the open window having a quick one before he came home from work. She'd had the radio on loud playing dance music and she had turned round to pour herself another cup of coffee and there he was standing in the doorway, huge and grim, staring down at her with those awful eyes, a little black dot of fury blazing in the centre of each.

For four weeks after that, he had paid the housekeeping bills himself and given her no money at all, but of course he wasn't to know that she had over six pounds stashed away in a soap-flake carton in the cupboard under the sink.

'What is it?' she had said to him once during supper. 'Are you worried about me getting lung cancer?'

'I am not,' he had answered.

'Then why can't I smoke?'

'Because I disapprove, that's why.'

He had also disapproved of children, and as a result they had never had any of them either.

Where was he now, this William of hers, the great disapprover?

Landy would be expecting her to call up. Did she *have* to call Landy?

Well, not really, no.

She finished her cigarette, then lit another one immediately from the old stub. She looked at the telephone that was sitting on the worktable beside the television set. William had asked her to call. He had specifically requested that she telephone Landy as soon as she had read the letter. She hesitated, fighting hard now against that old ingrained sense of duty that she didn't quite yet dare to shake off. Then, slowly, she got to her feet and crossed over to the phone on the worktable. She found a number in the book, dialled it, and waited.

'I want to speak to Dr Landy, please.'

'Who is calling?'

'Mrs Pearl. Mrs William Pearl.'

'One moment, please.'

Almost at once, Landy was on the other end of the wire.

'Mrs Pearl?'

'This is Mrs Pearl.'

There was a slight pause.

'I am so glad you called at last, Mrs Pearl. You are quite well, I hope?' The voice was quiet, unemotional, courteous. 'I wonder if you would care to come over here to the hospital? Then we can have a little chat. I expect you are very eager to know how it all came out.'

She didn't answer.

'I can tell you now that everything went pretty smoothly, one way and another. Far better, in fact, than I was entitled to hope. It is not only alive, Mrs Pearl, it is conscious. It recovered consciousness on the second day. Isn't that interesting?'

She waited for him to go on.

'And the eye is seeing. We are sure of that because we get an immediate change in the deflections on the encephalograph when we hold something up in front of it. And now we're giving it the newspaper to read every day.'

'Which newspaper?' Mrs Pearl asked sharply.

'*The Daily Mirror*. The headlines are larger.'

'He hates *The Mirror*. Give him *The Times*.'

There was a pause, then the doctor said, 'Very well, Mrs Pearl. We'll give it *The Times*. We naturally want to do all we can to keep it happy.'

'*Him*,' she said. 'Not *it*. *Him!*'

'Him,' the doctor said. 'Yes, I beg your pardon. To keep him happy. That's one reason why I suggested you should come along here as soon as possible. I think it would be good for him to see you. You could indicate how delighted you were to be with him again – smile at him and blow him a kiss and all that sort of thing. It's bound to be a comfort to him to know that you are standing by.'

There was a long pause.

'Well,' Mrs Pearl said at last, her voice suddenly very meek and tired. 'I suppose I had better come on over and see how he is.'

'Good. I knew you would. I'll wait here for you. Come straight up to my office on the second floor. Goodbye.'

Half an hour later, Mrs Pearl was at the hospital.

'You mustn't be surprised by what he looks like,' Landy said as he walked beside her down a corridor.

'No, I won't.'

'It's bound to be a bit of a shock to you at first. He's not very prepossessing in his present state, I'm afraid.'

'I didn't marry him for his looks, Doctor.'

Landy turned and stared at her. What a queer little woman this was, he thought, with her large eyes and her sullen, resentful air. Her features, which must have been quite pleasant once, had now gone completely. The mouth was slack, the cheeks loose and flabby, and the whole face gave the impression of having slowly but surely sagged to pieces through years and years of joyless married life. They walked on for a while in silence.

'Take your time when you get inside,' Landy said. 'He won't know you're in there until you place your face directly above his eye. The eye is always open, but he can't move it at all, so the field of vision is very narrow. At present we have it looking straight up at the ceiling. And of course he can't hear anything. We can talk together as much as we like. It's in here.'

Landy opened a door and ushered her into a small square room.

'I wouldn't go too close yet,' he said, putting a hand on her arm. 'Stay back here a moment with me until you get used to it all.'

There was a biggish white enamel bowl about the size of a washbasin standing on a high white table in the centre of the room, and there were half a dozen thin plastic tubes coming out of it. These tubes were connected with a whole lot of glass piping in which you could see the blood flowing to and from the heart machine. The machine itself made a soft rhythmic pulsing sound.

'He's in there,' Landy said, pointing to the basin, which was too high for her to see into. 'Come just a little closer. Not too near.'

He led her two paces forward.

By stretching her neck, Mrs Pearl could now see the surface of the liquid inside the basin. It was clear and still, and on it there floated a small oval capsule, about the size of a pigeon's egg.

'That's the eye in there,' Landy said. 'Can you see it?'

'Yes.'

'So far as we can tell, it is still in perfect condition. It's his right eye, and the plastic container has a lens on it similar to the one he used in his own spectacles. At this moment he's probably seeing quite as well as he did before.'

'The ceiling isn't much to look at,' Mrs Pearl said.

'Don't worry about that. We're in the process of working out a whole programme to keep him amused, but we don't want to go too quickly at first.'

'Give him a good book.'

'We will, we will. Are you feeling all right, Mrs Pearl?'

'Yes.'

'Then we'll go forward a little more, shall we, and you'll be able to see the whole thing.'

He led her forward until they were standing only a couple of yards from the table, and now she could see right down into the basin.

'There you are,' Landy said. 'That's William.'

He was far larger than she had imagined he would be, and darker in colour. With all the ridges and creases running over his surface, he reminded her of nothing so much as an enormous pickled walnut. She could see the stubs of the four big arteries and the two veins coming out from the base of him and the neat way in which they were joined to the plastic tubes; and with each throb of the heart machine, all the tubes gave a little jerk in unison as the blood was pushed through them.

'You'll have to lean over,' Landy said, 'and put your pretty face right above the eye. He'll see you then, and you can smile at him and blow him a kiss. If I were you I'd say a few nice things as well. He won't actually hear them, but I'm sure he'll get the general idea.'

'He hates people blowing kisses at him,' Mrs Pearl said. 'I'll do it my own way if you don't mind.' She stepped up to the edge of the table, leaned forward until her face was directly over the basin, and looked straight down into William's eye.

'Hallo, dear,' she whispered. 'It's me – Mary.'

The eye, bright as ever, stared back at her with a peculiar, fixed intensity.

'How are you, dear?' she said.

The plastic capsule was transparent all the way round so that the whole of the eyeball was visible. The optic nerve connecting the underside of it to the brain looked like a short length of grey spaghetti.

'Are you feeling all right, William?'

It was a queer sensation peering into her husband's eye when there was no face to go with it. All she had to look at was the eye, and she kept staring at it, and gradually it grew bigger and bigger, and in the end it was the only thing that she could see – a sort of face in itself.

There was a network of tiny red veins running over the white surface of the eyeball, and in the ice-blue of the iris there were three or four rather pretty darkish streaks radiating from the pupil in the centre. The pupil was large and black, with a little spark of light reflecting from one side of it.

'I got your letter, dear, and came over at once to see how you were. Dr Landy says you are doing wonderfully well. Perhaps if I talk slowly you can understand a little of what I am saying by reading my lips.'

There was no doubt that the eye was watching her.

'They are doing everything possible to take care of you, dear. This marvellous machine thing here is pumping away all the time and I'm sure it's a lot better than those silly old hearts all the rest of us have. Ours are liable to break down any moment, but yours will go on for ever.'

She was studying the eye closely, trying to discover what there was about it that gave it such an unusual appearance.

'You seem fine, dear, just fine. Really you do.'

It looked ever so much nicer, this eye, than either of his eyes used to look, she told herself. There was a softness about it somewhere, a calm, kindly quality that she had never seen before. Maybe it had to do with the dot in the very centre, the pupil. William's pupils used always to be tiny black pinheads. They used to glint at you, stabbing into your brain, seeing right through you, and they always knew at once what you were up to and even what you were thinking. But this one she was looking at now was large and soft and gentle, almost cowlike.

'Are you quite sure he's conscious?' she asked, not looking up.

'Oh yes, completely,' Landy said.

'And he *can* see me?'

'Perfectly.'

'Isn't that marvellous? I expect he's wondering what happened.'

'Not at all. He knows perfectly well where he is and why he's there. He can't possibly have forgotten that.'

'You mean he *knows* he's in this basin?'

'Of course. And if only he had the power of speech, he would probably be able to carry on a perfectly normal conversation with you this very minute. So far as I can see, there should be absolutely no difference mentally between this William here and the one you used to know back home.'

'Good *gracious* me,' Mrs Pearl said, and she paused to consider this intriguing aspect.

You know what, she told herself, looking behind the eye now and staring hard at the great grey pulpy walnut that lay so placidly under the water. I'm not at all sure that I don't prefer him as he is at present.

217

In fact, I believe that I could live very comfortably with this kind of a William. I could cope with this one.

'Quiet, isn't he?' she said.

'Naturally he's quiet.'

No arguments and criticisms, she thought, no constant admonitions, no rules to obey, no ban on smoking cigarettes, no pair of cold disapproving eyes watching me over the top of a book in the evenings, no shirts to wash and iron, no meals to cook – nothing but the throb of the heart machine, which was rather a soothing sound anyway and certainly not loud enough to interfere with television.

'Doctor,' she said. 'I do believe I'm suddenly getting to feel the most enormous affection for him. Does that sound queer?'

'I think it's quite understandable.'

'He looks so helpless and silent lying there under the water in his little basin.'

'Yes, I know.'

'He's like a baby, that's what he's like. He's exactly like a little baby.'

Landy stood still behind her, watching.

'There,' she said softly, peering into the basin. 'From now on Mary's going to look after you *all* by herself and you've nothing to worry about in the world. When can I have him back home, Doctor?'

'I beg your pardon?'

'I said when can I have him back – back in my own house?'

'You're joking,' Landy said.

She turned her head slowly around and looked directly at him.

'Why should I joke?' she asked. Her face was bright, her eyes round and bright as two diamonds.

'He couldn't possibly be moved.'

'I don't see why not.'

'This is an experiment, Mrs Pearl.'

'It's my husband, Dr Landy.'

A funny little nervous half-smile appeared on Landy's mouth.

'Well . . .' he said.

'It *is* my husband, you know.' There was no anger in her voice. She spoke quietly, as though merely reminding him of a simple fact.

'That's rather a tricky point,' Landy said, wetting his lips. 'You're a widow now, Mrs Pearl. I think you must resign yourself to that fact.'

She turned away suddenly from the table and crossed over to the window. 'I mean it,' she said, fishing in her bag for a cigarette. 'I want him back.'

Landy watched her as she put the cigarette between her lips and lit it. Unless he were very much mistaken, there was something a bit odd about this woman, he thought. She seemed almost pleased to have her husband over there in the basin.

He tried to imagine what his own feelings would be if it were *his* wife's brain lying there and *her* eye staring up at him out of that capsule.

He wouldn't like it.

'Shall we go back to my room now?' he said.

She was standing by the window, apparently quite calm and relaxed, puffing her cigarette.

'Yes, all right.'

On her way past the table she stopped and leaned over the basin once more. 'Mary's leaving now, sweetheart,' she said. 'And don't you worry about a single thing, you understand? We're going to get you right back home where we can look after you properly just as soon as we possibly can. And listen, dear . . .' At this point she paused and carried the cigarette to her lips, intending to take a puff.

Instantly the eye flashed.

She was looking straight into it at the time, and right in the centre of it she saw a tiny but brilliant flash of light, and the pupil contracted into a minute black pinpoint of absolute fury.

At first she didn't move. She stood bending over the basin, holding the cigarette up to her mouth, watching the eye.

Then very slowly, deliberately, she put the cigarette between her lips and took a long suck. She inhaled deeply, and she held the smoke inside her lungs for three or four seconds; then suddenly, *whoosh*, out it came through her nostrils in two thin jets which struck the water in the basin and billowed out over the surface in a thick blue cloud, enveloping the eye.

Landy was over by the door, with his back to her, waiting. 'Come on, Mrs Pearl,' he called.

'Don't look so cross, William,' she said softly. 'It isn't any good looking cross.'

Landy turned his head to see what she was doing.

'Not any more it isn't,' she whispered. 'Because from now on, my pet, you're going to do just exactly what Mary tells you. Do you understand that?'

'Mrs Pearl,' Landy said, moving toward her.

'So don't be a naughty boy again, will you, my precious,' she said, taking another pull at the cigarette. 'Naughty boys are liable to get punished most severely nowadays, you ought to know that.'

Landy was beside her now, and he took her by the arm and began drawing her firmly but gently away from the table.

'Goodbye, darling,' she called. 'I'll be back soon.'

'That's enough, Mrs Pearl.'

'Isn't he sweet?' she cried, looking up at Landy with big bright eyes. 'Isn't he darling? I just can't wait to get him home.'

William Wilson

BY EDGAR ALLAN POE

Great Ghost Stories *which NBC screened in 1961 is something of a curiosity. Firstly, because it is probably the only late night horror anthology series to have been specifically scheduled for the summer months; while in American television history it has been recorded as the last 'live' dramatic show to be aired in prime time. The series of mostly classic ghost stories which were shown from July to September between nine-thirty PM and ten PM, were slotted in as the summer replacement for the weekly entertainment show starring Country singer, Tennessee Ernie Ford! The series was able to draw on actors appearing on the New York stage for its casts, and although always restrained by a limited budget did feature some talented players whose best years lay ahead of them, including Arthur Hill, Lois Nettleton, Salome Jens, Richard Thomas, Kevin McCarthy, Joanne Linville, Vincent Gardenia, James Broderick and Robert Duvall. The stories were introduced by Frank Gallop, and among the highlights of the series were an adaptation of Saki's classic about the sinister little boy Conradin in 'Sredi Vashtar' (with Judith Evans and a youthful Richard Thomas) and 'William Wilson' by the great master of the horror short story, Edgar Allan Poe (1809–1849) without whom no anthology would be complete.*

Poe's stories have, of course, been adapted for the stage, broadcast on the radio and made into several dozen films for the cinema and television. Indeed, his influence is to be found throughout the whole genre of late night horror. William Wilson, the central character of this next tale, is a figure who has been seen in many guises in subsequent tales of the macabre, and in the 1961 Great Ghost Stories *version he was played by Robert Duvall in a foretaste of the style which has made him one of today's most highly paid and respected actors. It is a tragedy that no copy exists of his television peformance in this next story.*

LET me call myself, for the present, William Wilson. The fair page now lying before me need not be sullied with my real appellation. This has been already too much an object for the scorn, for the horror, for the detestation of my race. To the uttermost legions of the globe have not the indignant winds bruited its unparalleled infamy? O outcast of all outcasts most abandoned! to the earth art thou not for ever dead? to its honours, to its flowers, to its golden aspirations? – and a cloud, dense, dismal, and limitless, does it not hang eternally between thy hopes and heaven?

I would not, if I could, here or to-day, embody a record of my later years of unspeakable misery and unpardonable crime. This epoch – these later years – took unto themselves a sudden elevation in turpitude, whose origin alone it is my present purpose to assign. Men usually grow base by degrees. From me in an instant all virtue dropped bodily as a mantle. From comparatively trivial wickedness I passed, with the stride of a giant, into more than the enormities of an Elagabalus. What chance – what one event brought this evil thing to pass, bear with me while I relate. Death approaches, and the shadow which foreruns him has thrown a softening influence over my spirit. I long in passing through the dim valley for the sympathy, I had nearly said for the pity, of my fellow-men. I would fain have them believe that I have been in some measure the slave of circumstances beyond human control. I would wish them to seek out for me, in the details I am about to give, some little oasis of *fatality* amid a wilderness of error. I would have them allow, what they cannot refrain from allowing, that although temptation may have erewhile existed as great, man was never *thus* at least tempted before, certainly never *thus* fell. And is it therefore that he has never thus suffered? Have I not indeed been living in a dream? And am I not now dying a victim to the horror and the mystery of the wildest of all sublunary visions?

I am the descendant of a race whose imaginative and easily excitable temperament has at all times rendered them remarkable; and in my earliest infancy I gave evidence of having fully inherited the family character. As I advanced in years it was more strongly developed, becoming for many reasons a cause of serious disquietude to my friends, and of positive injury to myself. I grew self-willed, addicted to the wildest caprices, and a prey to the most ungovernable passions.

Weak-minded, and beset with constitutional infirmities akin to my own, my parents could do but little to check the evil propensities which distinguished me. Some feeble and ill-directed efforts resulted in complete failure on their part, and of course in total triumph on mine. Thenceforward my voice was a household law, and at an age when few children have abandoned their leading-strings, I was left to the guidance of my own will, and became in all but name the master of my own actions.

My earliest recollections of a school-life are connected with a large rambling Elizabethan house, in a misty-looking village of England, where were a vast number of gigantic and gnarled trees, and where all the houses were excessively ancient. In truth, it was a dream-like and spirit-soothing place that venerable old town. At this moment, in fancy, I feel the refreshing chilliness of its deeply-shadowed avenues, inhale the fragrance of its thousand shrubberies, and thrill anew with indefinable delight at the deep hollow note of the church-bell, breaking each hour with sullen and sudden roar upon the stillness of the dusky atmosphere in which the fretted Gothic steeple lay imbedded and asleep.

It gives me perhaps as much of pleasure as I can now in any manner experience to dwell upon minute recollections of the school and its concerns. Steeped in misery as I am – misery, alas! only too real – I shall be pardoned for seeking relief, however slight and temporary, in the weakness of a few rambling details. These, moreover, utterly trivial, and even ridiculous in themselves, assume to my fancy adventitious importance, as connected with a period and a locality when and where I recognize the first ambiguous monitions of the destiny which afterwards so fully overshadowed me. Let me then remember.

The house, I have said, was old and irregular. The grounds were extensive, and a high and solid brick wall, topped with a bed of mortar and broken glass, encompassed the whole. This prison-like rampart formed the limit of our domain: beyond it we saw but thrice-a-week, once every Saturday afternoon, when, attended by two ushers, we were permitted to take brief walks in a body through some of the neighbouring fields; and twice during Sunday, when we paraded in the same formal manner to the morning and evening service in the one church of the village. Of this church the principal of our school was pastor. With how deep a spirit of wonder and perplexity was I wont to regard him from our remote pew in the gallery, as with step solemn and slow he ascended the pulpit! This reverend man, with countenance so demurely benign, with robes so glossy and so clerically flowing, with wig so minutely powdered, so rigid and so vast – could this be he who, of late, with sour visage, and in snuffy habiliments, administered, ferule in hand, the Draconian laws of the academy? O gigantic paradox, too utterly monstrous for solution!

At an angle of the ponderous wall frowned a more ponderous gate. It was riveted and studded with iron bolts, and surmounted with jagged iron spikes. What impressions of deep awe did it inspire! It was never opened save for the three periodical egressions and ingressions already mentioned; then in every creak of its mighty hinges we found a plenitude of mystery, a world of matter for solemn remark, or for more solemn meditation.

The extensive enclosure was irregular in form, having many capacious recesses. Of these, three or four of the largest constituted the play-ground. It was level, and covered with fine hard gravel. I well remember it had no trees nor benches, nor anything similar within it. Of course it was in the rear of the house. In front lay a small parterre, planted with box and other shrubs, but through this sacred division we passed only upon rare occasions indeed, such as a first advent to school or final departure thence, or perhaps, when a parent or friend having called for us, we joyfully took our way home for the Christmas or Midsummer holidays.

But the house! – how quaint an old building was this! To me how veritably a palace of enchantment! There was really no end to its windings, to its incomprehensible subdivisions. It was difficult, at any given time, to say with certainty upon which of its two storeys one happened to be. From each room to every other there were sure to be found three or four steps either in ascent or descent. Then the lateral branches were innumerable, inconceivable, and so returning in upon themselves that our most exact ideas in regard to the whole mansion were not very far different from those with which we pondered upon infinity. During the five years of my residence here I was never able to ascertain with precision in what remote locality lay the little sleeping apartment assigned to myself and some eighteen or twenty other scholars.

The school-room was the largest in the house, I could not help thinking, in the world. It was very long, narrow, and dismally low, with pointed Gothic windows and a ceiling of oak. In a remote and terror-inspiring angle was a square enclosure of eight or ten feet, comprising the *sanctum*, 'during hours', of our principal, the Reverend Dr Bransby. It was a solid structure, with massy door, sooner than open which in the absence of the 'dominie' we would all have willingly perished by the *peine forte et dure*. In other angles were two other similar boxes, far less reverenced, indeed, but still greatly matters of awe. One of these was the pulpit of the 'classical' usher, one of the 'English and mathematical'. Interspersed about the room, crossing and recrossing in endless irregularity, were innumerable benches and desks, black, ancient, and time-worn, piled desperately with much-bethumbed books, and so beseamed with initial letters, names at full length, grotesque figures, and other multiplied efforts of the knife, as to have entirely lost what little of original form might have been their portion in days long departed. A huge bucket with water stood at one extremity of the room, and a clock of stupendous dimensions at the other.

Encompassed by the massy walls of this venerable academy, I passed, yet not in a tedium or disgust, the years of the third lustrum of my life. The teeming brain of childhood requires no external world of incident to occupy or amuse it; and the apparently dismal monotony of a school was replete with more intense excitement than my riper youth has derived from luxury, or my full manhood from crime. Yet I must believe that my first mental development had in it much of the uncommon – even much of the *outré*. Upon mankind at large the events of very early existence rarely leave in mature age any definite impression. All is grey shadow – a weak and irregular remembrance – an indistinct regathering of feeble pleasures and phantasmagoric pains. With me this is not so. In childhood I must have felt with the energy of a man what I now find stamped upon memory in lines as vivid, as deep, and as durable as the *exergues* of the Carthaginian medals.

Yet in fact – in the fact of the world's view – how little was there to remember! The morning's awakening, the nightly summons to bed; the connings, the recitations; the periodical half-holidays, and perambulations; the play-ground, with its broils, its pastimes, its intrigues – these, by a mental sorcery long forgotten, were made to involve a wilderness of sensation, a world of rich incident, a universe of varied emotion, of excitement the most passionate and spirit-stirring. '*O le bon temps, que ce siècle de fer!*'

In truth, the ardour, the enthusiasm, and the imperiousness of my disposition, soon rendered me a marked character among my schoolmates, and by slow but natural gradations gave me an ascendency over all not greatly older than myself – over all with a single exception. This exception was found in the person of a scholar, who, although no relation, bore the same christian and surname as myself, a circumstance, in fact, little remarkable; for notwithstanding a noble descent, mine was one of those every-day appellations which seem, by prescriptive right, to have been, time out of mind, the common property of the mob. In this narrative I have therefore designated myself as William Wilson – a fictitious title not very dissimilar to the real. My namesake alone, of those who in school phraseology constituted 'our set', presumed to compete with me in the studies of the class – in the sports and broils of the play-ground – to refuse implicit belief in my assertions, and submission to my will – indeed, to interfere with my arbitrary dictation in any respect whatsoever. If there is on earth a supreme and unqualified despotism, it is the despotism of the master-mind in boyhood over the less energetic spirits of its companions.

Wilson's rebellion was to me a source of the greatest embarrassment: the more so as, in spite of the bravado with which in public I made a point of treating him and his pretensions, I secretly felt that I feared him, and could not help thinking the equality which he maintained so easily with myself a proof of his true superiority, since not to be overcome cost me a perpetual struggle. Yet this superiority – even this equality – was in truth acknowledged by no one but myself; our associates, by some unaccountable blindness, seemed not even to suspect it. Indeed, his competition, his resistance, and especially his impertinent and dogged interference with my purposes, were not more pointed than private. He appeared to be destitute alike of the ambition which urged, and of the passionate energy of mind which enabled me to excel. In this rivalry he might have been supposed actuated solely by a whimsical desire to thwart, astonish, or mortify myself; although there were times when I could not help observing, with a feeling made up of wonder, abasement, and pique, that he mingled with his injuries, his insults, or his contradictions, a certain most inappropriate, and assuredly most unwelcome *affectionateness* of manner. I could only conceive this singular behaviour to arise from a consummate self-conceit assuming the vulgar airs of patronage and protection.

Perhaps it was this latter trait in Wilson's conduct, conjoined with our identity of name, and the mere accident of our having entered the school upon the same day, which set afloat the notion that we were brothers among the senior classes in the academy. These do not usually inquire with much strictness into the affairs of their juniors. I have before said, or should have said, that Wilson was not, in the most remote degree, connected with my family. But assuredly if we *had* been brothers we must have been twins; for, after leaving Dr Bransby's, I casually learned that my namesake was born on the nineteenth of January 1813 – and this is a somewhat remarkable coincidence, for the day is precisely that of my own nativity.

It may seem strange that in spite of the continual anxiety occasioned me by the rivalry of Wilson, and his intolerable spirit of contradiction, I could not bring myself to hate him altogether. We had, to be sure, nearly every day a quarrel, in which, yielding me publicly the palm of victory, he in some manner contrived to make me feel that it was he who had deserved it, yet a sense of pride on my part and a veritable dignity on his own, kept us always upon what are called 'speaking terms', while there were many points of strong congeniality in our tempers, operating to awake in me a sentiment which our position alone, perhaps, prevented from ripening into friendship. It is difficult indeed to define or even to describe my real feelings towards him. They formed a motley and heterogeneous admixture; some petulant animosity, which was not yet hatred, some esteem, more respect, much fear, with a world of uneasy curiosity. To the moralist it will be unnecessary to say in addition that Wilson and myself were the most inseparable of companions.

It was no doubt the anomalous state of affairs existing between us which turned all my attacks upon him (and they were many, either open or covert) into the channel of banter or practical joke (giving pain while assuming the aspect of mere fun), rather than into a more serious and determined hostility. But my endeavours on this head were by no means uniformly successful, even when my plans were the most wittily concocted; for my namesake had much about him in character of that unassuming and quiet austerity which, while enjoying the poignancy of its own jokes, has no heel of Achilles in itself, and absolutely refuses to be laughed at. I could find indeed but one vulnerable point, and that lying in a personal peculiarity, arising perhaps from constitutional disease, would have been spared by any antagonist less at his wit's end than myself; my rival had a weakness in the faucial or guttural organs which precluded him from raising his voice at any time *above a very low whisper*. Of this defect I did not fail to take what poor advantage lay in my power.

Wilson's retaliations in kind were many; and there was one form of his practical wit that disturbed me beyond measure. How his sagacity first discovered at all that so petty a thing would vex me is a question I never could solve, but having discovered, he habitually practised the annoyance. I had always felt aversion to my uncourtly patronymic and its very common, if not plebeian prænomen. The words were venom in my ears; and when, upon the day of my arrival, a second William Wilson came also to the academy, I felt angry with him for bearing the name, and doubly disgusted with the name because a stranger bore it, who would be the cause of its two-fold repetition, who would be constantly in my presence, and whose concerns, in the ordinary routine of the school business, must inevitably, on account of the detestable coincidence, be often confounded with my own.

The feeling of vexation thus engendered grew stronger with every circumstance tending to show resemblance, moral or physical, between my rival and myself. I had not then discovered the remarkable fact that we were of the same age; but I saw that we were of the same height, and I perceived that we were even singularly alike in general contour of person and outline of feature. I was galled, too, by the rumour touching a relationship, which had grown current in the upper forms. In a word, nothing could more seriously disturb me (although I scrupulously concealed such disturbance), than any allusion to a similarity of mind, person, or condition existing between us. But, in truth, I had no reason to believe that (with the exception of the matter of relationship, and in the case of Wilson himself) this similarity had ever been made a subject of comment, or even observed at all, by our school-fellows. That *he* observed it in all its bearings, and as fixedly as I, was apparent; but that he could discover in such circumstances so fruitful a field of annoyance can only be attributed, as I said before, to his more than ordinary penetration.

His cue, which was to perfect an imitation of myself, lay both in words and in actions, and most admirably did he play his part. My dress it was an easy matter to copy; my gait and general manner were without difficulty appropriated; in spite of his constitutional defect, even my voice did not escape him. My louder tones were of course unattempted, but then the key, it was identical; *and his singular whisper, it grew the very echo of my own.*

How greatly this most exquisite portraiture harassed me (for it could not justly be termed a caricature), I will not now venture to describe. I had but one consolation – in the fact that the imitation, apparently, was noticed by myself alone, and that I had to endure only the knowing and strangely sarcastic smiles of my namesake himself. Satisfied with having produced in my bosom the intended effect, he seemed to chuckle in secret over the sting he had inflicted, and was characteristically disregardful of the public applause which the success of his witty endeavours might have so easily elicited. That the school, indeed, did not feel his design, perceive its accomplishment and participate in his sneer, was for many anxious months a riddle I could not resolve. Perhaps the *gradation* of his copy rendered it not so readily perceptible, or more possibly I owed my security to the masterly air of the copyist, who, disdaining the letter (which in a painting is all the obtuse can see), gave but the full spirit of his original for my individual contemplation and chagrin.

I have already more than once spoken of the disgusting air of patronage which he assumed toward me, and of his frequent officious interference with my will. This interference often took the ungracious character of advice — advice not openly given, but hinted or insinuated. I received it with a repugnance which gained strength as I grew in years. Yet at this distant day, let me do him the simple justice to acknowledge that I can recall no occasion when the suggestions of my rival were on the side of those errors or follies so usual to his immature age and seeming inexperience; that his moral sense, at least, if not his general talents and worldly wisdom, was far keener than my own; and that I might to-day have been a better, and thus a happier man, had I less frequently rejected the counsels embodied in those meaning whispers which I then but too cordially hated and too bitterly despised.

As it was, I at length grew restive in the extreme under his distasteful supervision, and daily resented more and more openly what I considered his intolerable arrogance. I have said that in the first years of our connection as schoolmates, my feelings in regard to him might have been easily ripened into friendship; but, in the latter months of my residence at the academy, although the intrusion of his ordinary manner had, beyond doubt, in some measure abated, my sentiments in nearly similar proportion partook very much of positive hatred. Upon one occasion he saw this, I think, and afterwards avoided, or made a show of avoiding me.

It was about the same period, if I remember aright, that, in an altercation of violence with him, in which he was more than usually thrown off his guard, and spoke and acted with an openness of demeanour rather foreign to his nature, I discovered, or fancied I discovered, in his accent, his air, and general appearance, at something which first startled, and then deeply interested me, by bringing to mind dim visions of my earliest infancy — wild, confused, and thronging memories of a time when memory herself was yet unborn. I cannot better describe the sensation which oppressed me than by saying that I could with difficulty shake off the belief of my having been acquainted with the being who stood before me at some epoch very long ago, some point of the past even infinitely remote. The delusion, however, faded rapidly as it came, and I mention it at all but to define the day of the last conversation I there held with my singular namesake.

The huge old house, with its countless subdivisions, had several large chambers communicating with each other, where slept the greater number of the students. There were, however (as must necessarily happen in a building so awkwardly planned), many little nooks or recesses, the odds and ends of the structure, and these the economic ingenuity of Dr Bransby had also fitted up as dormitories, although, being the merest closets, they were capable of accommodating but a single individual. One of these small apartments was occupied by Wilson.

One night, about the close of my fifth year at the school, and immediately after the altercation just mentioned, finding every one wrapped in sleep, I arose from bed, and, lamp in hand, stole through a wilderness of narrow passages from my own bedroom to that of my rival. I had long been plotting one of those ill-natured pieces of practical wit at his expense in which I had hitherto been so uniformly unsuccessful. It was my intention now to put my scheme in operation, and I resolved to make him feel the whole extent of the malice with which I was imbued. Having reached his closet, I noiselessly entered, leaving the lamp, with a shade over it, on the outside. I advanced a step, and listened to the sound of his tranquil breathing. Assured of his being asleep, I returned, took the light, and with it again approached the bed. Close curtains were around it, which, in the prosecution of my plan, I slowly and quietly withdrew, when the bright rays fell vividly upon the sleeper, and my eyes, at the same moment, upon his countenance. I looked and a numbness, an iciness of feeling, instantly pervaded my frame. My breast heaved, my knees tottered, my whole spirit became possessed with an objectless yet intolerable horror. Gasping for breath, I lowered the lamp in still nearer proximity to the face. Were these – *these* the lineaments of William Wilson? I saw, indeed, that they were his, but I shook as if with a fit of the ague in fancying they were not. What *was* there about them to confound me in this manner? I gazed, while my brain reeled with a multitude of incoherent thoughts. Not thus he appeared, assuredly not *thus*, in the vivacity of his waking hours. The same name, the same contour of person, the same day of arrival at the academy; and then his dogged and meaningless imitation of my gait, my voice, my habits, and my manner. Was it, in truth, within the bounds of human possibility that *what I now saw* was the result merely of the habitual practice of this sarcastic imitation. Awe-stricken, and with a creeping shudder, I extinguished the lamp, passed silently from the chamber, and left at once the halls of that old academy, never to enter them again.

After a lapse of some months, spent at home in mere idleness, I found myself a student at Eton. The brief interval had been sufficient to enfeeble my remembrance of the events at Dr Bransby's, or at least to effect a material change in the nature of the feelings with which I remembered them. The truth, the tragedy, of the drama was no more. I could now find room to doubt the evidence of my senses, and seldom called up the subject at all but with wonder at the extent of human credulity, and a smile at the vivid force of the imagination which I hereditarily possessed. Neither was this species of scepticism likely to be diminished by the character of the life I led at Eton. The vortex of thoughtless folly into which I there so immediately and so recklessly plunged washed away all but the froth of my past hours, engulfed at once every solid or serious impression, and left to memory only the veriest levities of a former existence.

I do not wish, however, to trace the course of my miserable profligacy here – a profligacy which set at defiance the laws, while it eluded the vigilance of the institution. Three years of folly, passed without profit, had but given me rooted habits of vice, and added, in a somewhat unusual degree, to my bodily stature, when, after a week of soulless dissipation, I invited a small party of the most dissolute students to a secret carousal in my chambers. We met at a late hour of the night, for our debaucheries were to be faithfully protracted until morning. The wine flowed freely, and there were not wanting other and perhaps more dangerous seductions, so that the grey dawn had already faintly appeared in the east, while our delirious extravagance was at its height. Madly flushed with cards and intoxication, I was in the act of insisting upon a toast of more than wonted profanity, when my attention was suddenly diverted by the violent, although partial, unclosing of the door of the apartment, and by the eager voice of a servant from without. He said that some person, apparently in great haste, demanded to speak with me in the hall.

Wildly excited with wine, the unexpected interruption rather delighted than surprised me. I staggered forward at once, and a few steps brought me to the vestibule of the building. In this low and small room there hung no lamp, and now no light at all was admitted, save that of the exceedingly feeble dawn which made its way through the semi-circular window. As I put my foot over the threshold I became aware of the figure of a youth about my own height, and habited in a white kerseymere morning frock, cut in the novel fashion of the one I myself wore at the moment. This the faint light enabled me to perceive, but the features of his face I could not distinguish. Upon my entering he strode hurriedly up to me, and seizing me by the arm with a gesture of petulant impatience, whispered the words 'William Wilson!' in my ear.

I grew perfectly sober in an instant.

There was that in the manner of the stranger, and in the tremulous shake of his uplifted finger, as he held it between my eyes and the light, which filled me with unqualified amazement; but it was not this which had so violently moved me. It was the pregnancy of solemn admonition in the singular, low, hissing utterance, and, above all, it was the character, the tone, *the key*, of those few, simple, and familiar, yet *whispered* syllables, which came with a thousand thronging memories of by-gone days, and struck upon my soul with the shock of a galvanic battery. Ere I could recover the use of my senses he was gone.

Although this event failed not of a vivid effect upon my disordered imagination, yet was it evanescent as vivid. For some weeks, indeed, I busied myself in earnest inquiry, or was wrapped in a cloud of morbid speculation. I did not pretend to disguise from my perception the identity of the singular individual who thus perseveringly interfered with my affairs, and harassed me with his insinuated counsel. But who and what was this Wilson? – and whence came he? – and what were his purposes? Upon neither of these points could I be satisfied – merely ascertaining in regard to him, that a sudden accident in his family had caused his removal from Dr Bransby's academy on the afternoon of the day in which I myself had eloped. But in a brief period I ceased to think upon the subject, my attention being all absorbed in a contemplated departure for Oxford. Thither I soon went, the uncalculating vanity of my parents furnishing me with an outfit and annual establishment which would enable me to indulge at will in the luxury already so dear to my heart – to vie in profuseness of expenditure with the haughtiest heirs of the wealthiest earldoms in Great Britain.

Excited by such appliances to vice, my constitutional temperament broke forth with redoubled ardour, and I spurned even the common restraints of decency in the mad infatuation of my revels. But it were absurd to pause in the detail of my extravagance. Let it suffice, that among spendthrifts I out-Heroded Herod, and that giving name to a multitude of novel follies, I added no brief appendix to the long catalogue of vices then usual in the most dissolute university of Europe.

It could hardly be credited, however, that I had, even here, so utterly fallen from the gentlemanly estate as to seek acquaintance with the vilest arts of the gambler by profession, and having become an adept in his despicable science, to practise it habitually as a means of increasing my already enormous income at the expense of the weak-minded among my fellow-collegians. Such, nevertheless, was the fact; and the very enormity of this offence against all manly and honorable sentiment proved, beyond doubt, the main, if not the sole reason of the impunity with which it was committed. Who, indeed, among my most abandoned associates, would not rather have disputed the clearest evidence of his senses than have suspected of such courses the gay, the frank, the generous William Wilson – the noblest and most liberal commoner at Oxford – him whose follies (said his parasites) were but the follies of youth and unbridled fancy – whose errors but inimitable whim – whose darkest vice but a careless and dashing extravagance?

I had been now two years successfully busied in this way when there came to the university a young *parvenu* nobleman, Glendinning – rich, said report, as Herodes Atticus – his riches, too, as easily acquired. I soon found him of weak intellect, and of course marked him as a fitting subject for my skill. I frequently engaged him in play, and contrived with the gambler's usual art to let him win considerable sums, the more effectually to entangle him in my snares. At length, my schemes being ripe, I met him (with the full intention that this meeting should be final and decisive) at the chambers of a fellow-commoner (Mr Preston) equally intimate with both, but who, to do him justice, entertained not even a remote suspicion of my design. To give to this a better colouring I had contrived to have assembled a party of some eight or ten, and was solicitously careful that the introduction of cards should appear accidental, and originate in the proposal of my contemplated dupe himself. To be brief upon a vile topic, none of the low finesse was omitted, so customary upon similar occasions, that it is a just matter for wonder how any are still found so besotted as to fall its victim.

We had protracted our sitting far into the night, and I had at length effected the manoeuvre of getting Glendinning as my sole antagonist. The game, too, was my favourite *écarté*. The rest of the company, interested in the extent of our play, had abandoned their own cards, and were standing around us as spectators. The *parvenu*, who had been induced by my artifices in the early part of the evening to drink deeply, now shuffled, dealt, or played with a wild nervousness of manner for which his intoxication, I thought, might partially but could not altogether account. In a very short period he had become my debtor to a large amount, when, having taken a long draught of port, he did precisely what I had been coolly anticipating – he proposed to double our already extravagant stakes. With a well-feigned show of reluctance, and not until after my repeated refusal had seduced him into some angry words which gave a colour of *pique* to my compliance, did I finally comply. The result of course did but prove how entirely the prey was in my toils: in less than an hour he had quadrupled his debt. For some time his countenance had been losing the florid tinge lent it by the wine, but now, to my astonishment, I perceived that it had grown to a pallor truly fearful. I say to my astonishment. Glendinning had been represented to my eager inquiries as immeasurably wealthy; and the sums which he had as yet lost, although in themselves vast, could not, I supposed, very seriously annoy, much less so violently affect him. That he was overcome by the wine just swallowed was the idea which most readily presented itself; and, rather with a view to the preservation of my own character in the eyes of my associates, than from any less interested motive, I was about to insist peremptorily upon a discontinuance of the play, when some expressions at my elbow from among the company, and an ejaculation evincing utter despair on the part of Glendinning, gave me to understand that I had effected his total ruin under circumstances which, rendering him an object for the pity of all, should have protected him from the ill offices even of a fiend.

What now might have been my conduct it is difficult to say. The pitiable condition of my dupe had thrown an air of embarrassed gloom over all, and for some moments a profound silence was maintained, during which I could not help feeling my cheeks tingle with the many burning glances of scorn or reproach cast upon me by the less abandoned of the party. I will even own that an intolerable weight of anxiety was a brief instant lifted from my bosom by the sudden and extraordinary interruption which ensued. The wide heavy folding-doors of the apartment were all at once thrown open to their full extent, with a vigorous and rushing impetuosity that extinguished, as if by magic, every candle in the room. Their light, in dying, enabled us just to perceive that a stranger had entered, about my own height, and closely muffled in a cloak. The darkness, however, was now total, and we could only *feel* that he was standing in our midst. Before any one of us could recover from the extreme astonishment into which this rudeness had thrown all, we heard the voice of the intruder.

'Gentlemen,' he said, in a low, distinct, and never-to-be-forgotten whisper which thrilled to the very marrow of my bones, 'Gentlemen, I make no apology for this behaviour because in thus behaving, I am but fulfilling my duty. You are, beyond doubt, uninformed of the true character of the person who has to-night won at *écarté* a large sum of money from Lord Glendinning. I will therefore put you upon an expeditious and decisive plan of obtaining this very necessary information. Please to examine at your leisure the inner linings of the cuff of his left sleeve, and the several little packages which may be found in the somewhat capacious pockets of his embroidered morning wrapper.'

While he spoke, so profound was the stillness that one might have heard a pin drop upon the floor. In ceasing, he departed at once, and as abruptly as he had entered. Can I – shall I describe my sensations? Must I say that I felt all the horrors of the damned? Most assuredly I had little time for reflection. Many hands roughly seized me upon the spot, and lights were immediately reprocured. A search ensued. In the lining of my sleeve were found all the court cards essential in *écarté*, and in the pockets of my wrapper a number of packs, facsimiles of those used at our sittings, with the single exception that mine were of the species called, technically, *arrondées*; the honours being slightly convex at the ends, the lower cards slightly convex at the sides. In this disposition, the dupe who cuts, as customary, at the length of the pack, will invariably find that he cuts his antagonist an honour; while the gambler, cutting at the breadth, will as certainly cut nothing for his victim which may count in the records of the game.

Any burst of indignation upon this discovery would have affected me less than the silent contempt, or the sarcastic composure, with which it was received.

'Mr Wilson,' said our host, stooping to remove from beneath his feet an exceedingly luxurious cloak of rare furs, 'Mr Wilson, this is your property.' (The weather was cold; and, upon quitting my own room, I had thrown a cloak over my dressing wrapper, putting it off upon reaching the scene of play.) 'I presume it is supererogatory to seek here (eyeing the folds of the garment with a bitter smile) for any further evidence of your skill. Indeed, we have had enough. You will see the necessity, I hope, of quitting Oxford – at all events, of quitting instantly my chambers.'

Abased, humbled to the dust as I then was, it is probable that I should have resented this galling language by immediate personal violence, had not my whole attention been at the moment arrested by a fact of the most startling character. The cloak which I had worn was of a rare description of fur; how rare, how extravagantly costly, I shall not venture to say. Its fashion, too, was of my own fantastic invention, for I was fastidious to an absurd degree of coxcombry in matters of this frivolous nature. When, therefore, Mr Preston reached me that which he had picked up upon the floor, and near the folding doors of the apartment, it was with an astonishment nearly bordering upon terror that I perceived my own already hanging on my arm (where I had no doubt unwittingly placed it), and that the one presented me was but its exact counterpart in every, in even the minutest possible particular. The singular being who had so disastrously exposed me had been muffled, I remembered, in a cloak, and none had been worn at all by any of the members of our party with the exception of myself. Retaining some presence of mind, I took the one offered me by

235

Preston, placed it unnoticed over my own, left the apartment with a resolute scowl of defiance, and next morning, ere dawn of day, commenced a hurried journey from Oxford to the Continent in a perfect agony of horror and of shame.

I fled in vain. My evil destiny pursued me as if in exultation, and proved indeed that the exercise of its mysterious dominion had as yet only begun. Scarcely had I set foot in Paris ere I had fresh evidence of the detestable interest taken by this Wilson in my concerns. Years flew while I experienced no relief. Villain! – at Rome, with how untimely, yet with how spectral an officiousness, stepped he in between me and my ambition! At Vienna, too – at Berlin – and at Moscow! Where, in truth, had I *not* bitter cause to curse him within my heart? From his inscrutable tyranny did I at length flee, panic-stricken, as from a pestilence; and to the very ends of the earth *I fled in vain.*

And again and again, in secret communion with my own spirit, would I demand the questions, 'Who is he? – whence came he? – and what are his objects?' But no answer was there found. And now I scrutinized, with a minute scrutiny, the forms, and the methods, and the leading traits of his impertinent supervision. But even here there was very little upon which to base a conjecture. It was noticeable, indeed, that in no one of the multiplied instances in which he had of late crossed my path had he so crossed it except to frustrate those schemes, or to disturb those actions, which, if fully carried out, might have resulted in bitter mischief. Poor justification this, in truth, for an authority so imperiously assumed! Poor indemnity for natural rights of self-agency so pertinaciously, so insultingly denied!

I had also been forced to notice that my tormentor for a very long period of time (while scrupulously and with miraculous dexterity maintaining his whim of an identity of apparel with myself) had so contrived it, in the execution of his varied interference with my will, that I saw not at any moment the features of his face. Be Wilson what he might, *this* at least was but the veriest of affectation or of folly. Could he for an instant have supposed that in my admonisher at Eton – in the destroyer of my honour at Oxford – in him who thwarted my ambition at Rome, my revenge at Paris, my passionate love at Naples, or what he falsely termed my avarice in Egypt – that in this, my arch-enemy and evil genius, I could fail to recognise the William Wilson of my school-boy days – the namesake, the companion, the rival – the hated and dreaded rival at Dr Bransby's? Impossible! – But let me hasten to the last eventful scene of the drama.

Thus far had I succumbed supinely to this imperious domination. The sentiment of deep awe with which I habitually regarded the elevated character, the majestic wisdom, the apparent omnipresence and omnipotence of Wilson, added to a feeling of even terror, with which certain other traits in his nature and assumptions inspired me, had operated hitherto to impress me with an idea of my own utter weakness and helplessness, and to suggest an implicit, although bitterly reluctant submission to his arbitrary will. But of late days I had given myself up entirely to wine, and its maddening influence upon my hereditary temper rendered me more and more impatient of control. I began to murmur – to hesitate – to resist. And was it only fancy which induced me to believe that, with the increase of my own firmness, that of my tormentor underwent a proportional diminution? Be this as it may, I now began to feel the inspiration of a burning hope, and at length nurtured in my secret thoughts a stern and desperate resolution that I would submit no longer to be enslaved.

It was at Rome, during the Carnival of 18 – , that I attended a masquerade in the palazzo of the Neapolitan Duke Di Broglio. I had indulged more freely than usual in the excesses of the wine-table, and now the suffocating atmosphere of the crowded rooms irritated me beyond endurance. The difficulty, too, of forcing my way through the mazes of the company contributed not a little to the ruffling of my temper; for I was anxiously seeking (let me not say with what unworthy motive) the young, the gay, the beautiful wife of the aged and doting Di Broglio. With a too unscrupulous confidence she had previously communicated to me the secret of the costume in which she would be habited, and now, having caught a glimpse of her person, I was hurrying to make my way into her presence. At this moment I felt a light hand placed upon my shoulder, and that ever-remembered, low, damnable *whisper* within my ear.

In an absolute frenzy of wrath I turned at once upon him who had thus interrupted me, and seized him violently by the collar. He was attired, as I had expected, in a costume altogether similar to my own; wearing a Spanish cloak of blue velvet, begirt about the waist with a crimson belt sustaining a rapier. A mask of black silk entirely covered his face.

'Scoundrel!' I said, in a voice husky with rage, while every syllable I uttered seemed as new fuel to my fury; 'scoundrel! impostor! accursed villain! you shall not – you *shall not* dog me unto death! Follow me, or I will stab you where you stand!' – and I broke my way from the ball-room into a small ante-chamber adjoining, dragging him unresistingly with me as I went.

Upon entering, I thrust him furiously from me. He staggered against the wall, while I closed the door with an oath, and commanded him to draw. He hesitated but for an instant; then, with a slight sigh, drew in silence, and put himself upon his defence.

The contest was brief indeed. I was frantic with every species of wild excitement, and felt within my single arm the energy and power of a multitude. In a few seconds I forced him by sheer strength against the wainscoting, and thus, getting him at mercy, plunged my sword, with brute ferocity, repeatedly through and through his bosom.

At that instant some person tried the latch of the door. I hastened to prevent an intrusion, and then immediately returned to my dying antagonist. But what human language can adequately portray *that* astonishment, *that* horror which possessed me at the spectacle then presented to view? The brief moment in which I averted my eyes had been sufficient to produce apparently a material change in the arrangements at the upper or farther end of the room. A large mirror – so at first it seemed to me in my confusion – now stood where none had been perceptible before; and, as I stepped up to it in extremity of terror, mine own image, but with features all pale and dabbled in blood, advanced to meet me with a feeble and tottering gait.

Thus it appeared, I say, but was not. It was my antagonist – it was Wilson who then stood before me in the agonies of his dissolution. His mask and cloak lay where he had thrown them upon the floor. Not a thread in all his raiment – not a line in all the marked and singular lineaments of his face which was not, even in the most absolute identity, *mine own!*

It was Wilson; but he spoke no longer in a whisper, and I could have fancied that I myself was speaking while he said:

'*You have conquered and I yield. Yet, henceforward art thou also dead – dead to the World, to Heaven, and to Hope! In me didst thou exist – and, in my death, see by this image, which is thine own, how utterly thou hast murdered thyself.*'

The Duplicate Man

BY CLIFFORD D. SIMAK

The Outer Limits *is held in equal regard to* The Twilight Zone *by its admirers and, similarly is regularly re-run on late night television. Like* The Twilight Zone, *too, its title has become a catch-phrase for going to the furthest extremes, and now crops up as often in films and books as it does on television. (Curiously, though, the programme was originally going to be called* Please Stand By!*) The show also had an opening monologue which can be recited, word perfect, by its fans. 'There is nothing wrong with your television set,' the ethereal "Control Voice" would intone. 'Do not attempt to adjust the picture. We are controlling transmissions. If we wish to make it louder, we will bring up the volume. If we wish to make it softer, we will tune it to a whisper. We will control the horizontal. We will control the vertical. We can roll the image, make it flutter. We can change the focus to a soft blur, or sharpen it to crystal clarity. For the next hour, sit quietly, and we will control all that you see and hear. We repeat: There is nothing wrong with your television set. You are about to participate in a great adventure. You are about to experience the awe and mystery which reaches from the inner mind to . . .* The Outer Limits.'*

Masterminded by veteran producers Leslie Stevens and Joseph Stefano, the fifty minute, black and white series which ran for over two years was notable in the history of television for being probably the first show to be made by an independent production company (Daystar Productions of Los Angeles) specifically for TV (ABC in this instance) — a now commonplace arrangement in the world of broadcasting. As far as viewers were concerned, it was the programme's stylish monsters like the shimmering, mouthless Andromedan, the anti-like Zanti, and the amorphous, man-sized silver globe —

the Milkie, that made it memorable; not forgetting the excellent acting by guest stars of the calibre of Cliff Robertson, Robert Culp, Donald Pleasance, Martin Landau, Martin Sheen, Robert Duvall, Vera Miles, Lloyd Nolan, William Shatner, June Havoc and Adam West. The stories in the series were mostly fantasy tales presented in a kind of dark film noir style which frequently had reviewers comparing them to Gothic extravaganzas. Among the best remembered are the haunted house tale, 'The Form of Things Unknown' which paid tribute to Clouzot's Les Diaboliques and starred Vera Miles and Sir Cedric Hardwicke; and 'Don't Open Till Doomsday' which mixed horror and science Fiction in a story about an ageing heiress (Miriam Hopkins) whose husband is being kept forever young in their bridal suite by an Alien.

Some of the stories for The Outer Limits were commissioned from scriptwriters, while others were drawn from the work of established fantasy authors of the time including Arthur Leo Zagat, Louis Charbonneau, Earl and Otto Binder and Clifford D. Simak (1904–). Simak, a former journalist and prolific author of science fiction, has often mixed rural American folklore with stories of time travel and alien invasion. Such a tale is 'The Duplicate Man' which The Outer Limits screened in December 1964, directed by Gerald Oswald and featuring Ron Randell, Sean McClory and Constance Towers.

I

HE came alive from nothing. He became aware from unawareness. He smelled the air of the night and heard the trees whispering on the embankment above him and the breeze that had set the trees to whispering came down to him and felt him over with soft and tender fingers, for all the world as if it were examining him for broken bones or contusions and abrasions.

He sat up and put both his palms down upon the ground beside him to help him sit erect and stared into the darkness. Memory came slowly and when it came it was incomplete and answered nothing.

His name was Henderson James and he was a human being and he was sitting somewhere on a planet that was called the Earth. He was thirty-six years old and he was, in his own way, famous, and comfortably well-off. He lived in an old ancestral home on Summit avenue, which was a respectable address even if it had lost some of its smartness in the last twenty years or so.

On the road above the slope of the embankment a car went past with its tyres whining on the pavement and for a moment its headlights made the treetops glow. Far away, muted by the distance, a whistle cried out. And somewhere else a dog was barking with a flat viciousness.

His name was Henderson James and if that were true, why was he here? Why should Henderson James be sitting on the slope of an embankment, listening to the wind in the trees and to a wailing whistle and a barking dog? Something had gone wrong, some incident that, if he could but remember it, might answer all his questions.

There was a job to do.

He sat and stared into the night and found that he was shivering, although there was no reason why he should, for the night was not that cold. Beyond the embankment he heard the sounds of a city late at night, the distant whine of the speeding car and the far-off wind-broken screaming of a siren. Once a man walked along a street close by and James sat listening to his footsteps until they faded out of hearing.

Something had happened and there was a job to do, a job that he had been doing, a job that somehow had been strangely interrupted by the inexplicable incident which had left him lying here on this embankment.

He checked himself. Clothing . . . shorts and shirt, strong shoes, his wristwatch and the gun in the holster at his side.

A gun?

The job involved a gun.

He had been hunting in the city, hunting something that required a gun. Something that was prowling in the night and a thing that must be killed.

Then he knew the answer, but even as he knew it he sat for a moment wondering at the strange, methodical, step-by-step progression of reasoning that had brought him to the memory. First his name and the basic facts pertaining to himself, then the realization of where he was and the problem of why he happened to be there and finally the realization that he had a gun and that it was meant to be used. It was a logical way to think, a primer schoolbook way to work it out:

I am a man named Henderson James.

I live in a house on Summit avenue.

Am I in the house on Summit avenue?

No, I am not in the house on Summit avenue.

I am on an embankment somewhere.

Why am I on the embankment?

But it wasn't the way a man thought, at least not the normal way a normal man would think. Man thought in short-cuts. He cut across the block and did not go all the way around.

It was a frightening thing, he told himself, this clear-around-the-block thinking. It wasn't normal and it wasn't right and it made no sense at all . . no more sense than did the fact that he should find himself in a place with no memory of getting there.

He rose to his feet and ran his hands up and down his body. His clothes were neat, not rumpled. He hadn't been beaten up and he hadn't been thrown from a speeding car. There were no sore places on his body and his face was unbloody and whole and he felt all right.

He hooked his fingers in the holster belt and shucked it up so that it rode tightly on his hips. He pulled out the gun and checked it with expert and familiar fingers and the gun was ready.

He walked up the embankment and reached the road, went across it with a swinging stride to reach the sidewalk that fronted the row of new bungalows. He heard a car coming and stepped off the sidewalk to crouch in a clump of evergreens that landscaped one corner of a lawn. The move was instinctive and he crouched there, feeling just a little foolish at the thing he'd done.

The car went past and no one saw him. They would not, he now realized, have noticed him even if he had remained out on the sidewalk.

He was unsure of himself; that must be the reason for his fear. There was a blank spot in his life, some mysterious incident that he did not know and the unknowing of it had undermined the sure and solid foundation of his own existence, had wrecked the basis of his motive and had turned him, momentarily, into a furtive animal that darted and hid at the approach of his fellow men.

That and something that had happened to him that made him think clear around the block.

He remained crouching in the evergreens, watching the street and the stretch of sidewalk, conscious of the white-painted, ghostly bungalows squatting back in their landscaped lots.

A word came into his mind. *Puudly*. An odd word, unearthly, yet it held terror.

The *puudly* had escaped and that was why he was here, hiding on the front lawn of some unsuspecting and sleeping citizen, equipped with a gun and a determination to use it, ready to match his wits and the quickness of brain and muscle against the most bloodthirsty, hate-filled thing yet found in the Galaxy.

The *puudly* was dangerous. It was not a thing to harbour. In fact, there was a law against harbouring not only a *puudly*, but certain other alien beasties even less lethal than a *puudly*. There was good reason for such a law, reason which no one, much less himself, would ever think to question.

And now the *puudly* was loose and somewhere in the city.

James grew cold at the thought of it, his brain forming images of the things that might come to pass if he did not hunt down the alien beast and put an end to it.

Although beast was not quite the word to use. The *puudly* was more than a beast . . . just how much more than a beast he once had hoped to learn. He had not learned a lot, he now admitted to himself, not nearly all there was to learn, but he had learned enough. More than enough to frighten him.

For one thing, he had learned what hate could be and how shallow an emotion human hate turned out when measured against the depth and intensity and the ravening horror of the *puudly's* hate. Not unreasoning hate, for unreasoning hate defeats itself, but a rational, calculating, driving hate that motivated a clever and deadly killing machine which directed its rapacity and its cunning against every living thing that was not a *puudly*.

For the beast had a mind and a personality that operated upon the basic law of self-preservation against all comers, whoever they might be, extending that law to the interpretation that safety lay in one direction only . . . the death of every other living being. No other reason was needed for a *puudly's* killing. The fact that anything else lived and moved and was thus posing a threat, no matter how remote, against a *puudly*, was sufficient reason in itself.

It was psychotic, of course, some murderous instinct planted far back in time and deep in the creature's racial consciousness, but no more psychotic, perhaps, than many human instincts.

The *puudly* had been, and still was for that matter, a unique opportunity for a study in alien behaviourism. Given a permit, one could have studied them on their native planet. Refused a permit, one sometimes did a foolish thing, as James had.

And foolish acts backfire, as this one did.

James put down a hand and patted the gun at his side, as if by doing so he might derive some assurance that he was equal to the task. There was no question in his mind as to the thing that must be done. He must find the *puudly* and kill it and he must do that before the break of dawn. Anything less than that would be abject and horrifying failure.

For the *puudly* would bud. It was past its time for the reproductive act and there were bare hours left to find it before it had loosed upon the Earth dozens of baby *puudlies*. They would not remain babies for

243

long. A few hours after budding they would strike out on their own. To find one *puudly*, lost in the vastness of a sleeping city, seemed bad enough; to track down some dozens of them would be impossible.

So it was tonight or never.

Tonight there would be no killing on the *puudly's* part. Tonight the beast would be intent on one thing only, to find a place where it could rest in quiet, where it could give itself over, wholeheartedly and with no interference, to the business of bringing other *puudlies* into being.

It was clever. It would have known where it was going before it had escaped. There would be, on its part, no time wasted in seeking or in doubling back. It would have known where it was going and already it was there, already the buds would be rising on its body, bursting forth and growing.

There was one place, and one place only, in the entire city where an alien beast would be safe from prying eyes. A man could figure that one out and so could a *puudly*. The question was: Would the *puudly* know that a man could figure it out? Would the *puudly* underestimate a man? Or, knowing that the man would know it, too, would it find another place of hiding?

James rose from the evergreens and went down the sidewalk. The street marker at the corner, standing underneath a swinging street light, told him where he was and it was closer to the place where he was going than he might have hoped.

II

The zoo was quiet for a while, and then something sent up a howl that raised James' hackles and made his blood stop in his veins.

James, having scaled the fence, stood tensely at its foot, trying to identify the howling animal. He was unable to place it. More than likely, he told himself, it was a new one. A person simply couldn't keep track of all the zoo's occupants. New ones were coming in all the time, strange, unheard-of creatures from the distant stars.

Straight ahead lay the unoccupied moat cage that up until a day or two before had held an unbelievable monstrosity from the jungles of one of the Arctian worlds. James grimaced in the dark, remembering the thing. They had finally had to kill it.

And now the *puudly* was there . . . well, maybe not there, but one place that it could be, the one place in the entire city where it might be seen and arouse no comment, for the zoo was filled with animals that were seldom seen and another strange one would arouse only momentary wonder. One animal more would go unnoticed unless some zoo attendant should think to check the records.

There, in that unoccupied cage area, the *puudly* would be undisturbed, could quietly go about its business of budding out more *puudlies*. No one would bother it, for things like *puudlies* were the normal occupants of this place set aside for the strangers brought to Earth to be stared at and studied by that ferocious race, the humans.

James stood quietly beside the fence.

Henderson James. Thirty-six. Unmarried. Alien psychologist. An official of this zoo. And an offender against the law for having secured and harboured an alien being that was barred from Earth.

Why, he asked himself, did he think of himself in this way? Why, standing here, did he catalogue himself? It was instinctive to know one's self . . . there was no need, no sense of setting up a mental outline of one's self.

It had been foolish to go ahead with this *puudly* business. He recalled how he had spent days fighting it out with himself, reviewing all the disastrous possibilities which might arise from it. If the old renegade spaceman had not come to him and had not said, over a bottle of most delicious Lupan wine, that he could deliver, for a certain, rather staggering sum, one live *puudly*, in good condition, it never would have happened.

James was sure that of himself he never would have thought of it. But the old space captain was a man he knew and admired from former dealings. He was a man who was not averse to turning either an honest or a dishonest dollar, and yet he was a man, for all of that, you could depend upon. He would do what you paid him for and keep his lip buttoned tight once the deed was done.

James had wanted a *puudly*, for it was a most engaging beast with certain little tricks that, once understood, might open up new avenues of speculation and approach, might write new chapters in the tortuous study of alien minds and manners.

But for all of that, it had been a terrifying thing to do and now that the beast was loose, the terror was compounded. For it was not wholly beyond speculation that the descendants of this one brood that the escaped *puudly* would spawn might wipe out the population of the Earth, or at the best, make the Earth untenable for its rightful dwellers.

A place like the Earth, with its teeming millions, would provide a field day for the fangs of the *puudlies*, and the minds that drove the fangs. They would not hunt for hunger, nor for the sheer madness of the kill, but because of the compelling conviction that no *puudly* would be safe until Earth was wiped clean of life. They would be killing for survival, as a cornered rat would kill . . . except that they would be cornered nowhere but in the murderous insecurity of their minds.

If the posses scoured the Earth to hunt them down, they would be found in all directions, for they would be shrewd enough to scatter. They would know the ways of guns and traps and poisons and there would be more and more of them as time went on. Each of them would accelerate its budding to replace with a dozen or a hundred the ones that might be killed.

James moved quietly forward to the edge of the moat and let himself down into the mud that covered the bottom. When the monstrosity had been killed, the moat had been drained and should long since have been cleaned, but the press of work, James thought, must have prevented its getting done.

Slowly he waded out into the mud, feeling his way, his feet making sucking noises as he pulled them through the slime. Finally he reached the rocky incline that led out of the moat to the island cage.

He stood for a moment, his hands on the great, wet boulders, listening, trying to hold his breath so the sound of it would not interfere with hearing. The thing that howled had quieted and the night was deathly quiet. Or seemed, at first, to be. Then he heard the little insect noises that ran through the grass and bushes and the whisper of the leaves in the trees across the moat and the far-off sound that was the hoarse breathing of a sleeping city.

Now, for the first time, he felt fear. Felt it in the silence that was not a silence, in the mud beneath his feet, in the up-thrust boulders that rose out of the moat.

The *puudly* was a dangerous thing, not only because it was strong and quick, but because it was intelligent. Just how intelligent, he did not know. It reasoned and it planned and schemed. It could talk, though not as a human talks . . . probably better than a human ever could. For it not only could talk words, but it could talk emotions. It lured its victims to it by the thoughts it put into their minds; it held them entranced with dreams and illusions until it slit their throats. It could purr a man to sleep, could lull him to suicidal inaction. It could drive him crazy with a single flickering thought, hurling a perception so foul and alien that the mind recoiled deep inside itself and stayed there, coiled tight, like a watch that has been overwound and will not run.

It should have budded long ago, but it had fought off its budding, holding back against the day when it might escape, planning, he realized now, its fight to stay on Earth, which meant its conquest of

Earth. It had planned, and planned well, against this very moment, and it would feel or show no mercy to anyone who interfered with it.

His hand went down and touched the gun and he felt the muscles in his jaw involuntarily tightening and suddenly there was at once a lightness and a hardness in him that had not been there before. He pulled himself up the boulder face, seeking cautious hand- and toeholds, breathing shallowly, body pressed against the rock. Quickly, and surely, and no noise, for he must reach the top and be there before the *puuldly* knew there was anyone around.

The *puudly* would be relaxed and intent upon its business, engrossed in the budding forth of that numerous family that in days to come would begin the grim and relentless crusade to make an alien planet safe for *puudlies* . . . and for *puudlies* alone.

That is, if the *puudly* were here and not somewhere else. James was only a human trying to think like a *puudly* and that was not an easy or a pleasant job and he had no way of knowing if he succeeded. He could only hope that his reasoning was vicious and crafty enough.

His clawing hand found grass and earth and he sank his fingers deep into the soil, hauling his body up the last few feet of the rock face above the pit.

He lay flat upon the gently sloping ground, listening, tensed for any danger. He studied the ground in front of him, probing every foot. Distant street lamps lighting the zoo walks threw back the total blackness that had engulfed him as he climbed out of the moat, but there still were areas of shadow that he had to study closely.

Inch by inch, he squirmed his way along, making sure of the terrain immediately ahead before he moved a muscle. He held the gun in a rock-hard fist, ready for instant action, watching for the faintest hint of motion, alert for any hump or irregularity that was not rock or bush or grass.

Minutes magnified themselves into hours, his eyes ached with staring and the lightness that had been in him drained away, leaving only the hardness, which was as tense as a drawn bowstring. A sense of failure began to seep into his mind and with it came the full-fledged, until now unadmitted, realization of what failure meant, not only for the world, but for the dignity and the pride that was Henderson James.

Now, faced with the possibility, he admitted to himself the action he must take if the *puudly* were not here, if he did not find it here and kill it. He would have to notify the authorities, would have to attempt to alert the police, must plead with newspapers and radio to warn the citizenry, must reveal himself as a man who, through pride and self-

247

conceit, had exposed the people of the Earth to this threat against their hold upon their native planet.

They would not believe him. They would laugh at him until the laughter died in their torn throats, choked off with their blood. He sweated, thinking of it, thinking of the price this city, and the world, would pay before it learned the truth.

There was a whisper of sound, a movement of black against deeper black.

The *puudly* rose in front of him, not more than six feet away, from its bed beside a bush. He jerked the pistol up and his finger tightened on the trigger.

'Don't,' the *puudly* said inside his mind. 'I'll go along with you.'

His finger strained with the careful slowness of the squeeze and the gun leaped in his hand, but even as it did he felt the whiplash of terror slash at his brain, caught for just a second the terrible import, the mind-shattering obscenity that glanced off his mind and ricocheted away.

'Too late,' he told the *puudly*, with his voice and his mind and his body shaking. 'You should have tried that first. You wasted precious seconds. You would have got me if you had done it first.'

It had been easy, he assured himself, much easier than he had thought. The *puudly* was dead or dying and the Earth and its millions of unsuspecting citizens were safe and, best of all, Henderson James was safe . . . safe from indignity, safe from being stripped naked of the little defences he had built up through the years to shield him against the public stare. He felt relief flood over him and it left him pulseless and breathless and feeling clean, but weak.

'You fool,' the dying *puudly* said, death clouding its words as they built up in his mind. 'You fool, you half-thing, you duplicate . . .'

It died then and he felt it die, felt the life go out of it and leave it empty.

He rose softly to his feet and he seemed stunned and at first he thought it was from knowing death, from having touched hands with death within the *puudly's* mind.

The *puudly* had tried to fool him. Faced with the pistol, it had tried to throw him off his balance to give it the second that it needed to hurl the mind-blasting thought that had caught at the edge of his brain. If he had hesitated for a moment, he knew, it would have been all over with him. If his finger had slackened for a moment, it would have been too late.

The *puudly* must have known that he would think of the zoo as the first logical place to look and, even knowing that, it had held him in

248

enough contempt to come here, had not even bothered to try to watch for him, had not tried to stalk him, had waited until he was almost on top of it before it moved.

And that was queer, for the *puudly* must have known, with its uncanny mental powers, every move that he had made. It must have maintained a casual contact with his mind every second of the time since it had escaped. He had known that and . . . wait a minute, he hadn't known it until this very moment, although, knowing it now, it seemed as if he had always known it.

What is the matter with me, he thought. There's something wrong with me. I should have known I could not surprise the *puudly*, and yet I didn't know it. I must have surprised it, for otherwise it would have finished me off quite leisurely at any moment after I climbed out of the moat.

You fool, the *puudly* had said. You fool, you half-thing, you duplicate.

You duplicate!

He felt the strength and the personality and the hard, unquestioned identity of himself as Henderson James, human being, drained out of him, as if someone had cut the puppet string and he, the puppet, had slumped supine upon the stage.

So that was why he had been able to surprise the *puudly*!

There were two Henderson Jameses. The *puudly* had been in contact with one of them, the original, the real Henderson James, had known every move he made, had known that it was safe so far as that Henderson James might be concerned. It had not known of the second Henderson James that had stalked it through the night.

Henderson James, duplicate.

Henderson James, temporary.

Henderson James, here tonight, gone tomorrow.

For they would not let him live. The original Henderson James would not allow him to continue living, and even if he did, the world would not allow it. Duplicates were made only for very temporary and very special reasons and it was always understood that once their purpose was accomplished they would be done away with.

Done away with . . . those were the words exactly. Gotten out of the way. Swept out of sight and mind. Killed as unconcernedly and emotionlessly as one chops off a chicken's head.

He walked forward and dropped on one knee beside the *puudly*, running his hand over its body in the darkness. Lumps stood out all over it, the swelling buds that now would never break to spew forth in a loathsome birth a brood of *puudly* pups.

He rose to his feet.

The job was done. The *puudly* had been killed – killed before it had given birth to a horde of horrors.

The job was done and he could go home.

Home?

Of course, that was the thing that had been planted in his mind, the thing they wanted him to do. To go home, to go back to the house on Summit avenue, where his executioners would wait, to walk back deliberately and unsuspectingly to the death that waited.

The job was done and his usefulness was over. He had been created to perform a certain task and the task was now performed and while an hour ago he had been a factor in the plans of men, he was no longer wanted. He was an embarrassment and superfluous.

Now wait a minute, he told himself. You may not be a duplicate. You do not feel like one.

That was true. He felt like Henderson James. He was Henderson James. He lived on Summit avenue and had illegally brought to Earth a beast known as a *puudly* in order that he might study it and talk to it and test its alien reactions, attempt to measure its intelligence and guess at the strength and depth and the direction of its non-humanity. He had been a fool, of course, to do it, and yet at the time it had seemed important to understand the deadly, alien mentality.

I am human, he said, and that was right, but even so the fact meant nothing. Of course he was human. Henderson James was human and his duplicate would be exactly as human as the original. For the duplicate, processed from the pattern that held every trait and characteristic of the man he was to become a copy of, would differ in not a single basic factor.

In not a single basic factor, perhaps, but in certain other things. For no matter how much the duplicate might be like his pattern, no matter how full-limbed he might spring from his creation, he still would be a new man. He would have the capacity for knowledge and for thought and in a little time he would have and know and be all the things that his original was . . .

But it would take some time, some short while to come to a full realization of all he knew and was, some time to coordinate and recognize all the knowledge and experience that lay within his mind. At first he'd grope and search until he came upon the things that he must know. Until he became acquainted with himself, with the sort of man he was, he could not reach out blindly in the dark and put his hand exactly and unerringly upon the thing he wished.

That had been exactly what he'd done. He had groped and searched.

He had been compelled to think, at first, in simple basic truths and facts.

I am a man.

I am on a planet called Earth.

I am Henderson James.

I live on Summit avenue.

There is a job to do.

It had been quite a while, he remembered now, before he had been able to dig out of his mind the nature of the job.

There is a *puudly* to hunt down and destroy.

Even now he could not find in the hidden, still-veiled recesses of his mind the many valid reasons why a man should run so grave a risk to study a thing so vicious as a *puudly*. There were reasons, he knew there were, and in a little time he would know them quite specifically.

The point was that if he were Henderson James, original, he would know them now, know them as a part of himself and his life, without laboriously searching for them.

The *puudly* had known, of course. It had known, beyond any chance of error, that there were two Henderson Jameses. It had been keeping tab on one when another one showed up. A mentality far less astute than the *puudly's* would have had no trouble in figuring that one out.

If the *puudly* had not talked, he told himself, I never would have known. If it had died at once and not had a chance to, taunt me, I would not have known. I would even now be walking to the house on Summit avenue.

He stood lonely and naked of soul in the wind that swept across the moated island. There was a sour bitterness in his mouth.

He moved a foot and touched the dead *puudly*.

'I'm sorry,' he told the stiffening body. 'I'm sorry now I did it. If I had known, I never would have killed you.'

Stiffly erect, he moved away.

III

He stopped at the street corner, keeping well in the shadow. Halfway down the block, and on the other side, was the house. A light burned in one of the rooms upstairs, and another on the post beside the gate that opened into the yard, lighting the walk up to the door.

Just as if, he told himself, the house were waiting for the master to come home. And that, of course, was exactly what it was doing. An old lady of a house, waiting, hands folded in its lap, rocking very gently in a squeaky chair . . . and with a gun beneath the folded shawl.

His lip lifted in half a snarl as he stood there, looking at the house. What do they take me for, he thought, putting out a trap in plain sight and one that's not even baited? Then he remembered. They would not know, of course, that he knew he was a duplicate. They would think that he would think that he was Henderson James, the one and only. They would expect him to come walking home, quite naturally, believing he belonged there. So far as they would know, there would be no possibility of his finding out the truth.

And now that he had? Now that he was here, across the street from the waiting house?

He had been brought into being, had been given life, to do a job that his original had not dared to do, or had not wanted to do. He had carried out a killing his original didn't want to dirty his hands with, or risk his neck in doing.

Or had it not been that at all, but the necessity of two men working on the job, the original serving as a focus for the *puudly's* watchful mind while the other man sneaked up to kill it while it watched?

No matter what, he had been created, at a good stiff price, from the pattern of the man that was Henderson James. The wizardry of man's knowledge, the magic of machines, a deep understanding of organic chemistry, of human physiology, of the mystery of life, had made a second Henderson James. It was legal, of course, under certain circumstances . . . for example, in the case of public policy, and his own creation, he knew, might have been validated under such a heading. But there were conditions and one of these was that a duplicate not be allowed to continue living once it had served the specific purpose for which it had been created.

Usually such a condition was a simple one to carry out, for the duplicate was not meant to know he was a duplicate. So far as he was concerned, he was the original. There was no suspicion in him, no foreknowledge of the doom that was invariably ordered for him, no reason for him to be on guard against the death that waited.

The duplicate knitted his brow, trying to puzzle it out.

There was a strange set of ethics here.

He was alive and he wanted to stay alive. Life, once it had been tasted, was too sweet, too good, to go back to the nothingness from which he had come . . . or would it be nothingness? Now that he had known life, now that he was alive, might he not hope for a life after death, the same as any other human being? Might not he, too, have the same human right as any other human to grasp at the shadowy and glorious promises and assurances held out by religion and by faith?

He tried to marshal what he knew about those promises and

assurances, but his knowledge was illusive. A little later he would remember more about it. A little later, when the neutral book-keeper in his mind had been able to coordinate and activate the knowledge that he had inherited from the pattern, he would know.

He felt a trace of anger stir deep inside of him, anger at the unfairness of allowing him only a few short hours of life, of allowing him to learn how wonderful a thing life was, only to snatch it from him. It was a cruelty that went beyond mere human cruelty. It was something that had been fashioned out of the distorted perspective of a machine society that measured existence only in terms of mechanical and physical worth, that discarded with a ruthless hand whatever part of that society had no specific purpose.

The cruelty, he told himself, was in ever giving life, not in taking it away.

His original, of course, was the one to blame. He was the one who had obtained the *puudly* and allowed it to escape. It was his fumbling and his inability to correct his error without help which had created the necessity of fashioning a duplicate.

And yet, could he blame him?

Perhaps, rather, he owed him gratitude for a few hours of life at least, gratitude for the privilege of knowing what life was like. Although he could not quite decide whether or not it was something which called for gratitude.

He stood there, staring at the house. That light in the upstairs room was in the study off the master bedroom. Up there Henderson James, original, was waiting for the word that the duplicate had come home to death. It was an easy thing to sit there and wait, to sit and wait for the word that was sure to come. An easy thing to sentence to death a man one had never seen, even if that man be the walking image of one's self.

It would be a harder decision to kill him if you stood face to face with him . . . harder to kill someone who would be, of necessity, closer than a brother, someone who would be, even literally, flesh of your flesh, blood of your blood, brain of your brain.

There would be a practical side as well, a great advantage to be able to work with a man who thought as you did, who would be almost a second self. It would be almost as if there were two of you.

A thing like that could be arranged. Plastic surgery and a price for secrecy could make your duplicate into an unrecognizable other person. A little red tape, some finagling . . . but it could be done. It was a proposition that Henderson James, duplicate, thought would interest Henderson James, original. Or at least he hoped it would.

The room with the light could be reached with a little luck, with strength and agility and determination. The brick expanse of a chimney, its base cloaked by shrubs, its length masked by a closely growing tree, ran up the wall. A man could climb its rough brick face, could reach out and swing himself through the open window into the lighted room.

And once Henderson James, original, stood face to face with Henderson James, duplicate . . . well, it would be less of a gamble. The duplicate then would no longer be an impersonal factor. He would be a man and one that was very close to his original.

There would be watchers, but they would be watching the front door. If he were quiet, if he could reach and climb the chimney without making any noise, he'd be in the room before anyone would notice.

He drew back deeper in the shadows and considered. It was either get into the room and face his original, hope to be able to strike a compromise with him, or simply to light out . . . to run and hide and wait, watching his chance to get completely away, perhaps to some far planet in some other part of the Galaxy.

Both ways were a gamble, but one was quick, would either succeed or fail within the hour; the other might drag on for months with a man never knowing whether he was safe, never being sure.

Something nagged at him, a persistent little fact that skittered through his brain and eluded his efforts to pin it down. It might be important and then again, it might be a random thing, simply a floating piece of information that was looking for its pigeonhole.

His mind shrugged it off.

The quick way or the long way?

He stood thinking for a moment and then moved swiftly down the street, seeking a place where he could cross in shadow.

He had chosen the short way.

IV

The room was empty.

He stood beside the window, quietly, only his eyes moving, searching every corner, checking against a situation that couldn't seem quite true . . . that Henderson James was not here, waiting for the word.

Then he strode swiftly to the bedroom door and swung it open. His finger found the switch and the light went on. The bedroom was empty and so was the bath. He went back into the study.

He stood with his back against the wall, facing the door that led into the hallway, but his eyes went over the room, foot by foot, orientating himself, feeling himself flow into the shape and form of it, feeling familiarity creep in upon him and enfold him in its comfort of belonging.

Here were the books, the fireplace with its mantel loaded with souvenirs, the easy chairs, the liquor cabinet . . . and all were a part of him, a background that was as much a part of Henderson James as his body and his inner thoughts were a part of him.

This, he thought, is what I would have missed, the experience I never would have had if the *puudly* had not taunted me. I would have died an empty and unrelated body that had no actual place in the universe.

The phone purred at him and he stood there startled by it, as if some intruder from the outside had pushed its way into the room, shattering the sense of belonging that had come to him.

The phone rang again and he went across the room and picked it up.

'James speaking,' he said.

'That you, Mr James?'

The voice was that of Anderson, the gardener.

'Why, yes,' said the duplicate. 'Who did you think it was?'

'We got a fellow here who says he's you.'

Henderson James, duplicate, stiffened with fright and his hand, suddenly, was grasping the phone so hard that he found the time to wonder why it did not pulverize to bits beneath his fingers.

'He's dressed like you,' the gardener said, 'and I knew you went out. Talked to you, remember? Told you that you shouldn't? Not with us waiting for that . . . that thing.'

'Yes,' said the duplicate, his voice so even that he could not believe it was he who spoke. 'Yes, certainly I remember talking with you.'

'But, sir, how did you get back?'

'I came in the back way,' the even voice said into the phone. 'Now what's holding you back?'

'He's dressed like you.'

'Naturally. Of course he would be, Anderson.'

And that, to be sure, didn't quite follow, but Anderson wasn't too bright to start with and now he was somewhat upset.

'You remember,' the duplicate said, 'that we talked about it.'

'I guess I was excited and forgot,' admitted Anderson. 'You told me to call you, to make sure you were in your study, though. That's right, isn't it, sir?'

'You've called me,' the duplicate said, 'and I am here.'

'Then the other one out here is him?'

'Of course,' said the duplicate. 'Who else could it be?'

He put the phone back into the cradle and stood waiting. It came a moment after, the dull, throaty cough of a gun.

He walked to a chair and sank into it, spent with the knowledge of how events had so been ordered that now, finally, he was safe, safe beyond all question.

Soon he would have to change into other clothes, hide the gun and the clothes that he was wearing. The staff would ask no questions, most likely, but it was best to let nothing arouse suspicion in their minds.

He felt his nerves quieting and he allowed himself to glance about the room, take in the books and furnishings, the soft and easy . . . and earned . . . comfort of a man solidly and unshakably established in the world.

He smiled softly.

'It will be nice,' he said.

It had been easy. Now that it was over, it seemed ridiculously easy. Easy because he had never seen the man who had walked up to the door. It was easy to kill a man you have never seen.

With each passing hour he would slip deeper and deeper into the personality that was his by right of heritage. There would be no one to question, after a time not even himself, that he was Henderson James.

The phone rang again, and he got up to answer it.

A pleasant voice told him, 'This is Allen, over at the duplication lab. We've been waiting for a report from you.'

'Well,' said James, 'I . . .'

'I just called,' interrupted Allen, 'to tell you not to worry. It slipped my mind before.'

'I see,' said James, though he didn't.

'We did this one a little differently,' Allen explained. 'An experiment that we thought we'd try out. Slow poison in his bloodstream. Just another precaution. Probably not necessary, but we like to be positive. In case he fails to show up, you needn't worry any.'

'I am sure he will show up.'

Allen chuckled. 'Twenty-four hours. Like a time bomb. No antidote for it even if he found out somehow.'

'It was good of you to let me know,' said James.

'Glad to,' said Allen. 'Good night, Mr James.'

Random Quest

BY JOHN WYNDHAM

It was to be over a decade after the BBC's success with Nigel Kneale's horror serial, Quatermass, *before the Corporation produced its own anthology series devoted to the weird:* Out of the Unknown, *a fifty-minute, black and white production which ran for two years from 1965 to the winter of 1967. Perhaps not altogether unexpectedly, an early contribution was an original script by Nigel Kneale himself, 'The Shattered Eye', made with a typically bravure performance from Freddie Jones. In the main, though, producer Alan Bromly and his script editor, Roger Parkes, looked to contemporary fantasy literature for their source material and utilised tales by such luminaries as Clifford D. Simak ('Beachhead' adapted by Robert Muller with Edward Bishop and Helen Downing), Isaac Asimov ('Liar' dramatized by David Campton with Ian Ogilvy and Wendy Gifford), John Brunner ('The Last Lonely Man' adapted by Jeremy Paul with George Cole), Ray Bradbury ('The Fox and the Forest' dramatized by Terry Nation with Frederick Bartman and Liane Aukin) and no less than two contributions from Britain's leading author in the genre, John Wyndham.*

Wyndham (1903–1969) who had begun his writing career contributing stories under pen-names to the American SF pulp magazines shortly before World War Two, became internationally famous with his novel of alien invasion, The Day of the Triffids, *published in 1951, which was subsequently filmed in 1963 and in 1981 made into a television series by the BBC with John Duttine and Emma Relph. John Wyndham's story, 'No Place Like Earth' provided the first story for* Out of the Unknown, *directed by Alan Bromly and starring Terence Morgan. It generated excellent reviews for the acting, the sets, and especially the sound effects of the Radiophonics Workshop. 'Random*

Quest' which was made the following year was voted by many viewers the best in the entire series, and it was certainly faithfully adapted by Owen Holder, splendidly directed by Christopher Barry, and with excellent performances from Keith Barron, Tracy Reed and Noel Howlett in the leading roles.

THE sound of a car coming to a stop on the gravel caused Dr Harshom to look at his watch. He closed the book in which he had been writing, put it away in one of his desk drawers, and waited. Presently Stephens opened the door to announce: 'Mr Trafford, sir.'

The doctor got up from his chair, and regarded the young man who entered, with some care. Mr Colin Trafford turned out to be presentable, just in his thirties, with brown hair curling slightly, clean-shaven, a suit of good tweed well cut, and shoes to accord. He looked pleasant enough though not distinguished. It would not be difficult to meet thirty or forty very similar young men in a day. But when he looked more closely, as the doctor now did, there were signs of fatigue to be seen, indications of anxiety in the expression and around the eyes, a strained doggedness in the set of the mouth.

They shook hands.

'You'll have had a long drive,' said the doctor. 'I expect you'd like a drink. Dinner won't be for half an hour yet.'

The younger man accepted, and sat down. Presently, he said:

'It was kind of you to invite me here, Dr Harshom.'

'Not really altruistic,' the doctor told him. 'It is more satisfactory to talk than to correspond by letter. Moreover, I am an inquisitive man recently retired from a very humdrum country practice, Mr Trafford, and on the rare occasions that I do catch the scent of a mystery my curiosity urges me to follow it up.' He, too, sat down.

'Mystery?' repeated the young man.

'Mystery,' said the doctor.

The young man took a sip of his whisky.

'My inquiry was such as one might receive from – well, from any solicitor,' he said.

'But you are not a solicitor, Mr Trafford.'

'No,' Colin Trafford admitted, 'I am not.'

'But you do have a very pressing reason for your inquiry. So there is the mystery. What pressing, or indeed leisurely, reason could you have for inquiries about a person whose existence you yourself appear to be uncertain – and of whom Somerset House has no record?'

The young man regarded him more carefully, as he went on:

'How do I know that? Because an inquiry there would be your natural first step. Had you found a birth-certificate, you would not have pursued the course you have. In fact, only a curiously determined person would have persisted in a quest for someone who had no official existence. So, I said to myself: When this persistence in the face of reason addresses itself to me I will try to resolve the mystery.'

The young man frowned.

'You imply that you said that *before* you had my letter?'

'My dear fellow, Harshom is not a common name – an unusual corruption of Harvesthome, if you are interested in such things – and, indeed, I never yet heard of a Harshom who was not traceably connected with the rest of us. And we do, to some extent, keep in touch. So, quite naturally, I think, the incursion of a young man entirely unknown to any of us, but persistently tackling us one after another with his inquiries regarding an unidentifiable Harshom, aroused our interest. Since it seemed that I myself came low on your priority list I decided to make a few inquiries of my own. I —'

'But why should you judge yourself low on a list,' Colin Trafford interrupted.

'Because you are clearly a man of method. In this case, geographical method. You began your inquiries with Harshoms in the Central London area, and worked outwards, until you are now in Hereford-shire. There are only two further-flung Harshoms now on your list, Peter, down in the toe of Cornwall, and Harold, a few miles from Durham – am I right?'

Colin Trafford nodded, with a trace of reluctance.

'You are,' he admitted.

Dr Harshom smiled, a trifle smugly.

'I thought so. There is —' he began, but the young man interrupted him again.

'When you answered my letter, you invited me here, but you evaded my question,' he remarked.

'That is true. But I have answered it now by insisting that the person you seek not only does not exist, but never did exist.'

'But if you're quite satisfied on that, why ask me here at all?'

'Because —' The doctor broke off at the sound of a gong. 'Dear me, Phillips allows one just ten minutes to wash. Let me show you your room, and we can continue over dinner.'

A little later when the soup was before them, he resumed:

'You were asking me why I invited you here. I think the answer is that since you feel entitled to be curious about a hypothetical relative of mine, I feel no less entitled to be curious about the motives that impel your curiosity. Fair enough? – as they say.'

'Dubious,' replied Mr Trafford after consideration. 'To inquire into my motives would, I admit, be not unreasonable if you knew this person to exist – but, since you assure me she does not exist, the question of my motives surely becomes academic.'

'My interest *is* academic, my dear fellow, but none the less real. Perhaps we might progress a little if I might put the problem as it appears from my point of view?'

Trafford nodded. The doctor went on:

'Well, now, this is the situation: Some seven or eight months ago a young man, unknown to any of us, begins a series of approaches to my relatives. His concern, he says, is to learn the whereabouts, or to gain any clues which may help him to trace the whereabouts of a lady called Ottilie Harshom. She was born, he believes, in 1928, though it could be a few years to either side of that – and she may, of course, have adopted another surname through marriage.

'In his earlier letters there is an air of confidence suggesting his feeling that the matter will easily be dealt with, but as one Harshom after another fails to identify the subject of his inquiries his tone becomes less confident though not less determined. In one or two directions he does learn of young Harshom ladies – none of them called Ottilie, by the way, but he nevertheless investigates them with care. Can it be, that he is as uncertain about the first name as about everything else concerning her? But apparently none of these ladies fulfils his requirements, for he presses on. In the face of unqualified unsuccess, his persistence in leaving no Harshom stone unturned begins to verge upon the unreasonable. Is he an eccentric, with a curious obsession?

'Yet by all the evidence he was – until the spring of 1953, at any rate, a perfectly normal young man. His full name is Colin Wayland Trafford. He was born in 1921, in Solihull, the son of a solicitor. He went to Chartowe School 1934. Enlisted in the Army 1939. Left it, with the rank of Captain 1945. Went up to Cambridge. Took a good degree in Physics 1949. Joined Electro-Physical Industries on the managerial side that same year. Married Della Stevens 1950. Became a widower 1951. Received injuries in a laboratory demonstration accident early in 1953. Spent the following five weeks in St Merryn's Hospital. Began his first approaches to members of the Harshom family for information regarding Ottilie Harshom about a month after his discharge from hospital.'

Colin Trafford said coldly:

'You are very fully informed, Dr Harshom.'

The doctor shrugged slightly.

'Your own information about the Harshoms must by now be almost exhaustive. Why should you resent some of us knowing something of you?'

Colin did not reply to that. He dropped his gaze, and appeared to study the tablecloth. The doctor resumed:

'I said just now – has he an obsession? The answer has appeared to be yes – since sometime last March. Prior to that, there seems to have been no inquiry whatever regarding Miss Ottilie Harshom.

'Now when I had reached this point I began to feel that I was on the edge of a more curious mystery than I had expected.' He paused. 'I'd like to ask you, Mr Trafford, had you ever been aware of the name Ottilie Harshom before January last?'

The young man hesitated. Then he said, uneasily:

'How can one possibly answer that? One encounters a myriad names on all sides. Some are remembered, some seem to get filed in the subconscious, some apparently fail to register at all. It's unanswerable.'

'Perhaps so. But we have the curious situation that before January Ottilie Harshom was apparently not on your mental map, but since March she has, without any objective existence, dominated it. So I ask myself, what happened between January and March . . . ?

'Well, I practise medicine. I have certain connections, I am able to learn the external facts. One day late in January you were invited, along with several other people, to witness a demonstration in one of your Company's laboratories. I was not told the details, I doubt if I would understand them if I were: the atmosphere around the higher flights of modern physics is so rarefied – but I gather that during this demonstration something went amiss. There was an explosion, or an implosion, or perhaps a matter of a few atoms driven berserk by provocation, in any case, the place was wrecked. One man was killed outright, another died later, several were injured. You yourself were not badly hurt. You did get a few cuts, and bruises – nothing serious, but you were knocked out – right out . . .

'You were, indeed, so thoroughly knocked out that you lay unconscious for twenty-four days . . .

'And when at last you did come round you displayed symptoms of considerable confusion – more strongly, perhaps, than would be expected in a patient of your age and type, and you were given sedatives. The following night you slept restlessly, and showed signs of mental distress. In particular you called again and again for someone named Ottilie.

'The hospital made what inquiries they could, but none of your friends or relatives knew of anyone called Ottilie associated with you.

'You began to recover, but it was clear you had something heavily on your mind. You refused to reveal what it was, but you did ask one of the doctors whether he could have his secretary try to find the name Ottilie Harshom in any directory. When it could not be found, you became depressed. However, you did not raise the matter again – at least, I am told you did not – until after your discharge when you set out on this quest for Ottilie Harshom, in which, in spite of completely negative results, you continue.

'Now, what must one deduce from that?' He paused to look across the table at his guest, left eyebrow raised.

'That you are even better informed than I thought,' Colin said, without encouragement. 'If I were your patient your inquiries might be justified, but as I am not, and have not the least intention of consulting you professionally, I regard them as intrusive, and possibly unethical.'

If he had expected his host to be put out he was disappointed. The doctor continued to regard him with interested detachment.

'I'm not yet entirely convinced that you ought not to be someone's patient,' he remarked. 'However, let me tell you why it was I, rather than another Harshom, who was led to make these inquiries. Perhaps you may then think them less impertinent. But I am going to preface that with a warning against false hopes. You must understand that the Ottilie Harshom you are seeking *does not exist and has not existed*. That is quite definite.

'Nevertheless, there *is* one aspect of this matter which puzzled me greatly, and that I cannot bring myself to dismiss as coincidence. You see, the name Ottilie Harshom was not entirely unknown to me. No –' He raised his hand. '– I repeat, no false hopes. There *is no* Ottilie Harshom, but there has been – or, rather, there have in the past been, two Ottilie Harshoms.'

Colin Trafford's resentful manner had entirely dropped away. He sat, leaning a little forward, watching his host intently.

'But,' the doctor emphasized, 'It was all long ago. The first was my grandmother. She was born in 1832, married Grandfather Harshom in 1861, and died in 1866. The other was my sister: she, poor little thing, was born in 1884 and died in 1890 . . .'

He paused again. Colin made no comment. He went on:

'I am the only survivor of this branch so it is not altogether surprising that the others have forgotten there was ever such a name in the family, but when I heard of your inquiries I said to myself: There is something out of order here. Ottilie is not the rarest of names, but on any scale of popularity it would come a very long way down indeed; and Harshom is a rare name. The odds against these two being coupled by mere chance must be some quite astronomical figure. Something so large that I cannot believe it is chance. Somewhere there must be a link, some cause . . .

'So, I set out to discover if I could find out why this young man Trafford should have hit upon this improbable conjunction of names – and, seemingly, become obsessed by it. You would not care to help me at this point?'

Colin continued to look at him, but said nothing.

'No? Very well. When I had all the available data assembled the conclusion I had to draw was this: that as a result of your accident you underwent some kind of traumatic experience, an experience of considerable intensity as well as unusual quality. Its intensity one deduces from your subsequent fixation of purpose; the unusual quality partly from the pronounced state of confusion in which you regained consciousness, and partly from the consistency with which you deny recollecting anything from the moment of the accident until you awoke.

'Now, if that were indeed a blank, why did you awake in such a confused condition? There must have been some recollection to cause it. And if there was something akin to ordinary dream images, why this refusal to speak of them? There must have been, therefore, some experience of great personal significance wherein the name Ottilie Harshom was a very potent element indeed.

'Well, Mr Trafford. Is the reasoning good, the conclusion valid? Let me suggest, as a physician, that such things are a burden that should be shared.'

Colin considered for some little time, but when he still did not speak the doctor added:

'You are almost at the end of the road, you know. Only two more Harshoms on the list, and I assure you they won't be able to help – so what then?'

Colin said, in a flat voice:

'I expect you are right. You should know. All the same, I must see them. There might be something, some clue . . . I can't neglect the least possibility . . . I had just a little hope when you invited me here. I knew that you had a family . . .'

'I *had*,' the doctor said, quietly. 'My son Malcolm was killed racing at Brooklands in 1927. He was unmarried. My daughter married, but she had no children. She was killed in a raid on London in 1941 . . . So there it ends . . .' He shook his head slowly.

'I am sorry,' said Colin. Then: 'Have you a picture of your daughter that I may see?'

'She wasn't of the generation you are looking for.'

'I realize that, but nevertheless . . .'

'Very well – when we return to the study. Meanwhile, you've not yet said what you think of my reasoning.'

'Oh, it was good.'

'But you are still disinclined to talk about it? Well, I am not. And I can still go a little further. Now, this experience of yours cannot have been of a kind to cause a feeling of shame or disgust, or you would be trying to sublimate it in some way, which manifestly you are not. Therefore it is highly probable that the cause of your silence is fear. Something makes you afraid to discuss the experience. You are not, I am satisfied, afraid of facing it; therefore your fear must be of the consequences of communicating it. Consequences possibly to someone else, but much more probably to yourself . . .'

Colin went on regarding him expressionlessly for a moment. Then he relaxed a little and leaned back in his chair. For the first time he smiled faintly.

'You do get there, in the end, don't you, Doctor? But do you mind if I say that you make quite Germanically heavy-going of it? And the whole thing is so simple, really. It boils down to this. If a man, any man, claims to have had an experience which is outside all normal experience, it will be inferred, will it not, that he is in some way not quite a normal man? In that case, he cannot be entirely relied upon to react to a particular situation as a normal man should – and if his reactions may be non-normal, how can he be really dependable? He may be, of course – but would it not be sounder policy to put authority into the hands of a man about whom there is *no* doubt? Better to be on the safe side. So he is passed over. His failure to make the expected step is not unnoticed. A small cloud, a mere wrack, of doubt and risk begins to gather above him. It is tenuous, too insubstantial for him to disperse, yet it casts a faint, persistent shadow.

'There is, I imagine, no such thing as a normal human being, but there is a widespread feeling that there ought to be. Any organization has a conception of "the type of man we want here", which is regarded as the normal for its purposes. So every man there attempts more or less to accord to it – organizational man, in fact – and anyone who diverges more than slightly from the type in either his public, or in his private life does so to the peril of his career. There is, as you said, fear of the results to myself: it is, as I said, so simple.'

'True enough,' the doctor agreed. 'But you have not taken any care to disguise the consequence of the experience – the hunt for Ottilie Harshom.'

'I don't need to. Could anything be more reassuringly normal than "man seeks girl?" I have invented a background which has quite satisfied any interested friends – and even several Harshoms.'

'I dare say. None of them being aware of the "coincidence" in the conjunction of "Ottilie" with "Harshom". But I am.'

He waited for Colin Trafford to make some comment on that. When none came, he went on:

'Look, my boy. You have this business very heavily on your mind. There are only the two of us here. I have no links whatever with your firm. My profession should be enough safeguard for your confidence, but I will undertake a special guarantee if you like. It will do you good to unburden – and I should like to get to the bottom of this . . .'

But Colin shook his head.

'You won't, you know. Even if I were to tell you, you'd only be the more mystified – as I am.'

'Two heads are better than one. We could try,' said the doctor, and waited.

Colin considered again, for some moments. Then he lifted his gaze, and met the doctor's steadily.

'Very well then. I've tried. You shall try. But first I would like to see a picture of your daughter. Have you one taken when she was about twenty-five?'

They left the table and went back to the study. The doctor waved Colin to a chair, and crossed to a corner cupboard. He took out a small pile of cardboard mounts and looked though them. He selected three, gazed at them thoughtfully for a few seconds, and then handed them over. While Colin studied them he busied himself with pouring brandy from a decanter.

Presently Colin looked up.

'No,' he said. 'And yet there is something . . .' He tried covering parts of the full-face portrait with his hand. 'Something about the setting and shape of the eyes – but not quite. The brow, perhaps, but it's difficult to tell with the hair done like that . . .' He pondered the photographs a little longer, and then handed them back. 'Thank you for letting me see them.'

The doctor picked up one of the others and passed it over.

'This was Malcolm, my son.'

It showed a laughing young man standing by the forepart of a car which bristled with exhaust manifold and had its bonnet held down by straps.

'He loved that car,' said the doctor, 'but it was too fast for the old track there. It went over the banking, and hit a tree.'

He took the picture back, and handed Colin a glass of brandy.

Colin swirled it. Neither of them spoke for some little time. Then he tasted the brandy, and, presently, lit a cigarette.

'Very well,' he said again. 'I'll try to tell you. But first I'll tell you what *happened* – whether it was subjective, or not, it happened for me. The implications and so on we can look at later – if you want to.'

'Good,' agreed the doctor. 'But tell me first, do we start from the moment of the accident – or was there anything at all relevant before that?'

'No.' Colin Trafford said, 'that's where it *does* start.'

It was just another day. Everything and everybody perfectly ordinary – except that this demonstration was something a bit special. What it concerned is not my secret, and not, as far as I know, relevant. We all gathered round the apparatus. Deakin, who was in charge, pulled down a switch. Something began to hum, and then to whine, like a motor running faster and faster. The whine became a shriek as it went up the scale. There was a quite piercingly painful moment or two near the threshold of audibility, then a sense of relief because it was over and gone, with everything seeming quiet again. I was looking across at Deakin watching his dials, with his fingers held ready over the switches, and then, just as I was in the act of turning my head towards the demonstration again, there was a flash . . . I didn't hear anything, or feel anything: there was just this dazzling white flash . . . Then nothing but black . . . I heard people crying out, and a woman's voice screaming . . . screaming . . . screaming . . .

I felt crushed by a great weight. I opened my eyes. A sharp pain jabbed through them into my head, but I struggled against the weight, and found it was due to two or three people being on top of me; so I managed to shove a couple of them off, and sit up. There were several other people lying about on the ground, and a few more picking themselves up. A couple of feet to my left was a large wheel. I looked further up and found that it was attached to a bus – a bus that from my position seemed to tower like a scarlet skyscraper, and appeared, moreover, to be tilted and about to fall on me. It caused me to get up very quickly, and as I did I grabbed a young woman who had been lying across my legs, and dragged her to a safer place. Her face was dead white, and she was unconscious.

I looked around. It wasn't difficult to see what had happened. The bus, which must have been travelling at a fair speed, had, for some reason got out of control, run across the crowded pavement, and through the plate-glass window of a shop. The forepart of the top deck had been telescoped against the front of the building, and it was up there that the screaming was going on. Several people were still lying on the ground, a woman moving feebly, a man groaning, two or three more quite still. Three streams of blood were meandering slowly across the pavement among the crystals of broken glass. All the traffic had stopped, and I could see a couple of policemen's helmets bobbing through the crowd towards us.

I moved my arms and legs experimentally. They worked perfectly well, and painlessly. But I felt dazed, and my head throbbed. I put my hand up to it and discovered a quite tender spot where I must have taken a blow on the left occiput.

The policemen got through. One of them started pushing back the gaping bystanders, the other took a look at the casualties on the ground. A third appeared and went up to the top deck of the bus to investigate the screaming there.

I tried to conquer my daze, and looked round further. The place was Regent Street, a little up from Piccadilly Circus; the wrecked window was one of Austin Reed's. I looked up again at the bus. It was certainly tilted, but not in danger of toppling, for it was firmly wedged into the window opening to within a yard of the word 'General', gleaming in gold letters on its scarlet side.

At this point it occurred to me that I was supernumerary, and that if I were to hang around much longer I should find myself roped in as a witness – not, mind you, that I would grudge being a witness in the ordinary way, if it would do anyone any good, but I was suddenly and acutely aware that this was not at all in the ordinary way. For one thing I had no knowledge of anything whatever but the aftermath – and, for another, what was I doing here anyway . . . ? One moment I had been watching a demonstration out at Watford; the next, there was this. How the devil did I come to be in Regent Street at all . . . ?

I quietly edged my way into the crowd, then out of it again, zigzagged across the road amid the held-up traffic and headed for the Café Royal, a bit further down.

They seemed to have done things to the old place since I was there last, a couple of years before, but the important thing was to find the bar, and that I did, without difficulty.

'A double brandy, and some soda,' I told the barman.

He gave it me, and slid along the siphon. I pulled some money out of my pocket, coppers and a little small silver. So I made to reach for my notecase.

'Half a crown, sir,' the barman told me, as if fending off a note.

I blinked at him. Still, he had said it. I slid over three shillings. He seemed gratified.

I added soda to the brandy, and took a welcome drink. It was as I was putting the glass down that I caught sight of myself in the mirror behind the bar . . .

I used to have a moustache. I came out of the Army with it, but decided to jettison it when I went up to Cambridge. But there it was – a little less luxuriant, perhaps, but resurrected. I put up my hand and felt it. There was no illusion, and it was genuine, too. At almost the same moment I noticed my suit. Now, I used to have a suit pretty much like that, years ago. Not at all a bad suit either, but still, not quite the thing we organization men wear in EPI . . .

I had a swimming sensation, took another drink of the brandy, and felt, a little unsteadily, for a cigarette. The packet I pulled out of my pocket was unfamiliar – have you ever beard of Player's 'Mariner' cigarettes – No? Neither had I, but I got one out, and lit it with a very unsteady match. The dazed feeling was not subsiding; it was growing, rapidly . . .

I felt for my inside pocket. No wallet. It should have been there – perhaps some opportunist in the crowd round the bus had got it . . . I sought through the other pockets – a fountain-pen, a bunch of keys, a couple of cash receipts from Harrods, a cheque book – containing cheques addressed to the Knightsbridge branch of the Westminster Bank. Well, the bank was all right, but why Knightsbridge? – I live in Hampstead . . .

To try to get some kind of grip on things I began to recapitulate from the moment I had opened my eyes and found the bus towering over me. It was quite vivid. I had a sharp recollection of staring up at that scarlet menace, with the gilded word 'General' shining brightly . . . yes, in gleaming gold – only, as you know, the word 'General' hasn't been seen on London buses since it was replaced by 'London Transport' in 1933 . . .

I was getting a little rattled by now, and looked round the bar for something to steady my wits. On one table I noticed a newspaper that someone had discarded. I went across to fetch it, and got carefully back on to my stool before I looked at it. Then I took a deep breath and regarded the front page. My first response was dismay for the whole thing was given up to a single display advertisement. Yet there was some reassurance, of a kind, at the top, for it read: 'Daily Mail, London, Wednesday 27 January 1954.' So it was at least the right day – the one we had fixed for the demonstration at the labs.

I turned to the middle page, and read: 'Disorders in Delhi. One of the greatest exhibitions of Civil disobedience so far staged in India took place here today demanding the immediate release of Nehru from prison. For nearly all the hours of daylight the city has been at a standstill —' Then an item in an adjoining column caught my eye: 'In answer to a question from the Opposition front bench Mr Butler, the Prime Minister, assured the House that the Government was giving serious consideration —' In a dizzy way I glanced at the top of the page: the date there agreed with that on the front, 27 January 1954, but just below it there was a picture with the caption: 'A scene from last night's production of *The Lady Loves*, at the Laughton Theatre, in which Miss Amanda Coward plays the lead in the last of her father's many musical plays. *The Lady Loves* was completed only a few days before Noel Coward's death last August, and a moving tribute to his memory was paid at the end of the performance by Mr Ivor Novello who directed the production.'

I read that again, with care. Then I looked up and about, for reassurance, at my fellow drinkers, at the furniture, at the barman, at the bottles: it was all convincingly real.

I dropped the paper, and finished the rest of my brandy. I could have done with another, but it would have been awkward if, with my wallet gone, the barman should change his mind about his modest price. I glanced at my watch – and there was a thing, too! It was a very nice watch, gold, with a crocodile strap, and hands that stood at twelve-thirty, but I had never seen it before. I took it off and looked at the back. There was a pretty bit of engraving there; it said: 'C. for ever O. 10.x.50.' And it jolted me quite a little, for 1950 was the year I was married – though not in October, and not to anyone called O. My wife's name was Della. Mechanically I restrapped the watch on my wrist, and left.

The interlude and the brandy had done me some good. When I stepped out into Regent Street again I was feeling less dazed (though, if it is not too fine a distinction, more bewildered) and my head had almost ceased to ache, so that I was able to pay more attention to the world about me.

At first sight Piccadilly Circus gave an impression of being much as usual, and yet a suggestion that there was something a bit wrong with it. After a few moments I perceived that it was the people and the cars. Surprising numbers of the men and women, too, wore clothing that looked shabby, and the flower-girls below Eros seemed like bundles of rags. The look of the women who were not shabby took me completely aback. Almost without exception their hats were twelve-inch platter-like things balanced on the top of their heads. The skirts were long, almost to their ankles, and, worn under fur coats, gave an impression that they were dressed for the evening, at midday. Their shoes were pointed, over-ornamented, pin-heeled and quite hideous. I suppose all high-fashion would look ludicrous if one were to come upon it unprepared, but then one never does – at least one never had until now . . . I might have felt like Rip van Winkle newly awakened, but for the date line on that newspaper . . . The cars were odd, too. They seemed curiously high-built, small, and lacking in the flashy effects one had grown accustomed to, and when I paid more attention I did not see one make I could readily identify – except a couple of unmistakable Rolls.

While I stood staring curiously a plate-hatted lady in a well-worn fur-coat posted herself beside me and addressed me as 'dearie' in a somewhat grim way. I decided to move on, and headed for Piccadilly. On the way, I looked across at St James's Church. The last time I had seen it it was clothed in scaffolding, with a hoarding in the garden to help to raise funds for the rebuilding – that would have been about a fortnight before – but now all that had gone, and it looked as if it had never been bombed at all. I crossed the road to inspect it more closely, and was still more impressed with the wonderful job they had made of the restoration.

Presently I found myself in front of Hatchard's window, and paused to examine their contents. Some of the books had authors whose names I knew; I saw works by Priestley, C. S. Lewis, Bertrand Russell, T. S. Eliot, and others, but scarcely a title that I recognized. And then, down in the front, my eye was caught by a book in a predominantly pink jacket: *Life's Young Day*, a novel by Colin Trafford.

I went on goggling at it, probably with my mouth open. I once had ambitions in that direction, you know. If it had not been for the war I'd probably have taken an Arts degree, and tried my hand at it, but as things happened I made a friend in the regiment who turned me to science, *and* could put me in the way of a job with EPI later. Therefore it took me a minute or two to recover from the coincidence of seeing my name on the cover, and, when I did, my curiosity was still strong enough to take me into the shop.

There I discovered a pile of half a dozen copies lying on a table. I picked up the top one, and opened it. The name was plain enough on the title-page – and opposite was a list of seven other titles under 'author of'. I did not recognize the publisher's name, but overleaf there was the announcement: 'First published January 1954'.

I turned it over in my hand, and then all but dropped it. On the back was a picture of the author; undoubtedly me – and with the moustache . . . The floor seemed to tilt slightly beneath my feet.

Then, somewhere over my shoulder, there was a voice; one that I seemed to recognize. It said:

'Well met, Narcissus! Doing a bit of sales-promotion, eh? How's it going?'

'Martin!' I exclaimed. I had never been so glad to see anyone in all my life. 'Martin. Why we've not met since – when was it?'

'Oh, for at least three days, old boy,' he said, looking a little surprised.

Three days! I'd seen a lot of Martin Falls at Cambridge, but only run across him twice since we came down, and the last of those was two years ago. But he went on:

'What about a spot of lunch, if you're not booked?' he suggested.

And that wasn't quite right either. I'd not heard anyone speak of a *spot* of lunch for years. However, I did my best to feel as if things were becoming more normal.

'Fine,' I said, 'but you'll have to pay. I've had my wallet pinched.'

He clicked his tongue.

'Hope there wasn't much in it. Anyway, what about the club? They'll cash you a cheque there.'

I put the book I was still holding back on the pile, and we left.

'Funny thing,' Martin said. 'Just run into Tommy – Tommy Westhouse. Sort of blowing sulphur – hopping mad with his American agent. You remember that god-awful thing of Tommy's – *The Thornèd Rose* – kind of Ben Hur meets Cleopatra, with the Marquis de Sade intervening? Well, it seems this agent —' He rambled on with a shoppy, anecdotal recital full of names that meant nothing to me, but lasted through several streets and brought us almost to Pall Mall. At the end of it he said: 'You didn't tell me how *Life's Young Day*'s doing. Somebody said it was over-subscribed. Saw the Lit Sup wagged a bit of a finger at you. Not had time to read it myself yet. Too much on hand.'

I chose the easier – the non-committal way. It seemed easier than trying to understand, so I told him it was doing just about as expected.

The Club, when in due course we reached it, turned out to be the Savage. I am not a member, but the porter greeted me by name, as though I were in the habit of dropping in every day.

'Just a quick one,' Martin suggested. 'Then we'll look in and see George about your cheque.'

I had misgivings over that, but it went off all right, and during lunch I did my best to keep my end up. I had the same troubles that I have now – true it was from the other end, but the principle still holds: if things are *too* queer people will find it easier to think you are potty than to help you; so keep up a front.

I am afraid I did not do very well. Several times I caught Martin glancing at me with a perplexed expression. Once he asked: 'Quite sure you're feeling all right, old man?'

But the climax did not come until, with cheese on his plate, he reached out his left hand for a stick of celery. And as he did so I noticed the gold signet ring on his little finger, and that jolted me right out of my caution – for, you see, Martin doesn't have a little finger on his left hand, or a third finger, either. He left both of them somewhere near the Rhine in 1945 . . .

'Good God!' I exclaimed. For some reason that pierced me more sharply than anything yet. He turned his face towards me.

'What on earth's the matter, man? You're as white as a sheet.'

'Your hand —' I said.

He glanced at it curiously, and then back at me, even more curiously.

'Looks all right to me,' he said, eyes a little narrowed.

'But – but you lost the two last fingers – in the war,' I exclaimed. His eyebrows rose, and then came down in an anxious frown. He said, with kind intention:

'Got it a bit mixed, haven't you, old man? Why, the war was over before I was born.'

Well, it goes a bit hazy just after that, and when it got coherent again I was lying back in a big chair, with Martin sitting close beside, saying:

'So take my advice, old man. Just you trot along to the quack this afternoon. Must've taken a bit more of a knock than you thought, you know. Funny thing, the brain – can't be too careful. Well, I'll have to go now I'm afraid. Appointment. But don't you put it off. Risky. Let me know how it goes.' And then he was gone.

I lay back in the chair. Curiously enough I was feeling far more myself than I had since I came to on the pavement in Regent Street. It was as if the biggest jolt yet had shaken me out of the daze, and got the gears of my wits into mesh again. I was glad to be rid of Martin, and able to think.

I looked round the lounge. As I said, I am not a member, and did not know the place well enough to be sure of details, but I rather thought the arrangement was a little different, and the carpet, and some of the light fittings, from when I saw it last . . .

There were few people around. Two talking in a corner, three napping, two more reading papers; none taking any notice of me. I went over to the periodicals table, and brought back *The New Statesman*, dated 22 January 1954. The front page leader was advocating the nationalization of transport as a first step towards putting the means of production into the hands of the people and so ending unemployment. There was a wave of nostalgia about that. I turned on, glancing at articles which baffled me for lack of context. I was glad to find Critic present, and I noticed that among the things that were currently causing him concern was some experimental work going on in Germany. His misgivings were, it seemed, shared by several eminent scientists, for, while there was little doubt now that nuclear fission was a theoretical possibility, the proposed methods of control were inadequate. There could well be a chain reaction resulting in a disaster of cosmic proportions. A consortium which included names famous in the Arts as well as many illustrious in the sciences was being formed to call upon the League of Nations to protest to the German government in the name of humanity against reckless research . . .

Well, well . . . !

With returning confidence in myself I sat and pondered.

Gradually, and faintly at first, something began to glimmer . . . Not anything about the how, or the why – I still have no useful theories about those – but about *what* could conceivably have happened.

It was vague – set off, perhaps, by the thought of that random neutron which I knew in one set of circumstances to have been captured by a uranium atom, but which, in another set of circumstances, apparently had not . . .

And there, of course, one was brought up against Einstein and relativity which, as you know, denies the possibility of determining motion absolutely and consequently leads into the idea of the four-dimensional space-time continuum. Well, then, since you cannot determine the motions of the factors in the continuum, any pattern of motion must be illusory, and there cannot be any determinable consequences. Nevertheless, where the factors are closely similar – are composed of similar atoms in roughly the same relation to the continuum, so to speak – you *may* quite well get similar consequences. They can never be identical, of course, or determination of motion would be possible. But they could be very similar, and capable of consideration in terms of Einstein's Special Theory, and they *could* be determined further by a set of closely similar factors. In other words although the infinite point which we may call a moment in 1954 *must* occur throughout the continuum, it *exists* only in relation to each observer, and *appears* to have similar existence in relation to certain close groups of observers. However, since no two observers can be identical – that is, the same observer – each must perceive a different past, present, and future from that perceived by any other; consequently,

273

what he perceives arises only from the factors of his relationship to the continuum, and exists only for him.

Therefore I began to understand that *what* had happened must be this: in some way – which I cannot begin to grasp – I had somehow been translated to the position of a different observer – one whose angle of view was in some respects very close to my own, and yet different enough to have relationships, and therefore realities, unperceived by me. In other words, he must have lived in a world real only to him, just as I had lived in a world real only to me – until this very peculiar transposition had occurred to put me in the position of observing *his* world, with, of course, its relevant past and future, instead of the one I was accustomed to.

Mind you, simple as it is when you consider it, I certainly did not grasp the form of it all at once, but I did argue my way close enough to the observer-existence relationship to decide that whatever might have gone amiss, my own mind was more or less all right. The trouble really seemed to be that it was in the wrong place, and getting messages not intended for me; a receiver somehow hooked into the wrong circuit.

Well, that's not good, in fact, it's bad; but it's still a lot better than a faulty receiver. And it braced me a bit to realize that.

I sat there quite a time trying to get it clear, and wondering what I should do, until I came to the end of my packet of 'Mariner' cigarettes. Then I went to the telephone.

First I dialled Electro-Physical Industries. Nothing happened. I looked them up in the book. It was quite a different number, on a different exchange. So I dialled that.

'Extension one three three,' I told the girl on the desk, and then, on second thoughts, named my own department.

'Oh. You want Extension five nine.' she told me.

Somebody answered. I said:

'I'd like to speak to Mr Colin Trafford.'

'I'm sorry. We've no one of that name in this department,' the voice told me.

Back to the desk. Then a longish pause.

'I'm sorry,' said the girl. 'I can't find that name on our staff list.'

I hung up. So, evidently, I was not employed by EPI. I thought a moment, and then dialled my Hampstead number. It answered promptly. 'Transcendental Belts and Corsets,' it announced brightly. I put down the receiver.

It occurred to me to look myself up in the book. I was there, all right: 'Trafford, Colin W., 54 Hogarth Court, Duchess Gardens, S.W.7.

SLOane 67021.' So I tried that. The phone at the other end rang . . .
and went on ringing . . .

I came out of the box wondering what to do next. It was an
extremely odd feeling to be bereft of orientation, rather as if one had
been dropped abruptly into a foreign city without even a hotel room
for a base – and somehow made worse by the city being foreign only in
minor and personal details.

After further reflection I decided that the best protective colouration
would come from doing what this Colin Trafford might reasonably be
expected to do. If he had no work to do at EPI, he did at least have a
home to go to . . .

A nice block of flats, Hogarth Court, springy carpet and illuminated
floral arrangement in the hall, that sort of thing, but, at the moment no
porter in view, so I went straight to the lift. The place did not look big
enough to contain fifty-four flats, so I took a chance on the five
meaning the fifth floor, and sure enough I stepped out to find 54 on the
door facing me. I took out my bunch of keys, tried the most likely one,
and it fitted.

Inside was a small hall. Nothing distinctive – white paint, lightly
patterned paper, close maroon carpet, occasional table with telephone
and a few flowers in a vase, with a nice guilt-framed mirror above, the
hard occasional chair, a passage off, lots of doors. I paused.

'Hullo,' I said, experimentally. Then a little louder: 'Hullo! Anyone
at home?'

Neither voice nor sound responded. I closed the door behind me.
What now? Well – well, hang it, I was – am – Colin Trafford! I took off
my overcoat. Nowhere to put it. Second try revealed the coat closet . . .
Several other coats already in there. Male and female, a woman's
overshoes, too . . . I added mine.

I decided to get the geography of the place, and see what home was
really like . . .

Well, you won't want an inventory, but it was a nice flat. Larger
than I had thought at first. Well furnished and arranged; not with
extravagance, but not with stint, either. It showed taste, too; though
not my taste – but what is taste? Either feeling for period, or refined
selection from a fashion. I could feel that this was the latter, but the
fashion was strange to me, and therefore lacked attraction . . .

The kitchen was interesting. A fridge, no washer, single-sink, no
plate racks, no laminated tops, old-fashioned looking electric cooker,
packet of soap powder, no synthetic detergents, curious lighting panel
about three feet square in the ceiling, no mixer . . .

The sitting-room was airy, chairs comfortable. Nothing spindly. A large radiogram, rather ornate, no FM on its scale. Lighting again by ceiling panels, and square things like glass cake-boxes on stands. No television.

I prowled round the whole place. Bedroom feminine, but not fussy. Twin beds. Bathroom tiled, white. Spare bedroom, small double-bed. And so on. But it was a room at the end of the passage that interested me most. A sort of study. One wall all bookshelves, some of the books familiar – the older ones – others not. An easy-chair, a lighter chair. In front of the window a broad, leather-topped desk, with a view across the bare-branched trees in the Gardens, roofs beyond, plenty of sky. On the desk a covered typewriter, adjustable lamp, several folders with sheets of paper untidily projecting, cigarette box, metal ashtray, clean and empty, and a photograph in a leather frame.

I looked at the photograph carefully. A charming study. She'd be perhaps twenty-four – twenty-five? Intelligent, happy-looking, somebody one would like to know – but not anyone I did know . . .

There was a cupboard on the left of the desk, and, on it, a glass-fronted case with eight books in it; the rest was empty. The books were all in bright paper jackets, looking as new. The one on the right-hand end was the same that I had seen in Hatchard's that morning – *Life's Young Day*; all the rest, too, bore the name Colin Trafford. I sat down in the swivel chair at the desk and pondered them for some moments. Then, with a curious, schizoid feeling I pulled out *Life's Young Day*, and opened it.

It was, perhaps, half an hour, or more, later that I caught the sound of a key in the outer door. I laid down the book, and thought rapidly. I decided that, on the whole, it would be better to disclose myself than wait to be discovered. So I opened the door. Along at the end of the passage a figure in a three-quarter-length grey suède coat which showed a tweed skirt beneath was dumping parcels on to the hall table. At the sound of my door she turned her head. It was the original of the photograph, all right; but not in the mood of the photograph. As I approached, she looked at me with an expression of surprise, mixed with other feelings that I could not identify; but certainly it was not an adoring-wife-greets-devoted-husband look.

'Oh,' she said. 'You're in. What happened?'

'Happened?' I repeated, I repeated, feeling for a lead.

'Well, I understood you had one of those so-important meeting with Dickie at the BBC fixed for this afternoon,' she said, a little curtly I thought.

'Oh. Oh, that, yes. Yes, he had to put it off,' I replied, clumsily.

She stopped still, and inspected me carefully. A little oddly, too, I thought. I stood looking at her, wondering what to do, and wishing I had had the sense to think up some kind of plan for this inevitable meeting instead of wasting my time over *Life's Young Day*. I hadn't even had the sense to find out her name. It was clear that I'd got away wrong somehow the moment I opened my mouth. Besides, there was a quality about her that upset my balance altogether . . . It hit me in a way I'd not known for years, and more shrewdly than it had then . . . Somehow, when you are thirty-three you don't expect these things to happen – well, not to happen quite like that, any more . . . Not with a great surge in your heart, and everything coming suddenly bright and alive as if she had just switched it all into existence . . .

So we stood looking at one another; she with a half-frown, I trying to cope with a turmoil of elation and confusion, unable to say a word.

She glanced down, and began to unbutton her coat. She, too, seemed uncertain.

'If —' she began. But at that moment the telephone rang.

With an air of welcoming the interruption, she picked up the receiver. In the quiet of the hall I could hear a woman's voice ask for Colin.

'Yes,' she said, 'he's here.' And she held the receiver out to me, with a very curious look.

'Hullo,' I said. 'Colin here.'

'Oh, indeed,' replied the voice, 'and why, may I ask?'

'Er – I don't quite —' I began, but she cut me short.

'Now, look here, Colin, I've already wasted an hour waiting for you, thinking that if you couldn't come you might at least have had the decency to ring me up and tell me. Now I find you're just sitting at home. Not quite good enough, Colin.'

'I – um – Who is it? Who's speaking?' was the only temporizing move I could think of. I was acutely conscious that the young woman beside me was frozen stock-still in the act of taking off her coat.

'Oh, for God's sake,' said the voice, exasperated. 'What silly game is this? Who do you think it is?'

'That's what I'm asking,' I said.

'Oh, don't be such a clown, Colin. If it's because Ottilie's still there – and I bet she is – you're just being stupid. She answered the phone herself, so she knows it's me.'

'Then perhaps I'd better ask her who you are,' I suggested.

'Oh – you must be tight as an owl. Go and sleep it off,' she snapped, and the phone went dead.

I put the receiver back in the rest. The young woman was looking at me with an expression of genuine bewilderment. In the quietness of the hall she must have been able to hear the other voice almost as clearly as I had. She turned away, and busied herself with taking her coat off and putting it on a hanger in the closet. When she'd carefully done that she turned back.

'I don't understand,' she said. 'You aren't tight, are you? What's it all about? What has dear Dickie done?'

'Dickie?' I inquired. The slight furrow between her brows deepened.

'Oh, really, Colin. If you think I don't know Dickie's voice on the telephone by this time.'

'Oh,' I said. A bloomer of a peculiarly cardinal kind, that. In fact, it is hard to think of a more unlikely mistake than that a man should confuse the gender of his friends. Unless I wanted to be thought quite potty, I must take steps to clarify the situation.

'Look, can't we go into the sitting-room. There's something I want to tell you,' I suggested.

She watched me thoughtfully.

'I think perhaps I'd rather not hear it, Colin.'

'Please,' I said. 'It's important. It really is . . .'

She hesitated, and then consented, reluctantly.

'Oh, very well, if you must . . .'

We went in. She switched on the heater, and sat down. 'Well?' she asked.

I took the chair opposite, and wondered how to begin. Even if I had been clear in my own mind about what had happened, it would have been difficult enough. But how to convey that though the physical form was Colin Trafford's, and I myself was Colin Trafford, yet I was not that Colin Trafford; not the one who wrote books and was married to her, but a kind of alternative Colin Trafford astray from an alternative world? What seemed to be wanted was some kind of approach which would not immediately suggest a call for an alienist – and it wasn't easy to perceive.

'Well?' she repeated.

'It's difficult to explain,' I temporized, but truthfully enough.

'I'm sure it is,' she replied, without encouragement, and added: 'Would it perhaps be easier if you didn't look at me like that? I'd prefer it, too.'

'Something very odd has happened to me,' I told her.

'Oh dear, again?' she said. 'Do you want my sympathy, or something?'

I was taken aback, and a little confused.

'Do you mean it's happened to him before?' I asked.

She looked at me hard.

'Him? Who's him? I thought you were talking about you. And what I mean is last time it happened it was Dickie, and the time before that it was Frances, and before that it was Lucy . . . And now you've given Dickie a most peculiar kind of brush-off . . . Am I supposed to be surprised . . . ?

I was learning about my *alter ego* quite fast, but we were off the track. I tried:

'No, you don't understand. This is something quite different.'

'Of course not. Wives never do, do they? And it's always different. Well, if that's all that's so important . . .' She began to get up.

'No, please . . .' I said anxiously.

She checked herself, looking very carefully at me again. The half-frown came back.

'No,' she said. 'No, I don't think I do understand. At least, I – I hope not . . .' And she went on examining me, with something like growing uncertainty, I thought.

When you plead for understanding you can scarcely keep it on an impersonal basis, but when you don't know whether the best address would be 'my dear' or 'darling,' or some more intimate variant, nor whether it should be prefaced by first name, nickname, or pet name, the way ahead becomes thorny indeed. Besides, there was this persistent misunderstanding on the wrong level.

'Ottilie, darling,' I tried – and that was clearly no usual form, for, momentarily, her eyes almost goggled, but I ploughed on: 'It isn't at all what you're thinking – nothing a bit like that. It's – well, it's that in a way I'm not the same person . . .'

She was back in charge of herself.

'Oddly enough, I've been aware of that for some time,' she said. 'And I could remind you that you've said something like that before, more than once. All right then, let me go on for you; so you're not the same person I married, so you'd like a divorce – or is it that you're afraid Dickie's husband is going to cite you this time? Oh, God! How sick I am of all this . . .'

'No, no,' I protested desperately. 'It's not that sort of thing at all. Do please be patient. It's a thing that's terribly difficult to explain . . .' I paused, looking at her. That did not make it any easier. Indeed, it was far from helping the rational processes. She sat looking back at me, still with that half-frown, but now it was a little more uneasy than displeased.

'Something *has* happened to you . . .' she said.

'That's what I'm trying to tell you about,' I told her, but I doubt whether she heard it. Her eyes grew wider as she looked. Suddenly they avoided mine.

'No!' she said. 'Oh, *no!*' She looked as if she were about to cry, and wound her fingers tightly together in her lap. She half-whispered: 'Oh, no! . . . Oh, please God, no! . . . Not again . . . Haven't I been hurt enough? . . . I won't . . . I won't . . . !'

Then she jumped up, and, before I was halfway out of my chair, she was out of the room . . .

Colin Trafford paused to light a fresh cigarette, and took his time before going on. At length he pulled his thoughts back.

'Well,' he went on, 'Obviously you will have realized by now that *that* Mrs Trafford was born Ottilie Harshom. It happened in 1928, and she married that Colin Trafford in 1949. Her father was killed in a plane crash in 1938 – I don't remember her ever mentioning his first name. That's unfortunate – there are a lot of things that are unfortunate: had I had any idea that I might be jerked back here I'd have taken more notice of a lot of things. But I hadn't . . . Something exceedingly odd had happened, but that was no reason to suppose that an equally odd thing would happen, in reverse . . .

'I did do my best, out of my own curiosity, to discover when the schism had taken place. There must, as I saw it, have been some point where, perhaps by chance, some pivotal thing had happened, or failed to happen, and finding it could bring one closer to knowing the moment, the atom of time, that had been split by some random neutron to give two atoms of time diverging into different futures. Once that had taken place, consequences gradually accumulating would make the conditions on one plane progressively different from those on the other.

'Perhaps that is always happening. Perhaps chance is continually causing two different outcomes so that in a dimension we cannot perceive there are infinite numbers of planes, some so close to our own and so recently split off that they vary only in minor details, others vastly different. Planes on which some misadventure caused Alexander to be beaten by the Persians, Scipio to fall before Hannibal, Caesar to stay beyond the Rubicon; infinite, infinite planes of the random split and re-split by the random. Who can tell? But, now that we know the Universe for a random place, why not?

'But I couldn't come near fixing the moment. It was, I think, somewhere in late 1926, or early 1927. Further than that one seemed unable to go without the impossible data of quantities of records from both planes for comparison. Something happening, or not happening, about then had brought about results which prevented, among other things, the rise of Hitler, and thus the Second World War – and consequently postponed the achievement of nuclear fission on this plane of our dichotomy – if that is a good word for it.

'Anyway, it was for me, and as I said, simply a matter of incidental curiosity. My active concerns were more immediate. And the really important one was Ottilie . . .

'I have, as you know, been married – and I was fond of my wife. It was, as people say, a successful marriage, and it never occurred to me to doubt that – until this thing happened to me. I don't want to be disloyal to Della now, and I don't think she was unhappy – but I am immensely thankful for one thing: that this did not happen while she was alive: she never knew, because I didn't know then, that I had married the wrong woman – and I hope she never thought it . . .

'And Ottilie had married the wrong man . . . We found that out. Or perhaps one should put it that she had not married the man she thought she had. She had fallen in love with him; and, no doubt, he had loved her, to begin with – but in less than a year she became torn between the part she loved, and the side she detested . . .

'Her Colin Trafford looked like me – right down to the left thumb which had got mixed up in an electric fan and never quite matched the other side – indeed, up to a point, that point somewhere in 1926–27 he *was* me. We had, I gathered, some mannerisms in common, and voices that were similar – though we differed in our emphases, and in our vocabularies, as I learnt from a tape, and in details: the moustache, the way we wore our hair, the scar on the left side of the forehead which was exclusively his, yet, in a sense, I was him and he was me. We had the same parents, the same genes, the same beginning, and – if I was right about the time of the dichotomy – we must have had the same memory of our life, for the first five years or so.

'But, later on, things on our different planes must have run differently for us. Environment, or experiences, had developed qualities in him which, I have to think, lie latent in me – and, I suppose, vice versa.

'I think that's a reasonable assumption, don't you? After all, one begins life with a kind of armature which has individual differences and tendencies, though a common general plan, but whatever is modelled on that armature later consists almost entirely of stuff from contacts and influences. What these had been for the other Colin Trafford I don't know, but I found the results somewhat painful – rather like continually glimpsing oneself in unexpected distorting mirrors.

'There were certain cautions, restraints, and expectations in Ottilie that taught me a number of things about him, too. Moreover, in the next day or two I read his novels attentively. The earliest was not displeasing, but as the dates grew later, and the touch surer I cared less and less for the flavour; no doubt the widening streaks of brutality showed the calculated development of a selling-point, but there was something a little more than that – besides, one has a choice of selling-points . . . With each book I resented seeing my name on the title-page a little more.

'I discovered the current 'work in progress', too. With the help of his notes I could, I believe, have produced a passable forgery, but I knew I would not. If I had to continue his literary career, it would be with my kind of books, not his. But, in any case, I had no need to worry over making a living: what with the war and one thing and another, physics on my own plane was a generation ahead of theirs. Even if they had got as far as radar it was still someone's military secret. I had enough knowledge to pass for a genius, and make my fortune if I cared to use it . . .'

He smiled, and shook his head. He went on:

'You see, once the first shock was over and I had begun to perceive what must have happened, there was no cause for alarm, and, once I had met Ottilie, none for regret. The only problem was adjustment. It helped in general, I found, to try to get back to as much as I could remember of the pre-war world. But details were more difficult: unrecognized friends, lapsed friends, all with unknown histories, some of them with wives, or husbands, I knew (though not necessarily the same ones); some with quite unexpected partners. There were queer moments, too – an encounter with a burly cheerful man in the bar of the Hyde Park Hotel. He didn't know me, but I knew him; the last time I had seen him he was lying by a road with a sniper's bullet through his head. I saw Della, my wife, leaving a restaurant looking happy, with her arm through that of a tall legal-looking type; it was uncanny to have her glance at me as at a complete stranger – I felt as if both of us were ghosts – but I was glad she had got past 1951 all right on that plane. The most awkward part was frequently running into people that it appeared I should know; the other Colin's acquaintanceship was evidently vast and curious. I began to favour the idea of proclaiming a breakdown from overwork, to tide me over for a bit.

'One thing that did not cross my mind was the possibility of what I took to be a unique shift of plane occurring again, this time in reverse . . .

'I am thankful it did not. It would have blighted the three most wonderful weeks in my life. I thought it was, as the engraving on the back of the watch said: "C. forever O".

'I made a tentative attempt to explain to her what I thought had happened, but it wasn't meaning anything to her, so I gave it up. I think she had it worked out for herself that somewhere about a year after we were married I had begun to suffer from overstrain, and that now I had got better and become again the kind of man she had thought I was . . . something like that . . . but theories about it did not interest her much – it was the consequence that mattered . . .

'And how right she was – for me, too. After all, what else did matter? As far as I was concerned, nothing. I was in love. What did it matter *how* I had found the one unknown woman I had sought all my life. I was happy, as I had never expected to be . . . Oh, all the phrases are trite, but "on top of the world" was suddenly, half-ridiculously vivid. I was full of a confidence rather like that of the slightly drunk. I could take anything on. With her beside me I could keep on top of that, or any, world . . . I think she felt like that, too. I'm sure she did. She'd wiped out the bad years. Her faith was re-growing, stronger every day . . . If I'd only known – but how could I know? What could I do . . . ?

Again he stopped talking, and stared into the fire, this time for so long that at last the doctor fidgeted in his chair to recall him, and then added.

'What happened?'

Colin Trafford still had a faraway look.

'Happened?' he repeated. 'If I knew that I could perhaps – but I *don't* know. There's nothing *to* know . . . *It's* random, too. One night I went to sleep with Ottilie beside me – in the morning I woke up in a hospital bed – back here again . . . That's all there was to it. All there is . . . Just random . . .'

In the long interval that followed, Dr Harshom unhurriedly refilled his pipe, lit it with careful attention, assured himself it was burning evenly and drawing well, settled himself back comfortably, and then said, with intentional matter-of-factness:

'It's a pity you don't believe that. If you did, you'd never have begun this search; if you'd come to believe it, you'd have dropped the search before now. No, you believe that there is a pattern or rather, that there were two patterns, closely similar to begin with, but gradually, perhaps logically, becoming more variant – and that you, your psyche, or whatever you like to call it, was the aberrant, the random factor.

'However, let's not go into the philosophical, or metaphysical consideration of what you call the dichotomy now – all that stuff will keep. Let us say that I accept the validity of your experience, for you, but reserve judgement on its nature. I accept it on account of several features – not the least being, as I have said, the astronomical odds

283

against the conjunction of names, Ottilie and Harshom, occurring fortuitously. Of course, you could have seen the name somewhere and lodged it in your subconscious, but that, too, I find, so immensely improbable that I put it aside.

'Very well, then, let us go on from there. Now, you appear to me to have made a number of quite unwarrantable assumptions. You have assumed, for instance, that because an Ottilie Harshom exists on what you call that plane, she must have come into existence on this plane also. I cannot see that that is justified by anything you have told me. That she might have existed here, I admit, for the name Ottilie is in my branch of the family; but the chances of her having no existence at all are considerably greater – did not you yourself mention that you recognized friends who in different circumstances were married to different wives? – is it not, therefore, highly probable that the circumstances which produced an Ottilie Harshom there failed to occur here, with the result that she could not come into existence at all? And, indeed, that must be so.

'Believe me, I am not unsympathetic. I do understand what your feelings must be, but are you not, in effect, in the state we all have known – searching for an ideal young woman who has never been born? We must face the facts: if she exists, or did exist, I should have heard of her, Somerset House would have a record of her, your own extensive researches would have revealed *something* positive. I do urge you for your own good to accept it, my boy. With all this against you, you simply have no case.'

'Only my own positive conviction,' Colin put in. 'It's against reason, I know – but I still have it.'

'You must try to rid yourself of it. Don't you see there are layers of assumptions? If she did exist she might be already married.'

'But to the wrong man,' Colin said promptly.

'Even that does not follow. Your counterpart varied from you, you say. Well, her counterpart if she existed would have had an entirely different upbringing in different circumstances from the other; the probability is that there would only be the most superficial resemblance. You must see that the whole thing goes to holes wherever you touch it with reason.' He regarded Colin for a moment, and shook his head. 'Somewhere at the back of your mind you are giving houseroom to the proposition that unlike causes can produce like results. Throw it out.'

Colin smiled.

'How Newtonian, Doctor. No, a random factor is random. Chance therefore exists.'

'Young man, you're incorrigible,' the doctor told him. 'If there weren't little point in wishing success with the impossible I'd say your tenacity deserves it. As things are, I advise you to apply it to the almost attainable.'

His pipe had gone out, and he lit it again.

'That,' he went on, 'was a professional recommendation. But now, if it isn't too late for you, I'd like to hear more. I don't pretend to guess at the true nature of your experience, but the speculations your plane of might-have-been arouses are fascinating. Not unnaturally one feels a curiosity to know how one's own counterpart made out there – and failing that, how other people's did. Our present Prime Minister, for instance – did both of him get the job? And Sir Winston – or is he not *Sir* Winston over there? – how on earth did he get along with no Second World War to make his talents burgeon? And what about the poor old Labour Party . . . ? The thing provokes endless questions . . .'

After a late breakfast the next morning Dr Harshom helped Colin into his coat in the hall, but held him there for a final word.

'I spent what was left of the night thinking about this,' he said, earnestly. 'Whatever the explanation may be, you must write it down, every detail you can remember. Do it anonymously if you like, but do it. It may not be unique, someday it may give valuable confirmation of someone else's experience, or become evidence in support of some theory. So put it on record – but then leave it at that . . . Do your best to forget the assumptions you jumped at – they're unwarranted in a dozen ways. *She does not exist.* The only Ottilie Harshoms there have been in this world died long ago. Let the mirage fade. But thank you for your confidence. Though I am inquisitive, I am discreet. If there should be any way I can help you . . .'

Presently he was watching the car down the drive. Colin waved a hand just before it disappeared round the corner. Dr Harshom shook his head. He knew he might as well have saved his breath, but he felt in duty bound to make one last appeal. Then he turned back into the house, frowning. Whether the obsession was a fantasy, or something more than a fantasy, was almost irrelevant to the fact that sooner or later the young man was going to drive himself into a breakdown . . .

During the next few weeks Dr Harshom learned no more, except that Colin Trafford had not taken his advice, for word filtered through that both Peter Harshom in Cornwall and Harold in Durham had received requests for information regarding a Miss Ottilie Harshom who, as far as they knew, was non-existent.

After that there was nothing more for some months. Then a picture-postcard from Canada. On one side was a picture of the Parliament Buildings, Ottawa. The message on the other was brief. It said simply: 'Found her. Congratulate me. C.T.'

Dr Harshom studied it for a moment, and then smiled slightly. He was pleased. He had thought Colin Trafford a likeable young man; too good to run himself to pieces over such a futile quest. One did not believe it for a moment, of course, but if some sensible young woman had managed to convince him that she was the reincarnation, so to speak, of his beloved, good luck to her – and good luck for him . . . The obsession could now fade quietly away. He would have liked to respond with the requested congratulations, but the card bore no address.

Several weeks later there was another card, with a picture of St Mark's Square, Venice. The message was again laconic, but headed this time by an hotel address. It read:

'Honeymoon. May I bring her to see you after?'

Dr Harshom hesitated. His professional inclination was against it; a feeling that anything likely to recall the young man to the mood in which he had last seen him was best avoided. On the other hand, a refusal would seem odd as well as rude. In the end he replied on the back of a picture of Hereford Cathedral:

'Do. When?'

Half August had already gone before Colin Trafford did make his reappearance. He drove up looking sun-burnt and in better shape all round than he had on his previous visit. Dr Harshom was glad to see it, but surprised to find that he was alone in the car.

'But I understood the whole intention was that I should meet the bride,' he protested.

'It was – it is,' Colin assured him. 'She's at the hotel. I – well, I'd like to have a few words with you first.'

The doctor's gaze became a little keener, his manner more thoughtful.

'Very well. Let's go indoors. If there's anything I'm not to mention, you could have warned me by letter, you know.'

'Oh, it's not that. She knows about that. Quite what she makes of it, I'm not sure, but she knows, and she's anxious to meet you. No, it's – well, it won't take more than ten minutes.'

The doctor led the way to his study. He waved Colin to an easy-chair, and himself took the swivel-chair at the desk.

'Unburden yourself,' he invited.

Colin sat forward, forearms on knees, hands dangling between them.

'The most important thing, Doctor, is for me to thank you. I can never be grateful enough to you – never. If you had not invited me here as you did, I think it is unlikely I ever would have found her.'

Dr Harshom frowned. He was not convinced that the thanks were justified. Clearly, whoever Colin had found was possessed of a strong therapeutic quality, nevertheless:

'As I recollect, all I did was listen, and offer you unwelcome advice for your own good – which you did not take,' he remarked.

'So it seemed to me at the time,' Colin agreed. 'It looked as if you had closed all the doors. But then, when I thought it over, I saw one, just one, that hadn't quite latched.'

'I don't recall giving you *any* encouragement,' Dr Harshom asserted.

'I am sure you don't, but you did. You indicated to me the last, faintly possible line – and I followed it up – No, you'll see what it was later, if you'll just bear with me a little.

'When I did see the possibility, I realized it meant a lot of ground-work that I couldn't cover on my own, so I had to call in the professionals. They were pretty good, I thought, and they certainly removed any doubt about the line being the right one, but what they could tell me ended on board a ship bound for Canada. So then I had to call in some inquiry agents over there. It's a large country. A lot of people go to it. There was a great deal of routine searching to do, and I began to get discouraged, but then they got a lead and in another week they came across with the information that she was a secretary working in an office in Ottawa.

'Then I put it to EPI that I'd be more valuable after a bit of unpaid recuperative leave –'

'Just a minute,' put in the doctor. 'If you'd asked me I could have told you there are no Harshoms in Canada. I happen to know that because –'

'Oh, I'd given up expecting that. Her name wasn't Harshom – it was Gale,' Colin interrupted, with the air of one explaining.

'Indeed. And I suppose it wasn't Ottilie, either?' Dr Harshom said heavily.

'No. It was Belinda,' Colin told him.

The doctor blinked slightly, opened his mouth, and then thought better of it. Colin went on:

'So then I flew over, to make sure. It was the most agonizing journey I've ever made. But it was all right. Just one distant sight of her was

287

enough. I couldn't have *mistaken* her for Ottilie, but she was so very, very nearly Ottilie that I would have known her among ten thousand. Perhaps if her hair and her dress had been —' He paused speculatively, unaware of the expression on the doctor's face. 'Anyway,' he went on. 'I *knew*. And it was damned difficult to stop myself rushing up to her there and then, but I did just have enough sense to hold back.

'Then it was a matter of managing an introduction. After that it was as if there were – well, an inevitability, a sort of predestination about it.'

Curiosity impelled the doctor to say:

'Comprehensible, but sketchy. What, for instance, about her husband?'

'Husband?' Colin looked momentarily startled.

'Well, you did say her name was Gale,' the doctor pointed out.

'So it was, Miss Belinda Gale – I thought I said that. She was engaged once, but she didn't marry. I tell you there was a kind of – well, fate, in the Greek sense, about it.'

'But if –' Dr Harshom began, and then checked himself again. He endeavoured, too, to suppress any sign of scepticism.

'But it would have been just the same if she had had a husband,' Colin asserted, with ruthless conviction. 'He'd have been the wrong man.'

The doctor offered no comment, and he went on:

'There were no complications, or involvements – well, nothing serious. She was living in a flat with her mother, and getting quite a good salary. Her mother looked after the place, and had a widow's pension – her husband was in the RCAF; shot down over Berlin – so between them they managed to be reasonably comfortable.

'Well, you can imagine how it was. Considered as a phenomenon I wasn't any too welcome to her mother, but she's a fair-minded woman, and we found that, as persons, we liked one another quite well. So that part of it, too, went off more easily than it might have done.'

He paused there. Dr Harshom put in.

'I'm glad to hear it, of course. But I must confess I don't quite see what it has to do with your not bringing your wife along with you.'

Colin frowned.

'Well, I thought – I mean she thought – well, I haven't quite got to the point yet. It's rather delicate.'

'Take your time. After all, I've retired.' said the doctor, amiably.

Colin hesitated.

'All right. I think it'll be fairer to Mrs Gale if I tell it the way it fell out.

'You see, I didn't intend to say anything about what's at the back of all this – about Ottilie, I mean, and why I came to be over in Ottawa – not until later, anyway. You were the only one I had told, and it seemed better that way . . . I didn't want them wondering if I was a bit off my rocker, naturally. But I went and slipped up.

'It was on the day before our wedding. Belinda was out getting some last-minute things, and I was at the flat doing my best to be reassuring to my future mother-in-law. As nearly as I can recall it, what I said was:

' "My job with EPI is quite a good one, and the prospects are good, but they do have a Canadian end, too, and I dare say that if Ottilie finds she really doesn't like living in England –"

'And then I stopped because Mrs Gale had suddenly sat upright with a jerk, and was staring at me open-mouthed. Then in a shaky sort of voice she asked:

' "*What* did you say?"

'I'd noticed the slip myself, just too late to catch it. So I corrected: "I was just saying that if Belinda finds she doesn't like —"

'She cut in on that.

' "You didn't say Belinda. You said Ottilie."

' "Er – perhaps I did," I admitted, "but, as I say, if she doesn't –"

' "Why?" she demanded. "*Why* did you call her Ottilie?"

'She was intense about that. There was no way out of it.

' "It's well, it's the way I think of her," I said.

' "But why? *Why* should you think of Belinda as Ottilie?" she insisted.

'I looked at her more carefully. She had gone quite pale, and the hand that was visible was trembling. She was afraid, as well as distressed. I was sorry about that, and I gave up bluffing.

' "I didn't mean this to happen," I told her.

'She looked at me steadily, a little calmer.

' "But now it has, you *must* tell me. What do you know about us?" she asked.

' "Simply that if things had been – different she wouldn't be Belinda Gale. She would be Ottilie Harshom," I told her.

'She kept on watching my face, long and steadily, her own face still pale.

' "I don't understand,' she said, more than half to herself. 'You *couldn't* know. Harshom – yes, you might have found that out somehow, or guessed it – or did she tell you?" I shook my head. "Never mind, you could find out," she went on "But Ottilie . . . You *couldn't* know that – just that – just that one name out of all the thousands of names in the world . . . *Nobody* knew that – nobody but me . . ." She shook her head.

' "I didn't even tell Reggie . . . When he asked me if we could call her Belinda, I said yes; he'd been so very good to me . . . He had no idea that I had meant to call her Ottilie – nobody had. I've never told anyone, before or since . . . So how *can* you know."

'I took her hand between mine, and pressed it, trying to comfort her and calm her.

' "There's nothing to be alarmed about," I told her. "It was a – a dream, a kind of vision – I just knew . . ."

'She shook her head. After a minute she said quietly:

' "Nobody knew but me . . . It was in the summer in 1927. We were on the river, in a punt, pulled under a willow. A white launch swished by us, we watched it go, and saw the name on its stern. Malcolm said" ' – if Colin noticed Dr Harshom's sudden start, his only acknowledgement of it was a repetition of the last two words –

' "Malcolm said: 'Ottilie – pretty name, isn't it? It's in our family. My father had a sister Ottilie who died when she was a little girl. If ever I have a daughter I'd like to call her Ottilie.' " '

Colin Trafford broke off, and regarded the doctor for a moment. Then he went on:

'After that she said nothing for a long time, until she added:

' "He never knew, you know. Poor Malcolm, he was killed before even I knew she was coming . . . I did so want to call her Ottilie for him . . . He'd have liked that . . . I wish I had . . ." And then she began quietly crying . . .'

Dr Harshom had one elbow on his desk, one hand over his eyes. He did not move for some little time. At last he pulled out a handkerchief, and blew his nose decisively.

'I did hear there was a girl,' he said. 'I even made inquiries, but they told me she had married soon afterwards. I thought she – But why didn't she come to me? I would have looked after her.'

'She couldn't know that. She was fond of Reggie Gale. He was in love with her, and willing to give the baby his name,' Colin said.

After a glance towards the desk, he got up and walked over to the window. He stood there for several minutes with his back to the room until he heard a movement behind him. Dr Harshom had got up and was crossing to the cupboard.

'I could do with a drink,' he said. 'The toast will be the restoration of order, and the rout of the random element.'

'I'll support that,' Colin told him, 'but I'd like to couple it with the confirmation of your contention, Doctor – after all, you are right at last, you know; Ottilie Harshom *does not exist* – not any more – And then, I think, it will be high time you were introduced to your granddaughter, Mrs Colin Trafford.'

The Open Door

BY MARGARET OLIPHANT

It was perhaps only appropriate that ABC, the company which had launched the horror anthology on British television, should also be responsible for the first landmark series, Mystery and Imagination, which made its debut in January 1966 and continued at regular intervals until the last production, Robert Louis Stevenson's 'The Suicide Club', was transmitted in February 1970. The series, produced by Jonathan Alwyn, concentrated on classic horror literature and was responsible for two of the most faithful adaptations seen on TV of Frankenstein *and* Dracula. *The highly skilled director, Voytek, compressed Mary Shelley's novel into eighty engrossing minutes with Ian Holm, Neil Stacy and Ron Pember, while the accomplished Patrick Dromgoole directed Bram Stoker's vampire classic in which Denholm Elliott, playing Count Dracula, visibly disintegrated in the closing scene in a display of special effects unlike anything seen previously on television. Among other classics featured in the series were Joseph Sheridan Le Fanu's 'Uncle Silas' (starring Robert Eddison and Roy Godfrey), 'The Tell-Tale Heart' by Edgar Allan Poe (with Freddie Jones and Kenneth J.Warren), 'Fanthom Lover' by Vernon Lee (with Robert Hardy and Virginia McKenna) and 'The Canterville Ghost' by Oscar Wilde (with the extraordinary pairing of Bruce Forsyth and Eleanor Bron!).*

In the memory of many viewers of the series, however, the most dramatic of the productions was 'The Open Door' by the Victorian supernatural novelist Margaret Oliphant (1828–1897) which George Kerr adapted and Joan Kemp-Welsh directed. Jack Hawkins and Rachel Gurney starred in the story of a tragic haunting – but it was the poignancy of Hawkins' performance which gave the drama so much extra frisson, as The Daily Express *revealed shortly after the transmission on 19 February, 1966. 'This weekend's episode of Mystery and Imagination was incomparably more moving and dreadful than any we have seen or are likely to see. Not for the story itself, but for the untold theme simmering under the surface. That of an actor losing his voice. Speaking his lines through a tumour in his throat. 'The Open Door' starred Jack Hawkins and was recorded before his operation for throat cancer. And it was terribly evident.' Wondering whether the episode should have been shown at all in the circumstances, the paper added, 'There was much to admire in the acting and more to admire in the courage of the actor. He kicked and coaxed his voice to the last line which was, "All is well, thank God. All is well."' Jack Hawkins, of course, recovered from his operation and continued to appear in films and on television – although his voice was dubbed – until his death in 1973. He never, though, gave a subsequent performance to quite match the menace and magnificence of his part in 'The Open Door', of which* The Times *also wrote, 'The haunting voice in the ruins provided the most chilling experience the series has so far brought.'*

I TOOK the house of Brentwood on my return from India in 18 –, for the temporary accommodation of my family, until I could find a permanent home for them. It had many advantages which made it peculiarly appropriate. It was within reach of Edinburgh, and my boy Roland, whose education had been considerably neglected, could go in and out to school, which was thought to be better for him than either leaving home altogether or staying there always with a tutor. The first of these expedients would have seemed preferable to me, the second commended itself to his mother. The doctor, like a judicious man, took the midway between. 'Put him on his pony, and let him ride into the High School every morning; it will do him all the good in the world,' Dr Simson said; 'and when it is bad weather there is the train.' His mother accepted this solution of the difficulty more easily than I could have hoped; and our pale-faced boy, who had never known anything more invigorating than Simla, began to encounter the brisk breezes of the North in the subdued severity of the month of May. Before the time of the vacation in July we had the satisfaction of seeing him begin to acquire something of the brown and ruddy complexion of his schoolfellows. The English system did not commend itself to Scotland in these days. There was no little Eton at Fettes; nor do I think, if there had been, that a genteel exotic of that class would have tempted either my wife or me. The lad was doubly precious to us, being the only one left us of many; and he was fragile in body, we believed, and deeply sensitive in mind. To keep him at home, and yet to send him to school – to combine the advantages of the two systems – seemed to be everything that could be desired. The two girls also found at Brentwood everything they wanted. They were near enough to Edinburgh to have masters and lessons as many as they required for completing that never-ending education which the young people seem to require nowadays. Their mother married me when she was younger than Agatha, and I should like to see them improve upon their mother! I myself was then no more than twenty-five – an age at which I see the young fellows now groping about them, with no notion what they are going to do with their lives. However, I suppose every generation has a conceit of itself which elevates it, in its own opinion, above that which comes after it.

Brentwood stands on that fine and wealthy slope of country, one of the richest in Scotland, which lies between the Pentland Hills and the Firth. In clear weather you could see the blue gleam – like a bent bow, embracing the wealthy fields and scattered houses – of the great estuary on one side of you; and on the other the blue heights, not gigantic like those we had been used to, but just high enough for all the glories of the atmosphere, the play of clouds, and sweet reflections, which give to a hilly country an interest and a charm which nothing else can emulate. Edinburgh, with its two lesser heights – the Castle and the Calton Hill – its spires and towers piercing through the smoke, and Arthur's Seat, lying crouched behind, like a guardian no longer very needful, taking his repose beside the well-beloved charge, which is now, so to speak, able to take care of itself without him – lay at our right hand. From the lawn and drawing-room windows we could see all these varieties of landscape. The colour was sometimes a little chilly, but sometimes, also, as animated and full of vicissitude as a drama. I was never tired of it. Its colour and freshness revived the eyes which had grown weary of arid plains and blazing skies. It was always cheery, and fresh, and full of repose.

The village of Brentwood lay almost under the house, on the other side of the deep little ravine, down which a stream – which ought to have been a lovely, wild, and frolicsome little river – flowed between its rocks and trees. The river, like so many in that district, had, however, in its earlier life been sacrificed to trade, and was grimy with paper-making. But this did not affect our pleasure in it so much as I have known it to affect other streams. Perhaps our water was more rapid – perhaps less clogged with dirt and refuse. Our side of the dell was charmingly *accidenté*, and clothed with fine trees, through which various paths wound down to the river-side and to the village bridge which crossed the stream. The village lay in the hollow, and climbed, with very prosaic houses, the other side. Village architecture does not flourish in Scotland. The blue slates and the grey stone are sworn foes to the picturesque; and though I do not, for my own part, dislike the interior of an old-fashioned pewed and galleried church, with its little family settlements on all sides, the square box outside, with its bit of a spire like a handle to lift it by, is not an improvement to the landscape. Still a cluster of houses on differing elevations – with scraps of garden coming in between, a hedgerow with clothes laid out to dry, the opening of a street with its rural amiability, the women at their doors, the slow waggon lumbering along – gives a centre to the landscape. It was cheerful to look at, and convenient in a hundred ways. Within ourselves we had walks in plenty, the glen being always beautiful in all its phases, whether the woods were green in the spring or ruddy in the autumn. In the park which surrounded the house were the rains of the former mansion of Brentwood, a much smaller and less important house than the solid Georgian edifice which we inhabited. The ruins were picturesque, however, gave importance to the place. Even we, who were but temporary tenants, felt a vague pride in them, as if they somehow reflected a certain consequence upon ourselves. The old building had the remains of a tower, an indistinguishable maw of mason-work, overgrown with ivy, and the shells of walls attached to this were half filled up with soil. I had never examined it closely, I am ashamed to say. There was a large room, or what had been a large room, with the lower part of the windows still existing, on the principal floor, and underneath other windows, which were perfect, though half filled up with fallen soil, and waving with a wild growth of brambles and chance growths of all kinds. This was the oldest part of all. At a little distance were some very commonplace and disjointed fragments of building, one of them suggesting a certain pathos by its very commonness and the complete wreck which it showed. This was the end of a low gable, a bit of grey wall, all encrusted with lichens, in which was a common doorway. Probably it had been a servants' entrance, a back-door, or opening into what are called 'the offices' in Scotland. No offices remained to be entered – pantry and kitchen had all been swept out of being; but there stood the doorway open and vacant, free to all the winds, to the rabbits, and every wild creature. It struck my eye, the first time I went to Brentwood, like a melancholy comment upon a life that was over. A door that led to nothing – closed once, perhaps, with anxious care, bolted and guarded, now void of any meaning. It impressed me, I remember, from the first; so perhaps it may be said that my mind was prepared to attach to it an importance which nothing justified.

The summer was a very happy period of repose for us all. The warmth of Indian suns was still in our veins. It seemed to us that we could never have enough of the greenness, the dewiness, the freshness of the northern landscape. Even its mists were pleasant to us, taking all the fever out of us, and pouring in vigour and refreshment. In autumn we followed the fashion of the time, and went away for change which we did not in the least require. It was when the family had settled down for the winter, when the days were short and dark, and the rigorous reign of frost upon us, that the incidents occurred which alone could justify me in intruding upon the world my private affairs. These incidents were, however, of so curious a character, that I hope my inevitable references to my own family and pressing personal interests will meet with a general pardon.

I was absent in London when these events began. In London an old Indian plunges back into the interests with which all his previous life has been associated, and meets old friends at every step. I had been circulating among some half-dozen of these – enjoying the return to my former life in shadow, though I had been so thankful in substance to throw it aside – had missed some of my home letters, what with going down from Friday to Monday to old Benbow's place in the country, and stopping on the way back to dine and sleep at Sellar's and to take a look into Cross's stables, which occupied another day. It is never safe to miss one's letters. In this transitory life, as the Prayer-book says, how can one ever be certain what is going to happen? All was well at home. I knew exactly (I thought) what they would have to say to me: 'The weather has been so fine, that Roland has not once gone by train, and he enjoys the ride beyond anything.' 'Dear papa, be sure that you don't forget anything, but bring us so-and-so, and so-and-so' – a list as long as my arm. Dear girls and dearer mother! I would not for the world have forgotten their commissions, or lost their little letters, for all the Benbows and Crosses in the world.

But I was confident in my home-comfort and peacefulness. When I got back to my club, however, three or four letters were lying for me, upon some of which I noticed the 'immediate', 'urgent', which old-fashioned people and anxious people still believe will influence the post-office and quicken the speed of the mails. I was about to open one of these, when the club porter brought me two telegrams, one of which, he said, had arrived the night before. I opened, as was to be expected, the last first, and this was what I read: 'Why don't you come or answer? For God's sake, come. He is much worse.' This was a thunderbolt to fall upon a man's head who had one only son, and he the light of his eyes! The other telegram, which I opened with hands trembling so much that I lost time by my haste, was to much the same purport: 'No better; doctor afraid of brain-fever. Calls for you day and night. Let nothing detain you.' The first thing I did was to look up the time-tables to see if there was any way of getting off sooner than by the night-train, though I knew well enough there was not; and then I read the letters, which furnished, alas! too clearly, all the details. They told me that the boy had been pale for some time, with a scared look. His mother had noticed it before I left home, but would not say anything to alarm me. This look had increased day by day; and soon it was observed that Roland came home at a wild gallop through the park, his pony panting and in foam, himself 'as white as a sheet', but with the perspiration streaming from his forehead. For a long time he had resisted all questioning, but at length had developed such strange changes of mood, showing a reluctance to go to school, a desire to be fetched in the carriage at night – which was a ridiculous piece of luxury – an unwillingness to go out into the grounds, and nervous start at every sound, that his mother had insisted upon an explanation. When the boy – our boy Roland, who had never known what fear was – began to talk to her of voices he had heard in the park, and shadows that had appeared to him among the ruins, my wife promptly put him to bed and sent for Dr Simson – which, of course, was the only thing to do.

I hurried off that evening, as may be supposed with an anxious heart. How I got through the hours before the starting of the train, I cannot tell. We must all be thankful for the quickness of the railway when in anxiety; but to have thrown myself into a post-chaise as soon as horses could be put to, would have been a relief. I got to Edinburgh very early in the blackness of the winter morning, and scarcely dared look the man in the face, at whom I gasped 'What news?' My wife had sent the brougham for me, which I concluded, before the man spoke, was a bad sign. His answer was that stereotyped answer which leaves the imagination so wildly free – 'Just the same.' Just the same! What might that mean? The horses seemed to me to creep along the long dark country-road. As we dashed through the park, I thought I heard someone moaning among the trees, and clenched my fist at him (whoever he might be) with fury. Why had the fool of woman at the gate allowed any one to come in to disturb the quiet of the place? If I had not been in such hot haste to get home, I think I should have stopped the carriage and got out to see what tramp it was that had made an entrance, and chosen my grounds, of all places in the world – when my boy was ill! – to grumble and groan in. But I had no reason to complain of our slow pace here. The horses flew like lightning along the intervening path, and drew up at the door all panting, as if they had run a race. My wife stood waiting to receive me with a pale face, and a candle in her hand, which made her look paler still as the wind blew the flame about. 'He is sleeping,' she said in a whisper, as if her voice might wake him. And I replied, when I could find my voice, also in a whisper, as though the jingling of the horses' furniture and the sound of their hoofs must not have been more dangerous. I stood on the steps with her a moment, almost afraid to go in, now that I was here; and it seemed to me that I saw without observing, if I may say so, that the horses were unwilling to turn round, though their stables lay that way, or that the men were unwilling. These things occurred to me afterwards, though at the moment I was not capable of anything but to ask questions and to hear of the condition of the boy.

I looked at him from the door of his room, for we were afraid to go near, lest we should disturb that blessed sleep. It looked like actual sleep – not the lethargy into which my wife told me he would sometimes fall. She told me everything in the next room, which communicated with his, rising now and then and going to the door of communication; and in this there was much that was very startling and confusing to the mind. It appeared that ever since the winter began, since it was early dark, and night had fallen before his return from school, he had been hearing voices among the ruins – at first only a groaning, he said, at which his pony was as much alarmed as he was, but by degrees a voice. The tears ran down my wife's cheeks as she described to me how he would start up in the night and cry out, 'Oh, mother, let me in! oh, mother, let me in!' with a pathos which rent her heart. And she sitting there all the time, only longing to do everything his heart could desire! But though she would try to soothe him, crying, 'You are at home, my darling. I am here. Don't you know me? Your mother is here!' He would only stare at her, and after a while spring up again with the same cry. At other times he would be quite reasonable, she said, asking eagerly when I was coming, but declaring that he must go with me as soon as I did so, 'to let them in'. 'The doctor thinks his nervous system must have received a shock,' my wife said. 'Oh, Henry, can it be that we have pushed him on too much with his work – a delicate boy like Roland? – and what is his work in comparison with his health? Even you would think little of honours or prizes if it hurt the boy's health.' Even I! as if I were an inhuman father sacrificing my child to my ambition. But I would not increase her trouble by taking

298

any notice. After a while they persuaded me to lie down, to rest, and to eat – none of which things had been possible since I received their letters. The mere fact of being on the spot, of course, in itself was a great thing; and when I knew that I could be called in a moment, as soon as he was awake and wanted me, I felt capable, even in the dark, chill morning twilight, to snatch an hour or two's sleep. As it happened, I was so worn out with the strain of anxiety, and he so quieted and consoled by knowing I had come, that I was not disturbed till the afternoon, when the twilight had again settled down. There was just daylight enough to see his face when I went to him; and what a change in a fortnight! He was paler and more worn, I thought, than even in those dreadful days in the plains before we left India. His hair seemed to me to have grown long and lank; his eyes were like blazing lights projecting out of his white face. He got hold of my hand in a cold and tremulous clutch, and waved to everybody to go away. 'Go away – even mother,' he said, 'go away.' This went to her heart, for she did not like that even I should have more of the boy's confidence than herself; but my wife has never been a woman to think of herself, and she left us alone. 'Are they all gone?' he said eagerly. 'They would not let me speak. The doctor treated me as if I were a fool. You know I am not a fool, papa.'

'Yes, yes, my boy, I know; but you are ill, and quiet is so necessary. You are not only not a fool, Roland, but you are reasonable and understand. When you are ill you must deny yourself; you must not do everything that you might do being well.'

He waved his thin hand with a sort of indignation. 'Then, father, I am not ill,' he cried. 'Oh, I thought when you came you would not stop me – you would see the sense of it! What do you think is the matter with me, all of you? Simson is well enough, but he is only a doctor. What do you think is the matter with me? I am no more ill than you are. A doctor, of course, he thinks you are ill the moment he looks at you – that's what he's there for – and claps you in bed.'

'Which is the best place for you at present, my dear boy.'

'I made up my mind,' cried the little fellow, 'that I would stand it till you came home. I said to myself, I won't frighten mother and the girls. But now, father,' he cried, half jumping out of bed, 'it's not illness – it's a secret.'

His eyes shone so wildly, his face was so swept with strong feeling, that my heart sank within me. It could be nothing but fever that did it, and fever had been so fatal. I got him into my arms to put him back into bed. 'Roland,' I said, humouring the poor child, which I knew was the only way, 'if you are going to tell me this secret to do any good, you know you must be quite quiet, and not excite yourself. If you excite yourself, I must not let you speak.'

'Yes, father,' said the boy. He was quiet directly, like a man, as if he quite understood. When I had laid him back on his pillow, he looked up at me with that grateful sweet look with which children, when they are ill, break one's heart, the water coming into his eyes in his weakness. 'I was sure as soon as you were here you would know what to do,' he said.

'To be sure, my boy. Now keep quiet, and tell it all out like a man.' To think I was telling lies to my own child! for I did it only to humour him, thinking, poor little fellow, his brain was wrong.

'Yes, father. Father, there is some one in the park – some one that has been badly used.'

'Hush, my dear; you remember, there is to be no excitement. Well, who is this somebody, and who has been ill-using him? We will soon put a stop to that.'

'Ah,' cried Roland, 'but it is not so easy as you think. I don't know who it is. It is just a cry. Oh, if you could hear it! It gets into my head in my sleep. I heard it as clear – as clear – and they think that I am dreaming – or raving perhaps,' the boy said, with a sort of disdainful smile.

This look of his perplexed me; it was less like fever than I thought. 'Are you quite sure you have not dreamt it, Roland?' I said.

'Dreamt? – that!' He was springing up again when he suddenly bethought himself, and lay down flat with the same sort of smile on his face. 'The pony heard it too,' he said. 'She jumped as if she had been shot. If I had not grasped at the reins – for I was frightened, father —'

'No shame to you, my boy,' said I, though I scarcely knew why.

'If I hadn't held to her like a leech, she'd have pitched me over her head, and never drew breath till we were at the door. Did the pony dream it?' he said, with a soft disdain, yet indulgence for my foolishness. Then he added slowly: 'It was only a cry the first time, and all the time before you went away. I would not tell you, for it was so wretched to be frightened. I thought it might be a hare or a rabbit snared, and I went in the morning and looked, but there was nothing. It was after you went I heard it really first, and this is what he says.' He raised himself on his elbow close to me, and looked me in the face. ' "Oh, mother, let me in! oh, mother, let me in!" ' As he said the words a mist came over his face, the mouth quivered, the soft features all melted and changed, and when he had ended these pitiful words, dissolved in a shower of heavy tears.

Was it a hallucination? Was it the fever of the brain? Was it the

300

disordered fancy caused by great bodily weakness? How could I tell? I thought it wisest to accept it as if it were all true.

'This is very touching, Roland,' I said.

'Oh, if you had just heard it, father! I said to myself, if father heard it he would do something; but mamma, you know, she's given over to Simson, and that fellow's a doctor, and never thinks of anything but clapping you into bed.'

'We must not blame Simson for being a doctor, Roland.'

'No, no,' said my boy, with delightful toleration and indulgence; 'oh no; that's the good of him – that's what he's for; I know that. But you – you are different; you are just father: and you'll do something – directly, papa, directly – this very night.'

'Surely,' I said. 'No doubt it is some little lost child.'

He gave me a sudden, swift look, investigating my face as though to see whether, after all, this was everything my eminence as 'father' came to – no more than that? Then he got hold of my shoulder, clutching it with his thin hand: 'Look here,' he said, with a quiver in his voice; 'suppose it wasn't – living at all!'

'My dear boy, how then could you have heard it?' I said.

He turned away from me with a pettish exclamation – 'As if you didn't know better than that!'

'Do you want to tell me it is a ghost?' I said.

Roland withdrew his hand; his countenance assumed an aspect of great dignity and gravity; a slight quiver remained about his lips. 'Whatever it was – you always said we were not to call names. It was something – in trouble. Oh, father, in terrible trouble!'

'But, my boy,' I said – I was at my wits' end – 'if it was a child that was lost, or any poor human creature – but, Roland, what do you want me to do?'

'I should know if I was you,' said the child, eagerly. 'That is what I always said to myself – Father will know.' 'Oh, papa, papa, to have to face it night after night, in such terrible, terrible trouble! and never to be able to do it any good. I don't want to cry; it's like a baby, I know; but what can I do else? – out there all by itself in the ruin, and nobody to help it. I can't bear it, I can't bear it!' cried my generous boy. And in his weakness he burst out, after many attempts to restrain it, into a great childish fit of sobbing and tears.

I do not know that I ever was in a greater perplexity in my life; and afterwards, when I thought of it, there was something comic in it too. It is bad enough to find your child's mind possessed with the conviction that he has seen – or heard – a ghost. But that he should require you to go instantly and help that ghost, was the most

301

bewildering experience that had ever come my way. I am a sober man myself, and not superstitious – at least any more than everybody is superstitious. Of course I do not believe in ghosts; but I don't deny, any more than other people, that there are stories, which I cannot pretend to understand. My blood got a sort of chill in my veins at the idea that Roland should be a ghost-seer; for that generally means a hysterical temperament and weak health, and all that men most hate and fear for their children. But that I should take up his ghost and right its wrongs, and save it from its trouble, was such a mission as was enough to confuse any man. I did my best to console my boy without giving any promise of this astonishing kind; but he was too sharp for me. He would have none of my caresses. With sobs breaking in at intervals upon his voice, and the rain-drops hanging on his eyelids, he yet returned to the charge.

'It will be there now – it will be there all the night . . . Oh think, papa, think, if it was me! I can't rest for thinking of it. Don't!' he cried, putting away my hand – 'don't! You go and help it, and mother can take care of me.'

'But, Roland, what can I do?'

My boy opened his eyes, which were large with weakness and fever, and gave me a smile such, I think, as sick children only know the secret of. 'I was sure you would know as soon as you came. I always said – Father will know: and mother,' he cried, with a softening of repose upon his face, his limbs relaxing, his form sinking with a luxurious ease in his bed – 'mother can come and take care of me.'

I called her, and saw him turn to her with the complete dependence of a child, and then I went away and left them, as perplexed a man as any in Scotland. I must say, however, I had this consolation, that my mind was greatly eased about Roland. He might be under a hallucination, but his head was clear enough, and I did not think him so ill as everybody else did. The girls were astonished even at the ease with which I took it. 'How do you think he is?' they said in a breath, coming round me, laying hold of me. 'Not half so ill as I expected,' I said; 'not very bad at all.' Oh, papa, you are a darling!' cried Agatha, kissing me, and crying upon my shoulder; while little Jeanie, who was as pale as Roland, clasped both her arms round mine, and could not speak at all. I knew nothing about it, not half so much as Simson: but they believed in me; they had a feeling that all would go right now. God is very good to you when your chidren look to you like that. It makes one humble, not proud. I was not worthy of it; and then I recollected that I had to act the part of a father to Roland's ghost, which made me almost laugh, though I might just as well have cried. It was the strangest mission that ever was entrusted to mortal man.

It was then I remembered suddenly the looks of the men when they turned to take the brougham to the stables in the dark that morning: they had not liked it, and the horses had not liked it. I remembered that even in my anxiety about Roland I had heard them tearing along the avenue back to the stables, and had made a memorandum mentally that I must speak of it. It seemed to me that the best thing I could do was to go to the stables now and make a few inquiries. It is impossible to fathom the minds of rustics; there might be some devilry of practical joking, for anything I knew; or they might have some interest in getting up a bad reputation for the Brentwood avenue. It was getting dark by the time I went out, and nobody who knows the country will need to be told how black is the darkness of a November night under high laurel-bushes and yew-trees. I walked into the heart of the shrubberies two or three times, not seeing a step before me, till I came out upon the broader carriage-road, where the trees opened a little, and there was a faint grey glimmer of sky visible, under which the great limes and elms stood darkling like ghosts; but it grew black again as I approached the corner where the ruins lay. Both eyes and ears were on the alert, as may be supposed; but I could see nothing in the absolute gloom, and, so far as I can recollect, I heard nothing. Nevertheless there came a strong impression upon me that somebody was there. It is a sensation which most people have felt. I have seen when it has been strong enough to awake me out of sleep, the sense of someone looking at me. I suppose my imagination had been affected by Roland's story; and the mystery of the darkness is always full of suggestions. I stamped my feet violently on the gravel to rouse myself, and called out sharply, 'Who's there?' Nobody answered, nor did I expect any one to answer, but the impression had been made. I was so foolish that I did not like to look back, but went sideways, keeping an eye on the gloom behind. It was with great relief that I spied the light in the stables, making a sort of oasis in the darkness. I walked very quickly into the midst of that lighted and cheerful place, and thought the clank of the groom's pail one of the pleasantest sounds I had ever heard. The coachman was the head of this little colony, and it was to his house I went to pursue my investigations. He was a native of the district, and had taken care of the place in the absence of the family for years; it was impossible but that he must know everything that was going on, and all the traditions of the place. The men, I could see, eyed me anxiously when I thus appeared at such an hour among them, and followed me with their eyes to Jarvis's house, where he lived alone with his old wife, their children being all married and out in the world. Mrs Jarvis met me with anxious questions. How was the poor young gentleman? but the others knew, I could see by their faces, that not even this was the foremost thing in my mind.

'Noises? – ou ay, there'll be noises – the wind in the trees, and the water soughing down the glen. As for tramps, Cornel, no, there's little o' that kind o' cattle about here; and Merran at the gate's a careful body.' Jarvis moved about with some embarrassment from one leg to another as he spoke. He kept in the shade, and did not look at me more than he could help. Evidently his mind was perturbed, and he had reasons for keeping his own counsel. His wife sat by, giving him a quick look now and then, but saying nothing. The kitchen was very snug, and warm, and bright – as different as could be from the chill and mystery of the night outside.

'I think you are trifling with me, Jarvis,' I said.

'Triflin', Cornel? no me. What would I trifle for? If the deevil himsel was in the auld hoose, I have no interest in't one way or another —'

'Sandy, hold your peace!' cried his wife, imperatively.

'And what am I to hold my peace for, wi' the Cornel standing there asking a' thae questions? I'm saying, if the deevil himsel —'

'And I'm telling ye hold your peace!' cried the woman, in great excitement. 'Dark November weather and lang nichts, and us that ken a' we ken. How daur ye name – a name that shouldna be spoken?' She threw down her stocking and got up, also in great agitation. 'I tell't ye you never could keep it. It's no a thing that will hide; and the haill toun kens as weel as you or me. Tell the Cornel straight out – or see, I'll do it. I dinna hold wi' your secrets: and a secret that the haill toun kens!' She snapped her fingers with an air of large disdain. As for Jarvis, ruddy and big as he was, he shrank to nothing before this decided woman. He repeated to her two or three times her own adjuration, 'Hold your peace!' then, suddenly changing his tone, cried out, 'Tell him then, confound ye! I'll wash my hands o't. If a' the ghosts in Scotland were in the auld hoose, is that ony concern o' mine?'

After this I elicited without much difficulty the whole story. In the opinion of the Jarvises, and of everybody about, the certainty that the place was haunted was beyond all doubt. As Sandy and his wife warmed to the tale, one tripping up another in their eagerness to tell everything, it gradually developed as distinct a superstition as I ever heard, and not without poetry and pathos. How long it was since the voice had been heard first, nobody could tell with certainty. Jarvis's opinion was that his father, who had been coachman at Brentwood before him, had never heard anything about it, and that the whole thing had arisen within the last ten years, since the complete dismantling of the old house: which was a wonderfully modern date for a tale so well authenticated. According to these witnesses, and to several whom I questioned afterwards, and who were all in perfect agreement, it was only in the mouths of November and December that 'the visitation' occurred. During these months, the darkest of the year, scarcely a night passed without the recurrence of these inexplicable cries. Nothing, it was said, had ever been seen – at least nothing that could be identified. Some people, bolder or more imaginative than the others, had seen the darkness moving, Mrs Jarvis said, with unconcious poetry. It began when night fell, and continued, at intervals, until day broke. Very often it was only an inarticulate cry and moaning, but sometimes the words which had taken possession of my poor boy's fancy had been distinctly audible – 'Oh, mother, let me in!' The Jarvises were not aware that there had ever been any investigation into it. The estate of Brentwood had lapsed into the hands of a distant branch of the family, who had lived but little there; and of the many people who had taken it, as I had done, few had remained through two Decembers. And nobody had taken the trouble to make a very close examination into the facts. 'No, no,' Jarvis said, shaking his head, 'No, no, Cornel. Wha wad set themsels up for a laughin' stock to a' the country-side, making a wark about a ghost? Naebody believes in ghosts. It bid to be the wind in the trees, the last gentleman said, or some effec' o' the water wrastlin' among the rocks. He said it was a' quite easy explained: but he gave up the hoose. And when you cam, Cornel, we were awfu' anxious you should never hear. What for should I have spoiled the bargain and hairmed the property for nothing?'

'Do you call my child's life nothing?' I said in the trouble of the moment, unable to restrain myself. 'And instead of telling this all to me, you have told it to him – to a delicate boy, a child unable to sift evidence, or judge for himself, a tender-hearted young creature —'

I was walking about the room with an anger all the hotter that I felt it to be most likely quite unjust. My heart was full of bitterness against the stolid retainers of a family who were content to risk other people's children and comfort rather than let a house lie empty. If I had been warned I might have taken precautions, or left the place, or sent Roland away, a hundred things which now I could not do; and here I was with my boy in a brain-fever, and his life, the most precious life on earth, hanging in the balance, dependent on whether or not I could get to the reason of a commonplace ghost-story! I paced about in high wrath, not seeing what I was to do; for, to take Roland away, even if he were able to travel, would not settle his agitated mind; and I feared even that a scientific explanation of refracted sound, or reverberation, or any other of the easy certainties with which we elder men are silenced, would have very little effect upon the boy.

'Cornel,' said Jarvis solemnly, 'and *she'll* bear me witness – the young gentleman never heard a word from me – no, nor from either groom or gardener; I'll gie ye my word for that. In the first place, he's no a lad that invites ye to talk. There are some that are, and some that arena. Some will draw ye on, till ye've tellt them a' the clatter of the toun, and a' ye ken, and whiles mair. But Maister Roland, his minds fu' of his books. He's aye civil and kind, and a fine lad; but no that sort. And ye see it's for a' our interest, Cornel, that you should stay at Brentwood. I took it upon me mysel to pass the word – "No a syllable to Maister Roland, nor to the young leddies – no a syllable." The woman-servants, that have little reason to be out at night, ken little or nothing about it. And some think it grand to have a ghost so long as they're no in the way of coming across it. If you had been tellt the story to begin with, maybe ye would have thought so yourself.'

This was true enough, though it did not throw any light upon my perplexity. If we had heard of it to start with, it is possible that all the family would have considered the possession of a ghost a distinct advantage. It is the fashion of the times. We never think what a risk it is to play with young imaginations, but cry out, in the fashionable jargon, 'A ghost! – nothing else was wanted to make it perfect.' I should not have been above this myself. I should have smiled, of course, at the idea of the ghost at all, but then to feel that it was mine would have pleased my vanity. Oh yes, I claim no exemption. The girls would have been delighted. I could fancy their eagerness, their interest, and excitement. No; if we had been told, it would have done no good – we should have made the bargain all the more eagerly, the fools that we are. 'And there has been no attempt to investigate it,' I said, 'to see what it really is?'

'Eh, Cornel,' said the coachman's wife, 'wha would investigate, as ye call it, a thing that nobody believes in? Ye would be the laughin' stock of a' the country-side, as my man says.'

'But you believe in it,' I said, turning upon her hastily. The woman was taken by surprise. She made a step backward out of my way.

'Lord, Cornel, how ye frichten a body! Me! – there's awfu' strange things in this world. An unlearned person doesna ken what to think. But the minister and the gentry they just laugh in your face. Inquire into the thing that is not! Na, na, we just let it be.'

'Come with me, Jarvis,' I said, hastily, 'and we'll make an attempt at least. Say nothing to the men or to anybody. I'll come back after dinner, and we'll make a serious attempt to see what it is, if it is anything. If I hear it – which I doubt – you may be sure I shall never rest till I make it out. Be ready for me about ten o'clock.'

'Me, Cornel!' Jarvis said, in a faint voice. I had not been looking at him in my own preoccupation, but when I did so, I found that the greatest change had come over the fat and ruddy coachman. 'Me, Cornel!' he repeated, wiping the perspiration from his brow. His ruddy face hung in flabby folds, his knees knocked together, his voice seemed half extinguished in his throat. Then he began to rub his hands and smile upon me in a deprecating, imbecile way. 'There's nothing I wouldna do to pleasure ye, Cornel,' taking a step further back. 'I'm sure, *she* kens I've aye said I never had to do with a mair fair, weelspoken gentleman —' Here Jarvis came to a pause, again looking at me, rubbing his hands.

'Well?' I said.

'But eh, sir!' he went on, with the same imbecile yet insinuating smile, 'if ye'll reflect that I am no used to my feet. With a horse atween my legs, or the reins in my hand, I'm maybe nae worse than other men; but on fit, Cornel — It's no the – bogles — but I've been cavalry, ye see,' with a little hoarse laugh, 'a' my life. To face a thing ye didna understan' – on your feet, Cornel.'

'Well, sir, if *I* do it,' said I tartly, 'why shouldn't you?'

'Eh, Cornel, there's au awfu' difference. In the first place, ye tramp about the haill country-side, and think naething of it; but a walk tires me mair than a hunard miles' drive: and then ye're a gentleman, and do your ain pleasure; and you're no so auld as me; and it's for your ain bairn, ye see, Cornel; and then —'

'He believes in it, Cornel, and you dinna believe in it,' the woman said.

'Will you come with me?' I said, turning to her.

She jumped back, upsetting her chair in her bewilderment. 'Me!' with a scream, and then fell into a sort of hysterical laugh. 'I wouldna say but what I would go; but what would the folk say to hear of Cornel Mortimer with an auld silly woman at his heels?'

The suggestion made me laugh too, though I had little inclination for it. 'I'm sorry you have so little spirit, Jarvis,' I said. 'I must find someone else, I suppose.'

Jarvis, touched by this, began to remonstrate, but I cut him short. My butler was a soldier who had been with me in India, and was not supposed to fear anything – man or devil – certainly not the former;

307

and I felt that I was losing time. The Jarvises were too thankful to get rid of me. They attended me to the door with the most anxious courtesies. Outside, the two grooms stood close by, a little confused by my sudden exit. I don't know if perhaps they had been listening – at least standing as near as possible, to catch any scrap of the conversation. I waved my hand to them as I went past, in answer to their salutations, and it was very apparent to me that they also were glad to see me go.

And it will be thought very strange, but it would be weak not to add that I myself, though bent on the investigation I have spoken of, pledged to Roland to carry it out, and feeling, that my boy's health, perhaps his life, depended on the result of my inquiry – I felt the most unaccountable reluctance to pass these ruins on my way home. My curiosity was intense; and yet it was all my mind could do to pull my body along. I daresay the scientific people would describe it the other way, and attribute my cowardice to the state of my stomach. I went on; but if I had followed my impulse, I should have turned and bolted. Everything ill seemed to cry out against it; my heart thumped, my pulses all began, like sledge-hammers, beating against my ears and every sensitive part. It was very dark, as I have said; the old house, with its shapeless tower, loomed a heavy mass through the darkness, which was only not entirely so solid as itself. On the other hand, the great dark cedars of which we were so proud seemed to fill up the night. My foot strayed out of the path in my confusion and the gloom together, and I brought myself up with a cry as I felt myself knock against something solid. What was it? The contact with hard stone and lime, and prickly bramblebushes restored me a little to myself. 'Oh, it's only the old gable,' I said aloud, with a little laugh to reassure myself. The rough feeling of the stones reconciled me. As I groped about thus, I shook off my visionary folly. What so easily explained as that I should have strayed from the path in the darkness? This brought me back to common existence, as if I had been shaken by a wise hand out of all the silliness of superstition. How silly it was, after all! What did it matter which path I took? I laughed again, this time with better heart – when suddenly, in a moment, the blood was chilled in my veins, a shiver stole along my spine, my faculties seemed to forsake me. Close by me at my side, at my feet, there was a sigh. No, not a groan, not a moaning, not anything so tangible – a perfectly soft, faint, inarticulate sigh. I sprang back, and my heart stopped beating. Mistaken! no, mistake was impossible. I heard it as clearly as I hear myself speak; a long, soft, weary sigh, as if drawn to the utmost, and emptying out a load of sadness that filled the breast. To hear this in the solitude, in the dark, in the night (though it was still early), had an effect which I cannot describe. I feel it now – something cold creeping over me, up into my hair, and down to my feet, which refused to move. I cried out, with a trembling, voice, 'Who is there?' as I had done before – but there was no reply.

I got home I don't quite know how; but in my mind there was no longer any indifference as to the thing, whatever it was, that haunted these ruins. My scepticism disappeared like a mist. I was as firmly determined that there was something as Roland was. I did not for a moment pretend to myself that it was possible I could be deceived; there were movements and noises which I understood all about, cracklings of small branches in the frost, and little rolls of gravel on the path, such as have a very, eerie sound sometimes, and perplex you with wonder as to who has done it, *when there is no real mystery*; but I assure you all these little movements of nature don't affect you one bit *when there is something*. I understood *them*. I did not understand the sigh. That was not simple nature; there was meaning in it – feeling, the soul of a creature invisible. This is the thing that human nature trembles at – a creature invisible, yet with sensations, feelings, a power somehow of expressing itself. I had not the same sense of unwillingness to turn my back upon the scene of the mystery which I had experienced in going to the stables; but I almost ran home, impelled by eagerness to get everything done that had to be done, in order to apply myself to finding it out. Bagley was in the hall as usual when I went in. He was always there in the afternoon, always with the appearance of perfect occupation, yet, so far as I know, never doing anything. The door was open, so that I hurried in without any pause, breathless; but the sight of his calm regard, as he came to help me off with my overcoat, subdued me in a moment. Anything out of the way, anything incomprehensible, faded to nothing in the presence of Bagley. You saw and wondered how *he* was made: the parting of his hair, the tie of his white neckcloth, the fit of his trousers, all perfect as works of art; but you could see how they were done, which makes all the difference. I flung myself upon him, so to speak, without waiting to note the extreme unlikeness of the man to anything of the kind I meant. 'Bagley,' I said, 'I want you to come out with me tonight to watch —'

'Poachers, Colonel,' he said, a gleam of pleasure running all over him.

'No, Bagley; a great deal worse,' I cried.

'Yes, Colonel; at what hour, sir?' the man said; but then I had not told him what it was.

It was ten o'clock when we set out. All was perfectly quiet indoors.

My wife was with Roland, who had been quite calm, she said, and who (though, no doubt, the fever must run its course) had been better ever since I came. I told Bagley to put on a thick greatcoat over his evening coat, and did the same myself – with strong boots; for the soil was like a sponge, or worse. Talking to him, I almost forgot what we were going to do. It was darker even than it had been before, and Bagley kept very close to me as we went along. I had a small lantern in my hand, which gave us a partial guidance. We had come to the corner where the path turns. On one side was the bowling-green, which the girls had taken possession of for their croquet-ground – a wonderful enclosure surrounded by high hedges of holly, three hundred years old and more; on the other, the ruins. Both were black as night; but before we got so far, there was a little opening in which we could just discern the trees and the lighter line of the road. I thought it best to pause there and take breath. 'Bagley,' I said, 'there is something about these ruins I don't understand. It is there I am going. Keep your eyes open and your wits about you. Be ready to pounce upon any stranger you see – anything, man or woman. Don't hurt, but seize – anything you see.' 'Colonel,' said Bagley, with a little tremor in his breath, 'they do say there's things there – as is neither man nor woman.' There was no time for words. 'Are you game to follow me, my man? that's the question,' I said. Bagley fell in without a word, and saluted. I knew then I had nothing to fear.

We went, so far as I could guess, exactly as I had come, when I heard that sigh. The darkness, however was so complete that all marks, as of trees or paths, disappeared. One moment we felt our feet on the gravel, another sinking noiselessly into the slippery grass, that was all. I had shut up my lantern not wishing to scare any one, whoever it might be. Bagley followed, it seemed to me, exactly in my footsteps as I made my way, as I supposed, towards the mass of the ruined house. We seemed to take a long time groping along seeking this; the squash of the wet soil under our feet was the only thing that marked our progress. After a while I stood still to see, or rather feel, where we were. The darkness was very still, but no stiller than is usual in a winter's night. The sounds I have mentioned – the crackling of twigs, the roll of a pebble, the sound of some rustle in the dead leaves, or creeping creature on the grass – were audible when you listened, all mysterious enough when your mind is disengaged, but to me cheering now as signs of the livingness of nature, even in the death of the frost. As we stood still there came up from the trees in the glen the prolonged hoot of an owl. Bagley started with alarm, being in a state of general nervousness, and not knowing what he was afraid of. But to me the sound was encouraging and pleasant, being so comprehensible. 'An owl,' I said, under my breath. 'Y – es, Colonel,' said Bagley, his teeth chattering. We stood still about five minutes, while it broke into the still brooding of the air, the sound widening out in circles, dying upon the darkness. This sound, which is not a cheerful one, made me almost gay. It was natural, and relieved the tension of the mind. I moved on with new courage, my nervous excitement calming down.

When all at once, quite suddenly, close to us, at our feet, there broke out a cry. I made a spring backwards in the first moment of surprise and horror, and in doing so came sharply against the same rough masonry and brambles that had struck me before. This new sound came upwards from the ground – a low, moaning, wailing voice, full of suffering and pain. The contrast between it and the hoot of the owl was indescribable; the one with a wholesome wildness and natural-ness that hurt nobody – the other, a sound that made one's blood curdle, full of human misery. With a great deal of fumbling – for in spite of everything I could do to keep up my courage my hands shook – I managed to remove the slide of my lantern. The light leaped out like something living, and made the place visible in a moment. We were what would have been inside the ruined building had anything remained but the gable-wall which I have described. It was close to us, the vacant doorway in it going out straight into the blackness outside. The light showed the bit of wall, the ivy glistening upon it in clouds of dark green, the bramble-branches waving, and below, the open door – a door that led to nothing. It was from this the voice came which died out just as the light flashed upon this strange scene. There was a moment's silence, and then it broke forth again. The sound was so near, so penetrating, so pitiful, that, in the nervous start I gave, the light fell out of my hand. As I groped for it in the dark my hand was clutched by Bagley, who I think must have dropped upon his knees; but I was too much perturbed myself to think much of this. He clutched at me in the confusion of his terror, forgetting all his usual decorum. 'For God's sake, what is it, sir?' he gasped. If I yielded, there was evidently an end of both of us. 'I can't tell,' I said, 'any more than you; that's what we've got to find out: up, man, up!' I pulled him to his feet. 'Will you go round and examine the other side, or will you stay here with the lantern?' Bagley gasped at me with a face of horror. 'Can't we stay together, Colonel?' he said – his knees were trembling under him. I pushed him against the corner of the wall, and put the light into his hands. 'Stand fast till I come back; shake yourself together, man; let nothing pass you,' I said. The voice was within two or three feet of us, of that there could be no doubt.

I went myself to the other side of the wall, keeping close to it. The light shook in Bagley's hand, but, tremulous though it was, shone out through the vacant door, one oblong block of light marking all the crumbling corners and hanging masses of foliage. Was that something dark huddled in a heap by the side of it? I pushed forward across the light in the doorway, and fell upon it with my hands; but it was only a juniper-bush growing close against the wall. Meanwhile, the sight of my figure crossing the doorway had brought Bagley's nervous excitement to a height: he flew at me, gripping my shoulder. 'I've got him, Colonel! I've got him!' he cried, with a voice of sudden exultation. He thought it was a man, and was at once relieved. But at that moment the voice burst forth again between us, at our feet – more close to us than any separate being could be. He dropped off from me, and fell against the wall, his jaw dropping as if he were dying. I suppose, at the same moment, he saw that it was me whom he had clutched. I, for my part, had scarcely more command of myself. I snatched the light out of his hand, and flashed it all about me wildly. Nothing – the juniper-bush which I thought I had never seen before, the heavy growth of the glistening ivy, the brambles waving. It was close to my ears now, crying, crying, pleading as if for life. Either I heard the same words Roland had heard, or else, in my excitement, his imagination got possession of mine. The voice went on, growing into distinct articulation, but wavering, about, now from one point, now from another, as if the owner of it were moving slowly back and forward. 'Mother! mother!' and then an outburst of wailing. As my mind steadied, getting accustomed (as one's mind gets accustomed to anything), it seemed to me as if some uneasy, miserable creature was pacing up and down before a closed door. Sometimes – but that must have been excitement – I thought I heard a sound like knocking, and then another burst, 'Oh, mother! mother!' All this close, close to the space where I was standing with my lantern – now before me, now behind me: a creature restless, unhappy, moaning, crying, before the vacant doorway, which no one could either shut or open more.

'Do you hear it, Bagley? do you hear what it is saying?' I cried, stepping in through the doorway. He was lying against the wall – his eyes glazed, half dead with terror. He made a motion of his lips as if to answer me, but no sounds came; then lifted his hand with a curious imperative movement as if ordering me to be silent and listen. And how long I did so I cannot tell. It began to have an interest, an exciting hold upon me, which I could not describe. It seemed to call up visibly a scene any one could understand – a something shut out, restlessly wandering to and fro; sometimes the voice dropped, as if throwing itself down – sometimes wandered off a few paces, growing sharp and clear. 'Oh, mother, let me in! oh, mother, mother, let me in! oh, let me in!' every word was clear to me. No wonder the boy had gone wild with pity. I tried to steady my mind upon Roland, upon his conviction that I could do something, but my head swam with the excitement, even when I partially overcame the terror. At last the words died away, and there was a sound of sobs and moaning. I cried out, 'In the name of God who are you?' with a kind of feeling in my mind that to use the name of God was profane, seeing that I did not believe in ghosts or anything supernatural; but I did it all the same, and waited, my heart giving a leap of terror lest there should be a reply. Why this should have been I cannot tell, but I had a feeling that if there was an answer it would be more than I could bear. But there was no answer; the moaning went on, and then, as if it had been real, the voice rose a little higher again, the words recommenced, 'Oh, mother, let me in! oh, mother, let me in!' with an expression that was heartbreaking to hear.

As if it had been real! What do I mean by that? I suppose I got less alarmed as the thing went on. I began to recover the use of my senses – I seemed to explain it all to myself by saying that this had once happened, that it was a recollection of a real scene. Why there should have seemed something quite satisfactory and composing in this explanation I cannot tell, but so it was. I began to listen almost as if it had been a play, forgetting Bagley, who, I almost think, had fainted, leaning against the wall. I was startled out of this strange spectatorship that had fallen upon me by the sudden rush of something which made my heart jump once more, a large black figure in the doorway waving its arms. 'Come in! come in! come in!' it shouted out hoarsely at the top of a deep bass voice, and then poor Bagley fell down senseless across the threshold. He was less sophisticated than I – he had not been able to bear it any longer. I took him for something supernatural, as he took me, and it was some time before I awoke to the necessities of the moment. I remembered only after, that from the time I began to give my attention to the man, I heard the other voice no more. It was some time before I brought him to. It must have been a strange scene; the lantern making a luminous spot in the darkness, the man's white face lying on the black earth, I over him, doing what I could for him. Probably I should have been thought to be murdering him had any one seen us. When at last I succeeded in pouring a little brandy down his throat, he sat up and looked about him wildly. 'What's up?' he said; then recognizing me, tried to struggle to his feet with a faint 'Beg your pardon, Colonel.' I got him home as best I could, making him lean upon my arm. The great fellow was as weak as a child. Fortunately he did not for some time remember what had happened. From the time Bagley fell the voice had stopped, and all was still.

'You've got an epidemic in your house, Colonel,' Simson said to me next morning. 'What's the meaning of it all? Here's your butler raving about a voice. This will never do, you know; and so far as I can make out, you are in it too.'

'Yes, I am in it, doctor. I thought I had better speak to you. Of course you are treating Roland all right — but the boy is not raving, he is as sane as you or me. It's all true.'

'As sane as — I — or you. I never thought the boy insane. He's got cerebral excitement, fever. I don't know what you've got. There's something very queer about the look of your eyes.'

'Come,' said I, 'you can't put us all to bed, you know. You had better listen and hear the symptoms in full.'

The doctor shrugged his shoulders, but he listened to me patiently. He did not believe a word of the story, that was clear; but he heard it all from beginning to end. 'My dear fellow,' he said, 'the boy told me just the same. It's an epidemic. When one person falls a victim to this sort of thing, it's as safe as can be — there's always two or three.'

'Then how do you account for it?' I said.

'Oh, account for it! — that's a different matter; there's no accounting for the freaks our brains are subject to. If it's delusion; if it's some trick of the echoes or the winds — some phonetic disturbance or other —'

'Come with me to-night, and judge for yourself,' I said.

Upon this he laughed aloud, then said, 'That's not such a bad idea; but it would ruin me for ever if it were known that John Simson was ghost-hunting.'

'There it is,' said I; 'you dart down on us who are unlearned with your phonetic disturbances, but you daren't examine what the thing really is for fear of being laughed at. That's science!'

'It's not science — it's common-sense,' said the doctor. 'The thing has delusion on the front of it. It is encouraging an unwholesome tendency even to examine. What good could come of it? Even if I am convinced, I shouldn't believe.'

'I should have said so yesterday; and I don't want you to be convinced or to believe,' said I. 'If you prove it to be a delusion, I shall be very much obliged to you for one. Come; somebody must go with me.'

'You are cool,' said the doctor. 'You've disabled this poor fellow of yours, and made him — on that point — a lunatic for life; and now you want to disable me. But for once, I'll do it. To save appearance, if you'll give me a bed, I'll come over after my last rounds.'

314

It was agreed that I should meet him at the gate, and that we should visit the scene of last night's occurrences before we came to the house, so that nobody might be the wiser. It was scarcely possible to hope that the cause of Bagley's sudden illness should not somehow steal into the knowledge of the servants at least, and it was better that all should be done as quietly as possible. The day seemed to me a very long one. I had to spend a certain part of it with Roland, which was a terrible ordeal for me – for what could I say to the boy? The improvement continued, but he was still in a very precarious state, and the trembling vehemence with which he turned to me when his mother left the room filled me with alarm. 'Father?' he said, quietly. 'Yes, my boy; I am giving my best attention to it – all is being done that I can do. I have not come to any conclusion – yet. I am neglecting nothing you said,' I cried. What I could not do was to give his active mind any encouragement to dwell upon the mystery. It was a hard predicament, for some satisfaction had to be given him. He looked at me very wistfully, with the great blue eyes which shone so large and brilliant out of his white and worn face. 'You must trust me,' I said. 'Yes, father. Father understands,' he said to himself, as if to soothe some inward doubt. I left him as soon as I could. He was about the most precious thing I had on earth, and his health my first thought; but yet somehow, in the excitement of this other subject, I put that aside, and preferred not to dwell upon Roland, which was the most curious part of it all.

That night at eleven I met Simson at the gate. He had come by train, and I let him in gently myself. I had been so much absorbed in the coming experiment that I passed the ruins in going to meet him, almost without thought, if you can understand that. I had my lantern; and he showed me a coil of taper which he had ready for use. 'There is nothing like light,' he said, in his scoffing tone. It was a very still night, scarcely a sound, but not so dark. We could keep the path without difficulty as we went along. As we approached the spot we could hear a low moaning, broken occasionally by a bitter cry. 'Perhaps that is your voice,' said the doctor; 'I thought it must be something of the kind. That's a poor brute caught in some of these infernal traps of yours; you'll find it among the bushes somewhere.' I said nothing. I felt no particular fear, but a triumphant satisfaction in what was to follow. I led him to the spot where Bagley and I had stood on the previous night. All was silent as a winter night could be – so silent that we heard far off the sound of the horses in the stables, the shutting of a window at the house. Simson lighted his taper and went peering about, poking into all the corners. We looked like two conspirators lying in wait for some unfortunate traveller; but not a sound broke the quiet. The moaning had stopped before we came up; a star or two shone over us in the sky, looking down as if surprised at our strange proceedings. Dr Simson did nothing but utter subdued laughs under his breath. 'I thought as much,' he said. 'It is just the same with tables and all other kinds of ghostly apparatus; a sceptic's presence stops everything. When I am present nothing ever comes off. How long do you think it will be necessary to stay here? Oh, I don't complain; only, when *you* are satisfied, *I* am – quite.'

I will not deny that I was disappointed beyond measure by this result. It made me look like a credulous fool. It gave the doctor such a pull over me as nothing else could. I should point all his morals for years to come, and his materialism, his scepticism, would be increased beyond endurance. 'It seems, indeed,' I said, 'that there is to be no —' 'Manifestation,' he said, laughing; 'that is what all the mediums say. No manifestations, in consequence of the presence of an unbeliever.' His laugh sounded very uncomfortable to me in the silence; and it was now near midnight. But that laugh seemed the signal; before it died away the moaning we had heard before was resumed. It started from some distance off, and came towards us, nearer and nearer, like some one walking along and moaning to himself. There could be no idea now that it was a hare caught in a trap. The approach was slow, like that of a weak person with little halts and pauses. We heard it coming along the grass straight towards the vacant doorway. Simson had been a little startled by the first sound. He said hastily, 'That child has no business to be out so late.' But he felt, as well as I, that this was no child's voice. As it came nearer, he grew silent, and, going to the doorway with his taper, stood looking out towards the sound. The taper being unprotected blew about in the night air, though there was scarcely any wind. I threw the light of my lantern steady and white across the same space. It was in a blaze of light in the midst of the blackness. A little icy thrill had gone over me at the first sound, but as it came close, I confess that my only feeling was satisfaction. The scoffer could scoff no more. The light touched his own face, and showed a very perplexed countenance. If he was afraid, he concealed it with great success, but he was perplexed. And then all that had happened on the previous night was enacted once more. It fell strangely upon me with a sense of repetition. Every cry, every sob seemed the same as before. I listened almost without any emotion at all in my own person, thinking of its effect upon Simson. He maintained a very bold front on the whole. All that coming and going of the voice was, if our ears could be trusted, exactly in front of the vacant, blank doorway, blazing full of light, which caught and shone in the glistening leaves of the great hollies at a little distance. Not a rabbit could have crossed the turf without being seen – but there was nothing. After a time, Simson, with a certain caution and bodily reluctance, as it seemed to me, went out with his roll of taper into this space. His figure showed against the holly in full outline. Just at this moment the voice sank, as was its custom, and seemed to fling itself down at the door. Simson recoiled violently, as if someone had come up against him, then turned, and held his taper low as if examining something. 'Do you see anybody?' I cried in a whisper, feeling the chill of nervous panic steal over me at this action. 'It's nothing but a — confounded juniper-bush,' he said. This I knew very well to be nonsense, for the juniper-bush was on the other side. He went about after this round and round, poking his taper everywhere, then returned to me on the inner side of the wall. He scoffed no longer; his face was contracted and pale. 'How long does this go on?' he whispered to me, like a man who does not wish to interrupt someone who is speaking. I had become too much perturbed myself to remark whether the successions and changes of the voice were the same as last night. It suddenly went out in the air almost as he was speaking, with a soft reiterated sob dying away. If there had been anything to be seen, I should have said that the person was at that moment crouching on the ground close to the door.

We walked home very silent afterwards. It was only when we were in sight of the house that I said, 'What do you think of it?' 'I can't tell what to think of it,' he said, quickly. He took – though he was a very temperate man – not the claret I was going to offer him, but some brandy from the tray, and swallowed it almost undiluted. 'Mind you, I don't believe a word of it,' he said, when he had lighted his candle; 'but I can't tell what to think,' he turned round to add, when he was half-way upstairs.

All of this, however, did me no good with the solution of my problem. I was to help this weeping, sobbing thing, which was already to me as distinct a personality as anything I knew – or what should I say to Roland? It was on my heart that my boy would die if I could not find some way of helping this creature. You may be surprised that I should speak of it in this way. I did not know if it was man or woman; but I no more doubted that it was a soul in pain than I doubted my own being; and it was my business to soothe this pain – to deliver it, if that was possible. Was ever such a task given to an anxious father trembling for his only boy? I felt in my heart, fantastic as it may appear, that I must fulfil this somehow, or part with my child; and you may conceive that rather than do that I was ready to die. But even my

317

dying would not have advanced me – unless by bringing me into the same world with that seeker at the door.

Next morning Simson was out before breakfast, and came in with evident signs of the damp grass on his boots, and a look of worry and weariness, which did not say much for the night he had passed. He improved a little after breakfast, and visited his two patients, for Bagley was still an invalid. I went out with him on his way to the train, to hear what he had to say about the boy. 'He is going on very well,' he said; 'there are no complications as yet. But mind you, that's not a boy to be trifled with, Mortimer. Not a word to him about last night.' I had to tell him then of my last interview with Roland, and of the impossible demand he had made upon me – by which, though he tried to laugh, he was much discomposed, as I could see. 'We must just perjure ourselves all round,' he said, 'and swear you exorcised it;' but the man was too kind-hearted to be satisfied with that. 'It's frightfully serious for you, Mortimer. I can't laugh as I should like to. I wish I saw a way out of it, for your sake. By the way,' he added shortly, 'didn't you notice that juniper-bush on the left-hand side?' 'There was one on the right hand of the door. I noticed you made that mistake last night.' 'Mistake!' he cried, with a curious low laugh, pulling up the collar of his coat as though he felt the cold – 'there's no juniper there this morning, left or right. Just go and see.' As he stepped into the train a few minutes after, he looked back upon me and beckoned me for a parting word. 'I'm coming back to-night,' he said.

I don't think I had any feeling about this as I turned away from that common bustle of the railway which made my private preoccupations feel so strangely out of date. There had been a distinct satisfaction in my mind before that his scepticism had been so entirely defeated. But the more serious part of the matter pressed upon me now. I went straight from the railway to the manse, which stood on a little plateau on the side of the river opposite to the woods of Brentwood. The minister was one of a class which is not so common in Scotland as it used to be. He was a man of good family, well educated in the Scotch way, strong in philosophy, not so strong in Greek, strongest of all in experience – a man who had 'come across', in the course of his life, most people of note that had ever been in Scotland – and who was said to be very sound in doctrine, without infringing the toleration with which old men, who are good men, are generally endowed. He was old-fashioned; perhaps he did not think so much about the troublous problems of theology as many of the young men, nor ask himself any hard questions about the Confession of Faith – but he understood human nature, which is perhaps better. He received me with a cordial welcome. 'Come away, Colonel Mortimer,' he said; 'I'm all the more glad to see you, that I feel it's a good sign for the boy. He's doing well? – God be praised – and the Lord bless him and keep him. He has many a poor body's prayers – and that can do nobody harm.'

'He will need them all, Dr Moncrieff,' I said, 'and your counsel too.' And I told him the story – more than I had told Simson. The old clergyman listened to me with many suppressed exclamations, and at the end the water stood in his eyes.

'That's just beautiful,' he said. 'I do not mind to have heard anything like it; it's as fine as Burns when he wished deliverance to one that is prayed for in no kirk. Ay, ay! so he would have you console the poor lost spirit? God bless the boy! There's something more than common in that, Colonel Mortimer. And also the faith of him in his father! – I would like to put that into a sermon.' Then the old gentleman gave me an alarmed look, and said, 'No, no; I was not meaning a sermon; but I must write it down for the "Children's Record".' I saw the thought that passed through his mind. Either he thought, or he feared I would think, of a funeral sermon. You may believe this did not make me more cheerful.

I can scarcely say that Dr Moncrieff gave me any advice. How could any one advise on such a subject? But he said, 'I think I'll come too. I'm an old man; I'm less liable to be frighted than those that are further off the world unseen. It behoves me to think of my own journey there. I've no cut-and-dry beliefs on the subject. I'll come too: and maybe at the moment the Lord will put into our heads what to do.'

This gave me a little comfort – more than Simson had given me. To be clear about the cause of it was not my grand desire. It was another thing that was in my mind – my boy. As for the poor soul at the open door, I had no more doubt, as I have said, of its existence than I had of my own. It was no ghost to me. I knew the creature, and it was in trouble. That was my feeling about it, as it was Roland's. To hear it first was a great shock to my nerves, but not now; a man will get accustomed to anything. But to do something for it was the great problem; how was I to be serviceable to a being that was invisible, that was mortal no longer? 'Maybe at the moment the Lord will put it into our heads.' This is very old-fashioned phraseology, and a week before, most likely, I should have smiled (though always with kindness) at Dr Moncrieff's credulity; but there was a great comfort, whether rational or otherwise I cannot say, in the mere sound of the words.

The road to the station and the village lay through the glen – not by the ruins; but though the sunshine and the fresh air, and the beauty of the trees, and the sound of the water were all very soothing to the spirits, my mind was so full of my own subject that I could not refrain from turning to the right hand as I got to the top of the glen, and going straight to the place which I may call the scene of all my thoughts. It was lying full in the sunshine, like all the rest of the world. The ruined gable looked due east, and in the present aspect of the sun the light streamed down through the doorway as our lantern had done, throwing a flood of light upon the damp grass beyond. There was a strange suggestion in the open door – so futile, a kind of emblem of vanity – all free around, so that you could go where you pleased, and yet that semblance of an enclosure – that way of entrance, unnecessary, leading to nothing. And why any creature should pray and weep to get in – to nothing: or be kept out – by nothing! You could not dwell upon it, or it made your brain go round. I remembered, however, what Simson said about the juniper, with a little smile on my own mind as to the inaccuracy of recollection, which even a scientific man will be guilty of. I could see now the light of my lantern gleaming upon the wet glistening surface of the spiky leaves at the right hand – and he ready to go to the stake for it that it was the left! I went round to make sure. And then I saw what he had said. Right or left there was no juniper at all. I was confounded by this, though it was entirely a matter of detail: nothing at all: a bush of brambles waving, the grass growing up to the very walls. But after all, though it gave me a shock for a moment, what did that matter? There were marks as if a number of footsteps had been up and down in front of the door; but these might have been our steps; and all was bright, and peaceful, and still. I poked about the other ruin – the larger ruins of the old house – for some time, as I had done before. There were marks upon the grass here and there, I could not call them footsteps, all about; but that told for nothing one way or another. I had examined the ruined rooms closely the first day. They were half filled up with soil and *débris*, withered brackens and bramble – no refuge for any one there. It vexed me that Jarvis should see me coming from that spot when he came up to me for his orders. I don't know whether my nocturnal expeditions had got wind among the servants. But there was a significant look in his face. Something in it I felt was like my own sensation when Simson in the midst of his scepticism was struck dumb. Jarvis felt satisfied that his veracity had been put beyond question. I never spoke to a servant of mine in such a peremptory tone before. I sent him away 'with a flea in his lug', as the man described it afterwards. Interference of any kind was intolerable to me at such a moment.

But what was strangest of all was, that I could not face Roland. I did not go up to his room as I would have naturally done at once. This the girls could not understand. They saw there was some mystery in it. 'Mother has gone to lie down,' Agatha said; 'he has had such a good night.' 'But he wants you so, papa!' cried little Jeanie, always with her two arms embracing mine in a pretty way she had. I was obliged to go at last – but what could I say? I could only kiss him, and tell him to keep still – that I was doing all I could. There is something mystical about the patience of a child. 'It will come all right, won't it, father?' he said. 'God grant it may! I hope so, Roland.' 'Oh yes, it will come all right.' Perhaps he understood that in the midst of my anxiety I could not stay with him as I should have done otherwise. But the girls were more surprised than it is possible to describe. They looked at me with wondering eyes. 'If I were ill, papa, and you only stayed with me a moment, I should break my heart,' said Agatha. But the boy had a sympathetic feeling. He knew that of my own will I would not have done it. I shut myself up in the library, where I could not rest, but kept pacing up and down like a caged beast. What could I do? and if I could do nothing, what would become of my boy? These were the questions that, without ceasing, pursued each other through my mind.

Simson came out to dinner, and when the house was all still, and most of the servants in bed, we went out and met Dr Moncrieff, as we had appointed, at the head of the glen. Simson, for his part, was disposed to scoff at the Doctor. 'If there are to be any spells, you know, I'll cut the whole concern,' he said. I did not make him any reply. I had not invited him; he could go or come as he pleased. He was very talkative, far more so than suited my humour, as we went on. 'One thing is certain, you know, there must be some human agency,' he said. 'It is all bosh about apparitions. I never have investigated the laws of sound to any great extent, and there's a great deal in ventriloquism that we don't know much about.' 'If it's the same to you,' I said, 'I wish you'd keep all that to yourself, Simson. It doesn't suit my state of mind.' 'Oh, I hope I know how to respect idiosyncrasy,' he said. The very tone of his voice irritated me beyond measure. These scientific fellows, I wonder people put up with them as they do, when you have no mind for their cold-blooded confidence. Dr Moncrieff met us about eleven o'clock, the same time as on the previous night. He was a large man, with a venerable countenance and white hair – old, but in full vigour, and thinking less of a cold night walk than many a younger man. He had his lantern as I had. We were fully provided with means of lighting the place, and we were all of us resolute men. We had a rapid consultation as we went up, and the result was that we divided to different posts. Dr Moncrieff remained inside the wall – if you can call that inside where there was no wall but one. Simson placed himself on the side next the ruins, so as to intercept any communication with the old house, which was what his mind was fixed upon. I was posted on the other side. To say that nothing could come near without being seen was self-evident. It had been so also on the previous night. Now, with our three lights in the midst of the darkness, the whole place seemed illuminated. Dr Moncrieff's lantern, which was a large one, without any means of shutting up – an old-fashioned lantern with a pierced and ornamental top – shone steadily, the rays shooting out of it upward into the gloom. He placed it on the grass, where the middle of the room, if this had been a room, would have been. The usual effect of the light streaming out of the doorway was prevented by the illumination which Simson and I on either side supplied. With these differences, everything seemed as on the previous night.

And what occurred was exactly the same, with the same air of repetition, point for point, as I had formerly remarked. I declare that it seemed to me as if I were pushed against, put aside, by the owner of the voice as he paced up and down in his trouble – though these are perfectly futile words, seeing that the stream of light from my lantern, and that from Simson's taper, lay broad and clear, without a shadow, without the smallest break, across the entire breadth of the grass. I had ceased even to be alarmed, for my part. My heart was rent with pity and trouble – pity for the poor suffering human creature that moaned and pleaded so, and trouble for myself and my boy. God! if I could not find any help – and what help could I find? – Roland would die.

We were all perfectly still till the first outburst was exhausted, as I knew (by experience) it would be. Dr Moncrieff, to whom it was new, was quite motionless on the other side of the wall, as we were in our places. My heart had remained almost at its usual beating during the voice. I was used to it; it did not rouse all my pulses as it did at first. But just as it threw itself sobbing at the door (I cannot use other words), there suddenly came something which sent the blood coursing through my veins and my heart into my mouth. It was a voice inside the wall – the minister's well-known voice. I would have been prepared for it in any kind of adjuration, but I was not prepared for what I heard. It came out with a sort of stammering, as if too much moved for utterance. 'Willie, Willie! Oh, God preserve us! Is it you?'

These simple words had an effect upon me that the voice of the invisible creature had ceased to have. I thought the old man, whom I had brought into this danger, had gone mad with terror. I made a dash round to the other side of the wall, half crazed myself with the thought. He was standing where I had left him, his shadow thrown vague and large upon the grass by the lantern which stood at his feet. I lifted my own light to see his face as I rushed forward. He was very pale, his eyes wet and glistening, his mouth quivering with parted lips. He neither saw nor heard me. We that had gone through this experience before, had crouched towards each other to get a little strength to bear it. But he was not even aware that I was there. His whole being seemed absorbed in anxiety and tenderness. He held out his hands, which trembled, but it seemed to me with eagerness, not fear. He went on speaking all the time. 'Willie, if it is you – and it's you, if it is not a delusion of Satan – Willie, lad! why come ye here frighting them that know you not? Why came ye not to me?'

He seemed to wait for an answer. When his voice ceased, his countenance, every line moving, continued to speak. Simson gave me another terrible shock, stealing into the open doorway with his light, as much awe-stricken, as wildly curious, as I. But the minister resumed, without seeing Simson, speaking to someone else. His voice took a tone of expostulation –

'Is this right to come here? Your mother's gone with your name on her lips. Do you think she would ever close her door on her own lad? Do ye think the Lord will close the door, ye faint-hearted creature? No! – I forbid ye! I forbid ye!' cried the old man. The sobbing voice had begun to resume its cries. He made a step forward, calling out the last words in a voice of command. 'I forbid ye! Cry out no more to man. Go home, ye wandering spirit! go home! Do you hear me? – me that christened ye, that have struggled with ye, that have wrestled for ye with the Lord!' Here the loud tones of his voice sank into tenderness. 'And her too, poor woman! poor woman! her you are calling upon. She's no here. You'll find her with the Lord. Go there and seek her, not here. Do you hear me, lad? go after her there. He'll let you in, though it's late. Man, take heart! if you will lie and sob and greet, let it be at heaven's gate, and no your poor mother's ruined door.'

He stopped to get his breath: and the voice had stopped, not as it had done before, when its time was exhausted and all its repetitions said, but with a sobbing catch in the breath as if over-ruled. Then the minister spoke again, 'Are you hearing me, Will? Oh, laddie, you've liked the beggarly elements all your days. Be done with them now. Go home to the Father – the Father! Are you hearing me?' Here the old man sank down upon his knees, his face raised upwards, his hands held up with a tremble in them, all white in the light in the midst of the darkness. I resisted as long as I could, though I cannot tell why – then I, too, dropped upon my knees. Simson all the time stood in the doorway, with an expression in his face such as words could not tell, his under lip dropped, his eyes wild, staring. It seemed to be to him, that image of blank ignorance and wonder, that we were praying. All the time the voice, with a low arrested sobbing, lay just where he was standing, as I thought.

'Lord,' the minister said – 'Lord, take him into Thy everlasting habitations. The mother he cries to is with Thee. Who can open to him but Thee? Lord, when is it too late for Thee, or what is too hard for Thee? Lord, let that woman there draw him inower! Let her draw him inower!'

I sprang forward to catch something in my arms that flung itself wildly within the door. The illusion was so strong, that I never paused till I felt my forehead graze against the wall and my hands clutch the ground – for there was nobody there to save from falling, as in my foolishness I thought. Simson held out his hand to me to help me up. He was trembling and cold, his lower lip hanging, his speech almost inarticulate. 'It's gone,' he said, stammering – 'it's gone!' We leant upon each other for a moment, trembling so much both of us that the whole scene trembled as if it were going to dissolve and disappear; and yet as long as I live I will never forget it – the shining of the strange lights, the blackness all round, the kneeling figure with all the whiteness of the light concentrated on its white venerable head and uplifted hands. A strange solemn stillness seemed to close all round us. By intervals a single syllable, 'Lord! Lord!' came from the old minister's lips. He saw none of us, nor thought of us. I never knew how long we stood, like sentinels guarding him at his prayers, holding our lights in a confused dazed way, not knowing what we did. But at last he rose from his knees, and standing up at his full height, raised his arms, as the Scotch manner is at the end of a religious service, and solemnly gave the apostolical benediction – to what? to the silent earth, the dark woods, the wide breathing atmosphere – for we were but spectators gasping an Amen!

It seemed to me that it must be the middle of the night, as we all walked back. It was in reality very late. Dr Moncrieff put his arm into mine. He walked slowly, with an air of exhaustion. It was as if we were coming from a deathbed. Something hushed and solemnized the very air. There was that sense of relief in it which there always is at the end of a death-struggle. And nature, persistent, never daunted, came back in all of us, as we returned into the ways of life. We said nothing to each other, indeed, for a time; but when we got clear of the trees and reached the opening near the house, where we could see the sky, Dr Moncrieff himself was the first to speak. 'I must be going,' he said; 'it's very late, I'm afraid. I will go down the glen, as I came.'

'But not alone. I am going with you, Doctor.'

'Well, I will not oppose it. I am an old man, and agitation wearies more than work. Yes; I'll be thankful of your arm. To-night, Colonel, you've done me more good turns than one.'

I pressed his hand on my arm, not feeling able to speak. But Simson, who turned with us, and who had gone along all this time with his taper flaring, in entire unconsciousness, came to himself, apparently at the sound of our voices, and put out that wild little torch with a quick movement, as if of shame. 'Let me carry your lantern,' he said; 'it is heavy.' He recovered with a spring, and in a moment, from the awe-stricken spectator he had been, became himself, sceptical and cynical. 'I should like to ask you a question,' he said. 'Do you believe in Purgatory, Doctor? It's not in the tenets of the Church, so far as I know.'

'Sir,' said Dr Moncrieff, 'an old man like me is sometimes not very sure what he believes. There is just one thing I am certain of – and that is the loving-kindness of God.'

'But I thought that was in this life. I am no theologian —'

'Sir,' said the old man again, with a tremor in him which I could feel going over all his frame, 'if I saw a friend of mine within the gates of hell, I would not despair but his Father would take him by the hand still – if he cried like *yon*.'

'I allow it is very strange – very strange. I cannot see through it. That there must be human agency, I feel sure. Doctor, what made you decide upon the person and the name?'

The minister put out his hand with the impatience which a man might show if he were asked how he recognized his brother. 'Tuts!' he said, in familiar speech – then more solemnly, 'how should I not recognize a person that I know better – far better – than I know you?'

'Then you saw the man?'

Dr Moncrieff made no reply. He moved his hand again with a little impatient movement, and walked on, leaning heavily on my arm. And we went on for a long time without another word, threading the dark paths, which were steep and slippery with the damp of the winter. The air was very still – not more than enough to make a faint sighing in the branches, which mingled with the sound of the water to which we were descending. When we spoke again, it was about indifferent matters – about the height of the river, and the recent rains. We parted with the minister at his own door, where his old housekeeper appeared in great perturbation, waiting for him. 'Eh me, minister! the young gentleman will be worse?' she cried.

'Far from that – better. God bless him!' Dr Moncrieff said.

I think if Simson had begun again to me with his questions, I should have pitched him over the rocks as we returned up the glen; but he was silent, by a good inspiration. And the sky was clearer than it had been for many nights, shining high over the trees, with here and there a star faintly gleaming through the wilderness of dark and bare branches. The air, as I have said, was very soft in them, with a subdued and peaceful cadence. It was real, like every natural sound, and came to us like a hush of peace and relief. I thought there was a sound in it as of the breath of a sleeper, and it seemed clear to me that Roland must be sleeping, satisfied and calm. We went up to his room when we went in. There we found the complete hush of rest. My wife looked up out of a doze, and gave me a smile; 'I think he is a great deal better: but you are very late,' she said in a whisper, shading the light with her hand that the doctor might see his patient. The boy had got back something like his own colour. He woke as we stood all round his bed. His eyes had the happy half-awakened look of childhood, glad to shut again, yet pleased with the interruption and glimmer of the light. I stooped over him and kissed his forehead, which was moist and cool. 'All is well, Roland,' I said. He looked up at me with a glance of pleasure, and took my hand and laid his cheek upon it, and so went to sleep.

For some nights after, I watched among the ruins, spending all the dark hours up to midnight patrolling about the bit of wall which was associated with so many emotions; but I heard nothing, and saw nothing beyond the quiet course of nature: nor, so far as I am aware, has anything been heard again. Dr Moncrieff gave me the history of the youth, whom he never hesitated to name. I did not ask, as Simson did, how he recognized him. He had been a prodigal — weak, foolish, easily imposed upon, and 'led away', as people say. All that we had heard had passed actually in life, the Doctor said. The young man had come home thus a day or two after his mother died — who was no more than the housekeeper in the old house — and distracted with the news, had thrown himself down at the door and called upon her to let him in. The old man could scarcely speak of it for tears. To me it seemed as if — heaven help us, how little do we know about anything! — a scene like that might impress itself somehow upon the hidden heart of nature. I do not pretend to know how, but the repetition had struck me at the time as, in its terrible strangeness and incomprehensibility, almost mechanical — as if the unseen actor could not exceed or vary, but was bound to re-enact the whole. One thing that struck me, however, greatly, was the likeness between the old minister and my boy in the manner of regarding these strange phenomena. Dr Moncrieff was not

326

terrified, as I had been myself, and all the rest of us. It was no 'ghost', as I fear we all vulgarly considered it, to him – but a poor creature whom he knew under these conditions, just as he had known him in the flesh, having no doubt of his identity. And to Roland it was the same. This spirit in pain – if it was a spirit – this voice out of the unseen – was a poor fellow-creature in misery, to be succoured and helped out of his trouble, to my boy. He spoke to me quite frankly about it when he got better. 'I knew father would find out some way,' he said. And this was when he was strong and well, and all idea that he would turn hysterical or become a seer of visions had happily passed away.

I must add one curious fact which does not seem to me to have any relation to the above, but which Simson made great use of, as the human agency which he was determined to find somehow. We had examined the ruins very closely at the time of these occurrences; but afterwards, when all was over, as we went casually about them one Sunday afternoon in the idleness of that unemployed day, Simson with his stick penetrated an old window which had been entirely blocked up with fallen soil. He jumped down into it in great excitement, and called me to follow. There we found a little hole – for it was more a hole than a room – entirely hidden under the ivy and ruins, in which there was a quantity of straw laid in a corner, as if someone had made a bed there, and some remains of crusts about the floor. Someone had lodged there, and not very long before, he made out; and that this unknown being was the author of all the mysterious sounds we heard he is convinced. 'I told you it was human agency,' he said, triumphantly. He forgets, I suppose, how he and I stood with our lights seeing nothing, while the space between us was audibly traversed by something that could speak, and sob, and suffer. There is no argument with men of this kind. He is ready to get up a laugh against me on this slender ground. 'I was puzzled myself – I could not make it out – but I always felt convinced human agency was at the bottom of it. And here it is – and a clever fellow he must have been,' the Doctor says.

Bagley left my service as soon as he got well. He assured me it was no want of respect; but he could not stand 'them kind of things', and the man was so shaken and ghastly that I was glad to give him a present and let him go. For my own part, I made a point of staying out the time, two years, for which I had taken Brentwood; but I did not renew my tenancy. By that time we had settled, and found for ourselves a pleasant home of our own.

I must add that when the doctor defies me, I can always bring back gravity to his countenance, and a pause in his railing, when I remind him of the juniper-bush. To me that was a matter of little importance. I could believe I was mistaken. I did not care about it one way or other; but on his mind the effect was different. The miserable voice, the spirit in pain, he could think of as the result of ventriloquism, or reverberation, or – anything you please: an elaborate prolonged hoax executed somehow by the tramp that had found a lodging in the old tower. But the juniper-bush staggered him. Things have effects so different on the minds of different men.

The Kiss of Blood

BY SIR ARTHUR CONAN DOYLE

In 1967, shortly before the introduction of colour transmissions on BBC2, the Corporation started a practical training experiment to familiarize its staff in the use of the new equipment for the service. In a somewhat surprising decision considering the normally sober-sided nature of the BBC, the channel opted to produce a series of half-hour plays under the generic title of Late Night Horror *which it hoped would provide the necessary experience. The resultant use by producer Harry Moore and his scriptwriters of stories replete with colourful surroundings and lashings of blood and gore was, perhaps, hardly surprising! Amongst the tales adapted were H. Russell Wakefield's 'The Triumph of Death' about a crumbling, haunted mansion, dramatized by David Campton and starring Claire Bloom and Nora Nicholson; an unexpectedly erotic chiller, 'The Bells of Hell' by Robert Aickman, dramatized by Hugh Whitemore with Michele Dotrice and Ronald Hines; 'The Corpse Can't Play' by John Burke, adapted by Hugh Leonard, with Clare Austin and Frank Barry; and, for a second time on television, 'William and Mary' by Roald Dahl, which Richard Martin directed with Donald Sinden, Brenda Bruce and Andre van Gyseghem. Commenting on the series after its launch, Francis Hope wrote in the* New Statesman, *'We are all ready with scornful dismissals of green rubber monsters, diaphanous spooks and gouts of ketchup, but the series seems to me practically effective and artistically interesting. I was, indeed, horrified, but I wouldn't necessarily call that a success for the programme.'*

The episode to take most advantage of its new freedom to use colour was 'The Kiss of Blood' an adaptation of the short story, 'The Case of Lady Sannox' by Sir Arthur Conan Doyle (1859–1930), whose

Sherlock Holmes stories had already made a considerable impact on both British and American television. (See my companion volume, The Television Detectives' Omnibus, Orion 1992.) The story of the beautiful young wife of one of the richest men in London who horrifyingly discovers when she takes a lover that her husband is not the meek and mild man she believed, was stylishly adapted by John Hawksworth and directed with relish by Richard Martin. Diane Cilento was dazzling as Lady Sannox, Roy Dotrice dashing as her lover, and Charles Workman all determination and cunning as the cuckolded Lord Sannox. The episode was screened at eleven-fifty PM *on Friday, 16 May, 1968, after which the jangled nerves of viewers were allowed to settle with* Late Night Line-Up *'a last look around the daily scene' until midnight. . .*

THE relations between Douglas Stone and the notorious Lady Sannox were very well known both among the fashionable circles of which she was a brilliant member, and the scientific bodies which numbered him among their most illustrious *confrères*. There was naturally, therefore, a very widespread interest when it was announced one morning that the lady had absolutely and for ever taken the veil, and that the world would see her no more. When, at the very tail of this rumour, there came the assurance that the celebrated operating surgeon, the man of steel nerves, had been found in the morning by his valet, seated on one side of his bed, smiling pleasantly upon the universe, with both legs jammed into one side of his breeches and his great brain about as valuable as a cap full of porridge, the matter was strong enough to give quite a little thrill of interest to folk who had never hoped that their jaded nerves were capable of such a sensation.

Douglas Stone in his prime was one of the most remarkable men in England. Indeed, he could hardly be said to have ever reached his prime, for he was but nine-and-thirty at the time of this little incident. Those who knew him best were aware that famous as he was as a surgeon, he might have succeeded with even greater rapidity in any of a dozen lines of life. He could have cut his way to fame as a soldier, struggled to it as an explorer, bullied for it in the courts, or built it out of stone and iron as an engineer. He was born to be great, for he could plan what another man dare not do, and he could do what another man dare not plan. In surgery none could follow him. His nerve, his judgement, his intuition, were things apart. Again and again his knife cut away death, but grazed the very springs of life in doing it, until his assistants were as white as the patient. His energy, his audacity, his full-blooded self-confidence – does not the memory of them still linger to the south of Marylebone Road and the north of Oxford Street?

His vices were as magnificent as his virtues, and infinitely more picturesque. Large as was his income, and it was the third largest of all professional men in London, it was far beneath the luxury of his living. Deep in his complex nature lay a rich vein of sensualism, at the sport of which he placed all the prizes of his life. The eye, the ear, the touch, the palate, all were his masters. The bouquet of old vintages, the scent of rare exotics, the curves and tints of the daintiest potteries of Europe, it was to these that the quick-running stream of gold was transformed. And then there came his sudden mad passion for Lady Sannox, when a single interview with two challenging glances and a whispered word set him ablaze. She was the loveliest woman in London and the only one to him. He was one of the handsomest men in London, but not the only one to her. She had a liking for new experiences, and was gracious to most men who wooed her. It may have been cause or it may have been effect that Lord Sannox looked fifty, though he was but six-and-thirty.

He was a quiet, silent, neutral-tinted man, this lord, with thin lips and heavy eyelids, much given to gardening, and full of home-like habits. He had at one time been fond of acting, had even rented a theatre in London, and on its boards had first seen Miss Marion Dawson, to whom he had offered his hand, his title, and the third of a county. Since his marriage this early hobby had become distasteful to him. Even in private theatricals it was no longer possible to persuade him to exercise the talent which he had often shown that he possessed. He was happier with a spade and a watering-can among his orchids and chrysanthemums.

It was quite an interesting problem whether he was absolutely devoid of sense, or miserably wanting in spirit. Did he know his lady's ways and condone them, or was he a mere blind, doting fool? It was a point to be discussed over the teacups in snug little drawing-rooms, or with the aid of a cigar in the bow windows of clubs. Bitter and plain were the comments among men upon his conduct. There was but one who had a good word to say for him, and he was the most silent member in the smoking-room. He had seen him break in a horse at the University, and it seemed to have left an impression upon his mind.

But when Douglas Stone became the favourite all doubts as to Lord Sannox's knowledge or ignorance were set for ever at rest. There was no subterfuge about Stone. In his high-handed, impetuous fashion, he set all caution and discretion at defiance. The scandal became notorious. A learned body intimated that his name had been struck from the list of its vice-presidents. Two friends implored him to consider his professional credit. He cursed them all three, and spent forty guineas on a bangle to take with him to the lady. He was at her house every evening, and she drove in his carriage in the afternoons. There was not an attempt on either side to conceal their relations; but there came at last a little incident to interrupt them.

It was a dismal winter's night, very cold and gusty, with the wind whooping in the chimneys and blustering against the window-panes. A thin spatter of rain tinkled on the glass with each fresh sough of the gale, drowning for the instant the dull gurgle and drip from the eaves. Douglas Stone had finished his dinner, and sat by his fire in the study, a glass of rich port upon the malachite table at his elbow. As he raised it to his lips, he held it up against the lamplight, and watched with the eye of a connoisseur the tiny scales of beeswing which floated in its rich ruby depths. The fire, as it spurted up, threw fitful lights upon his bold, clear-cut face, with its widely-opened grey eyes, its thick and yet firm lips, and the deep, square jaw, which had something Roman in its strength and its animalism. He smiled from time to time as he nestled back in his luxurious chair. Indeed, he had a right to feel well pleased, for, against the advice of six colleagues, he had performed an operation that day of which only two cases were on record, and the result had been brilliant beyond all expectation. No other man in London would have had the daring to plan, or the skill to execute, such a heroic measure.

But he had promised Lady Sannox to see her that evening and it was already half-past eight. His hand was outstretched to the bell to order the carriage when he heard the dull thud of the knocker. An instant later there was the shuffling of feet in the hall, and the sharp closing of a door.

'A patient to see you, sir, in the consulting room,' said the butler.

'About himself?'

'No, sir; I think he wants you to go out.'

'It is too late,' cried Douglas Stone peevishly. 'I won't go.'

'This is his card, sir.'

The butler presented it upon the gold salver which had been given to his master by the wife of a Prime Minister.

' "Hamil Ali, Smyrna." Hum! The fellow is a Turk, I suppose.'

'Yes, sir. He seems as if he came from abroad, sir. And he's in a terrible way.'

'Tut, tut! I have an engagement. I must go somewhere else. But I'll see him. Show him in here, Pim.'

A few moments later the butler swung open the door and ushered in a small and decrepit man, who walked with a bent back and with the forward push of the face and blink of the eyes which goes with extreme short sight. His face was swarthy, and his hair and beard of the deepest black. In one hand he held a turban of white muslin striped with red, in the other a small chamois leather bag.

'Good evening,' said Douglas Stone, when the butler had closed the door. 'You speak English, I presume?'

'Yes, sir. I am from Asia Minor, but I speak English when I speak slow.'

'You wanted me to go out, I understand?'

'Yes, sir. I wanted very much that you should see my wife.'

'I could come in the morning, but I have an engagement which prevents me from seeing your wife tonight.'

The Turk's answer was a singular one. He pulled the string which closed the mouth of the chamois leather bag, and poured a flood of gold on to the table.

'There are one hundred pounds there,' said he, 'and I promise you that it will not take you an hour. I have a cab ready at the door.'

Douglas Stone glanced at his watch. An hour would not make it too late to visit Lady Sannox. He had been there later. And the fee was an extraordinarily high one. He had been pressed by his creditors lately, and he could not afford to let such a chance pass. He would go.

'What is the case?' he asked.

'Oh, it is so sad a one! So sad a one! You have not, perhaps, heard of the daggers of the Almohades?'

'Never.'

'Ah, they are Eastern daggers of a great age and of a singular shape, with the hilt like what you call a stirrup. I am a curiosity dealer, you understand, and that is why I have come to England from Smyrna, but next week I go back once more. Many things I brought with me, and I have a few things left, but among them, to my sorrow, is one of these daggers.'

'You will remember that I have an appointment, sir,' said the surgeon, with some irritation; 'pray confine yourself to the necessary details.'

'You will see that it is necessary. To-day my wife fell down in a faint in the room in which I keep my wares, and she cut her lower lip upon this cursed dagger of Almohades.'

'I see,' said Douglas Stone, rising. 'And you wish me to dress the wound?'

'No, no, it is worse than that.'

'What then?'

'These daggers are poisoned.'

'Poisoned!'

'Yes, and there is no man, East or West, who can tell now what is the poison or what the cure. But all that is known I know, for my father was in this trade before me, and we have had much to do with these poisoned weapons.'

'What are the symptoms?'

'Deep sleep, and death in thirty hours.'

'And you say there is no cure. Why then should you pay me this considerable fee?'

'No drug can cure, but the knife may.'

'And how?'

'The poison is slow of absorption. It remains for hours in the wound.'

'Washing, then, might cleanse it?'

'No more than in a snake bite. It is too subtle and too deadly.'

'Excision of the wound, then?'

'That is it. If it be on the finger, take the finger off. So said my father always. But think of where this wound is, and that it is my wife. It is dreadful.'

But familiarity with such grim matters may take the finer edge from a man's sympathy. To Douglas Stone this was already an interesting case, and he brushed aside as irrelevant the feeble objections of the husband.

'It appears to be that or nothing,' said he brusquely. 'It is better to lose a lip than a life.'

'Ah, yes, I know that you are right. Well, well, it is kismet, and it must be faced. I have the cab, and you will come with me and do this thing.'

Douglas Stone took his case of bistouries from a drawer, and placed it with a roll of bandage and a compress of lint in his pocket. He must waste no more time if he were to see Lady Sannox.

'I am ready,' said he, pulling on his overcoat. 'Will you take a glass of wine before you go out into this cold air?'

His visitor shrank away, with a protesting hand upraised.

'You forget that I am a Mussulman, and a true follower of the Prophet,' said he. 'But tell me what is the bottle of green glass which you have placed in your pocket?'

'It is chloroform.'

'Ah, that also is forbidden to us. It is a spirit, and we make no use of such things.'

'What! You would allow your wife to go through an operation without an anaesthetic?'

'Ah! She will feel nothing, poor soul. The deep sleep has already come on, which is the first working of the poison. And then I have given her of our Smyrna opium. Come, sir, for already an hour has passed.'

As they stepped out into the darkness, a sheet of rain was driven in upon their faces, and the hall lamp, which dangled from the arm of a marble Caryatid, went out with a fluff. Pim, the butler, pushed the heavy door to, straining hard with his shoulder against the wind, while the two men groped their way towards the yellow glare which showed where the cab was waiting. An instant later they were rattling upon their journey.

'Is it far?' asked Douglas Stone.

'Oh, no. We have a very little quiet place off the Euston Road.'

The surgeon pressed the spring of his repeater and listened to the little tings which told him the hour. It was a quarter past nine. He calculated the distances and the short time which it would take him to perform so trivial an operation. He ought to reach Lady Sannox by ten o'clock. Through the fogged windows he saw the blurred gas lamps dancing past, with occasionally the broader glare of a shop front. The rain was pelting and rattling upon the leathern top of the carriage, and the wheels swashed as they rolled through puddle and mud. Opposite to him the white headgear of his companion gleamed faintly through the obscurity. The surgeon felt in his pockets and arranged his needles, his ligatures and his safety-pins, that no time might be wasted when they arrived. He chafed with impatience and drummed his foot upon the floor.

But the cab slowed down at last and pulled up. In an instant Douglas Stone was out, and the Smyrna merchant's toe was at his very heel.

'You can wait,' said he to the driver.

It was a mean-looking house in a narrow and sordid street. The surgeon, who knew his London well, cast a swift glance into the shadows, but there was nothing distinctive – no shop, no movement, nothing but a double line of dull, flat-faced houses, a double stretch of wet flagstones which gleamed in the lamplight, and a double rush of water in the gutters which swirled and gurgled towards the sewer gratings. The door which faced them was blotched and discoloured, and a faint light in the fan pane above it served to show the dust and the grime which covered it. Above, in one of the bedroom windows, there was a dull yellow glimmer. The merchant knocked loudly, and, as he turned his dark face towards the light, Douglas Stone could see that it was contracted with anxiety. A bolt was drawn, and an elderly

335

woman with a taper stood in the doorway, shielding the thin flame with her gnarled hand.

'Is all well?' gasped the merchant.

'She is as you left her, sir.'

'She has not spoken?'

'No, she is in a deep sleep.'

The merchant closed the door, and Douglas Stone walked down the narrow passage, glancing about him in some surprise as he did so. There was no oil-cloth, no mat, no hat-rack. Deep grey dust and heavy festoons of cobwebs met his eyes everywhere. Following the old woman up the winding stair, his firm footfall echoed harshly through the silent house. There was no carpet.

The bedroom was on the second landing. Douglas Stone followed the old nurse into it, with the merchant at his heels. Here, at least, there was furniture and to spare. The floor was littered and the corners piled with Turkish cabinets, inlaid tables, coats of chain mail, strange pipes, and grotesque weapons. A single small lamp stood upon a bracket on the wall. Douglas Stone took it down, and picking his way among the lumber, walked over to a couch in the corner, on which lay a woman dressed in the Turkish fashion, with yashmak and veil. The lower part of the face was exposed, and the surgeon saw a jagged cut which zigzagged along the border of the under lip.

'You will forgive the yashmak,' said the Turk 'You know our views about woman in the East.'

But the surgeon was not thinking about the yashmak. This was no longer a woman to him. It was a case. He stooped and examined the wound carefully.

'There are no signs of irritation,' said he. 'We might delay the operation until local symptoms develop.'

The husband wrung his hands in uncontrollable agitation.

'Oh! sir, sir,' he cried. 'Do not trifle. You do not know. It is deadly. I know, and I give you my assurance that an operation is absolutely necessary. Only the knife can save her.'

'And yet I am inclined to wait,' said Douglas Stone.

'That is enough,' the Turk cried, angrily. 'Every minute is of importance, and I cannot stand here and see my wife allowed to sink. It only remains for me to give you my thanks for having come, and to call in some other surgeon before it is too late.'

Douglas Stone hesitated. To refund that hundred pounds was no pleasant matter. But of course if he left the case he must return the money. And if the Turk were right and the woman died, his position before a coroner might be an embarrassing one.

336

'You have had personal experience of this poison?' he asked.

'I have.'

'And you assure me that an operation is needful.'

'I swear it by all that I hold sacred.'

'The disfigurement will be frightful.'

'I can understand that the mouth will not be a pretty one to kiss.'

Douglas Stone turned fiercely upon the man. The speech was a brutal one. But the Turk has his own fashion of talk and of thought, and there was no time for wrangling. Douglas Stone drew a bistoury from his case, opened it and felt the keen straight edge with his forefinger. Then he held the lamp closer to the bed. Two dark eyes were gazing up at him through the slit in the yashmak. They were all iris, and the pupil was hardly to be seen.

'You have given her a very heavy dose of opium.'

'Yes, she has had a good dose.'

He glanced again at the dark eyes which looked straight at his own. They were dull and lustreless, but, even as he gazed, a little shifting sparkle came into them, and the lips quivered.

'She is not absolutely unconscious,' said he.

'Would it not be well to use the knife while it will be painless?'

The same thought had crossed the surgeon's mind. He grasped the wounded lip with his forceps, and with two swift cuts he took out a broad V-shaped piece. The woman sprang up on the couch with a dreadful gurgling scream. Her covering was torn from her face. It was a face that he knew. In spite of that protruding upper lip and that slobber of blood, it was a face that he knew. She kept on putting her hand up to the gap and screaming. Douglas Stone sat down at the foot of the couch with his knife and his forceps. The room was whirling round, and he had felt something go like a ripping seam behind his ear. A bystander would have said that his face was the more ghastly of the two. As in a dream, or as if he had been looking at something at the play, he was conscious that the Turk's hair and beard lay upon the table, and that Lord Sannox was leaning against the wall with his hand to his side, laughing silently. The screams had died away now, and the dreadful head had dropped back again upon the pillow, but Douglas Stone still sat motionless, and Lord Sannox still chuckled quietly to himself.

'It was really very necessary for Marion, this operation,' said he, 'not physically, but morally, you know, morally.'

Douglas Stone stooped forwards and began to play with the fringe of the coverlet. His knife tinkled down upon the ground, but he still held the forceps and something more.

'I had long intended to make a little example,' said Lord Sannox, suavely. 'Your note of Wednesday miscarried, and I have it here in my pocket-book. I took some pains in carrying out my idea. The wound, by the way, was from nothing more dangerous than my signet ring.'

He glanced keenly at his silent companion, and cocked the small revolver which he held in his coat pocket. But Douglas Stone was still picking at the coverlet.

'You see you have kept your appointment after all,' said Lord Sannox.

And at that Douglas Stone began to laugh. He laughed long and loudly. But Lord Sannox did not laugh now. Something like fear sharpened and hardened his features. He walked from the room, and he walked on tiptoe. The old woman was waiting outside.

'Attend to your mistress when she awakes,' said Lord Sannox.

Then he went down to the street. The cab was at the door, and the driver raised his hand to his hat.

'John,' said Lord Sannox, 'you will take the doctor home first. He will want leading downstairs, I think. Tell his butler that he has been taken ill at a case.'

'Very good, sir.'

'Then you can take Lady Sannox home.'

'And how about yourself, sir?'

'Oh, my address for the next few months will be Hotel di Roma, Venice. Just see that the letters are sent on. And tell Stevens to exhibit all the purple chrysanthemums next Monday, and to wire me the result.'

The Killing Bottle

BY L. P. HARTLEY

If viewers of Journey to the Unknown *saw certain similarities between this 1968 series and the psychological horror stories which Alfred Hitchcock had created for television a decade earlier the reason was not hard to find. For the producer was Joan Harrison who had been Hitch's personal secretary and script assistant from 1935 until the early Sixties. The series was created for Independent Television by the famous Hammer Studios in what was their first television venture, and they set out to offer according to the pre-publicity 'everything from devil worship to murder, from reincarnation to supernatural powers, and from terror to revenge' in the seventeen hour-long episodes. Appointed as producer, Joan Harrison and her story editor, John Gould, mostly drew their material from well-known writers whose work had already been utilized by TV such as Cornell Woolrich, (of* Suspense *fame), Robert Bloch (who, of course, had worked for Hitchcock), Charles Beaumont (ditto* Twilight Zone) *and Alfred Shaugnessy (creator of the hugely successful series* Upstairs, Downstairs). *The actors who starred were also familiar names: Patrick Allen, Adrienne Corri, Jane Asher, Joseph Cotton, Kenneth Haigh, Edward Fox, Paul Daneman, Dennis Waterman and Michael Gough. Talking about the influence of Hitchcock on her work before* Journey to the Unknown *was premiered in November 1968, Joan Harrison said, 'Neither Hitch nor myself is concerned with outlandish horrors. We deal in character horror and character terror. It is the warped mind that creates fear.'*

When shown in America, each episode of the series was introduced by a celebrity guest – among them Vincent Price and Patrick McGoohan – but when screened in Britain, these were inexplicably dropped. The attention-grabbing, opening credits were, though, retained on both sides of the Atlantic. A deserted fairground at midnight. An unseen hand pushing a turnstile. A slowly revolving, empty ferris wheel and, finally, a roller coaster plunging into a terrifying, steep descent. As to the stories themselves, viewers had difficulty selecting their favourites, though 'The Killing Bottle' adapted by Julian Bond featured on a good few lists. The original short story about a murder committed to obtain inheritance money was by L.P. Hartley (1895–1972), an accomplished teller of horror stories and the author of that classic novel of country life, The Go-Between *(1953). Roddy McDowell starred as Rollo Verdew, with Ingrid Brett as Vena Verdew and Barry Evans as Jimmy Rintoul.* Journey to the Unknown *is today regarded by some fans as one of the most underrated horror series of the Sixties, and although it has not been repeated on TV since, it did inspire two further anthologies,* Hammer House of Horror *(1980) and* Hammer House of Mystery and Suspense *which was screened in 1984.*

Though both of these later series using only original scripts were, in their own ways, ingenious and often suspenseful, neither quite matched the style or the terror content of the original.

UNLIKE the majority of men, Jimmy Rintoul enjoyed the hour or so's interval between being called and having breakfast; for it was the only part of the day upon which he imposed an order. From nine-fifteen onwards the day imposed its order upon him. The bus, the office, the hasty city luncheon; then the office, the bus, and the unsatisfactory interval before dinner: such a promising time and yet, do what he would with it, it always seemed to be wasted. If he was going to dine alone at his club, he felt disappointed and neglected; if, as seldom happened, in company, he felt vaguely apprehensive. He expected a good deal from his life, and he never went to bed without the sense of having missed it. Truth to tell, he needed a stimulus, the stimulus of outside interest and appreciation, to get the best out of himself. In a competitive society, with rewards dangled before his eyes, his nature fulfilled itself and throve. How well he had done at school, and even afterwards, while his parents lived to applaud his efforts. Now he was thirty-three; his parents were dead; there was no one close enough to him to care whether he made a success of his life or not. Nor did life hand out to grown-up men incontestable signs of merit and excellence, prizes bound in vellum or silver cups standing proudly on ebony pedestals. No, its awards were far less tangible, and

Jimmy, from the shelter of his solicitors' office, sometimes felt glad that its more sensational prizes were passing out of his reach – that he need no longer feel obliged, as he had once felt, to climb the Matterhorn, play the Moonlight Sonata, master the Spanish language, and read the Critique of Pure Reason, before he died. His ambition was sensibly on the ebb.

But not in the mornings. The early mornings were still untouched by the torpors of middle-age. Dressing was for Jimmy a ritual, and like all rituals it looked forward to a culmination. Act followed act in a recognized sequence, each stage contributing its peculiar thrill, opening his mind to a train of stimulating and agreeable thoughts, releasing it, encouraging it. And the culmination: what was it? Only his morning's letters and the newspaper! Not very exciting. But the newspaper might contain one of those helpful, sympathetic articles about marriage, articles that warned the reader not to rush into matrimony, but to await the wisdom that came with the early and still more with the late thirties; articles which, with a few tricks of emphasis, of skipping here and reading between the lines there, demonstrated that Jimmy Rintoul's career, without any effort of his own, was shaping itself on sound, safe lines. The newspaper, then, for reassurance; the letters for surprise! And this morning an interesting letter would be particularly welcome. It would distract his mind from a vexing topic that even the routine of dressing had not quite banished – the question of his holiday, due in a fortnight's time.

Must it be Swannick Fen again? Partly for lack of finding others to take their place he had cherished the interests of his boyhood, of which butterfly-collecting was the chief. He was solitary and competitive, and the hobby ministered to both these traits. But alas, he had not the patience of the true collector; his interest fell short of the lesser breeds, the irritating varieties of Wainscots and Footmen and what-nots. It embraced only the more sensational insects – the large, the beautiful, and the rare. His desire had fastened itself on the Swallow-tail butterfly as representing all these qualities. So he went to Swannick, found the butterfly, bred it, and presently had a whole hutch-full of splendid green caterpillars. Their mere number, the question of what to do with them when they came out, whether to keep them all in their satiating similarity, to give them away, or to sell them; to let them go free so that the species might multiply, to the benefit of all collectors; to kill all but a few, thus enhancing the value of his own – these problems vexed his youthful, ambitious, conscientious mind. Finally he killed them all. But the sight of four setting-boards plastered with forty identical insects destroyed by a surfeit his passion for the

Swallow-tail butterfly. He had coaxed it with tempting baits: the Pine Hawk moth, the Clifden Nonpareil; but it would not respond, would accept no *pis aller*, being, like many passions, monogamous and constant. Every year, in piety, in conservatism, in hope, he still went to Swannick Fen; but with each visit the emotional satisfaction diminished. Soon it would be gone.

However, there on his dressing-table (for some reason) stood the killing-bottle – mutely demanding prey. Almost without thinking he released the stopper and snuffed up the almond-breathing fumes. A safe, pleasant smell; he could never understand how anything died of it, or why cyanide of potassium should figure in the chemists' book of poisons. But it did; he had had to put his name against it. Now, since the stuff was reputed to be so deadly, he must add a frail attic to the edifice of dressing, and once more wash his hands before breakfast. In a fortnight's time, he thought, I shall be doing this twenty times a day.

On the breakfast-table lay a large, shiny blue envelope. He did not recognize the handwriting, nor, when he examined the post-mark, did it convey anything to him. The flap, gummed to the top and very strong, resisted his fingers. He opened it with a knife and read:

Verdew Castle.

My dear Rintoul,

How did you feel after our little dinner on Saturday? None the worse, I hope. However, I'm not writing to enquire about your health, which seems pretty good, but about your happiness, or what I should like to think would be your happiness. Didn't I hear you mutter (the second time we met, I think it was, at Smallhouse's) something about going for a holiday in the near future? Well, then, couldn't you spend it here with us, at Verdew? Us being my brother Randolph, my wife, and your humble servant. I'm afraid there won't be a party for you; but we could get through the day somehow, and play bridge in the evenings. Randolph and you would make perfect partners, you would be so kind to each other. And didn't you say you collected bugs? Then by all means bring your butterfly-net and your killing-bottle and your other engines of destruction and park them here; there are myriads of green-flies, bluebottle-flies, may-flies, dragon-flies, and kindred pests which would be all the better for your attentions. Now don't say no. It would be a pleasure to us, and I'm sure it would amuse you to see ye olde castle and us living in our medieval seclusion. I await the favour of a favourable reply, and will then tell you the best way of reaching the Schloss, as we sometimes call it in our German fashion.

Yours,
Rollo Verdew.

Jimmy stared at this facetious epistle until its purport faded from his mind, leaving only a blurred impression of redundant loops and twirls. Verdew's handwriting was like himself, bold and dashing and unruly. At least, this was the estimate Jimmy had formed of him, on the strength of three meetings. He had been rather taken by the man's bluff, hearty manner, but he did not expect Verdew to like him: they were birds of a different feather. He hadn't felt very well after the dinner, having drunk more than was good for him in the effort to fall in with his host's mood; but apparently he had succeeded better than he thought. Perhaps swashbucklers like Verdew welcomed mildness in others. If not, why this invitation? He considered it. The district might be entomologically rich. Where exactly was Verdew Castle? He had, of course, a general idea of its locality, correct to three counties; he knew it was somewhere near the coast. Further than that, nothing; and directly he began to sift his knowledge he found it to be even less helpful than he imagined. The note-paper gave a choice of stations: wayside stations they must be, they were both unknown to him. The postal, telegraphic, and telephonic addresses all confidently cited different towns – Kirton Tracy, Shrivecross, and Pawlingham – names which seemed to stir memories but never fully awakened recollection. Still, what did it matter? Verdew had promised to tell him the best route, and it was only a question of getting there, after all. He could find his own way back

Soon his thoughts, exploring the future, encountered an obstacle and stopped short. He was looking ahead as though he had made up his mind to go. Well, hadn't he? The invitation solved his immediate difficulty: the uncertainty as to where he should take his holiday. The charm of Swannick had failed to hold him. And yet, perversely enough, his old hunting-ground chose this very moment to trouble him with its lures: its willows, its alders, the silent clumps of grey rushes with the black water in between. The conservatism of his nature, an almost superstitious loyalty to the preferences of his early life, protested against the abandonment of Swannick – Swannick, where he had always done exactly as he liked, where bridge never intruded, and the politenesses of society were unknown. For Jimmy's mind had run forward again, and envisaged existence at Verdew Castle as divided between holding open the door for Mrs Rollo Verdew, and exchanging compliments and forbearances and com- miscration with Rollo's elder (or perhaps younger, he hadn't said) brother Randolph across the bridge-table, with a lot of spare time that wasn't really spare and a lot of being left to himself that really meant being left to everybody.

Jimmy looked at the clock: it was time to go. If it amused his imagination to fashion a mythical Verdew Castle, he neither authorized nor forbade it. He still thought himself free to choose. But when he reached his office his first act was to write his friend a letter of acceptance.

Four days later a second blue envelope appeared on his breakfast-table. It was evidently a two-days' post to Verdew Castle, for Rollo explained that he had that moment received Jimmy's welcome communication. There followed a few references, necessarily brief, to matters of interest to them both. The letter closed with the promised itinerary:

> So we shall hope to see you in ten days' time, complete with lethal chamber and big-game apparatus. I forget whether you have a car; but if you have, I strongly advise you to leave it at home. The road bridge across the estuary has been dicky for a long time. They may close it any day now, since it was felt to wobble the last time the Lord-Lieutenant crossed by it. You would be in a mess if you found it shut and had to go trailing thirty miles to Amplesford (a hellish road, since it's no one's interest to keep it up). If the bridge carried the Lord-Lieutenant it would probably bear you, but I shouldn't like to have your blood on my head! Come, then, by train to Verdew Grove. I recommend the four o'clock; it doesn't get here till after dark, but you can dine on it, and it's almost express part of the way. The morning train is too bloody for anything: you would die of boredom before you arrived, and I should hate that to happen to any of my guests. I'm sorry to present you with such ghastly alternatives, but the Castle was built here to be out of everyone's reach, and by Heaven, it is! Come prepared for a long stay. You must. I'm sure the old office can get on very well without you. You're lucky to be able to go away as a matter of course, like a gentleman. Let us have a line and we'll send to meet you, not my little tin kettle but Randolph's large, majestic Daimler. Good-bye.
>
> Yours,
> Rollo.

It was indeed a troublesome, tedious journey, involving changes of train and even of station. More than once the train, having entered a terminus head first, steamed out tail first, with the result that Rintoul lost his sense of direction and had a slight sensation of vertigo whenever, in thought, he tried to recapture it. It was half-past nine, and the sun was setting, when they crossed the estuary. As always in such places, the tide was low and the sun's level beams illuminated the too rotund and luscious curves of a series of mud-flats. The railway-line approached the estuary from its marshy side, by a steep embankment. Near by, and considerably below, ran the road bridge — an antiquated affair of many arches, but apparently still in use, though there seemed to be no traffic on it. The line curved inwards, and by straining his neck Rintoul could see the train bent like a bow, and the engine approaching a hole, from which a few wisps of smoke still issued, in the ledge of rock that crowned the further shore. The hole rushed upon him; Rintoul pulled in his head and was at once in darkness. The world never seemed to get light again. After the long tunnel they were among hills that shut out the light that would have come in, and stifled the little that was left behind. It was by the help of the station lantern that he read the name, Verdew Grove, and when they were putting his luggage on the motor he could scarcely distinguish between the porter and the chauffeur. One of them said:

'Did you say it was a rabbit?'

And the other: 'Well, there was a bit of fur stuck to the wheel.'

'You'd better not let the boss see it,' said the first speaker.

'Not likely.' And so saying, the chauffeur, who seemed to be referring to an accident, climbed into the car. As Rollo had said, it was a very comfortable one. Jimmy gave up counting the turns and trying to catch glimpses of the sky over the high hedges, and abandoned himself to drowsiness. He must have dozed, for he did not know whether it was five minutes or fifty before the opening door let in a gust of cool air and warned him that he had arrived.

For a moment he had the hall to himself. It did not seem very large, but to gauge its true extent was difficult, because of the arches and the shadows. Shaded lamps on the tables gave a diffused but very subdued glow; while a few unshaded lights, stuck about in the groining of the vault, consuming their energy in small patches of great brilliancy, dazzled rather than assisted the eye. The fact that the spaces between the vaulting-ribs were whitewashed seemed to increase the glare. It was curious and not altogether happy, the contrast between the brilliance above and the murk below. No trophies of the chase adorned the walls; no stags' heads or antlers, no rifles, javelins, tomahawks, assegais or krisses. Clearly the Verdews were not a family of sportsmen. In what did Randolph Verdew's interests lie? Rintoul wondered, and he was walking across to the open grate, in whose large recess a log-fire flickered, when the sound of a footfall startled him. It came close, then died away completely, then still in the same rhythm began again. It was Rollo.

Rollo with his black moustaches, his swaggering gait, his large expansive air, his noisy benevolence. He grasped Jimmy's hand.

345

But before he could say more than 'Damned glad,' a footman appeared. He came so close to Jimmy and Rollo that the flow of the latter's eloquence was checked.

'Mr Rintoul is in the pink room,' announced the footman.

Rollo put his little finger in his mouth and gently bit it.

'Oh, but I thought I said –'

'Yes, sir,' interrupted the footman. 'But Mr Verdew thought he might disturb Mr Rintoul in the onyx room, because sometimes when he lies awake at night he has to move about, as you know, sir. And he thought the pink room had a better view. So he gave orders for him to be put there, sir.'

The footman finished on a tranquil note and turned to go. But Rollo flushed faintly and seemed put out.

'I thought it would have been company for you having my brother next door,' he said. 'But he's arranged otherwise, so it can't be helped. Shall I take you to the room now, or will you have a drink first? That is, if I can find it,' he muttered. 'They have a monstrous habit of sometimes taking the drinks away when Randolph has gone to bed. And by the way, he asked me to make his excuses to you. He was feeling rather tired. My wife's gone, too. She always turns in early here; she says there's nothing to do at Verdew. But, my God, there's a lot that wants doing, as I often tell her. This way.'

Though they found the whisky and soda in the drawing-room, Rollo still seemed a little crestfallen and depressed; but Jimmy's spirits, which sometimes suffered from the excessive buoyancy of his neighbour's, began to rise. The chair was comfortable; the room, though glimpses of stone showed alongside the tapestries, was more habitable and less ecclesiastical than the hall. In front of him was an uncurtained window through which he could see, swaying their heads as though bent on some ghostly conference, a cluster of white roses. I'm going to enjoy myself here, he thought.

Whatever the charms of the only room, whatever virtue resided in the proximity of Mr Randolph Verdew, one thing was certain: the pink room had a splendid view. Leaning out of his window the next morning Jimmy feasted his eyes on it. Directly below him was the moat, clear and apparently deep. Below that again was the steep conical hill on which the Castle stood, its side intersected by corkscrew paths and level terraces. Below and beyond, undulating ground led the eye onwards and upwards to where, almost on the horizon, glittered and shone the silver of the estuary. Of the Castle were visible only the round wall of Jimmy's tower, and a wing of the Tudor period, the gables of which rose to the level of his bedroom window. It was half-past eight and he dressed quickly, meaning to make a little tour of the Castle precincts before his hosts appeared.

His intention, however, was only partially fulfilled, for on arriving in the hall he found the great door still shut, and fastened with a variety of locks and bolts, of antique design and as hard to open, it seemed, from within as from without. He had better fortune with a smaller door, and found himself on a level oblong stretch of grass, an island of green, bounded by the moat on the east and on the other sides by the Castle walls. There was a fountain in the middle. The sun shone down through the open end of the quadrangle, making the whole place a cave of light, flushing the warm stone of the Elizabethan wing to orange, and gilding the cold, pale medieval stonework of the rest. Jimmy walked to the moat and tried to find, to right or left, a path leading to other parts of the building. But there was none. He turned round and saw Rollo standing in the doorway.

'Good-morning,' called his host. 'Already thinking out a plan of escape?'

Jimmy coloured slightly. The thought had been present in his mind, though not in the sense that Rollo seemed to mean it.

'You wouldn't find it very easy from here,' remarked Rollo, whose cheerful humour the night seemed to have restored. 'Because even if you swam the moat you couldn't get up the bank: it's too steep and too high.'

Jimmy examined the further strand and realized that this was true.

'It would be prettier,' Rollo continued, 'and less canal-like, if the water came up to the top; but Randolph prefers it as it used to be. He likes to imagine we're living in a state of siege.'

'He doesn't seem to keep any weapons for our defence,' commented Jimmy. 'No arquebuses or bows and arrows; no vats of molten lead.'

'Oh, he wouldn't hurt anyone for the world,' said Rollo. 'That's one of his little fads. But it amuses him to look across to the river like one of the first Verdews and feel that no one can get in without his leave.'

'Or out either, I suppose,' suggested Jimmy.

'Well,' remarked Rollo, 'some day I'll show you a way of getting out. But now come along and look at the view from the other side; we have to go through the house to see it.'

They walked across the hall, where the servants were laying the breakfast-table, to a door at the end of a long narrow passage. But it was locked. 'Hodgson!' shouted Rollo.

A footman came up.

'Will you open this door, please?' said Rollo. Jimmy expected him to be angry, but there was only a muffled irritation in his voice. At his leisure the footman produced the key and let them through.

'That's what comes of living in someone else's house,' fumed Rollo, once they were out of earshot. 'These lazy devils want waking up. Randolph's a damned sight too easy-going.'

'Shall I see him at breakfast?' Jimmy enquired.

'I doubt it.' Rollo picked up a stone, looked round, for some reason, at the Castle, and threw the pebble at a thrush, narrowly missing it. 'He doesn't usually appear till lunch-time. He's interested in all sorts of philanthropical societies. He's always helping them to prevent something. He hasn't prevented you, though, you naughty fellow,' he went on, stooping down and picking up from a stone several fragments of snails' shells. 'This seems to be the thrushes' Tower Hill.'

'He's fond of animals, then?' asked Jimmy.

'Fond, my boy?' repeated Rollo. 'Fond is not the word. But we aren't vegetarians. Some day I'll explain all that. Come and have some bacon and eggs.'

That evening in his bath, a large wooden structure like a giant's coffin, Jimmy reviewed the day, a delightful day. In the morning he had been taken round the Castle; it was not so large as it seemed from outside – it had to be smaller, the walls were so thick. And there were, of course, a great many rooms he wasn't shown, attics, cellars, and dungeons. One dungeon he had seen: but he felt sure that in a fortress of such pretensions there must be more than one. He couldn't quite get the 'lie' of the place at present; he had his own way of finding his room, but he knew it wasn't the shortest way. The hall, which was like a Clapham Junction to the Castle's topographical system, still confused him. He knew the way out, because there was only one way, across a modernized drawbridge, and that made it simpler. He had crossed it to get at the woods below the Castle, where he had spent the afternoon, hunting for caterpillars, They had really left him alone – even severely alone! Neither of Rollo's wife nor his brother was there as yet any sign. 'But I shall see them at dinner,' he thought, wrapping himself in an immense bath-towel.

The moment he saw Randolph Verdew, standing pensive in the drawing-room, he knew he would like him. He was an etherealized version of Rollo, taller and slighter. His hair was sprinkled with grey and he stooped a little. His cloudy blue eyes met Jimmy's with extraordinary frankness as he held out his hand, and apologized for his previous non-appearance.

'It is delightful to have you here,' he added. 'You are a naturalist, I believe.'

His manner was formal but charming, infinitely reassuring.

'I am an entomologist,' said Jimmy, smiling.

'Ah, I love to watch the butterflies fluttering about the flowers – and the moths, too, those big heavy fellows that come in of an evening and knock themselves about against the lights. I have often had to put as many as ten out of the window, and back they come – the deluded creatures. What a pity that their larvae are harmful and in some cases have to be destroyed! But I expect you prefer to observe the rarer insects?'

'I'm hoping to catch sight of one or two rare ones while I'm here,' answered Jimmy, with an uneasy sense of being disingenuous.

'I'm sure I hope you will,' said Randolph Verdew with so much feeling in his voice that Jimmy nearly smiled. 'You must get Rollo to help you.'

'Oh,' said Jimmy. 'Rollo! —'

'I hope you don't think Rollo indifferent to Nature?' asked his brother, with distress in his voice and an engaging simplicity of manner. 'He has had rather a difficult life, as I expect you know. His affairs have kept him a great deal in towns and he has had little leisure – very little leisure.'

'He must find it restful here,' remarked Jimmy, again with the sense of being more tactful than truthful.

'I'm sure I hope he does. Rollo is a dear fellow; I wish he came here oftener. Unfortunately his wife does not care for the country – and Rollo himself is very much tied by his new employment – the motor business.'

'Hasn't he been with Scorcher and Speedwell's long?'

'Oh no; poor Rollo, he is always trying his hand at something new. He ought to have been born a rich man instead of me' – Rudolph spread his hands out with a gesture of helplessness. 'He could have done so much, whereas I – ah, here he comes. We were talking about you, Rollo.'

'No scandal, I hope; no hitting a man when he's down?'

'Indeed, no. We were saying we hoped you would soon come into a fortune.'

'Where do you think it's coming from?' demanded Rollo, screwing up his eyes as though the smoke from his cigarette had made them smart.

'Perhaps Vera could tell us,' rejoined Randolph mildly, making his way to the table, though his brother's cigarette was still unfinished. 'How is she, Rollo? I hoped she would feel sufficiently restored to make a fourth with us this evening,'

'Still moping,' said the husband. 'Don't waste your pity on her. She'll be all right to-morrow.'

They sat down to dinner.

The next day, or it might have been the day after, Jimmy was coming home to tea from the woods below the Castle. On either side of the path was a hayfield. They were mowing the hay. The mower was a new one, painted bright blue; the horse tossed its head up and down; the placid afternoon air was alive with country sounds, whirring, shouts, and clumping footfalls. The scene was full of an energy and gentleness that refreshed the heart. Jimmy reached the white iron fence that divided the plain from the Castle mound and, with a sigh, set his feet upon the zig-zag path. For though the hill was only a couple of hundred feet high at most, the climb called for an effort he was never quite prepared to make. He was tramping with lowered head, conscious of each step, when a voice hailed him.

'Mr Rintoul!'

It was a foreign voice, the *i*'s pronounced like *e*'s. He looked up and saw a woman, rather short and dark, and a stranger, watching him from the path above.

'You see I have come down to meet you,' she said, advancing with short, brisk, but careful and unpractised steps. And she added, as he still continued to stare at her:

'Don't you know? I am Mrs Verdew.'

By this time she was at his side.

'How could I know?' he asked, laughing, and shaking the hand she was already holding out to him. All her gestures seemed to be quick and unpremeditated.

'Let us sit here,' she said, and almost before she had spoken was sitting, and had made him sit, on the wooden bench beside them. 'I am tired from walking down-hill; you will be tired by walking up-hill: therefore we both need a rest.'

She decided it all so quickly that Jimmy, whose nature had a streak of obstinacy, wondered if he were really so tired after all.

'And who should I have been, who could I have been, but Mrs Verdew?' she demanded challengingly.

Jimmy saw that an answer was expected, but couldn't think of anyone who Mrs Verdew might have been.

'I don't know,' he said feebly.

'Of course you don't, silly,' said Mrs Verdew. 'How long have you been here?'

'I can't remember. Four or five days, I think,' said Jimmy, who disliked being nailed down to a definite fact.

'Four *or* five days? Listen to the man, how vague he is!' commented Mrs Verdew, with a gesture of impatience apostrophizing the horizon. 'Well, whether it's five days or only four, you must have learnt one thing – that no one enters these premises without leave.'

'Premises?' murmured Jimmy.

'Hillside, garden, grounds – premises,' repeated Mrs Verdew. 'How slow you are! But so are all Englishmen?'

'I don't think Rollo is slow,' remarked Jimmy, hoping to carry the war into her country.

'Sometimes too slow, sometimes too fast, never the right pace,' pronounced his wife. 'Rollo misdirects his life.'

'He married you,' said Jimmy gently.

Mrs Verdew gave him a quick look. 'That was partly because I wanted him to. But only just now, for instance, he has been foolish.'

'Do you mean he was foolish to come here?'

'I didn't mean that. Though I hate the place, and he does no good here.'

'What good could he do?' asked Jimmy, who was staring vacantly at the sky. 'Except, perhaps, help his brother to look after – to look after –'

'That's just it,' said Mrs Verdew. 'Randolph doesn't need any help, and if he did he wouldn't let Rollo help him. He wouldn't even have him made a director of the coal-mine!'

'What coal-mine?' Jimmy asked.

'Randolph's. You don't mean to say you didn't know he had a coal-mine? One has to tell you everything!'

'I like you to tell me things!' protested Jimmy.

'As you don't seem to find out anything for yourself, I suppose I must. Well, then: Randolph has a coal-mine, he is very rich, and he spends his money on nothing but charitable societies for contradicting the Laws of Nature. And he won't give Rollo a penny – not a penny, though he is his only brother, his one near relation in the world! He won't even help him to get a job!'

'I thought he had a job,' said Jimmy, in perplexity.

'You thought that! You'd think anything!' exclaimed Mrs Verdew, her voice rising in exasperation.

'No, but he told me he came here for a holiday,' said Jimmy pacifically.

'Holiday, indeed! A long holiday. I can't think why Rollo told you that. Nor can I think why I bore you with all our private troubles. A

351

man can talk to a woman about anything; but a woman can only talk to a man about what interests him.'

'But who is to decide that?'

'The woman, of course; and I see you're getting restless.'

'No, no. I was so interested. Please go on.'

'Certainly not. I am a Russian, and I often know when a man is bored sooner than he knows himself. Come along,' pulling him from the bench much as a gardener uproots a weed; 'and I will tell you something very interesting. Ah, how fast you walk! Don't you know it's less fatiguing to walk uphill slowly – and you with all those fishing-nets and pill-boxes. And what on earth is that great bottle for?'

'I try to catch butterflies in these,' Jimmy explained. 'And this is my killing-bottle.'

'What a horrible name. What is it for?'

'I'm afraid I kill the butterflies with it.'

'Ah, what a barbarian! Give it to me a moment. Yes, there are their corpses, poor darlings. Is that Randolph coming towards us? No, don't take it away. I can carry it quite easily under my shawl. What was I going to tell you when you interrupted me? I remember – it was about the terrace. When I first came here I used to feel frightfully depressed – it was winter and the sun set so early, sometimes before lunch! In the afternoons I used to go down the mound, where I met you, and wait for the sun to dip below that bare hill on the left. And I would begin to walk quite slowly towards the Castle, and all the while the sun was balanced on the hill-top like a ball! And the shadow covered the valley and kept lapping my feet, like the oncoming tide! And I would wait till it reached my ankles, and then run up into the night, and be safe for a moment. It was such fun, but I don't expect you'd enjoy it, you're too sophisticated. Ah, here's Randolph. Randolph, I've been showing Mr Rintoul the way home; he didn't know it – he doesn't know anything! Do you know what he does with this amusing net? He uses it to catch tiny little moths, like the ones that get into your furs. He puts it over them and looks at them, and they're so frightened, they think they can't get out; then they notice the little holes, and out they creep and fly away! Isn't it charming?'

'Charming,' said Randolph, glancing away from the net and towards the ground.

'Now we must go on. We want our tea terribly!' And Mrs Verdew swept Jimmy up the hill.

With good fortune the morning newspaper arrived at Verdew Castle in time for tea, already a little out of date. Jimmy accorded it, as a rule, the tepid interest with which, when abroad, one contemplates the English journals of two days ago. They seem to emphasize one's remoteness, not lessen it. Never did Jimmy seem further from England, indeed, further from civilization, than when he picked up the familiar sheet of *The Times*. It was like a faint rumour of the world that had somehow found its way down hundreds of miles of railway, changed trains and stations, rumbled across the estuary and threaded the labyrinth of lanes and turnings between Verdew Grove and the Castle. Each day its news seemed to grow less important, or at any rate less important to Jimmy. He began to turn over the leaves. Mrs Verdew had gone to her room, absent-mindedly taking the killing-bottle with her. He was alone; there was no sound save the crackle of the sheets. Unusually insipid the news seemed. He turned more rapidly. What was this? In the middle of page fourteen, a hole? No, not a mere hole: a deliberate excision, an operation performed with scissors. What item of news could anyone have found worth reading, much less worth cutting out? To Jimmy's idle mind, the centre of page fourteen assumed a tremendous importance, it became the sun of his curiosity's universe. He rose; with quick cautious fingers he searched about, shifting papers, delving under blotters, even fumbling in the more public-looking pigeon-holes.

Suddenly he heard the click of a door opening, and with a bound he was in the middle of the room. It was only Rollo, whom business of some kind had kept all day away from home.

'Enter the tired bread-winner,' he remarked. 'Like to see the paper? I haven't had time to read it.' He threw something at Jimmy and turned on his heel.

It was *The Times*. With feverish haste Jimmy turned to page fourteen and seemed to have read the paragraph even before he set eyes on it. It was headed:

'MYSTERIOUS OUTBREAK AT VERDEW

'The sequestered, little-known village of Verdew-le-Dale has again been the scene of a mysterious outrage, recalling the murders of John Didwell and Thomas Presland in 1910 and 1912, and the occasional killing of animals which has occurred since. In this instance, as in the others, the perpetrator of the crime seems to have been actuated by some vague motive of retributive justice. The victim was a shepherd-dog, the property of Mr J. R. Cross. The dog, which was known to worry cats, had lately killed two belonging to an old woman of the parish. The Bench, of which Mr Randolph Verdew is chairman, fined Cross and told him to keep the dog under proper control, but did not order its destruction. Two days ago the animal was found dead in a ditch, with its throat cut. The police have no doubt that the wound was made by the same weapon that killed Didwell and Presland, who, it will be remembered, had both been prosecuted by the R.S.P.C.A. for cruelty and negligence resulting in the deaths of domestic animals. At present no evidence has come to light that might lead to the detection of the criminal, though the police are still making investigations.'

'And I don't suppose it will ever come to light,' Jimmy muttered.

'What do you suppose won't come to light?' enquired a voice at his elbow. He looked up. Randolph Verdew was standing by his chair, and looking over his shoulder at the newspaper.

Jimmy pointed to the paragraph.

'Any clue to the identity of the man who did this.'

'No,' said Randolph after a perceptible pause. 'I don't suppose it will.' He hesitated a moment and then added:

'But it would interest me much to know how that paragraph found its way back into the paper.'

Jimmy explained.

'You see,' observed Randolph, 'I always cut out, and paste into a book, any item of news that concerns the neighbourhood, and especially Verdew. In this way I have made an interesting collection.'

'There seem to have been similar occurrences here before,' remarked Jimmy.

'There have, there have,' Randolph Verdew said.

'It's very strange that no one has even been suspected.'

Randolph Verdew answered obliquely:

'Blood calls for blood. The workings of justice are secret and incalculable.'

'Then you sympathize a little with the murderer?' Jimmy enquired.

'I?' muttered Randolph. 'I think I hate cruelty more than anything in the world.'

'But wasn't the murderer cruel?' persisted Jimmy. 'No,' said Randolph Verdew with great decision 'At least,' he added in a different tone, 'the victims appear to have died with the minimum of suffering. But here comes Vera. We must find a more cheerful topic of conversation. Vera, my dear, you won't disappoint us of our bridge to-night?'

Three days elapsed, three days rendered slightly unsatisfactory for Jimmy from a trivial cause. He could not get back his killing-bottle from Mrs Verdew. She had promised it, she had even gone upstairs to fetch it; but she never brought it down. Meanwhile, several fine specimens (in particular a large female Emperor moth) languished in match-boxes and other narrow receptacles, damaging their wings and even having to be set at liberty. It was very trying. He began to feel that the retention of the killing-bottle was deliberate. In questions of conduct he was often at sea. But in the domain of manners, though he sometimes went astray, he considered that he knew very well which road he ought to take, and the knowledge was a matter of pride to him. The thought of asking Mrs Verdew a third time to restore his property irked him exceedingly. At last he screwed up his courage. They were walking down the hill together after tea.

'Mrs Verdew,' he began.

'Don't go on,' she exclaimed. 'I know exactly what you're going to say. Poor darling, he wants to have his killing-bottle back. Well, you can't. I need it myself for those horrible hairy moths that come in at night.'

'But Mrs Verdew —!' he protested.

'And please don't call me Mrs Verdew. How long have we known each other? Ten days! And soon you've got to go! Surely you could call me Vera!'

Jimmy flushed. He knew that he must go soon, but didn't realize that a term had been set to his stay.

'Listen,' she continued, beginning to lead him down the hill; 'when you're in London I hope you'll often come to see us.'

'I certainly will,' said he.

'Well, then, let's make a date. Will you dine with us on the tenth? That's tomorrow week.'

'I'm not quite sure —' began Jimmy unhappily, looking down on to the rolling plain and feeling that he loved it.

'How long you're going to stay?' broke in Mrs Verdew, who seemed able to read his thoughts. 'Why do you want to stay? There's nothing to do here: think what fun we might have in London. You can't like this place and I don't believe it's good for you; you don't look half as well as you did when you came.'

'I feel very well,' said Jimmy.

'Feeling is nothing,' said Mrs Verdew. 'Look at me. Don't I look well?' She turned up to him her face: it was too large, he thought, and dull and pallid with powder; the features were too marked: but undeniably it had beauty. 'I suppose I do: I feel well. But in this place I believe my life might stop at any moment of its own accord! Do you never feel that?'

'No,' said Jimmy, smiling.

355

'Sit down,' she said suddenly, taking him to a seat as she had done on the occasion of their first meeting, 'and let me have your hand – not because I love you, but because I'm happier holding something, and it's a pretty hand.' Jimmy did not resist: he was slightly stupefied, but somehow not surprised by her behaviour. She held up his drooping hand by the wrist, level with her eyes, and surveyed it with a smile, then she laid it, palm upward, in her lap. The smile vanished from her face: she knitted her brows.

'I don't like it,' she said, a sudden energy in her voice.

'I thought you said it was a pretty hand,' murmured Jimmy.

'I did; you know I don't mean that. It is pretty: but you don't deserve to have it, nor your eyes, nor your hair; you are idle and complacent and unresponsive and ease-loving – you only think of your butterflies and your killing-bottle!' She looked at him fondly; and Jimmy, for some reason, was rather pleased to hear all this. 'No, I meant that I see danger in your hand, in the lines.'

'Danger to me?' murmured Jimmy.

'To whom else? Ah, God, the conceit of men! Yes, to you.'

'What sort of danger – physical danger?' enquired Jimmy, only moderately interested.

'*Danger de mort*,' pronounced Mrs Verdew.

'Come, come,' said Jimmy, bending forward and looking into Mrs Verdew's face to see if she was pretending to be serious. 'When does the danger threaten?'

'Now,' said Mrs Verdew.

Oh, thought Jimmy, what a tiresome woman! So you think I'm in danger, do you, Mrs Verdew, of losing my head at this moment? God, the conceit of women! He stole a glance at her; she was looking straight ahead, her lips pursed up and trembling a little, as though she wanted him to kiss her. Shall I? he thought, for compliance was in his blood and he always wanted to do what was expected of him. But at that very moment a wave of irritability flooded his mind and changed it: she had taken his killing-bottle, spoilt and stultified four precious days, and all to gratify her caprice. He turned away.

'Oh, I'm tougher than you think,' he said.

'Tougher?' she said. 'Do you mean your skin? All Englishmen have thick skins.' She spoke resentfully; then her voice softened. 'I was going to tell you ——' She uttered the words with difficulty, and as though against her will. But Jimmy, not noticing her changed tone and still ridden by his irritation, interrupted her.

'That you'd restore my killing-bottle?'

'No, no,' she cried in exasperation, leaping to her feet. 'How you do harp on that wretched old poison bottle! I wish I'd broken it!' She caught her breath, and Jimmy rose too, facing her with distress and contrition in his eyes. But she was too angry to heed his change of mood. 'It was something I wanted you to know – but you make things so difficult for me! I'll fetch you your bottle,' she continued wildly, 'since you're such a child as to need it! No, don't follow me; I'll have it sent to your room.'

He looked up; she was gone, but a faint sound of sobbing disturbed the air behind her.

It was evening, several days later, and they were sitting at dinner. How Jimmy would miss these meals when he got back to London! For a night or two, after the scene with Mrs Verdew, he had been uneasy under the enforced proximity which the dining-table brought; she looked at him reproachfully, spoke little, and when he sought occasions to apologize to her, she eluded them. She had never been alone with him since. She had, he knew, little control over her emotions, and perhaps her pride suffered. But her pique, or whatever it was, now seemed to have passed away. She looked lovely to-night and he realized he would miss her. Rollo's voice, when he began to speak, was like a commentary on his thoughts.

'Jimmy says he's got to leave us, Randolph,' he said. 'Back to the jolly old office.'

'That is a great pity,' said Randolph in his soft voice. 'We shall miss him, shan't we, Vera?'

Mrs Verdew said they would.

'All the same, these unpleasant facts have to be faced,' remarked Rollo. 'That's why we were born. I'm afraid you've had a dull time, Jimmy, though you must have made the local flora and fauna sit up. Have you annexed any prize specimens from your raids upon the countryside?'

'I have got one or two good ones,' said Jimmy with a reluctance that he partially attributed to modesty.

'By the way,' said Rollo, pouring himself out a glass of port, for the servants had left the room, 'I would like you to show Randolph that infernal machine of yours, Jimmy. Anything on the lines of a humane killer bucks the old chap up no end.' He looked across at his brother, the ferocious cast of his features softened into an expression of fraternal solicitude.

After a moment's pause Randolph said: 'I should be much interested to be shown Mr Rintoul's invention.'

'Oh, it's not my invention,' said Jimmy, a little awkwardly.

'You'll forgive me disagreeing with you, Rollo,' Mrs Verdew, who had not spoken for some minutes, suddenly remarked. 'I don't think it's worth Randolph's while looking at it. I don't think it would interest him a bit.'

'How often have I told you, my darling,' said Rollo leaning across the corner of the table towards his wife, 'not to contradict me? I keep a record of the times you agree with me: December, 1919, was the last.'

'Sometimes I think that was a mistake,' said Mrs Verdew, rising in evident agitation, 'for it was then I promised to marry you.' She reached the door before Jimmy could open it for her.

'Ah, these ladies!' moralized Rollo, leaning back and closing his eyes. 'What a dance the dear things lead us, with their temperaments.' And he proceeded to enumerate examples of feminine caprice, until his brother proposed that they should adjourn to the bridge table.

The next morning Jimmy was surprised to find a note accompanying his early-morning tea.

> *Dear Mr Rintoul* (it began), *since I mustn't say 'Dear Jimmy'.* ('I never said she mustn't,' Jimmy thought.) *I know it isn't easy for any man, most of all an Englishman, to understand moods, but I do beg you to forgive my foolish outburst of a few days ago. I think it must have been the air or the lime in the water that made me* un po' *nervosa, as the Italians say. I know you prefer a life utterly flat and dull and even – it would kill me, but there! I am sorry. You can't expect me to change,* à mon age! *But anyhow try to forgive me.*
>
> > *Yours,*
> > *Vera Verdew.*
>
> *PS– I wouldn't trouble to show that bottle to Randolph. He has quite enough silly ideas in his head as it is.*

What a nice letter, thought Jimmy drowsily. He had forgotten the killing-bottle. I won't show it to Randolph, Jimmy thought, unless he asks me.

But soon after breakfast a footman brought him a message: Mr Verdew was in his room and would be glad to see the invention (the man's voice seemed to put the word into inverted commas) at Mr Rintoul's convenience. 'Well,' reflected Jimmy, 'if he's to see it working it must have something to work on.' Aimlessly he strolled over the drawbridge and made his way, past blocks of crumbling wall, past grassy hummocks and hollows, to the terraces. They were gay with flowers; and looked at from above, the lateral stripes and bunches of colour, succeeding each other to the bottom of the hill, had a peculiarly brilliant effect. What should he catch? A dozen white butterflies presented themselves for the honour of exhibiting their death-agony to Mr Randolph Verdew, but Jimmy passed them by. His collector's pride demanded a nobler sacrifice. After twenty minutes' search he was rewarded; his net fell over a slightly battered but still recognizable specimen of the large Tortoiseshell butterfly. He put it in a pill-box and bore it away to the house. But as he went he was visited by a reluctance, never experienced by him before, to take the butterfly's life in such a public and cold-blooded fashion; it was not a good specimen, one that he could add to his collection; it was just cannon-fodder. The heat of the day, flickering visibly upwards from the turf and flowers, bemused his mind; all around was a buzzing and humming that seemed to liberate his thoughts from contact with the world and give them the intensity of sensations. So vivid was his vision, so flawless the inner quiet from which it sprang, that he came up with a start against his own bedroom door. The substance of his day-dream had been forgotten; but it had left its ambassador behind it – something that, whether apprehended by the mind as a colour, a taste, or a local inflammation, spoke with an insistent voice and always to the same purpose: 'Don't show Randolph Verdew the butterfly; let it go, here, out of the window, and send him an apology.'

For a few minutes, such was the force of this inward monitor, Jimmy did contemplate setting the butterfly at liberty. He was prone to sudden irrational scruples and impulses, and if there was nothing definite urging him the other way he often gave in to them. But in this case there was. Manners demanded that he should accede to his host's request; the rules of manners, of all rules in life, were the easiest to recognize and the most satisfactory to act upon. Not to go would clearly be a breach of manners.

'How kind of you,' said Randolph, coming forward and shaking Jimmy's hand, a greeting that, between two members of the same household, struck him as odd, 'You have brought your invention with you?'

Jimmy saw that it was useless to disclaim the honour of its discovery. He unwrapped the bottle and handed it to Randolph.

Randolph carried it straight away to a high window, the sill of which was level with his eyes and above the top of Jimmy's head. He held the bottle up to the light. Oblong in shape and about the size of an ordinary jam-jar, it had a deep whitish pavement of plaster, pitted with brown furry holes like an over-ripe cheese. Resting on the plaster, billowing and coiling up to the glass stopper, stood a fat column of cotton-wool. The most striking thing about the bottle was the word POISON, printed in large, loving characters on a label stuck to the outside.

'May I release the stopper?' asked Randolph at length.

'You may,' said Jimmy, 'but a whiff of the stuff is all you want.'

Randolph stared meditatively into the depths of the bottle. 'A rather agreeable odour,' he said. 'But how small the bottle is. I had figured it to myself as something very much larger.'

'Larger?' echoed Jimmy. 'Oh no, this is quite big enough for me. I don't need a mausoleum.'

'But I was under the impression,' Randolph Verdew remarked, still fingering the bottle, 'that you used it to destroy pests.'

'If you call butterflies pests,' said Jimmy, smiling.

'I am afraid that some of them must undeniably be included in that category,' pronounced Mr Verdew, his voice edged with a melancholy decisiveness. 'The cabbage butterfly, for instance. And it is, of course, only the admittedly noxious insects that need to be destroyed.'

'All insects are more or less harmful,' Jimmy said.

Randolph Verdew passed his hand over his brow. The shadow of a painful thought crossed his face, and he murmured uncertainly:

'I think that's a quibble. There are categories. . . I have been at some pains to draw them up. . . . The list of destructive lepidoptera is large, too large. . . . That is why I imagined your lethal chamber would be a vessel of considerable extent, possibly large enough to admit a man, and its use attended by some danger to an unpractised exponent.'

'Well,' said Jimmy, 'there is enough poison here to account for half a town. But let me show you how it works.' And he took the pill-box from his pocket. Shabby, battered and cowed, the butterfly stood motionless, its wings closed and upright.

'Now,' said Jimmy, 'you'll see.'

The butterfly was already between his fingers and half-way to the bottle when he heard, faint but clear, the sound of a cry. It was two-syllabled, like the interval of the cuckoo's call inverted, and might have been his own name.

'Listen!' he exclaimed. 'What was that? It sounded like Mrs Verdew's voice.' His swiftly-turning head almost collided with his host's chin, so near had the latter drawn to watch the operation, and chased the tail-end of a curious look from Randolph Verdew's face.

'It's nothing,' he said. 'Go on.'

Alas, alas, for the experiment in humane slaughter! The butterfly must have been stronger than it looked; the power of the killing-bottle had no doubt declined with frequent usage. Up and down, round and round flew the butterfly; its frantic flutterings could be heard through the thick walls of its glass prison. It clung to the cotton-wool, pressed itself into corners, its straining, delicate tongue coiling and uncoiling in the effort to suck in a breath of living air. Now it was weakening. It fell from the cotton-wool and lay with its back on the plaster slab. It jolted itself up and down and, when strength for this movement failed, it clawed the air with its thin legs as though pedalling an imaginary bicycle. Suddenly, with a violent spasm, it gave birth to a thick cluster of yellowish eggs. Its body twitched once or twice and at last lay still.

Jimmy shrugged his shoulders in annoyance and turned to his host. The look of horrified excitement, whose vanishing vestige he had seen a moment before, lay full and undisguised upon Randolph Verdew's face. He only said:

'Of what flower or vegetable is that dead butterfly the parasite?'

'Oh, poor thing,' said Jimmy carelessly, 'it's rather a rarity. Its caterpillar may have eaten an elm-leaf or two – nothing more. It's too scarce to be a pest. It's fond of gardens and frequented places, the book says – rather sociable, like a robin.'

'It could not be described as injurious to human life?'

'Oh no. It's a collector's specimen really. Only this is too damaged to be any good.'

'Thank you for letting me see the machine in operation,' said Randolph Verdew, going to his desk and sitting down. Jimmy found his silence a little embarrassing. He packed up the bottle and made a rather awkward, self-conscious exit.

The four bedroom-candles always stood, their silver flashing agreeably, cheek by jowl with the whisky decanter and the hot-water kettle and the soda. Now, the others having retired, there were only two, one of which (somewhat wastefully, for he still had a half-empty glass in his left hand) Rollo was lighting.

'My dear fellow,' he was saying to Jimmy, 'I'm sorry you think the new model insecticide fell a bit flat. But Randolph's like that, you know: damned undemonstrative cove, I must say, though he's my own brother.'

'He wasn't exactly undemonstrative,' answered Jimmy, perplexity written on his face.

'No, rather like an iceberg hitting you amidships,' said his friend. 'Doesn't make a fuss, but you feel it all the same. But don't you worry, Jimmy: I happen to know that he enjoyed your show. Fact is, he told me so.' He gulped down some whisky.

'I'm relieved,' said Jimmy, and he obviously spoke the truth. 'I've only one more whole day here, and I should be sorry if I'd hurt his feelings.'

'Yes, and I'm afraid you'll have to spend it with him alone,' said Rollo, compunction colouring his voice. 'I was coming to that. Fact is, Vera and I have unexpectedly got to go away to-morrow for the day.' He paused; a footman entered and began walking uncertainly about the room. 'Now, Jimmy,' he went on, 'be a good chap and stay on a couple of days more. You do keep us from the blues so. That's all right, Williams, we don't want anything,' he remarked parenthetically to the footman's retreating figure. 'I haven't mentioned it to Randolph, but he'd be absolutely charmed if you'd grace our humble dwelling a little longer. You needn't tell anyone anything: Just stay, and we shall be back the day after to-morrow. It's hellish that we've got to go, but you know this bread-winning business: it's the early bird that catches the worm. And talking of that, we have to depart at cock-crow. I may not see you again – that is, unless you stay, as I hope you will. Just send a wire to the old blighter who works with you and tell him to go to blazes.'

'Well,' said Jimmy, delighted by the prospect, 'you certainly do tempt me.'

'Then fall, my lad,' said Rollo, catching him a heavy blow between the shoulder-blades. I shan't say good-bye, but "au revoir". Don't go to bed sober; have another drink.'

But Jimmy declined. The flickering candles lighted them across the hall and up the stone stairs.

And it's lucky I have a candle, thought Jimmy, trying in vain the third and last switch, the one on the reading-lamp by the bed. The familiar room seemed to have changed, to be closing hungrily, with a vast black embrace, upon the nimbus of thin clear dusk that shone about the candle. He walked uneasily up and down, drew a curtain and let in a ray of moonlight. But the silver gleam crippled the candle-light without adding any radiance of its own, so he shut it out. This window must be closed, thought Jimmy, that opens on to the parapet, for I really couldn't deal with a stray cat in this localized twilight. He opened instead a window that gave on to the sheer wall. Even after the ritual of tooth-cleaning he was still restless and dissatisfied, so after a turn or two he knelt by the bed and said his prayers – whether from devotion or superstition he couldn't tell: he only knew that he wanted to say them.

*

'Come in!' he called next morning, in answer to the footman's knock.

'I can't come in, sir,' said a muffled voice. 'The door's locked.'

How on earth had that happened? Then Jimmy remembered. As a child he always locked the door because he didn't like to be surprised saying his prayers. He must have done so last night, unconsciously. How queer! He felt full of self-congratulation – he didn't know why. 'And – oh, Williams!' he called after the departing footman.

'Yes, sir?'

'The light's fused, or something. It wouldn't go on last night.'

'Very good, sir.'

Jimmy addressed himself to the tea. But what was this? Another note from Mrs Verdew!

Dear Jimmy (he read),

You will forgive this impertinence, for I've got a piece of good news for you. In future, you won't again be able to say that women never help a man in his career! (Jimmy was unaware of having said so.) *As you know, Rollo and I have to leave to-morrow morning. I don't suppose he told you why, because it's rather private. But he's embarking on a big undertaking that will mean an enormous amount of litigation! and lawyers' fees! Think of that! (Though I don't suppose you think of anything else.) I know he wants you to act for him: but to do so you positively MUST leave Verdew to-morrow. Make any excuse to Randolph; send yourself a telegram if you want to be specially polite: but you* must *catch the 8.30 p.m. to London. It's the chance of a lifetime! – of a life. You can get through to Rollo on the telephone next morning. Perhaps we could lunch together – or dine? A bientôt, therefore.*

Your friend,
Vera Verdew.

P.S. I shall be furious if you don't come.

Jimmy pondered Mrs Verdew's note, trying to read between its lines. One thing was clear: she had fallen in love with him. Jimmy smiled at the ceiling. She wanted to see him again, so soon, so soon! Jimmy smiled once more. She couldn't bear to wait an unnecessary day. How urgent women were! Jimmy smiled more indulgently. And, also, how exacting. Here was this cock-and-bull story, all about Rollo's 'undertaking' which would give him, Jimmy, the chance of a lifetime! And because she was so impatient she expected him to believe it! Luncheon, indeed! Dinner! How could they meet for dinner, when Rollo was to be back at Verdew that same evening? In her haste she had not even troubled to make her dates credible. And then: 'I shall be furious if you don't come.' What an argument! What confidence in her own powers did not that sentence imply! Let her be furious, then, as furious as she liked.

Her voice, just outside his door interrupted his meditation.

'Only a moment, Rollo, it will only take me a moment!'

And Rollo's reply, spoken in a voice as urgent as hers, but louder:

'I tell you there isn't time: we shall miss the train.'

He seemed to hustle her away downstairs, poor Vera. She had really been kind to Jimmy, in spite of her preposterous claims on his affection. He was glad he would see her again to-morrow. Verdew was so much nicer than London. He began to doze.

On the way back from the woods there was a small low church with a square tower and two bells – the lower one both cracked and flat. You could see up into the belfry through the slats in the windows. Close by the church ran a stream, choked with green scum except where the cattle went down to drink, and crossed by a simple bridge of logs set side by side. Jimmy liked to stand on the bridge and listen to the unmelodious chime. No one heeded it, no one came to church, and it had gone sour and out of tune. It gave Jimmy an exquisite, slightly morbid sense of dereliction and decay, which he liked to savour in solitude; but this afternoon a rustic had got there first.

'Good-day,' he said.

'Good-day,' said Jimmy.

'You're from the Castle, I'm thinking?' the countryman surmised.

'Yes.'

'And how do you find Mr Verdew?'

'Which Mr Verdew?'

'Why, the squire, of course.'

'I think he's pretty well,' said Jimmy.

'Ah, he may appear to be so,' the labourer observed; 'but them as has eyes to see and ears to hear, knows different.'

'Isn't he a good landlord?' asked Jimmy.

'Yes,' said the old man. 'He's a tolerable good landlord. It isn't that.' He seemed to relish his mysteriousness.

'You like Mr Rollo Verdew better?' suggested Jimmy.

'I wouldn't care to say that, sir. He's a wild one, Mr Rollo.'

'Well, anyhow, Mr Randolph Verdew isn't wild.'

'Don't you be too sure, sir.'

'I've never seen him so.'

'There's not many that have. And those that have – some won't tell what they saw and some can't.'

'Why won't they?'

'Because it's not their interest to.'

'And why can't the others?'

'Because they're dead.'

There was a pause.

'How did they die?' asked Jimmy.

'That's not for me to say,' the old man answered, closing his mouth like a trap. But this gesture, as Jimmy had already learned, was only part of his conversational technique. In a moment he began again:

'Did you ever hear of the Verdew Murders?'

'Something.'

'Well,'twasn't only dogs that was killed.'

'I know.'

'But they were all killed the same way.'

'How?'

'With a knife,' said the old man. 'Like pigs. From ear to ear,' he added, making an explanatory gesture; 'from ear to ear.' His voice became reminiscent. 'Tom Presland was a friend o' mine. I seed him in the evening and he said, he says, "That fine blamed donkey weren't worth a ten-pound fine." And I said, "You're lucky not to be in prison," for in case you don't know, sir, the Bench here don't mind fellows being a bit hasty with their animals, although Mr Verdew is the chairman. I felt nigh killing the beast myself sometimes, it was that obstinate. "ut, Bill," he says,"I don't feel altogether comfortable when I remember what happened to Jack Didwell." And sure enough he was found next morning in the ditch with his throat gapin' all white at the edges, just like poor old Jack. And the donkey was a contrary beast, that had stood many a knock before, harder than the one what killed him.'

'And why is Mr Verdew suspected?'

'Why, sir, the servants said he was in the Castle all night and must have been, because the bridge was drawed. But how do they know he had to use the bridge? Anyhow, George Wiscombe swears he saw him going through Nape's Spinney the night poor old Tom was done in. And Mr Verdew has always been cruel fond of animals, that's another reason.'

How easy it is, thought Jimmy, to lose one's reputation in the country!

'Tell me,' he said, 'how does Mr Verdew satisfy his conscience when he eats animals and chickens, and when he has slugs and snails killed in the garden?'

'Ah, there you've hit it,' said the old man, not at all nonplussed. 'But

365

they say Mr Rollo Verdew has helped him to make a mighty great list of what may be killed and what mayn't, according as it's useful-like to human beings. And anybody kills anything, they persuade him it's harmful and down it goes on the black list. And if he don't see the thing done with his own eyes, or the chap isn't hauled up before the Bench, he doesn't take on about it. And in a week or less it's all gone from his mind. Jack and Tom were both killed within a few days of what they'd done becoming known; so was the collie dog what was found here a fortnight back.'

'Here?' asked Jimmy.

'Close by where you're standing. Poor beast, it won't chase those b — y cats no more. It was in a mess. But, as I said, if what you've done's a week old, you're safe, in a manner of speaking.'

'But why, if he's really dangerous,' said Jimmy, impressed in spite of himself by the old man's tacit assumption of Randolph's guilt, 'doesn't Mr Rollo Verdew get him shut up?'

This simple question evoked the longest and most pregnant of his interlocutor's pauses. Surely, thought Jimmy, it will produce a monstrous birth, something to make suspicion itself turn pale.

'Now don't you tell nothing of what I'm saying to you,' said the old man at length. 'But it's my belief that Mr Rollo don't want his brother shut up; no, nor thought to be mad. And why? Because if people know he's mad, and he goes and does another murder, they'll just pop him in the lunatic asylum and all his money will go to Government and charity. But if he does a murder like you or me, and the circumstances are circumstantial, he'll be hanged for it, and all the money and the Castle and the coal-mine will go into the pockets of Mr Rollo.'

'I see,' said Jimmy. 'It sounds very simple.'

'I'm not swearing there's anything of the sort in Mr Rollo's mind,' said the old man. 'But that's the way I should look at it if I was him. Now I must be getting along. Good-night, sir.'

'Good-night.'

Of course it wasn't really night, only tea-time, five o'clock; but he and his acquaintance would meet no more that day, so perhaps the man was right to say good-night. Jimmy's thoughts, as he worked his way up the Castle mound, were unclear and rather painful. He didn't believe a tithe of what the old man said. It was not even a distortion of the truth; it was an ignorant and vulgar slander, that had no relation to the truth except by a kind of contiguity. But it infected his mood and gave a disagreeable direction to his thoughts. He was lonely; Randolph had not appeared at lunch, and he missed Rollo, and even

366

more he missed (though this surprised him) Rollo's wife. He hadn't seen much of them, but suddenly he felt the need of their company. But goodness knows where they are, thought Jimmy; I can't even telephone to them. In the midst of these uneasy reflections he reached his bedroom door. Walking in, he could not for a moment understand why the place looked so strange. Then he realized: it was empty. All his things had been cleared out of it.

'Evidently,' thought Jimmy, 'they've mistaken the day I was going away, and packed me!' An extraordinary sensation of relief surged up into his heart. Since his luggage was nowhere to be seen, it must have been stacked in the hall, ready for his departure by the evening train. Picturing himself already at the *guichet* of Verdew Grove station buying a ticket for London, Jimmy started for the hall.

Williams cut short his search.

'Were you looking for your things, sir?' he asked, with a slight smile. 'Because they're in the onyx room. We've moved you, sir.'

'Oh,' said Jimmy, following in the footman's wake. 'Why?'

'It was Mr Verdew's orders, sir. I told him the light was fused in your bedroom, so he said to move you into the onyx room.'

'The room next his?'

'That's right, sir.'

'Couldn't the fuse be mended?'

'I don't think it was the fuse, sir.'

'Oh, I thought you said it was.'

So this was the onyx room. Certainly its colours were dark and lustrous and laid on in layers, but Jimmy didn't care for them. Even the ceiling was parti-coloured. Someone must have been given a free hand here; perhaps Vera had done the decoration. The most beautiful thing in the room was the Chinese screen masking the door that communicated, he supposed, with Randolph's bedroom. What a clatter it would make if it fell, thought Jimmy, studying the heavy, dark, dully-shining panels of the screen. The door opening would knock it over. He heard the footman's voice.

'Is it for one night or more, sir? I've packed up some of your things.'

'I'm not sure yet,' said Jimmy. 'Williams, will this screen move?'

The footman took hold of the screen with both hands and telescoped it against his chest. There was revealed an ordinary-looking door covered with green baize. Jimmy could see the point of a key-head, so the door was probably not very thick.

'This used to be the dressing-room,' Williams volunteered, as though making a contribution to Jimmy's unspoken thoughts.

'Thank you,' said Jimmy 'and would you mind putting that screen back? . . . And, Williams!'

The footman stopped.

'There's still time to send a telegram?'

'Oh yes, sir. There's a form here.'

All through his solitary tea Jimmy debated with himself as to whether he should send the telegram – a telegram of recall, of course, it would be. The message presented no difficulty. 'Wire if Croxford case opens Tuesday.' He knew that it did, but his attendance was not at all necessary. He was undoubtedly suffering from a slight attack of nerves; and nowadays one didn't defy nerves, one yielded to them gracefully. 'I know that if I stay I shall have a bad night,' he thought; 'I might as well spend it in the train.' But of course he hadn't meant to go at all; he had even promised Rollo to stay. He had wanted to stay. And in a sense he still meant, he still wanted to stay. To leave abruptly to-night would be doubly rude: rude to Randolph, rude to Rollo. Vera alone would be pleased. Vera, whose clumsy attempt to lure him to London he had so easily seen through. Vera, whose 'I shall be furious if you don't come' rankled whenever he thought of it. Every moment added its quota to the incubus of indecision that paralysed his mind. Manners, duty, wishes, fears, all were contradictory, all pulled in different directions. A gust of apprehension sent him hot-foot to the writing-table. The telegram was ready written when, equally strong, an access of self-respect came and made him tear it up. At last he had an idea. At six o'clock he would send the telegram; the office might still be open. There would still be time to get a reply. If, in spite of this twofold obstacle he had an answer, he would take it as the voice of Fate, and leave that night . . .

At half-past seven Williams came in to draw the curtains; he also brought a message. Mr Verdew begged Mr Rintoul to excuse him, but he felt a little unwell, and was dining in his own room. He hoped to see Mr Rintoul to-morrow to say good-bye. 'You are going, then, sir?' added the footman.

Jimmy blindfolded his will, and took an answer at random from among the tablets of his mind.

'Yes. And – Williams!' he called out.

'Sir?'

'I suppose it's too late now for me to get an answer to my telegram?'

'I'm afraid so, sir.'

For a second Jimmy sunned himself in a warm glow of recovered self-esteem. Luck had saved him from a humiliating flight. Now his one regret was that his nerves had cheated him of those few extra days at Verdew. 'If there had been a bolt on my side of the green door,' he said to himself,' I should never have sent that telegram.'

How like, in some ways, was the last evening to the first. As bedtime approached, he became acutely conscious of his surroundings – of the stone floors, the vaulted passages, the moat, the drawbridge – all those concrete signs which seemed to recall the past and substitute it for the present. He was completely isolated and immured; he could scarcely believe he would be back in the real, living world to-morrow. Another glass of whisky would bring the centuries better into line. It did; and, emboldened by its heady fumes, he inspected, with the aid of his candle (for the ground-floor lights had been turned out) the defences of door and window, and marvelled anew at their parade of clumsy strength. Why all these precautions when the moat remained, a flawless girdle of protection?

But was it flawless? Lying in bed, staring at the painted ceiling, with its squares and triangles and riot of geometrical designs, Jimmy smiled to remember how Rollo had once told him of a secret entrance, known only to him. He had promised to show it to Jimmy, but he had forgotten. A nice fellow, Rollo, but he didn't believe they would ever know each other much better. When dissimilar natures come together, the friendship ripens quickly and as quickly falls. Rollo and Jimmy just tolerated each other – they didn't share their lives, their secrets, their secret passages . . .

Jimmy was lying on his back, his head sunk on the brightly-lit pillow, his mind drowsier than his digestion. To his departing consciousness the ceiling looked like a great five of diamonds spread over his head; the scarlet lozenges moved on hinges, he knew that quite well, and as they moved they gave a glimpse of black and let in a draught. Soon there would be a head poking through them all, instead of through this near corner one, and that would be more symmetrical. But if I stand on the bed I can shut them; they will close with a click. If only this one wasn't such a weight and didn't stick so . . .

Jimmy awoke in a sweat, still staring at the ceiling. It heaved and writhed like a half-dead moth on the setting-board. But the walls stood still, so that there was something more than whisky at the back of it. And yet, when he looked again, peace had descended on the ceiling.

The dream was right; he could touch the ceiling by standing on the bed. But only with the tips of his fingers. What he needed was a bar of some kind with which to prise it open. He looked round the room, and could see nothing suitable but a towel-horse. But there were plenty of walking-sticks downstairs. To light his candle and put on his dressing-gown and slippers was the work of a moment. He reached the

369

door in less time than it takes to tell. But he got no further, because the door was locked.

Jimmy's heart began to beat violently. Panic bubbled up in him like water in a syphon. He took a wild look round the room, ran to the bed-head, and pressed the bell-button as though he meant to flatten it in its socket. Relief stole into his heart. Already he heard in imagination the quick patter of feet in the corridor, the hurried, whispered explanations, the man's reassuring voice: 'I'll be with you in a moment, *sir.*' Already he felt slightly ashamed of his precipitate summons, and began to wonder how he should explain it away. The minutes passed, and nothing happened. He need not worry yet; it would take Williams some time to dress, and no doubt he had a long way to come. But Jimmy's returning anxiety cried out for some distraction, so he left the edge of the bed where he had been sitting, fetched the towel-horse, and, balancing unsteadily on the mattress, began to prod the ceiling. Down came little flakes and pellets of painted plaster; they littered the sheets and would be very uncomfortable to sleep on. Jimmy stooped to flick them away, and saw from the tail of his eye that since he rang five minutes had gone by. He resumed the muffled tattoo on the ceiling. Suddenly it gave; the red diamond shot upwards and fell back, revealing a patch of black and letting in a rush of cool air.

As, stupefied, Jimmy lowered his eyes, they fell upon the screen. It was moving stealthily outwards, toppling into the room. Already he could see a thin strip of the green door. The screen swayed, paused, seemed to hang by a hair. Then, its leaves collapsing inwards upon each other, it fell with a great crash upon the floor. In the opening stood Randolph, fully dressed; he had a revolver in his right hand, and there was a knife between his teeth. It was curved and shining, and he looked as though he were taking a bite out of the new moon.

The shot missed Jimmy's swaying legs, the knife only grazed his ankle, and he was safe in the darkness of the attic, with the bolt of the trap-door securely shut. He ran trembling in the direction the draught came from, and was rewarded first by a sense of decreasing darkness, and then by a glimpse, through a framed opening in the roof, of the stars and the night sky.

The opening was low down, and to climb out was easy. He found himself in a leaden gully, bounded on one side by a shallow parapet two feet high, and on the other, as it seemed, by the slope of the roof. Finding his way along the gully, he was brought up sharp against an octagonal turret, that clearly marked the end of the building. The moat was directly below him. Turning to the left, he encountered another similar turret, and turning to the left again he found himself up against a wall surmounted by tall chimneys. This wall appeared to be scored with projections and indentations – soot-doors he guessed them to be; he hoped to be able to use them to climb the wall, but they were awkwardly spaced, close to the parapet, and if he missed his footing he ran the risk of falling over its edge.

He now felt a curious lightheartedness, as though he had shuffled off every responsibility: responsibility towards his clothes, which were torn and dirty, towards his foot, which was bleeding, towards trains, letters, engagements – all the petty and important demands of life. Cold, but not unhappy, he sat down to await day-break.

The clock had just chimed three-quarters, which three-quarters he did not know, when he heard a scraping sound that seemed to come from the corresponding parapet beyond the roof. He listened, crouching in the angle between the chimney wall and the battlement. His fears told him that the sound was following the track by which he had come; the shuffling grew indistinct, and then, the first turret passed, began to draw nearer. It could only be Randolph, who clearly had some means of access to the roof other than the trap-door in Jimmy's bedroom. He must have, or he could not have reached it to spy on his victim while he was asleep. Now he was turning the last corner. Jimmy acted quickly and with the courage of desperation. At the corner where he crouched there projected above the battlement three sides of an octagonal turret, repeating the design of the true turrets at the end. Grasping the stone as well as he could, he lowered himself into space. It was a terrible moment, but the cautious shuffle of Randolph's approach deadened his fear. His arms almost at their full stretch, he felt the dripstone underneath his feet. It seemed about six inches wide, with a downward curve, but it sufficed. He changed his grip from the plain stone band of the parapet to the pierced masonry beneath it, which afforded a better purchase, and held his breath. Randolph could not find him unless he leant right over the balustrade. This he never did. He muttered to himself; he climbed up to the apex of the roof; he examined the flue-doors, or whatever they were. All this Jimmy could clearly see through the quatrefoil to which he was clinging. He heard Randolph say, 'I shall find him when the light comes,' and then he disappeared. The clock struck four, four-fifteen, four-thirty, and then a diffused pallor began to show itself in the eastern sky.

The numbness that had taken hold of Jimmy's body began to invade his mind, which grew dull and sleepy under the effort of compelling his tired hands to retain their hold. His back curved outwards, his head sank upon his breast; the changes of which his cramped position admitted were too slight to afford his body relief. So that he could not at once look round when he heard close above his head the sound of an opening door and the sharp rattle of falling mortar. He recognized the figure as it passed him – Rollo's.

Jimmy restrained his impulse to call out. Why had Rollo come back? Why was he swaggering over the roofs of Verdew Castle at daybreak looking as though he owned it? It was not his yet. Rollo turned, and in the same leisurely fashion walked back towards Jimmy's corner. His face was set and pale, but there was triumph in his eyes, and cruelty, and the marks of many passions which his every-day exterior had concealed. Then his eyebrows went up, his chin quivered, and his underlip shot out and seemed to stretch across his face. 'Just five minutes more, five minutes more; I'll give him another five minutes,' he kept muttering to himself. He leaned back against the wall. Jimmy could have touched the laces of his shoes, which were untied and dirty. 'Poor old Jimmy, poor old James!' Rollo suddenly chanted, in a voice that was very distinct, but quite unlike his own. To Jimmy's confused mind he seemed to be speaking of two different people. 'He came to Verdew Castle, and left it all in' – he paused – 'in flames. Never mind, Jimmy,' he added in the conciliatory tone of one who, overcome by his better nature, at last gives up teasing. 'Anyhow, it's ten to one against.' He stumbled down the gully and round the bend.

Jimmy never knew how he summoned strength to climb over the parapet. He found himself sprawling in the gully, panting and faint. But he had caught sight of a gaping hole like a buttery-hatch amid the tangle of soot-doors, and he began to crawl towards it. He was trying to bring his stiff knee up to his good one when from close by his left ear he heard a terrible scream. It went shooting up, and seemed to make a glittering arc of sound in the half-lit sky. He also thought he heard the words, 'Oh, God, Randolph, it's me!' but of this he was never certain. But through all the windings of Rollo's bolt-hole, until it discharged itself at the base of a ruined newell-staircase among the outbuildings, he still heard the agonized gasping, spasmodic, yet with a horrible rhythm of its own, that followed Rollo's scream. He locked the cracked, paintless door with the key that Rollo had left, and found himself among the lanes.

Late in the evening of the same day a policeman asked to see Mrs Verdew, who was sitting in a bedroom in the King's Head inn at Fremby, a market town ten miles from Verdew Castle. She had been sitting there all day, getting up from time to time to glance at a slip of paper pinned to one of the pillows. It was dated '7.30 a.m., July 10th,' and said, 'Back in a couple of hours. Have to see a man about a car. Sorry. – ROLLO.' She wouldn't believe the constable when he said that her husband had met with an accident, some time early that morning, probably about five o'clock. 'But look; but look!' she cried. 'See for yourself! It is his own handwriting! He says he went away at half-past seven. Why are all Englishmen so difficult to convince?'

'We have a statement from Mr Randolph Verdew,' said the policeman gently. 'He said that he . . . he . . . he met Mr Rollo at the Castle in the early hours of the morning.'

'But how can you be so stupid!' cried Mrs Verdew. 'It wasn't Rollo – it was Mr Rintoul who . . .'

'What name is that?' asked the policeman, taking out his note-book.

But Mrs Verdew did not answer; she had fainted.

Pickman's Model

BY H. P. LOVECRAFT

It was inevitable after the success of The Twilight Zone *that Rod Serling would sooner or later come up with an idea for another anthology series. Indeed, shortly after the last of the 156 episodes was screened in 1964, plans were afoot at ABC to revive it as* Witches, Warlocks and Werewolves *(after the title of a paperback anthology Serling had edited for Bantam Books) or alternatively as* Rod Serling's Wax Museum *in which models would represent the protagonist in each story. But neither idea got past the planning stage, and it was not until 1969 after Serling had done a lot of other television scriptwriting that he produced the basic idea for* Night Gallery. *To herald the series, a three-part 'special' was devised in which Serling introduced the respective stories by referring to three pictures hanging on a wall behind him. The stories, all of which he had written, were 'The Cemetery', a return-from-the dead revenge tale; 'Eyes' about a rich, blind woman's quest for sight; and 'Escape Route' in which a Nazi concentration camp survivor confronted his old tormentor. Impressive as the show was with its three featured stars, Roddy McDowall, Joan Crawford and Richard Kiley, it is better remembered for the man who directed the Joan Crawford segment, 'Eyes' – a twenty-one-year-old would-be film maker named Steven Spielberg. Although Spielberg has subsequently admitted he was nervous of the legendary Joan Crawford and not altogether happy with the script, with that one piece of filming he revealed to Hollywood – and the world – something of the talent which has since made him one of the most famous and successful directors. Undoubtedly, too, he contributed to the success of the* Night Gallery *pilot when it was shown on 8 November 1969, and which became the highest-rated programme of the evening as well as receiving an Edgar Award from the Mystery Writers of America. In the years which followed, the series ran to a total of ninety-five episodes which were screened, initially, on Wednesday evenings from ten PM to eleven PM, then later shifted to the same time spot on Sunday nights. Night Gallery drew on the work of many important writers of horror fiction for its episodes including Fritz Leiber, A.E. Van Vogt, David Ely, Conrad Aiken, Manly Wade Wellman, Robert Bloch and August Derleth, as well as a galaxy of guest stars.*

One story from the series has special memories for both Rod Sterling and his viewers: 'Pickman's Model', about an artist who specializes in grotesque paintings of monsters, written by the eccentric but widely influential H.P. Lovecraft (1890–1937). Adapted by Alvin Sapinsley and directed by Jack Laird, the episode featured Bradford Dillman and Louise Sorel with Robert Prohaska as 'The Creature' who, though only hinted at in the story, was the undoubted star of the TV adaptation, thanks to the make-up artistry of Leonard Engelman and John F. Chambers. According to Jack Laird the monster generated more letters from viewers than any other episode of Night Gallery and also won an Emmy Award nomination for 'best makeup in a single programme or series'. Even when viewed twenty years later, 'Pickman's Model' serves as a chilling reminder of Night Gallery – and as one of the best ever episodes of late night horror . . .

YOU needn't think I'm crazy, Eliot – plenty of others have queerer prejudices than this. Why don't you laugh at Oliver's grandfather, who won't ride in a motor? If I don't like that damned subway, it's my own business; and we got here more quickly anyhow in the taxi. We'd have had to walk up the hill from Park Street if we'd taken the car.

I know I'm more nervous than I was when you saw me last year, but you don't need to hold a clinic over it. There's plenty of reason, God knows, and I fancy I'm lucky to be sane at all. Why the third degree? You didn't used to be so inquisitive.

Well, if you must hear it, I don't know why you shouldn't. Maybe you ought to, anyhow, for you kept writing me like a grieved parent when you heard I'd begun to cut the Art Club and keep away from Pickman. Now that he's disappeared I go around to the club once in a while, but my nerves aren't what they were.

No, I don't know what's become of Pickman, and I don't like to guess. You might have surmised I had some inside information when I dropped him – and that's why I don't want to think where he's gone. Let the police find what they can – it won't be much, judging from the fact that they don't know yet of the old North End place he hired under the name of Peters. I'm not sure that I could find it again myself – not that I'd ever try, even in broad daylight! Yes, I do know, or am afraid I know, why he maintained it. I'm coming to that. And I think you'll understand before I'm through why I don't tell the police. They would ask me to guide them, but I couldn't go back there even if I knew the way. There was something there – and now I can't use the subway or (and you may as well have your laugh at this, too) go down into cellars any more.

I should think you'd have known I didn't drop Pickman for the same silly reasons that fussy old women like Dr Reid or Joe Minot or Bosworth did. Morbid art doesn't shock me, and when a man has the genius Pickman had I feel it an honour to know him, no matter what direction his work takes. Boston never had a greater painter than Richard Upton Pickman. I said it at first and I say it still, and I never swerved an inch, either, when he showed that *Ghoul Feeding*. That, you remember, was when Minot cut him.

You know, it takes profound art and profound insight into Nature to turn out stuff like Pickman's. Any magazine-cover hack can splash paint around wildly and call it a nightmare or Witches' Sabbath or a portrait of the devil, but only a great painter can make such a thing really scare or ring true. That's because only a real artist knows the actual anatomy of the terrible or the physiology of fear – the exact sort of lines and proportions that connect up with latent instincts or hereditary memories of fright, and the proper colour contrasts and lighting effects to stir the dormant sense of strangeness. I don't have to tell you why a Fuseli really brings a shiver while a cheap ghost-story frontispiece merely makes us laugh. There's something those fellows catch – beyond life – that they're able to make us catch for a second. Doré had it. Sime has it. Angarola of Chicago has it. And Pickman had it as no man ever had it before or – I hope to heaven – ever will again.

Don't ask me what it is they see. You know, in ordinary art, there's all the difference in the world between the vital, breathing things drawn from Nature or models and the artificial truck that commercial small fry reel off in a bare studio by rule. Well, I should say that the really weird artist has a kind of vision which makes models, or summons up what amounts to actual scenes from the spectral world he lives in. Anyhow, he manages to turn out results that differ from the pretender's mince-pie dreams in just about the same way that the life painter's results differ from the concoctions of a correspondence-school cartoonist. If I had ever seen what Pickman saw – but no! Here, let's have a drink before we get any deeper. Gad, I wouldn't be alive if I'd ever seen what that man – if he was a man – saw!

You recall that Pickman's forte was faces. I don't believe anybody since Goya could put so much of sheer hell into a set of features or a twist of expression. And before Goya you have to go back to the medieval chaps who did the gargoyles and chimeras on Notre Dame and Mont Saint-Michel. They believed all sorts of things – and maybe they saw all sorts of things, too, for the Middle Ages had some curious phases. I remember your asking Pickman yourself once, the year before you went away, wherever in thunder he got such ideas and visions. Wasn't that a nasty laugh he gave you? It was partly because of that laugh that Reid dropped him. Reid, you know, had just taken up comparative pathology, and was full of pompous 'inside stuff' about the biological or evolutionary significance of this or that mental or physical symptom. He said Pickman repelled him more and more every day, and almost frightened him toward the last – that the fellow's features and expression were slowly developing in a way he didn't like; in a way that wasn't human. He had a lot of talk about diet, and said Pickman must be abnormal and eccentric to the last degree. I suppose you told Reid, if you and he had any correspondence over it, that he'd let Pickman's paintings get on his nerves or harrow up his imagination. I know I told him that myself – then.

But keep in mind that I didn't drop Pickman for anything like this. On the contrary, my admiration for him kept growing; for that *Ghoul Feeding* was a tremendous achievement. As you know, the club wouldn't exhibit it, and the Museum of Fine Arts wouldn't accept it as a gift; and I can add that nobody would buy it, so Pickman had it right in his house till he went. Now his father has it in Salem – you know Pickman comes of old Salem stock, and had a witch ancestor hanged in 1692.

I got into the habit of calling on Pickman quite often, especially after I began making notes for a monograph on weird art. Probably it was his work which put the idea into my head, and anyhow, I found him a mine of data and suggestions when I came to develop it. He showed me all the paintings and drawings he had about; including some pen-and-ink sketches that would, I verily believe, have got him kicked out of the club if many of the members had seen them. Before long I was pretty nearly a devotee, and would listen for hours like a schoolboy to art theories and philosophic speculations wild enough to qualify him for the Danvers asylum. My hero-worship, coupled with the fact that people generally were commencing to have less and less to do with

377

him, made him get very confidential with me; and one evening he hinted that if I were fairly close-mouthed and none too squeamish, he might show me something rather unusual – something a bit stronger than anything he had in the house.

'You know,' he said, 'there are things that won't do for Marlborough Street – things that are out of place here, and that can't be conceived here, anyhow. It's my business to catch the overtones of the soul, and you won't find those in a parvenu set of artificial streets on made land. Back Bay isn't Boston – it isn't anything yet, because it's had no time to pick up memories and attract local spirits. If there are any ghosts here, they're the tame ghosts of a salt marsh and a shallow cove; and I want human ghosts – the ghosts of beings highly organized enough to have looked on hell and known the meaning of what they saw.

'The place for an artist to love is the North End. If any æsthete, were sincere, he'd put up with the slums for the sake of the massed traditions. God, man! Don't you realize that places like that weren't merely *made*, but actually *grew*? Generation after generation lived and felt and died there, and in days when people weren't afraid to live and feel and die. Don't you know there was a mill on Copp's Hill in 1632, and that half the present streets were laid out by 1650? I can show you houses that have stood two centuries and a half and more; houses that have witnessed what would make a modern house crumble into power. What do moderns know of life and the forces behind it? You call the Salem witchcraft a delusion, but I'll wager my four-times-great-grandmother could have told you things. They hanged her on Gallows Hill, with Cotton Mather looking sanctimoniously on. Mather, damn him, was afraid somebody might succeed in kicking free of this accursed cage of monotony – I wish someone had laid a spell on him or sucked his blood in the night!

'I can show you a house he lived in, and I can show you another one he was afraid to enter in spite of all his fine bold talk. He knew things he didn't dare put into that stupid *Magnalia* or that puerile *Wonders of the Invisible World*. Look here, do you know the whole North End once had a set of tunnels that kept certain people in touch with each other's houses, and the burying ground, and the sea? Let them prosecute and persecute above ground – things went on every day that they couldn't reach, and voices laughed at night that they couldn't place!

'Why, man, out of ten surviving houses built before 1700 and not moved since I'll wager that in eight I can show you something queer in the cellar. There's hardly month that you don't read of workmen finding bricked-up arches and wells leading nowhere in this or that old place as it comes down – you could see one near Henchman Street from the elevated last year. There were witches and what their spells summoned; pirates and what they brought in from the sea; smugglers; privateers – and I tell you, people knew how to live, and how to enlarge the bounds of life, in the old times! This wasn't the only world a bold and wise man could know – faugh! And to think of today in contrast, with such pale-pink brains that even a club of supposed artists gets shudders and convulsions if a picture goes beyond the feelings of a Beacon Street tea-table!

'The only saving grace of the present is that it's too damned stupid to question the past very closely. What do maps and records and guidebooks really tell of the North End? Bah! At a guess I'll guarantee to lead you to thirty or forty alleys and networks of alleys north of Prince Street that aren't suspected by ten living beings outside of the foreigners that swarm them. And what do those Dagoes know of their meaning? No, Thurber, these ancient places are dreaming gorgeously and overflowing with wonder and terror and escapes from the commonplace, and yet there's not a living soul to understand or profit by them. Or, rather, there's only one living soul – for I haven't been digging around in the past for nothing!

'See here, you're interested in this sort of thing. What if I told you that I've got another studio up there, where I can catch the night-spirit of antique horror and paint things that I couldn't even think of in Marlborough Street? Naturally I don't tell those cursed old maids at the club – with Reid, damn him, whispering even as it is that I'm a sort of monster bound down the toboggan of reverse evolution. Yes, Thurber, I decided long ago that one must paint terror as well as beauty from life, so I did some exploring in places where I had reason to know terror lives.

'I've got a place that I don't believe three living Nordic men besides myself have ever seen. It isn't so very far from the elevated as distance goes, but it's centuries away as the soul goes. I took it because of the queer old brick well in the cellar – one of the sort I told you about. The shack's almost tumbling down, so that nobody else would live there, and I'd hate to tell you how little I pay for it. The windows are boarded up, but I like that all the better, since I don't want daylight for what I do. I paint in the cellar, where the inspiration is thickest, but I've other rooms furnished on the ground floor. A Sicilian owns it, and I've hired it under the name of Peters.

'Now if you're game, I'll take you there to-night. I think you'd enjoy the pictures, for as I said, I've let myself go a bit there. It's no vast tour –

I sometimes do it on foot, for I don't want to attract attention with a taxi in such a place. We can take the shuttle at the South Station for Battery Street, and after that the walk isn't much.'

Well, Eliot, there wasn't much for me to do after that harangue but to keep myself from running instead of walking for the first vacant cab we could sight. We changed to the elevated at the South Station, and at about 12 o'clock had climbed down the steps at Battery Street and struck along the old waterfront past Constitution Wharf. I didn't keep track of the cross streets, and can't tell you yet which it was we turned up, but I know it wasn't Greenough Lane.

When we did turn, it was to climb through the deserted length of the oldest and dirtiest alley I ever saw in my life, with crumbling-looking gables, broken small-paned windows, and archaic chimneys that stood out half-disintegrated against the moon-lit sky. I don't believe there were three houses in sight that hadn't been standing in Cotton Mather's time – certainly I glimpsed at least two with an overhang, and once I thought I saw a peaked roof-line of the almost forgotten pre-gambrel type, though antiquarians tell us there are none left in Boston.

From that alley, which had a dim light, we turned to the left into an equally silent and still narrower alley with no light at all; and in a minute made what I think was an obtuse-angled bend toward the right in the dark. Not long after this Pickman produced a flashlight and revealed an antediluvian ten-panelled door that looked damnably worm-eaten. Unlocking it, he ushered me into a barren hallway with what was once splendid dark-oak panelling – simple, of course, but thrillingly suggestive of the times of Andros and Phips and the Witchcraft. Then he took me through a door on the left, lighted an oil lamp, and told me to make myself at home.

Now, Eliot, I'm what the man in the street would call fairly 'hard-boiled'. but I'll confess that what I saw on the walls of that room gave me a bad turn. They were his pictures you know – the ones he couldn't paint or even show in Marlborough Street – and he was right when he said he had 'let himself go'. Here – have another drink – I need one, anyhow!

There's no use in my trying to tell you what they were like, because the awful, the blasphemous horror, and the unbelievable loathsome-ness and moral fetor came from simple touches quite beyond the power of words to classify. There was none of the exotic technique you see in Sidney Sime, none of the trans-Saturnian landscapes and lunar fungi that Clark Ashton Smith uses to freeze the blood. The back-grounds were mostly old churchyards, deep woods, cliffs by the sea, brick tunnels, ancient panelled rooms, or simple vaults of masonry. Copp's Hill Burying Ground which could not be many blocks away from this very house, was a favourite scene.

The madness and monstrosity lay in the figures in the foreground – for Pickman's morbid art was pre-eminently one of demoniac portraiture. These figures were seldom completely human, but often approached humanity in varying degrees. Most of the bodies, while roughly bipedal, had a forward slumping, and a vaguely canine cast. The texture of the majority was a kind of unpleasant rubberiness. Ugh! I can see them now! Their occupations – well, don't ask me to be too precise. They were usually feeding – I won't say on what. They were sometimes shown in groups in cemeteries or underground passages, and often appeared to be in battle over their prey – or rather, their treasure-trove. And what damnable expressiveness Pickman some-times gave the sightless faces of this charnel booty! Occasionally the things were shown leaping through open windows at night, or squatting on the chests of sleepers, worrying at their throats. One canvas showed a ring of them baying about a hanged witch on Gallows Hill, whose dead face held a close kinship to theirs.

But don't get the idea that it was all this hideous business of theme and setting which struck me faint. I'm not a three-year-old kid, and I'd seen much like this before. It was the *faces*, Eliot, those accursed *faces*, that leered and slavered out of the canvas with the very breath of life! By God, man, I verily believe they *were* alive! That nauseous wizard had waked the fires of hell in pigment, and his brush had been a nightmare-spawning wand. Give me that decanter, Eliot!

There was one thing called *The Lesson* – heaven pity me, that I ever saw it! Listen – can you fancy a squatting circle of nameless doglike things in a churchyard teaching a small child how to feed like themselves? The price of a changeling, I suppose – you know the old myth about how the weird people leave their spawn in cradles in exchange for the human babes they steal. Pickman was showing what happens to those stolen babes – how they grow up – and then I began to see a hideous relationship in the faces of the human and non-human figures. He was, in all his gradations of morbidity between the frankly non-human and the degradedly human, establishing a sardonic linkage and evolution. The dog-things were developed from mortals!

And no sooner had I wondered what he made of their own young as left with mankind in the form of changelings, than my eye caught a picture embodying that very thought. It was that of an ancient Puritan interior – a heavily beamed room with lattice windows, a settle, and clumsy seventeenth century furniture, with the family sitting about while the father read from the Scriptures. Every face but one showed nobility and reverence, but that one reflected the mockery of the pit. It was that of a man young in years, and no doubt belonged to a supposed son of that pious father, but in essence it was the kin of the unclean things. It was their changeling – and in a spirit of supreme irony Pickman had given the features a very perceptible resemblance to his own.

By this time Pickman had lighted a lamp in an adjoining room and was politely holding open the door for me; asking me if I would care to see his 'modern studies'. I hadn't been able to give him much of my opinions – I was too speechless with fright and loathing – but I think he fully understood and felt highly complimented. And now I want to assure you again, Eliot, that I'm no mollycoddle to scream at anything which shows a bit of departure from the usual. I'm middle-aged and decently sophisticated, and I guess you saw enough of me in France to know I'm not easily knocked out. Remember, too, that I'd just about recovered my wind and got used to those frightful pictures which turned colonial New England into a kind of annexe of hell. Well, in spite of all this, that next room forced a real scream out of me, and I had to clutch at the doorway to keep from keeling over. The other chamber had shown a pack of ghouls and witches overrunning the world of our forefathers, but this one brought the horror right into our own daily life!

Gad, how that man could paint! There was a study called *Subway Accident*, in which a flock of the vile things were clambering up from some unknown catacomb through a crack in the floor of the Boylston Street subway and attacking a crowd of people on the platform. Another showed a dance on Copp's Hill among the tombs with the background of to-day. Then there were any number of cellar views, with monsters creeping in through holes and rifts in the masonry and grinning as they squatted behind barrels or furnaces and waited for their first victim to descend the stairs.

One disgusting canvas seemed to depict a vast cross-section of Beacon Hill, with antlike armies of the mephitic monsters squeezing themselves through burrows that honeycombed the ground. Dances in the modern cemeteries were freely pictured, and another conception somehow shocked me more than all the rest – a scene in an unknown vault, where scores of the beasts crowded about one who held a well-known Boston guidebook and was evidently reading aloud. All were pointing to a certain passage, and every face seemed so distorted with epileptic and reverberant laughter that I almost thought I heard the fiendish echoes. The title of the picture was *Holmes, Lowell and Longfellow Lie Buried in Mount Auburn*.

As I gradually steadied myself and got readjusted to this second room of deviltry and morbidity, I began to analyse some of the points in my sickening loathing. In the first place, I said to myself, these things repelled because of the utter inhumanity and callous cruelty they showed in Pickman. The fellow must be a relentless enemy of all mankind to take such glee in the torture of brain and flesh and the degradation of the mortal tenement. In the second place, they terrified because of their very greatness. Their art was the art that convinced – when we saw the pictures we saw the demons themselves and were afraid of them. And the queer part was, that Pickman got none of his power from the use of selectiveness or bizarrerie. Nothing was blurred, distorted, or conventionalized; outlines were sharp and life-like, and details were almost painfully defined. And the faces!

It was not any mere artist's interpretation that we saw; it was pandemonium itself, crystal-clear in stark objectivity. That was it, by heaven! The man was not a fantaisiste or romanticist at all – he did not even try to give us the churning, prismatic ephemera of dreams, but coldly and sardonically reflected some stable, mechanistic, and well-established horror-world which he saw fully, brilliantly, squarely and unfalteringly. God knows what that world can have been, or where he ever glimpsed the blasphemous shapes that loped and trotted and crawled through it; but whatever the baffling source of his images, one thing was plain. Pickman was in every sense – in conception and in execution – a thorough, painstaking, and almost scientific *realist*.

My host was now leading the way down cellar to his actual studio, and I braced myself for some hellish effects among the unfinished canvases. As we reached the bottom of the damp stairs he turned his flashlight to a corner of the large open space at hand, revealing the circular brick kerb of what was evidently a great well in the earthen floor. We walked nearer, and I saw that it must be five feet across, with walls a good foot thick and some six inches above the ground level – solid work of the seventeenth century, or I was much mistaken. That, Pickman said, was the kind of thing he had been talking about – an aperture of the network of tunnels that used to undermine the hill. I noticed idly that it did not seem to be bricked up, and that a heavy disk of wood formed the apparent cover. Thinking of the things this well must have been connected with if Pickman's wild hints had not been mere rhetoric, I shivered slightly; then turned to follow him up a step and through a narrow door into a room of fair size, provided with a wooden floor and furnished as a studio. An acetylene gas outfit gave the light necessary for work.

The unfinished pictures on easels or propped against the walls were as ghastly as the finished ones upstairs, and showed the painstaking methods of the artist. Scenes were blocked out with extreme care, and penciled guide lines told of the minute exactitude which Pickman used in getting the right perspective and proportions. The man was great – I say it even now, knowing as much as I do. A large camera on a table excited my notice, and Pickman told me that he used it in taking scenes for backgrounds, so that he might paint them from photographs in the studio instead of carting his outfit around the town for this or that view. He thought a photograph quite as good as an actual scene or model for sustained work, and declared he employed them regularly.

There was something very disturbing about the nauseous sketches and half-finished monstrosities that leered around from every side of the room, and when Pickman suddenly unveiled a huge canvas on the side away from the light I could not for my life keep back a loud scream – the second I had emitted that night. It echoed and echoed through the dim vaultings of that ancient and nitrous cellar, and I had to choke back a flood of reaction that threatened to burst out as hysterical laughter. Merciful Creator! Eliot, I don't know how much was real and how much was feverish fancy. It doesn't seem to me that earth can hold a dream like that!

It was a colossal and nameless blasphemy with glaring red eyes, and it held in bony claws a thing that had been a man, gnawing at the head as a child nibbles at a stick of candy. Its position was a kind of crouch, and as one looked one felt that at any moment it might drop its present prey and seek a juicier morsel. But, damn it all, it wasn't even the fiendish subject that made it such an immortal fountain-head of all panic – not that, nor the dog face with its pointed ears, bloodshot eyes, flat nose, and drooling lips. It wasn't the scaly claws nor the mould-caked body nor the half-hoofed feet – none of these, though any one of them might well have driven an excitable man to madness.

It was the technique, Eliot – the cursed, the impious, the unnatural technique! As I am a living being, I never elsewhere saw the actual breath of life so fused into a canvas. The monster was there – it glared and gnawed and gnawed and glared – and I knew that only a suspension of Nature's laws could ever let a man paint a thing like that without a model – without some glimpse of the nether world which no mortal unsold to the Fiend has ever had.

Pinned with a thumb-tack to a vacant part of the canvas was a piece of paper now badly curled up – probably, I thought a photograph from which Pickman meant to paint a background as hideous as the nightmare it was to enhance. I reached out to uncurl and look at it when suddenly I saw Pickman start as if shot. He had been listening with peculiar intensity ever since my shocked scream had waked unaccustomed echoes in the dark cellar, and now he seemed struck with a fright which, though not comparable to my own, had in it more of the physical than the spiritual. He drew a revolver and motioned me to silence, then stepped out into the main cellar and closed the door behind him.

I think I was paralysed for an instant. Imitating Pickman's listening, I fancied I heard a faint scurrying sound somewhere, and a series of squeals or bleats in a direction I couldn't determine. I thought of huge rats and shuddered. Then there came a subdued sort of clatter which somehow set me all in gooseflesh – a furtive, groping kind of clatter, though I can't attempt to convey what I mean in words. It was like heavy wood falling on stone or brick – wood on brick – what did that make me think of?

It came again, and louder. There was a vibration as if the wood had fallen farther than it had fallen before. After that followed a sharp grating noise, a shouted gibberish from Pickman, and the deafening discharge of all six chambers of a revolver, fired spectacularly as a lion-tamer might fire in the air for effect. A muffled squeal or squawk, and a thud. Then more wood and brick grating, a pause, and the opening of the door – at which I'll confess I started violently. Pickman reappeared with his smoking weapon, cursing the bloated rats that infested the ancient well.

'The deuce knows what they eat, Thurber,' he grinned, 'for those archaic tunnels touched graveyard and witch-den and seacoast. But whatever it is, they must have run short, for they were devilish anxious to get out. Your yelling stirred them up, I fancy. Better be cautious in these old places – our rodent friends are the one drawback, though I sometimes think they're a positive asset by way of atmosphere and colour.'

Well, Elliot, that was the end of the night's adventure. Pickman had promised to show me the place, and heaven knows he had done it. He led me out of that tangle of alleys in another direction, it seems, for when we sighted a lamp-post we were in a half-familiar street with monotonous rows of mingled tenements blocks and old houses. Charter Street it turned out to be, but I was too flustered to notice just where we hit it. We were too late for the elevated, and walked back downtown through Hanover Street. I remember that walk. We switched from Tremont up Beacon, and Pickman left me at the corner of Joy, where I turned off. I never spoke to him again.

Why did I drop him? Don't be impatient. Wait till I ring for coffee. We've had enough of the other stuff, but I for one need something.

No – it wasn't the paintings I saw in that place; though I'll swear they were enough to get him ostracized in nine-tenths of the homes and clubs of Boston, and I guess you won't wonder now why I have to steer clear of subways and cellars. It was – something I found in my coat the next morning. You know, the curled-up paper tacked to that frightful canvas in the cellar; the thing I thought was a photograph of some scene he meant to use as a background for that monster. That last scare had come while I was reaching to uncurl it, and it seems I had vacantly crumpled it into my pocket. But here's the coffee – take it black, Eliot, if you're wise.

Yes, that paper was the reason I dropped Pickman; Richard Upton Pickman, the greatest artist I have ever known – and the foulest being that ever leaped the bounds of life into the pits of myth and madness. Eliot – old Reid was right. He wasn't strictly human. Either he was born in strange shadow, or he'd found a way to unlock the forbidden gate. It's all the same now, for he's gone – back into the fabulous darkness he loved to haunt. Here, let's have the chandelier going.

Don't ask me to explain or even conjecture about what I burned. Don't ask me, either, what lay behind that mole-like scrambling Pickman was so keen to pass off as rats. There are secrets, you know, which might have come down from old Salem times, and Cotton Mather tells even stranger things. You know how damned life-like Pickman's paintings were – how we all wondered where he got those faces.

Well – that paper wasn't a photograph of any background, after all. What it showed was simply the monstrous being he was painting on that awful canvas. It was the model he was using – and its background was merely the wall of the cellar studio in minute detail. But, by God, Eliot, *it was a photograph from life*.

The Treasure of Abbot Thomas

BY M. R. JAMES

In 1971, the BBC began a Christmas tradition that has been continued uninterrupted on the channel to this day – the screening of a ghost story in the middle of the festive season, the majority of them adapted from the works of M.R. James (1862–1936). Of course, the idea of telling supernatural stories at Christmas is not a new one: Charles Dickens virtually invented the idea (along with the concept of a 'white' Christmas) in his books over a century ago, and radio stations on both sides of the Atlantic have been broadcasting chilling tales during the dark days of winter to listeners huddled beside their roaring fires, since the Thirties. Producer/director Laurence Gordon Clark was the man responsible for initiating the TV tradition on 23 December 1971, with M.R. James' 'The Stalls of Barchester Cathedral'. The success of the transmission led to more adaptations from the pages of his books including 'A Warning to the Curious' (1973), 'Lost Hearts' (1973), 'The Treasure of Abbot Thomas' (1974) and 'The Ash Tree' (1975). In 1976, with an acknowledgement to the founder of the tradition, Clark presented 'The Signalman' by Charles Dickens and a year later, 'Schalken the Painter' by Joseph Sheridan Le Fanu. Since then, the ever-reliable Mr James has filled the bill.

There are probably no finer ghost stories in the English language than those of M.R. James, who was a most appropriate writer to have been selected for this treatment as his tales were originally written for reading to friends at King's College, Cambridge, where he was a Fellow. In them, he manages to conjure up terror by inference and suggestion rather than through descriptions of supernatural manifestations. This has, of course, presented problems for those attempting to turn the stories into television dramas – and by general consensus the most successful adaptation so far has been 'The Treasure of Abbot Thomas', about a Victorian antiquarian's investigation into the death of a sinister Medieval monk, for which John Bowen wrote the script. Starring the subtle and commanding actor Michael Bryant, the photography was splendidly haunting, and the background of Wells Cathedral along with the spooky music by Geoffrey Burgeon made it one of the highlights of Christmas viewing, as Shaun Usher wrote in the Daily Mail *of 24, December 1974, 'Those among us flattered at being frightened in style, ever grateful to sup full on Cordon Bleu horrors, dined at the top table last night. "The Treasure of Abbot Thomas" was the best of Lawrence Gordon Clark's series thus far, and when the forerunners were outstanding of their kind, this acknowledges that Treasure was very good indeed.' The story upon which it was based is equally outstanding, as the reader may now discover for himself . . .*

I

'VERUM usque in præsentem diem multa garriunt inter se Canonici de abscondito quodam istius Abbatis Thomæ thesauro, quem sæpe, quanquam adhuc incassum quæsiverunt Steinfeldenses. Ipsum enim Thomam adhuc florida in ætate existentem ingentem auri massam circa monasterium defodisse perhibent; de quo multoties interrogatus ubi esset, cum risu respondere solitus erat: "Job, Johannes, et Zacharias vel vobis vel posteris indicabunt"; idemque aliquando adiicere se inventuris minime invisurum. Inter alia huius Abbatis opera, hoc memoria præcipue dignum iudico quod fenestram magnam in orientali parte alæ australis in ecclesia sua imaginibus optime in vitro depictis impleverit: id quod et ipsius effigies et insignia ibidem posita demonstrant. Domum quoque Abbatialem fere totam restauravit: puteo in atrio ipsius effosso et lapidibus marmoreis pulchre cælatis exornato. Decessit autem, morte aliquantulum subitanea perculsus, ætatis suæ anno lxxii^{do}, incarnationis vero Dominiæ mdxxix^{o}.'

'I suppose I shall have to translate this,' said the antiquary to himself, as he finished copying the above lines from that rather rare and exceedingly diffuse book, the *'Sertum Steinfeldense Norbertinum.'** 'Well, it may as well be done first as last,' and

* An account of the Premonstratensian abbey of Steinfeld, in the Eiffel, with lives of the Abbots, published at Cologne in 1712 by Christian Albert Erhard, a resident in the district. The epithet *Norbertinum* is due to the fact that St Norbert was founder of the Premonstratensian Order.

accordingly the following rendering was very quickly produced:

'Up to the present day there is much gossip among the Canons about a certain hidden treasure of this Abbot Thomas, for which those of Steinfeld have often made search, though hitherto in vain. The story is that Thomas, while yet in the vigour of life, concealed a very large quantity of gold somewhere in the monastery. He was often asked where it was, and always answered, with a laugh: "Job, John, and Zechariah will tell either you or your successors." He sometimes added that he should feel no grudge against those who might find it. Among other works carried out by this Abbot I may specially mention his filling the great window at the east end of the south aisle of the church with figures admirably painted on glass, as his effigy and arms in the window attest. He also restored almost the whole of the Abbot's lodging, and dug a well in the court of it, which he adorned with beautiful carvings in marble. He died rather suddenly in the seventy-second year of his age, AD 1529.'

The object which the antiquary had before him at the moment was that of tracing the whereabouts of the painted windows of the Abbey Church of Steinfeld. Shortly after the Revolution, a very large quantity of painted glass had made its way from the dissolved abbeys of Germany and Belgium to this country, and may now be seen adorning various of our parish churches, cathedrals, and private chapels. Steinfeld Abbey was among the most considerable of these involuntary contributors to our artistic possessions (I am quoting the somewhat ponderous preamble of the book which the antiquary wrote), and the greater part of the glass from that institution can be identified without much difficulty by the help, either of the numerous inscriptions in which the place is mentioned, or of the subjects of the windows, in which several well-defined cycles or narratives were represented.

The passage with which I began my story had set the antiquary on the track of another identification. In a private chapel – no matter where – he had seen three large figures, each occupying a whole light in a window, and evidently the work of one artist. Their style made it plain that that artist had been a German of the sixteenth century; but hitherto the more exact localizing of them had been a puzzle. They represented – will you be surprised to hear it? – JOB PATRIARCHA, JOHANNES EVANGELISTA, ZACHARIAS PROPHETA, and each of them held a book or scroll, inscribed with a sentence from his writings. These, as a matter of course, the antiquary had noted, and had been struck by the curious way in which they differed from any text of the Vulgate that he had been able to examine. Thus the scroll in Job's hand was inscribed: 'Auro est locus in quo absconditur' (for 'conflatur')*; on the book of John was: 'Habent in vestimentis suis scripturam quam nemo novit'† (for 'in vestimento scriptum', the following words being taken from another verse); and Zacharias had: 'Super lapidem unum septem oculi sunt'‡ (which alone of the three presents an unaltered text).

A sad perplexity it had been to our investigator to think why these three personages should have been placed together in one window. There was no bond of connection between them, either historic, symbolic, or doctrinal, and he could only suppose that they must have formed part of a very large series of Prophets and Apostles, which might have filled, say, all the clerestory windows of some capacious church. But the passage from the 'Sertum' had altered the situation by showing that the names of the actual personages represented in the glass now in Lord D —'s chapel had been constantly on the lips of Abbot Thomas von Eschenhausen of Steinfeld, and that this Abbot had put up a painted widow, probably about the year 1520, in the south aisle of his abbey church. It was no very wild conjecture that the three figures might have formed part of Abbot Thomas's offering; it was one which, moreover, could probably be confirmed or set aside by another careful examination of the glass. And, as Mr Somerton was a man of leisure, he set out on pilgrimage to the private chapel with very little delay. His conjecture was confirmed to the full. Not only did the style and technique of the glass suit perfectly with the date and place required, but in another window of the chapel he found some glass, known to have been bought along with the figures, which contained the arms of Abbot Thomas von Eschenhausen.

At intervals during his researches Mr Somerton had been haunted by the recollection of the gossip about the hidden treasure, and, as he thought the matter over, it became more and more obvious to him that if the Abbot meant anything by the enigmatical answer which he gave to his questioners, he must have meant that the secret was to be found somewhere in the window he had placed in the abbey church. It was undeniable, furthermore, that the first of the curiously-selected texts on the scrolls in the window might be taken to have a reference to hidden treasure.

---

* There is a place for gold where it is hidden.
† They have on their raiment a writing which no man knoweth.
‡ Upon one stone are seven eyes.

Every feature, therefore, or mark which could possibly assist in elucidating the riddle which, he felt sure, the Abbot had set to posterity he noted with scrupulous care, and, returning to his Berkshire manor-house, consumed many a pint of the midnight oil over his tracings and sketches. After two or three weeks, a day came when Mr Somerton announced to his man that he must pack his own and his master's things for a short journey abroad, whither for the moment we will not follow him.

II

Mr Gregory, the Rector of Parsbury, had strolled out before breakfast, it being a fine autumn morning, as far as the gate of his carriage-drive, with intent to meet the postman and sniff the cool air. Nor was he disappointed of either purpose. Before he had had time to answer more than ten or eleven of the miscellaneous questions propounded to him in the lightness of their hearts by his young offspring, who had accompanied him, the postman was seen approaching; and among the morning's budget was one letter bearing a foreign postmark and stamp (which became at once the object of an eager competition among the youthful Gregorys), and was addressed in an uneducated, but plainly an English hand.

When the Rector opened it, and turned to the signature, he realized that it came from the confidential valet of his friend and squire, Mr Somerton. Thus it ran:

'HONOURED SIR,

'Has I am in a great anxeity about Master I write at is Wish to Beg you Sir if you could be so good as Step over. Master Has add a Nastey Shock and keeps His Bedd. I never Have known Him like this but No wonder and Nothing will serve but you Sir. Master says would I mintion the Short Way Here is Drive to Cobblince and take a Trap. Hopeing I Have maid all Plain, but am much Confused in Myself what with Anxiatey and Weakfulness at Night. If I might be so Bold Sir it will be a Pleasure to see a Honnest Brish Face among all These Forig ones.

'I am Sir

'Your obed^t Servt

'WILLIAM BROWN.

'P.S. – The Villiage for Town I will not Turm. It is name Steenfeld.'

The reader must be left to picture to himself in detail the surprise, confusion and hurry of preparation into which the receipt of such a letter would be likely to plunge a quiet Berkshire parsonage in the year of grace 1859. It is enough for me to say that a train to town was caught in the course of the day, and that Mr Gregory was able to secure a cabin in the Antwerp boat and a place in the Coblentz train. Nor was it difficult to manage the transit from that centre to Steinfeld.

I labour under a grave disadvantage as narrator of this story in that I have never visited Steinfeld myself, and that neither of the principal actors in the episode (from whom I derive my information) was able to give me anything but a vague and rather dismal idea of its appearance. I gather that it is a small place, with a large church despoiled of its ancient fittings; a number of rather ruinous great buildings, mostly of the seventeenth century, surround this church; for the abbey, in common with most of those on the Continent, was rebuilt in a luxurious fashion by its inhabitants at that period. It has not seemed to me worth while to lavish money on a visit to the place, for though it is probably far more attractive than either Mr Somerton or Mr Gregory thought it, there is evidently little, if anything, of first-rate interest to be seen – except, perhaps, one thing, which I should not care to see.

The inn where the English gentleman and his servant were lodged is, or was, the only 'possible' one in the village. Mr Gregory was taken to it at once by his driver, and found Mr Brown waiting at the door. Mr Brown, a model when in his Berkshire home of the impassive whiskered race who are known as confidential valets, was now egregiously out of his element, in a light tweed suit, anxious, almost irritable, and plainly anything but master of the situation. His relief at the sight of the 'honest British face' of his Rector was unmeasured, but words to describe it were denied him. He could only say:

'Well, I ham pleased, I'm sure, sir, to see you. And so I'm sure, sir, will master.'

'How *is* your master, Brown?' Mr Gregory eagerly put in.

'I think he's better, sir, thank you; but he's had a dreadful time of it. I 'ope he's gettin' some sleep now, but –'

'What has been the matter – I couldn't make out from your letter? Was it an accident of any kind?'

'Well, sir, I 'ardly know whether I'd better speak about it. Master was very partickler he should be the one to tell you. But there's no bones broke – that's one thing I'm sure we ought to be thankful –'

'What does the doctor say?' asked Mr Gregory.

They were by this time outside Mr Somerton's bedroom door, and speaking in low tones. Mr Gregory, who happened to be in front, was feeling for the handle, and chanced to run his fingers over the panels.

Before Brown could answer, there was a terrible cry from within the room.

'In God's name, who is that?' were the first words they heard. 'Brown, is it?'

'Yes, sir – me, sir, and Mr Gregory,' Brown hastened to answer, and there was an audible groan of relief in reply.

They entered the room, which was darkened against the afternoon sun, and Mr Gregory saw, with a shock of pity, how drawn, how damp with drops of fear, was the usually calm face of his friend, who, sitting up in the curtained bed, stretched out a shaking hand to welcome him.

'Better for seeing you, my dear Gregory,' was the reply to the Rector's first question; and it was palpably true.

After five minutes of conversation Mr Somerton was more his own man, Brown afterwards reported, than he had been for days. He was able to eat a more than respectable dinner, and talked confidently of being fit to stand a journey to Coblentz within twenty-four hours.

'But there's one thing,' he said, with a return of agitation which Mr Gregory did not like to see, 'which I must beg you to do for me, my dear Gregory. Don't,' he went on, laying his hand on Gregory's to forestall any interruption – 'don't ask me what it is, or why I want it done. I'm not up to explaining it yet; it would throw me back – undo all the good you have done me by coming. The only word I will say about it is that you run no risk whatever by doing it, and that Brown can and will show you to-morrow what it is. It's merely to put back – to keep – something – No; I can't speak of it yet. Do you mind calling Brown?'

'Well, Somerton,' said Mr Gregory, as he crossed the room to the door, 'I won't ask for any explanations till you see fit to give them. And if this bit of business is as easy as you represent it to be, I will very gladly undertake it for you the first thing in the morning.'

'Ah, I was sure you would, my dear Gregory; I was certain I could rely on you. I shall owe you more thanks than I can tell. Now, here is Brown. Brown, one word with you.'

'Shall I go?' interjected Mr Gregory.

'Not at all. Dear me, no. Brown, the first thing to-morrow morning – (you don't mind early hours, I know, Gregory) – you must take the Rector to – *there*, you know' (a nod from Brown, who looked grave and anxious), 'and he and you will put that back. You needn't be in the least alarmed; it's *perfectly* safe in the daytime. You know what I mean. It lies on the step, you know, where – where we put it.' (Brown swallowed dryly once or twice, and, failing to speak, bowed.) 'And –

yes, that's all. Only this one other word, my dear Gregory. If you *can* manage to keep from questioning Brown about this matter, I shall be still more bound to you. To-morrow evening, at latest, if all goes well, I shall be able, I believe, to tell you the whole story from start to finish. And now I'll wish you good-night. Brown will be with me – he sleeps here – and if I were you, I should lock my door. Yes, be particular to do that. They – they like it, the people here, and it's better. Good-night, good-night.'

They parted upon this, and if Mr Gregory woke once or twice in the small hours and fancied he heard a fumbling about the lower part of his locked door, it was, perhaps, no more than what a quiet man, suddenly plunged into a strange bed and the heart of a mystery, might reasonably expect. Certainly he thought, to the end of his days, that he had heard such a sound twice or three times between midnight and dawn.

He was up with the sun, and out in company with Brown soon after. Perplexing as was the service he had been asked to perform for Mr Somerton, it was not a difficult or an alarming one, and within half an hour from his leaving the inn it was over. What it was I shall not as yet divulge.

Later in the morning Mr Somerton, now almost himself again, was able to make a start from Steinfeld; and that same evening, whether at Coblentz or at some intermediate stage on the journey I am not certain, he settled down to the promised explanation. Brown was present, but how much of the matter was ever really made plain to his comprehension he would never say, and I am unable to conjecture.

III

This was Mr Somerton's story:
'You know roughly, both of you, that this expedition of mine was undertaken with the object of tracing something in connection with some old painted glass in Lord D — 's private chapel. Well, the starting-point of the whole matter lies in this passage from an old printed book, to which I will ask your attention.'

And at this point Mr Somerton went carefully over some ground with which we are already familiar.

'On my second visit to the chapel,' he went on, 'my purpose was to take every note I could of figures, lettering, diamond-scratchings on the glass, and even apparently accidental markings. The first point which I tackled was that of the inscribed scrolls. I could not doubt that the first of these, that of Job – "There is a place for the gold where it is hidden" – with its intentional alteration, must refer to the treasure; so I applied myself with some confidence to the next, that of St John – "They have on their vestures a writing which no man knoweth." The natural question will have occurred to you: Was there an inscription on the robes of the figures? I could see none; each of the three had a broad black border to his mantle, which made a conspicuous and rather ugly feature in the window. I was nonplussed, I will own, and but for a curious bit of luck I think I should have left the search where the Canons of Steinfeld had left it before me. But it so happened that there was a good deal of dust on the surface of the glass, and Lord D —, happening to come in, noticed my blackened hands, and kindly insisted on sending for a Turk's head broom to clean down the window. There must, I suppose, have been a rough piece in the broom; anyhow, as it passed over the border of one of the mantles, I noticed that it left a long scratch, and that some yellow stain instantly showed up. I asked the man to stop his work for a moment, and ran up the ladder to examine the place. The yellow stain was there, sure enough, and what had come away was a thick black pigment, which had evidently been laid on with the brush after the glass had been burnt, and could therefore be easily scraped off without doing any harm. I scraped, accordingly, and you will hardly believe – no, I do you an injustice; you will have guessed already – that I found under this black pigment two or three clearly-formed capital letters in yellow stain on a clear ground. Of course, I could hardly contain my delight.

'I told Lord D — that I had detected an inscription which I thought might be very interesting, and begged to be allowed to uncover the whole of it. He made no difficulty about it whatever, told me to do exactly as I pleased, and then, having an engagement, was obliged – rather to my relief, I must say – to leave me. I set to work at once, and found the task a fairly easy one. The pigment, disintegrated, of course, by time, came off almost at a touch, and I don't think that it took me a couple of hours, all told, to clean the whole of the black borders in all three lights. Each of the figures had, as the inscription said, "a writing on their vestures which nobody knew".

'This discovery, of course, made it absolutely certain to my mind that I was on the right track. And, now, what was the inscription? While I was cleaning the glass I almost took pains not to read the lettering, saving up the treat until I had got the whole thing clear. And when that *was* done, my dear Gregory, I assure you I could almost have cried from sheer disappointment. What I read was only the most hopeless jumble of letters that was ever shaken up in a hat.

Here it is:

Job. DREVICIOPEDMOOMSMVIVLISLCAVIBASBATAOVT
St. John. RDIIEAMRLESIPVSPODSEEIRSETTAAESGIAVNNR
Zechariah. FTEEAILNQDPVAIVMTLEEATTOHIOONVMCAAT.
H.Q.E.

'Blank as I felt and must have looked for the first few minutes, my disappointment didn't last long. I realized almost at once that I was dealing with a cipher or cryptogram; and I reflected that it was likely to be of a pretty simple kind, considering its early date. So I copied the letters with the most anxious care. Another little point, I may tell you, turned up in the process which confirmed my belief in the cipher. After copying the letters on Job's robe I counted them, to make sure that I had them right. There were thirty-eight; and, just as I finished going through them, my eye fell on a scratching made with a sharp point on the edge of the border. It was simply the number xxxviii in Roman numerals. To cut the matter short, there was a similar note, as I may call it, in each of the other lights; and that made it plain to me that the glass-painter had had very strict orders from Abbot Thomas about the inscription, and had taken pains to get it correct.

'Well, after that discovery you may imagine how minutely I went over the whole surface of the glass in search of further light. Of course, I did not neglect the inscription on the scroll of Zechariah – "Upon one stone are seven eyes", but I very quickly concluded that this must refer to some mark on a stone which could only be found *in situ*, where the treasure was concealed. To be short, I made all possible notes and sketches and tracings, and then came back to Parsbury to work out the cipher at leisure. Oh, the agonies I went through! I thought myself very clever at first, for I made sure that the key would be found in some of the old books on secret writing. The "*Steganographia*" of Joachim Trithemius, who was an earlier contemporary of Abbot Thomas, seemed particularly promising; so I got that, and Selenius's "*Cryptographia*" and Bacon's "*de Augmentis Scientiarum*" and some more. But I could hit upon nothing. Then I tried the principle of "the most frequent letter", taking first Latin and then German as a basis. That didn't help, either; whether it ought to have done so, I am not clear. And then I came back to the window itself, and read over my notes, hoping almost against hope that the Abbot might himself have somewhere supplied the key I wanted. I could make nothing out of the colour or pattern of the robes. There were no landscape backgrounds with subsidiary objects; there was nothing in the canopies. The only resource possible seemed to be in the attitudes of the figures. "Job," I read: "scroll in left hand, forefinger of left hand extended upwards.

John: holds inscribed book in left hand; with right hand blesses, with two fingers. Zechariah: scroll in left hand; right hand extended upwards, as Job, but with three fingers pointing up." In other words, I reflected, Job has *one* finger extended, John has *two*, Zechariah has *three*. May not there be a numeral key concealed in that? My dear Gregory,' said Mr Somerton, laying his hand on his friend's knee, 'that *was* the key. I didn't get it to fit at first, but after two or three trials I saw what was meant. After the first letter of the inscription you skip *one* letter, after the next you skip two, and after that skip three. Now look at the result I got. I've underlined the letters which form words:

D̲R̲EVICIOPED̲MOOMSMV̲IV̲LISL̲CAV̲IB̲ASB̲ATAOV̲T
R̲DIIEAMR̲L̲ESIP̲V̲SPODSEEIR̲SETTA̲AESGIA̲V̲NNR̲
F̲TEEAIL̲NQDP̲VAIV̲MTLEEATTOHIOONVMCA̲AT.H.Q.E.

'Do you see it? "*Decem millia auri reposita sunt in puteo in at . . .*" (Ten thousand [pieces] of gold are laid up in a well in . . .), followed by an incomplete word beginning *at*. So far so good. I tried the same plan with the remaining letters; but it wouldn't work, and I fancied that perhaps the placing of dots after the three last letters might indicate some difference of procedure. Then I thought to myself, "Wasn't there some allusion to a well in the account of Abbot Thomas in that book the '*Sertum*'?" Yes, there was: he built a *puteus in atrio* (a well in the court). There, of course, was my word *atrio*. The next step was to copy out the remaining letters of the inscription, omitting those I had already used. That gave what you will see on this slip:

RVIIOPDOOSMVVISCAVBSBTAOTDIEAMLSIVSPDEERSETA
EGIANRFEEALQDVAIMLEATTHOOVMCA.H.Q.E.

'Now, I knew what the three first letters I wanted were – namely, *rio* – to complete the word *atrio*; and, as you will see, these are all to be found in the first five letters. I was a little confused at first by the occurrence of two *i*'s, but very soon I saw that every alternate letter must be taken in the remainder of the inscription. You can work it out for yourself; the result, continuing where the first "round" left off, is this:

"rio domus abbatialis de Steinfeld a me, Thoma, qui posui custodem super ea. Gare à qui la touche."

'So the whole secret was out:

"Ten thousand pieces of gold are laid up in the well in the court of the

Abbot's house of Steinfeld by me, Thomas, who have set a guardian over them. *Gare à qui la touche*."

'The last words, I ought to say, are a device which Abbot Thomas had adopted. I found it with his arms in another piece of glass at Lord D — 's, and he drafted it bodily into his cipher, though it doesn't quite fit in point of grammar.

'Well, what would any human being have been tempted to do, my dear Gregory, in my place? Could he have helped setting off, as I did, to Steinfeld, and tracing the secret literally to the fountain-head? I don't believe he could. Anyhow, I couldn't, and, as I needn't tell you, I found myself at Steinfeld as soon as the resources of civilization could put me there, and installed myself in the inn you saw. I must tell you that I was not altogether free from forebodings – on one hand of disappointment, on the other of danger. There was always the possibility that Abbot Thomas's well might have been wholly obliterated, or else that someone, ignorant of cryptograms, and guided only by luck, might have stumbled on the treasure before me. And then' – there was a very perceptible shaking of the voice here – 'I was not entirely easy, I need not mind confessing, as to the meaning of the words about the guardian of the treasure. But, if you don't mind, I'll say no more about that until – until it becomes necessary.

'At the first possible opportunity Brown and I began exploring the place. I had naturally represented myself as being interested in the remains of the abbey, and we could not avoid paying a visit to the church, impatient as I was to be elsewhere. Still, it did interest me to see the windows where the glass had been, and especially that at the east end of the south aisle. In the tracery lights of that I was startled to see some fragments and coats-of-arms remaining – Abbot Thomas's shield was there, and a small figure with a scroll inscribed "Oculos habent, et non videbunt" (They have eyes, and shall not see), which, I take it, was a hit of the Abbot at his Canons.

'But, of course, the principal object was to find the Abbot's house. There is no prescribed place for this, so far as I know, in the plan of a monastery; you can't predict of it, as you can of the chapter-house, that it will be on the eastern side of the cloister, or, as of the dormitory, that it will communicate with a transept of the church. I felt that if I asked many questions I might awaken lingering memories of the treasure, and I thought it best to try first to discover it for myself. It was not a very long or difficult search. That three-sided court south-east of the church, with deserted piles of building round it, and grass-grown pavement, which you saw this morning, was the place. And glad enough I was to see that it was put to no use, and was neither very far from our inn nor overlooked by any inhabited building; there were only orchards and paddocks on the slopes east of the church. I can tell you that fine stone glowed wonderfully in the rather watery yellow sunset that we had on the Tuesday afternoon.

'Next, what about the well? There was not much doubt about that, as you can testify. It is really a very remarkable thing. That curb is, I think, of Italian marble, and the carving I thought must be Italian also. There were reliefs, you will perhaps remember, of Eliezer and Rebekah, and of Jacob opening the well for Rachel, and similar subjects; but, by way of disarming suspicion, I suppose, the Abbot had carefully abstained from any of his cynical and allusive inscriptions.

'I examined the whole structure with the keenest interest, of course – a square well-head with an opening in one side; an arch over it, with a wheel for the rope to pass over, evidently in very good condition still, for it had been used within sixty years, or perhaps even later, though not quite recently. Then there was the question of depth and access to the interior. I suppose the depth was about sixty to seventy feet; and as to the other point, it really seemed as if the Abbot had wished to lead searchers up to the very door of his treasure-house, for, as you tested for yourself, there were big blocks of stone bonded into the masonry, and leading down in a regular staircase round and round the inside of the well.

'It seemed almost too good to be true. I wondered if there was a trap – if the stones were so contrived as to tip over when a weight was placed on them; but I tried a good many with my own weight and with my stick, and all seemed, and actually were, perfectly firm. Of course, I resolved that Brown and I would make an experiment that very night.

'I was well prepared. Knowing the sort of place I should have to explore, I had brought a sufficiency of good rope and bands of webbing to surround my body, and crossbars to hold to, as well as lanterns and candles and crowbars, all of which would go into a single carpet-bag and excite no suspicion. I satisfied myself that my rope would be long enough, and that the wheel for the bucket was in good working order, and then we went home to dinner.

'I had a little cautious conversation with the landlord, and made out that he would not be overmuch surprised if I went out for a stroll with my man about nine o'clock, to make (Heaven forgive me!) a sketch of the abbey by moonlight. I asked no questions about the well, and am not likely to do so now. I fancy I know as much about it as anyone in Steinfeld: at least' – with a strong shudder – 'I don't want to know any more.

'Now we come to the crisis, and, though I hate to think of it, I feel sure, Gregory, that it will be better for me in all ways to recall it just as it happened. We started, Brown and I, at about nine with our bag, and attracted no attention; for we managed to slip out at the hinder end of the inn-yard into an alley which brought us quite to the edge of the village. In five minutes we were at the well, and for some little time we sat on the edge of the well-head to make sure that no one was stirring or spying on us. All we heard was some horses cropping grass out of sight further down the eastern slope. We were perfectly unobserved, and had plenty of light from the gorgeous full moon to allow us to get the rope properly fitted over the wheel. Then I secured the band round my body beneath the arms. We attached the end of the rope very securely to a ring in the stonework. Brown took the lighted lantern and followed me; I had a crowbar. And so we began to descend cautiously, feeling every step before we set foot on it, and scanning the walls in search of any marked stone.

'Half aloud I counted the steps as we went down, and we got as far as the thirty-eighth before I noted anything at all irregular in the surface of the masonry. Even here there was no mark, and I began to feel very blank, and to wonder if the Abbot's cryptogram could possibly be an elaborate hoax. At the forty-ninth step the staircase ceased. It was with a very sinking heart that I began retracing my steps, and when I was back on the thirty-eighth – Brown, with the lantern, being a step or two above me – I scrutinized the little bit of irregularity in the stonework with all my might; but there was no vestige of a mark.

'Then it struck me that the texture of the surface looked just a little smoother than the rest, or, at least, in some way different. It might possibly be cement and not stone. I gave it a good blow with my iron bar. There was a decidedly hollow sound, though that might be the result of our being in a well. But there was more. A great flake of cement dropped on to my feet, and I saw marks on the stone underneath. I had tracked the Abbot down, my dear Gregory; even now I think of it with a certain pride. It took but a very few more taps to clear the whole of the cement away, and I saw a slab of stone about two feet square, upon which was engraven a cross. Disappointment again, but only for a moment. It was you, Brown, who reassured me by a casual remark. You said, if I remember right:

' "It's a funny cross; looks like a lot of eyes."

'I snatched the lantern out of your hand, and saw with inexpressible pleasure that the cross *was* composed of seven eyes, four in a vertical line, three horizontal. The last of the scrolls in the window was explained in the way I had anticipated. Here was my "stone with the seven eyes". So far the Abbot's data had been exact, and, as I thought of this, the anxiety about the "guardian" returned upon me with increased force. Still, I wasn't going to retreat now.

'Without giving myself time to think, I knocked away the cement all round the marked stone, and then gave it a prise on the right side with my crowbar. It moved at once, and I saw that it was but a thin light slab, such as I could easily lift out myself, and that it stopped the entrance to a cavity. I did lift it out unbroken, and set it on the step, for it might be very important to us to be able to replace it. Then I waited for several minutes on the step just above. I don't know why, but I think to see if any dreadful thing would rush out. Nothing happened. Next I lit a candle, and very cautiously I placed it inside the cavity, with some idea of seeing whether there were foul air, and of getting a glimpse of what was inside. There *was* some foulness of air which nearly extinguished the flame, but in no long time it burned quite steadily. The hole went some little way back, and also on the right and left of the entrance, and I could see some rounded light-coloured objects within which might be bags. There was no use in waiting. I faced the cavity, and looked in. There was nothing immediately in the front of the hole. I put my arm in and felt to the right, very gingerly . . .

'Just give me a glass of cognac, Brown. I'll go on in a moment, Gregory . . .

'Well, I felt to the right, and my fingers touched something curved, that felt – yes – more or less like leather; dampish it was, and evidently part of a heavy, full thing. There was nothing, I must say, to alarm one. I grew bolder, and putting both hands in as well as I could, I pulled it to me, and it came. It was heavy, but it moved more easily than I had expected. As I pulled it towards the entrance, my left elbow knocked over and extinguished the candle. I got the thing fairly in front of the mouth and began drawing it out. Just then Brown gave a sharp ejaculation and ran quickly up the steps with the lantern. He will tell you why in a moment. Startled as I was, I looked round after him, and saw him stand for a minute at the top and then walk away a few yards. Then I heard him call softly, "All right, sir," and went on pulling out the great bag, in complete darkness. It hung for an instant on the edge of the hole, then slipped forward on to my chest, and *put its arms round my neck*.

'My dear Gregory, I am telling you the exact truth. I believe I am now acquainted with the extremity of terror and repulsion which a man can endure without losing his mind. I can only just manage to tell you now the bare outline of the experience. I was conscious of a most horrible smell of mould, and of a cold kind of face pressed against my own, and moving slowly over it, and of several – I don't know how many – legs or arms or tentacles or something clinging to my body. I screamed out, Brown says, like a beast, and fell away backward from the step on which I stood, and the creature slipped downwards, I suppose, on to that same step. Providentially the band round me held firm. Brown did not lose his head, and was strong enough to pull me up to the top and get me over the edge quite promptly. How he managed it exactly I don't know, and I think he would find it hard to tell you. I believe he contrived to hide our implements in the deserted building near by, and with very great difficulty he got me back to the inn. I was in no state to make explanations, and Brown knows no German; but next morning I told the people some tale of having had a bad fall in the abbey ruins, which, I suppose, they believed. And now, before I go further, I should just like you to hear what Brown's experiences during those few minutes were. Tell the Rector, Brown, what you told me.'

'Well, sir,' said Brown, speaking low and nervously, 'it was just this way. Master was busy down in front of the 'ole, and I was 'olding the lantern and looking on, when I 'eard somethink drop in the water from the top, as I thought. So I looked up, and I see someone's 'ead lookin' over at us. I s'pose I must ha' said somethink, and I 'eld the light up and run up the steps, and my light shone right on the face. That was a bad un, sir, if ever I see one! A holdish man, and the face very much fell in, and larfin, as I thought. And I got up the steps as quick pretty nigh as I'm tellin' you, and when I was out on the ground there warn't a sign of any person. There 'adn't been the time for anyone to get away, let alone a hold chap, and I made sure he warn't crouching down by the well, nor nothink. Next thing I hear master cry out somethink 'orrible, and hall I see was him hanging out by the rope, and, as master says, 'owever I got him up I couldn't tell you.'

'You hear that, Gregory?' said Mr Somerton. 'Now, does any explanation of that incident strike you?'

'The whole thing is so ghastly and abnormal that I must own it puts me quite off my balance; but the thought did occur to me that possibly the – well, the person who set the trap might have come to see the success of his plan.'

'Just so, Gregory, just so. I can think of nothing else so – *likely*, I should say, if such a word had a place anywhere in my story. I think it must have been the Abbot. . . . Well, I haven't much more to tell you. I spent a miserable night, Brown sitting up with me. Next day I was no better; unable to get up; no doctor to be had; and, if one had been available, I doubt if he could have done much for me. I made Brown write off to you, and spent a second terrible night. And, Gregory, of this I am sure, and I think it affected me more than the first shock, for it lasted longer: there was someone or something on the watch outside my door the whole night. I almost fancy there were two. It wasn't only the faint noises I heard from time to time all through the dark hours, but there was the smell – the hideous smell of mould. Every rag I had had on me on that first evening I had stripped off and made Brown take it away. I believe he stuffed the things into the stove in his room; and yet the smell was there as intense as it had been in the well; and, what is more, it came from outside the door. But with the first glimmer of dawn it faded out, and the sounds ceased, too; and that convinced me that the thing or things were creatures of darkness, and could not stand the daylight; and so I was sure that if anyone could put back the stone, it or they would be powerless until someone else took it away again. I had to wait until you came to get that done. Of course, I couldn't send Brown to do it by himself, and still less could I tell anyone who belonged to the place.

'Well, there is my story; and, if you don't believe it, I can't help it. But I think you do.'

'Indeed,' said Mr Gregory, 'I can find no alternative. I *must* believe it! I saw the well and the stone myself, and had a glimpse, I thought, of the bags or something else in the hole. And, to be plain with you, Somerton, I believe my door was watched last night, too.'

'I dare say it was, Gregory; but, thank goodness, that is over. Have you, by the way, anything to tell about your visit to that dreadful place?'

'Very little,' was the answer. 'Brown and I managed easily enough to get the slab into its place, and he fixed it very firmly with the irons and wedges you had desired him to get, and we contrived to smear the surface with mud so that it looks just like the rest of the wall. One thing I did notice in the carving on the well-head, which I think must have escaped you. It was a horrid, grotesque shape – perhaps more like a toad than anything else, and there was a label by it inscribed with the two words, "Depositum custodi." '*

* 'Keep that which is committed to thee.'

The Summer House

BY A. M. BURRAGE

The success of the M.R. James' stories on television prompted imitations on both sides of the Atlantic. In America, the following year, NBC launched a Friday night series, Ghost Story; *then four years on the BBC also produced an anthology of late night tales called* Ghost Story *produced by Stephen Weeks who confessed to having been 'always haunted by the ghost stories of M.R. James'. All the episodes were, though, based on specially commissioned scripts, and despite being glossily filmed and packed with star names – including Patricia Neal, Leigh Lawson, Murray Melvin and Penelope Keith – did not make the anticipated impact on either viewers or critics. The American* Ghost Story *which went out from nine PM to ten PM from September 1972, had a far greater impact and ran for almost two years. Produced by the veteran Hollywood horror producer and director, William (Rosemary's Baby) Castle, it featured stories of ghosts, vampires, witches and various other manifestations of the supernatural and was hosted by the bulky British character actor, Sebastian Cabot, in the role of a wealthy psychic, Winston Essex. The narrator would start each episode by inviting the audience into Mansfield House, a mansion converted into a hotel, where, clasping a large brandy in one hand, he would introduce the story as something that could happen to anyone. The mixture of classic stories and accomplished new scripts – not to mention the relish of Cabot's introductions and the excellent* Ghost Story *theme music by Billy Goldenberg – was further strengthened by the performances of familiar names such as Janet Leigh, Martin Sheen, Helen Hayes, Tab Hunter, Rory Calhoun and Barry Nelson, the first actor to have played James Bond on television in the CBS version of* Casino Royale *shown in October 1954. The resulting series of* Ghost

Story *was a hit with both audiences and reviewers. Unwisely, as it transpired, the title was changed to* Circle of Fear *in 1973 and Sebastian Cabot was dropped as the host. Very few of the stories now dealt with the supernatural and within five months* Ghost Story *was only a memory.*

Among the shows which did linger on in the minds of viewers was 'The Summer House' based on a short story by the English writer A.M. Burrage (1889–1956), whose reputation has been ensured by such haunted house classics as 'The Sweeper', and the famous account of a reporter who spends a night in a Chamber of Horrors, 'The Waxwork'. In the American television adaptation of 'The Summer House', Carolyn Jones and Steve Forest starred in the story of a haunting resolved by a murder mystery . . .

IT is only fair to warn the unwary that this is an unsatisfactory sort of story, lacking in that completeness which, nowadays, is considered good money's worth. But I do not consider it my business to fill up the spaces between the lines. They are open to those who care to read.

Oliver was a stout young fellow of five when the family moved to Bitterne Hillside. The family consisted of himself and his father and mother, together with Annie, his nurse, and two more female servants. The small staff of servants was almost immediately increased to eight, including a middle-aged gentleman of magnificent presence, who now answered the front-door bell instead of Mary; for Mr Fowler had recently made money in leather.

Mr Fowler, Oliver's father, was middle-aged and lean and bald, and through long association with leather had grown to look a little like the foundation of his fortune, after the same subtle fashion that some people come to resemble their domestic pets. Mrs Fowler was colourless and stupid, one of Nature's nonentities. She had met before moving to Bitterne Hillside three titled women, all wives of City knights, and found occasion to mention their names at every tea-party. These brief details are given to show that young Oliver, if he were unduly imaginative, did not owe it to immediate heredity.

Probably he enjoyed more than anybody else the move to Bitterne Hillside from the conventionality of Upper Norwood. His father wanted to impress his City friends by mentioning that he was now a country squire. His mother intended to storm what she described as County Society. They both had their disappointments; not so Oliver. To his eyes the long red-brick Queen Anne house with its beautiful simplicity of architecture was a palace out of one of the fairy stories which were occasionally read to him. The gardens, the small ring park, the model farm, the friendly cattle that grazed on 'Daddy's estate', were all to him in their several ways more splendid than anything he had previously seen, even on his annual visit to the seaside. After- wards, when custom had staled much, he was left with an abiding love for Bitterne Hillside, as if his forefathers for many generations had lived and died there.

The new home, where one could get lost at first even without wanting to, was a heaven-devised place for pastimes like hide-and- seek when Annie could be made skittish enough to play a real game with him. But he had not so poverty-stricken a mind as to be unable to find amusement for himself when left alone. He had the space now to play at being the hero of every story he knew, and he began to develop an affection for parts of the house and grounds, much as a cat might. For some unexplained reason he loved the cedar tree in the garden behind the house – thenceforward not to be called the back-garden, as savouring of commonness. But his favourite spot and place of retreat was the summer-house.

This little house, with tiled floor and lattice walls supported by pillars, was in the most secluded part of that garden which daddy and mummy did not like to hear called the back-garden. Oliver spent much of his time there when left to himself, with toys and picture-books. The truth was, although he did not realize it at first, he did not feel so lonely in the summer-house.

It was about this time, shortly after his arrival at Bitterne Hillside, that he began to have dreams, formless and incoherent to his waking memory. In them, or rather after them, he was conscious of loving something feminine which was neither his mother nor Annie. Both his mother and Annie he loved, but secretly deplored in both a lack of responsiveness. Certainly his mother kissed him once or twice a day, and even picked him up and nursed him uncomfortably in the presence of visitors, but he was old enough now to detect and resent theatricals. Annie made no pretences at all. It was her duty to look after him, and she did it grudgingly. Her favourite expressions were 'Bless the boy!' and 'Drat the child!' and her flat, red hand could sting when exasperation drove her to use it. Her round, vividly-coloured face, which invariably smelt of yellow soap, was, somehow, unsatisfactory to kiss.

Yes, that was the truth. His mother and Annie were both, in their different ways, unsatisfactory to kiss. His mother's cheeks were flaccid and nearly always cold, her lips were hardened by some preparation which made them look red. And yet he began to be conscious of the

406

beauty and freshness of young girlhood, and of somebody loving him as he wanted to be loved.

He had met no girls who were grown-up or nearly grown-up. Perhaps, one might suggest, his busy little mind had materialized her out of some picture once seen and subsequently forgotten. Perhaps he had already created the ideal, of which, during his adolescence, he was to go vainly in search.

However that may be, he was conscious of a friendship, the incidents of which always just eluded his memory. He knew that sometimes he was drawn into a heaven of warm arms, and fresh girlish kisses covered his upturned face. Somehow, he could not remember her face – only just in glimpses which went out like sparks. And there was a fragrance about her, too – like a summer garden at night after a shower of rain.

It was all very puzzling to his small mind. He knew that he was not remembering somebody he had known when he was very little, for these vague impressions had not started until he came to Bitterne Hillside. The experiences were recent and continuous; he knew that they would go on happening.

Having nobody in whom he felt that he could confide, he hugged these vague memories to himself. It was his secret, a rather jolly secret, but, at the same time, a bit 'scary'. It made one go a bit chilly and caused one's eyes to water when one thought of it. For although he knew that he had nothing to fear, he was well aware that this friend did not belong to the same world as Mummy and Annie.

It would be hard to say when he first began to associate his 'friend' with the summer-house. Something drew him there to play, and gradually he realized that he was not playing alone. This feeling was very nice at first, until he stopped playing and began to think about it. Then it seemed all wrong that there should be somebody there whom he couldn't see. At that he would take fright, like some little wild thing at the sound of a man's foot-step, and run panic-stricken through the thicket to the friendly cedar on the lawn, which was overlooked by the long row of windows at the back of the house. The cedar was always 'home' when Annie played one of her rare games of hide-and-seek with him. It was 'home', too, in this queer game – which was something more than a game – that he played by himself.

But this was not the only sort of experience with which the summer-house provided him. Sometimes he felt the presence of two people there – two people who were tremendously real except that he could not see nor hear nor touch them. He was not more afraid on those occasions than on the others, although he always left more quickly. He knew, although panic hastened his little legs through the thicket, that nobody wanted to hurt him. The sensation was the same that he experienced in the presence of grown-ups who wanted him to go so that they could talk in private. Being a sensitive little boy he was quick to detect when his father and mother wanted to talk privately, and knew instinctively when they were going to tell him to 'run and find Annie'.

At five or six years old one learns things without realizing them. Instinct is there without much development of reasoning. Thus he discovered, without thinking it strange, that if Annie or any other grown-up accompanied him to the summer-house there was never any other presence there.

Once, when his father brought two noisy City gentlemen home for the week-end, they spent the whole of Sunday afternoon there, with cigars and funny-shaped bottles which contained vividly-coloured medicines. They had Oliver with them for a little while, and although they called him Old Chap, and enriched him by tossing him for pennies, he was resentful of their presence and went to sulk for the rest of the afternoon under the cedar. He was well aware that they had driven Her away. He did not mind their having driven away That Other who was sometimes with Her in the summer-house. He was jealous of Him. When He was there She was a grown-up and did not desire the presence of little boys. Somehow, he was sure that That Other was male, just as he knew that She was female. But the male presence, while he disliked it, was very dim to his perception. Without Hers he would not have noticed it at all.

During the long months which intervened before he arrived at the age of six he longed for somebody whom he could make a confidant, although, if he found one, he was miserably aware that he could not make himself understood. Grown-ups sometimes failed to understand him when he tried to explain the simplest things.

Mr Beale, who answered the front-door bell and waited at table, and knew what was going to win a race which he called the 'Durby', was the most consistently friendly and cheerful of the mortals with whom he came in contact. But instinct made him doubt Mr Beale's ability to grasp the situation. He was quite sure that Mr Beale would only whistle.

Mummy, daddy, and Annie were quite out of the question. He placed them in the same mental category as Mr Beale. Besides – and here caution whispered at his elbow – this was a direct way to getting the summer-house put out of bounds. Experience had taught him that the things he liked doing most were forbidden as soon as detected.

But although he would not tell anybody exactly what was in his small mind, he developed cunning and began to fish for information. This was not easy, for grown-ups detested to be asked irrelevant questions. But on his sixth birthday, when even Annie had to affect good humour with him, he took advantage of the occasion.

'Please, Annie, can you dream about what isn't really there?'

'Of course you can,' said Annie briefly.

He was sure she had not understood.

'Sometimes,' he explained, 'I dream about you and daddy and mummy. But you're really there. Well, can you dream about anybody who isn't there at all?'

'Of course you can,' said Annie. 'Why, I dreamed of a big monkey the other night.'

'But there are big monkeys.'

'Nothing like the one I dreamed about,' said Annie definitely. 'At least,' she added, with a reminiscent shiver. 'I 'ope to 'Eaven there isn't! Why, what have you been dreaming, Master Oliver?'

But Oliver had learned all he wanted to know for the time being. To say another word about dreams might cause the curtailment of his supper and possibly hasten his bedtime. He had learned caution. But his heart was heavy within him, and when Annie's back was turned he ran off to cry under the friendly cedar.

So perhaps She wasn't real, after all – only just a make-believe, the lovely, pretty lady who brought love and warmth and colour and perfume into his dreams.

But next morning he woke comforted, with more dim and rapidly-fading memories, and warm as if fresh from the embrace of Her enfolding arms.

When Oliver was six and a half his education began in earnest, and he was promoted to having a governess. Annie, who was a good needlewoman, and had been learning the arts and crafts of a lady's maid, became the personal attendant of his mother.

Miss Cartwright, who had been strongly recommended by Lady Somebody, was middle-aged, conscientious and efficient. She was not the sort of person to inspire affection in Oliver, but she did inspire trust, and she had the knack of understanding children.

Yet Oliver never told her about his dreams, or of the invisible people who came to the summer-house when he was there. She was too hard and practical to invite a confidence of that sort. For the dreams, which left only thin wavering traces of memory behind them, still continued, and the summer-house was still a place of delight, of awe, and sometimes of fear. Oliver only remembered fragments of his dreams until something in real life sharply reminded him of something that came into them.

One evening, at half-past seven, the usual hour of his bed-time, mummy was dressing for dinner. There were to be several guests that night, and she was making a more than usually elaborate toilet. Generally, she did not change her frock till after he had gone to bed, but tonight he was told to go to her room and say good-night to her.

Annie was brushing her hair when he arrived, and the dress she was to wear was laid out for her on the bed. The colour was peacock-blue, and more suitable for a young girl. Instantly it attracted Oliver's gaze. For him the bright lights blazing on the silver of the dressing-table shone in vain. He stood staring, and uttered two little quick gasps. It was the colour She wore, but in his waking life he had not known it until now.

'What's the matter?' his mother asked indifferently. 'Have you been running upstairs? Come and kiss me good-night.'

He went towards her uncertainly, glancing back over his shoulder at the dress. Then, as his face drew close to that of the woman in the chair, he uttered a little sobbing cry, and clung to her.

'Mummy, mummy!' he cried. 'The scent! The scent!'

Mrs Fowler had liberally anointed herself with White Heather. She had never used it before, but Oliver recognized it. One may be mistaken over many things, but not over scent. Nothing is quicker or more certain to awaken memory.

'Well, I never!' exclaimed Annie.

'You funny boy!' laughed Mrs Fowler. 'Don't you like it?'

But he clung to her tenaciously, sobbing. He was frightened without knowing what made him afraid. That scent of White Heather was part of Her. She wore a dress of that funny sort of blue. Bit by bit he was going to remember her. Bit by bit he was going to see her.

He longed then to tell his mother everything, only what was there to tell? Mummy would not believe, or understand. Besides, it wasn't as if he wasn't awfully fond of Her. He was; only he was afraid.

'He was just like that before he had measles, m'm,' said Annie, when Oliver had been chided and sent away.

Not long after that came the climax. Looking back on it from his maturity Oliver was aware that he knew even then that it must come, and that he himself would bring it about.

He was getting a big boy now in his own estimation. He bathed and dressed himself, and was old enough to resent it when Philistines addressed him as 'little man'. Jerry, the second-gardener, bowled to him with a hard ball, and he could ride his pony without anybody leading it. He was beginning to think that Master Oliver Fowler was a person of some consequence.

On a certain warm, sunny afternoon he took with him to the summer-house a box containing his new train, set of rails, station, arch, and signal. The train when wound up went round and round in a series of circles, and it was fascinating to see if one could so wind it as to make it stop at the station without checking it by hand. He was so engaged when the old sensation stole over him. She was there, and not only She but He as well. The old feeling of awe passed over him as he turned the key which wound up the spring.

He watched the train spin round and round, past the station, and through the arch. Three, four, five times round it went before its speed slackened, and it came to a halt, and he knew that other eyes watched it besides his own. That miserable snubbed feeling of being a little boy who was in the way overtook him, as it always did when He was there.

He was jealous and sulky, besides being awe-stricken. It was only when He was there that She wanted him to go. Well, this time he just wasn't going. He glowered defiance at the seats, which looked empty to his eyes, as once more he turned the key.

Off went the train once more on its monotonous journey. His gaze followed it while his lips pouted sullenly. The snubbed, hurt feeling grew and grew. He had never felt it so strongly before, except when a favourite aunt had told him that little boys who were gentlemen did not remain in the room when their elders wanted to talk.

'I don't care!' he said aloud. 'I'm not going! I'm not going!'

The train stopped, and he wound it up again, only this time he did not look towards the seats. He kept his eyes on the train, and on the shining circle of aluminium rails. The straining engine sped from his hand once more.

Then he felt his heart beating violently. Terror, a lurking beast, leapt out upon him from some ambush of the mind – terror such as he had never felt before. Time seemed to have slowed down so that moments stretched themselves into minutes. The whirring toy crawled instead of sped. He watched it in nightmare panic – watched it because he dared not lift his eyes.

Never before had he felt Their presence so keenly; never before had They seemed so real. Even when he had run frightened from the summer-house he had not expected to see Them with his naked eyes. Now he knew that one glance over his shoulder would reveal Them to him.

They meant him no harm, but now that he had defied Their wish

411

that he should go, They were there in some new and dreadful sense of being present. Between past experiences and this there was all the difference of shadow and substance. This time They were there to be seen, and he would rather have died than see Them.

For long moments he stood sweating, panting, sobbing, the spell of terror holding his feet to the floor, while the toy-train completed half a dozen circles. The sound of it stopping acted like some sound which breaks the spell of a nightmare. He clapped his hands to his eyes, uttered one long cry, and blundered out, striking his head against one of the pillars as he went. Half stunned, he could still run. Twice he fell, tripping over the roots of trees, but both times he picked himself up and ran the faster.

Miss Cartwright was reading a book in the shade of the cedar on the lawn when a little boy, with a chalk-white face, a cut forehead, and a smear of blood on his cheek, flung himself sobbing into the sanctuary of her arms, and buried his face in her lap.

'They're there! I nearly saw them. Oh, don't let me see them!' was all that she could get from him at first, and, being a woman of sense, she consoled instead of questioned until he was calm.

Later she gleaned from him a little – a very little – of what he had to tell. But for Miss Cartwright it was enough. Being a conscientious woman as well as a woman of sense, she interviewed his mother that same evening.

'Oliver is very imaginative,' she concluded. 'I don't think in his present state that Bitterne Hillside is good for him. I should not care to accept the responsibility. He is old enough now to go to a preparatory school.'

Next week Oliver left home for the first time to go to an establishment at Bournemouth, where he met other little boys, and was initiated into the mysteries of real cricket.

New and more vital interests entered Oliver's life and ousted the old. Back home for the holidays he still dreamed of Her, but not so often, nor did the formless impressions of the dreams remain with him so long. He still felt Her presence when he went to the summer-house alone, but not so acutely as before. He was losing touch with Her. As the age of innocence passed so did She pass with it.

He told nobody the whole story, although he was less diffident about it now, and would laugh with his mother about 'the time when I was frightened in the summer-house,' and add:

'What a silly kid I must have been!'

Very little of the age of innocence survived his first two terms at Harrow, where he went after leaving the Bournemouth school. He had lost Her entirely now. He knew that he had lived in a world of imagination. He was puzzled, and a little troubled when he thought about it, but he did not often think. He lived now in a brisk, virile, noisy world, in which eccentricities, even of the mind, were not permissible.

At the age of nineteen he went up to Trinity College, Cambridge, and there, for the first time, discussed his early experiences with a friend. They were both of the opinion that 'kids were rummy little devils' whom no adult could ever properly understand.

Oliver never guessed there was to be a sequel. When it came it took him completely unawares.

It was in the long vacation after his second year at Cambridge. On a summer afternoon Oliver was lounging in flannels under the cedar tree on the lawn. There was a tennis-court marked out now, and the net had been tightened for action. Beside Oliver was a tennis-racket in a press. His fingers screwed and unscrewed the swivels, and he kept asking himself impatiently why the devil Gladys always was so infernally late.

Gladys was the daughter of a neighbour, a girl in whom Oliver took a lukewarm interest. She came over to play tennis with him two or three afternoons a week. His mother, who had at last decided to be middle-aged, was resting. His father, now a bigger man than ever in the City, spent much of his time there, and only the week-ends saw him at Bitterne Hillside.

While Oliver was lamenting the unpunctuality of the fair Gladys, the butler – still the same Mr Beale, but older and stouter – opened the glass door which communicated with the hall, and set foot upon the garden-path. Oliver sprang up.

'Is that Miss Baker?' he called.

Beale, after his fashion, vouchsafed no sign of having heard him, and did not speak until he had arrived at the conventional speaking distance.

'There is a gentleman to see you, Mr Oliver,' he said. 'Colonel Warlow.'

Oliver frowned over the name. It seemed vaguely familiar.

'Perhaps,' he suggested, 'he wants my father.'

'He asked for Mr Fowler. Shall I tell him –'

'No,' said Oliver. 'I suppose I had better see him. Where is he? In the morning-room? Right!'

He found an upright old man, with a white moustache faintly tinged with yellow, standing by the window of the morning-room and looking down the drive. The visitor glanced at Oliver in some mystification, and Oliver said:

'I expect you want my father, sir. I'm afraid he's away in town. Is there anything that I can do?'

The old man stared at him, and smiled.

'Of course,' he said, 'you must be Mr Fowler's son. I heard that there was a son, but I pictured you as a child. As one grows older one loses count of time. You've probably heard of me, Mr Fowler. I sold the house to your father many, years ago.'

Oliver smiled broadly.

'Oh, yes!' he exclaimed. 'You've been abroad, haven't you, sir? It's jolly of you to come and call. The mater —'

The old man interrupted courteously.

'Pray don't disturb her. I had a whim to come back and look at the old house and gardens. I returned to England last week after sixteen years. Perhaps, if you have five minutes to spare —'

'I shall be delighted to —' Oliver stopped short with a chuckle. 'I was going to say, "Show you round", but as you know the house much better than I do —'

'You mean, accompany me. Thank you. The gardens must look charming now.'

'Would you like to see them? Or will you have some refreshment first?'

'A cup of tea presently, since you're so kind,' said the old man, 'but not just yet.'

Together they went to the glass door overlooking the rear of the house, and Colonel Warlow immediately began to exclaim:

'Ah, you've done away with two beds and lengthened that lawn over there. I thought of doing that myself. Tennis, I see. It used to be croquet in my day. The old cedar still looks fit enough. I heard cedars were dying all over England. I'm glad —'

It seemed to Oliver that the old man was fighting some emotion which he was afraid of becoming audible in his voice. He supposed it was poverty which had made him sell the place, and felt uncomfortable. He had no illusions about his origin, but he did not care to see himself as one of a race of monied interlopers.

Colonel Warlow's voice chimed in upon his thoughts.

'You were going to play tennis, I see. Please don't let me keep you.'

'No, no, sir. My opponent hasn't arrived yet. She's always about an hour late.'

Colonel Warlow smiled.

'It's good to know there are young people about here again. Tell me, have you knocked down the summer-house?'

'No, that still stands.' Oliver smiled reminiscently. 'It used to be a favourite spot of mine. Would you like to see it, sir?'

The old man led the way across the central lawn and through the shrubbery. Inside the summer-house he sat himself on the old worm-eaten bench.

'It's strange to be here again,' he said, in a muffled voice.

'People like to come back to places where they have been happy,' Oliver hazarded.

'A murderer cannot help returning to the scene of his crime.'

Oliver looked at the visitor in surprise: he had spoken so quietly and seriously.

'I killed my daughter, you know,' said Colonel Warlow. His voice thickened and he cleared his throat. 'It was through my fault. Haven't they told you that? I couldn't bear the house any longer without my Margery. Haven't they told you about it? If I hadn't been an obstinate old fool –'

His voice thickened again, and died away.

'This was a favourite retreat of hers,' he continued, after a pause. 'She grew up. It's strange how a father scarcely realizes when his daughter becomes a woman. Young men began to take a fancy to the house – you've heard about it all, perhaps?'

He spoke anxiously, as if fearful that Oliver would deny him the pleasure of tearing open his old wound. The young man shook his head, afraid lest his own voice might break the spell. He met the gaze of the old man's dim blue eyes and flinched before the sadness in them.

'Ah, well, it happened a long time ago! Little Margery was nineteen. There was one young fellow – it doesn't matter about his name – the people left here even before I did. Margery liked him, and I didn't. I'd nothing against him but my own dislike. I told them they were both too young. I suppose I didn't want to lose Margery. They – they used to meet in this summer-house.'

Oliver felt suddenly chilled, as if a cold draught had struck him. Old memories came back to him like a flock of birds on silent wings.

'I forbade any love-making,' the old man's dreary voice continued. 'I was used to seeing that my orders were obeyed. I found them here once and made a scene. I threatened to horsewhip him – poor fellow, he couldn't have lifted a hand against me. And do you know what I did? Do you know what I did, Mr Fowler?'

His shaken voice paused as if for a reply. There being none, he continued:

'I drove them to meet clandestinely. I thought she'd given up seeing him. I didn't realize then that I was trying to give commands to Nature. They met elsewhere, and used to go up the river. I didn't know it until – oh, surely you know what happened now! He couldn't swim well enough to –'

He broke off the thread of his speech once more, looked up, and nodded.

'Both of them!' he said.

Oliver was staring out through the trellis-work window at the foliage beyond.

Those strange experiences of childhood – were they, after all, imaginary? Or had there lingered about the place some woman-spirit who loved children and had made her presence real to a lonely little boy? It was never her fault when he had felt afraid –

'Used she to wear a dress of peacock blue?'

It was Oliver who spoke, although he scarcely recognized his own voice.

'That was the dress she was drowned in, sir. Somebody must have told you –'

There followed another spell of silence, which was broken at last by a girl's voice from the lawn.

'Oliver! Ol-i-ver!'

Miss Baker had arrived, had been shown out into the garden, and was now making her presence known. Colonel Warlow's features relaxed into the ghost of a smile.

'I think somebody wants you to play tennis,' he said. 'Please do. If you will allow me, I will sit here alone for a little while.'

The Monkey's Paw
BY W. W. JACOBS

The multi-talented Orson Welles is famous for, among other things, having perpetrated one of the most terrifying radio programmes which literally convinced thousands of listeners that America was being invaded by men from Mars! On the evening of Halloween, 1938, Welles played the leading role in a dramatization on the 'Mercury Theatre of the Air' of H.G. Wells' classic, The War of the Worlds. *So vividly did he and his co-stars describe an invasion by space creatures of Grovers Mill, New Jersey, that many listeners became panic-striken and started evacuating their homes – despite disclaimers that had been given earlier that the whole broadcast was fictional. The following morning, Welles was pilloried by the broadcasting authorities and the media – but another element of his fame was already in place. Welles, in fact, nursed an affection for the macabre all his life, and it is perhaps a surprise that he only once again associated himself with the genre as the host of the half-hour series* Orson Welles' Great Mysteries *which Anglia TV made in 1973. Produced by John Jacobs, the mostly grisly tales were introduced by Welles suitably attired in an enveloping black cloak and with the inevitable big cigar in his hand. It was just a pity that he himself chose not to appear in any of the stories.*

No episode matched 'The Monkey's Paw' by the English humorist and dramatist, W.W. Jacobs (1863–1943), about a dried paw that grants an old man three wishes – and what occurs when he asks for a dead son to be revived. The story had earlier been adapted for the stage and broadcast on BBC Radio in 1946 in the Valentine Dyall series, Appointment with Fear. *This broadcast, starring Laidman Brown, also so unnerved a large number of viewers that they were forced to switch off their receivers: some even complained to the BBC. The Orson Welles version of the story scripted by Alan P. Sloane was similarly atmospheric and gruesome with a compelling performance by Patrick Magee as the distraught old man. It is not without good reason that this tale of despair and mourning has been described as one of the most powerful in English literature.*

I

WITHOUT, the night was cold and wet, but in the small parlour of Laburnam Villa the blinds were drawn and the fire burned brightly. Father and son were at chess, the former, who possessed ideas about the game involving radical changes, putting his king into such sharp and unnecessary perils that it even provoked comment from the white-haired old lady knitting placidly by the fire.

'Hark at the wind,' said Mr White, who, having seen a fatal mistake after it was too late, was amiably desirous of preventing his son from seeing it.

'I'm listening,' said the latter, grimly surveying the board as he stretched out his hand. 'Check.'

'I should hardly think that he'd come tonight,' said his father, with his hand poised over the board.

'Mate,' replied the son.

'That's the worst of living so far out,' bawled Mr White, with sudden and unlooked-for violence; 'of all the beastly, slushy, out-of-the-way places to live in, this is the worst. Pathway's a bog, and the road's a torrent. I don't know what people are thinking about. I suppose because only two houses in the road are let, they think it doesn't matter.'

'Never mind, dear,' said his wife, soothingly; 'perhaps you'll win the next one.'

Mr White looked up sharply, just in time to intercept a knowing glance between mother and son. The words died away on his lips, and he hid a guilty grin in his thin grey beard.

'There he is,' said Herbert White, as the gate banged to loudly and heavy footsteps came toward the door.

The old man rose with hospitable haste, and opening the door, was heard condoling with the new arrival. The new arrival also condoled with himself, so that Mrs White said, 'Tut, tut!' and coughed gently as her husband entered the room, followed by a tall, burly man, beady of eye and rubicund of visage.

'Sergeant-Major Morris,' he said, introducing him.

The sergeant-major shook hands, and taking the proffered seat by the fire, watched contentedly while his host got out whisky and tumblers and stood a small copper kettle on the fire.

At the third glass his eyes got brighter, and he began to talk, the little family circle regarding with eager interest this visitor from distant parts, as he squared his broad shoulders in the chair and spoke of wild scenes and doughty deeds; of wars and plagues and strange peoples.

'Twenty-one years of it,' said Mr White, nodding at his wife and son. 'When he went away he was a slip of a youth in the warehouse. Now look at him.'

'He don't look to have taken much harm,' said Mrs White, politely.

'I'd like to go to India myself,' said the old man, 'just to look round a bit, you know.'

'Better where you are,' said the sergeant-major, shaking his head. He put down the empty glass, and sighing softly, shook it again.

'I should like to see those old temples and fakirs and jugglers,' said the old man. 'What was that you started telling me the other day about a monkey's paw or something, Morris?'

'Nothing,' said the soldier, hastily. 'Leastways nothing worth hearing.'

'Monkey's paw?' said Mrs White, curiously.

'Well, it's just a bit of what you might call magic, perhaps,' said the sergeant-major, off-handedly.

His three listeners leaned forward eagerly. The visitor absent-mindedly put his empty glass to his lips and then set it down again. His host filled it for him.

'To look at,' said the sergeant-major, fumbling in his pocket, 'it's just an ordinary little paw, dried to a mummy.'

He took something out of his pocket and proffered it. Mrs White drew back with a grimace, but her son, taking it, examined it curiously.

'And what is there special about it?' inquired Mr White as he took it from his son, and having examined it, placed it upon the table.

'It had a spell put on it by an old fakir,' said the sergeant-major, 'a very holy man. He wanted to show that fate ruled people's lives, and that those who interfered with it did so to their sorrow. He put a spell on it so that three separate men could each have three wishes from it.'

His manner was so impressive that his hearers were conscious that their light laughter jarred somewhat.

'Well, why don't you have three, sir?' said Herbert White, cleverly.

The soldier regarded him in the way that middle age is wont to

419

regard presumptuous youth. 'I have,' he said, quietly, and his blotchy face whitened.

'And did you really have the three wishes granted?' asked Mrs White.

'I did,' said the sergeant-major, and his glass tapped against his strong teeth.

'And has anybody else wished?' persisted the old lady.

'The first man had his three wishes. Yes,' was the reply; 'I don't know what the first two were, but the third was for death. That's how I got the paw.'

His tones were so grave that a hush fell upon the group.

'If you've had your three wishes, it's no good to you now, then, Morris,' said the old man at last. 'What do you keep it for?'

The soldier shook his head. 'Fancy, I suppose,' he said, slowly. 'I did have some idea of selling it, but I don't think I will. It has caused enough mischief already. Besides, people won't buy. They think it's a fairy tale; some of them, and those who do think anything of it want to try it first and pay me afterward.'

'If you could have another three wishes,' said the old man, eyeing him keenly, 'would you have them?'

'I don't know,' said the other. 'I don't know.'

He took the paw, and dangling it between his forefinger and thumb, suddenly threw it upon the fire. White, with a slight cry, stooped down and snatched it off.

'Better let it burn,' said the soldier, solemnly.

'If you don't want it, Morris,' said the other, 'give it to me.'

'I won't,' said his friend, doggedly. 'I threw it on the fire. If you keep it, don't blame me for what happens. Pitch it on the fire again like a sensible man.'

The other shook his head and examined his new possession closely. 'How do you do it?' he inquired.

'Hold it up in your right hand and wish aloud,' said the sergeant-major, 'but I warn you of the consequences.'

'Sounds like the *Arabian Nights*,' said Mrs White, as she rose and began to set the supper. 'Don't you think you might wish for four pairs of hands for me?'

Her husband drew the talisman from pocket, and then all three burst into laughter as the sergeant-major, with a look of alarm on his face, caught him by the arm.

'If you must wish,' he said, gruffly, 'wish for something sensible.'

Mr White dropped it back in his pocket, and placing chairs, motioned his friend to the table. In the business of supper the talisman was partly forgotten, and afterward the three sat listening in an enthralled fashion to a second instalment of the soldier's adventures in India.

'If the tale about the monkey's paw is not more truthful than those he has been telling us,' said Herbert, as the door closed behind their guest, just in time for him to catch the last train, 'we shan't make much out of it.'

'Did you give him anything for it, father?' inquired Mrs White, regarding her husband closely.

'A trifle,' said he, colouring slightly. 'He didn't want it, but I made him take it. And he pressed me again to throw it away.'

'Likely,' said Herbert, with pretended horror. 'Why, we're going to be rich, and famous and happy. Wish to be an emperor, father, to begin with; then you can't be henpecked.'

He darted round the table, pursued by the maligned Mrs White armed with an antimacassar.

Mr White took the paw from his pocket and eyed it dubiously. 'I don't know what to wish for, and that's a fact,' he said, slowly. 'It seems to me I've got all I want.'

'If you only cleared the house, you'd be quite happy, wouldn't you?' said Herbert, with his hand on his shoulder. 'Well, wish for two hundred pounds, then; that'll just do it.'

His father, smiling shamefacedly at his own credulity, held up the talisman, as his son, with a solemn face, somewhat marred by a wink at his mother, sat down at the piano and struck a few impressive chords.

'I wish for two hundred pounds,' said the old man distinctly.

A fine crash from the piano greeted the words, interrupted by a shuddering cry from the old man. His wife and son ran toward him.

'It moved,' he cried, with a glance of disgust at the object as it lay on the floor. 'As I wished, it twisted in my hand like a snake.'

'Well, I don't see the money,' said his son as he picked it up and placed it on the table, 'and I bet I never shall.'

'It must have been your fancy, father,' said his wife, regarding him anxiously.

He shook his head. 'Never mind, though; there's no harm done, but it gave me a shock all the same.'

They sat down by the fire again while the two men finished their pipes. Outside, the wind was higher than ever, and the old man started nervously at the sound of a door banging upstairs. A silence unusual and depressing settled upon all three, which lasted until the old couple rose to retire for the night.

'I expect you'll find the cash tied up in a big bag in the middle of your bed,' said Herbert, as he bade them good-night, 'and something horrible squatting up on top of the wardrobe watching you as you pocket your ill-gotten gains.'

He sat alone in the darkness, gazing at the dying fire, and seeing faces in it. The last face was so horrible and so simian that he gazed at it in amazement. It got so vivid that, with a little uneasy laugh, he felt on the table for a glass containing a little water to throw over it. His hand grasped the monkey's paw, and with a little shiver he wiped his hand on his coat and went up to bed.

II

In the brightness of the wintry sun next morning as it streamed over the breakfast table he laughed at his fears. There was an air of prosaic wholesomeness about the room which it had lacked on the previous night, and the dirty, shrivelled little paw was pitched on the sideboard with a carelessness which betokened no great belief in its virtues.

'I suppose all old soldiers are the same,' said Mrs White. 'The idea of our listening to such nonsense! How could wishes be granted in these days? And if they could, how could two hundred pounds hurt you, father?'

'Might drop on his head from the sky,' said the frivolous Herbert.

'Morris said the things happened so naturally,' said his father, 'that you might if you so wished attribute it to coincidence.'

'Well, don't break into the money before I come back,' said Herbert as he rose from the table. 'I'm afraid it'll turn you into a mean, avaricious man, and we shall have to disown you.'

His mother laughed, and following him to the door, watched him down the road; and returning to the breakfast table, was very happy at the expense of her husband's credulity. All of which did not prevent her from scurrying to the door at the postman's knock, nor prevent her from referring somewhat shortly to retired sergeant-majors of bibulous habits when she found that the post brought a tailor's bill.

'Herbert will have some more of his funny remarks, I expect, when he comes home,' she said, as they sat at dinner.

'I dare say,' said Mr White, pouring himself out some beer; 'but for all that, the thing moved in my hand; that I'll swear to.'

'You thought it did,' said the old lady soothingly.

'I say it did,' replied the other. 'There was no thought about it; I had just – What's the matter?'

His wife made no reply. She was watching the mysterious

movements of a man outside, who, peering in an undecided fashion at the house, appeared to be trying to make up his mind to enter. In mental connection with the two hundred pounds, she noticed that the stranger was well dressed, and wore a silk hat of glossy newness. Three times he paused at the gate, and then walked on again. The fourth time he stood with his hand upon it, and then with sudden resolution flung it open and walked up the path. Mrs White at the same moment placed her hands behind her, and hurriedly unfastening the strings of her apron, put that useful article of apparel beneath the cushion of her chair.

She brought the stranger, who seemed ill at ease, into the room. He gazed at her furtively, and listened in a preoccupied fashion as the old lady apologized for the appearance of the room, and her husband's coat, a garment which he usually reserved for the garden. She then waited as patiently as her sex would permit, for him to broach his business, but he was at first strangely silent.

'I – was asked to call,' he said at last, and stooped and picked a piece of cotton from his trousers. 'I come from "Maw and Meggins".'

The old lady started. 'Is anything the matter?' she asked, breathlessly. 'Has anything happened to Herbert? What is it? What is it?'

Her husband interposed. 'There, there, mother,' he said, hastily. 'Sit down, and don't jump to conclusions. You've not brought bad news, I'm sure, sir' and he eyed the other wistfully.

'I'm sorry –' began the visitor.

'Is he hurt?' demanded the mother, wildly.

The visitor bowed in assent. 'Badly hurt,' he said, quietly, 'but he is not in any pain.'

'Oh, thank God!' said the old woman, clasping her hands. 'Thank God for that! Thank –'

She broke off suddenly as the sinister meaning of the assurance dawned upon her and she saw the awful confirmation of her fears in the other's averted face. She caught her breath, and turning to her slower-witted husband, laid her trembling old hand upon his. There was a long silence.

'He was caught in the machinery,' said the visitor at length in a low voice.

'Caught in the machinery,' repeated Mr White, in a dazed fashion, 'yes.'

He sat staring blankly out at the window, and taking his wife's hand between his own, pressed it as he had been wont to do in their old courting-days nearly forty years before.

423

'He was the only one left to us,' he said, turning gently to the visitor. 'It is hard.'

The other coughed, and rising, walked slowly to the window. 'The firm wished me to convey their sincere sympathy with you in your great loss,' he said, without looking round. 'I beg that you will understand I am only their servant and merely obeying orders.'

There was no reply; the old woman's face was white, her eyes staring, and her breath inaudible; on the husband's face was a look such as his friend the sergeant might have carried into his first action.

'I was to say that Maw and Meggins disclaim all responsibility,' continued the other. 'They admit no liability at all, but in consideration of your son's services, they wish to present you with a certain sum as compensation.'

Mr White dropped his wife's hand, and rising to his feet, gazed with a look of horror at his visitor. His dry lips shaped the words, 'How much?'

'Two hundred pounds,' was the answer.

Unconscious of his wife's shriek, the old man smiled faintly, put out his hands like a sightless man, and dropped, a senseless heap, to the floor.

III

In the huge new cemetery, some two miles distant, the old people buried their dead, and came back to a house steeped in shadow and silence. It was all over so quickly that at first they could hardly realize it, and remained in a state of expectation as though of something else to happen – something else which was to lighten this load, too heavy for old hearts to bear.

But the days passed, and expectation gave place to resignation – the hopeless resignation of the old, sometimes miscalled, apathy. Sometimes they hardly exchanged a word, for now they had nothing to talk about, and their days were long to weariness.

It was about a week after that the old man, waking suddenly in the night, stretched out his hand and found himself alone. The room was in darkness, and the sound of subdued weeping came from the window. He raised himself in bed and listened.

'Come back,' he said, tenderly. 'You will be cold.'

'It is colder for my son,' said the old woman, and wept afresh.

The sound of her sobs died away on his ears. The bed was warm, and his eyes heavy with sleep. He dozed fitfully, and then slept until a sudden wild cry from his wife awoke him with a start.

'*The paw!*' she cried wildly. 'The monkey's paw!'

He started up in alarm. 'Where? Where is it? What's the matter?'

She came stumbling across the room toward him. 'I want it,' she said, quietly. 'You've not destroyed it?'

'It's in the parlour, on the bracket,' he replied, marvelling. 'Why?'

She cried and laughed together, and bending over, kissed his cheek.

'I only just thought of it,' she said, hysterically. 'Why didn't I think of it before? Why didn't *you* think of it?'

'Think of what?' he questioned.

'The other two wishes,' she replied, rapidly. 'We've only had one.'

'Was not that enough?' he demanded, fiercely.

'No,' she cried, triumphantly; 'we'll have one more. Go down and get it quickly, and wish our boy alive again.'

The man sat up in bed and flung the bed-clothes from his quaking limbs. 'Good God, you are mad!' he cried, aghast.

'Get it,' she panted; 'get it quickly, and wish – Oh, my boy, my boy!'

Her husband struck a match and lit the candle. 'Get back to bed,' he said, unsteadily. 'You don't know what you are saying.'

'We had the first wish granted,' said the old woman, feverishly; 'why not the second?'

'A coincidence,' stammered the old man.

'Go and get it and wish,' cried his wife, quivering with excitement.

The old man turned and regarded her, and his voice shook. 'He has been dead ten days, and besides he – I would not tell you else, but – I could only recognize him by his clothing. If he was too terrible for you to see then, how now?'

'Bring him back,' cried the old woman, and dragged him toward the door. 'Do you think I fear the child I have nursed?'

He went down in the darkness, and felt his way to the parlour, and then to the mantelpiece. The talisman was in its place, and a horrible fear that the unspoken wish might bring his mutilated son before him ere he could escape from the room seized upon him, and he caught his breath as he found that he had lost the direction of the door. His brow cold with sweat, he felt his way round the table, and groped along the wall until he found himself in the small passage with the unwholesome thing in his hand.

Even his wife's face seemed changed as he entered the room. It was white and expectant, and to his fears seemed to have an unnatural look upon it. He was afraid of her.

'*Wish!*' she cried, in a strong voice.

'It is foolish and wicked,' he faltered.

'*Wish!*' repeated his wife.

He raised his hand. 'I wish my son alive again.'

The talisman fell to the floor, and he regarded it fearfully. Then he sank trembling into a chair as the old woman, with burning eyes, walked to the window and raised the blind.

He sat until he was chilled with the cold, glancing occasionally at the figure of the old woman peering through the window. The candle-end, which had burned below the rim of the china candlestick, was throwing pulsating shadows on the ceiling and walls, until, with a flicker larger than the rest, it expired. The old man, with an unspeakable sense of relief at the failure of the talisman, crept back to his bed, and a minute or two afterward the old woman came silently and apathetically beside him.

Neither spoke, but lay silently listening to the ticking of the clock. A stair creaked, and a squeaky mouse scurried noisily through the wall. The darkness was oppressive, and after lying for some time screwing up his courage, he took the box of matches, and striking one, went downstairs for a candle.

At the foot of the stairs the match went out, and he paused to strike another; and at the same moment a knock, so quiet and stealthy as to be scarcely audible, sounded on the front door.

The matches fell from his hand and spilled in the passage. He stood motionless, his breath suspended until the knock was repeated. Then he turned and fled swiftly back to his room, and closed the door behind him. A third knock sounded through the house.

'*What's that?*' cried the old woman, starting up.

'A rat,' said the old man in shaking tones – 'a rat. It passed me on the stairs.'

His wife sat up in bed listening. A loud knock resounded through the house.

'It's Herbert!' she screamed. 'It's Herbert!'

She ran to the door, but her husband was before her, and catching her by the arm, held her tightly.

'What are you going to do?' he whispered hoarsely.

'It's my boy; it's Herbert!' she cried, struggling mechanically. 'I forgot it was two miles away. What are you holding me for? Let go. I must open the door.'

'For God's sake don't let it in,' cried the old man, trembling.

'You're afraid of your own son,' she cried, struggling. 'Let me go. I'm coming, Herbert; I'm coming.'

There was another knock, and another. The old woman with a sudden wrench broke free and ran from the room. Her husband followed to the landing, and called after her appealingly as she hurried downstairs. He heard the chain rattle back and the bottom bolt drawn slowly and stiffly from the socket. Then the old woman's voice, strained and panting.

'The bolt,' she cried, loudly. 'Come down. I can't reach it.'

But her husband was on his hands and knees groping wildly on the floor in search of the paw. If he could only find it before the thing outside got in. A perfect fusillade of knocks reverberated through the house, and he heard the scraping of a chair as his wife put it down in the passage against the door. He heard the creaking of the bolt as it came slowly back, and at the same moment he found the monkey's paw, and frantically breathed his third and last wish.

The knocking ceased suddenly, although the echoes of it were still in the house. He heard the chair drawn back, and the door opened. A cold wind rushed up the staircase, and a long loud wail of disappointment and misery from his wife gave him courage to run down to her side, and then to the gate beyond. The street lamp flickering opposite shone on a quiet and deserted road.

The Ferryman

BY KINGSLEY AMIS

Granada TV, the makers of such exemplary series as Coronation Street *and* The Adventures of Sherlock Holmes, *made their entry into the anthology genre in December 1976 with* Haunted *which drew from contemporary supernatural fiction. The producer was Derek Granger, the former theatre critic who would later become famous for his classic serial version of Evelyn Waugh's novel,* Brideshead Revisited *(1981). As a consultant on* Haunted, *I can vouch for the painstaking care that he gave to a wide range of material which produced two highly acclaimed episodes. One was 'Poor Girl', from a story by Elizabeth Taylor, directed by Michael Apted and starring Lynne Miller, Stuart Wilson and Matthew Pollock in the tale of an unhappy governess caught between the longings of a lovesick boy and the advances of his womanizing father. The second was 'The Ferryman' based on a curious supernatural story by Kingsley Amis (1922–) and starring the later-to-be Sherlock Holmes, Jeremy Brett.*

'The Ferryman' had its origins in a tall story which Kingsley Amis wrote in January 1973 about seeing a ghost while staying at a country inn that bore the most uncanny resemblence to the setting of one of his novels, The Green Man *(1969). Julian Bond adapted the tale for the series with Brett becoming Sheridan Owen, a young writer exhausted by the launching of his first bestseller who escapes for a weekend in the country with his wife, Alex (Natasha Parry). There the author and his wife find themselves plunged into the middle of a terrifying ordeal with an evil spirit. 'The Ferryman', which John Irvin directed, also co-starred Geoffrey Chater and Lesley Dunlop as Miles and Jill Attingham the couple running the inn, and it made superb late-night viewing when it was screened on 23, December 1976. In 1990, Amis'*

novel, The Green Man, *was also adapted as a series by Malcolm Bradbury for the BBC with Albert Finney as the hotel owner, Maurice Allington, whose three-in-a-bed sex scenes plus some terrifying special effect which made viewers' flesh creep, ignited a fierce press and public controversy after the screening of the first episode on Halloween night. Notwithstanding this, two years later the series was re-shown to even larger audiences. Like 'The Ferryman' it, too, now has a special place in the late-night horror tradition . . .*

I WANT to tell you about a very odd experience I had a few months ago – not so as to entertain you, but because I think it raises some very basic questions about, you know, what life is all about and to what extent we run our own lives. Rather worrying questions. Anyway, what happened was this . . .

My wife and I had been staying the weekend with her uncle and aunt in Westmorland, near a place called Milnethorpe. Both of us – Jane and I, that is – had things to do in London on the Monday morning, and it's a long drive from there down to Barnet, where we live, even though a good half of it is on the M6. So I said: 'Look, don't let's break our necks trying to get home in the light' (this was in August). 'Let's take it easy and stop somewhere for dinner and reckon to get home about half-past ten or eleven.' Jane said okay.

So we left Milnethorpe in the middle of the afternoon, took things fairly easily, and landed up about half-past seven or a quarter to eight at the place we'd picked out of one of the food guides before we started. I won't tell you the name of the place, because the people who run it wouldn't thank me if I did. Please don't go looking for it. I'd advise you not to.

Anyway, we parked the car in the yard and went inside. It was a nice-looking sort of place: pretty old, built a good time ago, I mean, done up in a sensible sort of way, no muzak and no bloody silly blacked-out lighting, but no olde-worlde nonsense either. I got us both a drink in the bar and went off to see about a table for dinner. I soon found the right chap, and he said: 'Table for two in half an hour – certainly, sir. Are you in the bar? I'll get someone to bring you the menu in a few minutes.' Pleasant sort of chap, a bit young for the job.

I was just going off when a sort of paunchy business-type came in and said something like 'Mr Allington not in tonight?' and the young fellow said: 'No, sir, he's taken the evening off.' 'All right, never mind.'

Well, I'll tell you why in a minute, but I turned back to the young

429

fellow and said, 'Excuse me, but is your name Palmer?' and he said: 'Yes, sir.' I said, 'Not David Palmer by any chance?' and he said: 'No, sir. Actually, the name's George.' I said, or rather burbled: 'A friend of mine was telling me about this place, said he'd stayed here, liked it very much, mentioned you – anyway, I got half the name right, and Mr Allington is the proprietor, isn't he?' 'That's correct, sir.'

I went straight back to the bar, went up to the barman and said: 'Fred?' He said: 'Yes, sir.' I said, 'Fred Soames?' and he said: 'Fred Browning, sir.' I just said 'Wrong Fred' – not very polite, but it was all I could think of. I went over to where my wife was sitting and I'd hardly sat down before she asked: 'What's the matter?'

What was the matter calls for a bit of explanation. In 1969 I published a novel called *The Green Man*, which was not only the title of the book but also the name of a sort of classy pub, or inn, where most of the action took place – very much the kind of establishment we were in that evening. Now the landlord of The Green Man was called Allington, and his deputy was called David Palmer, and the barman was called Fred Soames. Allington is a very uncommon name – I wanted that for reasons nothing to do with this story. The other two aren't, but to have got Palmer and Fred right, so to speak, as well as Allington was a thumping great coincidence – staggering, in fact. But I wasn't just staggered, I was very alarmed. Because The Green Man wasn't only the name of the pub in my book: it was also the name of a frightening creature, a sort of solid ghost, conjured up out of tree branches and leaves and so on, that very nearly kills Allington and his young daughter. I didn't want to find I was right about that too.

Jane was very sensible, as always. She said stranger coincidences had happened and still been just coincidences and mightn't I have come across an innkeeper called Allington somewhere, half-forgotten about it and brought it up out of my unconscious mind when I was looking for a name for an innkeeper to put in the book. and now the real Allington had moved from wherever I'd seen him before to this place. And Palmer and Fred really are very common names. And I'd got the name of the pub wrong. (I'm still not telling you what it's called, but one of the things it isn't called is The Green Man.) And my pub was in Hertfordshire and this place was . . . off the M6. All very reasonable and reassuring.

Only I wasn't very reassured. I mean, I obviously couldn't just leave it there. The thing to do was get hold of this chap Palmer and see if there was, well, any more to come. Which was going to be tricky if I wasn't going to look nosey or mad or something else that would shut him up. Neither of us ate much at dinner, though there was nothing wrong with the food. We didn't say much, either. I drank a fair amount.

Then, half-way through, Palmer turned up to do his everything-all-right routine, as I'd hoped he would, and as he would have done in my book. I said yes, it was fine, thanks, and then I said we'd be very pleased if he'd join us for a brandy afterwards if he'd got time, and he said he'd be delighted. Jolly good, but I was still stuck with this problem of how to dress the thing up.

Jane had said earlier on, why didn't I just tell the truth, and I'd said that since Palmer hadn't reacted at all when I gave him my name when I was booking the table, he'd only have my word for the whole story and might think I was off my rocker. She'd said that of course she'd back me up, and I'd said he'd just think he'd got two loonies on his hands instead of one. Anyway, now she said: 'Some people who've read *The Green Man* must have mentioned it – fancy that. Mr Palmer, you and Mr Allington and Fred are all in a book by somebody called Kingsley Amis.' Obvious enough when you think of it, but like a lot of obvious things, you have got to think of it.

Well, that was the line I took when Palmer rolled up for his brandy: I'm me and I wrote this book and so on. Oh really? he said, more or less. I thought we were buggered, but then he said, 'Oh yes, now you mention it, I do remember some chap saying something like that, but it must have been two or three years ago' – as if that stopped it counting for much. 'I'm not much of a reader, you see,' he said.

'What about Mr Allington.' I said, 'doesn't he read?' 'Not what you'd call a reader,' he said. Well, that was one down to me, or one up, depending on how you look at it, because *my* Allington was a tremendous reader – French poetry and all that. Still, the approach had worked after a fashion, and Palmer very decently put up with being cross-questioned on how far this place corresponded with my place in the book. Was Mrs Allington blonde? There wasn't a Mrs Allington any more: she'd died of leukemia quite a long time ago. Had he got his widowed father living here? (Allington's father, that is.) No, Mr Allington senior, and his wife, lived in Eastbourne. Was the house, the pub, haunted at all? Not as far as Palmer knew, and he'd been there three years. In fact, the place was only about two hundred years old, which completely clobbered a good half of my novel, where the ghosts had been hard at it more than a hundred years earlier still.

Nearly all of it was like that. Of course, there were some questions

431

I couldn't ask, for one reason or another. For instance, was Allington a boozer, like my Allington, and, even more so, had this Allington had a visit from God? In the book, God turns up in the form of a young man to give Allington some tips on how to deal with the ghosts, who he, God, thinks are a menace to him. No point in going any further into that part.

I said nearly all the answers Palmer gave me were straight negatives. One wasn't, or rather there were two points where I scored, so to speak. One was that Allington had a fifteen-year-old daughter called Marilyn living in the house. My Allington's daughter was thirteen, and called Amy, but I'd come somewhere near the mark – too near for comfort. The other thing was a bit harder to tie down. When I'm writing a novel, I very rarely have any sort of mental picture of any of the characters, what they actually look like. I think a lot of novelists would say the same. But, I don't know why, I'd had a very clear image of what my chap David Palmer looked like, and now I'd had a really good look at George Palmer, this one here, he was nearly the same as I'd imagined: not so tall, different nose, but still nearly the same. I didn't care for that.

Palmer, George Palmer, said he had things to see to and took off. I told Jane about the resemblance. She said I could easily have imagined that, and I said I supposed I might. 'Anyway,' she said, 'what do you think of it all?' I said it could still all be coincidence. 'What could it be if it isn't coincidence?' she asked. I'd been wondering about that while we were talking to Palmer. Not an easy one. Feeling a complete bloody fool, I said I thought we could have strayed into some kind of parallel world that slightly resembles the world I had made up – like in a Science Fiction story. She didn't laugh or back away. She looked round and spotted a newspaper someone had left on one of the chairs. It was that day's *Sunday Telegraph*. She said: 'If where we are is a world that's parallel to the real world. it's bound to be different from the real world in all sorts of ways. Now you read most of the *Telegraph* this morning, the real *Telegraph*. Look at this one and see if it's any different.' Well, I did, and it wasn't: same front page, same article on the trade unions by Perry, that's Peregrine Worsthorne, same readers' letters, same crossword down to the last clue. Well, that was a relief.

But I didn't stay relieved, because there was another coincidence shaping up. It was a hot night in August when all this happened, and Allington was out for the evening. It was on a hot night in August, after Allington had come back from an evening out, that the monster, the Green Man, finally takes shape and comes pounding up the road to tear young Amy Allington to pieces. That bit begins on page 225 in my book, if you're interested.

The other nasty little consideration was this. Unlike some novelists I could name, I invent all my characters, except for a few minor ones here and there. What I mean is, I don't go in for just renaming people I know and bunging them into a book. But, of course, you can't help putting *something* of yourself into all your characters, even if it's a surly bus-conductor who only comes in for half a page. Obviously, this comes up most of all with your heroes. None of my heroes, not even old Lucky Jim, are me, but they can't help having pretty fair chunks of me in them, some more than others. And Allington in that book was one of the same. I'm more like him than I'm like most of the others: in particular, I'm more like my Maurice Allington in my book than the real Allington, who, by the way, turned out to be called John, seemed (from what I'd heard) to be like my Maurice Allington. Sorry to be long-winded, but I want to get that quite clear.

So, if, by some fantastic chance, the Green Man, the monster, was going to turn up here, he, or it, seemed more likely to turn up tonight than most nights. Furthermore, I seemed better cast for the part of the young girl's father, who manages in the book to save her from the monster, than this young girl's father did.

I tried to explain all this to Jane. Evidently I got it across all right, because she said straight away: 'We'd better stay here tonight, then.' 'If we can,' I said, meaning if there was a room. Well, there was, and at the front of the house too – which was important, because in the book that's the side the monster appears on.

While one of the blokes was taking our stuff out of the car and upstairs, I said to Jane: 'I'm not going to be like a bloody fool in a ghost story who insists on seeing things through alone, not if I can help it – I'm going to give Bob Conquest a ring. 'Bob's an old chum of mine, and about the only one I felt I could ask to come belting up all this way (he lives in Battersea) for such a ridiculous reason. It was just after ten by this time, and the Green Man wasn't scheduled to put in an appearance till after one AM, so Bob could make it all right, if he started straight away. Fine, except his phone didn't answer: I tried twice.

Jane said: 'Get hold of Monkey. I'll speak to him.' Monkey, otherwise known as Colin, is her brother: he lives with us in Barnet. Our number answered all right, but I got my son Philip, who was staying the weekend there. He said Monkey was out at a party, he didn't know where. So all I could do was the necessary but not at all helpful job of saying we wouldn't be home till the next morning. So

433

that was that. I mean, I just couldn't start getting hold of George Palmer and asking him to sit up with us into the small hours in case a ghost came along. Could any of you? I should have said that Philip hasn't got a car.

We stayed in the bar until it closed. I said to Jane at one point: 'You don't think I'm mad, do you? Or silly or anything?' She said: 'On the contrary, I think you're being extremely practical and sensible.' Well, thank God for that. Jane believes in ghosts, you see. My own position on that is exactly that of the man who said: 'I don't believe in ghosts, but I'm afraid of them.'

Which brings me to one of the oddest things about this whole business. I'm a nervous type by nature: I never go in an aeroplane; I won't drive a car (Jane does the driving); I don't even much care for being alone in the house. But, ever since we'd decided to stay the night at this place, all the uneasiness and, let's face it, the considerable fear I'd started to feel as soon as these coincidences started coming up, it all just fell away. I felt quite confident, I felt I knew I'd be able to do whatever might be required of me.

There was one other thing to get settled. I said to Jane – we were in the bedroom by this time: 'If he turns up, what am I going to use against him?' You see, in the book, Maurice Allington has dug up a sort of magic object that sort of controls the Green Man. I hadn't. Jane saw what I was driving at. She said she'd thought of that, and took off and gave me the plain gold cross she wears round her neck, not for religious reasons: it was her grandmother's. That'll fix him, I thought, and, as before, I felt quite confident about it.

After that, we more or less sat and waited. At one point a car drove up and stopped in the car park. A man got out and went in the front door. It must have been Allington. I couldn't see much about him except that he had the wrong colour hair, but when I looked at my watch it was eight minutes to midnight, the exact time when the Allington in the book got back after his evening out the night he coped with the creature. One more bit of . . . call it confirmation.

I opened our bedroom door and listened. Soon I heard footsteps coming upstairs and going off towards the back of the house, then a door shutting, and then straight away the house seemed totally still. It can't have been much later that I said to Jane: 'Look, there's no point in me hanging round up here. He might be early, you never know. It's a warm night, I might as well go down there now.' She said: 'Are you sure you don't want me to come with you?'

'Absolutely sure,' I said, 'I'll be fine. But I do want you to watch from the window here.'

'Okay,' she said. She wished me luck and we clung to each other for a bit, and then off I went.

I was glad I'd left plenty of time, because getting out of the place turned out to be far from straightforward. Everything seemed to be locked and the key taken away. Eventually I found a scullery door with the key still in the lock. Outside it was quite bright, with a full moon, or not far off, and a couple of fairly powerful lights at the corners of the house. It was a pretty lonely spot, with only two or three other houses in sight. I remember a car went by soon after I got out there, but it was the only one. There wasn't a breath of wind. I saw Jane at our window and waved, and she waved back.

The question was, where to wait. If what was going to happen – assuming something was – went like the book, then the young girl, the daughter, was going to come out of the house because she'd thought she'd heard her father calling her (another bit of magic), and then this Green Man creature was going to come running at her from one direction or the other. I couldn't decide which was the more likely direction.

A bit of luck: near the front door there was one of those heavy wooden benches. I sat down on that and started keeping watch, first one way, then the other, half a minute at a time. Normally, ten minutes of this would have driven me off my head with boredom, but that night somehow it was all right. After some quite long time, I turned my head from right to left on schedule and there was a girl, standing a few yards away: she must have come round that side of the house. She was wearing light-green pyjamas – wrong colour again. I was going to speak to her, but there was something about the way she was standing . . .

She wasn't looking at me: in fact, I soon saw she wasn't looking at anything much. I waved my hand in front of her eyes, the way they do in films when they think someone's been hypnotized or something. I felt a perfect idiot, but her eyes didn't move. Sleepwalking, presumably: not in the book. Do people walk in their sleep? Apparently not: they only pretend to, according to what a psychiatrist chum told me afterwards, but I hadn't heard that then. All I knew, or thought I knew, was this thing everybody's heard somewhere about it being dangerous to wake a sleepwalker. So I just stayed close to the girl and went on keeping watch. A bit more time went by, and then, sure enough, I heard, faintly but clearly, the sound I'd written about: the rustling, creaking sound of the movement of something made of tree branches, twigs and clusters of leaves. And there it was, about a hundred yards away, not really much like a

435

man, coming up at a clumsy, jolting sort of jog-trot on the grass verge, and accelerating.

I knew what I had to do. I started walking to meet it, with the cross ready in my hand. (The girl hadn't moved at all.) When the thing was about twenty yards away I saw its face, which had fungus on it, and I heard another sound I'd written about coming from what I suppose you'd have to call its mouth, like the howling of wind through trees. I stopped and steadied myself and threw the cross at it, and it vanished – immediately. That wasn't like the book, but I didn't stop to think about it. I didn't stop to look for the cross, either. When I turned back, the girl had gone. So much the better. I rushed back into the inn and up to the bedroom and knocked on the door – I'd told Jane to lock it after me.

There was a delay before she came and opened it. I could see she looked confused or something, but I didn't bother with that, because I could feel all the calm and confidence I'd had earlier, it was all just draining away from me. I sat her down on the bed and sat down myself on a chair and just rattled off what had happened as fast as I could. I must have forgotten she'd been meant to be watching.

By the time I'd finished I was shaking. So was Jane. She said: 'What made you change your mind?'

'Change my mind – what about?'

'Going out there,' she said: 'getting up again and going out.'

'But,' I said, 'I've been out there all the time.'

'Oh no you haven't,' she said. 'You came back up here after about twenty minutes, and you told me the whole thing was silly and you were going to bed, which we both did.' She seemed quite positive.

I was absolutely shattered. 'But it all really happened,' I said. 'Just the way I told you.'

'It couldn't have,' she said. 'You must have dreamed it. You certainly didn't throw the cross at anything because it's here, you gave it back to me when you came back the first time.'

And there it was, on the chain round her neck.

I broke down then. I'm not quite clear what I said or did. Jane got some sleeping pills down me and I went off in the end. I remember thinking rather wildly that somebody or other with a funny sense of humour had got me into exactly the same predicament, the same mess, as the hero of my book had been in: seeing something that must have been supernatural and just not being believed. Because I knew I'd seen the whole thing: I knew it then and I still know it.

I woke up late, feeling terrible. Jane was sitting reading by the bed. She said: 'I've seen young Miss Allington. Your description of her fits

436

and, she said, she used to walk in her sleep.' I asked her how she'd found out, and she said she just had: she's good at that kind of thing. Anyway, I felt better straight away. I said it looked as if we'd neither of us been dreaming, even if what I'd seen couldn't be reconciled with what she'd seen, and she agreed. After that we rather dropped the subject in a funny sort of way. We decided not to look for the cross I'd thrown at the Green Man. I said we wouldn't be able to find it. I didn't ask Jane whether she was thinking what I was thinking: that looking would be a waste of time because she was wearing it at that very moment.

We packed up, made a couple of phone calls rearranging our appointments, paid the bill and drove off. We still didn't talk about the main issue. But then, as we were coming off the Mill Hill roundabout — that's only about ten minutes from home Jane said: 'What do you think happened to sort of make it all happen?' I said: 'I think someone was needed there to destroy that monster. Which means I was guided there at that time, or perhaps the time could be adjusted. I must have been, well, sent all that stuff about the Green Man and about Allington and the others.'

'To make sure you recognized the place when you got there and knew what to do,' she said. 'Who did all the guiding and the sending and so on?'

'The same chap who appeared in my book to tell Allington what he wanted done.'

'Why couldn't he have fixed the monster himself?'

'There are limitations to his power.'

'There can't be many,' she said, 'if he can make the same object be in two places at the same time.'

Yes, you see, she'd thought of that too. It's supposed to be a physical impossibility, isn't it? Anyway, I said, probably the way he'd chosen had been more fun. 'More fun,' Jane repeated. She looked very thoughtful.

As you'll have seen, there was one loose end, of a sort. Who or what was it that had taken on my shape to enter that bedroom, talk to Jane with my voice, and share her bed for at any rate a few minutes? She and I didn't discuss it for several days. Then one morning she asked me the question more or less as I've just put it.

'Interesting point,' I said. 'I don't know.'

'It's more interesting than you think,' she said. 'Because when . . . whoever it was got into bed with me, he didn't just go to sleep.'

I suppose I just looked at her.

'That's right,' she said. 'I thought I'd better go and see John before I told you.' (That's John Allison, our GP.)

'It was negative, then,' I said.

'Yes,' Jane said.

Well, that's it. A relief, of course. But in one way, rather disappointing.

BEASTS

The Tarroo-Ushtey

BY NIGEL KNEALE

Nigel Kneale (1922–) has been one of the most important creators of late night horror television in Britain during the last forty years – though he dislikes being categorized as either a supernatural or science fiction writer. His success was founded on his original series for the BBC, The Quatermass Experiment *(1953), and re-affirmed by the sequels,* Quatermass II *(1955),* Quatermass and the Pit *(1958) and* Quatermass *(1979). Kneale's 1954 television adaptation of George Orwell's* Nineteen Eighty-Four *with Peter Cushing and Yvonne Mitchell was also a television landmark and raised a storm of protest when it was first shown live on Sunday evenings. There were determined attempts to have the Thursday evening repeats – also live – banned, but a firm stand by Michael Barry, the head of drama, avoided this and the BBC chief even went on camera to introduce each of the second performances himself. Controversy has also surrounded some of the author's later TV plays such as* The Year of the Sex Olympics *(1969) and* The Stone Tape *(1972).*

The only horror anthology series Nigel Kneale has contributed to television is Beasts *which he wrote for ATV producer Nicholas Palmer in 1976. Each episode dealt with the different human attitudes towards animals and featured terrifying creatures that were either supernatural, psychological or from the realms of fantasy. They included rats ('During Barty's Party'), dolphins ('Buddyboy'), an imaginary chipmunk-like cartoon creature ('Special Offer'), and a nine-foot monster in a horror movie. The monster story, 'The Dummy', was one of Kneale's favourites. 'It was about this series of "Dummy" films being made at a place rather like Bray Studios with all the essential cosiness that emanates from the floor of a studio when they're making horror pictures,' he explained. 'The horror industry is actually a very cosy kind of industry, and that story provided me with a lot of fun. It was extremely well acted, too.' Nigel, in fact, drew his inspiration for the story from 'The Tarroo-Ushtey' a short tale he had written in 1949 about a fake monster specially created to ensure the survival of an old superstition. It appears hereunder as a reminder of* Beasts, *another late night series which well deserves reshowing . . .*

IN far-off days before the preachers and the school-masters came, the island held a great many creatures besides people and beasts. The place swarmed with monsters.

A man would think twice before answering his cottage door on a windy night, in dread of a visit from his own ghost. The high mountain roads rang in the darkness with the thunderous tiffs of the bugganes, which had unspeakable shapes and heads bigger than houses; while a walk along the sea-shore after the sun had set was to invite the misty appearance of a tarroo-ushtey, in the likeness of a monstrous bull, ready to rush the beholder into the sea and devour him. At harvest-time the hairy troll-man, the phynodderee, might come springing out of his elder-tree to assist in the reaping, to the farmer's dismay; for the best-intentioned of the beings were no more helpful than interfering neighbours, and likely to finish the day pulling the thatch off the house or trying to teach the hens to swim. What with the little people, the fairies themselves, so numerous that they were under everybody's feet, turning milk sour and jamming locks and putting the fire out; and with witches waiting at every other bend in the road with their evil eye ready to paralyse the horses, ordinary people led a difficult life. It was necessary to carry charm-herbs, or beads, and to remember warding-off rhymes that had been taught in early childhood.

As the generations went by and people took to speaking English on polite occasions, the old creatures grew scarcer. By the time that travellers from the packet boats had spread the story about a girl named Victoria being the new queen of the English, their influence was slipping; at night people put out milk for the fairies more from habit than fear, half-guessing it would be drunk by the cat; if they heard a midnight clamour from the henhouse, they reached for a musket, not a bunch of hawthorn. But back hair could still rise on a dark mountain road.

From the gradual loss of the old knowledge, came dependence on the wise men and women.

Charlsie Quilliam was one of these.

He was the fattest man on the island, said those who had travelled all over it and could speak with authority.

He carried his enormous body with special care, like a man with a brim-full jug; but he still stuck in doors and caused chairs to collapse; and people meeting him on a narrow path had to climb the hedge to let him pass. The right of way was always Charlsie's.

His fatness, coupled with a huge black beard, left little shape to his face, but his eyes were quick. Above them, like a heathery ledge, ran a single, unbroken line of eyebrow, which denoted second sight.

Whatever question was asked, he would be able to answer it. Even if he said nothing, the expression in his eyes showed that he knew, but considered the questioner would be better in ignorance. It was Charlsie who had had a vision of the potato blight crossing to Ireland in a black cloud, but he kept the frightening secret to himself until long afterwards, when the subsequent famine was common talk and nobody could be alarmed by what he had seen.

Old secret customs; birth-charms and death-charms, and rites for other dark days; Charlsie's big head held them all. Folk in trouble might set out for the minister's house, think better of it, and go to find Charlsie where he sat on a hump of earth outside his cottage, his thick fingers busy with scraps of coloured wool and feathers.

Ever since he became too fat for other work, his secret knowledge had supported him; and gifts of food from grateful clients kept his weight creeping up.

Many a winter night he would be at the centre of a fireside gathering. Charlsie's guttural, hoarse voice could hold a packed cottage in frightened suspense for hours as it laid horror upon horror. Personal experience of dealing with witches was his chief subject. Most of his stories had little point, which made them all the more uncanny and likely. People went home in groups after an evening with Charlsie.

Apart from the witches, he had only one open enemy.

This was a Scottish peddler named McRae. The man had lost a leg in the Crimea, and called himself a Calvinist. He sneered at the old beliefs and tried to tell his own war experiences instead; but people were chary of listening, in case Charlsie got to know. They bought Duncan McRae's buttons and shut the door quickly.

The little Scot hated it. At hardly a single house in the fat man's territory could he get himself invited inside for a free meal; even the news he brought from the towns was received with suspicion, when at all, as if he had made it up on the road. He would have cut the district out altogether, except that he sold more elastic there than anywhere else.

One hot afternoon in the late summer, the peddler sweated up the hill towards the village.

A dense sea-fog had smothered the sun, the air was close, and his pack wearied him. Time after time he had to rest his wooden leg.

Duncan McRae had news. A tit-bit he had picked up before he left town particularly pleased him, and had gone down well in two villages already. For once it was an item that people would be able to put to the proof themselves later on.

A new machine was to be tested on the English side of the channel, less than thirty miles away. It was said to be able to warn ships in fog.

McRae hastened. He had heard that when the new 'fog horn', as they called it, was tested, people on the island might be able to hear it blowing faintly. To-day's weather seemed very suitable for such an experiment, but even if nothing happened, surely this story at least had enough interest to call for hospitality.

At the top of the hill he leaned on a hedge to ease his leg. The air was heavy, and the quietness a relief after the clumping of his iron-tipped stump in the grit.

He held his breath, listening.

Far away there was a moan. He pulled himself up the hedge and faced towards the fog-blanketed sea.

The sound came again, faint and eerie; a growl so low-pitched that it could hardly be heard at all. It could only be one thing.

Excitedly, McRae slid down the hedge and straightened his pack. Within ten minutes, bursting with news, he had reached the first outlying cottage door. He rattled the latch and pushed it open.

'Hallo, there!' he called. 'D'ye hear the new invention yonder?'

There was silence; no one at home.

He hurried out, and on to the next fuchsia-hedged cabin. 'Hallo, missis! D'ye hear the wonders that's going on across the water – ?'

No one to be seen.

McRae frowned. He was at the top end of the village now, looking down the winding street as it sloped towards the sea. There was nobody moving in it, and no sound. Even the blacksmith's forge was silent.

The peddler shouted, 'Where is everybody? Is there no' a single body up the day?'

His voice went quietly away into the mist.

Charlsie Quilliam had been in his cottage when they came for him.

He was threading a dried caul on a neckband as a cure against shipwreck, working indoors because the damp grieved his chest.

People came clustering round his door, muttering.

'Come in or go out!' called Charlsie. He pricked his thumb. 'Devil take it! This caul is like the hide of a crocodile!'

They saw that he did not hear what they heard; he suffered at times from deafness. At last old Juan Corjeag persuaded him to come outside.

Charlsie was surprised to see nearly all the village assembled at his door.

'Just listen, Charlsie!' said old Juan.

The frightened faces seemed to be expecting something from him. 'Well, what is it at all?' he said after a moment.

'Oh – listen, do!'

Then Charlsie heard it. A sound that might have been made by a coughing cow far away on a calm night.

'Some beast that wants lookin' to,' he decided. 'Is that all? Whatever's got into everybody?'

Old Juan's face was too horrified to express anything. He pointed.

'Them sounds is from out at sea!' he said. There was a shocked murmur from the villagers at the speaking of the words.

Charlsie made no move. His little eyes sharpened.

'Tell us what it is, Charlsie! What've we got to do? Oh, an' it's far worse down by the water! The twist of the land smothers it here!'

Without a word Charlsie Quilliam turned back into his cottage; the crowd were alarmed by his stillness. When he reappeared, he had his big blackthorn walking-stick in one hand; in the other was a bunch of dried leaves.

'I'm goin' down there for a sight,' he said. 'Anybody that wants to, can come.'

He set ponderously off.

For a little space they hesitated, whispering among themselves. Old Juan licked his lips and went after Charlsie. When he looked round, a few dozen paces down the shore path, he saw the rest following behind him in a body on the sandy track.

Charlsie stopped for breath. Old Juan caught him up.

'Ye're right. It's clearer down here.'

Old Juan spoke slowly. 'Charlsie, I'm hopin' it won't put bad luck on me, but I was the first that heard it.' He swallowed, remembering. 'Down in the tide, diggin' for lug-worms.'

'Ah?' said Charlsie. He grunted. 'Let's get nearer.'

As they came over the low brow of the fore-shore, where the

yellow sandy grass ended and the pebbles began, the sound hit them. It travelled straight in along the surface of the water; still very far away, but plainer to the ear; so unnatural that it shocked everybody afresh. It ended with a throaty gulp.

Charlsie made his way slowly across the stones, picking his way with the stick among the puddles. They all followed in silence towards the water's edge.

There he stood, leaning and listening.

Again and again and again the distant cry came from the fog, and they shivered. Old Juan made to speak, but Charlsie silenced him.

'Yes,' said Charlsie, turning back casually, 'it's a tarroo-ushtey.'

A woman screamed and had a hand clapped across her mouth. People drew back hastily from the creamy water's edge.

'What'll happen?' whispered old Juan.

Charlsie's single brow bent in a frown. 'Queer thing for it to come out in the daylight,' he said. 'It goes to prove such creatures is no fancy.'

He turned to the crowd and addressed them.

'Now listen, all! It's a tarroo-ushtey out yonder. Hush, now, hush! It's in trouble over somethin' – maybe lost an' callin' out to another one.'

'Aye, its mate, likely!' said Juan.

Charlsie ignored him. 'For all that they're not of this world, they can get lost in thick fog like any other creature. It's a terrible long way off at present; so the best thing to do is be quiet and go home, and do nothin' to draw it this way.'

'An' I'll tell ye what he's like. They look like a tremendous big black bull, but their feet is webbed. An' in th' ould days they've had many a person eaten. So nobody must come down here tonight, for fear of the fog clearin' and it seein' him. There's no tellin' what it might do if it got up in the village.'

He showed the bunch of herbs in his left hand. 'Now everybody go home quiet, an' I'll see about layin' a charm on the water. Keep all the childher indoors!'

He sat on a low rock near the tide as they went.

Peering back at him, they saw him wave the leaves back and forth in his hand. He seemed to be chanting something. In the sight of old Juan, the last to cross the sandy bluff, he finished by tossing the bunch into the sea and turning abruptly away.

Charlsie laboured up the track without a look behind. The lowing sounds still continued. He felt satisfied with what he had done, but was checking the rites over in his mind to make sure. Ahead, the last stragglers reached the safety of the village.

444

But when he came to the houses, Charlsie found people still talking in small groups.

'Look here, I told ye to get the childher out of sight!' he said. 'An' it'd be just as well if everybody kept themselves –'

A commotion was going on farther up the street.

'What the devil is it now?' Charlsie shouted; he felt privileged to make a noise.

Old Juan hobbled towards him. 'It's that Scotch peddler!' he said. 'He's got some nonsense tale! Oh, ye'd better give him a word, Charlsie – he'll be puttin' foolishness in their heads!'

Charlsie scowled.

He came ponderously to where Duncan McRae sat on a wooden bench outside a cottage. People parted before him, but he felt that there was a questioning quality in their respect.

'What's goin' on here?' he said.

The little Scot grinned up, hands tucked comfortably behind his head.

'Och, I've been sitting here wondering if ye'd all fled awa' into a far country. I was thinking ye had a nice day for it,' he said.

'What are ye bletherin' about?'

'Have ye got a strait-jacket on yon sea monster?' The peddler chuckled. 'Look him in the eye, man. That's what they say; look him in the eye and put salt on his tail. I've a new brand of table salt in ma pack – would ye care to try some?' He began to laugh loudly.

Charlsie's face was purple. 'Is the feller crazy or what? Shut up, will ye!' He seized the little man by the hair and shook him violently. 'Stop laughin'! Haven't I ordered quiet!'

The peddler squealed as he tried to escape; his wooden leg skidded, and he thrashed about.

The staring villagers broke into explanation.

'He's got a tale that the noises is from a machine, Charlsie!'

'A warnin' of fog, for the ships!'

'That's what he said.'

There was dead silence, apart from the spluttering breath of the dazed peddler. Charlsie slowly released him.

They were all tense, watching Charlsie's face. It showed no expression; he might have been thinking, or working something out, or studying his victim, or listening. 'Juan,' he said at last, pointedly.

'Yes, Charlsie?'

'Can ye still hear it?'

They all waited, listening. The noise at sea had stopped.

'No, Charlsie. No! It's gone!'

It was Charlsie's moment. He glowered down at the wretched peddler, and took a chance.

'It's gone because I stopped it,' he said. 'I put a charm on the water to send it away. Now tell me somethin', me little Scotchman! Could I ha' done that if it was only some kind of a steam-engine across the water?'

He felt the awe all round him.

'Ye poor ignorant cuss, ye're not worth mindin'! I pity ye!' said Charlsie kindly.

'Och, look here! You go down to the town, and they'll tell ye there –'

Charlsie gave a laugh. It began deep inside him, where there was plenty of room, and rose in a throaty bellow.

'In the town! Oh – oh, my!' Charlsie was overcome. 'Ye'd better stick to sellin' buttons, master! He heard it in the town! An' he believed it! In the town! – where they're washin' themselves from mornin' to night, an' where they have to give each other little bits of cardboard to know who they are, an' get special knives out for t' eat a fish! There was a feller in the town thought he was Napoleon of the French! Oh, yes, the town! That's where they know everythin'! I'm sure!'

There was a howl of laughter.

It was a complete victory. The peddler protested and raged against their laughter, but he could do nothing to stop it; only Charlsie could do that, by a finger to his lips and a warning nod at the sea.

Charlsie watched McRae go stumping away in a fury without selling anything. His face was dark and thoughtful.

'Juan,' he said, loudly enough for others to hear, and with great conviction, 'this has given me an idea! Ye know, the sound of a tarroo-ushtey's voice would be a good thing t' imitate, as a warnin' to the ships; it needs a frightenin' sort of a noise. I've a mind to suggest that to th' English government! In fact I will; I'll send the letter now. An' describe how it can be done.'

He went indoors, where he felt weak now that the crisis was over; praying for the silence to continue, but ready to make another journey to the beach with a bunch of herbs. His luck held.

The foghorn did not sound again that day, or again for more than a week.

When at last it did, Charlsie reassured the village and bade them observe the sound: they would find, he said, that it was copied from the cry of the tarroo-ushtey, according to a simple invention of his own. They listened, and it was so.

446

He was often to be seen after that, sitting outside his home on foggy days, listening to the far-off hooting with a critical expression. When he went indoors, they said it was to write to the English government again, advising them.

Charlsie's fame as an inventor spread. He was rumoured to be working on a device for closing gates automatically, and another to condense water from clouds. Even strangers came to the village to have their ailments or troubles charmed away, or to undergo his new massage treatment.

But Duncan McRae did not sell another inch of elastic in the whole district.

Countess Ilona

BY ROBERT MULLER

Supernatural *is another fondly remembered late night series transmitted by the BBC in 1977. It was imaginatively made by its producer, Pieter Rogers, stylishly performed by its guest stars, and evocatively introduced to viewers: 'During the final years of the last century,' a sonorous voice would announce beneath the opening credits, 'there still stood a mansion in Limehouse, to the east of London, known as The House on the River. Here men with bizarre tastes would meet once a month in order to terrify each other by means of true stories of horror and the supernatural. Those story-tellers who failed to impress the assembly were – it is said – never seen again. Those who succeeded were permitted to join The Club of the Damned.' For each episode, the hosts Sir Francis Fell (Andre van Gyseghem) and Sir Charles (Esmond Knight) would receive the latest guest into the plush clubroom and then, after the sombre organ strains of the Poulene signature tune had faded away, invite them to begin. The stories included, 'Dorabella' a vampire tale set in Eastern Europe (starring Jeremy Clyde, Anna Marson and John Justin); 'Night of the Marionettes' about a descendent of Baron Frankenstein using the resurrected monster in a puppet show (with Gordon Jackson and Kathleen Byron); and a variation on the Jekyll and Hyde theme, 'Lady Sybil' (with Denholm Elliott and Cathleen Nesbitt). Jeremy Brett appeared as 'Mr Nightingale' a man haunted by a doppleganger who drives him to murder – but because his story was judged by the members to be the product of a deranged mind rather than a supernatural occurence he suffered the ultimate punishment of The Club of the Damned.*
Supernatural *was the creation of Robert Muller (1925–), a German-born former journalist and theatre critic, whose interest in*

Gothic literature had been fired while working on some of the adaptions for the ITV anthology Mystery and Imagination. *For his own series, however, he utilized the archetypal themes of Victorian ghost and horror stories but gave them modern and often nasty twists. Muller wrote all of the episodes except one, 'Viktoria' by Sue Lake, which recounted the story of a little girl avenging the death of her mother with the aid of black magic. The stars were Catherine Schell and Judy Cornwall – who became the only female to trick her way into the club to tell her story. Perhaps the very best of the stories was the one I have selected here, 'Countess Ilona', a werewolf tale directed by Simon Langton and starring Billie Whitelaw (who was Robert Muller's wife), Ian Hendry, John Fraser and Sandor Eles. An interesting footnote to this series was the appearance of Edward Hardwicke in 'Countess Ilona' where he came to an unpleasant end like Jeremy Brett – the actor with whom, of course, he would be reunited in 1986 in* The Adventures of Sherlock Holmes . . .

M R Pettifer was late. He hurried breathlessly down the corridor, a small, anxious, elderly man, followed rather more sedately by one of the Club servants who carried a candelabrum to light his way.

Grotesque shadows leapt and danced from flickering, dripping candles as the slight scurrying reached the door at the end of the passage. It led to the room where the more punctual members were assembled for the evening's meeting.

He tried the handle; the door was locked. Kneeling, he peered eagerly through the keyhole. The members had already taken their seats and a tall stocky stranger was standing on the dais, his back to the door. Mr Pettifer turned desperately to the sombre lackey: 'I must get in. I'm one of the judges. Can't you . . . ?'

The servant's face remained impassive, and his hand descended with finality on to Mr Pettifer's thin shoulder. Reluctantly, the little man dropped the handle and pressed his ear to the door. He could hear the new candidate begin his address:

'Gentlemen – my story, though it happened only a few years ago, will doubtless sound more appropriate to that pre-eminently superstitious era known as the Middle Ages, but I can guarantee its truth with my life; even with my honour, gentlemen, as a man whose very existence has been scarred – some would say, destroyed – by the horrendous facts I am about to relate.' The voice was pitched low and strong, with a faint mid-European accent . . .

*

449

An excellent example of Gothic architecture is Castle Tyrrh, which stands remote in the wild and rugged country-side of Eastern Hungary. It was built by the murderous robber-barons who infested that land long ago, and to them its grim aspect and inaccessibility, the danger to prying travellers from the wild beasts in the surrounding woods, were inestimable advantages.

The castle was – and is yet! – inhabited by the elegant Ilona, Countess Tyrrh. She presides over her estate as to the manner born, so that the most discerning observer might never guess her penurious origins; for Ilona was born the bastard daughter of a tradeswoman, and reared in the reeking slums of Budapest. From the first she was determined to rise from the slime of the streets, and being gifted with talent and beauty as well as intelligence, she managed to earn quite a reasonable living as a café entertainer. In this she was helped, as one might expect, by the numerous men she attracted, and eventually she entered an older and more lucrative profession. After all, such as she have little to lose.

During the course of her dubious career she shook off every trace of that squalid poverty to which she might have seemed destined from birth, and finally achieved respectable admission to the leisured class. For, following her childhood deprivation and ignominious success as the most desired and expensive courtesan of the city, came the unexpected arrangement of her calamitous marriage to the Count.

To Ilona, it seemed a fairy-tale climax in a life of hardship and struggle. At thirty she was not quite so attractive as before, and her future was uncertain. But now, thanks to a blessed quirk of fate, she could marry her prince and live happily ever after in peace and security. It was all she had ever wanted. Ask, and it shall be given – to your cost, usually, or too late.

Count Anton Tyrrh was a man whose evil nature made the worst reprobates in the land shudder. His peers shunned him, and despised him for a violent, uncivilized brute. As for the common folk, they regarded him with superstitious horror; in that unenlightened country myths and legends still cling in the popular imagination even as the new scientific theories fascinate modern minds here. The Count came from contaminated stock, and such tales were whispered of his bestial viciousness, of his unnatural, rabid cruelty, that his name became a byword in his province for all that was abhorrent and dreaded. This was the man Ilona, in her ignorance of his true nature, married. But he did not long survive the union; within twelve months he was dead, and ambiguous, fearful rumours surrounded that death.

The same year which brought the marriage and demise of the Count also saw the birth of Ilona's son Bela, the sole heir. And exactly ten years afterwards — that is, on 13 March 1880 — the Countess Ilona chose to invite four old friends to the castle for a very special reunion party.

That morning began as usual. At dawn Ilona took her dog, a giant docile wolfhound, for a walk through the wooded grounds. As she re-entered the Castle her highly-trained servants bowed dutifully. She passed through the main hall, and only her little maid Magda, who regarded the Countess with awed devotion, glanced around to see that no one was looking and quickly crossed herself as her mistress swept up the staircase to her room.

Magda felt apprehensive about the arrival of the expected guests. Downstairs it was whispered that there was a man from the past whom the Countess hated with a vindictive and implacable hatred, and Magda knew from painful experience that it was not wise to arouse the Countess's wrath. Still, maybe the Lady had decided to forgive and forget, though she'd heard even more terrible rumours about —

'Magda! Stop gawking, girl, and fetch the Countess's tray.'

The stern voice belonged to the major-domo, Andras. Magda dropped a curtsey and shot off to the kitchens like a startled rabbit.

In her room, Ilona stretched luxuriously on her bed in the half-darkness, sleek and contented. Maturity suited her. Her slender figure in the thin white negligé was a little more rounded than formerly, perhaps; but the vicissitudes of her life were etched only faintly in the fine lines around her large expressive eyes, which grew impenetrable as a cat's when she dreamed her secret dreams.

Presently there was a knock at her door and Andras entered with her breakfast. Quietly and methodically he set down the tray and poured her coffee into a Meissen cup. He broke a fresh egg on to the meal of steak tartare and sprinkled it with seasoning. Then he straightened. A tremor crossed his strong features; his gloved hands remained extended over the tray like a penitent's.

Languidly Ilona reached out and began to draw off the white gloves, finger by finger, in a half-playful, caressing gesture. It was the voluptuous, private ritual of two long-familiar lovers.

They did not hear the thunderous knocking on the main door, which Magda hastened to open. She admitted a tubby, buoyant teddy-bear of a man in a hairy overcoat who announced himself as Zoltan Vinzenz, grumbled good-naturedly over the discomfort of his journey and demanded the whereabouts of his hostess in a loud, wheezy, genial voice.

'The Countess is in her room, sir,' said Magda timidly, helping to relieve him of his hat and coat.

'What, not down yet? Shame on her! Ye gods, what a mausoleum.' He stopped short as he surveyed the great echoing hall which, in spite of its rich furnishings, still managed to sustain an atmosphere of medieval gloom. 'Poor Ilona, buried alive in such a place! Miles from anywhere civilized! Ah well, fortunes of war as they say. Now then girl, I've travelled all night and I'm hungry as a wolf. What do you propose to do about it? Eh?'

'There is a buffet for the gentlemen.' Magda indicated a long table laden with delicacies at the side of the hall.

'Splendid! That's more like it, eh? This country air gives one an appetite, what?' This last remark was addressed to no one in particular. In the course of it he strode across to the table, grabbing cutlery and napkins from one of the silent servants in attendance, and began heaping a plate with salmon. Just for a second, with a forkful half-way to his mouth, he paused. Some prickling instinct seemed to warn him that he was being watched by eyes other than the servants'. He glanced quickly and uneasily towards the gallery which ran the length of the hall. Nothing there, of course. Creepy places, these moribund old castles.

Zoltan shrugged and applied himself avidly to his favourite occupation. He had known Ilona for years, for they had both been born in the same grimy district. When revolutions had broken out all over Europe thirty years before, few had raised the flag of protest more enthusiastically than that thin, ragged idealist, Zoltan Vinzenz. In fact he had spent a year in a sordid Prussian jail as punishment for his subversive activities. It was here that Zoltan had learned his first lesson in expediency. Later he had managed to accommodate himself to an important fact of politics; that no matter what radical changes are made in policy or personnel, government ultimately means the oppression of the miserable majority by the happy few who rule. Quieting his conscience with the logics of self-interest, therefore, Zoltan decided he didn't want to be a member of the down-trodden masses any more.

He became a sort of mercenary-by-proxy, that is to say, an arms merchant; a dubious profession no doubt, but a very remunerative one. For a number of years now he had been a confidential agent of Otto von Bismarck who, given his head at that time, would willingly have shot dead the likes of Herr Vinzenz for their attempted revolt in 1848. This irony was not lost on Zoltan, and he congratulated himself frequently on his shrewdness and success – witness the valuable masterpieces, mistresses and mansions he had almost carelessly accumulated on his way to the top of his profession; all due to living at peace with his idealistic and, happily, volatile fellow men! After all, people always appreciated the painstaking suppliers of their basic needs. Give them the means to murder each other, and they were grateful for his contribution to whatever cause they supported! And a happy, sympathetic chap like him got on terribly well with most of his important customers. With a proper understanding of mankind, life was really very simple.

Suddenly a familiar scent assailed his nostrils. He wrinkled his nose in a disgusted, anticipatory grimace, then turned with a hearty smile on his round face to welcome the newcomer.

'Why, Felix! I might have known!'

'Zoltan, my dear fellow!' If the second guest also felt a qualm of repulsion at meeting his old acquaintance, it hardly showed. Dr Felix Kraus, a slim, well-preserved man, stepped forward eagerly and the two embraced with a convincing show of mutual enthusiasm.

'What a surprise! I had no idea you were invited!'

'You were an obvious choice,' said Zoltan, returning to his meal. 'Ilona's always adored you. But frankly, I'm surprised she asked me. D'you know what her last words to me were, when I saw her ten years ago? She said to me, she said, "Hell is too good for you, my dear Zoltan." She's planning something strange if you ask me.' He nodded wisely and spooned more caviare on to his plate.

Felix was hardly listening. He had just noticed the pretty Magda, who was standing demurely at the end of the table; his eyes gleamed for a moment with an expression of furtive lust. Zoltan noticed with distaste the subtle layer of make-up that the doctor had applied to his face, once handsome, but now bearing the marks of continual debauchery so plainly to experienced eyes. If there was one thing Zoltan detested more thoroughly than a prating moralist, it was a conceited and ageing fool.

Felix wrenched his attention back to Zoltan. 'Ah, yes, quite,' he said vaguely. 'Tell me, has our hostess put in an appearance yet? Who else is invited, do you know?'

'There's no guest list,' said Zoltan flatly. 'And it's too early for Ilona. She'll be making up or dressing I expect, you know what women are. None better, eh?' he spluttered, digging Felix clumsily in the ribs and spilling caviare on to his sleeve. 'But seriously, why don't you join me in some of this excellent food? You must be hungry after your journey.'

'No, thank you; my weight, you know,' said Felix, patting his taut stomach. He turned abruptly to Magda.

'My dear Fräulein, may I be shown to my room now?'

Magda glanced at Andras, who had entered the hall a few minutes before and was watching the guests with interest. He nodded to her curtly.

'Of course, sir.'

'How's the killing business?' was Felix's parting shot.

'It flourishes, my friend,' called Zoltan through a mouthful of fish. He glanced at the keen, intelligent face of the major-domo and chortled coarsely. 'Bread and murder!' he proclaimed. 'Two of mankind's indispensable commodities, son. Bakers and hangmen never starve. It's true, you needn't smile. Now then, is there any more of this delicious caviare?'

While Andras organized fresh supplies, Felix followed the maid up the wide staircase and along the gallery. The walls were adorned with the Tyrrh family portraits, and a haughty, sensual lot they looked, thought Felix. Some of the faces bore the unmistakeable stamp of depravity or insanity. 'Anton, Count Tyrrh. 1820–1870', read the metal plate fixed beneath the last portrait. Felix paused and glanced up expectantly; the canvas was blank. Gazing at the empty frame, an unpleasant feeling of insecurity assailed him. Perhaps Ilona couldn't bear to look at her deplorable husband's likeness? Well, he could understand that.

A sudden crash from a nearby room made him start and turn, but all was still. Only Magda was present, waiting patiently outside his room. He followed her into the comfortable apartment, marvelling at her downcast serenity. She reminded him, as did all the servants here, of the kind of human still life Vermeer had painted. Too long in the atmosphere of this castle, he reflected, would have excoriated the nerves of lesser mortals. Maybe they were simply too stupid and otiose to notice.

Magda watched him with covert admiration as he flung down his travelling-case and reclined carelessly on the large bed. His self-assured charm struck her not as vain and dissolute, but exotic and exciting, just as Felix had intended.

'Now then, my dear, tell me your name and why we have been invited here.'

'It's Magda, sir, and I don't know, I haven't asked,' she answered shyly, flattered at his interest.

'You have a charming voice, Magda. It's sensual but not vulgar. Will you visit me in the afternoon, at about three-thirty?' He smiled at her astonished look. 'We haven't time to equivocate, have we? You see, my dear, I am an erotomane, that is, an indefatigable pursuer of lovely women. I used to be a doctor, a nerve specialist, but I gave that up after an old and ugly aunt of mine died and left me a lot of money, which I squander at will on my favourite hobby. I usually get what I want, and I want you.'

'Sir?' Magda stared vapidly, bewildered at his frank attack.

'Unless, of course, you have some squalid arrangement with that strapping fellow downstairs?'

'Oh no, sir,' said Magda guilelessly. 'Andras is more ambitious you see, sir.'

Felix turned away to hide a grin. So Ilona hadn't changed. She hadn't really changed at all.

The Countess did not appear for lunch. The meal passed quietly and afterwards the guests sought their rooms, one sleepy, the other hopeful.

Over the distant Transylvanian mountains grey clouds gathered and muttered, threatening storms. The beasts and birds of the forest fell silent, sensing thunder in the clammy atmosphere. The castle too was silent. Everybody seemed to be taking an afternoon rest.

In his nursery three doors away from Felix's room, the little Count Tyrrh moped and yawned over his book. He was tired of studying and bored with staying in. It was all the fault of those friends of Mama's; he wasn't to disturb them by playing or making a noise. Bela had peeked at the two men from the gallery when they were in the hall and found the one with the loud laugh rather vulgar and frightening, and he hadn't much cared for the other one either, the one who smiled and didn't mean it.

It was very stuffy in the nursery and he had pins and needles in his left foot. He wished Andras would come in and tell him a story or play a game; Andras was his friend. If it hadn't been for Nanny sitting there watching him he would have been tempted to go in search of Andras. She seemed to be asleep but you could never tell with Nanny, she was so old and clever she could see even with her eyes closed, a feat Bela regarded as enviable and rather awe-inspiring.

Sylva had nursed the young Tyrrhs for three generations. She sat ancient and upright in her hard wooden chair, fragile with age, her will unswervingly directed to the protection of her young charge. Suddenly her eyes opened wide.

'You must read your book, my child.'

Bela started resentfully at the cadaverous, spindly figure. 'Why?' he muttered. 'I hate them! I hate all books, Nanny, this one most of all!' He flung the book angrily into the fireplace.

Sylva ignored the tantrum. 'You must read,' she insisted quietly, retrieving the book.

'But Nanny,' wailed the child, 'It makes me dream! Such awful dreams!'

The old woman softened. Bela had inherited his mother's classically perfect features and huge lustrous eyes; he was difficult to resist. Besides, his distress was genuine.

'Would you like a glass of milk, little one?'

Bela nodded, and Sylva went to fetch it. As soon as she was gone Bela scrambled up on to a high stool and took a colourful book of fairy-tales from the shelf. He started violently as the door swung open again – but it was only Andras.

'Come and look at this, Andras!' cried the child excitedly. Andras took the book from him. It fell open at the story of Little Red Riding Hood. There was a lurid illustration of the heroine on her way through the woods, with a huge and vicious-looking wolf skulking in the trees, its blood-red tongue hanging from jaws lined with jagged yellowish teeth. In the white spaces of the picture other wolves had been drawn by a childish hand.

Andras looked askance. 'What do you mean by this, Bela?'

'It's my dream,' explained the boy. 'Lots of wolves, with glowing eyes, hiding in the forest. But this story doesn't end how you tell it, Andras. The wolf became the grandmother; why was that? And it says the hunter killed the wolf with his knife but you always say it was killed with a silver bullet.'

Andras smiled grimly at the child's chatter. 'The wolf only pretended to be the grandmother,' he said. 'And the silver bullet is our secret.'

Suddenly Sylva appeared at the door, pale and angry. She shuffled into the room and put her arms protectively round Bela, staring at Andras with a look of mingled fear and loathing.

'Go!' she cried shrilly.

Andras's handsome, saturnine features twisted in a scowl. 'The boy is ten years old – he ought to be told! You, his nurse,' he added contemptuously, 'you understand nothing!'

Sylva glanced involuntarily at a huge antique cutlass which hung on the wall. Andras followed her gaze and laughed tauntingly. 'That thing's no use. Remember: the bullet made of silver!' He flung the book of fairy-tales contemptuously into the fire and strode out.

The door slammed behind him, and Bela began to cry.

'Bela, my precious, I will never let it harm you, never,' crooned the old woman, and she rocked the frightened child in her arms until he grew calmer.

*

456

A major tragedy had occurred while Ilona's third guest was walking from the railway station to the castle. Hugo Hoffman, the great musician, had stepped into a puddle and mud had splattered on to his new and costly beige trousers. The scarcely-suppressed rage and sorrow he experienced as a result of this sad accident was aggravated by the inordinate length of time it took him to reach his destination. He had miscalculated the distance by several miles. Also, the village lad he had hired to carry his luggage was panting tiresomely with fatigue before they had come half-way, and the stupid creature would stop, with such a look of terrified distress, every time a branch cracked in the forest, or a timber-wolf howled from the mountains! Really, it was too bad. Hugo reached the doors of Castle Tyrrh in a grievous state of exhausted vexation. He would not have undertaken such a journey again for a kingdom.

Andras opened the doors and Hugo tottered inside.

'Tip him,' he snapped, and Andras tossed a coin to the lad, who dumped all of Hugo's suitcases in the hall and raced off home as if the Devil were after him.

Hugo refused refreshment and was shown immediately to his room, where he threw himself on to the bed and endeavoured to rest and restore his ragged nerves. Instead he lay awake and fretted.

Why hadn't Ilona greeted him personally? Would these fools of provincial servants be able to understand that he must have his bath drawn at a temperature of 27° precisely? That he required white roses in his room because they soothed him? – In a word, were they capable of taking proper care of him? They looked a dumb and churlish lot, though the major-demo was rather attractive. Still, in general, he preferred women. Ilona had always appreciated that his genius must be protected and nurtured. She was the only person who had ever really understood him.

One day he would die, the flesh would fall from his bones with some frightful wasting disease, then they'd all be sorry, and serve them right, the philistines! No, artists simply must be given special consideration, for life treated them so cruelly. Heaven knew he did his best to preserve his talents for the world, but he did feel the need of a strong, sympathetic and loving personality to help him along his thorny path.

He'd never been robust. Geniuses seldom were. And what was it, two years now since he'd composed anything? Even his love life was on the wane. Maybe he was fading away already! He got off the bed to look, but as he reached the mirror a distant timber-wolf flung a long keening howl into the twilight. Hugo shuddered and drew the curtains. What kind of wilderness had he strayed into?

Returning to the mirror, he peered anxiously at his almost girlishly handsome face. Yes, he was showing signs of strain. Soon his youth would be gone. He sat on the bed disconsolately, his lip trembling.

Hugo had changed greatly from the lad of twenty-two Ilona had known, when he was striving for the recognition of his musical gifts in a harsh and indifferent world. Eventually he had found his fame, but success had proved catalytic to the vices and morbidities of his weak character.

Outside his door, Andras paused and listened. All was quiet. He made his way to Ilona's room and slipped inside. She was at the window, watching the rising moon.

'Only three of them have arrived so far.'

'There should be four,' answered Ilona regretfully. 'But it's too late for the other to come now. No coach will venture into this region after dusk.'

'There will be one to pay the price,' murmured Andras.

Ilona smiled.

In the great hall a long table had been set for dinner. The crystal and silver glittered in the light from the blazing chandeliers. Zoltan was the first down, warming himself at the enormous roaring fire and devouring the champagne and canapés which Andras and Magda were serving. He was joined a few minutes later by his fellow-guests.

'Any ideas as to why we've been invited?' asked Zoltan.

'We are all ex-friends of the Countess,' said Hugo, sipping critically at his wine.

'Ex-lovers, you mean,' said Zoltan blandly. 'And rich. We could afford her. I bought her the Esterhazy diamond, you know.'

Hugo wrinkled his delicate nose in distaste at this vulgarity.

'What puzzles me is the occasion,' persisted Zoltan. 'I mean, are we meant to be celebrating the tenth anniversary of her marriage, or old Tyrrh's death, or the child's birthday, or what? Eh!'

'I should think her husband's death must be the chief cause for rejoicing,' said Felix with a grimace.

'I think she killed him,' said Hugo unexpectedly.

Felix shook his head and Zoltan roared with laughter. 'Ilona? Nonsense! She couldn't kill a rabbit! – And here she is! My dear . . .'

He broke off quickly as he spied Ilona descending the staircase, proud and magnificent in an exquisite white evening gown. In her hair she wore the legendary Esterhazy diamond, as a compliment to Zoltan, perhaps, or to tease him. They greeted her effusively. After a great deal of hand-kissing and flattery, Ilona seated herself at the table and her guests followed suit. Their sense of nostalgia was keen; ten years seemed to have slipped away like a night's rest.

'I must apologize for the absence of our fourth guest, my friends,' said Ilona. 'Unfortunately the leader of his Majesty's unofficial opposition insists on travelling in his own coach, and I fear the heavy rains have delayed him.'

There was a general gasp.

'Von Haller? What, you and that – that devious rascal!'

'But Ilona, he's such a dreadful bore! All he ever talks about is politics!'

'How could you bear his company?'

Ilona laughed and changed the subject. 'It's good to see you all looking so prosperous!' She leaned back and raised her glass. 'What shall we all drink to? What do we hold most dear?'

'Why love, surely,' said Felix, with his charming smile.

'No, art,' exclaimed Hugo petulantly. 'It's the only thing that matters, ultimately.'

'Money,' contradicted Zoltan. 'People can provide both love and art, and people, thank God, can always be bought. Anyhow, here's to you, Ilona!'

'The great experience of all our lives,' supplied Felix hastily.

They raised their glasses and drank. The evening passed pleasantly enough with wine and laughter, and much re-living of old times.

Over coffee Zoltan, in his cups, began holding forth about his friend and hero, Bismarck.

'Say what you like,' he said dogmatically, waving his glass, 'democracies will never achieve the great feats despotism has produced. Blood and iron, that's what's needed today.'

'Yes, the Chancellor's managed to make a virtue out of ruthlessness,' yawned Felix. 'He seems to have bought peace and security with it. I can't see Germany ever embarking on another major war in Europe. But the blood-letting, my dear fellow! Atrocious!'

'The masses, what do they matter?' cried Zoltan heatedly. 'Most are born to die for the grand designs of tyrants, and they're happy to do so for a living wage!'

'All this must be very boring for our hostess. It's boring for me, at any rate,' Hugo interrupted truculently. 'Ilona, may I ask you about the late Count? Was he really as appalling as his reputation?'

Zoltan chuckled. 'He thinks you killed him.'

'Then Hugo is mistaken,' she replied calmly. 'The Count was killed in a hunting accident, attacked by wolves, you know. I'm afraid he suffered a great deal.'

The awkward pause this statement produced was broken by the appearance of Bela; the guests turned to the boy with relief, and Ilona introduced him.

'What an angel!' cried Felix.

Hugo, sensing competition, turned away. He did so hate to be out of the limelight.

'Here, little fellow!' shouted Zoltan boisterously, tossing the child a gold coin which he ignored, pressing close to his mother and regarding the strangers with round-eyed solemnity.

'Give him some candied fruit, Felix, he loves it,' suggested Ilona.

Felix assumed his best bedside manner. 'He will grow into a fine young man,' he pronounced, offering the sweets. Privately he thought that this oppressive, isolated old place was the worst possible environment for such a sensitive, intelligent-looking youngster. Still, it wasn't his problem . . . or was it?

When the child had accepted a candied pear and trotted obediently up to bed, Zoltan bluntly remarked that it was strange the boy had turned out so beautiful, the late Count having been quite the most hideous man he'd ever met.

'Really, you are so tactless, Zoltan,' Hugo snapped peevishly.

'It's true,' returned Ilona sweetly. 'Andras, Herr Hoffman's glass is empty. It seems unlikely, anyway, that my son was fathered by a man as repulsive as Anton.'

She paused while Hugo's glass was refilled, to let them absorb the implications of her remark. Andras handed her an old music-box with a little dancing couple on the lid. To the strains of a tinkling Strauss waltz she continued, smiling at no-one in particular.

'Do you remember that summer ten years ago, when we all behaved so . . . badly? The summer little Bela was conceived. And now, it is time to bid you all good-night, and may I wish you a restful first night under my roof.'

She snapped shut the lid of the box and rose. The men followed suit, and bowed as she left the table. Felix lit a cigar with a thoughtful air.

'Strange that Ilona should mention the Count's death like that,' he remarked. 'The way I heard it, he did not die immediately from his accident, but a few months later, of lycanthropy.'

'What the Devil's that?' demanded Zoltan.

'Clinically speaking, it's a disease in which the patient, usually a lunatic, suffers delusions of transformation into a wolf during the hours of darkness.'

Hugo paled. 'A werewolf, you mean? But there are no such things!'

'Precisely,' answered Felix. 'It's a mental affliction. Our ancestors, in their superstitious ignorance, would have called the sickness atavism, that is, devil-dealing in order to produce a throwback to the nature of a beast. The subject was supposed to absorb and develop the more savage qualities of the brute in question, for example its strength, its sexual prowess –'

'But that's absurd!' protested Hugo, badly upset. He took a gulp of wine, made a face and turned on Andras in sudden fury. 'This is inferior wine! Filthy stuff! How dare you serve it?' He flung his glass into the grate and glared at Felix as if it was all his fault.

'What are they said to look like, these creatures?'

'Oh, enormous and very hairy, half-man, half-beast. Their strength and aggression are abnormal, and so is their craving for human flesh. They have claws for hands, and their eyes –'

'That's enough! I won't listen to any more!' Hugo stood up abruptly and marched off to bed.

'Well, he did ask,' murmured Felix. He wondered with professional interest how long it would be before young Hugo developed some crippling disorder to match his emotional hypochondria. That's what usually happened to that type of neurotic, in Felix's experience.

'He's a pathetic creature.' Zoltan took a swig of brandy. 'Well, I think I'll turn in, too.'

When she was sure everybody had retired, Magda left her bed and tiptoed along the gallery to Felix's room. Suddenly she sensed a movement in the shadows; she stifled a scream as Andras's tall figure loomed before her. He spoke caustically:

'There's no need to wait up, the fourth guest won't be arriving tonight. You slut!' he added viciously; for a moment she thought he would strike her, but he strode past her and down the staircase. Trembling and bewildered, Magda hurried to Felix's door and opened it quietly. Felix turned with a look of expectation, which dissolved into ill-concealed disappointment. Magda stopped short.

'You expected my mistress,' she said flatly.

Felix shrugged, then smiled, and drew her into the room.

'Not another word from you, my dear,' he whispered, 'Till dawn.'

In his room Hugo, about to undress, suddenly felt strange. He swayed alarmingly and clutched his throbbing forehead. It was as though he'd been poisoned . . . the wine!

With an effort he staggered to the door, calling for Andras in a hoarse whisper; his throat was dry and burning. He found the staircase and wandered down it, weaving like a drunken man, reeling against the wall. It was all so weird and misty; he was sick, all the proportions were distorted, somebody had drugged him, the dying fire

461

and guttering candles throwing crazy red shadows in the dusky corners of the great hall, it was getting difficult to see, suddenly there was a door in front of him with a big brass handle, it was all getting senseless, any minute now he'd be on his knees asleep, no it couldn't be . . .

The organ case was Gothic, the gold embossed pipes extended to the high ceiling, there must be twenty steps leading up to the instrument and the whole vast room seemed like some unholy cathedral. Hugo stumbled and crawled towards the organ and half-fell upon the stool.

In his delirium he began to play wild discordant music, a requiem for a maniac. Then his sweating hands faltered over the cold white keys: something was behind him. Slowly, trembling, he turned.

It was Ilona, serene and beautiful in black, reclining gracefully upon the steps.

'My darling, I knew you would come!' he cried feverishly. 'You arranged all of this, didn't you? – This reunion, so that we could meet again! Ilona, I always loved you!'

'You loved so many things, Hugo,' she murmured. 'Wealth, fame, adulation, and now you have them all. Your musical genius is acknowledged; you're married to a rich princess. Strange that you cannot be content!'

'All my success is due to you, Ilona,' he said humbly. 'You sold yourself over and over again to keep me alive when I was starving in Budapest. You gave me your faith when nobody else believed. I had to leave you behind, my dearest friend, when I found acceptance in those exalted circles which would neither have understood nor welcomed you; such is the way of the world. And what has happened to me since? My genius, my zest for life, even my potency are diminishing with the years. My wife and I are separated; my fame withers. I am an artist, I have special needs, Ilona, and only you can supply them!' His voice rose to a childish wail, and tears of maudlin self-pity stood in his eyes. Covering her white hand with kisses, he begged,

'Come back to me, Ilona! Help me find peace!'

'Dear Hugo. For all you did for me, you shall have peace.' She rose and left him, and his eyes followed her with a kind of wondering adoration. To think he had once abandoned her to the streets, left her desolate and penniless while he wandered in the bright rich pastures of renown! And she had not uttered one word of blame; she would save him again! His fingers caressed the organ-keys, for only music could express his exuberance; his world was suddenly expanded, filled with elation and joy.

But what was that black hunched thing, looking out of the night to seek the lighted window? What kind of a creature was it that could stand upright to lunge its great bulk so savagely against the glass?

The night was very still. Hugo sat, frozen with shock, as the thick glass burst with a splintering crash and the beast scrambled like a dog into the room. It crouched, fixing him with burning yellow eyes, teeth bared in a venomous snarl; then it crept towards him, silently, closing for the kill. Hugo screamed, and ran like a madman for the door, but the thing was after him; it tore him down with an easy spring, and he felt its teeth fasten on his shoulder while the great claws gouged at his flesh.

The death agonies of Hugo Hoffman rang through the stillness like a scream of torment from the very depths of hell, arousing the sleepers in that silent castle from dreams to a nightmare.

It was Zoltan who found the room leading off from the main hall and discovered the corpse. His digestion was none the better for it. Felix Kraus had seen nothing like it since wartime, but experience and professionalism sustained his composure. He made a clinical examination of the badly-mauled body and concluded that the cause of death was a wild-beast attack. He and Zoltan refused to let Ilona view the sickening sight, and so she quieted and dismissed the frightened servants and went to reassure her little boy, who was shrieking with nightmares of prowling, yellow-eyed wolves.

Zoltan, when he had recovered sufficiently, whispered to Felix through chattering teeth that Ilona's motives were now clear, for Hugo, who, she had implied, was the father of her son, had paid the penalty for his past misuse of her. Felix agreed, evincing the belief that he had been invited so as to issue the necessary death certificate. As for Zoltan, he was presumably needed as a witness.

Considerably relieved, the two surviving guests took themselves to their beds, and passed the rest of the night peacefully enough, confident that they had found out the reason, or pretext, for Ilona's reunion party.

At the Club of the Damned, the story-teller briefly paused in his narrative.

'And perhaps they were right, although some of you may be wondering why Ilona had chosen to invite four guests and not three, if three were all she required for her purposes. But, gentlemen, I see that the hour is come when you generally take some refreshment, and I confess my throat is quite dry. May I propose a short interval?'

There was a murmur of agreement and much pushing back

of chairs, followed by subdued but intense discussion of the stranger's story.

Mr Pettifer turned impatiently to the patient lackey:

'Now will you open this door?'

A key was produced, the door was unlocked and Mr Pettifer was finally allowed to enter. He grabbed a glass of claret from a passing waiter and got as close as he could to the stranger, who was relaxing with his drink in a corner. He gazed earnestly at the man, and what he saw shocked him beyond measure. For sometimes the bereft of sight see clearer than their neighbours; Mr Pettifer, with only his two ears and his imagination to aid him, had built up certain mental images as he listened to the bizarre story. He shivered as he encountered the man's strange tawny-coloured eyes, and there was something odd about his mouth. Perversely, it was disfigured when he smiled, the front teeth were too long and somehow the grin gave a cold and menacing aspect to the otherwise handsome face, with its head of thick and prematurely-greying hair.

A terrifying suspicion gripped Mr Pettifer. Could this be the wolf, the werewolf? 'My life has been . . . destroyed . . .' The words bit into the old man's memory. What happened to that face when the moon was full?

Mr Pettifer glanced round frantically. He must warn the members of the monster in their midst; the creature must be stopped!

'To continue, gentleman.' The candidate resumed his place on the dais and the room grew still. Mr Pettifer sank into a chair, watching him with horrified fascination.

'I have said that the Countess Ilona invited four guests to her castle. The fourth, delayed by heavy rains you will recall, completed his journey in a hired coach and arrived the morning after the slaughter of Hugo Hoffman.'

Josef, Baron von Haller, was a man driven solely by a will to power. Is it possible to climb the grimy ladder of political success and remain untainted by corruption? Not if Josef was typical. His enemies considered him a person of unrivalled deceit, but to the public and his supporters he was known as 'the man of principle'. He looked the part, which helped: blond, monocled, erect, even somewhat military in appearance; a real Siegfried, and evidently a man of uncommon common sense. He was horrified beyond words to be greeted at the castle with the news of Hugo's gruesome death, and repelled by its sinister implications. A wild beast attack? Nonsense! Who ever heard of an animal actually breaking into a building? Josef did not quite

464

know what was going on, but he did know that a cool head and a firm hand were called for, and by Jove, he was the one to supply them! He was determined to conduct a proper investigation and get to the bottom of the whole affair. If there was a murderer loose, they might all be in danger!

He recoiled angrily from Zoltan's tales of werewolves. Such superstition was no more than one might expect from a newly-rich peasant like him. Equally repugnant were Dr Kraus's hints that he, or any of then, might be the father of Ilona's son.

'It's true,' insisted Felix, 'and she loved Hugo best, you know. He was more than a mere lover to her.'

'Do you think that's perhaps why . . . ?' Josef ventured.

'Why he was murdered?' Felix continued. 'It seems likely. But the fact is, Baron, poor Hoffman was torn apart and partly devoured. Nothing human could have done that. He was barely recognizable when we found him.'

Josef was at a loss for an answer to this; it wasn't making any sense.

'I knew of Hoffman, of course,' he mused. 'Heard him play once or twice. A bit showy, I thought. Socially dead for years, of course.'

'He's literally dead now, in any case,' repeated Zoltan patiently. 'Attacked by wolves. Sure you won't have any lunch?'

'Really, Herr Vinzenz, how can you eat at a time like this?' said Josef primly.

'You'll have to address me differently soon,' chuckled Zoltan. 'I'm buying a title, as you bought yours, Baron, some years ago. And I believe it's the bane of Christianity, this denigration of the normal desires. Drink, and we are told our livers will rot; fornicate – eh, Felix? – paralysis and insanity loom. "Thirsty evils", both! But if a man has a healthy appetite, will good food kill him?' He patted his enormous paunch complacently. 'Of course not! It's all scientific mumbo-jumbo and religious hypocrisy, this prudish holier-than-thou attitude adopted by some of our revered politicians! Still, I expect it catches a few votes.'

Josef did not deign to reply, but Felix remarked, in a moment of unusual gloom, 'It's true though, my friend. We do die of our pleasures.'

Andras approached them from the shadows of the hall and addressed the Baron.

'I have informed the Countess of your arrival, sir. The Countess hopes you will understand that she is most distressed by Herr Hoffman's death and wishes to keep to her bed today. But she will be delighted to dine with you this evening.'

465

'Just a minute, fellow,' said Josef sharply. 'Tell me, has anything like last night's tragedy happened here before? I heard that the late Count was also attacked by wild beasts. Some kind of hunting accident, I believe?'

'We all entered service here after the Count's death,' replied Andras stolidly. 'Nothing untoward has occurred since, to my knowledge, sir.'

'Send for the police,' Josef ordered, and the ghost of a smile crossed the servant's features.

'The police would not come here, Baron. It is a tradition.'

'Why, then, summon a coach from the village! Or saddle me a horse! I will go myself to make a proper report!'

Polite and impassive, Andras met the Baron's gaze.

'The coachman from the village regrettably met with an accident last night, sir, and we keep no horses here.'

'I think Andras is telling us that the Countess does not wish us to leave yet,' interrupted Felix. 'Am I right?'

'The Countess wishes your every order to be carried out to the letter, gentlemen.' Was there a trace of a sneer in the man's voice? He turned and left.

Josef muttered and fumed, marching up and down the room, no longer attempting to conceal his agitation.

'It's rather entertaining to see you so frightened, Josef,' remarked Felix with a wicked grin. 'Strange that Ilona shows no sign of fear, don't you think?'

Josef was, in fact, very disturbed by the events of the past twenty-four hours. First the harrowing journey to this God-forsaken place, and then to be met with the news of last night's tragedy! He did not care two pins for the dead Hugo, though it seemed likely that he had not had fair play, but his politician's instinct warned him away immediately from the scent of scandal. Ilona could murder half the province for all he cared; the important thing was to get out of this or any kind of dubious situation without calumny.

Besides, those machine-like, blank-eyed servants got on his nerves; he'd taken particular exception to Andras, with his quiet insolence. Altogether, the claustrophobic atmosphere of the castle was depressing. He had expected a gay party, not a gathering in a morgue. No, there was only one thing for it: coach or no coach, he must leave as soon as he could and if that dreadful old roué Kraus and his food-slobbering companion had any sense, they'd join him.

In the afternoon the two other guests went to their rooms. Zoltan was sleepy after his enormous lunch, and Felix evidently had his eye on that plump maid. All comforts supplied, thought Josef wryly. He

466

followed their example, tired after his journey. The air was close and clammy with the approaching storm, and he was soon asleep.

Bela left the nursery when all the guests had retired and went to stare at the blank frame which should have held his father's portrait. The sight of it always made him want to cry. He thrust his hands in his pockets and wandered back down the gallery, past the nursery where wizened old Sylva sat as if moulded to the furniture. She turned her head like a blind animal as he passed.

Ilona was still in bed when he entered her room. She took him in her arms and rocked him as if he had been ten months, and not ten years old, singing him lullabies and feeding him candied fruits from her own fingers.

'Mama, when shall we be alone again?' he asked wistfully. 'I don't like these visitors. I wish they'd go away!'

'Soon, very soon, my little love,' she murmured. 'But you mustn't worry about anything that happens. For you there is nothing to fear. Now, will you go back to the nursery? It's getting late and Mama must dress for dinner. Sylva will take good care of you.'

Her eyes followed the child with a kind of yearning despair as he left the room. She smiled bleakly at Magda, who had come to dress her:

'Never have a child!' she muttered, softly and intensely. 'Never have a child!'

The storm hung dry and brooding in the still air, until it burst in a fury as the guests were assembling for dinner. Ominous growls of thunder were preceded by vivid lightning flashes which lit the great hall with intermittent brilliance throughout the meal.

It was a gloomy enough occasion. Felix and Zoltan were experiencing an uneasy sensation of déjà-vu, though they tried to keep up some sort of social conversation. Josef, preoccupied and tense, picked at the sumptuous food and said little. All of Ilona's gaiety, for she was very high-spirited that evening, could not arouse him.

'Well, Josef,' she sighed, settling back in her chair when dinner was over, 'It's wonderful to see you looking so prosperous, so noble and handsome! Success suits you.'

Josef smiled frigidly, and answered with his usual decorum:

'I'm delighted to see you again, Ilona, and in spite of the tragedy, looking more lovely than ever.'

It was true. Her eyes were sparkling with youthful joy; radiant and sensuous, she turned to Felix.

'As for you, my friend, you're incorrigible! Poor Magda, she couldn't resist you, could she?'

Felix shrugged vainly, rather pleased at this public tribute to his virility.

'Did you know she had bad blood?' Ilona continued impishly.

'Bad blood . . . ?' Felix paled in sudden horror.

Zoltan shouted with laughter; it was exactly the sort of joke he relished. 'More than one way of killing a cat you now, old man,' he grinned.

'If that's so, perhaps it would have been wise to bring a food-taster, Zoltan,' she suggested mockingly.

Zoltan stopped in mid-chew and stared at her blankly. Josef frowned at this incongruous levity, and the mischief vanished from Ilona's eyes.

'Josef, you are not amused! We are not behaving conventionally, are we? You would prefer me to put on a show of grief for dear Hugo? Well, he was an extraordinary man, and he met an extraordinary death. But I will see to it personally that he has a proper burial, and his family are informed. Andras!'

The major-domo filled Josef's glass, then placed the music-box before her. Felix and Zoltan watched the miniature dancing couple on the lid with fascination as the tinkle of the waltz began, but Josef's sense of propriety was sadly affronted; he drained his glass and angrily pushed back his chair.

'Really Ilona, to countenance music, with poor Hoffman scarcely cold! It's intolerable!'

A sudden pain gripped his temples, and he rose unsteadily to his feet. Quietly Ilona closed the music-box.

'Why, Josef,' she said with concern, 'You are not well. I shall attend to you myself!'

She took his arm to support him as he staggered towards the staircase. Nervously Zoltan began to attack the chocolates. Felix shook his head and stared moodily into his glass.

Towards midnight, Josef was trying desperately to struggle out of his stupor. He was convinced that Ilona had tried to poison him. The sooner he was out of the place, the better. Hectic and clumsy, he was tossing his belongings haphazardly into a suitcase; he started violently at a quiet voice behind him.

'There are servants to pack for you, Josef. I never thought you a coward; but leave me, if that is your wish!'

Josef recovered his self-control with an effort. It didn't do to let things get out of proportion, and he might, of course, be misjudging her.

'Forgive me, Ilona, but something strange is happening here. If you are in any sort of danger, I will of course stay to protect you. But I . . .'

He stopped and rubbed his forehead. His vision was blurred and concentration difficult.

'I only wish,' he continued carefully, 'that certain misunder-standings between us could have been clarified before you married that abominable man.'

'But our problems resolved themselves, did they not, Josef? I was married off, and you became leader of the Party.'

'I could not marry you, Ilona,' he burst out. 'I know I spoke of it, but such a marriage – I'm sorry, my dear – it could have ruined my career. Real power was within reach, Ilona! It would have been unthinkable to let it slide from my grasp! Yes, I was ruthless over the Gregor affair, but you know he was a dangerous liberal; by eliminating him we saved the Party's unity, and the country from the rule of the mob!' He paused again, confused and sweating with fever.

'And so you arranged a scandal,' Ilona prompted softly. 'I spent the night with Gregor, and the next day all the country knew of it.'

Josef's composure crumbled; he could not meet her eyes. 'We *had* to ruin his career,' he cried passionately. 'It was imperative to discredit him, Ilona! And nobody could foresee that he would commit suicide, having first murdered his wife and children! The man's brain was unhinged!' He was shouting now; the 'man of principle' was no more. 'Ilona,' he continued pleadingly, 'you found him attractive, did you not? Perhaps we should have told you what we had planned, but we kept your name secret! You suffered no defamation for this – this one small act of political expediency! Ilona –'

He turned, but she was gone. He called her name once more in hysterical despair, then sank abjectly on to the bed, spent and wretched, while the high winds screamed around the castle and his head felt as if it would split.

A sudden movement outside the window jerked him out of his torpor. He hurried to the door and called for Andras. He was taking no chances after what had happened to Hoffman.

'Is something wrong, sir?' Andras regarded the quivering Josef with calm surprise.

'The window, man! Go and look!'

Andras obeyed. 'It's only a broken shutter, sir. It will be attended to first thing in the morning. Good night, Baron, I hope you will sleep soundly.' He bowed courteously and closed the door.

Josef stared at his shaking hands. What was the matter with his eyes? Images were blurred . . . his heart pounding. If only the wretched storm would stop and let him sleep. But the storm was at the height of its fury. It blustered and shrieked relentlessly round the castle, lashing the old stone walls with pelting rain, dementedly rattling the doors; it found out Josef's window and tore about it madly, until the catch broke and the windows flew open, filling the room with squalling tempest. Suddenly, the wind abated, the thunder ceased. There was only the patter of rain on the soaking carpet. Josef crouched on the bed as if mesmerized.

Was it a nightmare, the half-hazy familiar thing with the half-human face, whose huge shoulders filled nearly the whole of the window-frame? It flowed smoothly, silently over the sill, and skulked on all fours by his bed, gazing at him with preternatural yellow eyes.

'*You!* But it can't be – no – help! Help me, for pity's sake!' Josef flung himself, screaming, from the bed; but nothing in the world could have saved him as the slavering beast leapt swiftly and surely for his throat.

A rending crash of thunder drowned Josef's cries and the snarling, worrying sounds the creature made as it dragged its twitching prey into a corner and began, greedily, to feed.

Towards dawn Ilona rose and went for a walk with her wolfhound through the castle grounds. The storm-washed air was sweet and sparkling; the early sun dappled the trees and glittered in the dew. As she re-entered the castle, her servants were crossing the hall, bearing the body of Josef von Haller on a stretcher. Parts of the shroud were soaking red. Ilona smiled slightly and went to her bedroom, where she waited for Andras to bring her breakfast.

Zoltan rarely felt sick, but he could not touch his lunch that day. He kept pacing about, getting on Felix's nerves, muttering, 'Did you see his face, what was left of it? Did you see?' with obsessive stupidity.

'Look,' said Felix harshly. 'Hugo and Josef treated Ilona abominably; rejection, humiliation, betrayal, all the way. She may have arranged their deaths for revenge. But I will have to issue the death certificates, don't you see? And you are a witness. If she'd wanted to murder us she could have done it by now, and besides, why would she want to? I adored Ilona. Dogs and women,' he continued bitterly, 'Treat 'em properly and they'll never let you down. Give 'em affection and they'll respond with devotion. It never fails.'

'You still believe we're safe?' demanded Zoltan with a chattering laugh. 'You, of all people?' His voice rose hysterically. 'Don't you see yet, you vain fool, it's a plot to kill us all! She's got some kind of a wild animal chained up here, that madwoman – she's out to destroy us all!' In his agitation he grabbed a turkey-bone from the buffet and began to chew it furiously; spitting shreds of food as he cried, 'She's not getting rid of me! Not Zoltan Vinzenz! Why, I've survived everything, worse than this! Money, it can still buy life, my friend, you'll see!' He laid a trembling finger against his nose and resumed his caged-beast pacing.

'I doubt anyone in this house will take a bribe,' remarked Felix; he was considering his own form of bribery.

Zoltan wasn't listening. 'We'll pool our money,' he suggested eagerly. 'How much have you got?'

'Nothing, alas. I gave all I had to the delectable Magda.' Felix shut his ears to the uninhibited expression of Zoltan's opinion of him, and went in search of the delectable Magda.

In his room Felix carefully packed a special little case. He wasn't concerned about his clothes, but this case contained details of his female conquests; a lock of hair, a garter and a love letter from each, meticulously collated in a list with which he endeavoured to amuse his friends in Budapest. As he was adding Magda's name she came in to tidy the room, and Felix proposed that she secure him a horse so he could get to the station in the village, promising in return to send for her as soon as he reached home.

She listened to him very attentively, eyes downcast, as he enumerated the delights of city life, half his attention still given to the contents of his case; he had a superstitious fear that if ever he lost it, his potency would vanish.

'You know how fond of you I am, my dear. Sometimes the briefest affair can be the most intense,' he told her; it was a formula that usually worked. 'But it's imperative I leave at once, and you will help me, my dear little Magda.'

He turned to face her – she was gone, the stupid little slut! But she'd be back. No woman had ever let him down. Fighting off an insidious feeling of apprehension, Felix sat down to await her return, clutching his case as if for security.

Zoltan seemed to have similar luck. He had approached Andras and offered to make him a rich man in return for a coach to take him to the village. Andras pretended not to hear; Zoltan had been reduced to following the apparently oblivious servant through the hall, stuffing bank-notes in his pockets and promising the earth. There was not a man alive who could resist the lure of wealth. Andras would come through, all right. Still, it was as well to be circumspect – it was impossible to tell what that crazy woman would be up to next. Zoltan

471

hurried up to his room to make preparations for his departure. To hell with Felix! Let the optimistic fool look after himself! He tip-toed stealthily down the stairs and through the hall, intending to make his escape under cover of darkness.

No one was about. Quietly Zoltan reached for the handle of the great door.

'Must you leave us so soon, Zoltan?' The musical voice echoed clearly from the gallery. Holding her little son by the hand, Ilona began to walk down the staircase towards him. 'I am so sorry you're going! Bela, let us try and persuade your uncle to stay. Andras, forward!'

The tall figure of the major-domo appeared out of the shadows. Zoltan turned to him in a panic. 'Where is the coach, you fool? I gave you all my money . . . Ilona, I did not want to disturb you with my departure.'

'You are too kind, dear Zoltan,' she replied, drawing near. 'And I see you are determined to go. Will you embrace me, for the last time? No? Why then, goodbye, my friend.'

Zoltan's eyes darted from Ilona to Andras like a trapped animal's.

'Come, Ilona,' he wheedled clumsily, 'have I ever harmed you? I bought you everything you ever wanted!' Ilona merely smiled, and fright turned his cajolery to bullying:

'Damnation, woman, do you take me for an idiot? I saw through your sordid little plan from the beginning! Hunt down your enemies by all means, but Ilona, I never willingly injured you! All I ever did was to introduce you to that scoundrel Felix – with the best intentions; I had no inkling . . .'

He broke off as Andras politely handed him a basket full of food, and proceeded to unlock the great door.

'Herr Vinzenz is ready?'

'Your coach is waiting, Zoltan,' said Ilona sweetly. 'Bela, you may kiss your uncle goodbye.'

Zoltan backed away from the child as if he had been venomous, and with a last wild glance at the sinister trio he turned and ran for the open. A gentle gust of wind ruffled Ilona's hair as she and her son waved farewell; then the great doors crashed shut.

There was no sign of the coach. Somehow, he'd known there wouldn't be. From the depths of the forest came the tremulous call of a wolf, rising and dying on the still night air, hypnotic and mournful in its lonely ferocity. Zoltan felt the hairs at the back of his neck begin to prickle. Wolves! Wide-eyed and terrified, Zoltan ran for his life. He dropped his basket and the food scattered in the undergrowth as he stumbled, panting painfully, along the woodland path.

But then something far behind him sensed his vulnerable presence. It chased in a circle, grunting and snuffling, seeking out his scent: now upright, its arms outflung like an ape's, now on all fours; it found his trail and loped unerringly after him. A fit man could not have outrun it; Zoltan, gasping and sweating, heard the heavy swift foot-steps pounding behind him and turned at the moment it sprang upon him. The arms dealer's screams rose high above the wail of the wind as he was torn bloodily limb from limb.

The sounds of slaughter echoed through the night. Felix trembled, sick with horror; the killing of a pig was not comparable. The man who had sold death, grown fat on the profits of death, was now meeting his end as the food of a hungrier beast. The ghastly logic of it was more than Felix could stand. Nauseated, haggard, suddenly old, he rose and groped his way out of the room, grasping his case which was full of the keepsakes he prized above the women who had owned them, and which now represented his only link with the world he knew. Thank God, he could still be saved, he was not like the others! If only they had all resisted the frisson of the unexpected, if only vanity had not prevailed, and they had not accepted this invitation into the decaying jaws of hell! He would never get over the shock and the terror; he had aged ten years these last few hours.

Wearily, Felix walked down the great staircase, crossed the hall and plodded towards the doors of the castle. And then Ilona appeared before him, smiling her sweet and ready smile. He shrank from her, whimpering, clutching the handles of the huge doors. Outside he could hear shuffling, groping noises; something was trying to get in.

'You never used to be afraid of my husband, Felix,' said Ilona silkily.

'Anton is dead!' his voice was a muted scream. 'You buried him!'

Ilona shook her head.

'But, in the name of Christ, Ilona! Why did you not destroy him? Why did you let him live?' His eyes strayed fearfully to the door, and he grasped the handle convulsively.

The growling and snarling outside the door were getting louder. Ilona shook back her hair and gazed at him steadily.

'When the Count was alive, Felix, I was his creature. Do you understand? Look at me, don't wander! Do you now know what I'm saying? – And I was his because you arranged it thus, knowing what he was, Felix. Hugo and Josef abandoned me; what did I matter, so long as their careers were assured? Zoltan introduced me to you, like a good friend, and you arranged my splendid marriage. Think of it, to be discarded and passed on like a pair of slightly-soiled shoes! And I, so excited at the prospect of being wedded to a Count – and a rich one at that. What an innocent I was! But you knew, didn't you, Felix? You knew how far the Count's depravity extended – his bad blood, as the peasants call it. So far, so bad; the Count died some months afterwards, so why did I lust for revenge upon you all? I will tell you.'

She paused, smiling fixedly; Felix, realizing her purpose, shook with terror.

'I endured the Count's brutalities. No doubt you thought my upbringing sufficient preparation for that. But then I was pregnant with Anton's son. Sylva, his nanny, had only to touch the child to know that he was congenitally infected with his father's disease. She knew, and she told me, that it is only a matter of time before my lovely child develops his father's symptoms. There is nothing any living being can do to prevent my son being condemned, through his father's evil, to hell.' Her eyes burned.

'That is your legacy to me, Felix, yours and your friends. You are about to experience my gratitude. The years I have spent, planning and dreaming this moment! It is more than revenge to me.'

'But the Count *is* dead,' mumbled Felix stupidly; his wits were failing under the strain. 'You cannot mean that all of us – that we were all brought here to die!'

'Just so,' said Ilona quietly. 'I have said the Count died, and so he did, in a sense; his hunting accident was convenient, and averted popular suspicion. In fact, it was the beginning of his final state, which never ends. His humanity is lost, dissolved in the propensities of the beast; he is one of the Undead. Ever since he has been mine to command. I control him, as he once controlled me. And now I am sick of this discussion. Andras, open the doors!'

'*No!* Ilona, have pity!'

Andras appeared and brushed aside the gibbering Felix. He flung the doors wide open, then he and the Countess vanished into the shadows of the hall. Felix staggered backwards, stumbled and tried to crawl for the safety of the stairs, but it was too late. His dilated eyes were riveted to the gaping doorway as he cowered, shivering, at the sound of a shrill lingering wolf-howl outside the moonlit castle.

Silently it entered, his last enemy. The Wolf was bigger than he. Dark matted hair covered it all over, and the long claws scratched upon the polished floor as it advanced across the hall to the terrified doctor. But the brutish face was still recognizable; yes, even though the eyes were staring and mad, and the pendant tongue licked hungrily over the slavering jaws.

'I beg your mercy, Count Tyrrh!' Felix pleaded in a hoarse whisper.

474

The werewolf growled and skulked in the shadows, weaving before him like a nightmare-image. Felix grovelled before the evil and the power of this demoniac beast.

'Remember,' he whimpered, 'I gave that woman to you! I gave you that whore –'

The werewolf rounded on him in a sudden hellish fury, rearing upright; the slimy black lips curled in snarling savagery, the gleaming canine teeth snapping viciously as it struck, tearing, rending its helpless victim into oblivion with maniacal strength. The kill was over in seconds, and then the beast hunched jealously over its prey like some obscene living fungus, settling to gorge itself upon the bloody, half-dismembered corpse.

'You see, my darling, I said it would soon be over,' said Ilona to her little son. They were relaxing with Andras in front of a blazing fire. All traces of the guests were removed, and Magda had brought them some supper on a tray.

'It's good to be alone again,' said Andras, smiling at her fondly. He took a candied peach from the tray and offered it to Bela, who accepted it happily; Ilona sipped at a glass of wine, and sighed with contentment.

'Yes, just the three of us, dearest Andras – our little family!'

'Such is my tale, gentlemen.' The new candidate stretched his long arms and smiled at the gathering. 'I hope as a result of it you will see fit to favour me with membership of your renowned institution –'

'No! Impossible!' Trembling, Mr Pettifer rose to his feet. He glanced wildly round at his fellow-members. 'Can't you see what this man is?'

The shocked silence which greeted his outburst was broken by the stranger:

'Oh no, sir,' he said quietly. 'You are mistaken in you assumption; I am not that dreadful husband of the Countess Ilona. He was despatched some time ago by a silver bullet, a somewhat brutal but entirely effective method, I assure you. Now, gentlemen, if I could –'

'Then in God's name, what – who are you?' cried Mr Pettifer, ignoring caution and the disapproving frowns of his colleagues.

The man gazed at him with a cold, yellow-eyed stare, as if he were fixing the face and form of Mr Pettifer indelibly on his memory. Suddenly his stern features relaxed in a wolfish grin, and he turned to the room at large:

475

'May I be so bold as to ask you, gentlemen,' he enquired politely, 'for a glass of water and . . . a little candied fruit?'

Death Can Add

BY PHILIP KETCHUM

Tales of the Unexpected *was launched in 1979 and was the second TV series to utilize the stories of Roald Dahl. It became so popular with viewers on both sides of the Atlantic that a year later contributions were being sought by other leading thriller writers in order to keep the anthology on the small screen into the Eighties. The sardonic tales used in the series – 'They all tick like thirty-minute time bombs' was the verdict of the American magazine,* TV Guide *– made for memorable, sophisticated entertainment in which a plethora of well-known British and American actors appeared. Each of the half-hour programmes produced by John Woolf of Anglia TV ended with a sting in the tail and included some of the best adaptations of Roald Dahl's stories to be seen on TV. Among the most acclaimed of these Dahl episodes were* 'Man from the South' *(starring Jose Ferrer and Pamela Stephenson),* 'Lamb to the Slaughter' *(John Davies and Susan George),* 'Neck' *(Sir John Gielgud, Joan Collins and Peter Bowles),* 'Royal Jelly' *(Timothy West and Susan George),* 'Taste' *(Ron Moody) and yet another version of* 'William and Mary', *this time with Donald McWhinnie, Elaine Stritch and Marius Goring.*

I have a special affection for this late night horror series both as a viewer and as a story consultant, because I helped select material for the programme from 1980 up to the finale in 1984. Among the other authors whose work provided material in the Dahl mould were Stanley Ellin, Henry Slesar, Ruth Rendell, Julian Symons and two leading American mystery short story writers, Robert Arthur and Philip Ketchum. Indeed, among my own choices for the series were Robert Arthur's 'Completely Foolproof' *which starred Telly Savalas and Rita Gam, and* 'Death Can Add' *by Philip Ketchum (1940–).*

Ketchem has for years been a prolific contributor to American publications such as Alfred Hitchcock's Mystery Magazine *and* Ellery Queen's Mystery Magazine, *and it was from the pages of Hitch's magazine that I plucked 'Death Can Add' about an accountant who finally has to face the day of reckoning for his secret life of high living. The episode was shot in May 1981 and made newspaper headlines when a stunt for the finale nearly killed the film crew. While on location at Swaffham, Norfolk the unexpected really happened when a Mercedes car carrying two dummies went out of control at fifty mph, exploded in mid-air, and hurtled down a bank. It demolished a camera as the crew leaped for safety and then burned out in a field. Two men were hurt while fleeing from the fireball and had to be treated for burns in hospital. Unit manager Peter Durbridge said later, 'Unexpected is not the word for it. It was nearly a bloody disaster!' Small wonder, then, that this story has a special interest for me, both because of what is seen on the screen and what is not. It is a tale of the unexpected in every sense of the word!*

HIS mother was amazed, his father was startled. They could not seem to understand him. They looked at each other, then looked at him, and his father said, 'You really mean it, you don't want to go to college.'

Oliver shook his head. 'I want to go to a good business school. I want to study accounting.'

'You want to be a two-bit bookkeeper for the rest of your life?'

'That's where I might have to start,' Oliver admitted.

Ben Platt appealed to his wife, 'Olga, what did that highschool teacher say about Oliver?'

'She said he was a brilliant student, particularly in mathematics. She said this was basic to all science and that if he worked he could go to the top.'

Ben pointed at Oliver. 'Did you hear that?'

'I heard it,' Oliver said. 'I'll get to the top.'

'As a bookkeeper?'

'I won't always be a bookkeeper. That's just the first step.'

'What's the second?'

'I don't know, exactly,' Oliver said. 'But there will be a second step, and a third, and a fourth. I know what I want to do.'

Ben Platt scowled, glanced again at his wife, and shrugged. 'All right – it's your life but I wouldn't like it, chained to a bookkeeper's stool. I suppose the fifteen dollars I gave you for books this morning went for accounting books?'

'Two books,' Oliver said. 'The list price of each one was eight-fifty.'

'Then I owe you two bucks.'

'I was going to pay it out of my allowance.'

'Naw, I'll pay it,' Ben said and dug into his pocket to get the money.

Oliver took it, smiled. Very possibly his smile looked like a smile of appreciation. Actually he was amused that his father had accepted the list price without questioning it. The two books he had bought were second-hand, had cost him six-fifty. The profit to him was ten-fifty.

His mother stepped closer, put her arm around his shoulder. 'We want you to be happy, Oliver. Your father and I always hoped you would go to college – but if your heart is set on a business career, we want you to try it.'

'Thanks, Mom,' Oliver said. He hugged her, then smiled at his father. 'You are wonderful parents.'

Oliver Platt spent almost two years in a Business School. He took every course in mathematics, accounting, bookkeeping. He did a lot of outside reading, studying. Then he spent another year in business management, business law, and mathematical theory. By this time he was twenty-two. Tall, thin, a little pale but not unattractive, he was a quiet young man with an orderly mind, sharp blue eyes, tight, thin, lips. Long before he finished his schooling he had considered and rejected a number of jobs, and after his classes were ended he still waited for what he wanted. He finally got it – the job he was looking for – a job as a junior accountant for the Belmont Trust Company.

This was an old and respected firm, steeped in tradition, and well conditioned with money. Huge funds of money were placed there for careful and modest interest returns. The Belmont Trust Company did not gamble on the market. Securities were bought and sold but very conservatively. A number of bookkeepers and clerical workers were necessary, but only three accountants were listed. Oliver Platt replaced a man who was in his seventies. Both of the other accountants were growing old. In ten more years –

It took only five years for Oliver to rise to the position of chief accountant. One of the accountants above him retired, one died, and while two more accountants were hired, Oliver had the inside track, had made a good impression, and it was natural to give him the top job.

As chief accountant of the Belmont Trust, Oliver was now earning a respectable income. He could afford a respectable apartment, a respectable wife, and a respectable car. He bought two of those, the apartment and the car. The choosing of a wife was another matter. The world was filled with beautiful women. To pick what he wanted might take a little time, but of course there was no hurry. He could take his time, experimenting.

This was a pleasant diversion. The wining, dining and the entertainment of attractive women was exciting even if it was a little expensive. Now and then, in his mind, Oliver laughed at his father's observation that it would be horrible to be chained to a bookkeeper's stool. Definitely, he was not chained. In fact, he was doing very well financially. He had his respectable income – and his side-income. The side-income was what he was appropriating to himself. There was another, ugly word, to explain what he was doing. It was – *embezzlement*. But it was only called embezzlement if you were caught – and he was not going to be caught. He had worked out an almost fool-proof system for plucking the company for which he worked.

The next two years were delightful years. Oliver met a number of charming women. He took them out, but cautiously, and where he wouldn't be recognized. It would have been foolish to make a splash in society. A chief accountant could not afford it. And he did not ask any of the charming women to marry him. Once or twice he came close to it, but in time he backed off. The right woman, the woman he wanted, just had not shown up. He wanted beauty, spirit – and daring. Beauty was everywhere and sometimes with beauty there was a tinge of spirit. But the third ingredient, daring, was hard to find. Someday he was going to have to run, disappear to some spot half way around the world. The woman he wanted would have to risk a thing like that.

Even an old and traditional firm can find it necessary to reorganize its board and its executive staff. During the next year the Belmont Trust Company went through this process. Oliver Platt was retained as chief accountant, but a new executive vice-president was brought in as an administrative director. For possibly three months Oliver worried about the new man. He was in his late thirties, a big, physically powerful man, tall and heavy. He had a nice smile, had good connections. He seemed to know a little about accounting and if he had looked in the right places he might have disclosed something unpleasant for Oliver. But he didn't look in the right places, and gradually Oliver stopped worrying.

Another year passed. A pleasant year. In succeeding quarters of the year Oliver devoted himself outside of office hours, to Doris, Velma, Frances and Glory. They were delightful, but each one grew demanding and when he would not respond, they passed from his life. At the beginning of the next year, a new girl in the office caught his attention.

Lila Graham. She was a stenographer, tall, slender, graceful, with brown hair, brown eyes, a teasing smile. There were weeks when Oliver could have made a date with her, but he didn't. He avoided her eyes, avoided any attention to her. He had made a rule. He thought it a good rule. In order to escape any office complications, he would have no personal relationship with anyone on the staff. Sadly, this put Lila off bounds.

But Oliver thought about her – and thought about her – and thought about her. Then one afternoon something happened, something shattering, frightening. It made him almost forget about Lila. The executive vice-president, Howard Coburn, called him to his office, and in the matter of a few minutes pinned Oliver to the wall. At least it amounted to that.

'Platt, how much money do you make?' Coburn asked.

'Eight thousand, five hundred,' Oliver said. 'But you know that.'

'Yes I do,' Coburn said. 'You earn eight thousand, five hundred. Now, tell me how much you spend.'

Oliver frowned. He was suddenly uneasy. 'I imagine I spend most of it.'

'You spend that, and a great deal more,' Coburn said. 'At a guess, you have spent more than twenty thousand dollars during the past year. Twenty thousand – I wonder where it came from?'

'No – No – that's impossible,' Oliver gasped. 'There's been some terrible mistake –'

'I wouldn't call it that,' Coburn said, and he smiled but there wasn't anything pleasant in the curve of his lips. His eyes had narrowed, hardened.

'I – I don't quite know what you mean,' Oliver said.

'Then let me explain,' Coburn said. 'I have made a study of you. At a guess I have followed you in the evening at least a dozen times. You were never alone. You were always accompanied by a young woman, attractive, expensively dressed. And you spent money like water before the evening was over. Twice I saw you give jewellery to the woman with you. And it was not costume jewellery. It was the real stuff – expensive.'

Oliver was thoroughly frightened by now but he still shook his head, muttered a denial.

'I haven't finished,' Coburn said. 'I checked you and your activities, out of the office. Then I read and verified the information about you in your personnel record. Your parents are not wealthy. You haven't inherited a fortune. So I wondered where your money was coming from – and I found out. For three weeks now I've been working at the

481

office, late, studying the books, checking stock certificates. I'll have to admit you are clever. For two weeks I didn't find anything wrong. Possibly it was only by accident that I uncovered what you have been doing. Would it mean anything to you if I mentioned the Von Deiman holdings?'

Oliver took a long, deep breath. The Von Deiman holdings were no longer what they had been, or should have been. Of course he had such a complete control of the physical properties of a number of accounts that the differences in the records should never have been noticed. It was a sneaky thing Coburn had done, prying into the records, but what Oliver could do about it now he didn't know.

'Don't you think I ought to telephone the police?' Coburn asked.

Oliver moistened his lips. 'No – I'll make it up. I'll –'

'How would you make it up?'

'I don't know – but if you give me the chance –'

'If I give you the chance, in ten more years the assets of the Belmont Trust will have vanished.'

'No –'

'I'll tell you what I'm going to do,' Coburn said. 'I will give you a choice. One is to go to jail. Should I telephone the police?'

'No,' Oliver snapped, glaring at Coburn.

Coburn's smile had hardened into a grimace, twisted and confident. 'The other choice is this. Continue what you are doing. Line your own pockets *and mine!* I want sixty percent of every dollar you take – a full sixty percent. I will check your work very carefully. If you try to doublecross me, you're finished. I'll call in the police.'

This proposition Coburn had thrown at him was almost as startling as the knowledge that he had been discovered. He had expected to be arrested, to be thrown into jail. It had never occurred to him that there might be an alternative course he could follow. He never would have dreamed that Coburn was dishonest. It was hard to believe him now. He was a stuffy man, lived in a stuffy neighbourhood, had a stuffy wife and stuffy friends. He belonged to several dogooder committees. In fact his attitude was almost pious. That he would try anything crooked seemed impossible.

'Well, Oliver?' Coburn was asking. 'How about it?'

'I – I don't want to go to jail.' Oliver said.

'I'm sure you would rather be free,' Coburn nodded. 'That is easy to admit. But I want you to understand, clearly, the alternative course. I want sixty percent of every dollar you take, and to make it worth while, I want you to double what you are taking. I want to feel the money in my hands. No use being a piker.'

'We've got to be careful,' Oliver said.

'No. You have to be careful,' Coburn said. 'But I know how you work. I can use a little money over the weekend, say about six thousand. That's a take of ten thousand. Four thousand would be yours.'

Oliver frowned. He knew exactly where he could pick up the ten thousand. In fact he already had set up a number of situations, ready to be used. He had been saving them for later. His frown grew deeper, heavier. 'I'll see what I can do.'

'Have the money ready by Friday,' Coburn said crisply.

'But –'

'By Friday,' Coburn said. 'And I want the money in cash. That's all, Oliver. You can go.'

Oliver took another deep breath, swung around, and left Coburn's office. He bumped into Lila Graham on the way to his desk but he did not even notice her, did not see her. His world, momentarily, was in a cataclysmic state in which nothing made sense.

It took almost three months for Oliver to realize, completely, the situation into which he had fallen. It was hedged by fear, it smelled of bitterness, and within it were all the properties of a nightmare. He was clipping out more money than was safe. He was still being very careful, but now he had two dozen accounts he had to watch, and to keep under his own supervision. This took more time. It kept him busy into the evening. It occupied his weekends. He was putting away more and more money, but money, itself, was not exciting. As for interesting women, he had no opportunity to look for any. He was dead tired when he got back to his apartment, dragging, ready for bed. And of course he was not sleeping well.

Another thing annoyed him. He was taking all the risks. The false entries in his books were in his handwriting, the securities he had sold, unauthorized, he had ordered sold himself. The cheques received he had cashed through the firm, but without recording the transaction. If a very careful audit was made, the entire blame for any errors would land squarely on his shoulders. And Howard Coburn would go free. In no way was Coburn implicated. He took his money in cash, and he took the lion's share of the money. From the way things had worked out, Coburn was the one who was enjoying himself. All the money he wanted, but none of the risks.

Oliver was growing to hate Howard Coburn. He hated the man's jovial, friendly attitude around the office. He resented the man's fatuous goodness. He was even angered at the man's occasional symptoms of a hangover, an indication that he might have been out on the town. Without doing anything but put out his hand each Friday, he was collecting a modest fortune. Again and again Oliver tried to figure out how he could escape from the trap he was in. But there was no escape. If he refused to give Coburn any more money, the man would call in the police, and he would go to jail. If he ran away, Coburn would report the shortage and he would become a fugitive. If Coburn should die. . . .

Oliver shivered whenever he thought of that – Coburn's death. That would be perfect. That would save him. But Coburn looked healthy enough to live forever. As to murder, Oliver could not think of it. To steal was one matter but to take a man's life was horrible.

In the middle of his restless dreaming one night he awoke to a realization of what lay ahead. He was on a one-way road which was leading him to an inevitable destination. There was a definite limit to the amount of money he could steal without being caught. He was very near to that point now. When he reached it, the point of recklessness, one of two things would happen. He would be caught and sent to jail, or very possibly, and to protect himself, Howard Coburn would turn him in to the police. In any case, prison was just ahead. And not far off.

He had been going to the office early, and the next morning, for some reason or other, Lila Graham came in early. She nodded to him, but then frowned, and walked to her desk, a tall, slender girl, attractive. Good in her work, too. Efficient, quick-minded. For the past few months Oliver had been so introspective he had not found the time to think of anyone else, but there had been occasional lapses when he had looked at Lila and had noticed her as a woman, one it might be nice to know.

He stared at her now and it occurred to him abruptly that it might not hurt him at all if he ducked his responsibilities for at least one evening and enjoyed himself. A break like this might even clear up his foggy thinking. In the past he had lived by the hard rule of avoiding office complications, but somehow or other, that rule no longer seemed important.

He got up, walked to Lila's desk. 'Hello, there. Busy this morning?'

Her lips twitched. 'Have you finally admitted me to the human race?'

'I've been working too hard, and I've been worried, too,' Oliver admitted. 'But I've noticed you – and you know it.'

She laughed softly. 'You are an important man in the office.'

'Not really.'

'I think you are.'

This was one of the neatest compliments Oliver had ever received.

His weakened ego was suddenly fortified. He straightened just a little, glanced at the clock, realized that at any moment someone else might arrive. Before that happened he wanted to arrange to see more of this girl, continue their conversaion. Instinctively he lowered his voice. 'Doing anything tonight?'

She disappointed him. 'I have a date.'

'Break it,' Oliver said.

'But how can I?'

'Say that the chief accountant in your office is an old ogre, and he has loaded you up with a lot of work. I know a very nice place where we can go for dinner, a quiet place. The food is wonderful.'

Lila hesitated. 'I don't know that I should go out with you.'

'Then I'll make it an order,' Oliver said. And he grinned. 'Be ready by seven. We'll have a drive, cocktails, a delicious dinner. Then we do some dancing all in the name of good office relationships.'

Lila looked down but Oliver could see her lips twitch again. She nodded slowly. 'If it's an order, of course I'll have to agree. It might even be nice.'

He had a wonderful time that evening. Lila was pleasant, attentive, but she didn't hang on his arm. She had a nice laugh. They went to a dozen places. Several were ritzy, one or two were on the fringe of skidrow. Lila didn't seem to care about that. Oliver had a feeling she would enjoy herself anywhere.

Two nights later they tried it again. Oliver had even more fun. They went to an amusement park, tried everything there, acted like two kids, then back in Lila's apartment listened to chamber music over her hi fi. Oliver was afraid he was falling in love with her.

The next day, however, he was jolted back to reality. Howard Coburn sent for him, motioned to a chair, finished a telephone call to someone, maybe his wife, and then said, 'Well, Oliver, we've been doing very well.'

'We've been going too far, and too fast,' Oliver said. 'It's getting hard to cover up everything.'

Coburn's smile was irritating, but not his words. 'How would you like to get off the hook?'

'Get – off the hook?' Oliver gasped.

'That's it,' Coburn said. 'I'm going to move on, vanish. Do you know my wife?'

'I've seen her.'

'She's a lot worse than she looks, a real millstone. I've had enough. One more haul and I won't bother you anymore. But Oliver, next Friday I want a hundred thousand dollars.'

'A hundred thousand dollars!'

'Yes. That's my price. And I want it next Friday.'

'We would have to dip into our current operating funds.'

'I don't care how you get it,' Coburn said. 'That's your problem. I want one hundred thousand dollars, in cash. Start figuring on it now.'

Oliver went back to his desk. He was in an almost cataleptic state, but not quite. He could move. In a numb sort of way he could appreciate what would happen if he dug out a hundred thousand dollars. This would carry him far past the point of recklessness. He would be discovered, arrested, and would go to jail. Lila would be lost to him forever. In fact, his life was already over. There was no way he could escape. But Coburn would escape. No question of that. He would take the money, go somewhere, and enjoy himself. In his mind's eye Oliver could see the man in some South Pacific paradise, surrounded by beautiful women, living like a king, and laughing – laughing at the man who had made it possible, laughing at him.

He spent a miserable weekend. Lila was away, visiting her mother, and although Oliver might have found companionship, now that he wanted Lila he could think of no one else. There was one exception. He could think of Howard Coburn. He could hate him and hate him and hate him. But that did not seem to help. Next Friday afternoon, as usual, he would go into Coburn's office, carrying his briefcase. There, away from any other prying eyes he would substitute his briefcase for Coburn's. They were identical. But in the one he would leave would be Coburn's share of the money he was stealing. And next Friday was the big take – one hundred thousand dollars for a man who did nothing to help, a leech, a parasite. If he could only put a bomb in the briefcase. A bomb! One that would explode when –

Oliver shook his head. He tried to forget the sudden thought which had gripped him. He put it out of his mind, but it came back. It taunted him, teased him, nagged him. He had been good in physics, in chemistry. He was almost sure he could make a bomb, one that would work. He would have to check the possibility of available materials, but he could do that Monday. And he had until the next Friday to do what was necessary. A small but powerful bomb in the briefcase he gave Coburn, and at the proper time –

A shiver ran over his body, made his skin tingle. He spoke to himself aloud. 'No, I can't do it. I can't!' But even as he was saying that, in his mind he was building the bomb, testing in his thoughts just what he would have to do.

Monday evening he and Lila had dinner, and he tried to be cheerful. He was not very successful about it, and finally Lila asked him, directly, what was wrong. When he was evasive, she made a guess. 'You're having trouble with Mr Coburn.'

He was almost startled. 'How did you guess?'

She reached for his hand under the table. 'I've been watching you, and besides, I'm a clever girl.'

He frowned at her. 'Could I tell you something in strictest confidence?'

'Of course you can.'

'Coburn has been blackmailing me. Several months ago I was in financial trouble. I borrowed some money from the company's funds. Very easily I could have paid it back but before I did, Coburn found out what I had done. He threatened to call the police unless I stole more money from the company funds and gave the money to him.'

'So he's like that – a crook. He ought to be exposed.'

'If I do it, I suffer too. And the chances are he wouldn't be blamed at all.'

'Did you know he made a pass at me?'

'The stinker.'

'I walked away from him. Next time I'll claw his face.'

Oliver almost laughed, but then he grew serious. 'Coburn wants a big chunk of money, Friday. I've got to get it for him, but before anyone finds out I'm going to run, disappear. That's not being very brave, but I don't want to go to jail.'

Her voice was low. 'Where are you going?'

'Half way around the world,' Oliver said. 'Remember I told you I had an inheritance.'

'I don't care about that,' Lila said. 'Are you going away alone or would you like company?'

He looked straight at her. 'I'd like you to go with me, but Friday is not far off. We would have to leave directly from the office.'

She was still holding his hand under the table and now she squeezed it, and nodded. 'Friday afternoon – I'll be ready.'

Oliver straightened. His eyes had brightened. Probably he had never felt better in his life. Lila's offer to go with him was the final, determining factor, shaping up in his mind. He would make the bomb, a long, flattened bomb to fit into the bottom of his briefcase, money on top of it. Too bad to waste the money, but that could not be helped. Anyhow, to the money he had saved he would add as much as he could pick up, Friday. That was the inheritance money he had mentioned to Lila. No use to tell her everything.

The bomb he made was a thing of beauty, shallow, fitted to his briefcase, carefully and accurately timed. Coburn had told him, casually, that by five o'clock he expected to be at Cloverleaf Airport where he kept his private plane. By five-thirty he would be in the air and well on his way somewhere. Oliver had set the bomb to explode at exactly five-thirty.

Shortly after four o'clock in the afternoon he picked up the briefcase, glanced at Lila. She was watching him surreptitiously but that was natural. In just a few minutes, now, she would be leaving with him on a long, long journey. Oliver smiled, nodded to her, and headed for Coburn's office.

'Good. I've been expecting you,' Coburn said. He nodded toward the briefcase. 'Is it all there? One hundred thousand?'

'It's all there,' Oliver said. 'Want to count it?'

Coburn reached for the briefcase, looked inside, and grinned. 'It better be there. I'll count it later. I'm waiting for a telephone call, then I'll clear out. Will you miss me?'

'No,' Oliver said honestly.

Coburn laughed.'I'll miss you, even though I know what you're going to try.'

Oliver stiffened. 'What do you mean?'

'You're going to try to set up the books to indicate that I took the money. You will try it, but you won't be able to manage it. As chief accountant, you couldn't have been blind to what was going on. So I'm not worried.'

'I just hope the directors don't ask for an audit after you disappear.'

'They probably will,' Coburn said. 'So get to work, Oliver. Maybe you can save yourself.'

Oliver turned, left Coburn's office. He stopped at Lila's desk and said, 'Twenty minutes – at the side entrance.'

'I'll be there,' Lila said.

Oliver was carrying the substitute briefcase. He left it near his desk, walked to the cloak room, got his hat and coat and headed for the corridor. Five minutes later he was at a nearby garage where he kept his car. His bags, and all the possessions he wanted to keep, were in the trunk. Two of Lila's suitcases and a hat box were there. They would be travelling light but his pocket was wadded with money. Probably, in view of what he had taken for Coburn and for himself, the carefully conservative Belmont Trust was ready to collapse.

He watched the clock, left the garage just in time to meet Lila at the side entrance at precisely ten minutes to five. At a guess, Coburn was already on the way to the Cloverleaf Airport. He had said he was waiting for a telephone call but he was not the kind of person to be patient. Oliver caught a glimpse of Lila, waiting, but then watched

488

ahead, half sure he might see Howard Coburn driving away. He was a little tense.

Lila reached his car, opened the door, and climbed in. She twisted around to put her handbag and her coat in the back seat. She seemed breathless.

'Excited?' Oliver asked.

'A little,' her voice was shaky. 'Why don't you start?'

Oliver did. He slid his car into the moving traffic, headed for the expressway, and he drove very carefully. This was not the time to run into a traffic violation.

'We'll be able to relax tonight,' he mentioned, and he took a quick look at Lila. 'What are you worried about?'

'I guess I'm just not used to a thing like this.'

'You'll get over it,' Oliver said.

He was keeping an eye on the car's dashboard clock. It was five-twenty. Somewhere by now, probably already airborne, Coburn was headed away. But he wouldn't get far. He had only ten minutes to live.

The clock ticked on. Five twenty-three, five twenty-five, five twenty-seven.

His car moved smoothly down the expressway. The clock pointed to five twenty-eight, five twenty-nine –

'I didn't mean to do it,' Lila said. 'I mean, in a way it was an accident. That is –'

'Hold it a minute,' Oliver said. He was enjoying this moment. He wouldn't see the explosion but he could see it in his mind, the crashing sound, the blinding flash –

Lila interrupted his thoughts. 'I've got to tell you this. I wanted to tell you but I couldn't. Now, I've got to, for maybe you won't want me to go with you. After you left the office I went in to see Mr Coburn. I . . . think I killed him!'

This was such startling news Oliver could hardly speak. His car weaved toward the edge of the highway.

'I didn't think it was fair for him to take all that money,' Lila said. 'Mr Coburn was on the telephone when I entered his office. I walked around behind him and when he hung up the telephone I hit him over the head with a brass paperweight. I didn't mean to hit him too hard but I'm afraid I did.'

It was five-thirty by the car's dashboard clock. *Five-thirty!* Oliver wheeled his car to the grass bordering the highway. He jammed on the brakes, and he was almost shouting. *'The briefcase! What did you do with the briefcase!'*

'Why, it was full of money,' Lila said. 'So I took it with me. It's in the

489

back of the car. You didn't see it because my coat was draped over it –
Oliver, what's wrong?'

He twisted around, stared into the back seat and there it was, the
briefcase, loaded with money, loaded with death! If he could reach it,
hurl it out of the car – He stretched out his hand but suddenly all
about him was sound and flashing colours, an instant of pain and then
nothing –

DARKROOM

The Partnership

BY WILLIAM F. NOLAN

The tall, craggy-faced and sardonic James Coburn made an excellent host for the strange and often bizarre stories featured in Darkroom. *Produced by Peter S. Fisher for ABC, the series ran from nine PM to ten PM on Friday evenings and sometimes contained two or even three stories of the occult during the hour, as well as featuring a number of leading screen and television actors such as Steve Allen, Esther Rolle, June Lockhart and David Carradine. The stories, a number written by Robert Bloch and Jeffrey Bloom, varied from period settings to the present day. Among the best received by viewers were the tale of a French rogue trying to escape the guillotine by an ingenious plot to execute the executioner; a Vietnam veteran who gave his son an army of toy soldiers and then had to watch, horrified, as they came alive and attacked him; the quandry of an imaginative teenager who suspects that his sister's handsome boyfriend is a vampire; and the ruthless young hoodlum who finds himself being stalked by an eerie black cat . . .*

Among the story contributors to Darkroom *was William F. Nolan (1928–), the former commercial artist and magazine editor, who is perhaps best known for* Logan's Run *(1967) about a future world where no-one is allowed to live beyond their thirtieth birthday. It was first a lavish, special effects film (1976) directed by Michael Anderson, starring Michael York and Jenny Agutter, and then a CBS TV series with Gregory Harrison and Heather Menzies the following year. Bill shares with his great friend Ray Bradbury a fascination with old amusement parks and used this theme for his* Darkroom *story, 'The Partnership' transmitted in December 1981. It starred David Carradine and Lawrence Hilton-Jacobs, and like the story which begins hereunder, was creepy and not a little frightening . . .*

ME and Ed, we're in business together. Which is what I want to tell you about eventually because I think you folks will find it interesting. But this is also about the stranger with the beard. And he comes first.

You like ghost stories? Bet you do! Everybody does. But this isn't one of those. Not a ghost in it. Still, it's a little spooky, I'd guess. I mean, to some it will be. Strange – that's a good word for it.

Strange.

Anyhow, Ed and me, we got ourselves a real nice partnership going. For one thing, we trust each other, and that's the basis you build on. No trust, no partnership. Learned that long ago. My Irish grandaddy, bless him, came over from County Cork. Bought into a saloon in Virginia City with a partner who 'stole him blind'. That's how he always put it: 'That man stole me blind!'

Now, with Gramps long gone, I'm as old as he was when I was a tad. That's how I got my first name. Ralph's the legal one, but I've always been Tad since Gramps called me that. Tad Miller. Simple name for a simple man.

I grew up in Nevada, but we moved to Chicago when I was still a boy – but you don't really want to know all about how I got here to this little town stuck down in God-knows-where country. It's in Illinois, a good piece out from Chicago, and we're on the lake. That's what counts – not how I got here or what brought me.

I'm here. That's enough.

Name of this town's not important, so I won't give it out. If I did, some of you folks might come here one day, looking to say hello, and I wouldn't like that much since I'm not partial to meeting just anybody. No offence.

Ed's the same way. When he's ready to meet a stranger he'll go all out, but in between he's like me. Keeps to home.

Don't get me wrong. When a stranger comes to town, and I see he's lonely, I'll strike up a conversation as quick as the next fellow. I just don't *advertise*, if you know what I mean.

This town's on a spur highway into Chicago, and we get our share of hitchers. Road bums, sometimes. Others – like kids on the run from home, heading for life in the big city. Some on vacation. All kinds, drifting in for coffee and grub at Sally Anne's. They all end up at Sal's. Only eatery left in town, so she gets the business.

Real nice sort, too. You'd like her. Kind eyes. I always notice a person's eyes, first off. And hers are soft and liquidy, like a deer.

Me and Sally kid each other a lot, but we're both too old to have it mean anything. But she likes me. Most folks do. And that's nice.

Person wants to know he's liked, even if he keeps mostly to home.

Well, before I tell you about the bearded stranger I met at Sal's last month you need to know some things about this town.

For instance, it's dying fast. Getting smaller every year. Most of the young ones are gone now. Us diehards are still hanging on. Me and Ed, we'll have to split up one of these days because this town's due to just wink out like a star in the sky. Bound to happen. Be a sad day for me. Ed, too. We're not that close, understand, but there's a lot between us. Still, like my mama used to say, nothing lasts forever.

Anyhow, the town's slowed down a hellish lot since I first moved here from Chicago after Mama and Pop died. Expressway gets most of the traffic. Puts us in the backwash. The big change came when Moffitt Paper closed their factory. Town lost its main source of revenue, and things slowed way down.

That's when I had to leave Happyland. It's what they call the amusement park on the lake. Closed now. Boarded up. Left to rust and rain.

I ran the Funhouse out at Happyland. For twenty years. Slept there on summer nights. Knew every turn and twist of the place, every creaking board and secret passage and blind tunnel in it. Still do, for that matter. Which is where the stranger comes in, but I'll get to that.

First, a little more about me and this town if you don't mind. (I'm in no hurry, are you?)

I got married here. Surprise, eh? Guess, on paper, I don't come across as the romantic type – even though Sally still kids me that way. But married I was, and to a good woman who never liked kids so we didn't have any. When she died I was left alone. No family, not even cousins. (I didn't know Ed then.)

Her heart gave out. One day, fine, the next she's gone. Hit me hard. Made me kind of wacky for a while. But I got over it. We get over things, or things get over us, take your choice. Nowdays I'm used to being on my own, and I do fine. Enjoy my privacy. Enjoy the woods and some fishing in the fall. Like I said, a simple man. I miss her bad some nights, just like I do Happyland. But they're both gone – and everything has to die. Nature's way. Accept it. Flow with the tide.

She's buried out at Lakeside. Strangers think it odd, us having our cemetery right there on the lake, smack next to Happyland. Graveyard and amusement park snug-a-bug together on the lake. Odd, they say. Or *used* to, when Happyland was still open. 'Spooky' is what they called it, having them together that way. But I never saw a ghost in twenty years out there. Oh, once in a while some big rats would wander in and give the ladies a real scare in the dark. (I'd always refund when it happened.) They'd come from the burrows under the cemetery, the rats, that is. Big suckers. And scared of nothing. That's the way of a rat; he scares you, you don't scare him.

Anyhow, my good wife's buried out there, or was. Guess the rats have her by now, though that isn't very nice to think about, is it? They got mighty sharp teeth, can gnaw right through the side of a coffin unless you can afford a steel one. Me, I've never had one extra dime to rub against another! Spend what I earn. To the penny. But I pay my way. No debts for Tad Miller.

Better get on with telling you about the big stranger who passed through here last month . . .

I was at Sally's, kidding with her – and we didn't see him walk in. She was joshing me about a new ring I had on. Big shiny thing, and Sal said it looked like I was wearing a streetlight. I was joshing her back about her new hairdo, saying it looked like a hive of bees could make honey in there. That kind of stuff. Just kidding around, passing the time of day.

Next thing, the stranger is banging the counter and yelling for some service. Sal broke off quick and moved over there to ask him what he'd have.

'Coffee and your special,' he growled. 'The coffee now. And a small tomato juice.'

She told him no tomato juice, just orange. That made him madder than before.

He was big and mean looking. Maybe a lumber man. Had one of those shoulder-hike rigs, which he'd taken off and put on the counter next to him. Man of about forty, I'd guess. Muscled arms and a wide back. Thick dark beard. But honest eyes. I noticed his eyes right off.

He wore one of those space-age wristwatches with all kinds of dials and dates on it and little panels that light up. I'd never seen one like it before, and was plain curious, so I took the empty stool next to him. He gave me a scowl for doing that, because the rest of the counter was empty, and I guess he didn't want company.

'Hello, mister,' I said. 'My name's Tad Miller.'

'So what's that to me?'

Hard-voiced. Not friendly at all.

'Want to apologize for all that jawing I was into when you came in. Customers come *first* in this place.'

He grumbled 'all right' while stirring his coffee, but he didn't look at me. Ignored me. Hoped I'd go away.

I leaned toward him. 'Couldn't help but notice that timepiece you're wearing. Handsome thing. Never saw one quite like it.'

He swung around slowly, holding up his left wrist. 'Got it in Chi,' he said. 'You like it, eh?'

'Prettiest damn watch I ever did see.'

He was warming up fast. Like a woman will do when you tell her how cute her kid is. Works every time.

'What are all those little dials and things?' I asked.

He worked back his sleeve so I could get a better look. 'Tells you the time in ten parts of the world,' he said. 'Tells you the month of the year and the day of the week.'

'Well, I'll be jinged!'

He twisted a doodad at the side of the watch. 'Set this,' he said proudly, 'and it rings every hour on the hour.'

By now Sally was spreading out his lunch special, and she couldn't resist getting into the conversation. 'What's a thing like that cost?' she asked him.

Bad manners. I'd never have asked it that way, straight out. And he didn't like it. He scowled at her. 'That's my business.'

Watch could have been stolen, for all I knew. You just don't ask folks about how they get hold of a thing like that or how much they paid for it. But Sal was never one for laying back.

She huffed into the kitchen, all tight-faced.

He was eating in silence now. Sally's question had put him back into his sour mood. I felt bad about that.

'Look . . .' I said, 'don't mind her. She don't see many new folks around here. Sticks her nose in too far, is all.'

He grunted, kept eating. Really shovelling it in. It was beef stew. I knew Sally made good beef stew, so he was bound to be enjoying it. I tried him again.

'You just . . . passing through?'

'Yeah. Hitching. Can't hitch on the express so I'm on the spur. Not many cars, I'll tellya. Waited two hours for a ride this morning.'

I nodded in sympathy. 'Like you say, not many cars. But the fruit trucks go through this time of year. In the afternoons. One of those'll stop for you. Those truckers are good people. Just you give 'em a wave, they'll stop.'

'Thanks for the tip,' he said. 'Usually, with trucks, I don't even try. Regulations about riders and all.'

'Just give 'em a wave,' I repeated.

There was some silence then. Him finishing Sally's stew, me sitting there sipping at my own lukewarm coffee. (I drink too much of the stuff, so I've learned to nurse a cup. Can't sleep nights if I don't.)

Then I said to him, 'You ever go to amusement parks as a kid?'

495

He nodded. 'Sure. Who hasn't? Every kid has.'

'I ran the Funhouse in one,' I told him. 'Down by the lake just this side of town.'

His face brightened. A smile creased it. His first of the day, I'd wager.

'Hell, I loved those frigging funhouses! Used to sneak into 'em when my allowance was all spent and I couldn't afford to buy a ticket. They had an air vent inside that blew the girls' skirts up. Used to hide in there and watch.' He scrubbed at the side of his dark beard. 'Haven't been in one since I was eleven – back in Omaha.'

'Never made it to Nebraska, but I hear it's a nice state.'

'Used to scare myself half to death in those places. Bumping around in the dark . . . Couldn't see a thing. Scary as hell!'

'Folks like to be scared,' I said. 'Guess it's part of human nature.'

'Trick doors . . . blind tunnels leading nowhere . . . things that popped out at you!' He chuckled. 'One place had a big gorilla with red eyes . . . I musta jumped ten feet when that ape popped outa the floor at me! Had gorilla nightmares for a month after that. Wouldn't go to bed unless Ma left the light on.'

I've noticed one thing in the years with Happyland: people love to talk about funhouses. It's a subject everybody just plain likes to talk about – how scared they got as kids, lost in the dark tunnels, with things jumping at them. Funhouses are just that – *fun*.

'I miss running the place,' I told him honestly. 'Used to get a real kick out of scaring the folks. I'd work all the trick effects . . . and how they'd yell and scream! Especially the girls. Young girls love to scream.'

He nodded agreement.

Suddenly I turned to him, grinning. 'I got me an idea.'

'What's that?' he said, pushing away his last empty plate. He put his hand on his stomach and belched.

'Why don't you and me go out there – to Happyland? I can take you through the Funhouse!'

He blinked at me, a little confused. 'You mean – right *now?*'

'Sure. The park's closed, has been for years, but I can get in. Be no problem for me to show you through my Funhouse. Be proud to!'

The big man shook his head. 'Well . . . I dunno. That stuff's for kids.'

'Hell, *we're* kids, aren't we? Just wearing adult bodies. No man ever stops being a boy. Not inside. Not all the way.' I grinned at him. 'Want to have a go? . . . give it a try?'

'Sounds a little crazy.'

'Funhouse is for fun!' I said. 'It's not even noon yet. You can take the tour with me, come out of the park and still grab a hitch with one of the truckers.'

He slapped the countertop. 'Why not? Why the hell not?'

I grinned at him. 'Be fun for me, too. Haven't been out to Happyland for a longish while. Be like going home.'

I own a Ford pickup. Old, like I am. Got a missing tail-light. Clutch is bad. Needs a ring job. Tires are mostly bald. And the paint's gone altogether. But it putters along. Gets me where I have to go.

Happyland's only ten minutes out from town. As I said, right on the lake, at the deepend. Lot of boats used to be on the lake, but it's quiet now. Just black water, and too cold to swim in most of the year. Deep and black and quiet.

I parked next to the gate and we slipped under the rusted chain fence. The park was sad to see, all deserted and boarded up and with old newspapers and empty beer cans and trash everywhere. Vines growing right into the boards. Holes in the ground. I told the stranger to watch where he walked.

'Break an ankle out here at night,' I said.

'I'll bet.'

We passed the old Penny Arcade. All the machines were gone. It was like a dirty barn inside. No colour or movement or sound in there now. Just a rat or two, maybe. Or a spider trapping flies.

Sad.

We walked on in the noon heat, past the Loop and the Whip and the Merry-go-Round, with broken holes in the floor where all the painted horses had galloped.

'No gorillas today,' I said as we approached the Funhouse. 'Electricity's shut down, and they took all the trick stuff away to Chicago. But at least we can run the tunnels. They're still the same.'

'This is crazy,' said the bearded man. 'I've gotta be nuts, doing a thing like this.'

'Be proud of yourself!' I told him. 'You're not afraid to let out the boy in you! Every man would like to, but most are chicken about it. You've got guts.'

We stood outside, looking at the place. The big laughing fatman at the entrance was gone. I can still hear his booming Ha-Ha-Ha-Ha like it was yesterday. Twenty years of a laugh you don't forget.

The ticket booth was shaped like the jaws of a shark – but now most of the teeth were missing and the skin was peeling in big curling blisters along the sides. The broken glass in the booth had two boards nailed over it, like a pair of crossed arms.

'How do we get in?' the stranger asked me.

'There's bound to be a loose board,' I told him. 'Let's take a look.'

'Oke,' he nodded with a grin. 'Lead on.'

I found the loose board, pulling some brush away to clear it. Illinois is a green state; we get a lot of rain here, and things grow fast. The Funhouse was being choked by vines and creepers and high grass. It looked a thousand years old.

Sad.

The sky was clouding over. Late summer storm coming. They just pop up on you. It would be raining soon.

More rain, more growth. At this rate, in another fifty years, Happyland would be covered over – like those jungle temples in Mexico. No one could ever find it.

'Watch that nail near the top,' I warned, as the stranger stooped to squeeze through with me. 'Tear your shirt easy on a nail like that.'

'Thanks.'

'Got to watch out for my customers,' I said.

Now we were inside. It was absolutely tar-pit black in the Funhouse. A jump from daylight to the dark side of the moon. And hot. Muggy hot inside.

'Can't see an inch in front of me,' the stranger said.

'Don't worry, I'll walk you through. I've got a flash. It could use a new battery. Kind of dim, but we should be all right with it.'

For emergencies, I always keep a flash in the Ford's glove compartment, with a couple of spare batteries. Never know when a tire might let go on you at night. But I keep forgetting to put in the new batteries when the old ones wear out. I guess nobody's perfect!

'Lot of cobwebs in here,' I said, as we moved along. 'Hope you don't mind spiders.'

'I'm not in love with 'em,' said the big man. 'Not poisonous, are they?'

'No, no. Not these. Mostly little fellers. I'll clear the way for you.'

And I did that, using a rolled newspaper to sweep the tunnel as I moved through it.

'Where are we?' he asked. 'I mean – what part of the Funhouse?'

'About midway through from where you start,' I said. 'But the fun part is ahead. You haven't missed anything.'

'This is crazy,' he repeated again, half to himself. Then: 'Ouch!'

I stopped, flashed the dimming light back at him. He was down on one knee.

'Hurt yourself?'

'I'm okay. Just stumbled. A loose board.'

'Lots of those in here,' I admitted. 'Not dangerous, though. Not the way I'm taking you.'

As we moved down the narrow wooden tunnel there was a wet, sliding sound.

'What's that?' he asked.

'The lake,' I told him. 'This part of the tunnel is built over the shore. That's the sound the lake water makes, hitting the pilings. The wind's up. Storm's coming.'

We kept walking – going down one tunnel, turning, entering another, twisting, turning, reversing in the wooden maze. Maze to him, not to me. It was my world.

The rain had started, pattering on the wooden roof, dripping down into the tunnels. And the end-of-summer heat had given way to a sudden chill.

'This is no fun,' said the stranger. 'It's not what I remembered. I don't like it.'

'The fun's up ahead,' I promised him.

'You keep saying that. Look, I think we'd better –'

Suddenly my flash went out.

'Hey!' he shouted. 'What happened?'

'Battery finally died,' I said. 'Don't worry. I've got another in the pickup. Wait here and I'll get it.'

'Not on your life,' the stranger protested. 'I'm not staying alone here in the pitch dark in this damned place.'

'You *afraid* of the dark?' I asked him.

'No, dammit!'

'Then wait for me. I can't lead you back without a flash. Not through all the twists and turns. But I know the way. I can move fast. Won't be ten minutes.'

'Well . . . I –'

'One thing, though. I want to warn you carefully about one thing. *Don't* try to move. Just stay right where you are, so I'll know where to find you. Some of the side tunnels are dangerous. Rotting boards. You could break a leg. The tunnels are tricky. You have to know which ones to stay out of.'

'Don't worry, I'll stick right here like a bug on a wall.'

'Ten minutes,' I said.

And I left him there in the tunnel.

*

Of course I didn't go back to the pickup for any batteries. Instead, I went to the control room at the end of B Tunnel.

The door was padlocked, but I had the key. Inside, feeling excited about the stranger, I let Ed know I was here. Which was easy. I'd rigged a low-voltage generator in the control room, and when I pulled down a wall switch a red light went on under the tunnels and Ed knew I was back with a stranger.

I'll bet he was excited, too. Hard to tell with Ed. But *I* sure was. My heart was pounding.

Fun in the Funhouse!

I didn't waste any time here. I'd done this many times before, so it was routine now: unlock the door, go inside, throw the switch for Ed, then activate the trap.

Trapdoor.

Right under the bearded stranger's feet. Even if he moved up or down the tunnel for a few yards (some of the nervous ones did that) there was no problem because the whole section of flooring was geared to open and send whoever was inside the tunnel down onto the slide. And the slide ended on the sand at the lakefront.

Where Ed was.

He would come up out of the lake when he saw the light. It would shine on the black water and he would see it from where he lived down there in the deep end and he would come slithering up.

Ed wasn't much to look at. Kind of weird, really. His father was one of those really big rats that live in the burrows under the cemetery, and his mother was something from deep in the lake. Something big and ugly and leathery.

They'd made love – the rat and the lake thing – and Ed was the result. Their son. He doesn't really have a name, but I call him Ed the way Gramps called me Tad. It fits him somehow, makes him more appealing. More . . . human.

Ed and me, we get along fine as partners. I bring him things to eat, and he saves the 'goodies' for me. Like wallets, and cash and rings (that big one Sally was joshing me about came from one of Ed's meals) and whatever else the strangers have that I can use.

Ed is smart.

He seems to know that I need these things to keep going now that the factory's shut down and I've lost my job here and all. That's why the partnership works so well. We each get our share. After I take what I want (one time I got a fine pair of leather boots) he drags the body back into the lake.

Then he eats.

Lucky for me, one meal lasts Ed for almost a month. So I don't have to worry if no stranger shows up at Sally's for two, three, even four weeks. One always ambles along sooner or later. Like Mama always said, Everything comes to those that wait. Mama was a very patient woman. But she could be nasty. I can testify to that.

It gets bad in winter – for strangers, I mean – when the roads are closed, but that's when Ed sleeps anyhow, so things even out.

By the time I got back to the stranger's tunnel that afternoon it was really coming down. Rain, I mean. Dripping and sliding along the cold wood, and getting under my collar. Most uncomfortable. Somehow, rain always depresses me. Guess I'm too moody.

The stranger was down there with Ed where I expected him to be. Sometimes there's a little yelling and screaming, but nobody ever hears it, so that's no problem either. One fellow tried to use a knife on Ed, but Ed's skin is very tough and rubbery and doesn't cut easy. The stranger was just wasting his time, trying to use a knife on Ed.

I took a ladder down to the sand where the body was.

Ed was off by the water's edge, kind of breathing hard, when I got there. His jaw was dripping and his slanted black eyes glittered. Ed never blinked. He was watching me the way he always does, with his tail kind of moving, snakelike. He looked kind of twitchy, so I hurried. I don't think Ed likes the rain. Ed makes me nervous when it rains. He's not like himself. I never hang around the Funhouse when he's like that.

The bearded stranger was already dead, of course. Most of his head was gone, but Ed had been careful not to muss up his clothes – so it was no problem getting his wallet, rings, cash, coins . . .

When I climbed the ladder again Ed was already sliding toward the body.

Guess he was hungry.

Three and a half weeks later the stranger at the counter in Sally's was looking at my watch.

'I've never seen one like that,' he said.

'Tells you the time in ten parts of the world,' I said. 'Tells you the month of the year and the day of the week. And it rings every hour on the hour.'

The stranger was impressed.

After a while, I grinned, leaned toward him across the counter and said, 'You ever go to amusement parks as a kid?'

Gramma

BY STEPHEN KING

In 1982, two fans of the original Twilight Zone *TV series, the wunderkind directors Steven Spielberg and John Landis, convinced Warner Brothers and CBS that they should revive 'The Zone' – as it had become known amongst its admirers – first as a movie and then as a television series. Rod Serling had, however, died almost a decade earlier in 1975 and two new producers were required to get the project moving: Frank Marshall was selected for* Twilight Zone: The Movie *and Philip De Guere to oversee the small screen version. The name De Guere was to prove uncannily apposite, for a few weeks into shooting, the film made newspaper headlines all over the world when the actor Vic Morrow and two children, Renee Shinn Chen and My-ca Dinh Le, were killed in an accident while shooting a war scene for one of the picture's four segments. This occurred on 23 July when a Bell military helicopter lost its rear motor and fell onto the trio as they were filming at the Santa Clara River near Los Angeles. Despite the tragedy, the film became a box office success, and was followed in 1985 by the new TV series on American screens. It was evident that* New Twilight Zone *was aiming at a higher intellectual level than its predecessor and that the criterion for the stories in the hour-long shows – sometimes there was as many as three of them – was that each had a twist in the tail.*

The most memorable – and probably most grisly – story adapted for the series was 'Gramma' by the world's biggest selling author of horror fiction, Stephen King (1946–), about a little boy left in the care of his old, blind and terrifyingly obese grandmother. The screenplay was suitably entrusted to the enfant terrible *of fantasy writers, Harlan Ellison. Afterwards, Stephen King explained how he had come to write the story. 'My grandmother died when I was in the house alone* with her,' he said. 'I was the same age as the boy in the story. Obviously, she didn't get up and walk or anything like that, but it was my first experience of death. I was always afraid of her because the only time that I knew her was when my mother moved back to take care of her and she was, by that time, senile. And she was – to me – very frightening. She was this huge, grossly fat woman with all these billows of snow white hair. She had no eyesight . . . the eyes had been blown out by high blood pressure, glaucoma, diabetes. God knows what. No, she was not a love object of mine. She was horrible!' Harlan Ellison also claimed that his script version of the story was passed through several typists' hands on its way to production. 'They got terrified,' he explained, 'and had to stop and pass it on to someone else because they couldn't go any further on the first reading.' Just how terrifying the horrible the old lady might be, the reader is now invited to find out for himself . . .

GEORGE'S mother went to the door, hesitated there, came back, and tousled George's hair. 'I don't want you to worry,' she said. 'You'll be all right. Gramma, too.'

'Sure, I'll be okay. Tell Buddy to lay chilly.'

'Pardon me?'

George smiled. 'To stay cool.'

'Oh. Very funny.' She smiled back at him, a distracted, going-in-six-directions-at-once smile. 'George, are you sure –'

'I'll be *fine*.'

Are you sure what? Are you sure you're not scared to be alone with Gramma? Was that what she was going to ask?

If it was the answer is no. After all, it wasn't like he was six any more, when they had first come here to Maine to take care of Gramma, and he had cried with terror whenever Gramma held out her heavy arms toward him from her white vinyl chair that always smelled of the poached eggs she ate and the sweet bland powder George's mom rubbed into her flabby, wrinkled skin; she held out her white-elephant arms, wanting him to come to her and be hugged to that huge and heavy old white-elephant body. Buddy had gone to her, had been enfolded in Gramma's blind embrace, and Buddy had come out alive . . . but Buddy was two years older.

Now Buddy had broken his leg and was at the CMG Hospital in Lewiston.

'You've got the doctor's number if something *should* go wrong. Which it won't. Right?'

'Sure,' he said, and swallowed something dry in his throat. He smiled. Did the smile look okay? Sure. Sure it did. He wasn't scared of Gramma anymore. After all, he wasn't six anymore. Mom was going up to the hospital to see Buddy and he was just going to stay here and lay chilly. Hang out with Gramma awhile. No problem.

Mom went to the door again, hesitated again, and came back again, smiling that distracted, going-six-ways-at-once smile. 'If she wakes up and calls for her tea —'

'I know,' George said, seeing how scared and worried she was underneath that distracted smile. She was worried about Buddy, Buddy and his dumb *Pony League*, the coach had called and said Buddy had been hurt in a play at the plate, and the first George had known of it (he was just home from school and sitting at the table eating some cookies and having a glass of Nestlé's Quik) was when his mother gave a funny little gasp and said, *Hurt? Buddy? How bad?*

'I know *all* that stuff, Mom. I got it knocked. Negative perspiration. Go on, now.'

'You're a good boy, George. Don't be scared. You're not scared of Gramma anymore, are you?'

'Huh-uh,' George said. He smiled. The smile felt pretty good; the smile of a fellow who was laying chilly with negative perspiration on his brow, the smile of a fellow who Had It Knocked, the smile of a fellow who was most definitely not six anymore. He swallowed. It was a great smile, but beyond it, down in the darkness behind his smile, was one very dry throat. It felt as if his throat was lined with mitten-wool. 'Tell Buddy I'm sorry he broke his leg.'

'I will,' she said, and went to the door again. Four-o'clock sunshine slanted in through the window. 'Thank God we took the sports insurance, Georgie. I don't know what we'd do if we didn't have it.'

'Tell him I hope he tagged the sucker out.'

She smiled her distracted smile, a woman of just past fifty with two late sons, one thirteen, one eleven, and no man. This time she opened the door, and a cool whisper of October came in through the sheds.

'And remember, Dr Arlinder —'

'Sure,' he said. 'You better go or his leg'll be fixed by the time you get there.'

'She'll probably sleep the whole time,' Mom said. 'I love you, Georgie. You're a good son.' She closed the door on that.

George went to the window and watched her hurry to the old '69 Dodge that burned too much gas and oil, digging the keys from her purse. Now that she was out of the house and didn't know George was looking at her, the distracted smile fell away and she only looked

504

distracted – distracted and sick with worry about Buddy. George felt bad for her. He didn't waste any similar feelings about Buddy, who liked to get him down and sit on top of him with a knee on each of George's shoulders and tap a spoon in the middle of George's forehead until he just about went crazy (Buddy called it the Spoon Torture of the Heathen Chinee and laughed like a madman and sometimes went on doing it until George cried), Buddy who sometimes gave him the Indian Rope Burn so hard that little drops of blood would appear on George's forearm, sitting on top of the pores like dew on blades of grass at dawn, Buddy who had listened so sympathetically when George had one night whispered in the dark of their bedroom that he liked Heather MacArdle and who the next morning ran across the schoolyard screaming *GEORGE AND HEATHER UP IN A TREE, KAY-EYE-ESS-ESS-EYE-EN-GEE! FIRST COMES LOVE AN THEN COMES MARRITCH! HERE COMES HEATHER WITH A BABY CARRITCH!* like a runaway fire engine. Broken legs did not keep older brothers like Buddy down for long, but George was rather looking forward to the quiet as long as this one did. *Let's see you give me the Spoon Torture of the Heathen Chinee with your leg in a cast, Buddy. Sure, kid – EVERY day.*

The Dodge backed out of the driveway and paused while his mother looked both ways, although nothing would be coming; nothing ever was. His mother would have a two-mile ride over washboards and ruts before she even got to tar, and it was nineteen miles to Lewiston after that.

She backed all the way out and drove away. For a moment dust hung in the bright October afternoon air, and then it began to settle.

He was alone in the house.

With Gramma.

He swallowed.

Hey! Negative perspiration! Just lay chilly, right?

'Right,' George said in a low voice, and walked across the small, sunwashed kitchen. He was a towheaded, good-looking boy with a spray of freckles across his nose and cheeks and a look of good humour in his darkish grey eyes.

Buddy's accident had occurred while he had been playing in the Pony League championship game this 5 October. George's Pee Wee League team, the Tigers, had been knocked out of their tournament on the first day, two Saturdays ago (*What a bunch of babies!* Buddy had exulted as George walked tearfully off the field. *What a bunch of PUSSIES!*) . . . and now Buddy had broken his leg. If Mom wasn't so worried and scared, George would have been almost happy.

There was a phone on the wall, and next to it was a note-minder board with a grease pencil hanging beside it. In the upper corner of the board was a cheerful country Gramma, her cheeks rosy, her white hair done up in a bun; a cartoon Gramma who was pointing at the board. There was a comic-strip balloon coming out of the cheerful country Gramma's mouth and she was saying, 'REMEMBER *THIS* SONNY!' Written on the board in his mother's sprawling hand was *Dr Arlinder*, 681–4330. Mom hadn't written the number there just today, because she had to go to Buddy; it had been there almost three weeks now, because Gramma was having her 'bad spells' again.

George picked up the phone and listened.

'– so I told her, I said, "Mable, if he treats you like that –" '

He put it down again. Henrietta Dodd. Henrietta was always on the phone, and if it was in the afternoon you could always hear the soap opera stories going on in the background. One night after she had a glass of wine with Gramma (since she started having the 'bad spells' again, Dr Arlinder said Gramma couldn't have the wine with her supper, so Mom didn't either – George was sorry, because the wine made Mom sort of giggly and she would tell stories about her girlhood), Mom had said that every time Henrietta Dodd opened her mouth, all her guts fell out. Buddy and George laughed wildly, and Mom put a hand to her mouth and said *Don't you EVER tell anyone I said that,* and then she began to laugh too, all three of them sitting at the supper table laughing, and at last the racket had awakened Gramma, who slept more and more, and she began to cry *Ruth! Ruth! ROO-OOOTH!* in that high, querulous voice of hers, and Mom had stopped laughing and went into her room.

Today Henrietta Dodd could talk all she wanted, as far as George was concerned. He just wanted to make sure the phone was working. Two weeks ago there had been a bad storm, and since then it went out sometimes.

He found himself looking at the cheery cartoon Gramma again, and wondered what it would be like to have a Gramma like that. *His* Gramma was huge and fat and blind; the hypertension had made her senile as well. Sometimes, when she had her 'bad spells', she would (as Mom put it) 'act out the Tartar', calling for people who weren't there, holding conversations with total emptiness, mumbling strange words that made no sense. On one occasion when she was doing this last, Mom had turned white and had gone in and told her to shut up, shut up, *shut up*! George remembered that occasion very well, not only because it was the only time Mom had ever actually yelled at Gramma, but because it was the next day that someone discovered that the

Birches cemetery out on the Maple Sugar Road had been vandalized — gravestones knocked over, the old nineteenth-century gates pulled down, and one or two of the graves actually dug up — or something. *Desecrated* was the word Mr Burdon, the principal, had used the next day when he convened all eight grades for Assembly and lectured the whole school on Malicious Mischief and how some things Just Weren't Funny. Going home that night, George had asked Buddy what *desecrated* meant, and Buddy said it meant digging up graves and pissing on the coffins, but George didn't believe that . . . unless it was late. And dark.

Gramma was noisy when she had 'bad spells', but mostly she just lay in the bed she had taken to three years before, a fat slug wearing rubber pants and diapers under her flannel nightgown, her face runneled with cracks and wrinkles, her eyes empty and blind — faded blue irises floating atop yellowed corneas.

At first Gramma hadn't been totally blind. But she had been going blind, and she had to have a person at each elbow to help her totter from her white vinyl egg-and-baby-powder-smelling chair to her bed or the bathroom. In those days, five years ago, Gramma had weighed well over two hundred pounds.

She had held out her arms and Buddy, then eight, had gone to her. George had hung back. And cried.

But I'm not scared now, he told himself, moving across the kitchen in his Keds. *Not a bit. She's just an old lady who has 'bad spells' sometimes.*

He filled the teakettle with water and put it on a cold burner. He got a teacup and put one of Gramma's special herb tea bags into it. In case she should wake up and want a cup. He hoped like mad that she wouldn't, because then he would have to crank up the hospital bed and sit next to her and give the tea a sip at a time, watching the toothless mouth fold itself over the rim of the cup, and listen to the slurping sounds as she took the tea into her dank, dying guts. Sometimes she slipped sideways on the bed and you had to pull her back over and her flesh was *soft*, kind of *jiggly*, as if it was filled with hot water, and her blind eyes would look at you . . .

George licked his lips and walked toward the kitchen table again. His last cookie and half a glass of Quik still stood there, but he didn't want them anymore. He looked at his schoolbooks, covered with Castle Rock Cougars bookcovers, without enthusiasm.

He ought to go in and check on her.

He didn't want to.

He swallowed and his throat still felt as if it was lined with mitten-wool.

I'm not afraid of Gramma, he thought. *If she held out her arms I'd go right to her and let her hug me because she's just an old lady. She's senile and that's why she has 'bad spells'. That's all. Let her hug me and not cry. Just like Buddy.*

He crossed the short entryway to Gramma's room, face set as if for bad medicine, lips pressed together so tightly they were white. He looked in, and there lay Gramma, her yellow-white hair spread around her in a corona, sleeping, her toothless mouth hung open, chest rising under the coverlet so slowly you almost couldn't see it, so slowly that you had to look at her for a while just to make sure she wasn't dead.

Oh God, what if she dies on me while Mom's up to the hospital?
She won't. She won't.
Yeah, but what if she does?
She won't, so stop being a pussy.

One of Gramma's yellow, melted-looking hands moved slowly on the coverlet: her long nails dragged across the sheet and made a minute scratching sound. George drew back quickly, his heart pounding.

Cool as a moose, numbhead, see? Laying chilly.

He went back into the kitchen to see if his mother had been gone only an hour, or perhaps an hour and a half – if the latter, he could start reasonably waiting for her to come back. He looked at the clock and was astounded to see that not even twenty minutes had passed. Mom wouldn't even be into the city yet, let alone on her way back out of it! He stood still, listening to the silence. Faintly, he could hear the hum of the refrigerator and the electric clock. The snuffle of the afternoon breeze around the corners of the little house. And then – at the very edge of audibility – the faint, rasping susurrus of skin over cloth . . . Gramma's wrinkled, tallowy hand moving on the coverlet.

He prayed in a single gust of mental breath:
'PleaseGoddon'tletherwakeupuntilMomcomeshomeforJesus's-sake-Amen.'

He sat down and finished his cookie, drank his Quik. He thought of turning on the TV and watching something, but he was afraid the sound would wake up Gramma and that high, querulous, not-to-be-denied voice would begin calling *Roo-OOTH! RUTH! BRING ME M'TEA! TEA! ROOO-OOOOOTH!*

He slicked his dry tongue over his drier lips and told himself not to be such a pussy. She was an old lady stuck in bed, it wasn't as if she could get up and hurt him, and she was eighty-three years old, she wasn't going to die this afternoon.

George walked over and picked up the phone again.

508

'— that same day! And she even knew he was married! Gorry, I hate these cheap little corner-walkers that think they're so smart! So at Grange I said —'

George guessed that Henrietta was on the phone with Cora Simard. Henrietta hung on the phone most afternoons from one until six with first *Ryan's Hope* and then *One Life to Live* and then *All My Children* and then *As the World Turns* and then *Search for Tomorrow* and then God knew what other ones playing in the background, and Cora Simard was one of her most faithful telephone correspondents, and a lot of what they talked about was 1) who was going to be having a Tupperware party or an Amway party and what the refreshments were apt to be, 2) cheap little corner-walkers, and 3) what they had said to various people at 3-a) the Grange, 3-b) the monthly church fair, or 3-c) K of P Hall Beano.

'— that if I ever saw her up that way again, I guess I could be a good citizen and call —'

He put the phone back in its cradle. He and Buddy made fun of Cora when they went past her house just like all the other kids — she was fat and sloppy and gossipy and they would chant, *Cora-Cora from Bora-Bora, ate a dog turd and wanted more-a!* and Mom would have killed them both if she had known that, but now George was glad she and Henrietta Dodd were on the phone. They could talk all afternoon, for all George cared. He didn't mind Cora, anyway. Once he had fallen down in front of her house and scraped his knee — Buddy had been chasing him — and Cora had put a Band-Aid on the scrape and gave them each a cookie, talking all the time. George had felt ashamed for all the times he had said the rhyme about the dog turd and the rest of it.

George crossed to the sideboard and took down his reading book. He held it for a moment, then put it back. He had read all the stories in it already, although school had only been going for a month. He read better than Buddy, although Buddy was better at sports. *Won't be better for a while, he thought with momentary good cheer, not with a broken leg.*

He took down his history book, sat down at the kitchen table, and began to read about how Cornwallis had surrendered up his sword at Yorktown. His thoughts wouldn't stay on it. He got up, went through the entryway again. The yellow hand was still. Gramma slept, her face a grey, sagging circle against the pillow, a dying sun surrounded by the wild yellowish-white corona of her hair. To George she didn't look anything like people who were getting old and getting ready to die were supposed to look. She didn't look peaceful, like a sunset. She looked crazy and . . .

(and dangerous)

. . . yes, okay, and *dangerous* – like an ancient she-bear that might have one more good swipe left in her claws.

George remembered well enough how they had come to Castle Rock to take care of Gramma when Granpa died. Until then Mom had been working in the Stratford Laundry in Stratford, Connecticut. Granpa was three or four years younger than Gramma, a carpenter by trade, and he had worked right up until the day of his death. It had been a heart attack.

Even then Gramma had been getting senile, having her 'bad spells'. She had always been a trial to her family, Gramma had. She was a volcanic woman who had taught school for fifteen years, between having babies and getting in fights with the Congregational Church she and Granpa and their nine children went to. Mom said that Granpa and Gramma quit the Congregational Church in Scarborough at the same time Gramma decided to quit teaching, but once, about a year ago, when Aunt Flo was up for a visit from her home in Salt Lake City, George and Buddy, listening at the register as Mom and her sister sat up late, talking, heard quite a different story. Granpa and Gramma had been kicked out of the church and Gramma had been fired off her job because she did something wrong. It was something about *books*. Why or how someone could get fired from their job and kicked out of the church just because of *books*, George didn't understand, and when he and Buddy crawled back into their twin beds under the eave, George asked.

There's all kinds of books, Señor El-Stupido, Bobby whispered.

Yeah, but what kind?

How should I know? Go to sleep!

Silence. George thought it through.

Buddy?

What? An irritated hiss.

Why did Mom tell us Gramma quit the church and her job?

Because it's a skeleton in the closet, that's why! Now go to sleep!

But he hadn't gone to sleep, not for a long time. His eyes kept straying to the closet door, dimly outlined in moonlight, and he kept wondering what he would do if the door swung open, revealing a skeleton inside, all grinning tombstone teeth and cistern eye sockets and parrot-cage ribs; white moonlight skating delirious and almost blue on whiter bone. Would he scream? What had Buddy meant, *a skeleton in the closet?* What did skeletons have to do with books? At last he had slipped into sleep without even knowing it and had dreamed he was six again, and Gramma was holding out her arms, her blind eyes searching for him; Gramma's reedy, querulous voice was saying, *Where's the little one, Ruth? Why's he crying? I only want to put him in the closet . . . with the skeleton.*

George had puzzled over these matters long and long, and finally, about a month after Aunt Flo had departed, he went to his mother and told her he had heard her and Aunt Flo talking. He knew what a skeleton in the closet meant by then, because he had asked Mrs Redenbacher at school. She said it meant having a scandal in the family, and a scandal was something that made people talk a lot. *Like Cora Simard talks a lot?* George had asked Mrs Redenbacher, and Mrs Redenbacher's face had worked strangely and her lips had quivered and she had said, *That's not nice, George, but . . . yes, something like that.*

When he asked Mom, her face had gotten very still, and her hands had paused over the solitaire clockface of cards she had been laying out.

Do you think that's a good thing for you to be doing, Georgie? Do you and your brother make a habit of eavesdropping over the register?

George, then only nine, had hung his head.

We like Aunt Flo, Mom. We wanted to listen to her a little longer. This was the truth.

Was it Buddy's idea?

It had been, but George wasn't going to tell her that. He didn't want to go walking around with his head on backwards, which might happen if Buddy found out he had tattled.

No, mine.

Mom had sat silent for a long time, and then she slowly began laying her cards out again. *Maybe it's time you did know, she had said. Lying's worse than eavesdropping, I guess, and we all lie to our children about Gramma. And we lie to ourselves too, I guess. Most of the time, we do.* And then she spoke with a sudden, vicious bitterness that was like acid squirting out between her front teeth – he felt that her words were so hot they would have burned his face if he hadn't recoiled. *Except for me. I have to live with her, and I can no longer afford the luxury of lies.*

So his Mom had told him that after Granpa and Gramma had gotten married, they had had a baby that was born dead, and a year later they had another baby, and that was born dead too, and the doctor told Gramma she would never be able to carry a child to term and all she could do was keep on having babies that were dead or babies that died as soon as they sucked air. That would go on, he said, until one of them died inside her too long before her body could shove it out and it would rot in there and kill her, too.

The doctor told her that.

Not long after, the *books* began.

Books about how to have babies?

But Mom didn't – or wouldn't – say what kind of books they were, or where Gramma got them, or how she *knew* to get them. Gramma got pregnant again, and this time the baby wasn't born dead and the baby didn't die after a breath or two; this time the baby was fine, and that was George's Uncle Larson. And after that, Gramma kept getting pregnant and having babies. Once, Mom said, Granpa had tried to make her get rid of the books to see if they could do it without them (or even if they couldn't, maybe Granpa figured they had enough yowwens by then so it wouldn't matter) and Gramma wouldn't. George asked his mother why and she said: 'I think that by then having the books was as important to her as having the babies.'

'I don't get it,' George said.

'Well,' George's mother said, 'I'm not sure I do, either . . . I was very small, remember. All I know for sure is that those books got a hold over her. She said there would be no more talk about it and there wasn't, either. Because Gramma wore the pants in our family.'

George closed his history book with a snap. He looked at the clock and saw that it was nearly five o'clock. His stomach was grumbling softly. He realized suddenly, and with something very like horror, that if Mom wasn't home by six or so, Gramma would wake up and start hollering for her supper. Mom had forgotten to give him instructions about that, probably because she was so upset about Buddy's leg. He supposed he could make Gramma one of her special frozen dinners. They were special because Gramma was on a salt-free diet. She also had about a thousand different kinds of pills.

As for himself, he could heat up what was left of last night's macaroni and cheese. If he poured a lot of ketchup on it, it would be pretty good.

He got the macaroni and cheese out of the fridge, spooned it into a pan, and put the pan on the burner next to the teakettle, which was still waiting in case Gramma woke up and wanted what she sometimes called 'a cuppa cheer'. George started to get himself a glass of milk, paused, and picked up the telephone again.

'– and I couldn't even believe my eyes when . . .' Henrietta Dodd's voice broke off and then rose shrilly: 'Who keeps listening in on this line, I'd like to know!'

George put the phone back on the hook in a hurry, his face burning. *She doesn't know it's you, stupe. There's six parties on the line!*

All the same, it was wrong to eavesdrop, even if it was just to hear another voice when you were alone in the house, alone except for Gramma, the fat thing sleeping in the hospital bed in the other room; even when it seemed almost necessary to hear another human voice because your Mom was in Lewiston and it was going to be dark soon and Gramma was in the other room and Gramma looked like

(yes oh yes she did)

a she-bear that might have just one more murderous swipe left in her old clotted claws.

George went and got the milk.

Mom herself had been born in 1930, followed by Aunt Flo in 1932, and then Uncle Franklin in 1934. Uncle Franklin had died in 1948, of a burst appendix, and Mom sometimes still got teary about that, and carried his picture. She had liked Frank the best of all her brothers and sisters, and she said there was no need for him to die that way, of peritonitis. She said God had played dirty when He took Frank.

George looked out the window over the sink. The light was more golden now, low over the hill. The shadow of their back shed stretched all the way across the lawn. If Buddy hadn't broken his dumb *leg*, Mom would be here now, making chilli or something (plus Gramma's salt-free dinner), and they would all be talking and laughing and maybe they'd play some gin rummy later on.

George flicked on the kitchen light, even though it really wasn't dark enough for it yet. Then he turned on LO HEAT under his macaroni. His thoughts kept returning to Gramma, sitting in her white vinyl chair like a big fat worm in a dress, her corona of hair every crazy whichway on the shoulders of her pink rayon robe, holding out her arms for him to come, him shrinking back against his Mom, bawling.

Send him to me, Ruth. I want to hug him.

He's a little frightened, Momma. He'll come in time. But his mother sounded frightened, too.

Frightened? Mom?

George stopped, thinking. Was that true? Buddy said your memory could play tricks on you. Had she really sounded frightened?

Yes. She had.

Gramma's voice rising peremptorily: *Don't coddle the boy, Ruth! Send him over here; I want to give him a hug.*

No. He's crying.

And as Gramma lowered her heavy arms from which the flesh hung in great, doughlike gobbets, a sly, senile smile had overspread her face

513

and she had said: *Does he really look like Franklin, Ruth? I remember you saying he favoured Frank.*

Slowly, George stirred the macaroni and cheese and ketchup. He hadn't remembered the incident so clearly before. Maybe it was the silence that made him remember. The silence, and being alone with Gramma.

So Gramma had her babies and taught school, and the doctors were properly dumbfounded, and Granpa carpentered and generally got more and more prosperous, finding work even in the depths of the Depression, and at last people began to talk, Mom said.

What did they say? George asked.

Nothing important, Mom said, but she suddenly swept her cards together. *They said your Gramma and Granpa were too lucky for ordinary folks, that's all.* And it was just after that the books had been found. Mom wouldn't say more than that, except that the school board had found some and that a hired man had found some more. There had been a big scandal. Granpa and Gramma had moved to Buxton and that was the end of it.

The children had grown up and had children of their own, making aunts and uncles of each other; Mom had gotten married and moved to New York with Dad (who George could not even remember). Buddy had been born, and then they had moved to Stratford in 1969 George had been born, and in 1971 Dad had been hit and killed by a car driven by the Drunk Man Who Had to Go to Jail.

When Granpa had his heart attack there had been a great many letters back and forth among the aunts and uncles. They didn't want to put the old lady in a nursing home. And she didn't want to go to a home. If Gramma didn't want to do a thing like that, it might be better to accede to her wishes. The old lady wanted to go to one of them and live out the rest of her years with that child. But they were all married, and none of them had spouses who felt like sharing their home with a senile and often unpleasant old woman. All were married, that was, except Ruth.

The letters flew back and forth, and at last George's Mom had given in. She quit her job and came to Maine to take care of the old lady. The others had chipped together to buy a small house in outer Castle View, where property values were low. Each month they would send her a cheque, so she could 'do' for the old lady and for her boys.

What's happened is my brothers and sisters have turned me into a sharecropper, George could remember her saying once, and he didn't know for sure what that meant, but she had sounded bitter when she

514

said it, like it was a joke that didn't come out smooth in a laugh but instead stuck in her throat like a bone. George knew (because Buddy had told him) that Mom had finally given in because everyone in the big, far-flung family had assured her that Gramma couldn't possibly last long. She had too many things wrong with her – high blood pressure, uremic poisoning, obesity, heart palpitations – to last long. It would be eight months, Aunt Flo and Aunt Stephanie and Uncle George (after whom George had been named) all said; a year at the most. But now it had been five years, and George called that lasting pretty long.

She had lasted pretty long, all right. Like a she-bear in hibernation, waiting for . . . what?

(You know how to deal with her best Ruth you know how to shut her up.)

George, on his way to the fridge to check the directions on one of Gramma's special salt-free dinners, stopped. Stopped cold. Where had that come from? That voice speaking inside his head?

Suddenly his belly and chest broke out in gooseflesh. He reached inside his shirt and touched one of his nipples. It was like a little pebble, and he took his finger away in a hurry.

Uncle George. His 'namesake uncle', who worked for Sperry-Rand in New York. It had been his voice. He had said that when he and his family came up for Christmas two – no, three – years ago.

She's more dangerous now that she's senile.
George, be quiet. The boys are around somewhere.

George stood by the refrigerator, one hand on the cold chrome handle, thinking, remembering, looking out into the growing dark. Buddy hadn't been around that day. Buddy was already outside, because Buddy had wanted the good sled, that was why; they were going sliding on Joe Camber's hill and the other sled had a buckled runner. So Buddy was outside and here was George, hunting through the boot-and-sock box in the entryway, looking for a pair of heavy socks that matched, and was it his fault his mother and Uncle George were talking in the kitchen? George didn't think so. Was it George's fault that God hadn't struck him deaf, or, lacking the extremity of that measure, at least located the conversation elsewhere in the house? George didn't believe that, either. As his mother had pointed out on more than one occasion (usually after a glass of wine or two), God sometimes played dirty.

515

You know what I mean, Uncle George said.

His wife and his three girls had gone over to Gates Falls to do some last-minute Christmas shopping, and Uncle George was pretty much in the bag, just like the Drunk Man Who Had to Go to Jail. George could tell by the way his uncle slurred his words.

You remember what happened to Franklin when he crossed her.

George, be quiet, or I'll pour the rest of your beer right down the sink!

Well, she didn't really mean to do it. Her tongue just got away from her. Peritonitis —

George, shut up!

Maybe, George remembered thinking vaguely, *God isn't the only one who plays dirty.*

Now he broke the hold of these old memories and looked in the freezer and took out one of Gramma's dinners. Veal. With peas on the side. You had to preheat the oven and then bake it for forty minutes at 300 degrees. Easy. He was all set. The tea was ready on the stove if Gramma wanted that. He could make tea, or he could make dinner in short order if Gramma woke up and yelled for it. Tea or dinner, he was a regular two-gun Sam. Dr Arlinder's number was on the board, in case of an emergency. Everything was cool. So what was he worried about?

He had never been left alone with Gramma, that was what he was worried about.

Send the boy to me, Ruth. Send him over here.

No. He's crying.

She's more dangerous now . . . you know what I mean.

We all lie to our children about Gramma.

Neither he nor Buddy. Neither of them had ever been left alone with Gramma. Until now.

Suddenly George's mouth went dry. He went to the sink and got a drink of water. He felt . . . funny. These thoughts. These memories. Why was his brain dragging them all up now?

He felt as if someone had dumped all the pieces to a puzzle in front of him and that he couldn't quite put them together. And maybe it was *good* he couldn't put them together, because the finished picture might be, well, sort of boogery. It might —

From the other room, where Gramma lived all her days and nights, a choking, rattling, gargling noise suddenly arose.

A whistling gasp was sucked into George as he pulled breath. He turned towards Gramma's room and discovered his shoes were tightly

516

nailed to the linoleum floor. His heart was spike-iron in his chest. His eyes were wide and bulging. *Go now*, his brain told his feet, and his feet saluted and said *Not at all, sir!*

Gramma had never made a noise like that before.

Gramma had *never* made a noise like that before.

It arose again, a choking sound, low and then descending lower, becoming an insectile buzz before it died out altogether. George was able to move at last. He walked toward the entryway that separated the kitchen from Gramma's room. He crossed it and looked into her room, his heart slamming. Now his throat was *choked* with wool mittens; it would be impossible to swallow past them.

Gramma was still sleeping and it was all right, that was his first thought; it had only been some weird *sound*, after all; maybe she made it all the time when he and Buddy were in school. Just a snore. Gramma was fine. Sleeping.

That was his first thought. Then he noticed that the yellow hand that had been on the coverlet was now dangling limply over the side of the bed, the long nails almost but not quite touching the floor. And her mouth was open, as wrinkled and caved-in as an orifice dug into a rotten piece of fruit.

Timidly, hesitantly, George approached her.

He stood by her side for a long time, looking down at her, not daring to touch her. The imperceptible rise and fall of the coverlet appeared to have ceased.

Appeared.

That was the key word. *Appeared.*

But that's just because you are spooked, Georgie. You're just being Señor El-Stupido, like Buddy says — it's a game. Your brain's playing tricks on your eyes, she's breathing just fine, she's —

'Gramma?' he said, and all that came out was a whisper. He cleared his throat and jumped back, frightened of the sound. But his voice was a little louder. 'Gramma? You want your tea now? Gramma?'

Nothing.

The eyes were closed.

The mouth was open.

The hand hung.

Outside, the setting sun shone golden-red through the trees.

He saw her in a positive fullness then; saw her with that childish and brilliantly unhoused eye of unformed immature reflection, not here, not now, not in bed, but sitting in the white vinyl chair, holding out her arms, her face at the same time stupid and triumphant. He found himself remembering one of the 'bad spells' when Gramma began to shout, as if in a foreign language – *Gyaagin! Gyaagin! Hastur degryon Yos-soth-oth!* – and Mom had sent them outside, had screamed '*Just GO!*' at Buddy when Buddy stopped at the box in the entry to hunt for his gloves, and Buddy had looked back over his shoulder, so scared he was walleyed with it because their mom never shouted, and they had both gone out and stood in the driveway, not talking, their hands stuffed in their pockets for warmth, wondering what was happening.

Later, Mom had called them in for supper as if nothing had happened.

(You know how to deal with her best Ruth you know how to shut her up.)

George had not thought of that particular 'bad spell' from that day to this. Except now, looking at Gramma, who was sleeping so strangely in her crank-up hospital bed, it occurred to him with dawning horror that it was the next day they had learned that Mrs Harham, who lived up the road and sometimes visited Gramma, had died in her sleep that night.

Gramma's 'bad spells'.

Spells.

Witches were supposed to be able to cast spells. That's what made them witches, wasn't it? Poisoned apples. Princes into toads. Ginger-bread houses. Abracadabra. Presto-chango. *Spells*.

Spilled-out pieces of an unknown puzzle flying together in George's mind, as if by magic.

Magic, George thought, and groaned.

What was the picture? It was Gramma, of course, Gramma and her *books*, Gramma who had been driven out of town, Gramma who hadn't been able to have babies and then had been able to, Gramma who had been driven out of the *church* as well as out of town. The picture was Gramma, yellow and fat and wrinkled and sluglike, her toothless mouth curved into a sunken grin, her faded, blind eyes somehow sly and cunning; and on her head was a black, conical hat sprinkled with silver stars and glittering Babylonian crescents; at her feet were slinking black cats with eyes as yellow as urine, and the smells were pork and blindness, pork and burning, ancient stars and candles as dark as the earth in which coffins lay; he heard words spoken from ancient books, and each word was like a stone and each sentence like a crypt reared in some stinking boneyard and every paragraph like a nightmare caravan of the plague-dead taken to a place of burning; his eye was the eye of a child and in that moment it opened wide in startled understanding on blackness.

Gramma had been a witch, just like the Wicked Witch in the *Wizard of Oz*. And now she was dead. That gargling sound, George thought with increasing horror. That gargling, snoring sound had been a . . . a . . . a '*death rattle*'.

'Gramma?' he whispered, and crazily he thought: *Ding-dong, the wicked witch is dead.*

No response. He held his cupped hand in front of Gramma's mouth. There was no breeze stirring around inside Gramma. It was dead calm and slack sails and no wake widening behind the keel. Some of his fright began to recede now, and George tried to think. He remembered Uncle Fred showing him how to wet a finger and test the wind, and now he licked his entire palm and held it in front of Gramma's mouth.

Still nothing.

He started for the phone to call Dr Arlinder, and then stopped. Suppose he called the doctor and she really wasn't dead at all? He'd be in dutch for sure.

Take her pulse.

He stopped in the doorway, looking doubtfully back at that dangling hand. The sleeve of Gramma's nightie had pulled up, exposing her wrist. But that was no good. Once, after a visit to the doctor when the nurse had pressed her finger to his wrist to take his pulse, George had tried it and hadn't been able to find anything. As far as his own unskilled fingers could tell, he was dead.

Besides, he didn't really want to . . . well . . . to touch Gramma. Even if she was dead. *Especially* if she was dead.

George stood in the entryway, looking from Gramma's still, bedridden form to the phone on the wall beside Dr Arlinder's number, and back to Gramma again. He would just have to call. He would –

– *get a mirror!*

Sure! When you breathed on a mirror, it got cloudy. He had seen a doctor check an unconscious person that way once in a movie. There was a bathroom connecting with Gramma's room and now George hurried in and got Gramma's vanity mirror. One side of it was regular, the other side magnified, so you could see to pluck out hairs and do stuff like that.

George took it back to Gramma's bed and held one side of the mirror until it was almost touching Gramma's open, gaping mouth. He held it there while he counted to sixty, watching Gramma the whole time. Nothing changed. He was sure she was dead even before he took the mirror away from her mouth and observed its surface, which was perfectly clear and unclouded.

Gramma was dead.

George realized with relief and some surprise that he could feel sorry for her now. Maybe she had been a witch. Maybe not. Maybe she had only *thought* she was a witch. However it had been, she was gone now. He realized with an adult's comprehension that questions of concrete reality became not unimportant but less vital when they were examined in the mute bland face of mortal remains. He realized this with an adult's comprehension and accepted with an adult's relief. This was a passing footprint, the shape of a shoe, in his mind. So are all the child's adult impressions; it is only in later years that the child realizes that he was being *made; formed;* shaped by random experiences; all that remains *in the instant* beyond the footprint is that bitter gunpowder smell which is the ignition of an idea beyond a child's given years.

He returned the mirror to the bathroom, then went back through her room, glancing at the body on his way by. The setting sun had painted the old dead face with barbaric, orange-red colours, and George looked away quickly.

He went through the entry and crossed the kitchen to the telephone, determined to do everything right. Already in his mind he saw a certain advantage over Buddy; whenever Buddy started to tease him, he would simply say: *I was all by myself in the house when Gramma died, and I did everything right.*

Call Dr Arlinder, that was first. Call him and say, 'My Gramma just died. Can you tell me what I should do? Cover her up or something?'

No.

'I *think* my Gramma just died.'

Yes. Yes, that was better. Nobody thought a little kid knew anything anyway, so that was better.

Or how about:

'I'm pretty sure my Gramma just died –'

Sure! That was best of all.

And tell about the mirror and the death rattle and all. And the doctor would come right away, and when he was done examining Gramma he would say, *'I pronounce you dead, Gramma,'* and then say to George, *'You laid extremely chilly in a tough situation, George. I want to congratulate you.'* And George would say something appropriately modest.

George looked at Dr Arlinder's number and took a couple of slow deep breaths before grabbing the phone. His heart was beating fast, but that painful spike-iron thud was gone now. Gramma had died. The worst had happened, and somehow it wasn't as bad as waiting for her to start bellowing for Mom to bring her tea.

The phone was dead.

He listened to the blankness, his mouth still formed around the words *I'm sorry, Missus Dodd, but this is George Bruckner and I have to call the doctor for my Gramma.* No voices. No dial tone. Just dead blankness. Like the dead blankness in the bed there.

Gramma is –

– is –

(oh she is)

Gramma is laying chilly.

Gooseflesh again, painful and marbling. His eyes fixed on the Pyrex teakettle on the stove, the cup on the counter with the herbal tea bag in it. No more tea for Gramma. Not ever.

(laying so chilly)

George shuddered.

He stuttered his finger up and down on the Princess phone's cutoff button, but the phone was dead. Just as dead as –

(just as chilly as)

He slammed the handset down hard and the bell tinged faintly inside and he picked it up in a hurry to see if that meant it had magically gone right again. But there was nothing, and this time he put it back slowly.

His heart was thudding harder again.

I'm alone in this house with her dead body.

He crossed the kitchen slowly, stood by the table for a minute, and then turned on the light. It was getting dark in the house. Soon the sun would be gone; night would be here.

Wait. That's all I got to do. Just wait until Mom gets back. This is better, really. If the phone went out, it's better that she just died instead of maybe having a fit or something, foaming at the mouth, maybe falling out of bed –

Ah, that was bad. He could have done very nicely without *that* horse-pucky.

Like being alone in the dark and thinking of dead things that were still lively – seeing shapes in the shadows on the walls and thinking of death, thinking of the dead, those things, the way they would stink and the way they would move toward you in the black: thinking this: thinking that: thinking of bugs turning in flesh: burrowing in flesh: eyes that moved in the dark. Yeah. That most of all. Thinking of eyes that moved in the dark and the creak of floorboards as something came across the room through the zebra-stripes of shadows from the light outside. Yeah.

In the dark your thoughts had a perfect circularity, and no matter what you tried to think of – flowers or Jesus or baseball or winning the gold in the 440 at the Olympics – it somehow led back to the form in the shadows with the claws and the unblinking eyes.

'*Shittabrick!*' he hissed, and suddenly slapped his own face. And hard. He was giving himself the whimwhams, it was time to stop it. He wasn't six anymore. She was dead, that was all, dead. There was no more thought inside her now than there was in a marble or a floorboard or a doorknob or a radio dial or –

And a strong alien unprepared-for voice, perhaps only the unforgiving unbidden voice of simple survival, inside him cried: *Shut up Georgie and get about your goddam business!*

Yeah, okay. Okay, but –

He went back to the door of her bedroom to make sure.

There lay Gramma, one hand out of bed and touching the floor, her mouth hinged agape. Gramma was part of the furniture now. You could put her hand back in bed or pull her hair or pop a water glass into her mouth or put earphones on her head and play Chuck Berry into them full-tilt boogie, and it would be all the same to her. Gramma was, as Buddy sometimes said, out of it. Gramma had had the course.

A sudden low and rhythmic thudding noise began, not far to George's left, and he started, a little yipping cry escaping him. It was the storm door, which Buddy had put on just last week. Just the storm door, unlatched and thudding back and forth in the freshening breeze.

George opened the inside door, leaned out, and caught the storm door as it swung back. The wind – it wasn't a breeze but a wind – caught his hair and riffled it. He latched the door firmly and wondered where the wind had come from all of a sudden. When Mom left it had been almost dead calm. But when Mom left it had been bright daylight and now it was dusk.

George glanced in at Gramma again and then went back and tried the phone again. Still dead. He sat down, got up, and began to walk back and forth through the kitchen, pacing, trying to think.

An hour later it was full dark.

The phone was still out. George supposed the wind, which had now risen to a near-gale, had knocked down some of the lines, probably out by the Beaver Bog, where the trees grew everywhere in a helter-skelter of deadfalls and swampwater. The phone dinged occasionally, ghostly and far, but the line remained blank. Outside the wind moaned along the eaves of the small house and George reckoned he would have a story to tell as the next Boy Scout Camporee, all right . . . just sitting in the house alone with his dead Gramma and the phone out and the wind pushing rafts of clouds fast across the sky, clouds that were black on top and the colour of dead tallow, the colour of Gramma's claw-hands, underneath.

It was, as Buddy also sometimes said, a Classic.

He wished he was telling it now, with the actuality of the thing safely behind him. He sat at the kitchen table, his history book open in front of him, jumping at every sound . . . and now that the wind was up, there were a lot of sounds as the house creaked in all its unoiled secret forgotten joints.

She'll be home pretty quick. She'll be home and then everything will be okay. Everything.

(you never covered her)

will be all r—

(never covered her face)

George jerked as if someone had spoken aloud and stared wide-eyed across the kitchen at the useless telephone. You were supposed to pull the sheet up over the dead person's face. It was in all the movies.

Hell with that! I'm not going in there!

No! And no reason why he should! Mom could cover her face when she got home! Or *Dr Arlinder* when he came! Or the *undertaker*!

Someone, anyone, but him.

No reason why he should.

It was nothing to him, and nothing to Gramma.

Buddy's voice in his head:

If you weren't scared, how come you didn't dare to cover her face?

It was nothing to me.

Fraidycat!

Nothing to Gramma, either.

CHICKEN-GUTS fraidycat!

Sitting at the table in front of his unread history book, considering it, George began to see that if he didn't pull the counterpane up over Gramma's face, he couldn't claim to have done everything right, and thus Buddy would have a leg (no matter how shaky) to stand on.

Now he saw himself telling the spooky story of Gramma's death at the Camporee fire before taps, just getting to the comforting conclusion where Mom's headlights swept into the driveway — the reappearance of the grown-up, both reestablishing and reconfirming the concept of Order — and suddenly, from the shadows, a dark figure arises, and a pine-knot in the fire explodes and George can see it's Buddy there in the shadows, saying: *If you was so brave, chicken-guts, how come you didn't dare to cover up HER FACE?*

523

George stood up, reminding himself that Gramma was out of it, that Gramma was *wasted*, that Gramma was *laying chilly*. He could put her hand back in bed, stuff a tea bag up her nose, put on earphones playing Chuck Berry full blast, etc., etc., and none of it would put a buzz under Gramma, because that was what being dead was about, nobody could put a buzz under a dead person, a dead person was the ultimate laid-back cool, and the rest of it was just dreams, ineluctable and apocalyptic and feverish dreams about closet doors swinging open in the dead mouth of midnight, just dreams about moonlight skating a delirious blue on the bones of disinterred skeletons, just –

He whispered, 'Stop it, can't you? Stop being so – '

(gross)

He steeled himself. He was going to go in there and pull the coverlet up over her face, and take away Buddy's last leg to stand on. He would administer the few simple rituals of Gramma's death perfectly. He would cover her face and then – his face lit at the symbolism of this – he would put away her unused tea bag and her unused cup. Yes.

He went in, each step a conscious act. Gramma's room was dark, her body a vague hump in the bed, and he fumbled madly for the light switch, not finding it for what seemed to be an eternity. At last it clicked up, flooding the room with low yellow light from the cut-glass fixture overhead.

Gramma lay there, hand dangling, mouth open. George regarded her, dimly aware that little pearls of sweat now clung to his forehead, and wondered if his responsibility in the matter could possibly extend to picking up that cooling hand and putting it back in bed with the rest of Gramma. He decided it did not. Her hand could have fallen out of bed any old time. That was too much. He couldn't touch her. Everything else, but not that.

Slowly, as if moving through some thick fluid instead of air, George approached Gramma. He stood over her, looking down. Gramma was yellow. Part of it was the light, filtered through the old fixture, but not all.

Breathing through his mouth, his breath rasping audibly, George grasped the coverlet and pulled it up over Gramma's face. He let go of it and it slipped just a little, revealing her hairline and the yellow creased parchment of her brow. Steeling himself, he grasped it again, keeping his hands far to one side and the other of her head so he wouldn't have to touch her, even through the cloth, and pulled it up again. This time it stayed. It was satisfactory. Some of the fear went out of George. He had *buried* her. Yes, that was why you covered the dead person up, and why it was right: it was like *burying* them. It was a statement.

524

He looked at the hand dangling down, unburied, and discovered now that he could touch it, he could tuck it under and bury it with the rest of Gramma.

He bent, grasped the cool hand, and lifted it.

The hand twisted in his and clutched his wrist.

George screamed. He staggered backward, screaming in the empty house, screaming against the sound of the wind reaving the eaves, screaming against the sound of the house's creaking joints. He backed away, pulling Gramma's body askew under the coverlet, and the hand thudded back down, twisting, turning, snatching at the air . . . and then relaxing to limpness again.

I'm all right, it was nothing, it was nothing but a reflex.

George nodded in perfect understanding, and then he remembered again how her hand had turned, clutching his, and he shrieked. His eyes bulged in their sockets. His hair stood out, perfectly on end, in a cone. His heart was a runaway stamping-press in his chest. The world tilted crazily, came back to the level, and then just went on moving until it was tilted the other way. Every time rational thought started to come back, panic goosed him again. He whirled, wanting only to get out of the room to some other room — or even three or four miles down the road, if that was what it took — where he could get all of this under control. So he whirled and ran full tilt into the wall, missing the open doorway by a good two feet.

He rebounded and fell to the floor, his head singing with a sharp, cutting pain that sliced keenly through the panic. He touched his nose and his hand came back bloody. Fresh drops spotted his green shirt. He scrambled to his feet and looked around wildly.

The hand dangled against the floor as it had before, but Gramma's body was not askew; it also was as it had been.

He had imagined the whole thing. He had come into the room, and all the rest of it had been no more than a mind-movie.

No.

But the pain had cleared his head. Dead people didn't grab your wrist. Dead was dead. When you were dead they could use you for a hat rack or stuff you in a tractor tire and roll you downhill or et cetera, et cetera, et cetera. When you were dead you might be acted *upon* (by, say, little boys trying to put dead dangling hands back into bed), but your days of acting upon — so to speak — were over.

Unless you're a witch. Unless you pick your time to die when no one's around but one little kid, because it's best that way, you can . . . can . . .

Can what?

Nothing. It was stupid. He had imagined the whole thing because he had been scared and that was all there was to it. He wiped his nose with his forearm and winced at the pain. There was a bloody smear on the skin of his inner forearm.

He wasn't going to go near her again, that was all. Reality or hallucination, he wasn't going to mess with Gramma. The bright flare of panic was gone, but he was still miserably scared, near tears, shaky at the sight of his own blood, only wanting his mother to come home and take charge.

George backed out of the room, through the entry, and into the kitchen. He drew a long, shuddery breath and let it out. He wanted a wet rag for his nose, and suddenly he felt like he was going to vomit. He went over to the sink and ran cold water. He bent and got a rag from the basin under the sink – a piece of one of Gramma's old diapers – and ran it under the cold tap, snuffling up blood as he did so. He soaked the old soft cotton diaper-square until his hand was numb, then turned off the tap and wrung it out.

He was putting it to his nose when her voice spoke from the other room.

'Come here, boy,' Gramma called in a dead buzzing voice. 'Come in here – *Gramma wants to hug you.*'

George tried to scream and no sound came out. No sound at all. But there were sounds in the other room. Sounds that he heard when Mom was in there, giving Gramma her bed-bath, lifting her bulk, dropping it, turning it, dropping it again.

Only those sounds now seemed to have a slightly different and yet utterly specific meaning – it sounded as though Gramma was trying to . . . to get out of bed.

'*Boy! Come in here, boy! Right NOW! Step to it!*'

With horror he saw that his feet were answering that command. He told them to stop and they just went on, left foot, right foot, hay foot, straw foot, over the linoleum; his brain was a terrified prisoner inside his body – a hostage in a tower.

She IS a witch, she's a witch and she's having one of her 'bad spells', oh yeah, it's a 'spell' all right, and it's bad, it's REALLY bad, oh God oh Jesus help me help me help me –

George walked across the kitchen and through the entryway and into Gramma's room and yes, she hadn't just tried to get out of bed, she was out, she was sitting in the white vinyl chair where she hadn't sat for four years, since she got too heavy to walk and too senile to know where she was, anyway.

But Gramma didn't look senile now.

Her face was sagging and doughy, but the senility was gone – if it had ever really been there at all, and not just a mask she wore to lull small boys and tired husbandless women. Now Gramma's face gleamed with full intelligence – it gleamed like an old, stinking wax candle. Her eyes drooped in her face, lacklustre and dead. Her chest was not moving. Her nightie had pulled up, exposing elephantine thighs. The coverlet of her deathbed was thrown back.

Gramma held her huge arms out to him.

'I want to hug you, Georgie,' that flat and buzzing dead voice said. *'Don't be scared old crybaby. Let your Gramma hug you.'*

George cringed back, trying to resist that almost insurmountable pull. Outside, the wind shrieked and roared. George's face was long and twisted with the extremity of his fright; the face of a woodcut caught and shut up in an ancient book.

George began to walk toward her. He couldn't help himself. Step by dragging step toward those outstretched arms. *He would show Buddy that he wasn't scared of Gramma, either. He would go to Gramma and be hugged because he wasn't a crybaby fraidycat. He would go to Gramma now.*

He was almost within the circle of her arms when the window to his left crashed inward and suddenly a wind-blown branch was in the room with them, autumn leaves still clinging to it. The river of wind flooded the room, blowing over Gramma's pictures, whipping her nightgown and her hair.

Now George could scream. He stumbled backward out of her grip and Gramma made a cheated hissing sound, her lips pulling back over smooth old gums; her thick, wrinkled hands clapped uselessly together on moving air.

George's feet tangled together and he fell down. Gramma began to rise from the white vinyl chair, a tottering pile of flesh; she began to stagger toward him. George found he couldn't get up; the strength had deserted his legs. He began to crawl backward, whimpering. Gramma came on, slowly but relentlessly, dead and yet alive, and suddenly George understood what the hug would mean; the puzzle was complete in his mind and somehow he found his feet just as Gramma's hand closed on his shirt. It ripped up the side, and for one moment he felt her cold flesh against his skin before fleeing into the kitchen again.

He would run into the night. Anything other than being hugged by the witch, his Gramma. Because when his mother came back she would find Gramma dead and George alive, oh yes . . . but George would have developed a sudden taste for herbal tea.

527

He looked back over his shoulder and saw Gramma's grotesque, misshapen shadow rising on the wall as she came through the entryway.

And at that moment the telephone rang, shrilly and stridently.

George seized it without even thinking and screamed into it; screamed for someone to come, to please come. He screamed these things silently; not a sound escaped his locked throat.

Gramma tottered into the kitchen in her pink nightie. Her whitish-yellow hair blew wildly around her face, and one of her horn combs hung askew against her wrinkled neck.

Gramma was grinning.

'Ruth?' It was Aunt Flo's voice, almost lost in the whistling wind-tunnel of a bad long-distance connection. 'Ruth, are you there?' It was Aunt Flo in Minnesota, over two thousand miles away.

'Help me!' George screamed over the phone, and what came out was a tiny, hissing whistle, as if he had blown into a harmonica full of dead reeds.

Gramma tottered across the linoleum, holding her arms out for him. Her hands snapped shut and then open and then shut again. Gramma wanted her hug; she had been waiting for that hug for five years.

'Ruth, can you hear me? It's been storming here, it just started, and I . . . I got scared. Ruth, I can't hear you –'

'Gramma,' George moaned into the telephone. Now she was almost upon him.

'George?' Aunt Flo's voice suddenly sharpened; became almost a shriek. 'George, is that you?'

He began to back away from Gramma, and suddenly realized that he had stupidly backed away from the door and into the corner formed by the kitchen cabinets and the sink. The horror was complete. As her shadow fell over him, the paralysis broke and he screamed into the phone, screamed it over and over again: *'Gramma! Gramma! Gramma!'*

Gramma's cold hands touched his throat. Her muddy, ancient eyes locked on his, draining his will.

Faintly, dimly, as if across many years as well as many miles, he heard Aunt Flo say: 'Tell her to lie down, George, tell her to lie down and be still. Tell her she must do it in your name and the name of her father. The name of her taken father is *Hastur*. His name is power in her ear, George – tell her *Lie down in the Name of Hastur – tell her –*'

The old, wrinkled hand tore the telephone from George's nerveless grip. There was a taut pop as the cord pulled out of the phone. George collapsed in the corner and Gramma bent down, a huge heap of flesh above him, blotting out the light.

George screamed: *'Lie down! Be still! Hastur's name! Hastur! Lie down! Be still!'*

Her hands closed around his neck –

'You gotta do it! Aunt Flo said you did! In my name! In your *Father's* name! Lie down! Be sti –'

– and squeezed.

When the lights finally splashed into the driveway an hour later, George was sitting at the table in front of his unread history book. He got up and walked to the back door and opened it. To his left, the Princess phone hung in its cradle, its useless cord looped around it.

His mother came in, a leaf clinging to the collar of her coat. 'Such a wind,' she said. 'Was everything all – George? *George, what happened?'*

The blood fell from Mom's face in a single, shocked rush, turning her a horrible clown-white.

'Gramma,' he said. 'Gramma died. Gramma died, Mommy.' And he began to cry.

She swept him into her arms and then staggered back against the wall, as if the act of hugging had robbed the last of her strength. 'Did . . . did anything happen?' she asked. *'George, did anything else happen?'*

'The wind knocked a tree branch through her window,' George said.

She pushed him away, looked at his shocked, slack face for a moment, and then stumbled into Gramma's room. She was in there for perhaps four minutes. When she came back, she was holding a red tatter of cloth. It was a bit of George's shirt.

'I took this out of her hand,' Mom whispered.

'I don't want to talk about it,' George said. 'Call Aunt Flo, if you want. I'm tired. I want to go to bed.'

She made as if to stop him, but didn't. He went up to the room he shared with Buddy and opened the hot-air register so he could hear what his mother did next. She wasn't going to talk to Aunt Flo, not tonight, because the telephone cord had pulled out; not tomorrow, because shortly before Mom had come home, George had spoken a short series of words, some of them bastardized Latin, some only pre-Druidic grunts, and over two thousand miles away Aunt Flo had dropped dead of a massive brain haemorrhage. It was amazing how those words came back. How *everything* came back.

George undressed and lay down naked on his bed. He put his hands behind his head and looked up into the darkness. Slowly, slowly, a sunken and rather horrible grin surfaced on his face.

Things were going to be different around here from now on.

Very different.

Buddy, for instance. George could hardly wait until Buddy came home from the hospital and started in with the Spoon Torture of the Heathen Chinee or an Indian Rope Burn or something like that. George supposed he would have to let Buddy get away with it – at least in the daytime, when people could see – but when night came and they were alone in this room, in the dark, with the door closed . . .

George began to laugh soundlessly.

As Buddy always said, it was going to be a Classic.

The Doll

BY RICHARD MATHESON

In 1985 life turned full circle for Steven Spielberg when NBC offered him the chance to produce his own late night TV horror anthology series in the same mould as the Twilight Zone *where he had begun his dazzling career all those years earlier. With co-producer David E. Vogel he was given a budget approaching one million dollars per episode for a total of forty-four stories which, it was hoped, would recapture some of the magic that had made 'The Zone' – and the other Sixties' series he and many others had enjoyed,* Outer Limits *and* One Step Beyond – *so memorable. Sparing no cost on scripts and sets, the production team also hired some notable directors including Martin Scorsese, Joe Dante, Clint Eastwood, Burt Reynolds as well as Steven himself. The guest star list was equally impressive: Kevin Costner, Sid Caesar, Drew Barrymore, Mark Hamill, Sam Waterstone, Milton Berle, David Carradine, Stan Freberg and Charlie Sheen. Perhaps not surprisingly, the films proved to be a mixture of all the elements that had made Spielberg's fantasy films, such as* ET, Close Encounters of the Third Kind *and* Poltergeist, *such huge box office successes, but were also infused with the sense of mood and suspense that the director had first revealed when filming Joan Crawford in 'Eyes'.*

The most intriguing episode to be included in Amazing Stories *was unquestionably, 'The Doll' by Richard Matheson (1926–) one of the leading writers of horror for television, and the author of the classic vampire novel,* I Am Legend *(1954). Matheson, who has been writing for TV anthology shows since* Thriller *in the Sixties and scripted a trilogy of supernatural tales for a pilot transmitted as* Dead of Night *in 1977, had originally produced a script around his story about a lonely bachelor whose life is poignantly changed by a beautiful doll for*

Twilight Zone in 1964. However, the story was replaced in favour of another which also dealt with a mysterious toy, 'Living Doll' by Charles Beaumont, and it had remained in his files thereafter until the advent of Amazing Stories. This time when submitted, the decision to film the script was confirmed – and after two decades a unique and touching story that linked two anthology shows at last went before the cameras in Hollywood with John Lithgow as the bachelor, and Annie Helm as his co-star. After the filming, Matheson explained how his remarkable fantasy had come to be written in the first place. 'We bought a doll for one of our daughters,' he explained, 'and the doll's face was so mature and so lovely that the idea evolved: What if a man who was not married bought a doll like that for his niece, and the niece didn't care for it and he had to take it back – only he didn t want to take it back, because the face just looked so fascinating . . .'

THE poet screamed, 'Devil spawn! Scrabbling lizard! Maniacal kangaroo!'

His scraggy frame went leaping through the doorway, then locked into paralysis. *'Fiend!'* he gagged.

The object of this mottled-faced abuse squatted oblivious in a snow-bank of confettied manuscript. Manuscript delivered of sweaty gestation, typewritten in quivering agony.

'Foaming moonstruck *octopus*! Shovel-handed *ape*'! The blood-laced eyes of Ruthlen Beauson bagged gibbously behind their horn-rimmed lenses. At hipless sides, his fingers shook like leprous stringbeans in a gale. Ulcers within ulcers throbbed.

'Hun!' he raged anew, '*Goth*! *Apache*! Demented nihilist!'

Saliva dribbling from his teething maw, little Gardner Beauson bestowed a one-toothed grin upon his palsied sire. Shredded poetry filtered through his stubby fists as the semi-spheroid of his bottom hovered dampishly above each lacerated amphibrach with iambic variation.

Ruthlen Beauson groaned a soul-wracked groan. '*Confusion*,' he lamented in a trembling voice, 'Untrammeled farrago.'

Then, suddenly, his eyes embossed into metallic orbs, his fingers petrified into a strangler's pose. 'I'll do him in,' he gibbered faintly, 'I'll snap his hyoid with a brace of thumbs.'

Upon this juncture, Athene Beauson, smock bespattered, hands adrip with soppy clay, swept into the room like a wraith of vengeance resurrected from the mud.

'What *now*'? she asked, acidulous through gritted teeth.

'Look! *Look!*' Ruthlen Beauson's forefinger jabbed fitfully as he pointed toward their sniggering child. 'He's destroyed my *Songs of Sconce*! His 20–90 eyes went bulgy mad. 'I'll carve him,' he foreboded in a roupy whisper, 'I'll *carve* the shriveled viper!'

'Oh . . . *look out,*' Athene commanded, pulling back her butcher-bent spouse and dragging up her son by his drool-soaked undershirt.

Suspended over heaps of riven muse, he eyed his mother with a saucy aspect.

'*Whelp!*' she snapped, then let him have one, soundly, on his bulbous rump.

Gardner Beauson screeched in inflammatory protest, was shown the door and exited, his little brain already cocked for further action. A residue of clay upon his diaper, he waddled, saucer-eyed into the plenitude of breakables which was the living room as Athene turned to see her husband on his knees, aghast, in the rubble of a decade's labour.

'I shall destroy myself,' the poet mumbled, sagging shouldered. 'I'll inject my veins with lethal juices.'

'Get up, get up,' said Athene crisply, face a sour mask.

Ruthlen floundered to his feet. 'I'll kill him, yes, I'll kill the wizened beast,' he said in hollow-hearted shock.

'That's *no* solution,' said his wife, 'Even though . . .'

Her eyes grew soft a moment as she dreamed of nudging Gardner into a vat of alligators. Her full lips quivered on the brink of tremulous smiling.

Then her green eyes flinted. 'That's *no* solution,' she repeated, 'and it's time we solved this goddam thing.'

Ruthlen stared with dumb-struck eyes upon the ruins of his composition. 'I'll kill him,' he divulged to the scattered fragments, 'I'll –'

'*Ruthlen listen to me,*' said his wife, clay-soaked fingers clenching into fists.

His spiritless gaze lifted for moment.

'Gardner needs a playmate,' she declared. 'I read it in a book. He needs a playmate.'

'I'll kill him,' mumbled Ruthlen.

'Will you *listen*!'

'Kill him.'

'I tell you Gardner has to have a playmate! I don't care whether we can afford it or not, he needs a playmate!'

'Kill,' the poet hissed. 'Kill.'

'I don't care if we haven't got a cent! You want time for poetry and I want time for sculpturing!'

'My *Songs of Sconce.*'

'*Ruthlen Beauson!*' Athene screamed, a moment's time before the deafening shatter of a vase.

'Good God, what *now*'! Athath exclaimed.

They found him dangling from the mantelpiece, caterwauling for succor and immediate change of diaper . . .

THE DOLL THAT DOES EVERYTHING!

Athene stood before the plate glass window, lips pursed in deep deliberation. In her mind, a vivid balance see-sawed – grave necessity on the one side, sterile income on the other. Implastic contemplation ridged her brow. They had no money, that was patent. Nursey school was out, a governess impossible. And yet, there had to be an answer; there *had* to be.

Athene braced herself and strode into the shop.

The man looked up, a kindly smile dimpling his apple cheeks, welcoming his customer.

'That doll,' Athene inquired. 'Does it really do the things your placard says it does?'

'That doll,' the salesman beamed, 'is quite without comparison, the nonpareil of toycraft. It walks, it talks, it eats and drinks, dispenses body wastes, snores while it sleeps, dances a jig, rides a see-saw and sings the choruses of seven childhood favourites.' He caught his breath. 'To name a few,' he said. 'It sings "Molly Andrews" –'

'What is the cost of –'

'It swims the crawl for fifty feet, it reads a book, plays thirteen simplet etudes on the pianoforte, mows the lawn, changes its own diapers, climbs a tree and burps.'

'What is the price of –'

'And it grows,' the salesman said.

'It . . .'

'*Grows*,' the man reiterated, slit-eyed. 'Within its plastic body are all the cells and protoplasms necessary for a cycle of maturation lasting up to twenty years.'

Athene gaped.

'At one-oh-seven-fifty, an obvious bargain,' the man concluded. 'Shall I have it wrapped or would you rather walk it home?'

A swarm of eager hornets, each a thought, buzzed inside the head of Athene Beauson. It was the perfect playmate for little Gardner. One-hundred-seven-fifty though! Ruthlen's scream would shatter windows when he saw the tag.

'You can't go wrong,' the salesman said.

He *needs* a playmate!

'Time payments can easily be arranged.' The salesman guessed her plight and fired his *coup de grâce*.

All thoughts disappeared like chips swept off a gambling table. Athene's eye caught fire; a sudden smile pulled up her lip ends.

'A boy doll,' she requested eagerly, 'One year old.'

The salesman hurried to his shelves . . .

No windows broke but Athene's ears rang for half an hour after.

'Are you *mad?*' her husband's scream had plunged its strident blades into her brain. 'One-hundred-seven fifty!'

'We can pay on time.'

'With *what?*' he shrieked. 'Rejection slips and clay!'

'Would you rather,' Athene lashed out, 'have your son alone all day? Wandering through the house – *tearing – cracking – ripping – crushing?*'

Ruthlen winced at every word as if they were spiked shillelagh blows crushing in his head. His eyes fell shut behind the quarter-inch lenses. He shuddered fitfully.

'Enough,' he muttered, pale hand raised, surrendering. 'Enough, enough.'

'Let's bring the doll to Gardner,' Athene said excitedly.

They hurried to the little bedroom of their son and found him tearing down the curtains. A hissing, taut-cheeked Ruthlen jerked him off the windowsill and knuckles rapped him on the skull. Gardner blinked once his beady eyes.

'Put him down,' Athene said quickly. 'Let him see.'

Gardner stared with one toothed mouth ajar at the little doll that stood so silently before him. The doll was just about his size, dark-haired, blue-eyed, flesh-coloured, diapered, exactly like a real boy.

He blinked furiously.

'Activate the mechanism,' Ruthlen whispered and Athene, leaning over, pushed the tiny button.

Gardner toppled back in drooling consternation as the little boy doll grinned at him. 'Bah-bi-bah-bah!' Gardner cried hysterically.

'Bah-bi-bah-bah,' echoed the doll.

Gardner scuttled back, wild-eyed, and, from a wary crouch, observed the little boy doll waddling toward him. Restrained from further retreat by the wall, he cringed with tense astonishment until the doll clicked to a halt before him.

'Bah-bi-bah-bah.' The boy doll grinned again, then burped a single time and started into a jig on the linoleum.

Gardner's pudgy lips spread out, abruptly, in an idiotic grin. He gurgled happily. His parents' eyes went shut as one, beatific smiles creasing their grateful faces, all thoughts of financial cavilling vanished.

'*Oh,*' Athene whispered wonderingly.

'I can't believe it's true,' her husband said, guttural with awe . . .

For weeks, they were inseparable, Gardner and his motor-driven friend. They squatted down together, exchanging moon-eyed glances, chuckling over intimate jollities and, in the general, relishing to the full their drooly tête à têtes. Whatever Gardner did, the doll did too.

As for Ruthlen and Athene, they rejoiced in this advent of near-forgotten peace. Nerve-knotting screams no longer hammered malleus on incus and the sound of breaking things was not upon the air. Ruthlen poesied and Athene sculpted, all in a bliss of sabbath privacy.

'You see?' she said across the dinner table one evening. 'It was all he needed; a companion,' and Ruthlen bowed his head in solemn tribute to his wife's perspicacity.

'True, 'tis true,' he whispered happily.

A week, a month. Then, gradually, the metamorphosis.

Ruthlen, bogged in sticky pentameter, looked up one morning eyes marbleized. 'Hark,' he murmured.

The sound of dismemberment of plaything. Ruthlen hastened to the nursery to find his only begotten ripping cotton entrails from a heretofore respected doll.

The gloom-eyed poet stood outside the room, his heartbeat dwindling to the sickening thud of old while, in the nursery, Gardener disembowelled and the doll sat on the floor, observing.

'No,' the poet murmured, sensing it was *yes*. He crept away, somehow managing to convince himself it was an accident.

However, early the following afternoon at lunch, the fingers of both Ruthlen and his wife press in so sharply on their sandwiches that slices of tomato popped across the air and into the coffee.

'What,' said Athene horribly, 'is that?'

Gardner and his doll were found ensconced in the rubble of what had been, in happier times, a potted plant.

The doll was watching with a glassy interest as Gardner heaved up palmfuls of the blackish earth which rained in dirty crumbs upon the rug.

'No,' the poet said, ulcers revivified and, 'No,' the echo fell from Athene's paling lips.

Their son was spanked and put to bed, the doll was barricaded in the closet. A wounded caterwauling in their ears, the wife and husband twitched through wordless lunch while acids bred viler acids in their spasmed stomachs.

One remark alone was spoken as they faltered to their separate works and Athene said it.

'It was an accident.'

But, in the following week, they had to leave their work exactly eighty-seven times.

Once it was Gardner trashing in pulled-down draperies in the living room. Another time it was Gardner playing piano with a hammer in respondence to the doll's performance of a Bach gavotte. Still another time and time after time it was a rash of knocked-down objects ranging from jam jars to chairs. In all, thirty breakables broke, the cat disappeared and the floor showed through the carpet where Gardner had been active with a pair of scissors.

At the end of two days, the Beausons poesied and sculpted with eyes embossed and white lips rigid over grinding teeth. At the end of four, their bodies underwent a petrifying process, their brains began to ossify. By the week's end, after many a flirt and flutter of their viscera, they sat or stood in palsied silence, waiting for new outrages and dreaming of violent infanticide.

The end arrived.

One evening, suppering on a pitcherful of stomach-easing seltzers, Athene and her husband sat like rigor-mortised scarecrows in their chairs, their eyes four balls of blood-threaded stupor.

'What are we to *do*?' a spirit-broken Ruthlen muttered.

Athene's head moved side to side in negating jerks. 'I thought the doll —' she started, then allowed her voice to drift away.

'The doll has done no good,' lamented Ruthlen. 'We're right back where we started. And deeper still by one-oh-seven-fifty, since you say the doll cannot be exchanged.'

'It can't,' said Athene, 'It's —'

She was caught in mid-word by the noise.

It was a moist and slapping sound like someone heaving mud against a wall. Mud or —

'No.' Athene raised her soul-bruised eyes. 'Oh, *no*.'

The sudden spastic flopping of her sandals on the floor syncopated with the blood-wild pounding of her heart. He husband followed on his broomstick legs, lips a trembling circle of misgiving.

'*My figure!*' Athene screamed, standing a stricken marble in the studio doorway, staring ashen-faced upon the ghastly sight.

Gardner and the doll were playing *Hit the Roses on the Wallpaper*, using for ammunition great doughy blobs of clay ripped from Athene's uncompleted statue.

Athene and Ruthlen stood in horror-struck dumbness staring at the doll who, in the metal doming of its skull had fashioned new synaptic joinings and, to the jigging and the climbing and the burping, added flinging of clay.

And, suddenly it was clear – the falling plant, the broken vases and jars on high shelves – *Gardner needed help for things like that!*

Ruthlen Beauson seered a grisly future; i.e., the grisly past times two; all the Guignol torments of living with Gardner but multiplied by the presence of the doll.

'Get that metal monster from his house,' Ruthlen mumbled to his wife through concrete lips.

'But there's no exchange!' she cried hysterically.

'Then it's me for the can opener!' the poet rasped, backing away on rocklike legs.

'It's not the doll's fault!' Athene shouted. 'What good will tearing up the doll do? It's *Gardner*. It's that horrid thing we made together!'

The poet's eyes clicked sharply in their sockets as he looked from doll to son and back again and knew the hideous truth of her remark. It *was* their son. The doll just imitated, the doll would do whatever it was –

– *made to do*.

That was, precisely, to the second, when the idea came and, with it, peace unto the Beauson household.

From the next day forth, their Gardner was a model of deportment, the house became a sanctuary for blessed creation.

Everything was perfect.

It was only twenty years later, when a college-going Gardner Beauson met a wriggly sophomore and blew thirteen gaskets and his generator that the ugly truth came out, to the horror of everyone.

Distant Signals

BY ANDREW WEINER

One of the most famous horror movies of recent years is The Night
of the Living Dead *(1968), made by George A. Ronero, which not
only inspired two sequels,* Dawn of the Dead *(1968) and* Day of the
Dead *(1985), but also spawned a host of imitation zombie pictures
from studios in America and Europe. The success of Romero's films
enabled him to begin collaborating with Stephen King on movie
versions of his novels as well as fulfilling a long-held ambition to
create a late night TV horror series. He had been an enthusiast of
these programmes since his childhood and had a brief working
encounter with Alfred Hitchcock while Hitch was filming* North by
Northwest *in New York in 1959.* Tales of the Darkside *set its sights
on using material with the same kind of trick endings as those found
in the work of the great American short story writer, O. Henry, and
when transmissions began in 1985, reviewers felt the series was 'not
unlike a macabre* Twilight Zone'. *To add to the horror writers
Romero recruited for the programme – including Stephen King
(with 'Sorry, Right Number' and 'Word Processor of the Gods'),
Britain's Clive Barker (with an episode based on his* Books of
Blood) *and James Houghton, son of the original producer of*
Twilight Zone *(who wrote 'Unhappy Medium' and 'Choice of
Dreams') – the series also attracted an impressive roster of guest
stars in the ninety, half-hour shows which have so far been
screened. Among these were Connie Stevens, Keenan Wynn,
Arnold Stang, Fritz Weaver, Eddie Bracken, Jean Marsh, Harry
Anderson and Phyllis Diller. Each episode was introduced by the
wry and often cynical narrator, Paul Sparer.*

Among the most stylish episodes seen in Tales from the Darkside *was 'Distant Signals' by Canadian fantasy author Andrew Weiner (1952–), first shown in November 1985, which offered a nostalgic portrait of a man who wants to revive the bad-old, good-old days of Fifties television. The story was directed by Romero's co-producer William Teitler and contained an outstanding performance by Darren McGavin, who had earlier appeared in* Alfred Hitchcock Presents, *and also become something of a cult figure for his role as Kolchak,* The Night Stalker, *a blackly humorous vampire story set in Las Vegas written by Richard Matheson. This was first shown on television in 1971, and three years later became a spin-off series lasting twenty-two episodes.*

THERE was something not quite right about about the young man. His suit appeared brand new. Indeed, it glistened with an almost unnatural freshness and sharpness of definition. Yet it was made in a style that had not been fashionable since the late 1950s. The lapels were too wide, the trousers too baggy; the trouser legs terminated in one-inch cuffs. The young man's hair was short – too short. It was parted neatly on the left-hand side and plastered down with some sort of grease. And his smile was too wide. Too wide, at least, for nine o'clock on a Monday morning at the Parkdale Public Library.

Out for the day, was the librarian's first and last thought on the matter. Out, that is, from the state-run mental health centre just three blocks away.

'I would like,' said the young man, 'to be directed to the TV and film section.'

His voice, too, had an unnatural definition, as if he was speaking through some hidden microphone. It projected right across the library. Several patrons turned their heads to peer at him.

'Over there,' said the librarian, in a very pointed whisper. 'Just over there.'

STRANGER IN TOWN. Series, 1960. Northstar Studios for NBC-TV. Produced by KEN ODELL. From an original idea by BILL HURN. Directors included JASON ALTBERG, NICK BALL, and JIM SPIEGEL 26 b/w episodes. Running time: 50 minutes.

Horse opera following the exploits of Cooper aka The Stranger (VANCE MACCOBY), an amnesiacal gunslinger who wanders from town to town in search of his lost identity, stalked always by the mysterious limping loner Loomis (TERRY WHITE) who may or may not know his real name.

Despite this promisingly mythic promise, the series quickly degenerated into a formulaic pattern, with Cooper as a Shane-style saviour of widows and orphans. The show won mediocre ratings, and NBC declined to pick up its option for a second season. The identity of Cooper was never revealed.

See also: GUNSLINGERS; HOLLYWOOD EXISTENTIALISM; LAW AND ORDER; WESTERNS.

MACCOBY, VANCE (1938?–). Actor. Born Henry Mulvin in Salt Lake City, Utah. Frequent guest spots in WAGON TRAIN, RIVERBOAT, CAPTAIN CHRONOS, THE ZONE BEYOND, etc., 1957–59. Lead in the 1960 oater STRANGER IN TOWN and the short-lived 1961 private eye show MAX PARADISE, cancelled after 6 episodes. Subsequent activities unknown. One of dozens of nearly interchangeable identikit male stars of the first period of episodic TV drama, Maccoby had a certain brooding quality, particularly in b/w, that carried him far, but apparently lacked the resources for the long haul.

See also: STARS AND STARDOM.

– From *The Complete TV Encyclopedia*, Chuck Gingle, editor

There was something distinctly odd about the young man in the white loafers and pompadour hairstyle, the young man who had been haunting the anteroom of his office all day.

Had the Kookie look come back, Feldman wondered?

'Look, kid,' he said, not unkindly, 'as my secretary told you, I'm not taking on any more clients. I have a full roster right now. You'd really be much better off going to Talentmart, or one of those places. They specialize in, you know, unknowns.'

'And as I told your secretary,' the young man said, 'I don't want to be an actor, I want to hire one. One of your clients. This is strictly a business proposition.'

Business proposition my ass, Feldman thought. *Autograph hunter, more like.* But he said wearily, 'Which one would that be? Lola Banks? Dirk Raymond?'

'Vance Maccoby.'

'Vance Maccoby?' For a moment he had to struggle to place the name. 'Vance Maccoby?' he said again. 'That bum? What the hell do you want with Vance Maccoby?'

'Mr Feldman, I represent a group of overseas investors interested in independently producing a TV series for syndicated sale. We want Mr Maccoby to star. However, we have so far been unable to locate him.'

'I haven't represented him in years. No one has. He hasn't *worked* in years. Not since ... what was that piece of crap called? *Max Paradise*? I don't like to speak ill of former clients, but the man was impossible, you know. A drunk. Quite impossible. No one could work with him.'

'We're aware of that,' the young man said. 'We've taken all that into consideration, and we are still interested in talking to Mr Maccoby. We think he is the only man for the part. And we believe that if anyone can find him, you can.'

The young man opened his briefcase and fumbled inside it. 'We would like,' he continued, 'to retain your services towards that end. And we are prepared to make suitable remuneration whether or not a contract should be signed with Mr Maccoby and whether or not you choose to represent him as agent of record in that transaction.'

'Kid,' Feldman began, 'what you need is a private detective –' He stopped and stared at the bar-shaped object in the young man's hand. 'Is that gold?'

'It certainly is, Mr Feldman. It certainly is.'

The young man laid the bar on the desk between them.

'An ounce of gold?'

'One point three four ounces,' said the young man. 'We apologize for the unusual denomination.'

He held open the briefcase. 'I have twenty-four more such bars here. At the New York spot price this morning, this represents a value of approximately fifteen thousand dollars.'

'Fifteen thousand dollars to find Vance Maccoby?' Feldman said.

He got up and paced around the desk.

'Is this stuff hot?' he asked, pointing to the briefcase, feeling like a character in one of the more banal TV shows into which he booked his clients.

'Hot?' echoed the young man. He reached out and touched the gold bar on the desk. 'A few degrees below room temperature, I would say.'

'Cute,' Feldman said. 'Don't be cute. Just tell me, is this on the level?'

'Oh, I see,' said the young man. 'Yes, absolutely. We have a property which we wish to develop, to which we have recently purchased the rights from the estate of the late Mr Kenneth Odell. There is only one man who can star in this show, and that is Vance Maccoby.'

'What property?'

'*Stranger in Town*,' said the young man.

'I knew it,' she said. 'I knew you would come back.'

'You knew more than I did,' Cooper said. 'I was five miles out of

542

town and heading west. But something . . . something made me turn around and come back here and face the Kerraway Brothers.'

'You're a good man,' she said. 'You couldn't help yourself.'

'I don't know if I'm a good man,' Cooper said. 'I don't know what kind of man I am.' He stared morosely at the corpses strewn out on the ground around the ranch house. 'I just couldn't let the Kerraways take your land.'

He mounted his horse. 'Time to be moving on,' he said. 'You take good care of yourself and little Billy now.'

'Will you ever come back?'

'Maybe,' he said. 'Maybe after I find what I'm looking for.'

'I think you found it already,' she said. 'You just don't know it yet. You found yourself.'

'That may be so,' Cooper said. 'But I still gotta put a name to it.'

He rode off into a rapidly setting sun.

The video picture flickered, then resolved itself into an antique Tide commercial. Hurn cut the controls. He turned to the strange young man in the too-tweedy jacket and the heavy horn-rimmed glasses.

'That?' he said, gesturing at the screen. 'You want to remake that . . . *garbage*?'

'Not remake,' the young man said. 'Revive. Continue. Conclude. Tell the remainder of the story of the stranger Cooper, and of the reacquisition of his memory and identity.'

'Who cares?' Hurn asked. 'Who the hell cares who Cooper is or what he did? Certainly not the viewers. Do you know how many letters we got after we carded the series? Sixteen. Sixteen letters. That's how many people cared.'

'That is our concern, Mr Hurn. We believe that we to have a market for this property. That is why we are making this proposition. We are prepared to go ahead with or without you. But certainly we would much rather have you with us. As the main creative force behind the original series —'

'Creative?' Hurn said. 'Frankly, that whole show to me was nothing but an embarrassment. And I was glad when they cancelled it, actually. I wrote those scripts for one reason, and one reason alone. Money.'

'We can offer you a great deal of money, Mr Hurn.'

Hurn gestured, as though to indicate the oriental rugs on the floor, the rare books in the shelves on the wall, the sculptures and the paintings, the several-million-dollar Beverly Hills home that contained all this.

'I don't need money, Mr — what did you say your name was?'

'Smith.'

'Mr Smith, I have all the money I could ever want. I have done well in this business, Mr Smith. Quite well. I am no longer the struggling writer who conceived *Stranger in Town*. These days I choose my projects on the basis of quality.'

'You disparage yourself unnecessarily, Mr Hurn. We believe that *Stranger in Town* was a series of the highest quality. In some ways, in fact, it represented the very peak of televisual art. The existential dilemma of the protagonist, the picaresque nature of his journeyings, the obsessive fascination with the nature of memory . . . That scene . . .' The young man's eyes came alive. 'That scene when Cooper bites into a watermelon and says, "*I remember a watermelon like this. I remember summer days, summer nights, a cool breeze on the porch, the river rushing by. I remember a woman's lips, her eyes, her deep blue eyes. But where, damn it? Where?*" '

Hurn stared, open-mouthed. 'You remember that? Word for word? Oh, my God.'

'Art, Mr Hurn. Unabashed art.'

'Adolescent pretension. Fakery. Bullshit,' Hurn said. 'Embarrassing. Oh, my God, how embarrassing.'

'In some ways trite,' the young man conceded. 'Brash. Even clumsy sometimes. But burning with an inner conviction. Mr Hurn, you must help us. You must help us bring back *Stranger in Town*.'

'You can't,' Hurn said. 'You can't bring it back. Even if I agreed it was worth bringing back – and I'll admit to you that I've thought about it on occasion, though not in many years. I've always had a sense of it as a piece of unfinished business. . . . But even if I wanted to help you, it couldn't be done. Not now. It's too late, much too late. You can't repeat the past, Smith. You can't bring it back. It's over, finished, a dead mackerel.'

'Of course you can,' Smith said. 'Of course you can repeat the past. We have absolutely no doubt on that question.'

'Boats against the current,' Hurn said. 'But no, no, I can't agree. It's like when those promoters wanted to reunite the Beatles.'

'Beetles?' Smith asked. 'What beetles?'

'The Beatles,' Hurn said, astonished. '"She Loves You." "I Want to Hold Your Hand." Like that.'

'Oh, yes,' Smith said vaguely.

Where is this guy from? Hurn wondered. *Mongolia*?

'What exactly is your proposition, Mr Smith?'

The young man became businesslike. He pulled a sheaf of notes from his briefcase. 'One episode of Stranger was completed but not edited when the cancellation notice came from the network. We have acquired that footage, and it would be a simple matter to put it together. We have also acquired five scripts for the second season, commissioned prior to the cancellation. And we have an outline of your proposal for subsequent episodes, including a concluding episode in which the identity of Cooper is finally revealed. We would like you to supervise the preparation of these unwritten scripts and to write the final episode yourself. We are looking at a season of twenty-six fifty-minute episodes. For these services we are prepared to pay you the equivalent of two million dollars.'

'The equivalent, Mr Smith?'

'In gold, Mr Hurn.' The young man picked up the large suitcase he had brought with him into the writer's house. He opened it up. It was packed with yellowish metallic bars.

'My God,' Hurn said. 'That suitcase must weigh a hundred pounds.'

'About one hundred and twenty-five pounds,' said Mr Smith. 'Or the equivalent of about one million dollars at this morning's London gold fixing.'

The young man, Hurn recalled, had carried in this suitcase without the slightest sign of exertion. He hefted it now as though it was full of feathers. Obviously he was not as frail as he looked.

'Tell me, Mr Smith. Who is going to star in this show?'

'Oh, Vance Maccoby. Of course.'

'Vance Maccoby, if he is even still alive, is a hopeless alcoholic, Mr Smith. He hasn't worked in this town in twenty years. I don't even know where he is. Have you signed up Vance Maccoby, Mr Smith?'

'Not yet,' the young man said. 'But we will. We will.'

'My name's Loomis,' said the tall man with the limp, as he stood beside Cooper at the bar. He picked up the shot glass and stared into it thoughtfully.

'First or last?' Cooper asked.

'Just Loomis,' said the man.

'I'm Cooper,' said the other. 'Or at least that's what I call myself. One name's as good as another. There was a book in my saddlebag by a man named Cooper . . .'

'You forgot your name?'

'I forgot everything,' he said. 'Except how to speak and ride and shoot.'

Loomis drained his drink. 'Some things a man don't forget,' he said.

Cooper stared at him intently. 'Have I seen you in here before? There's something familiar . . .'

'I don't think so,' Loomis said. 'I'm a stranger here myself.'

The edges of the TV screen grew misty, then blurred. The picture dissolved. Another took shape. A bright, almost hallucinatorily bright summer day. A farm house. Chickens in a coop. The door of the house open, banging in the wind.

The camera moved through the door, into a parlor. Signs of struggle, furniture upended, a broken dish on the floor. A man stooped to pick up the fragments.

'Aimee?' he called. 'Aimee?'

The camera moved on, into a bedroom. A woman's body sprawled brokenly across the bed. The window open, the curtain blowing. And then a face, a man's face, staring into the room. His arm, holding a gun. A gunshot.

Darkness closed in. Outside, the shadow of a man running away. A shadow with a kind of limp.

And back, suddenly, to the bar.

'You all right, Cooper?'

'I'm all right,' he said, gripping the bar tightly. 'I'm all right.'

'Yeah,' said the fat bald man in the armchair. 'Let's hear it, for the strong silent ones.'

He picked up his glass from the TV table in front of him, made a mocking toast to the blank screen, then winked to his old agent, Feldman, sitting on the couch next to the young man. There was something a little odd about the young man, but the fat man was too drunk to put his finger on it. Maybe it was the Desi Arnaz haircut . . .

'Vance,' Feldman said. 'Vance I – I hate to see you like this.'

'Like what?' said the fat man who had once been Vance Maccoby. 'And the name is Henry. Henry Mulvin.'

He raised his bulk from the armchair and waddled into the tiny kitchen of the trailer to refreshen his drink.

Feldman looked helplessly at the young man.

'I told you, Smith. I told you this was pointless. You're going to have to find yourself another boy. Jesus, there must be hundreds in this town.'

'There's only one Vance Maccoby,' the young man said firmly. 'Mr Feldman, would you leave us together for a while? I promise you that I'll be in touch in the morning in regard to contractual arrangements.'

'Contractual arrangements? You're whistling in the wind.'

'I can be quite persuasive, Mr Feldman. Believe me.'

I believe you, Feldman thought. Or *what would I be doing in this trailer?*

When the sound of Feldman's Mercedes had disappeared into the distance, the young man turned to Vance Maccoby.

'Mr Maccoby,' he said almost apologtically, 'we have to have a serious talk. And in order to do that you will have to be sober.'

'Sober?' The fat man laughed. 'Never heard of it.'

'This won't hurt,' the young man said, producing a flat, boxlike device from his pocket and pointing it at the fat man. 'It will merely accelerate the metabolization of the alcohol in your bloodstream.' He pushed a button.

'But I don't want to be sober,' the fat man said. He began to cry.

'When this is all over, Mr Maccoby,' the young man said soothingly, 'you need never be sober nor unhappy ever again.'

'Guess I should ride on,' Cooper said. 'You got a nice little town here and I could easily settle in it. Easily. But a man can't settle anyplace until he knows who he is.'

'You think he knows?' the girl asked. 'You think that limping man knows who you are?'

'Yes, he does,' Cooper said. 'He knows, and he's going to tell me. Fact is, he's itching to tell me. He thinks he just wants to kill me, but first of all he wants to tell me. Otherwise he would have just finished me off back at Oscar's barn. Him and me, reckon we got ourselves a piece of unfinished business. But he's got the better of me, because he knows what it is.'

'He may kill you yet,' the girl said, dabbing at the tears that had begun to well up in her eyes.

'I can take care of myself.'

'Will you come back?' she asked. 'Afterward?'

'Maybe so,' he said. 'Maybe so.'

He rode off into the distanee.

'Print it,' said the director. 'And see you all to-morrow.'

Carefully, Vance Maccoby dismounted from his horse and began to walk back to his dressing room. Bill Hurn fell in step with him.

'That was good stuff, Vance,' he said.

Maccoby smiled, although it was more like a tic. The skin of his face had been stretched tight by the facelift operations, so that his usual expression was even blanker than it had been in his heyday. He took off his hat and ran his hand through his recently transplanted hair. Under the supervision of the strange young man called Smith, he had lost close to a hundred pounds in the three months prior to shooting.

For all of these changes, Maccoby close up looked every one of his forty-six years. The doctors could do little about the lines around his eyes, and nothing at all about the weariness in them. And yet the camera was still good to him, particularly in black and white. Hurn had argued fiercely on the subject of film stock, but Smith had been adamant. 'It must be black and white. Just like the original. Cost is not the question. This is a matter of aesthetics.'

Black and white helped hide the ravages of time. It just made Maccoby look more intense, more haunted. Perhaps that was why Smith had been so insistent. But Hurn doubted that. In many ways Smith was astonishingly ignorant of the mechanics of film-making.

'I didn't know,' Maccoby said, 'that he was still in here.' He pointed to his chest.

'Cooper?'

'Maccoby,' he said. 'Vance Maccoby. Inside me, Henry Mulvin. Still there, after all these years. I thought I'd finished him off for good. But he was still in there.'

Maccoby had not, to Hurn's knowledge, touched a drop of alcohol in six months. He was functioning well on the set, with none of the moodiness or tantrums that had marked his final days in Hollywood. But the stripping away of that alcoholic haze had only revealed the deeper sickness beneath: his unbearable discomfort with himself, or rather with the fictional person he had become – Vance Maccoby, TV star. Isolated, cut off, torn away from his roots, existing only on a million TV screens and in the pages of mass-circulation magazines.

Was that, Hurn wondered – and not for the first time – why he had made such a great Cooper? Despite his mediocrity as an actor, there had never been anyone else to play the role.

'Vance,' he said. 'Henry . . .'

'Call me Vance. You always did. That's who I am here. For this little command performance.'

'Vance, why did you agree to do this?'

'Why did you agree, Bill? And don't tell me it was the money. You don't care about the money any more than I do. You have all you want. I had all I needed to stay drunk.'

'I don't know,' Hurn said. 'Smith . . . He just made it seem so *important*. Like there were millions of people just sitting around waiting for a new season of *Stranger in Town*. He flattered me. And he tempted me. This was my baby, remember, and the network killed it. And I suppose there was a part of me that always wanted to do this. Finish it properly, tie up all those loose ends. And yet I know the whole thing is crazy. This show will never run on a US network. Not in black and white. Unless we put it straight into reruns.' He snickered.

'Maybe that's the plan. I mean, who would even know the difference? This whole thing is so – 1960.'

They had reached Maccoby's dressing room.

'Well,' Maccoby said, 'Smith is telling the truth, in a way. There *are* millions of people waiting for this.'

'In Hong Kong? North Korea? I mean, where does he expect to sell this stuff? Who are these overseas investors of his? How can he piss so much money away like water, and how does he expect to ever recoup it? The whole thing is bizarre.'

'Oh, it's bizarre all right,' Maccoby said. 'It sure is bizarre.' He glanced up briefly into the hard blue sky. Then he said, 'Well, I better get cleaned up.'

'You killed her,' Cooper said. 'You killed her and you tried to kill me. But somehow I survived. And I crawled out of there, halfway out of my mind. And I crawled into the desert. And a wagon train found me. And they carried me along with them, and nursed me. And when I woke up, I didn't even know my name. You took it. You took away my name.'

'Stevens,' Loomis said. 'Brad Stevens.' His hand did not waver on the gun.

'Oh, I remember that now,' he said. 'I remember it all. I remember Aimee . . . I remember it all.'

'I'm glad about that,' Loomis said. 'I truly am. I've been waiting for you to remember for the most wearisome time. Not much sense in killing a person when he doesn't even know why.'

He tightened his grip on the trigger. 'But there's something more,' he said. 'More than that. Something you couldn't remember, because you never knew. Something I been meaning to tell you for a long time. Longer than you could could imagine.'

'Make sense,' said the man who called himself Cooper. 'Make some kind of sense.'

'Your name,' Loomis said. 'It ain't really Stevens. Not really. The name you've been trying so hard to remember isn't even your real name. Isn't that a hoot? Isn't that the funniest thing you ever heard?' He laughed.

'Make sense,' said the man on the ground. 'You're still not making any.'

'Stevens,' Loomis said. 'That's just a name they gave you. The folks who picked you out at the orphanage. Picked out the pretty little baby. That was their name. Good God-fearing folks. But they only wanted the one, and they wanted a baby, not a full-grown child. And for sure they didn't want a gimp.'

'I was adopted? You're saying I was adopted? How could you know that?'

'I was there, little brother. I was there. I was the gimp they passed over for the pretty little baby. I was only four years old at the time. But some things you really don't forget.'

'Brother?'

'Right,' Loomis said. 'You and me, we're children of the very same flesh. Arnold and Mary Jane Loomis. Nobody ever changed my name. Nobody wanted the poor little cripple boy.'

'Our parents . . .'

'Dead,' Loomis said. 'Indians. They killed Pa. Killed Ma, too, after they got through with her. Would have killed us, too, except they got interrupted.'

Slowly, deliberately, the man who had been called Cooper climbed to his feet. 'We were separated?' he said.

'For nearly thirty years. You eating your good home cooking and me eating the poorhouse gruel. You growing into a solid citizen and marrying and farming. And me drifting from town to town like a piece of dried-up horse dung blown around by the wind. Never finding a place I could call home. And looking, looking for my little brother. And finally I found you . . .'

'Why?' he asked. 'Why did you do it?'

'I didn't mean to . . .' Loomis faltered. 'It was like a kind of madness came over me. Seeing your house and your farm and your wife, everything you had and I didn't, everything I hated you for having . . . But I don't know. Maybe that was what I was intending all along, intending to make you suffer just a little of what I had to suffer. I don't know. I don't think I meant to kill Aimee, but when I did I knew I would have to kill you, too. And I thought I did. And then I saw you alive. And I realized that you didn't remember, didn't remember a single thing. So I just waited, watched and waited, until you did start to remember. So you would know why I had to kill you. And now it's time. It's time.'

'You can't stand yourself, brother, can you?' said the man who had been called Cooper. 'You and you, they don't get along at all. I can understand that. I been through a little of that myself. Not knowing who the hell I was or what I might have done or what I should be doing. But you find out. Maybe not your name, but how you should be living. If you're any good at all, you find that out.'

He took a step toward Loomis. 'But you're not any good, brother, and you never were. Sure, you had some lousy breaks, sure you did. But that isn't any kind of excuse for what you did. You're just no good to anyone, not even yourself. And if you kill me, you'll have nothing to live for. Nothing. Because nobody will know your name and nobody will care.'

Another step.

'But I care, brother. I care in the worst way. You made me care. Buzzing around me like some housefly waiting to be swatted. Waiting for me to remember. Trying to make me remember. Remember you.'

Another step. He was only a few paces from Loomis now. He glanced down to his own gun on the floor of the stable. It was nearly within reach.

'Stay there,' Loomis said. 'Stay right where you are.'

He took another step.

'I remember you, brother. For what you did to me. No one else will. Kill me and you'll be all alone again, alone with yourself, the way you always were. Run away now and you'll have something to keep you going. Fear, brother. Fear. That's a kind of something. Something to make you feel alive. And me, too. I'll have something to keep me going, too.'

Loomis took a step backward. 'Don't move,' he said. 'Don't move or I'll kill you now.'

'What are you waiting for?' his brother asked him.

The gun wavered in his hand.

The man who had called himself Cooper stopped swiftly and scooped up his own gun from the floor.

Two guns blared.

Loomis stood straight for a moment. A strange smile spread over his face. And then, slowly, he crumpled to the floor of the stable.

The other continued to stand, in the clearing smoke, holding his wounded left arm.

'Damn,' he said softly. 'Damn.'

The lights in the screening room came up. One man was applauding vigorously. Smith. All heads turned toward him.

'Bit of an anticlimax,' Hurn said, 'don't you think? We were afraid it might be. I think, in a way, we were afraid of having to finish it.'

'On the contrary, Mr Hurn,' Smith said. 'On the contrary. It's absolutely perfect. Perfect. Real mythic power. A glimpse into the human condition. Into a world in which brother must slay brother, even as Cain slew Abel. *Archetypal*, Mr Hurn. Archetypal.'

He stood up and addressed the small crowd.

'I want to thank all of you,' he said, 'for making this possible. In particular I want to thank Mr Hurn and the one and only Vance Maccoby, without whom none of this would have been possible.'

Maccoby grinned in a spaced-out way. Hurn could smell the drink on his breath from two rows away.

The cure didn't take, he thought. *Well, it took for long enough.*

'I will be leaving town tomorrow,' Smith said, 'and I will not be returning in the near future. So let me just say what a wonderful group of people you have been to work with, and what a great, great privilege this has been for me.'

There was still, Hurn reflected, something rather odd about the young man. He was dressed now in what could pass as the uniform of the young Hollywood executive – safari jacket, open-collar sports shirt, gold medallion, aviator shades – and yet there was still something not quite right about it. He looked as if he had just stepped out of central casting.

'The show,' Hurn said, as Smith headed toward the door. 'When is the show going to run?'

'Oh, soon,' Smith said. 'Not in this country, at the present time, but we have plenty of interest overseas.'

A Canadian tax shelter? Hurm wondered. *One of those productions that never actually play anywhere? But surely they would not have gone to so much trouble.*

'Where?' he persisted. 'Where will it run?'

'Oh, faraway places,' Smith said, fingering his aviator shades. 'Far, far away.' He disappeared through the door. Hurn would not see him again.

'Far away,' Hurn repeated to himself.

'Very far,' Maccoby said, staggering a little as he rose from his seat in the back row. He was quite drunk.

'You know something I don't know?' Hurn asked, following him from the screening room.

'Very far,' Maccoby repeated, as they stepped into the parking lot. The smog was thin that night. Stars twinkled faintly in the sky. 'About twenty light years,' he said, looking up.

'What?'

'Twenty light years,' he repeated. 'Twenty years for the signals to reach them. Distant, distant signals. And then they stop. The signals stop. Before the story ends. And they don't like that.'

'They?'

'Smith's people. Our overseas investors. Our faraway fans.'

'Wait a minute,' Hurn said. 'You're telling me that our show was picked up . . . out there?'

Now he, too, craned his head to look up into the night sky. He shivered.

'I don't believe it,' he said.

'Sure you do,' Maccoby said.

'But it's crazy,' Hurn said. 'The whole thing is incredible. Up to and including the fact that they picked on our show.'

'I wondered about that myself,' Maccoby said. 'But you've got to figure that their tastes are going to be, well . . . *different*.'

'Then he really meant it,' Hurn said. 'When he said that our show was – what did he call it? The peak of televisual art.'

Maccoby nodded. 'He really meant it.'

'Art.' Hurn tested the word on his tongue. 'Life is short but art is long. Isn't that what they say? Something like that, at any rate.'

'Right,' Maccoby said absently. 'Art. Or something like that.'

He was staring now at the great mast of the TV antenna on the hill above the studio.

'Signals,' he said again. 'Distant, distant signals.'

The Coffin

BY RAY BRADBURY

*Few American writers have have more of their short stories used on
TV horror anthologies than Ray Bradbury (1920–), author of some of
the best collections of macabre tales published this century, as well as a
succession of outstanding novels like* The Martian Chronicles *(1950),*
Fahrenheit 451 *(1951) and, most recently,* A Graveyard For Lunatics
*(1990) about the horror movie-making business in Hollywood.
Indeed, Ray made his mark on the genre early on, when his tale of
something unspeakable residing in 'The Jar' was filmed for Alfred
Hitchcock Presents in 1956. So gruesome was this episode, and such
emotions did it stir up in viewers, that it has rarely been shown again in
re-runs of the series. This did not prevent Ray's work being used again
in the programme, however, nor from being selected for adaptation in
several other prestigious anthologies such as* Lights Out, Suspense,
The Twilight Zone, Tales of Tomorrow, *etc. One of his short stories,
'The Screaming Woman' was also made into an hour-long special in
1971 for TVM with the impressive cast of Olivia de Havilland, Joseph
Cotton and Walter Pidgeon*

*In 1988 Ray was accorded the distinction of having an entire series
built around his work in a unique co-production deal involving
Granada TV in England, Ellipse Programme (France) and Atlantic
Films of Canada. What made the deal unusual in TV terms was that
once the stories for filming had been chosen each of the companies
produced a third of the episodes in their own studios and with their
own actors. Ray, his wife, his agent and the production companies
were responsible for the selections. 'We all went through my books,'
Ray recalls, 'and made lists of our choices. Then I compared the
selections. It was remarkable how often we came up with the same*

stories!' Among those upon which all were agreed were 'The Crowd',
'The Coffin', 'Marionettes, Inc.', 'Banshee', 'Tyrannosaurus Rex', 'The
Man Upstairs' and 'The Small Assassin'. Ray himself adapted the
stories and also acted as host for the half-hour episodes which were
filmed with a number of well-known actors including Donald
Pleasance, Alan Bates, Robert Vaughn, Helen Shaver, Denholm
Elliott and Eugene Levy. In America and Canada the anthology has
been shown under the generic title Ray Bradbury Theatre, *while in*
Britain and France it is known as A Twist in the Tale.

It is generally felt by viewers that the Granada productions are the
most stylish, while the episode from the Manchester studios which
attracted the best reviews was 'The Coffin', directed by Tom Cotter and
starring Denholm Elliott and Dan O'Herlihy. It was a story every bit
as atmospheric and ultimately frightening on the small screen as it is
on the printed page . . .

THERE was any amount of banging and hammering for a number
of days; deliveries of metal parts and oddments which Mr Charles
Braling took into his little workshop with a feverish anxiety. He was a
dying man; a badly dying man and he seemed to be in a great hurry,
between racking coughs and spittlings, to piece together one last
invention.

'What are you doing?' inquired his younger brother, Richard
Braling. He had listened with increasing difficulty and much curiosity
for a number of days to that banging and rattling about, and now he
stuck his head through the work-room door.

'Go far far away and let me alone,' said Charles Braling, who was
seventy, trembly and wet-lipped most of the time. He trembled nails
into place and trembled a hammer down with a weak blow upon a
large timber and then struck a small metal ribbon down into an
intricate machine, and, all in all, was having a carnival of labour.

Richard looked on, bitter-eyed, for a long moment. There was a
hatred between them. It had gone on for some years and now was
neither any better or any worse for the fact that Charlie was dying.
Richard was delighted to know of the impending death, if he thought
of it at all. But all this busy fervour of his old brother's stimulated him.

'Pray tell,' he said, not moving from the door.

'If you must know,' snarled old Charles, fitting in an odd thing-
umabob on the box before him. 'I'll be dead in another week and I'm –
I'm building my own coffin!'

'A coffin, my dear Charlie. That doesn't *look* like a coffin. A coffin isn't that complex. Come on now, what are you up to?'

'I tell you it's a coffin! An odd coffin, yes, but nevertheless,' the old man shivered his fingers around in the large box, ' – nevertheless a coffin!'

'But it would be easier to buy one.'

'Not one like this! You couldn't buy one like this any place, ever. Oh, it'll be a real fine coffin, all right.'

'You're obviously lying.' Richard moved forward. 'Why, that coffin is a good twelve feet long. Six feet longer than normal size!'

'Oh, yes?' The old man laughed quietly.

'And that transparent top; who ever heard of a coffin lid you can see through? What good is a transparent lid to a corpse?'

'Oh, just never you mind at all,' sang the old man heartily. 'La!' And he went humming and hammering about the shop.

'This coffin is terribly thick,' shouted the young brother over the din. 'Why, it must be five feet thick; how utterly unnecessary!'

'I only wish I might live to patent this amazing coffin,' said old Charlie. 'It would be a god-send to all the poor peoples of the world. Think how it would eliminate the expenses of most funerals. Oh, but, of course, you don't know how it would do that, do you? How silly of me. Well, I shan't tell you. If this coffin could be mass-produced – expensive at first, naturally – but then when you finally got them made in vast quantities gah, but the money people would save.'

'To hell with you!' And the younger brother stormed out of the shop.

It had been an unpleasant life. Young Richard had always been such a bounder he never had two coins to clink together at one time; all of his money had come from old brother Charlie, who had the indecency to remind him of it at all times. Richard spent many hours with his hobbies; he dearly loved piling up bottles with French wine labels, in the garden. 'I like the way they glint,' he often said, sitting and sipping, sipping and sitting. He was the only man in the county who could hold the longest grey ash on a fifty cent cigar for the longest recorded time. And he knew how to hold his hands so his diamonds jangled in the light. But he had not bought the wine, the diamonds, the cigars – no! They were all gifts. He was never allowed to buy anything himself. It was always brought to him and given to him. He had to ask for everything, even writing paper. He considered himself quite a martyr to have put up with taking things from that rickety old brother for so long a time. Everything Charlie ever laid his hand to turned to money; everything Richard had ever tried in the way of a career had failed.

And now, here was this old mole of a Charlie whacking out a new invention which would probably bring Charlie additional specie long after his bones were slotted in the earth!

Well, two weeks passed.

One morning the old brother toddled upstairs and stole the insides out of the electric phonograph. Another morning he raided the gardener's greenhouse. Still another time he received a delivery from a medical company. It was all young Richard could do to sit and hold his long grey cigar ash steady while these murmuring excursions took place.

'I'm finished!' cried old Charlie on the fourteenth morning, and dropped dead.

Richard finished out his cigar, and, without showing his inner excitement, he laid down his cigar with its fine long whitish ash, two inches long, a real record, and arose.

He walked to the window and watched the sunlight playfully glittering among the fat beetle-like champagne bottles in the garden.

He looked toward the top of the stairs where old dear brother Charlie lay peacefully sprawled against the banister. Then he walked to the phone and perfunctorily dialled a number.

'Hello, Green Lawn Mortuary? This is the Braling residence. Will you send around a wicker, please? Yes. For Brother Charlie. Yes. Thank you. Thank you.'

As the mortuary people were taking brother Charles out in their wicker they received instructions. 'Ordinary casket,' said young Richard. 'No funeral service. Put him in a pine coffin. He would have preferred it that way – simple. Good bye.'

'Now!' said Richard, rubbing his hands together. 'We shall see about this "coffin" built by dear Charlie. I do not suppose he will realize he is not being buried in his "special" box. Ah.'

He entered the downstairs shop.

The coffin sat before some wide-flung French windows, the lid shut, complete and neat, all put together like the fine innards of a Swiss watch. It was vast, and it rested upon a long long table with rollers beneath for easy manoeuvring.

The coffin interior, as he peered through the glass lid, was six feet long. There must be a good three feet of false body at both head and foot of the coffin, then. Three feet at each end which, covered by secret panels that he must find some way of opening, might very well reveal – exactly what?

Money, of course. It would be just like Charlie to suck his riches into his grave with himself, leaving Richard with not a cent to buy a bottle with. The old bastard!

He raised the glass lid and felt about, but found no hidden buttons. There was a small sign studiously inked-on white paper, thumbtacked to the side of the satin-lined box. It said:

THE BRALING ECONOMY CASKET. Copyright, April, 1946. Simple to operate. Can be used again and again by morticians and families with an eye to the future.

Richard snorted thinly. Who did Charlie think he was fooling? There was more writing:

DIRECTIONS: SIMPLY PLACE BODY IN COFFIN.

What a fool thing to say. Put body in coffin! Naturally! How else would one go about it? He peered intently and finished out the directions:

SIMPLY PLACE BODY IN COFFIN – AND MUSIC WILL START.

'It can't be –' Richard gaped at the sign. 'Don't tell me all this work has been for a –' He went to the open door of the shop, walked out upon the tiled terrace and called to the gardener in his greenhouse. 'Rogers!' The gardener stuck his head out. 'What time is it?' asked Richard. 'Twelve o'clock, sir,' replied Rogers. 'Well, at twelve fifteen, you come up here and check to see if everything is all right, Rogers,' said Richard. 'Yes, sir,' said the gardener. Richard turned and went back into the shop. 'We'll find out –' he said, quietly.

There would be no harm in lying in the box, testing it. He noticed small ventilating holes in the sides. Even if the lid were closed down there'd be air. And Rogers would be up in a moment or two. SIMPLY PLACE BODY IN COFFIN – AND MUSIC WILL START. Really, how naive of old Charlie! Richard hoisted himself up.

He was like a man getting into a bath-tub. He felt naked and watched over. He put one shiny shoe into the coffin and crooked his knee and eased himself up and made some little remark to nobody in particular, then he put in his other knee and foot and crouched there, as if undecided about the temperature of the bath-water. Edging himself about, chuckling softly, he lay down, pretending to himself (for it was fun pretending) that he was dead, that people were dropping tears on him, that candles were fuming and illuminating and that the world was stopped in mid-stride because of his passing. He put on a long pale expression, shut his eyes, holding back the laughter in himself behind pressed, quivering lips. He folded his hands and decided they felt waxen and cold.

Whirr. Spung! Something whispered inside the box-wall. *Spung!*

The lid slammed down on him!

From outside, if one had just come into the room, one would have imagined a wild man was kicking, pounding, blathering, and shrieking inside a closet! There was a sound of a body dancing and cavorting. There was a thudding of flesh and fists. There was a squeaking and a kind of wind from a frightened man's lungs. There was a rustling like paper and a shrilling as of many pipes simultaneously played. Then there was a real fine scream. Then – silence.

Richard Braling lay in the coffin and relaxed. He let loose all his muscles. He began to chuckle. The smell of the box was not unpleasant. Through the little perforations he drew more than enough air to live on, comfortably. He need only push gently up with his hands, with none of this kicking and screaming and the lid would open. One must be calm. He flexed his arms.

The lid was locked.

Well, still there was no danger. Rogers would be up in a minute or two. There was nothing thing to fear.

The music began to play.

It seemed to come from somewhere inside the head of the coffin. It was green music. Organ music, very slow and melancholy, typical of Gothic arches and long black tapers. It smelled of earth and whispers. It echoed high between stone walls. It was so sad that one almost cried listening to it. It was music of potted plants and crimson and blue stained glass windows. It was late sun at twilight and a cold wind blowing. It was a dawn with only fog and a far away fog-horn moaning.

'Charlie, Charlie, Charlie, you old fool you! So this is your odd coffin!' Tears of laughter welled into Richard's eyes. 'Nothing more than a coffin which plays its own dirge. Oh, my sainted Grandma!'

He lay and listened critically, for it was beautiful music and there was nothing he could do until Rogers came up and let him out. His eyes roved aimlessly, his fingers tapped soft little rhythms on the satin cushions. He crossed his legs idly. Through the glass lid he saw sunlight shooting through the French windows, dust particles dancing on it. It was a lovely blue day.

The sermon began.

The organ music quieted and a gentle voice said:

'We are gathered together, those who loved and those who knew the deceased, to give him our homage and our due –'

'Charlie, bless you, that's *your* voice!' Richard was delighted. 'A mechanical funeral, by God. Organ music and lecture. And Charlie giving his own oration for himself!'

The soft voice said, 'We who knew and loved him are grieved at the passing of –'

'What was *that*?' Richard raised himself, startled. He didn't quite believe what he had heard. He repeated it to himself just the way he had heard it:

'We who knew and loved him are grieved at the passing of Richard Braling.'

That's what the voice had said.

'Richard Braling,' said the man in the coffin. 'Why, *I'm* Richard Braling.'

A slip of the tongue, naturally. Merely a slip. Charlie had meant to say 'Charles' Braling. Certainly. Yes. Of course. Yes. Certainly Yes. Naturally. Yes.

'Richard was a fine man,' said the voice, talking on. 'We shall see no finer in our time.'

'My name again!'

Richard began to move about uneasily in the coffin.

Why didn't Rogers come?

It was hardly a mistake, using that name twice. Richard Braling. Richard Braling. We are gathered here. We shall miss – We are grieved. No finer man. No finer in our time. We are gathered here. The deceased. *Richard* Braling. Richard Braling.

Whirrrr. Spung!

Flowers! Six dozen bright blue, red, yellow, sun-brilliant flowers leaped up from behind the coffin on concealed springs!

The sweet odour of fresh cut flowers filled the coffin The flowers swayed gently before his amazed vision, tapping silently on the glass lid. Others sprang up until the coffin was banked with petals and color and sweet odours. Gardenias and dahlias and daffodils, trembling and shining.

'Rogers!'

The sermon continued.

'– Richard Braling, in his life, was a connoisseur of great and good things –'

The music sighed, rose and fell, distantly.

'Richard Braling savoured of life, as one savours of a rare wine, holding it upon the lips –'

A small panel in the side of the box flipped open. A swift bright metal arm snatched out. A needle stabbed Richard in the thorax, not very deeply. He screamed. The needle shot him full of a coloured liquor before he could seize it. Then it popped back into a receptacle and the panel snapped shut.

'Rogers!'

A growing numbness. Suddenly he could not move his fingers or his arms or turn his head. His legs were cold and limp.

'Richard Braling loved beautiful things. Music. Flowers,' said the voice,

'Rogers!'

This time he did not scream it. He could only think it. His tongue was motionless in his anaesthetized mouth.

Another panel opened. Metal forceps issued forth on steel arms. His left wrist was pierced by a huge sucking needle.

His blood was being drained from his body.

He heard a little pump working somewhere.

' – Richard Braling will be missed among us –'

The organ sobbed and murmured.

The flowers looked down upon him, nodding their bright-petalled heads.

Six candles, black and slender, rose up out of hidden receptacles, and stood behind the flowers, flickering and glowing.

Another pump started to work. While his blood drained out one side of his body, his right wrist was punctured, held, a needle shoved into it, and the second pump began to force formaldehyde into him.

Pump, pause, *pump*, pause, *pump*, pause, *pump*, pause.

The coffin moved.

A small motor popped and chugged. The room drifted by on either side of him. Little wheels revolved. No pallbearers were necessary. The flowers swayed as the casket moved gently out upon the terrace under a blue clear sky.

Pump, pause. *Pump*, pause.

'Richard Braling will be missed –'

Sweet soft music.

Pump, pause.

'Ah, sweet mystery of life, at last –' Singing.

'Braling, the gourmet –'

'Ah, at last I have the secret of it all –'

Staring, staring, his eyes egg-blind, at the little card out of the corners of his eyes: *The Braling Economy Casket . . .*

DIRECTIONS: SIMPLY PLACE BODY IN COFFIN – AND MUSIC WILL START.

A tree swung by overhead. The coffin rolled gently through the garden, behind some bushes, carrying the voice and the music with it.

'Now it is the time when we must consign this part of this man to the earth –'

Little shining spades leaped out of the sides of the casket.

They began to dig.

He saw the spades toss up dirt. The coffin settled. Bumped, settled, dug, bumped and settled, dug, bumped and settled again.

Pulse, pause, *pulse*, pause. *Pump*, pause, *pulse*, *pump*, pause.

'Ashes to ashes, dust to dust –'

The flowers shook and jolted. The box was deep. The music played.

The last thing Richard Braling saw was the spading arms of the Braling Economy Casket reaching up and pulling the hole in after it.

'Richard Braling, Richard Braling, Richard Braling, Richard Braling, Richard Braling . . .'

The record was stuck.

Nobody minded. Nobody was listening.

The Legacy

BY ROBERT BLOCH

Robert Bloch (1917–) has also been a prolific contributor to TV horror anthologies from Alfred Hitchcock Presents *in the Sixties by way of* Thriller, Journey to the Unknown, Night Gallery, Darkroom, Tales from the Darkside *and the most recent,* Monsters, *which premiered on Cable TV in 1988. His name, though, is inextricably linked with that of Hitchcock, for it was after buying the rights to Bob's novel,* Psycho *(1959), and producing the classic shock film which ensured them both a place in cinema history, that Hitch offered the Chicago-born writer a chance to work on his television series. The invitation opened the doors of Hollywood to Bloch, who had actually begun his writing career some years earlier in the late Thirties by emulating the bizarre stories of H.P. Lovecraft – with whom he had corresponded – in the pages of the pulp magazine* Weird Tales. *This film break lead to a constant stream of TV and work and there has been many a television episode in the last quarter of a century which has been enlivened by his black humour and devilish imagination.*

Monsters *– a concept not unlike that devised by Nigel Kneale with* Beasts *– was co-produced by Richard P. Rubinstein and Mitchel Gatlin, and aimed to offer viewers a new and different creature each week. 'Our defininon of creature is pretty broad,' Rubinstein explained when the series began, 'and the stories will range from arch comedy to the Gothic. They'll be scary, too, like those in* Tales from the Darkside.' *Among the writers featured in the series of half-hour episodes have been Stephen King, Manly Wade Wellman, William Nolan and, of course, Robert Bloch. Amongst Bob's contributions that have already been screened are 'Everybody Needs a Little Love',*

'A Case of the Stubborns', 'Mannikins of Horror' and 'The Legacy'. This last story, which Mitchel Gatlin directed with Eddie Bracken and Matthew Engell, has a special place in Bob's affections because his life-long interest in horror stemmed from a visit as a child to the cinema where he saw the 1925 Lon Chaney version of The Phantom of the Opera. *He was, he recalls, terrifed and fascinated by the face that glowered at him from the screen. The story of 'The Legacy', upon which the episode in* Monsters *was based, contains more than a little of that same terror and fascination to which he owes a lifetime of creativity in films and on television. It also, I believe, offers a gripping finale to this collection. So, Goodnight . . . sleep well!*

NOBODY thought Dale was crazy until the trouble started. True, he'd been a film buff ever since he was a kid, the way other youngsters sometimes get hung-up on baseball, football, or even chess. If they follow their hobby into adult life such interests can become an obsession, yet no one thinks it's a sign of insanity.

In Dale's case his studies led him into teaching a course on film history at the university, which seemed sensible enough. Certainly he appeared to be normal; he wasn't one of those wimpy professors seen in comedy films aimed at the junk-food generation.

Actually Dale was rather attractive. Debbie Curzon thought so. She was a newscaster on local radio where she met and interviewed many of the stud celebrities in sports or films; Dale must have had some *charisma* for her to choose him as a lover.

The two of them might have ended up together on a permanent basis if Dale hadn't leased the Chaney house.

That's what the realtor called it – 'the Chaney house' – although Dale couldn't verify the claim and the ancient escrow was clouded. The place was really just a small cottage halfway up Nichols Canyon in the Hollywood hills. Huddled amidst a tangle of trees and underbrush on a dirt side-road which turned to quicksand during the rainy season, the weatherbeaten frame dwelling offered no exterior charm or interior comfort. Debbie's reluctance to share it was understandable, but once he found it Dale couldn't wait to move in.

'All right, do as you please,' Debbie told him. 'If that dump is more important to you than sharing a brand-new condo with me –'

'It's not just a dump,' Dale protested. 'This is the *Chaney* house. Can't you understand?'

'Frankly, no. What makes you want to hole up in a place like this just because some dumb actor may or may not have hung out here sixty years ago?'

'Lon Chaney wasn't dumb,' Dale said. 'He happens to be one of the finest performers in silent films, perhaps the greatest of them all.'

'Who cares?' Debbie's voice honed to a cutting-edge. 'I just hope your wonderful Mr Chaney knows how to cook and is good in bed, because from now on you'll be living with him, not me.'

It was open warfare, but Dale found no weapon to pierce the armour of feminine logic. In the end Debbie told him to bug off, and he had no choice but to obey the entomological injunction.

A week later Dale moved into the Chaney house and by then everybody thought he'd flipped out. Turning down a renewal of his teaching contract now at the end of the fall semester meant losing his chance at tenure, and that certainly was a crazy decision, because he gave no reason for leaving.

But Dale knew exactly what he was going to do. He would vindicate himself in the eyes of Debbie and the academic world by writing a Hollywood history of his own – a definitive work which would answer the questions which lurked behind the legends. Who killed William Desmond Taylor, and why? Did Thomas Ince meet his death because of illness or was it murder? What really kept Garbo from returning to the screen? Had there been cover-ups in the case of Thelma Todd or Marilyn Monroe? So much had been surmised, so little verified. And for a starter, he meant to solve the Chaney mystery.

Of all the stars of silent films, Lon Chaney was by far the most mysterious. There were books on his films but no full-length biographies except for a reporter's inaccurate magazine series following Chaney's untimely death from cancer in 1930. Chaney's first wife died without breaking silence and his second left no memoir. His son Creighton, who later changed his name to Lon Chaney, Jr., was estranged from his father for many years and avoided painful memories. To this day Chaney's private life remains an enigma. 'Between pictures,' he told reporters, 'there is no Lon Chaney.'

The coincidence of moving into one of the actor's former residences challenged Dale. Come what may, he meant to learn Lon Chaney's secret.

But first there were more practical questions to deal with. Once furniture arrived and utilities were installed, he had to renovate his surroundings. The cottage had been unoccupied for many years – no wonder the realtor offered him such a bargain rental – and it was time for a thorough housecleaning.

So Dale called an agency and secured the services of a Hispanic lady named Juanita. She was short, plump, but surprisingly strong; perched on a rickety ladder she scrubbed away at the ceiling and side-walls, then descended to attack the floors with mop and brush. And on the second day she made her discovery.

Finishing up her work, she cleared out old boxes and empty cartons from the bedroom closet. The last carton, wedged in back under a jumble of debris, was not entirely empty.

'Look what I find,' Juanita said, holding up her trophy for Dale's inspection.

He took the tin box from her, hefting it with both hands. Then he lifted the lid and his eyes widened.

'What is it?' Juanita asked.

The box was empty but its interior was divided into a number of small compartments lined with smudged cloth. And the underside of the lid was covered by a mirror.

'Some kind of a kit,' Dale said.

It was hard to keep his voice from quavering, hard to conceal rising excitement as he paid and dismissed Juanita. When she left, Dale picked up the box again and now his hands were trembling. His hands, holding Lon Chaney's makeup kit.

Dale had seen publicity stills of Chaney displaying a different and much larger kit with side-trays, so this obviously wasn't the only one. What made it unique was that this box was here, in Chaney's secret hideaway.

Or was it?

Dale forced himself to face facts. In spite of the realtor's claim, he couldn't be certain that Lon Chaney ever lived here. For all he knew, the kit might have belonged to any one of a thousand actors residing in these hills when Hollywood was young.

What Dale needed was proof. And staring at the bottom of the box, he found it.

Wedged against the base was a coil of paper, a small square scrap which must have peeled off after being pasted below the mirror. Dale picked it up, smoothed it out, then read aloud the lettering typed across its surface.

'Property of Leonidas Chaney.'

Leonidas!

This was proof and no mistake. While the general public knew the actor as Lon and most filmographies listed his first name as Alonzo, Dale was one of the few aware that the star's birth-certificate identified him as Leonidas.

Chaney, born on April Fool's Day, had fooled his public. And considering his passion for privacy it seemed odd he'd put his real name here. But perhaps he'd fixed on his deception later in his career. Dale's inspection told him that this battered box was old, perhaps dating back to pre-Hollywood days when Chaney was a struggling actor in travelling shows. Could this actually be his very first makeup kit?

One thing seemed certain – Chaney had lived here. But when?

Dale pondered the question as he sat in gathering darkness alone, with the makeup kit on the table before him.

From what little he knew, Chaney's homes were modest by Hollywood standards, even after he attained stardom, but he would never have settled his family here. Which left only one other plausible answer.

Suppose this place was really a hideaway, a place his family didn't know about, a place he came to secretly and alone? According to publicity he did have a cabin up in the mountains where he went fishing between films. Could it be that he actually spent some of that time here, perhaps even without his wife's knowledge?

And if so, why? Dale quickly dismissed the notion of a secret love-life; Chaney was never a womanizer, and even had he been, this was hardly the setting for a romantic rendezvous. Nor was he a closet alcoholic or drug-addict. In any case there'd be no reason for him to keep a makeup kit hidden here.

Dale leaned forward, peering at the box through the twilight shadows which fell across its murky mirror.

But the mirror wasn't murky now. As he stared, something in the mirror stared back.

For a moment Dale thought it was his own face, distorted by a flash of fading sunlight amidst the coming of the dark. Even so, he realized that what he saw was not a reflection. There was another face, a face in the mirror, a ghastly white face with painted features that glowed and grinned.

With a shock he realized what it was – the face of a clown. And before Dale's widened eyes the face was melting, changing, so that now a second clown loomed leering out at him – cheeks spotted with paint and tufts of hair suddenly sprouting above a bony brow.

Dale turned, seeking a glimpse of someone else, some intruder who must have stolen silently into the bedroom to stare over his shoulder.

But save for himself the room was empty. And when his eyes sought the mirror again the face – or faces – had vanished. All he saw now was his own face reflected in the glass, its features fading in the dark.

Dale rose, stumbling across the room to switch on the overhead light. In its welcome glare he saw the makeup box and the perfectly ordinary mirror mounted within.

The clown-images were gone. They had existed only in his imagination – or was it his memory? For there had been two clowns in Chaney's life.

Hastily Dale sought his bookshelves, fumbling and finding the volume containing Lon Chaney's filmography. He riffled through it until a page fell open upon a photograph of the actor in the title role of *He Who Gets Slapped*. And now it was Dale who felt the slap of recognition. The picture showed the face of the first clown he'd seen in the mirror.

Turning pages, he located the still photo of another clown with daubed cheeks and patches of hair clumped on the bone-white skull. Chaney again, in *Laugh, Clown, Laugh*.

But there was no mirth in the painted face, and none in Dale's as he banged the book shut and left the room. Left the room, left the cottage, left the canyon to drive down to the shelter and sanity of lighted streets below.

He parked on Fairfax and entered a restaurant, taking comfort in its crowded quarters and the presence of a friendly waitress who urged him to try tonight's special. But when his order came he had no appetite for it.

Tonight had already been too special for him, and he couldn't forget his confrontation at the cottage. Had he really glimpsed those faces in the mirror, or had the images been evoked from memories of the films seen in retrospective showings long ago? A mirror is just a sheet of silvered glass, and what it reflected must have come from his mind's eye.

Dale forced himself to eat and gradually the tension ebbed. By the time he finished and drove back up the canyon his composure returned.

Inside the cottage the lights still blazed upon commonplace surroundings, safeguarding against shadows and dispelling doubts. If Chaney had lived here at all, that time was long-gone and the actor himself was long-dead. There were no ghosts, and the box on the bedroom table was merely an old makeup kit, not a miniature haunted house.

For a moment Dale had an impulse to lift the lid and examine the mirror for added reassurance, then dismissed it. There was no point in dignifying his apprehensions; what he needed was a good night's sleep and a clear head for to-morrow.

Truth to tell, he felt drained after the emotional stress of the day, and once he undressed and sought his bed Dale quickly fell into dreamless slumber.

Just when the change occurred he did not know, but there was a change, and the dream came.

In the dream he found himself awakened, sitting up in bed and staring through darkness at the black blur of the box on the table. And now the impulse he'd rejected upon entering the bedroom returned with an urgency he could not deny.

Sometimes dreams seem oddly like films – movies of the mind in which one's own movements are silently commanded by an unseen director – a series of jump-cuts and sudden shifts in which one is both actor and audience.

Thus it was that Dale both felt and saw himself rise from the bed, captured in a full shot as he moved across the room. Now a cut to another angle, showing him poised above the makeup kit. Then came a close shot of his hand moving down to raise the lid.

Moonlight from the window sent a silvery shaft to strike the surface of the makeup mirror, flooding it with a blinding brightness that seethed and stirred.

Faces formed in the glass – contoured countenances which seemed frighteningly familiar, even in the depths of dream. Faces changed, and yet there was a lurking linkage between them, for all were oriental.

Some Dale had seen before only in photographs – the evil Chinaman from the lost film *Bits of Life*, the benevolent laundryman in *Shadows*. Then, in rapid shifts, the vengeful mandarin of *Mr Wu*, the bespectacled elderly image of Wu's father, and a final, frightening glimpse of the chinless, sunken cheeked, shrivelled face of the aged grandfather. They formed and faded, smiling their secret smiles.

Now others appeared – the two pirates, Pew and Merry, from *Treasure Island*, a bearded Fagin out of *Oliver Twist*, followed by figures looming full-length in the mirror's depths. Here were the fake cripples of *The Miracle Man, The Blackbird, Flesh and Blood*. Then the real cripple of *The Shock* and the legless Blizzard in *The Penalty*. Now came a derby-hatted gangster, a French-Canadian trapper, a tough sergeant of Marines, a scarred animal-trapper, an elderly railroad engineer, and Echo, the ventriloquist of *The Unholy Three*.

In his dream Dale stood frozen before the glass as faces flashed forth in faster flickerings – the faces of madmen. Here was a crazed wax-museum attendant, a bearded victim of senile delusions, a deranged Russian peasant, the insane scientists of *A Blind Bargain* and *The Monster*. They were laughing at him, grinning in glee as Dale closed his eyes, hands clawing out to close the lid of the makeup kit.

Then he staggered back to the bed. There were no images here, only the darkness, and Dale fell into it, fleeing the faces and seeking surcease in sleep.

It was morning when Dale's eyes blinked open, welcoming the sanity of sunlight. He stirred, conscious now that last night had been a dream, knowing he'd seen nothing in the mirror; indeed, he had never even left his bed.

As he rose he glanced over at the box resting on the table, remembering how he'd closed it in reality before retiring, then closed it again in his nightmare.

But now the lid was up.

For a moment Dale recoiled, fighting the irrational explanation until sunlight and common sense prevailed.

The makeup kit was old, its hinges worn or even sprung. Sometime during the night the catch must have loosened and the lid popped up.

It was a logical answer, but even so he had to force himself toward the table, steel himself to gaze down into the mirror set inside the lid and gaze on what was reflected there.

Sunshine formed a halo around the image in its glassy surface – the image of his own face.

And as his features formed a smile of rueful relief, Dale turned away. The mirror in the makeup kit held no terrors for him now, any more than the one he faced as he shaved. He dressed and sought the makeshift kitchen, taking comfort in the familiar ritual of preparing his breakfast, then eating eggs and toast with a copy of the morning *Times* propped up before his coffee-cup. Even the news offered an odd comfort of its own – the familiar headlines and stories of wars, terrorist bombings, political corruption, street crime, drug-busts, accidents, epidemics, natural and unnatural disasters that filled the newspaper pages. However grim, these were realities; realities which he and everyone else in the world faced with fortitude born of long familiarity. They had nothing to do with the unhealthy fantasies which took form when Lon Chaney stalked the screen – fantasies which existed now only in Dale's imagination.

Glancing at his watch, he folded the paper and rose quickly. There was a busy day ahead, and time was already running short.

Leaving the cottage, he drove down to Hollywood Boulevard, turned right, then made a left on Fairfax. He reached Wilshire and headed west, weaving through noonday traffic until he found a parking-space before the imposing structure of the Motion Picture Academy of Arts and Sciences.

Here, upstairs in the Margaret Herrick Library, he turned his attention to the files he requested. Lon Chaney wasn't the only movie monster he meant to deal with in his projected history; there was research to be done on other stars of the horror film. And unlike the case with Chaney, there was ample material on men like Karloff, Lorre and Lugosi.

But even as he scribbled notes Dale found something lacking in the interviews and biographical data of these celebrated actors who seemingly made no mystery of their careers.

The one missing element common to all was that of explanation. Why had a gentle gentleman like Boris ended up playing monsters? What led Peter Lorre, the rabbi's grandson, to the portrayal of psychopaths? How did Bela Lugosi, who played parts ranging from Romeo to Jesus Christ in early European appearances, transform himself into the dreaded Count Dracula?

William Henry Pratt, Laszlo Loewenstein, Béla Blasko – all three men had changed their names, but what had changed their natures?

Dale found no answer in the files, but the last item he read before leaving the Academy offered a hint. It was an interview with an actress who toured with Lugosi in *Dracula*.

She told of how the genial cigar-smoking Hungarian prepared for his famous role, sitting before his dressing-room mirror and donning the costume and makeup of the vampire. But that was only a preliminary to performing. The next and most crucial step came as he rose, wrapped in the black cape, face contorted and eyes blazing. As he confronted himself in the mirror his deep voice invoked an incantation. 'I am Dracula,' he intoned. 'I am Dracula. I am Dracula.' Over and over again he repeated the words, and by the time he strode out upon the stage the words became reality. Lugosi was Dracula.

'He psyched himself up,' the actress explained. And as the years passed, a part of him became the part he played; when he died he was buried in Dracula's cape, with Dracula's ring on his finger.

Dale jotted down his notes, then hurried out into the afternoon sunshine. Now it was time to drive into Beverly Hills for a medical appointment.

It had been made a month ago, just an annual checkup, as a matter of routine. But now, as he arrived and took a seat in the crowded waiting-room, Dale felt uptight. He felt no worry about possible physical illness, but what about psychological stress? Last night's dreams might be a symptom of mental disturbance. What if Dr Pendleton told him he was cracking up?

By the time the receptionist called his name and a nurse led him to the examining-room he knew his pulse was pounding and his blood-pressure had risen. So it came as a pleasant surprise when the doctor made no comment on his readings other than remarking he thought Dale was underweight and seemed overtired. Reports on blood-tests and urine-specimen would be available in a few days, but nothing indicated cause for concern.

'Slow down a little,' Dr Pendleton said. 'Pace yourself. And it won't hurt if you put on a few pounds.'

Armed with that advice Dale left. Relieved, he headed for a seafood restaurant on Brighton Way and there he ordered and actually enjoyed his meal. The doctor was probably right, Dale decided; he *had* been working too hard, and the tension flaring up after his break with Debbie took an added toll. He resolved to follow orders, rest and relax. Then, perhaps, it might be possible to come to terms with himself, and with Debbie too. He really missed her, missed the hours they spent together, and the breach must be mended. All in good time.

As Dale left the restaurant he sensed a change in the air; the chill breeze hinted at rain and a muted murmur of distant thunder confirmed its coming.

The first drops spattered the windshield as he turned onto the canyon side-road, and by the time he parked in the driveway a flicker of lightning heralded the downpour that followed. Dale hurried into the cottage beneath the wind-tossed trees. Once inside he flipped the light-switches as he moved from room to room. It was only upon reaching the bedroom that he halted when its overhead light came on.

Standing in the doorway he stared at the open makeup box on the table, forehead furrowed in doubt.

Hadn't he closed the lid before he left? Dale shrugged in uncertainty. Perhaps the loose catch was the culprit once again; he'd better examine it and put his mind to rest.

Rain drummed the rooftop in a faster tempo and lightning flashed outside the window as he crossed to the table. Then, as he reached it, a clap of thunder shook the walls and the lights went off, overhead and throughout the cottage.

Power-outages were not uncommon hereabouts during a storm and Dale wasn't alarmed; perhaps the lights would come back on in a moment. He waited, but the darkness persisted and prevailed. Maybe he'd better look for his flashlight.

Then its illumination was unnecessary as the lightning-bolt struck somewhere close outside the window, filling the bedroom with a greenish glare. As it did so Dale peered down at the mirror inside the lid of the makeup kit and froze.

The reflection peering up at him was not his own.

It was the face of Singapore Joe – the role Chaney played in *The Road to Mandalay* – the half-blind man whose left eye was covered with a ghastly white cast.

But the image seemed strangely blurred; Dale blinked to clear his vision as lightning faded and the room plunged into darkness again.

Dale's shudder wasn't prompted by the roar of thunder. It was what he'd seen that traumatized him. *The Road to Mandalay* was one of the lost films; he knew of no print in existence. But Singapore Joe existed, in the mirror, existed in an indelible image leering up at him through the dark.

And the dark must be dispelled. Dale turned and blundered his way into the hall. Reaching the kitchen he stooped and opened the cabinet beneath the sink. Lightning outside the kitchen window came to his aid and in its moment of livid life he found and grasped the flashlight. It was not just an ordinary cylinder-type but one which terminated in a square base, projecting a strong beam of almost lantern-like intensity.

Dale switched it on, and the ray guided him back to the bedroom. As he walked his relief faded with the realization that his vision had faded too.

He was seeing only with his right eye now. The left was blind. Blind – like the eye of Singapore Joe.

You're having a nightmare, he told himself. But he wasn't asleep, and if there was a nightmare it had to be in the mirror of the makeup kit. Unless, of course, he was hallucinating.

There was only one way to find out, and Dale knew what he must do. Rain swept across the rooftop above, doors creaked and groaned against the onslaught of the wind, lightning glimmered, thunder growled. Only the light he gripped in his hand was reassurance; a magic lantern to protect him on his way. *Magic lantern* – that's what they called the movies in the old days. Was there such a thing as magic?

Forcing himself toward the bedroom table, he gazed down at the glass reflected in the lantern-light.

Half-blind he stared, but what he saw with his right eye was just a mirror after all. A shining surface reflecting his own familiar face.

And now his left eye cleared and he could see again. Dale took a deep breath, then expelled it hastily – for now the mirror blurred and a piercing pain shot through his lower limbs, causing him to crouch. Something pressed heavily against his spine, bowing his back.

He was changing, and the image in the mirror was changing too. He saw the tousled hair, the gargoyle grimace, the twisted limbs, the body bent beneath the hideous hump. No need to ask the identity of this image – he was gazing at Quasimodo, the Hunchback of Notre Dame.

573

It was Chaney he saw in the glass but he himself felt the weight of the hump, the constriction of the harness binding it to his body, the pain inflicted by the mass of makeup covering his face, the jagged teeth wired into his mouth, the mortician's wax masking his right eye.

Realization brought relief. It was makeup, and only makeup after all. Gradually the image diffused and Dale's feeling of physical restraint faded until once again he stood erect.

Thunder rolled as the image dispelled. Dale sighed with relief; now was the time to slam down the lid of the kit once and for all.

He started to reach for it, but his hands were gone.

His hands – and his arms.

Illusion, of course, like the illusion of Chaney's face and form coming into focus beneath the mirror's shiny surface. Dale's eyes met those of the visage peering out at him from under the broad brim of a Spanish sombrero. Chaney was armless, and now Dale felt the agony of numbed circulation, the constriction of his own arms bound against his body by a tight, concealing corset. That, he remembered, had been Chaney's device when portraying the armless knife-thrower in *The Unknown*.

With the recollection his panic ebbed, and once more features and form receded into the mirror's depths. The numbness was gone from his arms now; he could lift his hands and close the lid.

Then he fell.

His legs gave way and he slumped to the floor, sprawling helplessly, the box on the table beyond his reach. All he could do was elevate his gaze, see the shaven-headed creature crawling across the glass, dead legs dragging behind him. It was Phroso, the paralysed cripple in *West of Zanzibar*.

No makeup had been involved in the simulation of the man who had lost the use of his lower limbs; it had been Chaney's artistry which made the role seem reality.

Knowing that, Dale strove to rise, but there was no feeling in his legs – he couldn't command them. The face in the mirror glowered at him in the lamplight, bursting into brightness as lightning flashed outside the window. The eyes were mocking him, mocking his plight, and now Dale realized that the mirror's monsters sensed his purpose and were summoned to prevent it. Their appearance in the mirror gave them life, his awareness gave them strength to survive, and that strength was growing. Closing the kit would condemn them to darkness and it was this they fought against. They knew he couldn't close the lid, not if he were blind, armless, or paralysed.

Frantically Dale balanced himself on the palm of his left hand, extending his right arm upward, inching to the table-top. Then his fingers gripped the lid of the makeup kit, wrenching it down. With a rasp of rusty hinges the box slammed shut.

The mirror disappeared from view, but Dale's paralysis persisted. Try as he would, he couldn't raise himself. All he could do was wriggle, wriggle across the floor like a snake with a broken back, and lever his arms against the side of the bed. Pulling his body upward, he lifted himself, gasping with effort, then collapsed upon the cool sheets which dampened with the sweat of fear pouring from his fevered forehead.

Fever. That was the answer; it had to be. The doctor was wrong in his diagnosis. Dale was coming down with something, something that twisted mind and body. Labelling it psychosomatic brought no relief.

Dale rolled over to face the telephone resting on the night-stand beside the bed. If he could reach it he could call the paramedics. But as his hand moved forward he felt a sudden tingling in his legs, then kicked out with both feet. The paralysis, real or imaginary, was gone.

No reason to summon paramedics now, but he still needed help. In the dim light cast by the flash-lantern standing on the table across the room he dialled Dr Pendleton's number. The ringing on the line gave way to the mechanical message of an answering-service.

'Dr Pendleton is not in. Please leave your name and number and he will get back to you —'

Dale cradled the receiver, frowning in frustration. Sure, the doctor would get back to him, perhaps in an hour, maybe two or three. And then what?

How could he explain all this? If he minimized his condition he'd get that take-two-aspirins-and-call-me-in-the-morning routine. And if he came on too strong the doctor would probably order up an ambulance on his own. Pendleton was a practitioner of modern medicine; he wouldn't come out in the storm to make a house-call merely to humour a hysterical patient with his presence.

But Dale had to have someone's presence here, someone to talk to, someone like —

'Debbie?'

He'd dialled her number automatically, and now the very sound of her voice brought relief.

'Dale! I was hoping you'd call.'

Then she *did* care. Thank God for that! He listened intently as the warmth of her response gave way to concern.

'What's wrong? Are you sick or something?'

'Something,' Dale said. 'That is, I'm not sure. No, I can't explain it on the phone. If you could just come over —'

'Tonight? In all this rain?'

'Debbie, please. I know it's asking a lot, but I need you. I need you now –'

'And I need you.' Debbie sighed. 'All right. Give me half an hour.'

The phone went dead, but as he replaced the receiver Dale came alive again. She was coming and he'd told the truth; he did need her, needed her desperately.

Listening, he realized the rain was slowing. It was a good sign. Perhaps by the time she arrived the storm would be over and they could talk without the punctuation of thunder. He'd tell her what had happened, make her understand.

But just what *had* happened – and why?

Dale rolled over on his back, staring at the shadows on the ceiling, facing up to the shadows surrounding the question in his own mind.

And the answer came.

He'd found it today at the Academy, found it when he read the actress's description of Bela Lugosi preparing for his portrayal.

'He psyched himself up.' That was her explanation of how Lugosi became Dracula, and that was what Lon Chaney must have done.

No wonder he'd established a secret hideaway! Here, in this very room, he did more than experiment with physical disguise. Dale pictured him sitting alone on a night like this, creating contrivances to deform his body, refashioning his face, staring into the mirror at the creature reflected there. And then, the final transformation.

'Make up your mind.' A figure of speech, but Chaney had given it a literal application, one beyond the mere application of makeup from his kit. Seated here in the shadowed silence, this man of mystery – this son of deaf-mute parents whom he communicated with through the power of pantomime – confronted the reflections of monsters in the mirror and whispered the words. 'I am the Frog. I am Blizzard. I am Dr Ziska, Sergei, Alonzo the Armless, the Blackbird, Mr Wu.' Each time a different incarnation, each time a new *persona*, each time a litany repeated hour after hour from midnight to dawn, willing himself into the role until the role became reality.

And psyching himself up, he'd psyched-up the mirror too. The intensity of total concentration had been captured in the glass forever, just as it was later captured on the blank surface of nitrate film used for silent pictures. The filmed images decayed in time but the makeup kit mirror preserved Chaney's psychic power forever – a long-latent power revived by Dale's own glimpses into the glass, a power that grew greater with each succeeding gaze.

Dale remembered the first apparitions – how fleetingly they

appeared and how little effect they had beyond the initial shock of recognition. It was his repeated viewing which gave strength to the shifting shapes until they transformed his body into a semblance of what he saw.

But he wouldn't repeat the mistake. From now on the makeup kit would remain closed and he'd never look into that mirror again.

The rain had ended now and so had his fear. Thunder and lightning gave way to a calm matching his own. Knowing the truth was enough; he wouldn't repeat all this to Debbie or try to convince her. Instead he'd just tell how much he needed her, and that was true too.

But first he must dispose of the kit.

Dale shifted himself over to the side of the bed, sitting up and swinging his feet to the floor. The power-outage hadn't ended; he'd shut the kit away in the closet, then take the flash-lantern with him and guide Debbie up the path when she arrived.

All was quiet as he crossed the room to the table where the lantern-light shone on the closed box beside it. That's what the kit was, really; just a battered old box. Lon Chaney's box – Pandora's box, which opened for evils to emerge. But not to worry; the lid was down and it would stay down forever.

His hand went to the flash-lantern.

At least that was his intention, until he felt the chill of cold metal at his fingertips and found them fixed upon the lid of the makeup kit.

He tried to pull away but his hand remained fixed, fixed by a force commanding his movement and his mind, a power he could not control.

It was the power that raised the lid of the box, a power that seethed and surged, and in the uptilted mirror he saw its source.

Two eyes blazed from a face surmounted by a beaver hat and framed by matted hair; a face that grinned to display the cruel, serrated teeth. But it was from the cruel eyes that the power poured – the burning eyes of the vampire in *London After Midnight*. Dale knew the film, though he'd never seen a print; knew its original title was *The Hypnotist*. And it was a hypnotist who glared up at him, a hypnotist's power which had compelled him to open the box and stand transfixed now by the vision in the glass.

Then suddenly the face was fading and for a moment Dale felt a glimmer of hope. But as the face disappeared into the mirror's distorted depths, another face took form.

It was a face Dale knew only too well, one which had lain buried in his brain since childhood when he'd first seen it fill the screen from behind a ripped-away mask. The face of madness, the face of Death

577

incarnate, the face of Chaney's supreme horror; the face of Erik in *The Phantom of the Opera.*

No wonder he'd blotted out all memory of the terror which tormented his nightmares as a child, the terror he'd hidden away in adulthood but which still survived in his unconscious. It was suppressed fear that lay behind his inexplicable interest in Lon Chaney, a fright disguised as fascination which guided him to this ultimate, inevitable confrontation with the gaping fangs, the flaring nostrils, the bulging eyes of a living skull.

The Phantom stared and Dale felt the flooding force of the death's-head's overwhelming power, to which he responded with a power of his own, born of utter dread.

For an instant, for an eternity, his gaze locked with that of the monster and he realized a final fear. The face was looming larger, moving forward – attempting to emerge from the mirror!

And then, with savage strength, Dale gripped the box in both hands, raising it high; panting, he dashed it down upon the floor. The makeup kit landed with a crash as the Phantom's image shattered into shards of splintered glass glinting up in the lantern-light.

Chaney's power was broken at last, and with it the power of the Phantom. Dale gasped, shuddering in relief as he felt full control return.

As the knocking sounded its summons he picked up the flash-lantern and carried it with him down the hall to the front door. Debbie was here now, his hope, his angel of salvation. And he went to her proudly and unafraid because he was free of Chaney, free of the mirror's magic, free of the Phantom forever. This was the beginning of a new life, a life of love and beauty.

Dale opened the door and saw her standing there, smiling up at him. It was only when he lifted the lantern and Debbie saw his face that she began to scream.